TALLINU!

He needs to be focused on us.

He's not listening! Tallinu! Tallinu!

He calls himself Kaid now.

Kaid, dammit! Kaid!

Confused, Kaid's chanting faltered as he tried to sense who was calling him.

He's not responding. We can't keep this up much longer.

Get the doctor to do it. He's supposed to be the god, after all. Maybe he'll listen to him.

God? What was this talk of gods?

I can't! The voice woke more memories.

You'd better, because we can't bring him back otherwise!

Kaid heard the implicit threat, and he began to mentally back away. This didn't feel right. Whatever it was, he didn't want to know. Then his mind was grasped and held. Powerless, he now heard a voice he recognized only too well.

Kaid, we're not finished yet. There's work still to do.

No! I've done enough for you! No more, Vartra, no more!

You will return once more. You're at the heart of matters both here and in the future. You have to return!

NO!

As if from a great height, he saw his body slump foward onto the floor. A white rime of frost began to form over his robe, then, as panic began to take hold, the image vanished as he swept into a maelstrom of sound and heat and pain. . . .

DAW BOOKS
is proud to present
LISANNE NORMAN'S
SHOLAN ALLIANCE Novels:

TURNING POINT (#1)

FORTUNE'S WHEEL (#2)

FIRE MARGINS (#3)

RAZOR'S EDGE (#4)

RAZOR'S EDGE

Lisanne Norman

DAW BOOKS, INC.
DONALD A. WOLLHEIM, FOUNDER
375 Hudson Street, New York, NY 10014

ELIZABETH R. WOLLHEIM
SHEILA E. GILBERT
PUBLISHERS

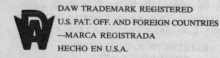

This book is dedicated to you, Ken, as my tribute to your 50th year in British SF Fandom.

I'd also like to thank all at DAW Books, and Marsha Jones and Ira Stoller, for their support and help. Without it you would not be reading this!

A few Guild personnel need a mention, too. So many thanks to:

Sholan Research and Development	-Merlin aka James Charlton
Sholan Communications	-Judith Faul
Sholan Medical Guild Research	-Helen Lofting
Alien Relations	
	-Pauline Dungate
	-Chris Morgan
Brotherhood of Vartra	-Sherrie Powell
Sholan Sciences	-Andrew Stephenson
	-Miavir
Sholan Archeology	-Ruth Blake

A further mention of Ken is, I think in order, because Ken Slater and I go back a long time, to the days when first I discovered Science Fiction Fandom and Conventions. His belief in me made me continue to chase my dreams of being a published writer. I'm not the only fan turned writer he's helped and inspired. The list of names is long and would surprise you. This year marks his fiftieth since starting Operation Fantast, a service not only to bring Science Fiction books and magazines to fans, but a fanzine to keep them in touch with each other. Happy fiftieth, Ken.

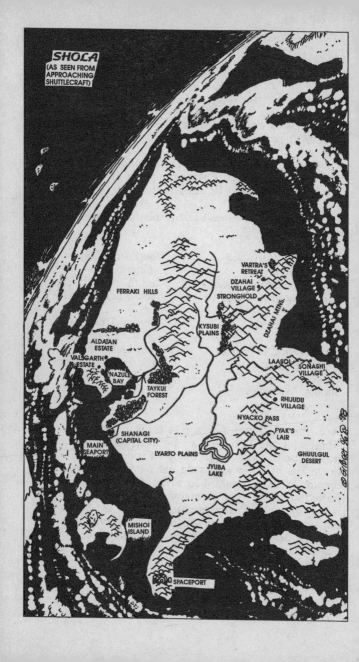

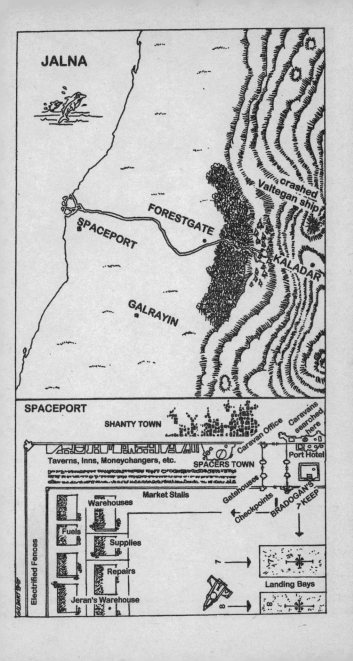

PROLOGUE

Rezac lunged past the alien for the floor of the stasis cube base unit, trying to reach a pistol that lay there. The alien reached out and stopped him.

No, don't. He'll have us killed before you reach it. You're weak from being inside that cube. You both nearly died. Wait for now.

Shocked not only by the sending from the stranger, but by his sudden weakness, Rezac let himself be pulled back till he sat on the ground by his Leska.

"Search, then bind them. Bring them up to the Lesser Hall," ordered the one in charge.

One at a time, Kris and Davies were taken from the small chamber, searched for weapons, then bound. There were cries of delight when a gun was found on the latter. Then Jo's turn came.

"Hey, this one's a woman!" yelled the guard searching her.

Jo struggled in the grasp of her captor as he began to search her again, an ugly leer on his face.

"What's a woman doing with a bunch of thieves? One of them your master, eh?"

"Leave me alone!" said Jo, pulling frantically away from his grasping hands.

Help came from an unexpected quarter—Zashou. With a rumble of anger that quickly rose to a growl, she pushed aside their guard and leaped into the corridor. Her lips pulled back from her teeth revealing large canines as she loomed protectively over the smaller Human female.

Jo felt a stab of pain as her mental shields were ruthlessly penetrated by Rezac and her mind quickly read. Then he was gone, leaving her confused and even more terrified.

"Leave her! Or lose your life!" said Zashou in halting

Jalnian. Her claws were extended, the deadly talons curved toward the guard.

Jo was suddenly released as the man stepped back in fear, fumbling for the crossbow slung on his shoulder.

The two holding Kris and Davies instantly came forward, quarrels pointed directly at Zashou and Jo.

"Enough! Turn around with your hands behind your backs," ordered the lead one.

We must comply. They will kill us otherwise, came the quick mental command from Zashou. The two females did as they were ordered.

Rezac was another matter. Realizing his Leska was being bound was enough for him. With an ear-splitting roar, he emerged from the room at full tilt, looking for someone to attack. What would have been a bloodbath ended abruptly as the lead guard stepped to one side, allowing the enraged Sholan to run past before hitting him soundly on the back of the head with his crossbow stock. Rezac fell like a stone.

By the time they'd been dragged through the great hall and up the stone steps to the Lord's private hall, Rezac, held securely by two burly guardsmen, was beginning to come round.

"Untie our guests," ordered Lord Killian, lifting his arm to allow his attendant to continue stripping off his padded body armor.

"Excuse the harsh welcome, but I didn't want you leaving before we'd time to get better acquainted."

At the sound of the voice, Rezac raised his head just enough to peer at the speaker through the hair that fell over his face. A growl began to build low in his throat as he tugged at his bonds.

"May I suggest you reassure your large friends they're in no danger. I'd prefer not to have to shoot them to preserve the lives of myself and my men." As the protective jacket was slipped from his chest, he indicated the half-dozen crossbowmen ranged at the top of the stairwell down to the main hall.

"I understand you," growled Rezac, lifting his head fully and shaking it till his mane of hair was cleared from his face. It settled like a dark cloud around his shoulders. "Release me, then we will listen to you."

Killian gestured to the guards, and Rezac's bonds were

cut. Pulling his arms forward, he ripped the remaining ropes free and massaged his wrists.

"I'm Lord Killian. Please, be seated," the burly man said, gesturing to the large wooden table that dominated the center of the room.

As Rezac moved toward the far end of the table, he glanced around the room, quickly assessing its windows and exits.

Opposite the opening for the stairs was a fireplace in which burned a generous log fire. There were two large windows, paned with small rectangles of thick glass. The other four, spaced along the outer wall, were mere narrow arrow slits covered by wooden shutters. Two doors flanked by tied-back curtains led off from either side of the fireplace. Against the third wall, the one with the arrow slits, a similar curtain was closed. Even as he looked at it, the lower edge flared outward. Probably a third door, Rezac surmised. One to the outside.

Facing the stairwell, its back to the fire, was a large, ornately carved high-backed chair. Obviously Killian's seat.

As Rezac sat down, he saw the Human female begin to move as well, the others following her. She was their leader, then. Strange that it wasn't one of the males. Quickly he searched through the information he'd taken from her downstairs. There was more than he'd realized at the time—too much to make sense of yet.

Later, sent Zashou. *Let's focus on now.*

Rezac turned to look more closely at their three Human companions. The differences between them and the Jalnians were subtle. He only noticed them because he'd touched the female's mind. They were newly into space, these Humans, and by their own endeavors: far more advanced than the Jalnians. Their skin had a slightly different cast to it, and their bodies moved differently, hinting at a dissimilar musculature and possibly skeleton beneath the flesh.

Movement by Lord Killian drew his attention away from them, and he watched the large male as he circled the table to take his seat. Placing hands almost as big as Rezac's own on the table, Killian looked at them all in turn.

"Time for you to introduce yourselves," he said, his voice deceptively mild. "Perhaps even to tell me why you're here."

Jo tried not to glance at her two male companions before she began to speak. "I'm afraid you've made a mistake,

Lord Killian. We're nothing more than thieves. . . ." Her voice trailed off into silence as the guard Killian gestured to approached the table and spilled onto it the bundle of possessions taken from them during the search.

"I think not," said Killian, picking up the energy pistol lying in the midst of the pile. "This doesn't belong to Jalna."

He fiddled with the weapon for a moment or two, then pointed it at Davies who was sitting opposite him.

"Don't point it at me, it's got a hair trigger!" he exclaimed, visibly blanching. "It'll discharge at the slightest pressure!"

Killian turned the gun on its side and studied it again before replacing it on the table. "Indeed. Then let's hope I don't have to use it on any of you. We were discussing your names and why you'd come to my castle."

Jo had let out an angry exclamation at the sight of the pistol. Now that it was no longer threatening him, Davies glanced over at her.

"Sorry, Jo," he muttered. "I know I shouldn't have brought it."

"So you're called Jo, and you're the leader. Now we're getting somewhere," said Killian, sitting back in his chair and clasping his hands across his stomach. "Please continue."

Rezac could sense his satisfaction.

Jo indicated them each in turn. "Davies, Kris, Zashou, and Rezac." She hesitated before continuing and Rezac could feel her uncertainty, then her acceptance that there was nothing to be gained from lying when the truth was obvious. "We aren't from Jalna. We came to find out what was on the crashed scouter."

"Not to rescue these furred ones?"

"Sholans," Jo corrected him. "We didn't know they were in the stasis cube."

"What is *stasis cube*?" Killian copied the Human words carefully.

"The cube you brought here. Inside it, time was frozen for our friends. In stasis."

"Frozen?"

In his mind, Rezac echoed the word. So that was what had happened to them! The last thing he remembered was them running from the Valtegan palace guards.

The lab! We ran into a laboratory! sent Zashou. *The cube must have been there!*

Later, replied Rezac, refocusing on the audible conversation. *It's difficult enough to follow them without getting sidetracked.*

"A person is a stasis cube has no idea of the passing of time," said Kris, looking to Rezac and Zashou for confirmation.

Rezac flicked an ear in assent.

"For them, when they're released, it's as if nothing has happened. Rezac and Zashou have also been moved. They're no longer where they were when they were imprisoned in the cube."

Killian scratched at his beard. "How long were they in this cube?"

Rezac was suddenly aware of Jo's compassion for them and her reluctance to say more. She looked at them before answering. "We think one thousand and five hundred years," she said quietly.

Rezac's ears flattened in shock and briefly the room began to fade around him. *How* long? He could barely comprehend what she'd said.

"A long time," said Killian, his voice slightly faint at the concept of that many years. "I presume your enemies placed you there. You must be formidable warriors indeed if that was the only way to remove you. Who were you fighting?"

"A species called the Valtegans," Jo replied. "They trade at the Spaceport occasionally."

Zashou's sudden despair swept through Rezac. *It was all for nothing! We failed!*

Enough! Rezac's mental tone was harsh.

Killian shook his head. "Never heard of them. No matter. What were you hoping to find on this crashed vehicle? Weapons?"

"Information," said Jo. "Information about the Valtegans—where they come from, what they left behind on Jalna, where they were going."

"And did you find this information?"

"Ah." Again Jo looked over at Rezac. "Partly."

"Obviously you found out what they left," said Killian, gesturing toward the two Sholans. "But the rest?"

"No," said Kris. "We found nothing. The craft was too badly damaged."

"There were no bodies. How can such a vehicle move with no one to drive it?"

"Remotes," said Rezac. "From a distance," he added, realizing how inadequate the Jalnian language was to explain technical matters.

Thoughtfully, Killian sat back in his chair and began stroking his beard while his gaze flicked from one to the other of them. "Now, I presume, you wish to return to the Spaceport and leave Jalna for your own worlds."

"That was the general idea," said Davies, speaking for the first time.

"Unfortunately that won't be possible," said Killian, his tone regretful. "Another blizzard is due tonight and the pass will be blocked by morning. I'm afraid you'll have to accept my hospitality until the weather improves."

He's lying, Kris sent to Jo.

We can't prove it, Rezac replied.

The only outward sign of both Kris' and Jo's surprise at Rezac joining the conversation was a slight tensing of their bodies.

Good, thought Rezac to himself. *At least they're skilled in concealment.*

Jo's reply, when it came, was slower and fainter. *What do we do, then?*

Go along with him for now. We have no other options yet, Rezac replied while sending a private thought to Kris.

Later, the Human replied.

"In return for my hospitality, perhaps you can help me," said Killian, oblivious to their mental exchange.

"In what way?" asked Kris.

"Bradogan, who rules the Spaceport and its surrounding lands, is hungry for power. Those Lords he can't ally to himself with bribes of off-world goods, he wages war on. It's only a matter of time till his eyes fall on Kaladar. I want an edge, something to keep him away from my lands. Something like this weapon here." He indicated the pistol. "You could help me by making more of them."

"Those weapons are highly sophisticated, Lord Killian," said Kris. "They require manufacturing methods not available on Jalna. We couldn't make them for you, even if we knew how."

Killian raised an eyebrow quizzically.

"We know how to use them, but we don't know how to make them," said Jo.

"You know how they work, you can make them." Killian's voice had grown cold.

"You misunderstand us, Lord," said Kris. He pointed to one of the guardsmen behind them. "They can use their crossbows, but could they make one?"

"You misunderstand *me*. You *will* provide me with off-world weapons," said Killian uncompromisingly. "If not that one, then others that fulfill a similar purpose."

He pushed himself to his feet. "Escort my guests to their chambers," he ordered his guards. "Think about it overnight. I'm sure you'll see the wisdom of mutual cooperation. We'll talk again in the morning."

They were escorted through the curtained doorway out onto an external balcony. The air was bitter as it blew fresh flurries of snow into their faces. Dressed as they were, Rezac could feel the cold hit Zashou and he moved closer to her, holding an arm out in invitation to her to share his warmth.

He felt her mental retreat as she shied physically back from him. Only a step, but it was enough. Their long sleep hadn't changed anything then, he thought with a sigh.

Are they going to lock us in some dungeon? asked Jo, trying to control the chattering of her teeth. *Maybe he wasn't lying about the blizzard after all!*

I don't think he'll put us in a dungeon tonight, sent Kris. *Likely it'll be somewhere comfortable. He's reminding us how cold it is to persuade us that cooperation is worthwhile. If we don't, then tomorrow it'll be the dungeons.*

I agree, sent Rezac.

The two males proved to be right. The rooms they were shown to were in a small tower set near the center of the castle. A suite for visiting dignitaries, or noble prisoners.

The main chamber boasted a fire almost as large as that in Killian's private quarters. Opening off it were two smaller bedrooms, both of which had beds hung with heavy drapes and fires burning in the grates. There was also a small closet that served as a privy. In the larger, a pile of blankets and three pallets lay next to the fire.

Once their escort had left, a search of the suite showed that the exit was guarded. The windows were shuttered, but in any case they were too far above ground level to make escape through them a practical proposition.

In front of the main fire, the table was set with food and wine.

"Ever get the feeling you were expected?" asked Davies, strolling over to the food and helping himself to a piece of meat from some type of fowl.

"We weren't betrayed," said Jo shortly.

Rezac turned to his Leska. "You should eat, Zashou. It's been a long time since our last meal."

She flicked an ear in reply and headed slowly for one of the dining chairs by the fire. He could feel her tiredness affecting him.

"You, too," he said, looking at the remaining two Humans. "We must all keep our strength up. No telling when or where our next meal will come from." As he turned toward the table, he felt a hand on his arm. Abruptly he turned back, teeth partially bared in a snarl.

Jo didn't flinch, but she did release him very slowly. "We're allies of Shola," she said in his language. "They brought us here undercover to examine the Valtegan scouter. There are four more Sholans imprisoned on Jalna. We have to work together, Rezac."

He turned away from her and continued over to the table. Lifting the flimsy knife, he began trying to hack some meat from the cold joint in the center.

"You've been to Shola?"

"Yes, briefly," replied Jo.

"Where?"

"Valsgarth Telepath Guild and the Warrior Guild in Nazule."

"What about Ranz, on the plains?" He sensed Kris joining him at the table.

"Don't you mean in the Dzahai Mountains? I've been to Vartra's Retreat too."

Startled, Rezac looked round. "Vartra's Retreat? So he did go to the temple at Stronghold after all."

"The temple at Valsgarth is the main one now, but yes, there's also a temple of Vartra at Stronghold."

"Temple?" asked Zashou, looking up at Jo and Kris. "What has Vartra to do with temples?"

Rezac watched the two Humans exchange glances.

"You've a helluva lot of catching up to do," observed Davies sitting down. "On the Shola we know, Vartra is the major god of warriors and telepaths. He was responsible for saving them from the Cataclysm." He reached out for another piece of meat.

"He was a person? You knew him?" Jo sat down opposite Zashou.

Shocked once more to the core, Rezac let the knife fall from his grasp and sat down heavily. "A god? How?"

"It seems we've outlived ourselves," said Zashou. "You were right the first time, Rezac. Let's eat. We can talk of these matters later, when we're stronger." *They can't tell us much if they were only there briefly.*

"I lived there for six months, Zashou," said Kris, taking the seat next to Jo.

"You can hear us mind-speak to each other?" demanded Rezac.

Kris smiled. "We Terrans have one or two Talents of our own. That's why I was living on Shola."

A small chirrup of sound drew Rezac's gaze to Kris' jacket pocket. From its depths popped a white-furred face, muzzle and ears tipped with brown, large eyes glancing rapidly round the assembled faces. A trill of pleasure as it saw Jo, and a sniff of disdain at the two Sholans, and Scamp emerged. Scrambling up Kris' arm to his neck, it raised its front paws to pat his face then leaped down to the table to run to Jo.

"A jegget!" exclaimed Zashou. "You brought a jegget with you?"

Rezac began to laugh. "You've got more than Talents if you can befriend a jegget!" Now he knew they came from Shola—and more: as the only other telepathic species on their world, no jegget would go near a person it didn't trust. In fact, the little creatures were notorious for that. Get a nest of jeggets in your barn, and you'd never get rid of them! They knew when you were coming, knew where your traps were.

Scamp, meanwhile, was twining himself and his dark-tipped bushy tail round Jo's neck, chirruping and purring for all he was worth.

Aware of his pet's feelings, and a large part of the reason for them, Kris glanced over at Rezac.

*Please, say nothing. The Valtegans ruled Jo's world, using
females like her for sex. I need her trust. If she realized what
I feel for her . . .*

Rezac cut him short with an affirmative gesture. *It's not
my business.*

Reassured all was well with Jo, Scamp returned to Kris,
looking and sniffing hopefully in the direction of the meat.

"Feed him," said Rezac, gesturing at the plate as feelings
of ravenous hunger stole into their minds. *She doesn't sense
him. Why not?*

*Jo is only a latent telepath. She chooses not to train her
Talent. She's a linguist—she studies languages and was responsible for compiling the first Valtegan lexicon.*

So the Valtegans are still at large.

*There are no Valtegans on Shola. Your people came
across them on our first colony world, Keiss. They rescued
the colonists—Jo was one of them. We don't know where
the Valtegans are now, or what they're doing, that's why
we're on Jalna. That's how we found you.*

Rezac, later, sent Zashou. *Catching up is not important.
Eating and sleeping is, so is deciding what to do about Killian and the weapons he wants.*

You're right.

"How did you avoid Scamp being found when we were
searched?" Zashou asked Kris as she tore off a lump of
bread from the loaf and handed the rest to Jo.

Kris grinned as he pushed some small pieces of meat to
one side for Scamp. "I suggested to the guard that he didn't
really want to touch me. Strangely enough, he agreed."

"They'll find out soon enough," warned Davies.

"I don't think they'll care," said Kris.

"You said you'd trained at a warrior guild. We had something similar in our time, but it taught you to fight unarmed
and with traditional bladed weapons."

"Now it also teaches you the use of modern energy weapons. I can strip and maintain most Sholan weapons with
the best of them, but build one from scratch?" He shook
his head.

"Davies is the electronics genius," said Jo.

Rezac looked at him. "Could you build a weapon?"

"Depends what they've brought here from the shuttle.
The good Lord Killian had the craft stripped of just about

everything that might have been useful, and naturally, they didn't know what they were doing!"

"What kind of vessel was it?"

"A scouter. Space to ground vehicle."

"From a Valtegan warship?"

"Do they have any other kind?" asked Jo wryly.

Rezac grinned slightly. "No. Then the scouter will be armed. It will have its own weapons system. We could dismantle and use that."

"Should we even be thinking of giving them a weapon at all?" asked Zashou. "I'm sure they've discovered enough efficient ways of killing each other on their own."

"We haven't a choice," said Kris. "You heard Killian."

"Besides, it doesn't have to work for long," said Davies. "Just long enough for us to get out of this place!"

"Fuel sources alone will limit its life," agreed Rezac. "Unless I'm mistaken, there should be a backup battery that stores energy for it to use."

"You know a fair bit about the Valtegans, don't you?" said Jo.

"Should. We were prized pets of theirs for a year," growled Rezac, the grin vanishing.

"You mentioned a palace. What palace?"

"The Emperor's. God-King of the Four Realms." He tried, but couldn't control his hate and anger at what they'd suffered during their captivity.

Zashou winced. "Rezac," she said warningly. "He's dust now, they all are. Let the rage go."

With an effort, Rezac pushed the anger to the back of his mind and refocused on the business at hand.

"That was fifteen hundred years ago, though," said Davies. "How much use is that knowledge to us now?"

"How much can a people change in that time?" Jo asked Rezac.

"Valtegans, not at all," he said shortly.

"You seem much the same as your modern counterparts," said Kris. "I imagine the basic Valtegan species traits will have remained unchanged too."

"Well, you'll be able to tell, won't you?" said Rezac, aware his tone was somewhat snappish but unable to stop himself.

"I was sent on this mission because I understand the Valtegans more than anyone else at present," said Jo.

"Your knowledge is invaluable. Will you both share it with me?"

"If it'll help, of course," said Zashou, glancing angrily at her Leska.

"Assuming this shuttle is military and has a weapons system on board, then we'll need to look for it, with no guarantee that the Jalnians haven't ripped it apart," said Kris. "That should buy us some time at least."

"Agreed," said Rezac. "However, it will be bolted into the structure of the vehicle and I doubt the Jalnians would have been able to work those panels loose."

"Were your people in space when the Valtegans came?" asked Davies.

"Only just. They arrived without warning and in such vast numbers that there was little we could do to fight them."

"So how come you know so much about their spacecraft?"

"I don't, but I was communicating with those of our people who were on warships in space."

Zashou leaned forward to touch Davies on the arm. "On Shola, telepaths were hunted by the Valtegans as live trophies and kept to show how important a person was. Anyone of high standing had a Sholan telepath as a pet," she said quietly. "That was the crux of their downfall. It took time, but eventually there were enough of us on the four Valtegan home worlds and in their galactic fleet to strike. It was we who coordinated the communications between the ships and the worlds—the slave worlds, too. We gave the order to strike."

"To strike?" asked Davies. "You're supposed to be unable to fight!"

Zashou shook her head. "Rezac can, for a short time, then the nausea gets to him, too. But I didn't mean that way. The nontelepath slaves and the other species, they fought. What we had done was to subvert the Valtegans' minds, cause them to doubt one another, Challenge for position—and more. We used our abilities to destroy them, weaken them for the civil war that followed. We turned Valtegan against Valtegan. So we know them, know their weaknesses—and their strengths." She shuddered briefly at the memories, still fresh for them, and sat back.

"Did you say the Valtegans had four home worlds?" asked Jo.

"Yes, plus some three other slave worlds."

She moaned quietly. "Four worlds full of Valtegans! There's no way we can possibly win against them!"

"We thought that, but you say Shola's free of them now," said Rezac. "It wasn't how many we killed, it was who we killed. Take out the bridge crew of a warship, barricade the doors, and within minutes you can crash the ship into the rest of that fleet and all for the loss of one person."

"That's suicide on a mass scale!"

Rezac looked calmly at Jo. "Yes, it was, and it was the price we all, us included, expected and were willing to pay."

"You communicated over interplanetary space?" Kris asked quietly.

"Were we not answered by telepaths from Shola?" asked Rezac. "The skill has obviously lived on."

"Those who answered you weren't exactly Sholan telepaths," said Jo.

Rezac frowned. "Of course they were. Who else could it have been? Not Humans—the minds were Sholan."

"They would seem so," said Kris. "The one who answered you was Human, a Human female with a Sholan Leska."

"Impossible!"

Jo shook her head. "No. He's telling you the truth. There are several Sholans with Human Leska partners now, but Carrie and Kusac Aldatan were the first."

"Aldatan?" exclaimed Zashou. "That's my family name! But how . . . ?"

"Vartra," said Rezac. "His tinkering with our genes led to that. Your sister must have been enhanced, too."

"Sister?" asked Jo.

"My sister Zylisha was Vartra's Companion when we were taken by the Valtegans," said Zashou. "The enhanced genes must have passed on to their children. Vartra did what he originally set out to do."

"He did more than that from the sound of it," said Davies dryly. "Carrie and Kusac would have had a child if she hadn't lost it when she was injured. Another mixed Leska pair were expecting one when we left Shola."

"Cubs," said Zashou faintly. "Human and Sholan cubs."

"No wonder he's achieved godhood!" said Rezac.

"Maybe Shanka had the right of it after all. Without Vartra playing god with our lives, none of this would have happened."

"Leave Shanka out of this, Rezac! Just remember, when I offered you the serum, you chose to take it! You could have refused."

Rezac snorted angrily. "What good would it have done? Once you'd taken it, we were all going to catch it."

"What does it matter now anyway! It's history—ancient history!"

At that moment, a knock came at the door. It opened to admit an obviously self-important man dressed in long robes, followed by a peasant woman carrying a large pile of clothing.

"I am Durvan, in charge of the smooth running of Lord Killian's house," he said, gesturing to the woman to follow him as he approached their table. "My master has asked me to bring you these clothes. He insists that you wear them as he doesn't want to advertise the fact that he's, shall we say, entertaining off-world visitors." His mouth split into a too-cheery smile that showed off his teeth.

Rezac began to growl low in his throat.

Humanoids show their teeth when they smile, sent Kris. *It isn't threatening—usually. In his case, I'd make an exception.*

"Put them down on a chair," Durvan said sharply to the woman as he strolled over to Jo, eyes roving across her face and those parts of her anatomy he could see. "The red dress, I think, for this lady," he said, holding his hand out for the garment.

Hurriedly the peasant pulled the dress from the pile and handed it to him.

Taking it from her, he advanced on Jo, ready to hold it against her.

Kris rose to his feet in front of him. "I'll take that," he said, reaching out for the garment.

Durvan frowned but handed it over. "I was merely going to hold it against her to see if it suited her coloring." He stepped back and looked around the little group. "I was told there were two ladies. Where is the other?"

"Just leave the clothes," said Kris. "We're capable of working out who should wear what ourselves."

"I'm sure you are," said Durvan. "However, the servant

will remain to show the ladies how the dresses are fastened."

"We can manage ourselves," said Jo.

Still angry, Rezac decided to put an end to the intrusion. Slowly he stood up, stretched his arms, and flexed his claws. "I think you should leave," he said, his voice a low rumble that carried to every part of the room. "We're tired and wish to sleep."

Durvan had begun to back away from the table as soon as the Sholan moved. The servant fled with a squeal of terror. Realizing he was alone, the steward beat a hasty retreat. "Should you need help, ask the guard," he said before closing the door behind him.

Rezac reached for the clothing and began sorting through it. A dress of blue he handed to Zashou, the rest he put over the backs of the nearest chairs.

"Help yourselves," he said. "They're all robes such as that character was wearing. Nothing practical, I'm afraid, but at least they're warm, which is more than can be said for what we're wearing." He looked down at his own clothing, then over at Zashou.

Both of them were dressed in garments that offered very little in the way of either covering or warmth. Rezac's consisted of a brightly colored woven belt from which hung two short panels of the same patterned material; one larger one in front, the one over his rear partially split to accommodate his tail. It most closely resembled a loincloth. From both ears hung gold rings, and on his wrists were broad bracelets inset with jewel-colored enameling.

Zashou was similarly clad, but her garments included a short tabard top, and her earrings were larger.

"What favored Valtegan drone slaves wear at the Emperor's court," said Rezac.

"Drones? They have drones?" asked Jo, getting up to examine her dress.

"Who do you think does all the domestic work? You know their females are feral, don't you? They keep very few females because of that. Once they've mated, they'll fight off any other male that comes near them until they've laid that clutch of eggs. The drones are the only ones who can get close to them most of the time," said Rezac.

Jo looked at him. "You're serious, aren't you? I'd figured

they were egg layers, but they have such a high sex drive that I'd assumed females were common."

"The males have a high sex drive because they need a high incentive to mate. Without the control collars on the females, the males would be ripped to shreds even approaching a female, let alone trying to mate with one. They are seriously feral. Mindless eating and laying machines that have to be separated from their eggs just before they hatch, or they'd eat them, too."

"So that's why they put those damned pleasure cities on Keiss," said Davies as he reached out to pick up the green robe. "They need to direct that sex drive elsewhere. On Keiss, it was our women in Geshader and Tashkerra."

"That's what they use the females of the slave races and some drones for," agreed Rezac, then he felt the sudden flare of fear mixed with pain and revulsion that came from Jo. It was gone almost immediately.

"Excuse me," she said, dropping the dress and heading for one of the bedrooms.

Rezac looked to Kris for an explanation.

"Look, guys," said Davies, drawing their attention. "It wasn't for me to say before, and still isn't, but I think you should know that Jo did undercover work with Elise, Carrie's twin, in one of the pleasure cities. I wouldn't have had the guts to do what they did with the Valtegan officers to get information for our movement. When Elise got caught and tortured to death, it hit Jo very hard."

"Yet she tries to understand these . . . creatures," said Zashou.

"Hey, it's her way of coping with it," said Davies. "I know how you feel about her, Kris, just go easy, hear me? She still has nightmares about those damned lizards pawing her. If you wouldn't mind, Zashou, it might help if you went to her. Another female, that kind of thing. We males just can't imagine what it was like for her."

"I can," said Rezac grimly. "Zashou . . . ?"

"I'll go," she said, getting to her feet. "Perhaps it might be better if she spent the night with me."

Kris looked at Rezac. "If you wouldn't mind, just for tonight?"

Rezac nodded briefly, keeping his personal feelings under control. *Tonight only, Zashou. Do not shame me in front of these people. We are Leskas.*

I know only too well what we are. Nothing has changed, Rezac. We will share the room, but not the bed, she replied as she made her way into the room where Jo had fled.

"I suggest for tonight we use the other room," said Kris. "Tomorrow we can see if Jo is willing for us to share the larger room with her, then you two can have the smaller one. I think we should avoid leaving her alone, if possible. The Jalnian attitude toward females is archaic, to say the least, and she's too easily mistaken for one of them."

CHAPTER 1

Landing the aircar immediately in front of the Valsgarth estate house, Kaid powered down the engine then took a moment to rest his head on his forearms. Kusac's voice from the rear of the craft roused him.

"Kaid, would you carry Kashini in for us?"

He pushed himself away from the console. He was dead tired; all he wanted to do was sleep. "Coming." Getting up, through the side window he caught sight of the small group of people waiting impatiently outside. "You've got a welcoming committee."

As he bent down to take the newborn infant from Carrie's arms, Kusac put a restraining hand on his arm. "Kaid, everyone's going to want to debrief us on what we saw in the Margins. I think your origin should remain your business; it should be your decision whether or not to reveal it."

Surprised, Kaid looked at him. Kusac flicked an ear, then tightened his grip briefly on his friend's arm before releasing him.

"I would prefer it to remain unknown," Kaid agreed as he took the sleeping cub from Carrie.

Kusac, Carrie cradled in his arms, was the first to leave the craft. Kaid and their cub followed behind.

Rhyasha was at her son's side instantly. "Thank Vartra you're all safe!" she said. "We've been so afraid for you!" She leaned forward to touch Carrie's cheek. "Are you all right, cub? Yes, you are: I can feel it. Kusac, let your father carry her upstairs. You look as exhausted as she is!"

Kusac looked across at his father. "I can manage, thank you," he said, holding Carrie a little closer, ears dipping in acknowledgment of Konis' more reserved concern.

"Let him be, Rhyasha," Konis said. "They're a family now. Of course he wants to carry the mother of his cub

into their home! I was just the same when you gave birth
to him!"

Kusac started walking up the steps, his mother still beside
him as his father fell in step with Kaid.

Noni's here, she sent. *She and Vanna—exchanged opinions!*
Noni? But she doesn't travel for anyone!

*She's here nonetheless. She says not only does she want
to see to the cub as Carrie requested, but that Kaid needs
her attention, too.*

He does. His hand was injured again.

I'll see Noni, sent Carrie, resting her hand on her bond-
mother's arm. *Rhyasha, go and look at Kashini. She's so
beautiful!*

I will! Again the fleeting touch for both of them, then,
with a smile, his mother went over to Kaid and her
husband.

Noni was waiting for them upstairs in the lounge adjacent
to their bedroom. She raised her hand in a negative gesture
before either Kusac or Carrie could speak. "A lucky
guess," she said. "Not all of life is visions and portents!
Now, young Human. Who do you want—me, or your
physician?"

"You, Noni," said Carrie, smiling tiredly, "but let Vanna
come, too."

"Hmpf! I hope you're not too tired for our arguments,
then," she grumbled, following them into the bedroom. She
looked over at Kaid. "You're next, so don't bother leaving
the suite."

At the side of the bed, a crib now stood, and it was in
this that Kaid placed the still sleeping cub. From where
she'd been laid on the bed, Carrie reached out to stop him
from leaving. "What can I say but thank you," she said,
gently squeezing his hand.

Mumbling an appropriate reply, Kaid escaped to the
lounge as quickly as he could. There he found Dzaka waiting for him. They stood looking at each other for a moment, then Kaid took hold of his son by the shoulders and
pulled him close.

"Thank Vartra you're safe," said Dzaka as they em-
braced. "When I heard you were at Chezy, with Fyak
and Ghezu . . ."

"Fyak's dead," said Kaid, letting him go and moving over

to the nearest chair. Gratefully he sank down into it. "The tribes executed him and Vraiyou." His voice took on a hard edge. "Ghezu I killed myself. That nightmare is over for both of us." He closed his eyes, resting his head against the back of the seat, aware now of the tension in his neck and shoulders.

"The Gods be praised," his son said with feeling. "Do you want to sleep now or eat first?"

Kaid opened his eyes. "Eat. We could all do with food. And c'shar for me, coffee for them."

"I'll get it."

"Tell Vanna that Carrie's asked her to join them," Kaid called out after him.

Dzaka stopped in the doorway. "Diplomatic of her. Did you hear Noni and Vanna had a heated discussion over who would treat Carrie and the cub?"

"No, I didn't. I pity our physician."

"Don't." Dzaka's mouth opened in a grin. "Vanna held her own."

Kaid sat back, closing his eyes again. He woke with a start a few minutes later as someone touched his knee. Still groggy, he found himself staring at a smaller version of Rhyasha. Golden-pelted like her mother, the young female's blonde hair fell below her shoulders in a mass of unbound waves.

"You're Kaid, Dzaka's father, aren't you?" she asked.

He nodded, memory beginning to return as he recognized her.

"I'm Kitra, his Companion," she said. "We haven't been properly introduced because last time you came back, you'd been ill. I think we should meet now, before Dzaka decides you're too ill again." She offered him her hand, palm uppermost.

Totally nonplussed, Kaid reached out to touch fingertips with her. "Well met, Liegena Kitra," he said.

She wrinkled her nose at him. "You don't call my brother or Carrie by their titles," she said. "I don't think you should use mine either, since we're sort of connected."

"If that's what you wish, Kitra," he said, just succeeding in hiding a grin. "Is there something I can do for you?" He watched as she headed for a nearby footstool and brought it over beside his chair.

"No. I just wanted to meet you formally," she said, settling herself on it and leaning against him. "Now I can come and talk to you whenever I want. We can get to know each other."

Dzaka returned carrying a tray loaded with cut meats, bread, and cheese as well as a jug each of c'shar and coffee. "I see Kitra's keeping you company," he said, carefully placing it down on the low table beside his father.

"Yes. You should have introduced us earlier, Dzaka," he said. "It isn't every day my son finds a Companion."

Dzaka frowned as he held a couple of the plates out. "But you know her! She's Kusac's sister."

"You didn't introduce her as your Companion, though," Kaid chided him gently.

"Ah. You're right," he said, tail swaying slightly with embarrassment. "Sorry, Kitra."

The door from the bedroom opened, and Kusac came through. He smelled the food immediately. "Is there enough for all of us?" he asked, pulling over another chair.

"For you and Kaid, yes. The Clan Leader intends to bring something more suitable up for the Liegena as soon as she's allowed to," replied Dzaka. "I've a message for you from T'Chebbi, Father. She says that General Raiban and Father Lijou wish full reports from you at the earliest possible moment. She told them that you were all suffering from exhaustion and minor injuries and that you'd need to see your physician first. She said you'd not be likely to have the reports ready before the end of the week at the earliest."

"Vartra bless her!" said Kaid with feeling as he reached for the c'shar jug.

"She's held everyone together since you disappeared," said Dzaka quietly.

"A female of hidden talents," murmured Kusac.

Kaid glanced over at him. "That's why I chose her. T'Chebbi never pushes herself forward, but she's a more than able member of the Brotherhood."

"Of the En'Shalla Brothers," Kusac reminded him. "We bought our freedom—and theirs—in the Fire Margins, Kaid."

The riding beasts had shied away as General Kezule was brought to the tethering line: His scent scared them. It was

good to know some things hadn't changed even if the Sholans were no longer the docile slaves of his day.

While two of his captors held the beast, one of the males
had mounted and then reached down for him. With his
hands bound behind him, he couldn't assist even had he
wanted to. They had to thrust him up to the rider.

The beast danced unhappily from side to side, terrified
at having the scent of an alien predator so close to its nostrils. He was thrown against its neck, the bony nodules on
its spine pressing into his chest uncomfortably. The rider
hauled on the reins, pulling its head up as the two on the
ground got a better grip on the halter. Once it was still
again, a rope was passed round his waist and the beast's
neck, tethering him in place.

Their leader, the one wearing the broad bracelet that
controlled his slave collar, mounted one of the other waiting creatures. There were twelve of them, and all but his
rider were heavily armed. They were taking no chances
with him. That was his only comforting thought—that they
considered him a formidable enemy even in captivity.

With a single cry of command, the group began to move.
As his rider took hold of the cord binding his wrists, the
beast was given its head. Once again he was flung forward
against its neck, this time violently enough to wind him.

The ride was unpleasant. Bounced continually not only
against the creature's painful spine, but also from side to
side, it wasn't long before he began to feel extremely
queasy. By the time they arrived at the rendezvous more
than an hour later, he was in no state to make a bid for
freedom even if the opportunity had presented itself.

It seemed an age before they hauled him down and he felt
firm ground under his feet again. He staggered and would
have fallen had he not stumbled into one of the tribe's males.
The sudden strong alien scent was the last straw, and as he
was grabbed by the wrists and hauled upright, he began to
retch. Doubling over, he was unable to stop his stomach
from expelling its contents all over the sand.

"What's wrong with him?" he heard a voice demand. "Is
he ill?"

"He's not used to land beasts," came the laughing reply
as, still retching, he was thrust forward.

"When he's done, Lieutenant, give him some water and
take him to the medical unit. They're expecting him."

"Aye, General Raiban."

Now rid of what little had been in it, his stomach spasms began to ease, and he was able to straighten up. Still shaking, he was temporarily beyond embarrassment. His bonds were cut and he slowly pulled his arms round in front of him. Then metal cuffs were snapped on his wrists. A canteen was handed to him. He could smell the water and took it gratefully.

"Does he understand Sholan?"

"Oh, yes," was the reply. "He spoke to Fyak. *He* was Kezule!"

"So you're the god, are you?"

He drank deeply, already feeling better, before even looking at the speaker. He'd recognized the scent as female. They still hadn't learned to keep their females decently locked in the breeding room. He considered not replying, or insisting that he speak only to a male, then decided on a safer option instead.

"I only speak to Commander." He hated their language almost as much as he hated them.

"I am the commander," was the soft reply. "I'm General Raiban."

He closed his eyes as the canteen was taken from him, trying to force himself not to react, not to let them see his revulsion at the presence of the female. It would be viewed by them as a weakness.

"I am General Kezule," he admitted, opening his eyes.

"Well come to the future, General. I think you'll find it somewhat different from the Shola you so recently left behind." She turned away abruptly and began to walk toward one of the larger vehicles accompanied by three of the desert males.

A tug on his arm brought his attention back to his immediate situation.

"You've an appointment with the physician," said the trooper, leading him toward one of the larger tents. Two armed guards followed close behind.

Here the indignities to his person started. His hands were released, and when, scenting yet another female present, he refused to remove his clothing for the medical examination, they held him and forcibly stripped him. He was dragged to a table and held there prone while they prodded and poked at him until they were satisfied he had no broken bones or internal injuries.

Released and allowed to get to his feet, his clothes were held out to him by the female. He snatched them from her, his crest rising and his tongue flicking out in anger.

"How dare you treat me like this! Don't you know who I am?" he demanded of the nearest male guard. "Not even the basest criminal is exposed to females and not only do you let this one see me naked, but you allow her to touch me!"

With one backhanded blow of his arm, he sent the female flying across the room till she collided with a metal cabinet. "Get her stinking body away from me!" he roared.

The room exploded into activity. He was instantly grabbed by the guards as the physician ran to the side of the unconscious female.

He struggled against them, this time using what he could muster of his full strength. Then he felt the coldness of a gun muzzle at the base of his neck and froze.

"That's better," a voice purred in his ear. "I wouldn't kill you, but a stunner shot right here would be excruciating, don't you think?"

"Get a stretcher in here on the double!" the physician was shouting. "I want the theater ready immediately, we've got a fractured skull here!" He paused to look up at Kezule. "Take that tree-climbing bastard out of here! There's nothing wrong with him an execution wouldn't cure!"

He was dragged out of the tent into the sunlight, then across the site to the vehicle where their commander had gone.

"What is it, Myule?" Raiban asked her aide, not bothering to look up from her comm.

"Lieutenant Naada, General. There's been an incident involving the Valtegan captive."

"What happened?" she demanded, her attention instantly on the lieutenant.

"One of the medics. Rashou Vrenga. The general hit her. It's serious, I'm afraid, General Raiban."

"Hit her? What d'you mean *hit her*? What the hell was she doing in there in the first place?"

"She's one of the on-duty staff, I imagine, General," Naada said, taken aback by her question. "The physician thinks her skull's fractured. She's been rushed to the theater."

"Of all the incompetent, idiotic . . ." She stopped, obviously remembering herself. "Why weren't my orders that no female personnel were to be allowed near him carried out?" she demanded coldly as she got to her feet.

"I've no idea, General Raiban," Naada stammered, taking a step backward. "I wasn't aware of the orders myself." The general's temper was legendary and he was not enjoying being this close to it.

"Where's Kezule now?"

"Outside your office, General. They'd finished the medical before he attacked the medic," he added.

"Bring him in, then when he's been escorted to the brig, you will find out who's responsible for not implementing my orders. By Vartra, I'll have the hide of the person responsible for this!"

"Yes, General Raiban," he said.

"Myule!" she called. "Myule, I want to be kept informed about the condition of Medic Rashou Vrenga," she said when her aide appeared. "I don't care what I'm doing, you keep me updated. You heard what's happened?"

Myule nodded.

"See that those on duty in the brig are aware that no female personnel are to be allowed near the area while we have Kezule on board—in fact, clear that section for the next three hours!"

"Yes, General."

"Bring in your prisoner, Lieutenant," she ordered. "I'll see him now.

Eyes still hurting from the rapid changes in light, he stood blinking in front her. Owlishly he watched her get to her feet.

"Where are his clothes?" she demanded. "I ordered him examined, not brought here naked!"

One of his guards held them out to her.

"I don't want his damned clothing! Take the General to the brig and let him dress himself! See he's fed and given whatever it is he drinks." She turned her attention back to him. "General, I apologize for the indignity you've suffered. It won't happen again, I assure you," she said with stiff formality. "However, while you are our guest, I expect

you to refrain from lashing out at my staff. Medical personnel are not warriors; in any conflict, they are recognized by
both sides as neutral. I hope I've made myself clear."

He said nothing. What was there to say? Every time he
was brought into the company of these females, they insulted him. Worse; he, one of the Emperor's Faithful, had
let his disgust overcome his senses. He'd made a tactical
error in letting them realize just how much the presence of
their females angered him.

She made a gesture of dismissal and the guards pulled
him away.

"General Raiban, what do we feed him?" he heard her
aide ask her as they left the room.

"How the hell should I know! The data from High Command should be here by now. That's your job, Myule, not
mine!"

As he was led through the echoing corridors to the de-
tention area, he realized that he was on no military atmospheric vehicle. This craft was space going as well. He could
feel his fear glands begin to tighten and fought to control
them. The Sholans were capable of reading his scent messages, and he would be damned before he'd let them know
he was afraid.

So it hadn't been the hairless female's species who had
found the Sholans as he'd surmised. It had been the Sholans themselves who had advanced to this technological
level. Obviously his own kind had never returned to reclaim
this world. Why not? The Empire had desperately needed
the raw materials this system had to offer. What could have
happened to prevent them returning?

They knew his kind, though, and in this time, but they
were obviously not a current worry of theirs. What did they
want from him? What could he know that would be of use
to them after all these years? If they found what they
wanted, it would mean his end—ripped to shreds by an
angry mob such as had dealt with Fyak and his companion
in the desert before they left. There was no real difference
between the sharpness of the Sholans' teeth and claws and
the ferocity of Valtegan females at mating time.

Again he felt his fear gland muscles tighten, but this time
he was unable to prevent them emitting their telltale scent.

He tensed, waiting for the inevitability of their attack on him.

"By Varta, he stinks!" said one of the troopers. "Another like the Touibans! Pity he doesn't smell as pleasant!"

"Shut up! You know he understands us," warned the other, pulling him to a halt in front of a broad windowed cell. Slapping his hand on the palm lock, he gave a voice code and the door slid open.

He was pushed into the cell, his clothing thrust into his arms, and the door sealed.

"They'll feed you soon," said the first guard, his voice sounding slightly remote through the speaker. "Water's in the faucet by the basin, and behind that half-door you'll find sanitary facilities."

Left alone, he was confused at their reaction. They hadn't turned on him as would his own kind. Why not? Still puzzled, he walked over to the bed. Doubtless he'd have plenty of time ahead of him to find out more about his captors. Now he regretted being stationed out in the desert rather than in one of the Sholan cities. At least if he'd been there, he'd have had more experience of this species. Throwing his clothes down on the bed, he turned his mind to other things and proceeded to check out his cell.

* * *

Once they'd eaten, Carrie and Kusac fell into an exhausted sleep that was broken only by the need to feed their daughter. Rhyasha sat by the crib late into the night, watching her granddaughter, hardly any more able to credit the miracle of her existence than Carrie and Kusac themselves. She left only when urged to do so by Konis.

But, Konis! Our first grandchild, she protested as he led her away.

And their first child. Let them enjoy her alone. Soon enough they'll want your help!

By morning, Noni's advice had proved to be sound, and the mother of a newborn on the estate was hired as a milk nurse. Just as Carrie had needed to supplement her own diet while carrying Kashini, so now did the cub need more than her Human mother's milk alone provided.

When Kusac finally awoke around the middle of the day,

he left Carrie sleeping and went in search of Kaid. He found him sitting at his desk comm eating breakfast and writing his report

"Mind if I join you?"

Kaid indicated a chair with his fork. "Please do."

"What did Noni say about your injuries?" Kusac asked, sitting down beside him.

"She says I'm fine now. Gave me a pot of ointment for my hand to help bring down the new swelling." He indicated that Kusac should help himself from his plate.

Kusac flicked an ear in a negative. "If I can use your comm for a moment, I'll send down for some more food. D'you want anything?"

Kaid's ears pricked forward. "I could eat a second breakfast," he said hopefully. "Don't know when I've been so hungry."

"Time travel," said Kusac. "Noni said it had depleted our energy reserves, so we have to eat as much as possible in the next few days to build ourselves up again. Carrie's been hit worst by it. She hadn't the weight to lose in the first place; neither has Kashini. She was developing at an alarming rate those last four days before she was born. Did I tell you that maintaining the gateway we used to come back destroyed the crystal Carrie wore?"

"It did?" asked Kaid, eye ridges meeting in concern as he turned his comm round for Kusac. "It didn't harm mine. What about the cub? Did it affect her?"

"Not that we can tell. Both Noni and Vanna said she was as healthy as any newborn they'd ever seen. I can't help worrying, though. If the energy drain could destroy Carrie's crystal, it must have had some effect on them beyond Carrie's weight loss." He leaned forward and keyed into the kitchen, asking Zhala for hot food and coffee to be sent up.

Returning the screen to its normal position, he sat back. "I think we should tell everyone concerned that the way to the past has been sealed."

Kaid nodded slowly. "Our success may encourage more people to try. We want to avoid that. Whatever the reasons, too many people have died that way already. And the gateway *has* been destroyed, in our time."

"Kezule will be able to tell us if other travelers arrived at the temple while he was there."

"It didn't need Kezule and his warriors to kill them. All they had to do was arrive as the temple collapsed," said Kaid. "But you're right. We should say the way is closed. Apart from any other consideration, we don't want the past altered any more than it has been."

"How much of the truth do we tell Lijou?"

Kaid hesitated. "Let's play that one by ear. See how our debriefing with him goes. The series of events that enabled us to go back are unlikely to recur, but if they become common knowledge, someone could try to duplicate them."

"They couldn't duplicate your contribution, Kaid. It's unique. There are no other telepathic warriors from the past living on Shola."

Kaid stopped what he was doing and reached for his pack of stim twigs. "There is one other. Rezac," he said quietly. "If the message Carrie—and others—received is to be believed."

"He's not on Shola. Who else is aware of the sending?"

"I checked through the messages as usual this morning. Lijou heard it, and I'm pretty sure that your father did."

"What does Lijou say?"

"To contact him as soon as possible. I wouldn't bother. Given the time of day, I'll warrant he's on his way over here already."

Kusac grunted. "If he is, he can wait till we've eaten."

Some ten minutes later, true to Kaid's prediction, Lijou's imminent arrival was announced by Ni'Zulhu, followed by Lijou himself shortly afterward.

"You both look thinner, not that that'll last from the size of the meals you two are eating," he said, staring critically at them.

"Join us," said Kusac. "You must be missing your second meal by coming out here."

"I am. Your young sister Kitra—who seems to be growing up remarkably quickly all of a sudden—appears to have assumed the position of house-head. She said she'd see a meal was sent up for me," he said, pulling up a chair to join them. "Your son's been good for her, Kaid—in fact, they've been good for each other. I'm glad. I was afraid he'd never recover from the loss of Nnya and his son."

"They're only Companions, Lijou," said Kaid. "It's a little early to be seeing a long-term relationship."

"The Aldatan females know exactly who they want from the first, and tend to stay with that choice, unfortunately," Lijou sighed. "Not that you males are much different! Mind if I have some coffee, Kusac?"

"Help yourself. How do you mean 'unfortunately'?"

"Rhyasha broke many hearts when she forced her choice of Konis as a life-mate on the Clan Lord, that's all." He poured himself a drink. "Kitra's so like her. She'll have Dzaka, mark my words. I'd stake money on it."

"My sister's barely left childhood, Lijou," objected Kusac, helping himself to more bread. "She's not ready to choose a life-mate yet."

"You've news for us, Lijou. What is it?" asked Kaid.

"While you slept this morning, Konis and I've been busy," he said, sipping his drink. "He convened a special meeting of the Clan Council and between us, we pushed through the ratification of your new Clan. It's been done as you asked, you're an official sub-sect of the Aldatan Clan and are to be known as the En'Shalla Aldatans or just the En'Shalla Clan. At the next meeting, you'll be Invested and can take your seat on the Council of Seventeen."

"Seventeen?" Kusac frowned. "Oh. Sixteen plus ours." Suddenly it felt like the society he'd grown up in was changing too rapidly—yet he realized he was the one who'd initiated the changes. He shook his head to dispel the somber mood and grinned over at Kaid. "We did it, Kaid. We won our freedom from the Guilds and Clans!" He turned back to Lijou. "How are the members of our Clan chosen?"

"You choose those friends and colleagues you want to be part of your family. If they agree, they must formally accept your invitation and take the Aldatan name. Then they will have En'Shalla status like you. Choose carefully, Kusac," Lijou warned. "Being a member of your Clan will confer great privileges which could be misused."

"You needn't worry, Lijou. I intend to set it up so only the immediate family, those with Human Leskas, and our Brothers, will have the En'Shalla status. Apart from new mixed Leskas, we're not recruiting for members. As you know, we have all the people I want living here on this estate. I also intend to set up a ruling council with myself as head to see to all matters of discipline and policy."

"That should help ensure that future generations will find it difficult to abuse the responsibilities that come with power. This afternoon, Governor Nesul will pass a bill giving all lay-Brothers and -Sisters the rank of priest. Unlike Esken's priests, we all belong to one faith—the only faith with its own college of priests. We're also being granted the right to wear black as our designated color. When acting as warriors of the Brotherhood, our people will wear gray trimmed with black and drop the use of the Warrior Guild's red."

"I said this would happen," Kusac reminded Lijou. "It's going to mean a lot of reorganizing for you."

"It's work I will relish," said Lijou, sitting back in his chair. "Even as we speak, because you are now En'Shalla, your status within the lay-Brotherhood is being altered to show that you are priests. That includes you, Kaid."

Kusac watched his friend's thoughtful expression. Had he realized that now Lijou could ask for his own Guild? The Guild of Priests? It would take yet another portion of Esken's power away from him, making all priests subject to Lijou.

Yes. It occurred to Konis, too, the Head Priest sent to him. *And Nesul and Raiban. I've been told to apply for it at the next All-Guilds' meeting.*

What about the joint leadership of the Brotherhood?

It'll remain unchanged. Esken's priests will simply belong to me instead. Switching to speech, Lijou looked toward Kaid. "The council selecting the candidate for Guild Leader of the Warrior Brothers wish to reinstate you as a Brother."

Startled, Kaid stared at him. "Reinstate me?"

"As if Ghezu had never expelled you," agreed the Head Priest.

Kaid was silent for a moment, then began to laugh softly. "No, thank you, Lijou. The past happened, it can't be undone. Besides, being En'Shalla, what more do I need?"

"I said that would be your answer. It's never good to dwell on the past. Now," he demanded sitting forward. "Tell me your news!"

"Our news?" Kusac gave Kaid a humorous glance. "Who says we have news?"

Lijou made an exasperated noise. "Don't wrong-spoor me! I gave you my news. Start with Carrie and the cub."

"Both fine. Vanna's scanner and Noni both agreed on that. About the only thing they did agree on," said Kusac wryly, remembering the females' attitudes toward each other.

"Noni's here?" Lijou looked startled.

"For a day or two. She'll be staying at the main house with my parents until after Kashini's Validation."

"I'm impressed. Now the Margins. What did you find? Did you see Him?"

"We found Vartra," said Kaid. "He's not what you'd expect, Lijou."

"Just tell me!" There was a glint in his eyes.

"Things were different then, Lijou, very diferent. No Guilds. Instead they had places of learning where many things were taught all under the same roof. Vartra was a physician who worked there teaching genetics to younglings. Not a Physician like we have, but a doctor of research. There were a few telepaths then, too few in Vartra's eyes. He was working on a way to enhance their abilities and increase the likelihood of Leska links happening so as to breed more. He thought himself unTalented, but he wasn't. Carrie said he forced the genes into the patterns he wanted. Which is why the result was unstable, and also why no one can duplicate it."

Lijou let out his breath with a hiss. "So what are we, the very fabric of our being as Telepaths, is due to Him, and it's unstable?"

"Not necessarily," said Kusac, putting a reassuring hand on the Head Priest's arm. "When we left, he was working on a way to stabilize us. We may well be the result of that stabilization."

"Where do the Humans fit in?"

"He took a blood sample from Carrie. Going back to the Margins contributed to our future and my own Link with her."

Lijou sat silently for a moment. "It's ironic, isn't it? Our fears of the future you and Carrie represented are what drove you back to the past to create what we feared."

"It had to happen, Lijou, because it did," said Kaid.

"I know," he sighed. "And I was right about you," he said, wagging a finger in his direction. "You *were* chosen before them!"

"Not quite, but I won't argue the point," Kaid murmured, trying not to let Kusac catch his eye.

"So how did He become a God—or is he?" This was Lijou's crucial question and they could see and feel his anxiety. Was their whole faith based on sand—or rock?

"He's a God now, that's indisputable," said Kaid. "I believe it was a mixture of guilt and His Talent that caused it. I don't know how Gods are formed, Lijou. That's your department."

"Guilt?" Lijou looked from one to the other.

"It wasn't completely his fault," said Kusac. "His students used the serum before it was fully tested. It's as well they did, because that generation of enhanced telepaths were all that stood between Shola and the Valtegans. He had to send his best people out on what was virtually a suicide mission. He hated having to do that."

Kaid stirred in his seat. "Lijou, there wasn't time to ask many questions. What we did gather was that the telepaths allowed themselves to be captured by the Valtegans, then somehow managed to place themselves next to important leaders. It was Rezac and Zashou who gave the signal for their attack to begin. What the nature of their attack was, we don't know, but a Valtegan starship, out of control because the telepaths on board created dissension among the command crew, hit our lesser moon. That caused the wholesale destruction on Shola that we call the Cataclysm."

"Fyak wasn't that far wrong, was he? We were significantly involved in causing the Cataclysm," said Lijou thoughtfully. "When you say Rezac and Zashou, you do mean the same Rezac who sent the message to Shola that Carrie intercepted, don't you?"

"The same," said Kusac. "They're on Jalna, with Jo, Davies, and Kris."

"Konis said they'd been captured by the Lord there. We must get them back safely to Shola. What they can tell us will be invaluable! Most of what we've discussed must not go beyond these walls," he said, looking from one to the other. "These are matters for our Order, not for the world at large."

"Raiban will know about some of them already, Lijou. We brought back a Valtegan general—Kezule. The one who convinced Fyak he was a god."

"Then we must decide now what Raiban should be told,"

he said. "More, we must talk, in depth, of what our Order should know of your meeting with Vartra."

A knock on the door heralded the arrival of Lijou's meal.

* * *

Carrie stood looking down at the freshly bathed cub lying on the padded nursery surface. The infant—her daughter—lay on her stomach, limbs splayed slightly out from her body, hands spread wide. Her skin, still pink from her bath, showed through the blonde down that covered her. The tiny tail, barely more than a short, stubby triangle, was held close to her rear. It was hard to think that she'd given birth to this small furred scrap.

The cub lifted her head an inch or two off the mat and sniffed the air, blindly searching for her mother. She gave a soft mewl of distress.

"Well, pick up your daughter, child," said Noni brusquely. "Don't let her get upset or she'll not settle properly for her feed."

Leaning down, Carrie carefully folded the cloth around her cub, picked her up and carried her over to the bed. Noni watched as she settled herself.

"So Tallinu delivered her, did he? A novel experience for all of you, I'll not doubt! A useful male to have about." She peered sharply at Carrie as she began to feed her infant. "You do intend to keep him, don't you?"

"Yes, Noni, I do," she said, wincing as Kashini's hands, claws splayed, began to open and close against her breast. "Ouch! Her teeth are bad enough, but those claws of hers!"

"It's only for a few weeks, child. You should wrap her arms tight in her blanket if it's that painful."

"No, I couldn't do that to her," she said, gently caressing her cub's head with her free hand. "She'd feel trapped. She needs to be free to move as *she* wants." She looked over to where the old Sholan sat. "You know, I wasn't sure how I'd feel about her, but somehow it doesn't seem important that she isn't like me. She's my daughter and that's all that matters." Reflexively she held her baby closer, feeling a surge of love welling up within her.

"That's blood talking to blood, child," Noni laughed gently. "Would you listen to her? I can hear her purring from here! You and she have bonded all right!"

Despite their talk about Kashini, Carrie could sense Noni

was more interested in Kaid. Now that the old Sholan knew she and her cub were bonded, she'd turned her mind to other matters. Well, if she wanted to know, she could damned well ask! Noni had been enigmatic with all of them often enough, now it was her turn.

After a few minutes of silence, Noni finally let her curiosity get the better of her.

"And how did your night with Tallinu go? You left before I had chance to ask you. It has only been the once so far, hasn't it?"

"So far," agreed Kaid from the open doorway. "As for how our night went, shame on you for asking, Noni!"

Carrie looked up, smiling in pleasure to see him. They were so different, he and Kusac. Her husband, the telepath and scholar, as dark-pelted as midnight, and Kaid, the highly disciplined warrior-priest, his fur the color of the desert soil at Khezy'ipik. How could she care so deeply for two such different males?

"Have you no more respect for your elders than to go sneakin' up on them like that?" Noni demanded tartly.

"Not a lot," he replied, coming over to Carrie. "Kusac will be here in a few minutes to escort you down to the aircar." He reached out impulsively to touch Carrie's cheek.

"Hmpf!" said Noni, pushing herself slowly up from her chair. "So you're not a lovesick youngling! You do a fair job of imitating one!"

"You'll not goad me today, Noni," he said.

Carrie took his hand in hers and urged him to sit beside her. As he did, his larger hand enveloped hers, keeping it within his grasp. "I've come to spend a little time with Carrie, if she doesn't mind, not to argue with you."

"I'd like that," said Carrie, aware of his grip tightening gently as she spoke.

"I suppose I'd better leave you in peace," Noni grumbled, turning away from them and making her way slowly to the door.

When she'd gone, Carrie gently eased her hand away. "Kashini's heavier than she looks," she explained, using it to help support her cub's weight. "How's it going with Lijou?"

"He'll be here for a while yet," said Kaid. "Kusac asked

me to keep you company, and I, reluctantly of course, agreed."

"Of course." She matched his grin. "Tell me some more about the Triads, Tallinu. I know they formed so the warrior could protect the Leska pair, but there was more to their Link than that, wasn't there?"

"Some," he agreed. "You have to see them in relation to their time. The needs they fulfilled then don't exist now."

She could sense his evasion. "Historically," she conceded, watching the muscles of his face and ears relax. She found Sholans so much easier to read than Humans.

"Historically, after the Cataclysm, there were only a few telepaths left on this continent. Those that remained had to breed, to provide future generations. We know Vartra was trying to increase the number of Leska bondings, and that his virus, like our ni'uzu, affected those with nontelepathic talents, too. The result was that some warriors were drawn to Leska pairs and formed a bond—a Triad—with them. More often it was the female who had two lovers, or life-mates. Because few females could be spared to fight then, it was important that they be adequately defended."

"*Two* life-mates?"

He nodded. "All telepathic links, be they Leska ones or minor ones, started out as a way for the strongest talents to be drawn together—natural selection. With so few pure telepaths, they had to keep track of the family bloodlines, and the Triads meant that the inclusion of some warriors with minor talents made the gene pool larger. Later generations of Triads recognized that only one life-mate was needed so long as the cubs were parented and nurtured by all three."

"That's why Kusac registered our Triad at the temple," nodded Carrie. She felt his mind begin to retreat from her as he broke eye contact.

"There's very little likelihood of us becoming genetically compatible," he said quietly. "I think Kusac was being overly cautious. Even with Leska pairs, it takes a gestalt."

"You've been exposed to a gestalt, Tallinu."

He looked sharply at her. "Never!"

"Mara's, when we were at the ruins the day you left Valsgarth to find Khemu," she reminded him.

He looked away again. "That doesn't count. It has to belong to your own Triad."

"There isn't time for more cubs anyway," she said, changing the tone of the conversation. "We've got friends to rescue. Vanna says that now she and Jack are working together with access to both our species data banks, they're much nearer a breakthrough for this common contraceptive for the mixed Leska females. And while we were in the Margins, the military gave her all the equipment and people she wanted. It seems they're determined nothing will delay us going on this rescue mission, which suits me."

"You know about it?"

"Of course," she said calmly. "Once Kusac figured it out, then naturally I knew. I picked it up from you as well."

"Me?" His whole body showed his surprise.

"I've been able to pick up your occasional unguarded surface thoughts since before you and Dzaka fought."

He grunted noncommittally.

She nodded. "With Rezac and Zashou and three Humans stranded on Jalna, that makes five people. There's no way two of us can locate that many people, let alone rescue them, Tallinu."

In her arms, Kashini began to make tiny mewling sounds of distress as she lifted her head and turned to look up at her mother. They both felt the sudden burst of hunger and fretfulness.

Kaid winced. "She's very sensitive to your emotions. Dzaka's talent wasn't this developed even by the age of six."

"We've noticed," she said, lifting the cub up and holding her out to him. "Take her for a moment, please."

Cautiously Kaid accepted the infant.

Carrie laughed, feeling his confusion and reluctance. "I'd get used to it, Tallinu. You're her secondary father after all!"

He gave her a horrified look. "Her uncle!" he said, a pained tone in his voice. "Only her uncle!"

The cub clutched at his arms, sniffing curiously.

"I'll take her back now," Carrie said.

As she settled Kashini against her other breast, Carrie was aware of Kaid watching her. *You males are all the same,* she sent. *Fascinated by newborns!*

Not newborns, by their mothers feeding them, he responded, ears dipping in embarrassment. *You do realize I've been waiting nearly fifty years to see Kashini born, don't you? And I was right. She is very special.*

He reached toward Carrie, gently running the sensitive tips of his fingers across the curve of her breast, then lower, till he touched the cub's cheek.

I have to confess I'm no different from Kusac. His hand moved again, his fingers first touching hers then twining round them where they supported the child.

"How so? Surely you've seen other females feeding their cubs?"

"Never. Only the closest of male clan members are allowed to be present."

"For such a liberated species, you have some strange customs," she murmured, feeling a warm lassitude begin to creep over her. "Don't make me feel tired, Kaid. When I've finished feeding her, I want to go downstairs and join you."

"You should rest. You've got the Validation ceremony the day after tomorrow."

"I've rested enough for now. I've seen too much of the nursery and my bedroom."

Kaid laughed and leaned forward across Kashini to nuzzle Carrie's cheek.

The gesture was slightly clumsy and reminded her how unused he was to moments of affection. Turning her face to his, she brushed his lips with hers. She found the kiss returned with an urgency she hadn't expected, then, just as suddenly, he pulled back from her, ears slightly laid back.

"I'm sorry," he said. "I shouldn't have done that while you're nursing. Tell me, are you really unharmed by the birth? You were in so much pain, and I could do nothing to help you. I should have studied birthing when I knew we were going to the Margins while you were still pregnant."

She tightened her hand around his, mentally sending reassurances to him. "How could you, Tallinu? You were barely able to move when we brought you out of Stronghold. You were the one who had to study the Margin rituals at the shrine with Ghyan, you had to lead us back into the past. That was far more important than learning about birthing when we thought I still had another eight or more weeks left. Yes, I really am fine! Noni herself could have done no more for me than you and Kusac did."

"What about Kashini?"

"She's fine, too. She *is* too mentally aware for her age. She may even have been born with her Talent fully awake instead of growing into it as is normal. It may be due to me having to control the vortex, but we don't know. Whatever it was, although it's inconvenient for us, it hasn't seemed to bother her yet."

"Being your and Kusac's child, I'd be surprised if she wasn't unusual from the first," he said with a grin, easing his hand away from her and beginning to get up. "I must go now. We've still a lot to discuss with Lijou. I"ll see you when you come downstairs."

*   *   *

That night, the first of the winter storms came, and with it, the nightmares. Though the environmental screens cut out most of the noises, Kaid could still hear the wind howling round the villa. No house was silent, especially not one as newly constructed as this. He tossed and turned, listening to the creakings and soft rattlings, trying to identify their source until at last he fell into an exhausted sleep.

Even then, for him the sounds didn't stop. They grew louder, deeper in pitch till he was trapped within a roaring sea of noise. Heat enveloped him; burning particles ripped their way through his pelt, searing the flesh below. As terror gripped his throat in its jaws, he realized he was caught within the vortex of the gateway to the past.

If only he could make a sound—cry out, anything—he *knew* he could end it! He fought against the terror, against the paralysis that held his body rigid and constricted his throat. This couldn't be happening! He couldn't possibly be traveling back to the past again! The drug dreams were supposed to be over!

A strangled noise escaped his lips: It was a beginning. He tried again, this time managing a low mewl. The world righted itself with a sickening lurch and suddenly he was sitting up in bed, drenched in sweat and gasping for air. The echo of a sigh was sounding in his ears.

The door slid open and, framed by the light from the other room, he saw Kusac. A curt hand signal to someone obviously behind him, then his Liege came over to his bedside. With a murmured apology, Kusac reached down and touched his fingertips to the pulse at the side of Kaid's neck.

"I'm fine," said Kaid, turning his head aside.

Kusac let his hand drop. "May I sit?"

Flicking his right ear briefly in agreement, Kaid worked on slowing his breathing as Kusac perched on the edge of the bed.

"Carrie said you'd cried out."

"A dream, nothing more," said Kaid. "I'm surprised that with the dampers on she noticed."

"She sensed it through your crystal."

Against his throat, Kaid became aware of the warmth of the crystal and her concern for him. He didn't respond: she'd know how he was through Kusac. He pushed aside the cover and got up, heading to the dispenser for a drink of water.

"I'm sorry I disturbed her," he said, keeping his back to Kusac. "I know she needs her sleep. I'll stop wearing it."

"No need to do that, Kaid. This wasn't a complaint: We were concerned for you, that's all."

Feeling Kusac's hesitation, he turned. "I think tomorrow it might be better if I moved into the Brotherhood accommodation across the street."

"Why?"

"I'm healed now, there's no need for me to live here unless I'm on duty. And I'm less likely to disturb Carrie."

He watched Kusac's ears flick backward in surprise. "Kaid, I told you at Chezy, you're not my Liegeman, you're my friend, part of our family. Surely by now you know that our friendship goes beyond the need we had to form a Triad. There's no reason for you to leave. Your home is here, with us—if you want it. As for being on duty, I know you, you always consider yourself on duty, but there's no need for that now. These are your rooms, here for you whether you choose to use them or not."

Turning, Kaid returned to his bed, placing the mug on his nightstand. "I never apologized for leaving the way I did," he said quietly. "Nor thanked you for getting me out of Stronghold."

"There's no need. We understood why you needed to go," said Kusac, standing up. "We were just damned glad to get you back alive."

"You have my thanks anyway. I'll not disturb you again. It was probably that cheese Zhala served tonight."

Kusac grimaced. "It was a little strong, certainly not to

my taste. Look, Kaid, the last week has been unimaginable.
We traveled back fifteen hundred years and Varta knows
how many thousand odd miles as well as everything else
you've been through. We're all exhausted. Not just that,
time itself has played some awful tricks on us, you especially. We all need to take it easy, come to terms with
what's happened, what we've seen and done. At least we
have each other, and our Talents. If you have any problems, don't try to cope alone. Remember, Telepaths share
the bad times as well as the good."

Kaid nodded. "I'll remember. Thank you for coming.
You'd best go before your cub wakes."

Kusac rejoined his mate, still concerned about Kaid. Sitting beside her, he leaned over the crib, looking down at
their sleeping daughter. Carefully he placed his finger
against the tiny half-curled hand, feeling the gentle twitch
as the cub gradually came closer to waking.

"I still can't believe she's real," he said, moving his hand
to stroke the tiny blonde head with its closely furled ears.

"Oh, she's real," said Carrie dryly, pushing herself up
into a sitting position. "Every time I feed her, I know she's
real! Her teeth are like needles!"

Instantly his attention was on her. "I thought it would
be easier for you now we had the nurse."

"It is, but that doesn't blunt those teeth! My skin isn't
quite as thick as yours, you know."

He leaned forward to place his cheek against hers as she
smothered a yawn. "Then give yourself a break tomorrow.
Let the nurse feed her. Have the day to yourself."

"No thanks! I'd rather have the teeth than the pain I get
if I miss more than one feed. Thank goodness it's only for
a few weeks. Tell me, how's Kaid?"

"You know you're the only one who can sense him, Carrie. You know as much as I do."

"You saw him, though. How did he look? What did his
body language tell you?"

"As usual, not much. He put it down to Zhala's cheese,
which might not be far wrong considering it gave me
indigestion."

"I'm glad I couldn't have any! What did your instincts
tell you?"

"That it was the cheese."

"Not that! You know what I mean." She grinned, batting his hand away as he stroked her cheek.

"That whatever it was, he's keeping it to himself. There's not a lot we can do, cub, except keep an eye on him. At least the drug dreams are over."

"It should all be over now Ghezu's dead," she murmured.

"You've got me worried now, Carrie," he said, sitting back and regarding her. "You said Ghezu hadn't broken him. Was that the truth, or were you protecting him?"

"Kaid has to have some privacy, Kusac. We've learned how to create our own despite the closeness of our Link. He hasn't. His mind's still an open book, and I can't betray those involuntary confidences." She stopped for a moment. "It was the truth."

"A near thing, then?"

She nodded slowly. "Near. But that's not all he's coming to terms with. Learning that he was responsible for sending himself forward to live in our time, and worse, responsible for giving his child-self his adult memories of me, did hit him hard. I think it still troubles him."

He reached out to take her face between both hands, looking deep into her eyes. "If he needs you, cub, go to him. I don't begrudge what you and he share, because we have so much. I'm glad you chose him as your lover and our third. There's no one I could trust the way I trust him." He urged her closer, his mouth touching hers in a gentle Terran kiss that gradually became more purposeful.

Beside them, in her crib, Kashini began to mewl. With a sigh, Carrie and Kusac parted.

* * *

He was two years old again, racing down the tunnel from the upper level to the lower caverns when he collided with her. Papers went flying everywhere. Then she reached out and grabbed hold of him. He froze, hardly believing what he saw. She was so different, not like them at all. Her face, surrounded by a cloud of hair the color of sunlight, was as furless as her hands. Then she grasped him by the other arm and held him even closer. For the first time, he could smell her scent.

He woke with a start, breath coming fast and sweat again coating his palms. Sitting up, he rubbed at his eyes, pushing his hair back from his face in an effort to be sure he was awake. Gods! It had been so real! As if he'd been there. Reaching out with a shaking hand, he picked up the mug of water from his night table. Their trip to the past had released all the memories he'd tried to hide so long ago, and now they were making themselves felt. He took a long drink before returning the mug to the stand.

Determinedly he lay down. He wasn't going to let this dream worry him. So what if he remembered her from back then? It didn't mean that what he felt for her now was based solely on what had happened to him as a cub. The nightmare earlier must have triggered the memory.

It took some time to succumb to sleep again, and when he did, it was only to return to the past.

They stood in front of the entrance to the lab, an area that Tallinu had never been allowed near. He was excited, could hardly contain himself. So much rushing around! Everything was being moved—all their belongings. He was too young to help, so he amused himself running round seeing what everyone was doing. He spent the most time watching their visitors, the two Sholans and the strange female.

Running into her had frightened him, because he knew enough to realize she'd been expecting a cub herself and he'd been afraid he'd hurt her. They'd taken her to the doctor, but she must have been all right as she'd not been kept in the infirmary for long.

When it came time to leave, he went with Dr. Vartra to see the door to the lab sealed. He'd been shown the collar, given it, in fact, to put into the control panel recess.

"We have to leave it here, Tallinu," the doctor said.

"Why?"

"Because it has to be found there."

He thought about this for a moment. "Like a present?"

"Yes, just like a present." He heard the note of surprised pleasure in the doctor's voice.

"For her? For the stranger? Can we leave it for her?" he'd asked.

"If you wish."

"We have to leave now," said Goran. "There's no more time left, Vartra."

"We're coming," the doctor said, looking over his shoulder. "Are our travelers safe?"

"Yeah, all loaded up like you said. Have you put the collar in yet?"

"We're just doing it now."

He felt himself being lifted and held level with the control panel. "Put the collar in, Tallinu. We have to go now."

He'd placed the collar into the recess, watching while the doctor pressed the button to seal the lab doors. As the panel itself slid shut, Vartra took his hand and placed it against the rock wall, letting him feel the slight indentations that marked the concealed mechanism.

"That's where you press to open the panel, Tallinu. You'll need to remember this, so feel carefully over the rock."

"I'll remember," he said. He felt proud that an important adult like Dr. Vartra would entrust him with the secret of how to unlock the doors.

They turned away, the doctor still carrying him. A sweet was handed to him as they made their way down the corridors to the outside where the vehicles were waiting for them. By the time he was handed into their truck, his eyelids were beginning to feel heavy and it was difficult to keep them open. He was passed from person to person till at last he felt himself come to rest on a soft lap. He sniffed. The scent was familiar. Opening his eyes with an effort, he looked up to see the strange female.

Her hand rubbed against his cheek as she gathered him more comfortably on what was left of her lap. "Settle down now," she said quietly. "Go to sleep, Tallinu. It's going to be a long journey."

His heavy eyelids closed as he pulled himself closer, leaning his head against her belly. He fell asleep listening to the gentle rhythm of her unborn cub's heartbeat.

*   *   *

His troubled night had left him disoriented and tired. He kept to his rooms, working on his report, coming down only for second meal and then retreating to the sanctuary of his rooms again. The day seemed to be full of shadows for him—shadows and whispers—to the point where he began to wonder if the balance of his mind had been affected. By evening, he felt as if he were inhabiting a world of half-reality that was neither here in his present nor belonging to the past.

After third meal, he excused himself, saying he was going to visit the shrine and that he might remain there overnight.

Ghyan was surprised to see him. "I thought you'd still be resting," he said.

"I've had a bellyful of resting," Kaid growled, sinking his hands deeper into the pockets of the long winter coat he wore. "I want to meditate, Ghyan. Can I use the room I had before?"

"It's your room, Kaid," said Ghyan. "Can I get you a drink?"

Kaid shook his head. "Nothing, thanks. The peace of this shrine is all I need."

"How long do you plan to stay?"

"Maybe overnight, if you have no objection."

"None. As I said, the room is yours." The priest stopped, obviously choosing his next words carefully. "Before you go, can you speak yet of what you saw in the Margins?"

"Not yet. Father Lijou has asked us to mention it to no one as yet," said Kaid, turning to leave. "I mean you no insult, Ghyan," he added.

"None taken, Kaid. I'll see you're not disturbed till morning. If you leave during the night, would you stop by our night watch and let him know?"

"I will."

It was with relief that he closed the door of the small room behind him and switched on the psychic damper field. Now he felt that he'd truly left the world outside. He started setting out the oil lamp and the incense, taking comfort from the familiar tasks. There had been too much in his life lately that had been beyond his control. He needed this time of solitude and old familiarity—and isolation from the constant background awareness of the minds around him.

Thankfully, the room was heated. Shrugging off his coat, he looked in the chest at the foot of the bed for something more comfortable to wear. In it he found a black priest's robe—one of the Brotherhood's. Surprised, he lifted it out and unfolded it. It had his scent on it—old, but unmistakably his. Then he recognized it. It had belonged to him all those years ago in Stronghold. How in all the Gods' names had it come here? Then it dawned on him. Kusac had said that Dzaka had kept the room tended while he'd been missing in the hope that Vartra would guide him home. He must have kept the robe these ten years past, and brought it here for him.

A wave of emotion came over him at the thought behind the gesture. Despite their unresolved quarrels and stormy relationship, his son had cared enough to not only keep the robe, but to place it here against his return. He took off his jacket and slipped his arms into it, fastening it with the cord that hung from the waist. A sense of premonition, swiftly followed by disquiet, came over him as he did, but resolutely he pushed it aside.

He settled on the mat, lighting the ornate bronze lamp and crumbling the incense onto the hot charcoal. Scented smoke filled the air, swirling lazily as he began to chant the litanies. Gradually the tension began to drop away from him as he let himself sink deeper and deeper into the mediative trance.

For some time he stayed like this, at peace with himself as he repeated the teaching litanies of Vartra, examining each of them in the new light of what he'd learned in the Margins.

It began almost subliminally at first, sounding like the whispers that had followed him all day. Then it became louder, finally intruding into his consciousness.

Tallinu!

He needs to be focused on us.

He's not listening! Tallinu! Tallinu!

Calls himself Kaid now.

Kaid, dammit! Kaid!

Confused, his chanting began to falter as he tried to sense who was calling him.

He's not responding. We can't keep this up much longer!

Get him to do it. He's supposed to be the god, after all.

Maybe he'll listen to the doctor.

God? What talk was this of gods?

I can't!

You'd better, because we can't get him otherwise!

He heard the implicit threat. Litanies, chants, all forgotten, he began to mentally back away. This didn't feel right. Whatever it was, he didn't want to know. Then his mind was grasped and held. Powerless, he had no choice but to listen.

Kaid, we're not finished yet. There's work still to be done.

No! I've done enough for you! No more, Vartra, no more! His mind shouted the refusal.

You will return once more. You are at the heart of matters both here and in the future. You will return!

NO!

The room started to recede, and he felt himself pulled toward a heat and fire he recognized only too well.

Got him!

As if from a great height, he saw his body slump, then fall forward onto the floor. A white rime began to form over his robe, then, as panic started to take hold, the image faded and he was swept into a maelstrom of sound and heat and pain.

Fire licked along his limbs, burning and consuming him. The smell of seared fur and flesh filled his nostrils, and as he opened his mouth to scream, flames gushed out. Mercifully, his senses left him.

He woke to find himself lying on the floor wrapped in a damp robe. The lamp flame began to flicker as he pushed himself upright. Groggily he peered at it. The oil reservoir was nearly empty. He must have been asleep for several hours. Stiffly he got to his feet, wincing as his groin muscles complained. Too tired to be concerned, he blew out the meditation lamp and limped over to the bedside to activate the light. Stripping off his robe, he hung it over a chair to dry. With a shiver, he pulled back the covers and climbed into bed, passing his hand over the sensor to douse the light. Almost instantly, he was asleep.

Morning brought a vague feeling of disquiet and uncertainty. His meditation the night before had resulted only in half a night's sleep on the floor and the stiff and sore muscles that accompanied it.

Getting out of bed, he dropped down onto all four limbs. It would be easier and less painful to ease his muscles this way. Arching his back upward, he stretched his spine first, all the way down to the tip of his tail. Then he leaned backward till his forearms touched the floor, straightening his spine and flexing the large muscles in his shoulders and neck, easing the kinks in his upper back. Standing up again, he extended first his left, then his right leg behind him. Before he reached full stretch, though, the tenderness in his groin made itself felt once more.

Rearing upright, he gently pressed the inner surfaces of both thighs: definitely tender, which was both surprising and worrying as he'd not been with a female since the night he'd spent with Jaisa in the Margins. Even if he'd had company the night before, for those muscles to be painful was not normal.

Something had caused it, but what? Using the skills Kusac had been teaching him, he searched his memory, finding nothing to give him even a clue as to what had happened the night before. He remembered meditating, then nothing until he'd wakened cold and damp in the early hours of the morning. He shivered, knowing it had nothing to do with the chill air. Resolutely he put it from his mind. Whatever the cause, a hot bath would help ease the aching muscles.

A note from Ghyan inviting him to join him for first meal was waiting when he returned. Inevitably the conversation centered round Vartra and the Fire Margins.

"Matters have gone beyond the point where we can discuss them on a personal basis, Ghyan. You'll have to wait till Lijou briefs you himself."

"What can you tell me, then?" Ghyan asked in exasperation. "Tell me about the person!"

Again the shiver as wisps of memory seemed to drift briefly through his mind. They were gone before he could pursue them. "He's like us—subject to the same fears and self-doubt." Yesterday he could have said more, now he felt unsure, as if the person he'd met in the past had retreated within the legend. The whole topic disturbed him deeply.

He got to his feet. "I have to go, Ghyan. Thank you

for your hospitality, but I've things I must do before the Validation ceremony starts."

He returned to his room, changing back into his ordinary clothes. Looking at the discarded robe, he reached for it, and folding it, placed it in the small bag he'd brought. The gap in his memory troubled him, as had the faint voices the day before. Was his mind becoming unstable? Was it, despite what Carrie said, due to his newly awakened Talent? His blood ran cold at the thought. To be rogue, with an unstable Talent! He *had* to go to Stronghold. He was a danger to himself and everyone, especially her and the cub.

*   *   *

The afternoon sun had warmed the air, and Carrie found she wasn't as cold as she'd feared. The Validation ceremony, because of its unique nature in their case, was being taken by Father Lijou himself at the Valsgarth Estate. Her attention, though she stood facing the Head Priest, wasn't focused on him or the ceremony he was conducting. It was on her daughter, lying in the priest's arms. Kashini was fretful, disliking being separated from her mother. Though silent, she was moving restlessly.

It couldn't last much longer, Carrie thought. Lijou had already confirmed that their new Clan was a legally designated branch of the Aldatan family, all that remained was the Validation of her daughter's birth.

Flanked by Kusac on one side and Kaid on the other, she was brought back to the present by a nudge in the ribs from each of them.

"Since the time of the Cataclysm, the Validation of every cub has been important, but especially so when she is the firstborn and Heir of her Clan. So it is with Kashini," Lijou was saying.

Carrie took a deep breath and forced her mind into stillness, aware of the concern for her emanating from the two male Sholans at her sides. She could feel their mental presences supporting and encouraging her for the part she must now play in the proceedings.

"It is time for Kashini's mother to come forward and claim her daughter."

She could feel her heartbeat start to quicken as she took her first steps away from her life-mates and the anonymity she'd had during her pregnancy.

Lijou's mouth opened in a gentle, encouraging smile as she slowly walked toward him and held out her arms to receive her cub.

With a purring trill of contentment, Kashini's ears flicked in pleasure and her hands, tiny claws extended, reached out to catch hold of her mother's long hair.

This was the part she was dreading. Holding Kashini close, she turned to face the gathering, trying not to see the sea of faces now in front of her. The inhabitants of both estates had gathered to witness the ceremony. A flash of sunlight on metal drew her eyes briefly upward to where the autovid hovered above Rhaema Vorkoh of Infonet. She looked away, trying not to think of the fact that her image was being broadcast all over Shola—and beyond, to Keiss, where her father and brother would also be watching.

Look at me, cub, sent Kusac. *Forget everyone else. Remember only us and our family.*

Her eyes met his, then flicked briefly to Kaid. From both of them she felt the same support.

"Carrie Aldatan, will you name Kashini's father?" Lijou was asking.

Moistening her lips, she glanced at Lijou before looking back to her mate. "My life-mate, Kusac Aldatan," she said, aware of and annoyed by the tremor in her voice. To one side of the Clan gathering, she could see the visiting Humans standing watching. Suddenly light-headed, she gave a small shudder, then Kusac was standing in front of her, blocking her view.

He touched her cheek with his hand before leaning forward to fold back the blanket that covered their cub.

You're doing fine, he sent. *It's almost over now.*

They're both so different from me, she thought involuntarily as she watched his dark-furred hands reaching down for their child.

The differences are only skin deep, you know that. His thoughts were a mental caress. Carefully he took hold of the cub, then turning, he lifted their newborn high above his head so the Clans could see her.

Kusac's voice rang out across the grounds. "Look well, Clansfolk, so that you'll know your Liegena, Heir to the only En'Shalla Clan."

The roar of acceptance from the throats of the several hundred Sholans gathered there was deafening. Kashini added her comments by beginning to whimper and squirm, ears flattened to her skull in distress. After the warmth of her blanket, the cold of the afternoon air on her uncovered pelt was disquieting.

Carrie had felt the mental sigh of relief from all the Sholans present as Kusac had held up their daughter: she was their Liegena no matter what her outward form, but in this time of rapid change, they were relieved that she appeared Sholan like themselves.

Kusac cradled Kashini in his arms before turning back to his mate and holding out a hand for the blanket. As they wound her back in its comforting warmth, Carrie was aware of Lijou calling Kaid forward.

"As the third in this Triad, Kaid Tallinu," Lijou said to him, "you have a responsibility to this cub. Since her parents are Leskas, should anything happen to them, it will fall to you to raise their daughter."

Kaid nodded briefly as Kusac handed Kashini to him. Cautiously, he accepted the small bundle.

"She'll be like a daughter to me," he said, holding her close for a moment before returning her to Carrie. As he did, he leaned toward her, one hand touching her neck as he placed his cheek against hers.

Startled, she moved back slightly before checking herself. For him to touch her neck was to admit publicly to a physical intimacy with her.

"It's part of the ceremony," Kaid murmured. "You need to do the same."

She returned the gesture, then, as he moved to her other side, she felt him retreat even farther behind his mental shields and cursed herself for inadvertently hurting him. Having their relationship announced so openly had taken her by surprise. It was too new for her to feel at ease with it yet.

After the ceremony, they left the Clans feasting and returned to the main house with a small number of guests and close family members for their own quieter celebrations.

Carrie settled herself in a large comfortable chair, Kusac standing beside her while their friends and guests came over to see the cub and exchange a few words with them. Kaid hovered nearby.

She was concerned about him. He'd been quiet and distant all morning, but since the incident at the ceremony, he'd retreated behind the barriers he'd had when they'd first met. Then she saw Lijou detach himself from Rhyasha and Konis and begin heading toward her. Passing Kaid, he stopped, and after addressing a few words to him, took him by the arm and brought him over, too.

"I've a small gift for the three of you," he said, looking from one to the other, mouth open in a grin. "Kha'Qwa found a reference to them in one of our ancient records and we had them made up to give to you today." Reaching into the pocket of his robe, he drew out a small wooden box which he opened before passing it to Carrie.

With her free hand, she took it from him. Nestling on a bed of black plush cloth lay three identical silver pendants. The motif was of three interlaced spirals, and in the center lay a small, blue-white faceted crystal.

"Lijou, they're lovely," she said. "Are the crystals from Stonghold?"

"From Vartra's Retreat to be exact," said Lijou. "Triad members exchanged them to show their commitment to each other, but we thought you wouldn't take them amiss as a gift from us."

Kusac bent down to see them more closely. "They are beautiful," he said, holding the box for his mate so she could pick one up.

As she held it up, the light from the main windows glinted through it, painting a rainbow across her face. "It even incorporates the spirit of the gateway," she murmured.

"The design is as it was described, even down to the number of facets on the crystals," said Lijou equally quietly.

Carrie held the pendant out to Kusac. "This one is yours," she said. Reaching into the box, she picked up the next one and held it out to Kaid. "And this, yours."

He reached out and, taking it from her, looped the chain around his hand. "My thanks to you and Kha'Qwa," he said, his voice barely audible as he watched Kusac put his own pendant on, then take Carrie's from her and fasten it round her neck.

"I'm glad our gift pleases you," said Lijou. "They can be worn as necklaces or set into the ear. We thought this way you could choose for yourselves."

"Thank you both, Lijou," said Carrie, fingering the tiny crystal. "You must have been very sure of our success."

"I knew the God had marked you all," he said. "And I know you. If it was possible for any mortals to succeed, then I knew it would be you."

"Thank you, Lijou," said Kusac. "You should have brought Kha'Qwa with you. Be sure to tell her how much we appreciate the pendants."

"You have enough people here today," said Lijou. "Kha'Qwa preferred to remain at Stronghold in the hope she could visit you another time under less formal circumstances."

"She's welcome any time, Lijou," said Carrie.

Lijou inclined his head. "I'll pass on your invitation, Carrie," he said, as he moved away to rejoin the rest of the guests.

When she looked back at Kaid, Carrie saw he was still holding the pendant clasped within his hand. *Don't feel compelled to wear it, Kaid,* she sent, handing him the box. *Keep it in here.*

Silently he accepted it from her, but, surprisingly, he put it in his pocket. *I'll wear it for now.* Opening the catch, he reached up and fastened the pendant round his neck, letting it drop down to lie on the breast of his tunic. That done, with a nod to them both, he turned back to his unconscious surveillance of the room.

What's up with Kaid? Kusac's sending was concerned.

I think the past's catching up with him. Then the time for any private communication was gone as she saw Tutor Sorli advance on them.

Glancing at Kusac for permission, he crouched down at Carrie's feet so his face was level with her cub's.

He reached a tentative hand out toward the infant, his expression hopeful. "May I?" he asked.

She nodded, watching him carefully as he reached toward Kashini. The little one grasped the proffered finger with both hands, extending her claws to get a better grasp, and pulled it toward her mouth.

"She's like your bond-mother," he said, mouth opening in a small grin. "And yourself," he added. "You're as fair as she is."

Carrie smiled. "You're the first one outside our family to notice," she said.

"I've been keeping up to date with Physician Kyjishi's work on genetics," he said. "It's different for you, though. Your daughter is the first cub born to a Human mother. Our Sholan genes might be dominant, but Kashini's adaptation to your body has been different from Marak's. His mother is Sholan, after all."

He stopped, looking up at her. "But you don't care about any of that for now, do you?" His grin became deeper. "All you care about is that you have her safe in your arms. And what else should concern a new mother? May she bring blessings to your Clan, Liegena Carrie," he said, extricating his hand and getting to his feet.

"About time!" came a voice Carrie knew well.

Noni came limping over to stand beside Sorli. "About time you left," said Noni tartly. "Look at her! Carrie's almost asleep where she sits! Kusac, send for the nurse for your daughter," she ordered. "And Tallinu," she said, fixing Kaid with a glower, "carry the Liegena upstairs to her room. She needs to rest. She can come down and join us later," she said, forestalling Kusac's unspoken objection.

Carrie could feel the tension in his body as Kaid carried her upstairs. She knew she was partly to blame. "Tallinu, I'm sorry. I didn't intend to pull away from you during the ceremony. It just took me by surprise."

"It's nothing to worry about, Carrie," he said. "It wasn't important."

"It matters to me. I don't like feeling you so distant. You're treating me almost as if I were a stranger."

"Things are different now," he said quietly, stopping at the door into Carrie's and Kusac's old suite. "We're home. We've done what we set out to do. You have your En'-Shalla Clan, and your cub—and I've got to pick up my life again." He took her through the lounge to the bedroom. "I've asked Father Lijou to let me return to Stronghold for a while. He's agreed. It's time I began to study how to use my Talent properly."

"You're leaving?" The news stunned her. It was the last thing she'd anticipated.

"In a few days," he said, laying her gently down on the bed. "You've got Dzaka and T'Chebbi to guard you, you don't need me, too." He stood up, not looking at her. "I need time to make sense of what I've been through, Carrie. Time for meditation."

"You might not return." She could feel the thought there on the edges of his mind, unresolved as yet, but a possibility that he hadn't rejected.

"I don't know what I want to do," he said, turning away from her, tail swaying slightly. "But I'll always be part of you both because of our Triad."

"I thought you'd found peace with yourself when we were in the Margins. You said you had. What's happened, Tallinu? You had none of these doubts two days ago."

"That was then. I belong to the past, Carrie, fifteen hundred years ago, not now." His tail was flicking from side to side as he turned round to face her. "Can't you understand that I'm not the same person I was? I need to find out who I am now."

"I know who you are," she said quietly. "You're who you've always been, Kaid Tallinu, our friend—and more."

His eyes caught and held hers, his tail stilling. "Don't make it difficult for me, Carrie," he said, his voice barely audible. "I have to leave—for a while at least."

She could tell his mind was made up. "I won't try to persuade you to stay, but at least promise you'll talk to me before you make a final decision on whether or not to return. Don't just disappear like the last time."

"When I've had some time alone and know my own mind, then yes, I'll talk to you. I owe you that at least," he said reluctantly, looking away again.

Tiredly, Carrie lay back against the pillows, watching him. Perhaps that was what they all needed: time. They'd been through so much in the last few weeks, Tallinu more than either her or Kusac. He'd become so much a part of their lives that it was difficult to imagine him not being there. But what of him? So much of his life had been spent serving others, yet he deserved the opportunity to build a life of his own, too.

"I have to go now. Kusac needs me downstairs."

She nodded. "Don't let them exhaust you," she said. "You're not long out of your own sickbed."

When the opportunity presented itself, Kaid took Lijou aside for a private word.

"How soon may I come to Stronghold?" he asked. "We

need to discuss Vartra, and it's time I learned how to use my Talent."

Lijou regarded him shrewdly. "Something's changed, hasn't it? You, better than anyone, Kaid, should know Stronghold's no retreat. No one comes to us to escape from the decisions they should be making out in the world. There's no rush to set our policy regarding Vartra yet. En'-Shalla, Kaid. You have to play out the hand the God has dealt you. Besides," he added more prosaically, "we're still debating over who should become the new Brotherhood Guild Master for our warriors. It would be inappropriate for non-Brotherhood personnel to be with us at this time."

Kaid growled softly. "I'm not trying to escape from anything, and you know it. You're stringing me along, Lijou."

"Not so!" Lijou reached out to lay his fingertips briefly on Kaid's arm, his gesture one of concern. "I'm telling you no more than the truth. Visit me by all means. I'll help you any way I can, but until you've been back for at least a few weeks and tried to adapt, as your Head Priest, I cannot let you turn your back on the world and stay at Stronghold. Ghyan can continue teaching you here."

Kaid growled softly again and turned away from him. It was a long time since any institution had held authority over him, and already it rankled. He saw Noni staring disapprovingly at him from the other side of the room.

Going back to hide in that dark corner, are you, Tallinu? she sent. *How long before you face the problem this time? Another thirty-four years? D'you think she'll wait that long for you? When the Gods set a Triad together, it isn't easily broken apart, as you'll doubtless find out!*

Mentally he retreated deeper within himself, refusing to even acknowledge he'd heard her. Seeing Meral standing by the doorway out into the family gardens, he caught his eye and went over to join him.

"I'm relieving you," he said. "Report in to Ni'Zulhu, then you can go off duty. I don't see why I should be the only one to suffer!" His slight grin made a joke out of the words. "Besides, Taizia looks lonely," he added, nodding in the direction of the young male's heavily pregnant mate. "How long now?"

"Any time, Vanna says. The sooner the better, frankly. She's finding it almost impossible to get comfortable these days."

"Value your sleep while you can, lad. Your cub will arrive soon enough. At least Dzaka was four when he came to me—a much more civilized age!"

Meral looked at him curiously. "Don't you want more cubs? I was sure you would now that you're part of a Triad."

Kaid shook his head, mentally shying away from any thought of that. "I have a son to be proud of in Dzaka, I don't need any more. Now the sooner you go, the sooner you can join Taizia!"

As he stood looking over the gardens, he felt Noni's presence behind him.

"What is it now?" he sighed.

"There will be cubs, Tallinu, prepare yourself for that," she said quietly, coming up to stand beside him. "Your cubs. I saw them before, and I've seen them since."

"Leave me alone, Rhuna!" he said, fighting to keep his ears from flattening sideways in anger. "Will you never be done with your meddling? I don't want cubs! You don't know what you're talking about anyway. We aren't fully compatible."

"I only tell you what I see, not how it'll happen. In Vartra's name, Tallinu, live the life you've been given! Don't analyze or agonize over it. You've discovered your origins, you have the respect and love of those who matter to you, and your son is finally safe from Ghezu—what more could you ask for?"

"Peace from your meddling!" he snarled, losing his battle for self-control and storming off into the grounds.

From upstairs, despite her tiredness, Carrie had sensed his increasing mental turmoil and had kept a discreet link to him. He'd become as distant as if he'd returned to the old relationship of bodyguard and Liegeman, abandoning the closeness they'd all three found through the Triad and the shared experience of their journey to the Fire Margins.

Getting up, she slipped on her loose outer robe and fished under the bed for her shoes. Somebody needed to be close enough to help him, and the only suitable person she could think of was T'Chebbi.

CHAPTER 2

As Kusac left their suite to go down for first meal, he saw that beyond the environmental shields, the first snow had begun to fall. The inner courtyard, open to the sky above, was already covered by a blanket of white. Winters could be bitter and this one, if the recent gales were anything to go by, looked set to be such a one. On Jalna, where Jo and her party were, it would be spring; by the time they got there, it would be summer. It was almost worth going for the change of climate alone, he thought irreverently as a small shiver ran through him.

He was hoping to catch Kaid in the kitchen rather than disturb him in his rooms. Kaid had been in a strange mood for the last couple of days. All Dzaka could tell them was what they already knew, that his father felt distant and withdrawn—even from him. Kusac was hoping that what he planned to suggest they do today would help focus him on the present rather than worry about what was long past.

Pushing open their family kitchen door, he saw Kaid still sitting at the table, his meal just finished.

"Just the person I want to see," he said, sitting down opposite him. "We've been considering this mission to Jalna that no one's told us about yet, and we can't see how it can be accomplished by just the two of us. Especially now that there are two more people to rescue."

"Not two more, nine in all," murmured Kaid.

"Nine!" Kusac was shocked. "How did nine people . . ." He broke off to start again. "I think it's time you told us about Jalna, don't you?"

Kaid regarded him from under lowered brows. "I only found out for sure days before I left for Rhijudu. I didn't want to spoil your joy in Carrie's pregnancy."

Kusac made a gesture of denial. "That's unimportant. Just tell me now."

"It seems the Valtegan starship orbiting Keiss had four Sholan captives on board. Where they got them, we don't know, but it's likely they were picked up either at Khyaal or Szurtha. We do know that the Valtegans sold them on Jalna in exchange for supplies."

"Jo and Davies were sent down to rescue them."

"No," said Kaid, reaching out to refill his mug as Zhala came in with a tray bearing Kusac's meal and a jug of coffee. He waited till the cook had left before continuing.

"Jo Edwards, Gary Davies, and a Terran telepath called Kris Daniels were sent to find a Valtegan craft that crashed on the planet's surface after takeoff—crashed on interdicted ground. The High Command wanted anything they could find on the Valtegans, including any indication of what that craft was doing there. The four Sholans were to be left for you and Carrie to locate, and hopefully rescue."

Kusac poured himself coffee and began to eat. "Go on," he said. "Apart from the impossibility of the two of us locating and rescuing four people on our own, how did they plan to get round the fact that the Jalnians are humanoid and I'm obviously not."

"Jalna is beyond Chemerian home space. I don't need to remind you how paranoid they are about allowing the other Alliance races access to their sector. Apparently they've been trading at Jalna for the last fifty years. In keeping the existence of the world secret, they've also hidden the fact that it's a trading point for several other previously unknown species. It wasn't till the Valtegans called in there with the Sholan captives that they began to panic and confessed to the Alliance. Not that they're concerned about the captive Sholans, of course: They're demanding we go in and find out what those they call *our enemies* are up to."

"Nice of them," said Kusac wryly. "So once again I'm reduced to playing the role of a forest cat. Great."

His words brought a grin from Kaid. "Hardly. One of the species that trades there is similar to us—felinoid as you call it—but all of them are black furred. Given that two of the missing Sholans are telepaths, with your abilities and appearance, you make the ideal team. And," he let out his breath in a long sigh, "they want to field-test you as agents."

Kusac nodded. "It had to come, didn't it? That's why

we've gotten all the financing we've needed for security and setting up the specialized medical facilities here on my estate."

"Got it in one," said Kaid, looking down at his mug as he swirled the last of its contents around. "The Valtegan craft that crashed was illegally landing some object on the planet's surface, presumably for collection later. Jo and her group were trying to find out what it was."

"And did they?"

Kaid looked up. "You know they did. Rezac and Zashou."

Kusac frowned. "The Valtegans sold four Sholans into slavery yet landed Rezac and Zashou, free, on the surface? That doesn't make sense, Kaid."

"Not them, as such," Kaid amended. "They landed what could only be some kind of stasis cube. Inside it were Rezac and Zashou. Jo's group must have been captured as they opened it and released them."

"How d'you know all this?"

Kaid raised an eye ridge. "I have my sources," he said. "News of the stasis cube was picked up by our telepath on the Chemerian ship that took them to Jalna. If they weren't being held in some Lord's castle, the Sumaan troops on that craft would have gotten them out by now, but a castle in the middle of a busy town is a little too public. We aren't ready yet for an official First Contact with four new species."

"It's going to take a damned sight more than the two of us to get that many people out of captivity. Do we have *any* idea where the four Sholans are?"

Kaid's ear flicked in a negative. "None."

Kusac ate in silence for a few minutes. "Have some coffee. You've been nursing those dregs for long enough," he said absently, pushing his empty plate aside. "Carrie promised Rezac we'd come for them, so we're committed whether or not we want to be. The only questions now are how many will go, and who they'll be. If we're dong this, we'll do it on our terms, not theirs. It's our lives at stake, after all." He looked sharply at Kaid as the other helped himself to the coffee. "You're coming with us?"

Kaid hesitated, spooning sweetener and whitener into his drink, then stirring it. "Did Carrie tell you I'm planning to go to Stronghold?"

"Yes, but I got the impression it was for a short while."
Kusac tried not to let his surprise show. That Kaid might
not wish to be part of this mission hadn't occurred to him.
Perhaps it should have.

"I need some time to myself," Kaid continued. "I want
to learn how to use my Talent properly, and that I can do at
Stronghold. I don't intend to put myself in Esken's hands."

"Does that mean you're considering remaining on
Shola?"

There was a small silence before Kaid asked, "Why do
you want me to come?"

Kusac couldn't hide his surprise this time. "Because
there's no one apart from Carrie that I'd rather have at my
side. Surely by now you know how much I—and she—
trust you?"

"Trust. It comes down to that in the end, doesn't it?"
The question was rhetorical. "If I'm finished with Stronghold, yes, I'll come," he said.

Something was wrong, really wrong, Kusac realized suddenly. This was so unlike Kaid, even the Kaid from the
days on the *Khalossa*. "You'll help me plan for this mission, though?"

Kaid nodded. "I'll help, yes, and suggest personnel for
you. You'll want several Sholans if you can disguise them
as these aliens, but the bulk of people involved may have
to be Humans, with at least two or three telepaths. I can
find out who among the Terrans would be the best
choices."

At least he'd piqued his interest; that was a start. Perhaps
he'd change his mind nearer the time. Kusac pushed his
chair back. "Then let's get started."

Reluctantly Kaid nodded and got to his feet.

When they broke for second meal, Kusac remained in
his office. Switching the room's psychic dampers on, he
keyed in Stronghold's number on his comm. He felt guilty
at going behind Kaid's back like this, but he really was
concerned for his friend's health.

The speed with which he was routed through to the Head
Priest's private unit convinced him his call had come as no
surprise, and that he'd made the right decision.

"I've been expecting you to contact me," said Lijou. "It's
Kaid, isn't it?"

"You've noticed, too. He's cutting himself off from us, Lijou. Creating those mental barriers again."

"What's caused that?"

"I don't know, that's the problem. As to when, he started acting strangely a couple of days before the Validation. The day after the first storm, in fact."

"Could the storm have triggered it?"

"No idea, but he woke Carrie because of some nightmare or something."

"Nightmare? What about?"

"He didn't say—blamed it on something he'd eaten, but he woke again later. Did you know he spent the night before the ceremony at the Shrine?"

"Ghyan mentioned it. He said he seemed restless and uneasy: His eyes were heavy from lack of sleep the next day. Kaid definitely felt strained during and after the ceremony yesterday. Are you sure the la'quo's out of his system?"

"I checked with Vanna. She says he's clear of the drug."

"If not that, then what? A vision?"

"That wouldn't make him behave like a stranger to us, Lijou."

"He's asked me if he can come here to study. I told him he'd have to come to terms with the world outside Stronghold first."

"Let him come. Staying here won't make the situation any better. Perhaps he's right and he needs some time to himself. He's been through too much in the last few weeks."

"I'm not sure it's wise for him to be allowed to turn his back on his problems," began the Head Priest.

"I'm asking you as his Clan Leader, Lijou," said Kusac. "He's a priest of Vartra and a telepath, doubly your concern. It may be the only way to let him catch his breath again. Concentrating on studying his Talent may help him feel he's achieving something worthwhile and is in control of his life again."

Lijou chose his words carefully. "Do you think his mind has become unstable because of what Ghezu did to him?"

"I don't think so. Carrie will say very little about it. She says, and she's right, that he's entitled to his privacy, but she did admit he had been close to the edge."

Lijou sighed. "As you say, he's my responsibility, and I have no option but to agree. The Brotherhood always looks after its own. However, if I contact him about this, he'll become suspicious, which is the very thing we want to avoid. I'll wait till he gets in touch with me again."

Kusac nodded. "Thank you, Lijou. Do what you can to help him. He's close family now."

"Of course he is. He's your third, after all."

"Even without that. I've a feeling our Triad Link is involved somehow in what's bothering him. He was talking about trust earlier. What could have happened to affect his trust of us?"

"I've no idea, Kusac, but you have my word that I'll do what I can to help."

"Thank you, Lijou."

After the call, Kusac sat in silence for a few minutes. Had Kaid had a vision of the future, one he was so desperate to avoid that he was going to turn his back on them? What could be so awful as to make him do that? Sighing, he switched off the dampers and got to his feet. Time to join them downstairs for second meal.

*　　*　　*

Rhyaz of the Brotherhood was closeted with General Raiban.

"So you want us to handle the interrogation. What do you hope to find out from him?"

"The vital information we need is the location of his homeworld," said Raiban, getting up and going over to her dispenser. "Second is finding out what they were doing here in the first place." She selected two vassas, a strong Sholan distillation of wines and fruit, and returned to her desk, passing one to the newly inaugurated Brotherhood Guild Master. It had been a long day for her, if not for him.

"Lastly, I want to know what kind of people we're dealing with, what motivates them, what hurts them, what their world's like."

"You want to understand them," nodded Rhyaz, ignoring his drink for the moment. "The Keissians know more about this species than anyone. I'll need some personnel from there transferred to any team we set up. Who have you got?"

"The main Keissian expert is on Jalna at the moment, more's the pity," said Raiban, sipping her drink.

"Jo Edwards."

"You're well informed."

"Of course. We make it our business to be. Who else have you got?"

Raiban pulled a folder from her desk drawer and opened it, quickly scanning through the dozen or so pages within it. "We have Dr. Jack Reynolds, currently on the Valsgarth Estate. He was the main medic on Keiss during the Valtegan occupation. He works with Physician Vanna Kyjishi who's also there. Between them they have the best working knowledge of Valtegan physiology. All the other experts are theorists as they've never seen a live Valtegan."

"A start," said Rhyaz, taking a small sip from his glass.

"Of course, Carrie and Kusac Aldatan are only available for a limited time due to their forthcoming mission to Jalna. Still, we can perhaps utilize their Talents while they are still here. Then there's Consultant Chiort and Mentor Mnya from the *Khalossa* who were involved in interrogating most of the captured Valtegans."

"All of whom died. I think not, General Raiban. We'll leave them on the *Khalossa*."

"All the modern day Valtegans on Keiss were terrified of us," said Raiban. "Not Kezule. He's a different class of Valtegan entirely. Chiort and Mnya could well be successful."

"They dealt with corpses, not living beings," said Rhyaz. "We need a permanent mixed Leska team. Who is available?"

Raiban's ears tilted, and her tone was sardonic. "*I* have no one. The En'Shalla Telepaths all owe allegiance only to your temple. Kusac Aldatan will allow them to hire themselves out as contractees, however."

Rhyaz lifted an eye ridge as he put his own glass down. Father Lijou was right: Kusac was no one's fool. "I'll have to deal directly with them, then. However, I'm sure your files include likely employees." He gestured to Raiban's folder.

"There's Interpreter Zhyaf and his Leska Mara Ryan, if Kusac will release them from the estate."

"Oh, I think he will," smiled Rhyaz. "From all accounts it will keep Interpreter Zhyaf interested and give him a break from young Mara. Anyone else?"

Raiban shrugged. "There are others, but they're still in a period of assessment, and we've been given no data on their Talents as yet."

Again Rhyaz was impressed. "No information comes from the estate to you, Raiban? You surprise me."

"That place has tighter security than a demon-fish's ass," she snapped, letting a brief flash of her frustration show through. "My people don't last there. On one pretext or another, they're recycled back here by Ni'Zulhu!"

"Very well. You make the initial approaches to Kusac regarding this pair, and I'll take it from there. The Brotherhood will want full authority over how the questioning is conducted, naturally."

Raiban growled. "And will therefore take full responsibility if anything happens to him!"

Rhyaz smiled and picked up his glass. "Of course. Standard procedure, General. Standard procedure." If Raiban thought him an easy mark because he was newly appointed to his position of Guild Master, she could think again. He'd survived Ghezu's rule unscathed, and managed to keep some degree of higher ethics going in the schoolrooms. He was well able to Challenge Raiban, and win.

*   *   *

For Kusac, the afternoon had been spent in the ruins working with the Touibans again. While he'd been there, he'd examined the lab, trying to see if he could identify any of the ancient equipment now that he'd actually seen some of it working while they were in the Margins.

His arrival had caused a stir, and he'd been treated with an unwonted degree of awe by several of the Sholans there—including a couple of the Brothers. He'd done his best to dispel it, not least because he didn't feel any different for having been to the Margins—only damned grateful he lived now rather than in that troubled time.

Kaid had remained at the villa with Carrie. Vanna and her sister Sashti had arrived before Kusac left and swept his mate off to the main bathing room for a pampering session, including a massage. Kaid had been invited to join them but had hastily backed out on the grounds that someone was needed to keep watch over the cub in case of intruders.

The late night feeding over, Carrie was unable to settle their daughter. Kashini wriggled and squirmed, mewling fretfully in her tiny, high-pitched voice.

"I'll take her for a while," offered Kusac, sitting on the edge of the bed beside her.

Gratefully, Carrie handed over the cub. "I don't know what's gotten into her," she said, rubbing her arms. "She was like this when I fed her this morning. The nurse said she's been fine with her, though. And she's growing so fast! She weighs a ton, Kusac."

"Hardly," he laughed, holding his daughter upright against his chest so she could see over his shoulder. "Cubs do grow quickly at first. She'll slow down soon, I promise you."

As if by magic, Kashini's mewling stopped to be replaced by a low, trilling purr. Carrie watched as the infant's hands clutched hold of Kusac's pelt and the small body began to relax against his.

"Great," she said "It's your fur she's after. Well, there's no competition, is there?"

Kusac reached out with his free hand to run his fingertips across Carrie's face. "You like my fur, why shouldn't she? She's only taking after her mother." His tone, both mental and verbal, held a teasing note and Carrie had to smile.

"That's better," he said, resting his hand on her shoulder. "You're tense. If you're finding Kashini so heavy, you should do what Vanna does. Lay Kashini down on the bed beside you and feed her like that. Then her weight won't matter."

Carrie grunted, making herself more comfortable against the pillows. "And how do you suggest I get round the problem of being unfurred?"

"You don't need to. What Kashini is responding to now is being held upright. Lying on her back isn't a natural position for her, it's one of surrender, of acknowledging you've lost a Challenge, or," he said, hand clasping the back of her neck firmly as he leaned toward her, "accepting your lover."

"I like that one," she said, leaning forward to meet him.

Their kiss was gentle, a stolen moment as their child began to settle. Reluctantly they parted.

"I think she's been picking up the physical tension her weight's causing, and that plus the fact she doesn't want to be on her back, are all that's wrong," Kusac said, reaching up to gently caress his daughter's tiny head.

"You're probably right," Carrie conceded. "I'll try what

you suggest tomorrow. By the way, shouldn't we have had a Link day round about now?"

"Not necessarily. Mother said you might not feel the Link compulsion just after Kashini's birth because of your hormone levels. It isn't dangerous so long as we stay close during this period."

"Will you go to Vanna?"

He hesitated, then decided to get up and put the cub in her crib before answering. He knew by the infant's slow mental rhythms that she was close to sleep.

"Not for the moment," he said, returning to his mate's side. "Vanna's becoming more involved in her own life at last. I'm hoping Kaid will settle with someone so that when you and he are together ..." He tailed off as he saw the expression on her face. "What is it? Is there another problem with Kaid?"

"Have you seen him since third meal?"

"No. Why?"

"He's wearing one of the Brotherhood robes."

"It's cold, Carrie. Even I'm feeling it," he said reasonably.

"That's not why he's wearing it. He's begun to create a physical barrier between us now, I can feel it."

Kusac sighed and climbed into bed beside her. "Then it's probably just as well I contacted Lijou. Don't let it upset you, cub," he said. "I'm sure we're as much victims of what's troubling Kaid as he is." He wrapped his arm across her waist and gently urged her closer.

"I'm not upset," she said. "I just wish I knew what had happened. It was so sudden. One day he was gentle and affectionate in his own way, the next, it was as if there was a wall of ice between us. Did I tell you I asked T'Chebbi to keep an eye on him?"

"Sensible. They're old friends. Her concern won't make him feel like his privacy's being invaded or that we're keeping a watch on him," he said, nuzzling the side of her neck.

"More than that, if there is anything wrong, she'll spot it quicker than anyone. The pity is she won't be able to go to Stronghold with him."

"Lijou and Kha'Qwa will watch over him, don't worry about that. I think our esteemed Head Priest regards Kaid as God-marked. He doesn't want any harm to come to him either."

Carrie turned to face him. "Dim the light," she said. "Kashini's asleep now." She began to gently stroke the short, soft fur that covered his face. "Have I told you what a good father you are?" she asked drowsily. "If I haven't, I meant to. I love watching you two."

A wave of pride swept through him and he began to gently lick along the edge of her jaw. *I try,* he sent. *You and Kashini mean everything to me.* He wanted her so much, but he knew she wasn't ready yet for a more intimate contact.

Soon, she replied, running her hand across his chest. *The magic will awaken me soon.*

I know. It's just so damned hard to wait! Resolutely he suppressed his lustful thoughts and contented himself with breathing her scent and holding her close within his arms.

* * *

T'Chebbi watched Kaid from behind a pillar in the garden. He stood looking out toward the woodland beyond the front gate. He'd been standing ankle-deep in the snow like this for the last half hour; it worried her.

"What is it, T'Chebbi?" he asked quietly, turning round to look at her hiding place.

She came out from behind the pillar and plowed through the snow to join him, pulling her coat tighter around her. "Should have expected that." She stopped a few feet in front of him.

"Why are you watching me?"

"She asked me to."

Kaid's ears flicked, once. "She?"

"The Liegena. Said you might need company at night."

"Company?" His ears laid themselves backward, flat against his skull.

She shrugged. "Talk. Company."

His eye ridges met. "She . . . told you what?"

T'Chebbi's ears flicked a negative. "Nothing."

"She's wrong," he said abruptly, turning away from her, raising his ears with an obvious effort. "I don't need anything."

T'Chebbi watched him stalk off into the villa, robe billowing behind him in the wind. "Wrong, Brother Tallinu," she sighed, waiting till he was out of sight before following him. "You need her. You just won't, or can't, admit it."

* * *

He paced angrily round his room, holding the Triad pendant tightly in his damaged hand. He felt used, but by whom he didn't know. The same with his anger—there was no one at whom he could rightly direct it. Part of him wanted to wear the pendant as openly as did Carrie and Kusac, but the other side . . . He flung the piece of jewelry at the far wall with all the force he could muster, hearing it hit and fall to the floor. Against the base of his throat, the crystal began to warm. He'd pull it off, too if he could bear to touch it, but touching it would bring back memories—and worse, enhance her presence in his mind.

He growled deep in his throat. Memories. He wanted none of them! His mind was playing tricks on him, hiding something from him. Why had Vartra reached out from the past and touched him in his new life? Why couldn't He have left him alone? He laughed, knowing the sound wasn't pleasant even as he made it. The life of a renegade hadn't been so bad. There had been no feelings, no memories to hurt and plague him, until Garras had contacted him. And no alien female to . . . what?

Flinging himself down on his bed, he pulled the cover over himself. He winced slightly as a fold caught on the edge of his right hand where his smallest finger had been. Ghezu. There were times when he woke with the smell of his own freshly spilled blood in his nostrils and the memory of Ghezu holding him upright by the hair. But Ghezu was dead. He'd personally killed him.

The memory wouldn't leave him though. *If I have to cut the information from you an inch at a time, I'll do it.* He could hear his voice, smell his scent. The room seemed to darken around him as he struggled to break free of the memory and the fear.

Another rushed up on him, banishing the first. Noni.

There will be cubs, Tallinu, prepare yourself for that. Your cubs. I saw them before, and I've seen them since.

"Not if I can help it," he growled, pushing himself up and lifting his head and shaking it in an effort to dispel the memory of her words. "Not if I can help it, you old crone! Not even if Vartra Himself orders it!"

Vartra. The God had used him—for what? He tried to remember, but it was becoming difficult to think straight. Half a lifetime of service to Him in return for . . . betrayal.

Betrayal? Harsh words, Tallinu. He knew the voice—knew it only too well. *What is one when balanced against the future of a species?*

Once more the beginnings of fear rushed through him, and determinedly he pushed them back.

"You're not a God. You're a male, no different from me!" His voice was low but intense in his anger.

I was. Who do you think speaks to you? How do I, dead these thousand and more years, speak to you if I'm not a God?

"Varza! He was the God, not you!"

Gently mocking laughter echoed inside his head as he put his hands up to his ears. "I won't listen to you any more, Vartra! It's over! I've done what you asked!"

Varza once lived, too. He was fragmented, first by the collapse of His Temple, then by His monastery. The people wouldn't let me sleep. They used Him to see me, Tallinu. They disturbed my peace, condemning me to live on, to exist without rest till I am as you know me now.

Kaid looked frantically round the room. "I'm imagining this," he growled. "You aren't real!" He began to shiver and cautiously let go of his head to pull the cover up again.

Not real? Look at me! A sigh sounded in his ears as he shut his eyes, afraid to look. *What's real, Tallinu? You helped create me! You and the generations of worshipers who demanded that I be there for them! You are my link to the future and the past, Tallinu. I cannot release you. Our work is not yet done. Look at me!*

He could feel the cold seeping into the room, making him shiver till his teeth began to chatter, chilling him to the very soul.

Look at me! The voice sounded loudly in his ears. He could smell the scent of the nung incense, of the world of the Margins.

He opened his eyes, afraid of what might happen if he didn't. Before him, at the foot of his bed, stood the image of the God. He sucked his breath in, trying not to cry out in terror. It was Vartra, the Vartra of the Margins, but dressed in traditional Warrior gear, complete with the two swords held in the back-slung harnesses. Gods! He was hallucinating! He really was losing his mind.

The soft laugh, mocking yet not unkind. *A male like you, lose your mind? I hope not, Tallinu. You, one day, will find peace. But not until our work is finished; we have our people to save. Trust, Tallinu. Now you must really trust me! Remember this meeting, remember what I've told you.*

He watched, frozen in fear, as the apparition turned. Beyond it a flicker of light shone, and it was toward this that Vartra seemed to walk. A few steps and he was gone. In his head Kaid heard the echo of the God's last words as he lost consciousness.

Remember this meeting.

He woke to feel a hand shaking his arm. He hadn't the strength to do more than let out a strangled cry before the light came on and he saw it was T'Chebbi. He lay there shivering convulsively as she leaned over him and took hold of his hand.

"Excuse," she said apologetically, reaching for his neck and placing her hand against his pulse. "You're burning up." She pulled the cover aside to feel his robe. "You went to bed damp," she said, frowning. "No wonder you have a fever."

He lay there watching as she went to the bathing room and returned with a large towel. It hurt to breathe and his joints ached. All he wanted to do was lie still till he felt better. Pulling him upright despite his feeble protests, she efficiently stripped off his robe and began to towel him briskly.

"Standing in snow for so long, then sleeping in damp clothes. You trying to die, Kaid?" she demanded, lowering him back to the bed. "Easier ways!" She left him and went to the wardrobe to fetch another woolen robe. Flinging it over the bed, she took hold of him and began to pull his legs off the bed until they touched the floor.

"Get up," she ordered. "Put robe on. I fetch Vanna."

At last he felt impelled to make the effort to speak. "No," he said hoarsely. "Not Vanna. She's got a cub, too. Take me to Jack."

She looked at him in disgust. "You mad? Take you out in this state? You die for sure!"

"No. Must leave. Mustn't give it to them or the cub," he insisted, taking hold of the robe with shaking hands. He knew without doubt that this time he was beyond dosing himself. "Take me, T'Chebbi."

She made a dismissive sound and turned to leave.

He caught hold of her. "T'Chebbi, I must leave here. This ever's dangerous, I know it! Could kill Kashini. Trust me!"

She searched his face, then nodded slowly. "Very well." She helped him get to his feet and put on his robe.

"Tell Jack, cleanse the room," he said, keeping his head turned from her as slowly they began to make for the door. "You must be isolated, too. Jack won't get it, nor any Humans except Leskas."

She grunted. "How you know so much? If you so sensible, why stand in snow?"

"Cold helps reduce the temperature. Tell Jack that, too." He leaned against her, trying not to cough as they made their way slowly toward the staircase.

Fifteen minutes later, they were knocking on the door of Jack's private quarters in the medical unit.

"God Almighty . . . What's up with him?" Jack demanded, flinging his door wide open.

"Fever," said T'Chebbi, supporting the almost unconscious Kaid. "Said bring him here. Contagious to Sholans and Human Leskas. He's burning up, Physician."

Jack ran his hands through his hair, thinking rapidly. "Take him to the ward on this level," he said. "Give me five minutes to get dressed."

"Where?"

"Back the way you came, second door on your left. Take the first room you come to and get him into bed." He turned back into his room then stopped. "Get that robe off him. Can you take his temperature?"

T'Chebbi raised an eye ridge. "I'm a paramedic," she said. "I'll do it."

Jack hurried into his bedroom and hastily got dressed, cursing himself briefly for assuming that because T'Chebbi used words sparingly, she wasn't the equal of any other Brotherhood member.

When he joined T'Chebbi in the single room, she silently held out the diagnostic unit to show him Kaid's temperature.

"He said use ice," she said. "Was more lucid than I thought."

Jack went over to the wall-mounted comm and called the medic on duty. "We've got a fever patient. I need as much ice as you can get and as fast as you can get it. Get buckets

and collect snow if you have to. I'm in room five." H
turned back to T'Chebbi. "Right. What d'you know abou
this? What kind of fever is it?"

"None I know," she said. "He kept saying *Carri
knows.*"

"Use the comm. Wake them and find out what you can,'
he said, going over to where Kaid lay on the bed. He pulle·
back the thin sheet that T'Chebbi had used to cover him
then proceeded to open both the windows.

"We'll have to put up with the cold until the ice arrives,"
he said. "Unless we get his temperature down fast, he coul·
go into convulsions."

Bleary eyed, Kusac answered the comm. "T'Chebb·
what is it?" Then he saw the hospital room behind her
"What's happened?" he demanded, instantly awake.

"Kaid has a fever," she said. "Serious. One he says you
and Liegena could catch. Says Liegena knows what th·
fever is."

"Carrie knows? How could she know? Are you sure i·
isn't the fever talking?"

She shook her head. "Not. Ask Liegena. Temperature
dangerously high. She knows, he says."

"I'll get her." He left the lounge and returned to the
bedroom at a run. Carrie was already half out of bed.

"I picked it up," she said, pulling on an overrobe and
hurrying into the lounge. "T'Chebbi, Kaid says I know the
fever. Did he say how?"

"No. Only other things he said was ice. He wants ice to
lower his temperature. Says only Sholans and Human
Leskas can catch it."

Kusac watched Carrie turn white and put her hand to
her mouth. "Oh, Gods, no!"

"What?" he demanded, grabbing hold of her and turning
her round to face him. "What is it?"

"The fever! The first fever he never caught! Vartra's serum!
He must have caught it while we were in the Margins!"

"The dream you had! That's got to be it! T'Chebbi, let
me speak to Jack." He waited impatiently till Jack came to
the screen. "Jack, back in the past, Vartra used a strain of
ni'uzu to carry his genetic enhancements. It triggered a
fever, but it was stronger than normal. It raised the temperature to the point where some patients suffered convulsions

nd brain damage. A lot of them died. You've got to bring
is temperature down!"

"I intend to, lad, don't worry," said Jack, glancing over
is shoulder. "The ice has just arrived, I've got to go."

Carrie pushed Kusac aside. "I'm coming over, Jack," she
aid. "The fever is a stronger variant of the one we caught.
Ve should be immune."

"You'll come nowhere near the center, Carrie," he said
ternly. "It's under quarantine as of now."

"Jack!"

"You've got a young baby to care for, lass. If you catch
t, then I've three patients to care for instead of one! Now
et me get on."

"Jack, he'll get violent," she said. "Rezac did. He may
eed to be restrained."

"What did they do with Rezac?"

"He had a Leska. They put her beside him. Jack, don't
et him die!"

"I'll do my best, lass. Now, I must go." The screen
olanked out.

"Kaid's had the modern fever, Carrie. He should have
some resistance to this one," said Kusac, putting his arms
round her.

"I hope so. God, I do hope so," she said, letting him
lead her back to their bedroom.

"T'Chebbi, you're going to get yourself settled in the
room next door," said Jack as he and the medic, now wearing face masks, began to pack the snow around Kaid's still
form. "You've been exposed, so I want you isolated, too.
With any luck, you might not have caught it."

"I'm staying. I'll help," she said firmly, helping herself
to a mask. "If I have it, then nothing now will stop it. Must
take a week to incubate since they've been back that long."
She picked up the empty buckets. "You stay with him. I
get more snow."

"Let her, Doctor Reynolds," said the medic. "It's the
dead of night, no one's about. One we've got him packed
in ice and his temperature starts to drop, then we can all
get into bio-suits. It makes little difference if the Sister
helps, so long as she isolates herself from Sholan telepaths."

Jack began to mutter imprecations. "I suppose you're

right. We could do with talking to Vanna as well. Her first
hand knowledge of the modern virus will be of great help."

"She'll be safe enough once we've set the room up as a
quarantine zone."

"Very well. How's his temperature doing?"

"Falling slowly."

"Put the sheet over him again. We'll try a layer of snow
over that and see if it's enough. I want that temperature
down fast!"

* * *

Half-formed images haunted Rezac, making it difficult to know what was real and what was not. Voices
faded one minute and were amplified the next as he
moved restlessly in his bed. The sheets were pulling
at his fur, pushing it against the lie, making each folli-
cle burn with discomfort. Every movement hurt his
joints, yet he had to try and move away from the
pressure of the sheet.

He dreamed he was made of fire, a fire that burned
from deep within him. He opened his eyes only to see
beams of flame streaming from them. Devastation followed his gaze, burning and searing everything
around. Fear touched him then, his own fear, and
instinctively he fought against it, lashing out at it with
taloned hands until he was held down forcibly.

"Get that wound dressed immediately," Dr. Nyaam
ordered as the nurse staggered back holding his
slashed and bleeding forearm. Nyaam continued to
fasten Rezac's limbs to the bed frame as Goran
grabbed for the arm that he'd managed to pull free.
Maro held on grimly to the other limb until Nyaam had
finished, then began picking up the scattered ice
packs and replacing them around Rezac's body.

"This'll only make him struggle more," said Goran
dispassionately.

"I hardly think you're qualified to give a medical
opinion," said Nyaam, moving beside the security
chief. "He's as much a danger to himself as to us in
this state."

"I know my people, Nyaam, which is more than you

do. You sent for me because you couldn't control him.
I've told you already, put the female in his bed."

"Don't talk rubbish," the doctor snapped. "Look at
what he did to my nurse! One blow from him and his
Leska would be dead. Then we'd lose them both."

"He'd quiet down," said Goran. "He'd know she
was there and he'd stop fighting. They're linked mentally, right? So why're you treating them separately?
What have you got to lose, Nyaam? At this rate they'll
both die. You can't get their temperatures down, and
he's exhausting himself by fighting your restraints."

"If he weren't so violent, I might consider it, but
look at him," said Nyaam.

Rezac, already pulling frantically at the restraining
bands, had lifted his head as high as he could and
was leaning over trying to snap at those holding his
wrists.

"We haven't got a bed wide enough for both of
them, even if I was prepared to countenance the risk,"
Nyaam added.

"I told you it would make him worse," said Goran,
stepping back to allow Maro in to replace the ice
packs. "He's a warrior, Nyaam. Restrain him, and he'll
fight all the harder against it. That's going to give him
convulsions faster than a high temperature."

"Goran's right," said Vartra abruptly. "Try it. We've
nothing to lose. If we can't get their temperatures
down within the next hour, Rezac is certainly going
to go into convulsions."

"I'm telling you, he'll kill her," said Nyaam, looking
over to where Dr. Kimin was beginning to unfasten
Zashou's bonds. The young female was lying semico-
matose and panting, having exhausted herself with
her own struggles.

"Fix the two beds together," said Dr. Kimin. "Use
the restraint straps, anything. We know nothing about
these new Leska pairs. We've all seen how Zashou's
condition has paralleled Rezac's, something that
doesn't happen with normal Leskas. For all we know,
we could be making the situation worse by keeping
them apart."

Maro pushed Zashou's bed over beside Rezac's
while the other nurse took the restraints from Dr.

Kimin and dived under the beds to lash the legs together.

"I'm advising you to keep the restraints on Rezac for the moment," said Nyaam. "I think you're taking a foolish risk, and I refuse to help you. However, I've no doubt you're going to ignore my opinion."

Goran began moving the ice packs from what was now the middle of one large bed, making room for Zashou to be placed beside Rezac. The sheet, dried out by his body heat, was taken off him and as he flinched away from contact with the others, he lurched briefly against Zashou. He froze, then as Zashou was moved closer so the contact was maintained, his body went into spasm.

"What did I tell you?" demanded Nyaam, grabbing his hypo off the treatment trolley behind them. "Just touching her has made him worse! Give her an anticonvulsant before she starts, too! Hold him still for the God's sake," he said, trying to get a grip on Rezac.

Goran took hold of Rezac's head. "Hold his arm," he ordered Maro.

Nyaam stuck the needle in Rezac's arm while the two males held him as still as possible.

Almost as they watched, the spasms that wracked his body began to diminish until suddenly, Rezac relaxed and lay there limp and panting, his tongue partially protruding from his mouth.

"Give him some water, Layul," said Dr. Kimin, leaning forward to unfasten the restraints.

Nyaam frowned. "What do you think you're doing?" he demanded, reaching out to stop her. "You should be moving the female away! That's what started the convulsions!"

"For the God's sake, Nyaam, look at his wrists!" she said, batting his hand aside with one of hers. "The leather has already lacerated him, he's bleeding. Goran's right, Rezac can't help but fight against your restraints. That's what made him convulse, not Zashou! Do something useful, pass me the dressings," she added. "We're working blind with these two, we've no idea what will help them since they're not responding to our treatment like any of the other telepaths. They're suffering identical symptoms, as if they were one person, not two." She took the dressings that Goran held out.

"I'd put money on it that they're amplifying each other's fever dreams. If they're touching, it might just give them the reassurances they need to cope with the hallucinations," she said, wiping the blood from the cuts with an antiseptic pad.

Vartra began unfastening Rezac's other arm.

"On your head be it, then," snapped Nyaam, standing back.

Kimin looked up from bandaging Rezac's wrist. "This isn't a competition, Nyaam," she said quietly. "If you want me to take sole responsibility, then I will. I have a gut feeling that Goran is right, and this will work."

Maro poured a small amount of water onto Rezac's tongue, and when he swallowed reflexively, gave him a little more. When his panting began to decrease, Goran released him.

Rezac moved his head slightly, his face creasing in pain. He opened and closed his hands, automatically checking to see if they were free.

"We telepaths learn to trust gut feelings and instincts, Dr. Nyaam," said Maro quietly as he replaced the water container and then began dressing Rezac's other wrist.

Nyaam grunted in disbelief. "We've got the damper on, Maro. Neither you nor Dr. Kimin can be picking anything up from him."

"We're inside its influence, Doctor," said Kimin, releasing Rezac's ankles. "Our thoughts don't escape the field, that's all."

It was Zashou who moved first, turning on her side to lie close against Rezac. The anticonvulsant had sedated him, and he continued to lie still save for a slight movement of his head and the blinking of his eyes.

He fought against the lassitude, trying to make sense of what was going on around him. His eyes refused to focus: everything was a blur that made his stomach tighten with nausea. The touch of her body against his was somehow helping the fire in his body die down. When a damp sheet was laid over them, it no longer made him burn, and the coolness that surrounded him, except for where they touched, was welcome.

He was tired, and his eyes began to close. His arm was too heavy to move more than a few centimeters. His hand touched her, reflexively closing on her arm. Now he could sense her mind, feel his heartbeat slowing till it matched hers. All he wanted now was to join her in sleep.

*   *   *

This was the memory of the dream that Kusac relayed to Vanna at her request. Armed with that information, Vanna had Kaid placed in an IC unit with freezing air ventilating it. Within the formfitting chamber, he was effectively restrained, unable to harm himself or anyone else. His every function was monitored, and they were able to accurately gauge the effects of the febrifuge they were using.

Kaid hovered on the edge of crisis for four hours before his fever broke. By the next day, conventional nursing was all that was needed. Though very weak, he was on the way to recovery.

For the first two days, he just lay there, too weak to do anything but eat the food they fed him and sleep. He was allowed no visitors apart from Jack and his nontelepathic nurse until on the third day he was pronounced well enough to be returned to the villa.

He tried saying he ought to move into the Brotherhood accommodation, but when Carrie heard of it, she threatened dire consequences if he didn't return home.

When T'Chebbi did succumb to the virus three days later, it only took the form of a heavy cold, and she was released a couple of days later.

Despite the fact that with so short an incubation period, it was unlikely Kaid could have contracted it in the Margins, Jack and Vanna ran DNA tests on both him and T'Chebbi.

"Well, looks like we've got our gene pool," said Vanna, turning away from her analyzer to look at Jack. "He's fully compatible with us mixed Leskas now, and T'Chebbi is definitely altering. There is, however, a subtle difference in their DNA compared to ours."

"Different, lass?" Jack looked at her over the top of his \[gla\]sses. "How different?"

"If I was speculating, I'd say we have in them an im\[pr\]oved version of our DNA. He *must* have caught it in the \[m\]argins; there isn't any other logical answer. I'll have to \[do\] an in-depth analysis to find out more. At least we have \[a\] vaccine. I think we should start inoculating now rather \[th\]an wait for an epidemic."

"If Kaid was the original carrier, we've contained it, lass. \[T\]here isn't going to be an epidemic. Besides, we don't \[kn\]ow how it will react with your and Carrie's newborn \[cu\]bs—or the Human Leskas for that matter. It might not \[b\]e so benign for them."

Vanna sighed. "You're right, of course. I should've thought \[of\] that."

"We're both tired, Vanna," said Jack, closing down his \[co\]mm. "I think we should call it a day now. The night \[sh\]ift's on duty. Relax and get some rest yourself."

"It's only a couple of hours till third meal," she admitted, \[ch\]ecking her wrist unit. "Will you join us, Jack? You should \[co\]me over more often. It isn't good for you to spend so \[m\]uch time on your own."

"Well actually," said Jack, looking slightly sheepish as \[h\]e pushed his glasses up onto the bridge of his nose, "I \[w\]on't be alone this evening. A rather nice young lady called \[K\]szoe has offered to cook a meal for me."

"Ah. Fieldwork, Jack?" She grinned as she got down \[fr\]om her stool and went over to her desk for her coat.

"Excuse me?"

"You were always curious about physical relationships \[b\]etween our species. Now you'll find out for yourself, \[w\]on't you?"

"I beg your pardon, Vanna, but the young lady's only \[o\]ffered to make a meal. Nothing else was implied, believe \[m\]e." He sounded faintly offended.

"What did she say to you, Jack? Her exact words."

"Just that she'd like to cook for me, so I could sample \[s\]ome real Sholan home cooking."

"Did she say she wanted to spend some time with you?"

"I believe she may have, but what difference does . . ."

Laughing gently, Vanna put her hand on his arm. "She \[w\]as telling you she wanted to pair with you, Jack. By ac\[c\]epting, you told her you were also interested. Since she's

offering to cook for you, she's interested in a longer re~~la~~
tionship. It may not happen tonight, but she'll make h~~er~~
invitation soon."

Jack's mouth opened in a wide "O" of surprise. "But .~~..~~
but . . . what do I do?"

"Enjoy your meal, of course," she chuckled, moving pa~~st~~
him toward the door, "and let nature take its course." S~~he~~
stopped in front of the door and turned back to look ~~at~~
him. "Unless you're not interested in that kind of relatio~~n~~
ship with her, in which case, get in touch with her now an~~d~~
tell her so. You wouldn't want to cause her embarrassmen~~t,~~
I'm sure."

"No, of course not! But I couldn't call her and cance~~l~~
Vanna!"

"Then have a nice evening," she said, leaving him alon~~e.~~

* * *

It was Kaid's first day up and about, but when Kusa~~c~~
reached the aircar, he was already waiting for him.

"I appreciate your company," said Kusac as he took o~~ff~~
and turned the craft toward the capital, Shanagi. "Are yo~~u~~
sure you're well enough?"

"I'm fine. I'd rather be doing something than sittin~~g~~
around, and we have to see Raiban."

"It's good to know you're coming to Jalna with us. Wha~~t~~
changed your mind?" He was curious. Kaid was still re~~-~~
served since his illness, but now he seemed to have som~~e~~
sense of purpose, though what it was, Kusac had no idea.

"I could do with some time off-world," Kaid said. "Be~~-~~
sides, I'm curious about anyone who can mind-speak acros~~s~~
space when most telepaths can't broadcast even the lengt~~h~~
of this continent."

"Raiban's as interested as we are, believe me. Thankfull~~y~~
she's not registered the fact that Carrie did the same whe~~n~~
she replied to him."

"Probably assumes, and Esken or Lijou will have con~~-~~
firmed it, that her reply backpacked, so to speak, on Re~~-~~
zac's sending. Isn't that what usually happens?"

Kusac turned to look at him. "Yes. It is. You've bee~~n~~
doing a fair bit of study already, haven't you?"

Kaid shrugged. "The lessons with you and Ghya~~n~~
rubbed off."

"Raiban will want us to leave as soon as possible."

'She'll not want us leaving with Carrie only partly
ined. If you've no objection, I'd like to have the final
y as to when we're all ready."

"By all means. You can take charge of the whole training
ogram if you want to."

"No. I'll leave that to the Warrior Guild and the Brother-
od. They know what they're doing. If we present them
th our plan, they'll train you in the best ways to imple-
ent it. I'll be kept informed while I'm at Stronghold."

They flew on in silence for a while, Kusac debating with
mself on the wisdom of trying to draw Kaid out and dis-
ver what was wrong. He'd just decided to do so when
aid picked up the folder lying on the console shelf.

"I think I'll go over Raiban's dossier again, if you don't
ind," he said quietly. "The fever left me tired enough
at I forget details now and then."

Kusac made an appropriate reply, cursing his timing. A
oment or two earlier and . . . or had Kaid known what
e intended to say? A moment's reflection, and he realized
at his next move had been predictable. So be it. Kaid
oviously didn't want to discuss the matter.

"Why don't you remind me of the salient points?" he
iggested. "Won't do any harm to be as thoroughly conver-
nt with the background information on Jalna as possible."

"We'll be efficient," said Kaid. "I don't intend to risk
ur lives or liberty on Jalna. I knew I was walking into a
ap at Rhijudu; I didn't foresee Dzaka nearly being
aught, too."

"No criticism intended, Kaid," said Kusac, hearing the
light chill in his companion's voice. "Some things can't be
voided, and I'm sure your capture was one. Without it,
e wouldn't have solved the problem concerning Fyak or
he Margins."

"I don't believe in fatalism," Kaid growled, opening
he folder.

*   *   *

"Clan Leader," said General Raiban, standing up as they
vere ushered into her office. "Kaid. Please, take a seat."
She indicated the two chairs set slightly to one side of her
lesk. "Clan Leader what, Kusac? Or is it Brother Kusac
ow?"

Kaid answered her. "Both are correct, General Raiban,"

he said smoothly. "It avoids confusion between my Lie
and his mother."

Raiban looked back at him, registering the black ro
he wore, and raised a questioning eye ridge. "You're
Brotherhood Priest again," she observed. "I'm glad to s
you've recovered from your stay with Ghezu. Perhaps
was for the best he eluded us that night at Stronghold."

"As you say," he murmured, sitting down. "My than
for allowing my Liege the time to liberate me."

"A debt repaid, Kaid," she said, then turned back
Kusac. "I know you've been fully briefed on the bac
ground to this situation. This meeting is to bring you up
date and tell you what our campaign is."

"With respect, General Raiban," said Kusac, settli
himself in the somewhat uncomfortable chair, "I think th
campaign is better organized by ourselves. We need a pla
that's flexible enough to adapt to the conditions we'll act
ally find on Jalna. The Chemerians consider the native po
ulation of the world to be extremely violent. That has
be taken at face value until we can assess it in person."

"I disagree. This is a military operation and . . ."

Kaid stirred, but Kusac gestured him to silence. "W
have the right to refuse," said Kusac quietly. "En'Shalla.

"You *are* a member of the Forces . . ."

Again Kusac interrupted. "Not anymore, General. En
Shalla negates that."

Raiban regarded him in stony silence.

"However, if you'd care to draft contracts for my people
I'm sure many of them would consent to being retained a
specialists in their field. As far as this mission is concernec
our terms would be total control over personnel and plan
ning—in consultation with you, of course."

"You've taught him too damned well," growled Raibar
looking over at Kaid with an angry glare.

"He has his own abilities, General," murmured Kaid
working hard to hide his amusement. Indeed, Kusac
showed every sign of surpassing what he had hoped he'c
become.

She reached forward and activated her comm. "Bring ir
the contracts, and the maps of Jalna," she said, then pushec
a folder toward each of them. "These are the proposec
personnel and the campaign. We'll look them over wher

ve shown you the maps and you've been brought up to
ate on the current situation."

Without thinking, Kusac reached mentally for Kaid. *That
ily old she-jegget knew all along what we'd do!*

Of course.

Realizing that not only had Kaid received him unassisted
or the first time, but had answered him as well, he glanced
narply at him. His companion appeared as self-contained
; ever, even his mental tone had been urbane. The old
.aid had returned completely. There wasn't a trace of the
oseness they'd shared over the past few weeks. He pushed
is concern aside and concentrated on Raiban.

Her aide entered carrying a folder and a large laminated
nap. The latter she spread on the desk in front of her, then
anded the folder to Kusac before leaving.

"I regret I have a short meeting I must attend during
econd meal," said Raiban. "Read the contracts then, and
e'll discuss them after we've eaten."

Kusac nodded as he and Kaid rose and joined Raiban at
er side of the desk to examine the map. Surreptitiously
Kaid turned up the setting on his personal damper. If he
ould receive Kusac, then it wasn't working properly. He
nust have knocked it during the night.

*   *   *

Tutor Sorli was in the Guild library when he sensed Mas-
er Esken approaching. With a sigh, he blanked his comm
and turned to the students at their workplaces.

"Take an early meal," he said. "We'll reconvene at four-
eenth hour."

As the young people collected their belongings and
began to leave, Sorli sat back to wait. When would the
Guild Master realize that the political influence he'd lost
over the last few months had never legitimately been his
n the first place? Ever since contact with the Humans had
been established, winds of change had been howling round
not only their Guild House, but the whole of their society.
Shola would never be the same, and it was as logical for
Master Esken to try and halt the changes as to attempt
to stop the winter storms. He wondered what it would be
this time.

Esken came over to where he sat at one of the long
study tables.

"Have you heard what's happened now?" he demande[d] voice taut with barely checked anger as he sat down. "N[o] of course you haven't! I've only just been informed m[y] self!" He waved an official letter in front of Sorli's nos[e] "Nesul has not only given the Brotherhood full priest[ly] status, but has appointed Lijou in ultimate control over *a[ll]* priests! That includes mine! They will no longer answer t[o] me, but to Lijou!"

"May I see the letter, Master Esken?" Sorli asked, hol[d]-ing his hand out for the offending document.

"Here!" Esken all but threw it at him.

Sorli scanned the contents. It was as his Guild Maste[r] had said. Father Lijou was being appointed in charge of a[ll] priests. Meticulously he folded the letter and handed [it] back. "It makes sense, Master Esken," he said. "He dea[ls] exclusively with religious matters. We can only give thos[e] who wish to become priests the most general of instruc[-] tion."

"So can Lijou!"

"He trains his priests not only for pastoral duties, bu[t] also in the mysteries of Vartra. And three of his Guil[d] members have traveled back to the time of the God, Maste[r] Esken. The existence of Vartra has been proved beyon[d] doubt. The same cannot be said of any other religion."

"So what? It didn't take the Aldatan cub going back t[o] the Fire Margins to tell us that!"

Sorli hesitated. "Then might this not be Vartra's will, Master Esken?"

Esken growled. "Vartra's will! More likely it's the Alda-tan will!"

Inwardly Sorli sighed. He had hoped his esteemed superio[r] had gotten over his conviction that the Aldatans intended to destroy him politically, especially in view of the new agreement between themselves and Kusac Aldatan.

"Master Esken, this solution is better for our priests. You have said many times we cannot provide either the people or the time to train them to the level they really need."

"They manage, don't they?" demanded Esken acerbi-cally. "We have very few complaints."

"They manage," agreed Sorli, "but I suggest that's more to do with their strength of character than our training methods. What will probably happen is that Master Lijou will set up a training center for them where they will re-

:ive a course in pastoral care, and from there they will go
n to a specific center for their own religion. I don't see him
ble or wanting to take on the whole task singlehandedly."

"I don't care how he plans to do it, it shouldn't be hap-
ening, Sorli! Priests traditionally come under the Tele-
ath Guild!"

"I realize that, Master Esken, but surely the people who
lo the most in the way of pastoral care in a variety of
ircumstances, be it on Shola or in space, are those best
uited to train priests?"

"It's not just that issue at stake, Sorli. It's also the fact
hat come the next All-Guild meeting, they will insist Lijou
las his own guild!"

Sorli felt an uncharacteristic flash of rage, and this time
lid not suppress it. "Then we bow to the inevitable, Master
Esken. If we fight it, we look like fools!"

Stunned, Esken sat back in his chair, ears tilting back. "I
lidn't realize you felt so strongly."

Sorli got to his feet and paced round the table till he
eaned over the seated Guild Master.

"Since we first heard the news of Kusac and his Human
Leska, you've changed. From the reasonable Master I was
pleased to serve under, you have become one I can no
longer support! You have let Khafsa influence you far too
much! I tell you, Master Esken, give it up, accept what fate
the God sends us, or today I leave the Guild and apply to
join the Brotherhood!"

"The Brotherhood," murmured Esken. "Surely you are
overreacting, Sorli."

"It would be preferable to remaining here, Guild Master," said Sorli, straightening up. He turned and stalked
from the library, not stopping till he reached the sanctuary
of his own room. He no longer cared about his position as
the next Guild Master. If Esken continued like this, it could
take more years than Sorli had left to repair public opinion
regarding the integrity of the Telepath Guild. Lying down
on his bed, he wondered whether the afternoon would see
him packing, or working with his students in the library.

* * *

Third meal over, Kaid decided to retire early. The day
at Shanagi had gone better than he'd thought it would, he
realized as he shut the door to his suite behind him. A

large part of that was due to the personal damper he was now wearing. It gave him a measure of self-confidence and peace of mind. It stopped the headaches and the intrusive snatches of mental noise he kept hearing—and might even help limit the involuntary visions he kept having.

Switching off the tiny device on his wrist, he activated the main room unit. With it on, he couldn't sense her at the edges of his mind—couldn't affect her or her cub with his confused mental state. At least since his fever there had been no more of the whispering voices that had haunted him.

Sighing, he walked through to his bedroom, pausing to pick up the contract folder from the top of the drawer unit. As he did, the room lights glinted off something lying beneath the unit. Bending down, he picked it up. The Triad pendant from Lijou and Kha'Qwa. Turning it over in his hand, he went to his bed and sat down.

He wouldn't forget that night in a hurry. He was still half-convinced it had been a fever dream. His fingers traced the intricate spirals, coming naturally to rest on the crystal in the center.

Remember this meeting. The echo of His voice filled Kaid's mind. With a shiver, he hastily set the pendant on his night table. Was he never to be left in peace? His life seemed to belong to everyone but him. Suddenly he longed for the uncomplicated days of his youth, before he'd met Khemu, before what he was had mattered. He pushed the thought aside. It did no good to dwell on issues he couldn't change.

Pulling the pillows from under the cover, he propped himself against the head of the bed and picked up the folder. Surprisingly, the contract had needed only a small amount of negotiation before both he and Kusac had been satisfied with it. Opening the folder, he began to read through it once more.

The room seemed to lurch and he was looking at the newborn cub in Noni's arms, unsure what to do or say.

"She's yours, Tallinu," the familiar old voice said. "Your daughter. Take her from me, for Vartra's sake! Let her know you accept your child!"

He reached down to take the child from her, holding the little one awkwardly in his arms.

She gave a soft mewl, mind and hands reaching out for him. He offered her a finger, and she took it, holding onto him firmly as she began to purr. He was totally unprepared for the flood of emotions that rushed through him as he stroked the tiny brown-furred hand. Gathering her closer, he laid his face against her tiny head, taking in her scent, bonding to her. Suddenly, this cub he'd tried so hard to avoid conceiving because of his love for her mother, was even more precious.

"A daughter," he said, looking over to where she lay, exhausted from the birth. "We share a daughter."

Light, streaming in from the small window in Noni's main room, blinded him.

"I know," she said, her voice tired but holding a purr beneath the words.

Still dazzled, he moved his head in an effort to see her clearly. As he blinked, his vision cleared and he realized that he was back in his room at the villa—and he wasn't alone.

Someone was holding him firmly by the shoulders and shaking him. Instinctively he reached up for his assailant's throat, but even as he did, he recognized the scent. T'Chebbi. His hands settled on hers instead.

Her grip slackened, and she would have released him if he hadn't been holding her.

"Slipping, Kaid. Not long ago, couldn't get this close."

His ears flicked back in annoyance, staying there. "I know." His tone was sharp and bitter. He grasped her hands within his, pulling them down. "How'd you get in?"

She shrugged. "Standard surveillance procedure."

"I change the code daily. No one should be able to enter."

Her mouth opened in a grin. "Didn't say it was easy. I know you, others don't."

He growled deep in his throat, hackles round his neck rising as he tightened his grip on her hands.

She winced. "Orders from my Liegena, Kaid."

That superseded his privacy. With a sigh, he released her.

"Is that why you're here?" he demanded, pushing her away.

T'Chebbi settled herself on the edge of the bed, massaging her hands. "Partly. Knew you were in. When no answer I was concerned."

His eyes flicked across her, taking in the off-duty clothing she wore, noticing the subtle difference in her scent: perfume? His eye ridges creased as he looked more closely at her appearance.

"Meeting someone?"

She shrugged, looking away from him. "Why not?"

Her voice was quiet, so quiet he had to sit up to hear her.

"Don't let me delay you, then. I'm fine."

She looked back. "I've time yet. What was it, Tallinu? A dream? A vision?"

"Vision," he said briefly, not wanting to discuss it.

"You weren't meditating."

"I know. I don't need to these days. Leave it, T'Chebbi." Belatedly. "Please." His mind was drifting off into irrelevancies and he couldn't stop it. What *was* that scent she was wearing? Not one of the common ones, that was for sure, because it was enhancing her personal scent, not changing it. He gave his head a small shake and leaned back against his pillows.

"What have you been doing these past years? I never did ask," he said. His head was clearing a little now that he was farther away from her.

"Worked for Ghezu mainly, some military contracts. Priest things aren't for me." Again the slight grin as she rearranged herself more comfortably.

"What about your personal life. Any Companions?" Why the hell was he asking her that? This was no more like him than her appearance was usual for her.

"None. Never met the male I reckoned could cope with me."

He heard the underlying irony in her tone. She still hadn't healed from her time with the packs, then.

The question was out before he had a chance to stop it. "So who're you meeting?"

"Friend."

He swung his legs over the opposite side of the bed from her and got to his feet. Her presence was unsettling him, but he couldn't be inhospitable. "Have you time for a drink?"

"A little. Vassa, please."

As he headed over to the dispenser, he wondered what the hell was wrong with him. He didn't want T'Chebbi to leave yet. He'd never seen her in off-duty clothes; he'd never known her to have any kind of social life. The Brotherhood had become her sanctuary after her time in the Fleet Pack.

From the cupboard beside the dispenser, he got out the bottle of spirits and poured them each a measure. A faint sound made him turn around. T'Chebbi was coming toward him, and he could only stand and stare.

The dark cerise paneled tunic reaching to her calves was certainly flattering against her silver-brown pelt. What made it out of the ordinary was the silver chain round her waist, the ends of which hung down provocatively over her exposed thighs. As he looked lower, he saw a similar chain round her left ankle.

He held out the glass to her, trying to ignore the freshly heightened awareness of her scent that her passage across the room had caused. Irrelevancies caught his attention, and he noticed that across her shoulder, her hair hung in a single long braid, unbound at the end.

"This friend must be special," he said. In the twenty years they'd been colleagues this was the first time he'd seen her wearing something feminine since he'd snatched her from the heart of the Fleet den. But it was no bedraggled and beaten qwene who stood before him now. This was a sophisticated, self-assured female.

"Very." She took a sip of the drink.

He sidestepped her, moving toward the door into his lounge. "Perhaps we'd be more comfortable next door," he said, suddenly feeling awkward being with her in his bedroom.

"If you wish." She walked past him, tail gently swaying, and waited at the door.

He found himself resenting this friend of hers, worried that not knowing her past he'd take advantage of her. He tried to review who was in the house at present, but he could think of no one beyond Kusac and Dzaka. Her perfumed scent was too potent a distraction.

Reaching past her, he put his hand on the door plate.

She turned and looked up at him, fingers reaching out to touch his face.

"You're the friend," she said quietly. "I came to you."

"Me?" He stood frozen in surprise. This was the last thing he'd have expected.

She moved her hand, taking the drink from his slack grasp, holding it up to his lips. "Drink. You need it."

He did as she said, too surprised to do anything else, watching while she drank hers. She dropped the empty glasses to the floor, then reached up to put her hands on his shoulders.

Ice-gray eyes regarded him calmly, but what he was sensing from her was anything but calm: It was like a hunger.

Looking away, hesitantly he touched her hair, his hand sliding down it, teasing the unbound braid free until he could run his hand through its length.

"Your hair's longer now," he murmured, knowing it sounded inane but unable to think of anything else.

"You said long was nice."

He felt a jolt of surprise. "You remembered that after all this time?" Though true, it had been the only compliment he could think of at a time when she'd needed that kind of reassurance.

"You came back. Never spoke before. Should have. Realized when you went missing." She stopped, watching his face. "Now you're a Triad, I can ask. Couldn't before." Seeing no negative signs, she continued. "Were my superior at Stronghold. Not now. Now only you—and me."

Tentatively she laid her palm against his neck. "You remembered a promise made to one like me." Her voice was low as she laid her head against the fold of his robe and began to nuzzle it open.

He remained still, forcing himself to answer her. "Like what, T'Chebbi? You were a victim, a prisoner of theirs. How could I leave you?" He sucked in a breath as unexpectedly her teeth closed on his flesh and she nipped him. His hand slipped round her waist, feeling the hardness of the silver chain beneath his fingers.

"Everyone else did," she said, lifting her head briefly to push his robe open wider.

As her mouth closed on him again, his hand tightened convulsively in her hair. Her scent was warm, inviting, and sending all thoughts of anything but her from his mind. The heat of desire flicked through his limbs, spread through his body till with a suddenness that surprised him, he was erect and ready for her.

"Wanted you then, Tallinu, even with all my fears." She took a step back from him and pulled his head down on a level with hers, beginning to nip and lick her way along his jawline to his ear. "Couldn't. You'd see me wrong."

"No, I wouldn't have," he protested, hands closing on her maddeningly provocative thighs. As he caressed them, he realized they were every bit as muscular and firm as they looked.

"We nearly lost you, Tallinu!"

He felt her fear as if it was his own, and the courage it had taken to be this open with him. She clutched him tighter as her mouth closed on his. Before he realized, he was responding in kind, her kiss so like Carrie's it shocked him.

"Human kisses," he murmured, pushing her against the door, holding her there while his free hand roamed across her hips and lower back.

"Was taught it long before the Humans were found," she said, reaching for his tie belt and releasing it. "Thirty years and more. Only you know my past."

"I knew you were a qwene," he began.

"Not that," she said, her tail twining round his leg and gently tugging him closer. "More. That's why the Fleet took me."

As her tail snaked higher, its feathery tip flicking against the more sensitive parts of his anatomy, he moaned with pleasure. Burying his head against her neck, he pushed her tunic skirt aside. "Tell me later," he mumbled. Her perfume enveloped him now, robbing him of any purpose other than pairing with her immediately.

Suddenly her hands tightened like vises on his forearms, claws penetrating enough to hurt as she pushed him back.

"*Not* Pack way." Her ears were lying aslant.

Letting her go, he growled deep in his throat, angry with himself. She deserved better. "You're right." Stepping back, he took a deep breath and indicated the waiting bed. "Will you share it with me?"

Her ears righted themselves as she stepped away from the door.

Curbing his impatience, he waited till she'd curled up in

the central depression of the bed before joining her, discarding his robe on the way.

"Are you sure this is what you want?" he asked, touching her ear gently.

She leaned closer, hair falling forward about her shoulders. Once more her scent rose to meet his nostrils. "Yes."

As she laid the flat of her palms against his chest, he felt his nipples instantly harden at her light touch. Then her hands moved, one to lose itself in the hair on his neck, the other to play games with claw tips up and down his spine, making him shiver in delight.

Tipping her down onto the bed, he reached for the seals on her tunic, pulling it free till all she wore was the silver chain. As his hands ran through her fur, he was momentarily surprised at the flatness of her chest and belly. He leaned closer, burying his nose in her pelt, breathing the perfume in deeply. He didn't want to remember Carrie at this moment. His tongue searched for her nipples and teased each of them in turn while his uninjured hand reached below her belly for the soft inner surface of her thighs.

Gentle, unexpectedly female mewls of pleasure escaped her as her hands began to knead his flesh. When he lifted his head, she sought his mouth, her tongue flicking between his teeth in a kiss as deep as any of Carrie's had been. Then her hand closed round the base of his tail.

Instantly he reared back, hands held facing her at shoulder level. "I cannot submit." His voice was hoarse, but it was the only response he could make when two warriors such as they met to pair.

The light had cast her face into a pool of shadow from which her eyes glittered up at him. She blinked slowly. "I will." Her voice was barely audible.

This he hadn't expected. He reached down, flipping her over onto her stomach, waiting for her to fold her legs up under her belly. As she rose to meet him, with one arm he encircled her hips while the other reached for the scruff of her neck. Pulling her firmly back against him, they joined. The relief was instant as her inner warmth closed tightly around him. He withdrew slowly, beginning to move rhythmically within her. Unable to move, T'Chebbi gave a sudden whimper of distress.

Automatically his mind reached for hers, and what he

sensed was enough to make him release his grasp on her neck. Whatever she'd said, it had been too soon for her to submit to him. She'd had no lovers till now—her period of celibacy had been almost as long as his. They needed to pair as equals since they were not lovers.

Letting his hand slide down her chest, he sat back on his haunches, supporting her as he pulled her upright against himself. Ignoring the fire in his blood, he leaned forward, gently licking her shoulder and the side of her throat in an effort to show her he understood.

It was enough, and with a low mewl of pleasure, she pushed herself free and turned on him. Seconds later, he was on his back and she was covering his body with a barrage of gentle bites as her hands began to stroke and coax him toward his secondary arousal.

"Wait!" He tried to fend her off. "We need to be joined first. I'll be too large!"

Her laugh held a trill of amusement as she used her not inconsiderable body weight to pin his forearms and chest against the bed. "No. Trust me. I learned this before you taught me the sword."

His view blocked by her body, there was nothing he could do but wait. Then he felt her tongue. At first lightly, then with its coarsest surface, it flicked across his groin, his belly, then the soft area at the top of his thighs, always close to his genitals but never touching them. It was driving him wild. Unable to stop himself, he twisted and turned his body, desperately trying to meet her.

She stopped and began to nip him instead, her bites sharp, almost painful, making him now flinch away in anticipation of the next one. A wave of pleasure began to build, and though he tried again to stop her, this time he was the one unable to move. Suddenly, with a cry, his body arched upward, lifting them both off of the bed as his erection swelled for the second time.

He'd barely collapsed back when he felt her move. Then she was lowering herself onto him. Almost whimpering in pleasure, he lay there, claws ripping the bedding as his hands clenched in spasms. It was agony and ecstasy at the same time as his hypersensitive flesh was so very slowly surrounded by her. This was a chancy thing to do, the risk of hurt to both of them being high.

Reaching up, he clutched her by the waist, tumbling them

both over till he lay on top. He could hear the blood pounding in his head as he tried to slow down, but she'd taken him so high that now all he could do was finish it.

She dragged her claws up the back of his thighs, letting them come to rest on the fleshy part of his buttocks. He reached out mentally, sharing everything he was experiencing with her, but there was no time to regret he couldn't sense her as he began to climax. Her arms held him so tightly her claws began to penetrate his flesh. At the last moment, he flinched and found himself falling off the bed.

She gave a yowl of surprise, letting him go to grab at the bedcover as she followed him onto the floor. They landed in a heap, the cover tangled round them. As T'Chebbi fought her way free, he began to laugh quietly. She glowered at him.

Still chuckling, he reached up for her and pulled her down beside him again. Carefully he pushed her hair from her face, stroking the soft fur on her cheek. "Spend tonight with me," he said, his touch becoming a caress. "I find I like your company."

Her face softened. "Perhaps."

"So you were an Exotic. I always knew you were talented," he murmured, catching her lower lip briefly with his teeth. "But I never would have guessed at the fire you carry in your belly. Or the power of that scent," he added dryly.

"Have talents of your own, Tallinu. Now I know why telepaths prefer their own kind."

He became still. "What is my own kind, T'Chebbi? Telepath? Brother? Then there's Carrie. I don't know what I am." His present problems loomed ahead of him again. Wisps of what might be memories flitted through his head. "I should be long dead by now," he murmured without thinking.

"You're from the past," she said. "Guessed that when I heard you were telepath." She touched his arm. "You're alive. Here and now, where you belong, Tallinu. Hold onto that. Is all you need. Did you meet her as a cub back then?"

He looked sharply at her. "How did you find out?"

"Research. Checked the Brotherhood and the Retreat."

"Damn! If you can do it, others can!" He was angry now, angry that he hadn't foreseen it.

"No." She shook her head. "I altered the records. Now shows you as orphaned."

He sat up, eye ridges meeting as he regarded her. The T'Chebbi he thought he knew bore only passing resemblance to the female he found himself with.

She looked away from him, down at the silver belt that still encircled her waist. Idly she toyed with the end that lay across her knee.

Faintly he heard the cry of Kashini from the suite next door. He shivered, remembering the vision, and reached out for T'Chebbi, winding his fingers through the chain where it encircled her waist. He pulled her up till she was in his arms again. She was part of the present, and he needed that right now. "I seem to have a taste for the exotic," he said.

As she lay in his arms later that night, her fingers twined through those of his damaged hand, she said, "When she can't come to you, and darkness brings memories you don't want, we could share the night."

"Perhaps," he said, barely aware of her as the haunting echoes of what might be memories played within his mind.

CHAPTER 3

Kaid waited impatiently to be put through to the Guild Master's office. Finally the Brotherhood sigil cleared from his screen and was replaced by the image of Lijou.

"Father Lijou," he began, but the priest cut him short.

"Kaid, when do you want to come to Stronghold? We need to discuss in detail your meeting with Vartra, and I could do with your help regarding setting up training centers for priests of all denominations."

He sat back, totally nonplussed. Lijou wanted his help?

Lijou frowned. "You were going to ask when you could come here, weren't you?"

"Yes, but . . ."

"You worked closely with Jyarti in the priesthood for a good many years, didn't you?"

"Yes."

"Then you must be aware of how he organized his teaching. I was appointed to this position, not trained to it. Your input would be invaluable."

"You plead an eloquent case, Father Lijou," said Kaid. "However, I have my own reasons for wanting . . ."

"Of course, but your own studies shouldn't occupy all your time."

"I've other work to attend to as well. I'm going to Jalna with Carrie and Kusac. I'll be peripherally involved in the training and planning of this mission."

"Any help at all would be welcome, Kaid. Think of it this way. You want to avoid Esken and train here rather than at the Telepath Guild. I wish I could avoid him but I'll be fighting him uphill all the way. An aide of your caliber would make life easier for me."

Out of sight, Kaid began to drum the fingers of his right hand on the desk. His rhythm faltered, then stopped as he realized he'd tried to tap the missing finger. The damage that Ghezu had done to innocent people was impossible to measure. Was Esken another Ghezu?

"What help I can give is yours, Father Lijou," he said.

"Thank you, Tallinu. I'll organize your instruction personally. Your training will be complete by the time you're due to leave for Jalna, that I promise."

"What was all that about needing his help?" asked Kha'Qwa from her perch on the settee in the informal area of her Companion's office.

Lijou got up from his desk and joined her. "It's not entirely fictitious. His help will not only be useful but will shorten the time it takes me to get our proposed college up and running. However, it does make sure that he doesn't have the opportunity to cut himself off from the world while he's here. I want him to be kept busy, but without pressure. It's too easy for someone who's been through the trauma he has to cut himself off from reality."

"And Kaid is a visionary as well. I see what you mean."

Lijou leaned his head against her shoulder. "I've need of your skills, Kha'Qwa. I want you to monitor him, be aware of the state of mind he's in. You'll be tutoring him as well, so it shouldn't be too difficult. From what I can gather, Kusac's worried that he might be heading for a mental breakdown. That, coupled with Tallinu's new awareness of his telepathic abilities, could be enough to make him dangerously unstable."

"Surely not! He has his Brotherhood training to fall back on, and at least we know he had a good grounding there."

"Don't make the mistake of overestimating him. I've seen for myself how his self-control has become a thin facade lately. Do you know his background?"

"Beyond the fact he was born fifteen hundred years ago? No. You've never mentioned it."

Lijou grunted. "He was found at Vartra's Retreat and sent here to the temple to be fostered in the village. You know the M'zushi family? They offered to take him in as an act of charity. By the time anyone knew what was going on there, he'd become wild, uncontrollable by anyone except Noni. Always getting into trouble, disappearing for days on end till finally he never came back. A recruitment team picked him up from one of the packs, the Claws, if memory serves me."

"What is his Talent?" asked Kha'Qwa, reaching for her mug of c'shar.

"Apart from telepathy, he has several, all of them making sense only when you realize that he's unique, quite literally a throwback—one of the original fighting telepaths from the past."

"So what are they?" She prodded him in the side with her elbow. "If I'm to get close to him, understand him, I need to know, Lijou."

"Hunting and killing skills, basically. The Talents he used to survive in Ranz. He can sense his prey, follow their unique mental pattern till he's caught them. He has the patience of a rock if he needs it, and can assess potential Talents quite uncannily. He'll do whatever it takes, for as long as it takes, to get what he's after. He's capable of being as cold and calculating as the Liege of Hell Himself. We can thank Vartra he's not ambitious with it. Ghezu was bad enough, and he was only cunning."

"The perfect Special Operative," she said thoughtfully, finishing her drink. "How much of it's innate, though, and how much is a protection against his childhood and early youth?"

"That's what you need to find out. If we have to, I'll send for one of the telepath medics who heal the mind."

"No. Don't do that," she said, replacing her mug. "He'll see it as a betrayal, and we're his only chance now. Kaid must be capable of trust, or else he wouldn't have worked with Garras. Leave it to me. I'll speak to Noni about it if we think it's necessary." She looked down at him, mouth opening slightly in a smile. "Sounds like he's always been on the verge of becoming a kzu-shu warrior. I'm surprised you're willing to let him come here at all."

"I haven't heard that one before. What's it mean?"

"A red-mist warrior—one locked in the hunter/kill state. I'm not saying he'll become one, just that the potential is there."

"On that I can't comment because it's outside my experience, but letting him come here is a matter of faith for me, Kha'Qwa," he said, sitting up. "I'd say he's been touched by Vartra, but it doesn't quite have the same ring when applied to him, does it?"

She laughed, reaching out to pat his hand affectionately. "But he has, Lijou, and years before he actually went back o meet him again as an adult. I've been over your records, and you know I agree wholeheartedly with your conclusions. From the time he started training under Jyarti in the ways of the priests, he became a focus for the God's attention. The pattern is there, believe me. We'll cope somehow. The Brotherhood looks after its own, and Kaid Tallinu is one of us."

*   *   *

Later that morning, Kaid sat in the kitchen with Kusac and Carrie. In front of them were several piles of papers and a map of Jalna. He pushed two personnel records in front of them.

"Here are the Human telepaths who'll accompany us. Both of them are male, both are unexceptional when it comes to resembling the natives of Jalna. I chose them because they're ex-military and in their late thirties—old enough to have the experience we need yet young enough for the strength and stamina."

Carrie picked up Conrad's file, studying the attached photograph carefully. The face was rectangular; mid-brown eyes evenly spaced, the nose straight, and the mouth generous. Short, curly brown hair topped it, giving him a more youthful appearance than the age suggested. Then she checked the data concerning him.

Handing it to Kusac, she looked at the other file. He was quite different. The face was squarer with heavy brows and deep-set eyes. The nose was broad, suggesting that at some time it had been broken. The mouth was set in a hard line.

She pointed to the closely cropped hair. "They'll both have to grow their hair longer, him especially."

"Already seen to. Anything else?"

Quickly she scanned his qualifications. "Beyond the fact that I'd be surprised if they don't both still work for the Human military, no. They'll do."

"They did for the first few months," said Kaid. "What made you think that?"

She shrugged. "Just a hunch. And now? Do they work for us?"

"Let's say the atmosphere at the Warrior Guild is more to their taste than that of their Forces. There are a few Human agents both in the Telepath Guild and the Warrior Guild. One we know was put there for us to find, the rest

suspect nothing. It's difficult for them to be mentally cover
when they don't have much faith in their own abilities as
telepaths to start with," said Kaid with a snort of amusement. "All it needs is a couple of good telepaths and a
Brother or three. When it comes to interspecies spying, the
Telepath Guild will swallow its high moral stance with the
rest of us, especially since Esken is so suspicious of the
Humans in the first place. We make sure the agents tell
Earth what we want it to know."

"These two," said Kusac, tapping the files, "how did they
come to be military telepaths? I understood Earth didn't
recognize telepathy at all."

"Turns out they did, at least within certain top secret
military units. They'd done work previously on seeing and
describing locations from a remote source, sometimes half
a planet away—analogous to what you and Carrie did when
you looked for the life pod on Keiss. It's all down in the
files," said Kaid. "I'm leaving them with you."

"Have you actually met these men?" asked Carrie.

Kaid's ears flicked momentarily before righting themselves. "Of course. I foresee no problems in our being able
to work together."

Carrie reached out to put her hand over his. "I was only
asking, Kaid. I wanted your own assessment of them."

"I've chosen them," he said. "They both have previous
covert mission experience and seem genuine enough."

"Apart from you, are any other Sholans going with us?"
asked Kusac.

"No. We're pushing credibility having me on the outside
anyway. If I'm caught, it could start the interspecies incident we're trying to avoid."

"Why can't you come with us as a U'Churian?"

"I'm not black-furred, and we haven't any operatives
near enough the right color and build who are," said Kaid

"I don't see the problem. All you have to do is dye your
pelts black. They've already developed a drug which will
increase the growth of Kusac's fur so it matches the U'Churians'. Surely including you with us reduces the risk."

Kaid stared at her openmouthed.

"What did you say?" demanded Kusac.

"Excuse me?" She looked from one to the other in
surprise.

"Dye." He repeated the English word. "What is dye?"

She realized she'd used the English term as no Sholan equivalent existed. "It's a permanent color for hair. It grows out eventually, but if you keep getting the roots of your hair touched up, no one could tell it wasn't your natural color. Don't Sholans change the color of their hair?"

"No. Never," said Kusac. "It's considered immoral to conceal your identity. The younger females will occasionally use a brightly colored paintlike substance on their hair, but it brushes or washes out the next day."

"Check at the Telepath and Warrior Guilds as well as among the archaeologists. There's bound to be one of the Human females who uses a hair dye."

"It's so simple a solution, it's brilliant," said Kaid, leaning his chin on his hand. "If we can get hold of some of this chemical, then our scientists will be able to reproduce it."

"You'll have to test it first," Carrie warned them. "Different hair types absorb dyes at different rates and sometimes the color goes badly wrong."

"Badly? How badly?" asked Kaid.

"Blondes going green overnight, or bleached hair becoming so porous in certain areas that the color goes on unevenly. That kind of thing."

He relaxed. That level of problem would be easily solved.

"We need more people anyway," said Carrie. "There's the five out at Kaladar to rescue, and the four the Valtegens sold to locate. I'd say we need two sizable groups."

"Has there been any contact with the telepaths in Kaladar yet?" asked Kusac.

"None since they were first taken prisoner. It has to be said that they may already be dead," Kaid said quietly. "I'm sorry, Carrie. I know you liked Jo."

"They're not dead," she said firmly. "We'd know if they were. I, at least, would have sensed something from Rezac."

"You've been otherwise occupied since our return," said Kaid, busying himself with the papers.

"It hasn't affected my Talents," she said, a little sharply.

"It has tired you, though," Kusac said placatingly. "Kaid's right. You might have missed it."

"Think what you want, but I know they're alive," she muttered, slouching back in her chair. "And tell me why we're going in after them if we think they're dead?"

"They might not all be dead," said Kaid. "It's only the telepath, Kris, we've lost contact with."

"What about the four Sholans? There's no mention of any contact with their two telepaths at all."

"Jo's group were told not to try and contact them."

"I still consider it strange that out of five telepaths, not one has been heard from recently. What about our folk in orbit above Jalna? Haven't they tried reaching the two captured by the Valtegans—Rezac and Zashou?"

"They've tried over the last few days, but without result." Kaid looked up. "Yes, I agree it's strange, but given the fact that the planet has been called hostile, we have to assume the telepaths, for one reason or another, haven't survived, or are incapable of broadcasting. And yes, we're facing the same risks."

"I only asked." Carrie's tone was mild now.

"Worrying, though," said Kusac. "What about finding the four sold as slaves? How do you propose we approach the problem of locating them?"

Kaid grinned, human-style, all teeth. "That's your contribution, Kusac. T'Chebbi, Dzaka, and Garras are going to teach you both some specialized Brotherhood skills. Concealment, surveillance, information gathering, that type of thing. Then you'll work out a plan, and we'll discuss it. You've already got a start through your AlRel training. It isn't that different in certain areas. Meral can join you. It's a good opportunity for him to begin his training, too."

"Uh huh." He looked dubious.

"Field agents, that's one of the prices of our freedom, and what the Brotherhood of Vartra do, unless you want to be based at one of the temples or the Retreat?"

"Not really."

"Thought not. Carrie," he looked over at her. "You can't start the physical training yet, but you can work on the other Brotherhood skills."

She nodded and pulled the map toward her. "Explain this to me."

"These are the maps made by the *Summer Bounty* while it was in orbit, that Jo, Davies, and Kris were using," said Kusac. "The spaceport is there, by the coast," he pointed to the anonymous mark. "That's the trade route they followed to Forestgate at the edge of the mountain range. From there to the end of the tree line is about sixty miles. After that, it's uphill to Kaladar in the mountains."

"Do we have to go via the crash site?"

"No. They got whatever there was to be had from there," said Kaid. "We go straight to the city, hopefully across the plains. It's an easier route."

"Then what?"

"Then we observe the situation and try to get them out."

"Who's going in?"

Kaid sighed. "Well, we can have two teams. You inside the spaceport and us on the outside. Hopefully our four enslaved Sholans are close to the port, which means you can concentrate on that area while we—Conrad, Quin, and I—head out for Kaladar. That's a working hypothesis, at least. The reality is going to be wait and see till we arrive on Jalna."

"We've got to be flexible," said Kusac. "A major consideration is how violent these people are."

"They've got to have a system for dealing with it, though, or they wouldn't have evolved to even this level," said Carrie. "What about Jo? Surely she observed their culture long enough to draw some conclusions and report them?"

"She saw nothing to support the Chemerians' allegations," said Kaid. "However, the indisputable fact remains that all the species that trade there want the Jalnians to remain planet-bound."

"Have we a detailed map of the spaceport?"

Kaid handed it to her. "It's a fairly standard layout, given that they're providing the combined facilities of an orbiting satellite and a ground port facility. The main difference is that the traders and spacers only have access to the port itself and the traders' town, the planet being interdicted by the Port Lord. Just as the alien traders don't want the Jalnians in space, so Bradogan doesn't want aliens and off-world goods freely available on his world. He controls what goes in and out of Jalna."

"Sounds more bother than it's worth."

"According to the Chemerians, it's a convenient meeting point for trade for the species involved."

"So we're almost as much in the dark as Jo's team was. What happens if we get caught, too?" Carrie looked at both of the males in turn. "I realize the Alliance doesn't want any kind of incident at Jalna—presumably they'll make contact at some point—but how dispensable are we?"

"We aren't. Raiban says there are two main options. One, send in the Sumaan and get us out by force, or two,

First Contact. Her people approach the leader of the alien Port police and negotiate our rescue. However . . ."

"We make sure we don't get caught in the first place," interrupted Kusac, reaching out to clasp Carrie's hand with his. "The basic approach is that I, as a U'Churian, am traveling with a Chemerian trader learning his craft. Apparently some Chemerians do this. Since you can't pass as a Jalnian with those eyes, you're a member of a new species we've just contacted, a Solnian. You're their representative to Jalna, checking out the trading opportunities there."

Carrie looked skeptical. "What about the other U'Churians? Won't they wonder why they've never heard of my people?"

"We met you at the Chemerian home world. Our ship is still there," said Kaid smoothly. "Kusac's family was offered a contract to escort you here, let you meet the people, see the goods, and assess the potential markets. All acceptable practice according to the Chemerians."

She made a noise not unlike a growl. "Too much depends on what the Chemerians say. They got us into this mess with their double standards! If they'd been honest about Jalna in the first place, none of this would have been necessary. How do we know they aren't still lying?"

"Again, we don't. So far, what they've said has either been accurate or not disproved, like the issue of violence."

"We're going in too blind," said Carrie. "I don't like it."

"Most missions aren't much different," said Kaid, leaning back and stretching his neck and shoulder muscles. He was feeling cramped from sitting studying the papers for so long. He'd have to put up with it, though. At least at Stronghold there was the exercise yard and the gym. "You'll get used to it. If it were straightforward, the Brotherhood wouldn't be needed."

Zhala came in with a tray of sweet pastries and coffee which she put down at the end of the table for them.

"Impeccable timing. Thank you," said Carrie, grinning at Kusac as she pulled the tray closer.

Kaid tidied the papers and maps back into their folders. "I'm leaving for Stronghold after second meal," he said quietly. "Father Lijou's expecting me."

"How long will you be away?" asked Kusac, passing the plate of pastries over to him as Carrie began refilling their mugs.

"Several months." Despite his personal damper, he felt the crystal warm against his chest, and with it came the shock Carrie felt at what he'd just said. She didn't show it though, he thought with pride. She'd paid attention to his tuition. "I'll be helping to set up the new curriculum for training priests. It's important work. Garras will keep me posted. If there's a problem, I'll get in touch."

Carrie handed him his mug. "Will you be living there?"

"Yes. As I said, I need some time to straighten things out in my own mind as well as learn how to use my telepathic abilities properly."

"The time will pass quickly for all of us," said Kusac. "We've got a lot to do."

Something drew Kaid's attention toward the door and, as he looked toward it, a familiar wave of dizziness swept over him. The door burst open. Dzaka stood there, Kashini held close against his chest, pistol in his free hand. Even as Kaid leaped to his feet, gun drawn, the scene had begun to fade.

"What is it?" demanded Kusac, instantly at his side. "What do you hear?"

"The wind," he muttered, reholstering his gun. "It must have been the wind." It was getting worse! The episodes were more frequent now, and so short, they were of no use to him as a guide to what might happen. In the past, they had only come when he was meditating. Now he couldn't guarantee one wouldn't dominate him during a life or death situation.

The door opened, making him swing his head round sharply again. Dzaka entered—but he wasn't carrying the cub, and there was no sense of urgency about him. Kaid's blood ran cold at the thought of what could have happened had his son arrived a moment or two earlier.

"The aircar from Stronghold's here, Father," he said. "I've put your bag on board."

If anything else was needed to convince him he had to leave the estate, this had. He had to go to a place where he'd cause the least harm if things went badly wrong for him—somewhere where they could deal with him quickly, where they wouldn't hesitate to do what was necessary.

Relieved, he nodded and turned to say his good-byes.

Carrie came forward to hug him. She felt soft in his arms,

smelled of milk and motherhood. It awakened memories of other visions and hurriedly he let her go.

"Take care," she said. "Stay in touch."

She'd neither said nor sent anything, but still he'd felt her hurt as he'd held her. Flicking an ear in acknowledgment of what she said, he held out his palm to Kusac.

His Liege looked at him, then slowly shook his head. "No," he said, coming closer to embrace him. "I've told you before, Kaid. You're family, an Aldatan if you wish it. My brother." He grinned as he let him go. "Hell, I need one with all the females around me! Even Taizia's and Meral's cub was a female!"

Kaid's mouth opened in a small grin despite himself.

"Have you seen T'Chebbi?" he asked once they'd left the kitchen.

"Passed her on her way to the ruins," Dzaka said. "Told her you wanted a word, but she said later. Is there a problem?"

"No." They hadn't spoken privately since their night together, but perhaps it was better this way.

*   *   *

The Valtegans or the Jalnians, it made little difference to Rezac. They'd won free of one set of guards only to wake up to another. Both species had stolen his liberty, abused him and his Leska, and forced them to do their will. Anger surged through him again, and this time he didn't need to conceal it. On the other side of the room, Zashou lay deeply asleep. For now there was none of her disapproving presence at the center of his mind and thoughts, no criticism of him for the effort wasted in hating their captors.

Tail flicking in irate jerky movements, he pushed himself away from the castle window and began to pace up and down his end of the room. It had been a bad day, but then it often was in the run up to their Link day. Zashou had never been good at hiding her resentment of their Link. At best he always felt a cool distancing and reserve from her, at worst, out-and-out dislike, though thank the Gods, those occasions were rarer since they'd awakened on this strange world.

Today he'd gotten into a row with her over the Humans. He was still suspicious of them, they looked too like the

Jalnians for comfort, whereas she believed implicitly in
them, even down to the frankly ridiculous claim that the
mind that had answered his cry had been a Human mind,
Leska-linked to a Sholan! Whoever had sent had been un-
deniably Sholan, of that he had no doubt. He'd touched
enough alien minds in the last year to know the difference.
Even Zashou hadn't been able to argue against that reality
despite what the Humans said. The one thing that they all
clung to like a lifeline was that the Sholans would come
for them. But when? At least so far, this Lord Killian had
been reasonable. They were bring held in decent rooms
and fed palatable food. Now they waited for better weather
so that they could go to the crash site and examine the
scouter for onboard weapons.

Agony shot through his foot as he stubbed a toe against
the chest by the window. Biting back the cry of pain, he
flung himself down on the pallet by the fire. Soon enough
he'd be able to share the bed with her again. Lying there,
massaging his foot, he let go of the anger and allowed the
heat from the fire to warm him into a reluctant drowsiness,
wondering for the thousandth time how it had all gone so
wrong from the start.

Tiernay stood near enough the window to look out
without being seen. Of the six in the lab, he had the
longest telepathic range, able to pick up the alien
presences from nearly a kilometer away.

They sky was clear, the sharp, bright blue of winter.
The Valtegan airborne troop carriers would be visible
long before he could hear or sense them—if they
came from that direction.

At the doorway, he stood with Jaisa and Shanka,
Jaisa watching through the side window, he and Shanka
keeping an eye on the corridor.

"Hurry up, Dr. Vartra," said Tiernay. "I want us out
of here as soon as possible. You should have moved
into the monastery with us days ago. You know how
risky this is for all of us, you especially."

"While the equipment at the monastery is adequate, Tiernay, since I still have access to the college
analyzer it makes sense to use it. It's saved me
weeks of testing and correlation," said Vartra, continuing to pack each vial in its rack bed in his briefcase.

"Zashou, have you got the last of my notes and the computer data from the safe?" he asked.

"All done," she said, resting the cardboard box on the bench beside him. It was heavy. She examined a clawtip, and finding the snag, chewed it off absently as she watched the genticist.

"They're coming," said Tiernay. "Three aircars—about twenty soldiers, I reckon."

Zashou reached forward for a slim box lying beside Vartra's case. "How long?" she asked, opening the box. Inside lay the faculty's only pressurized hypoderm gun.

"Maybe five minutes," he said.

Zashou sensed the others getting ready, swinging guns off their shoulders, switching off the safety catches.

"There's three more craft coming from this direction," said Rezac from the side window. "They're definitely here for you, Doctor."

"Almost finished," Vartra said, reaching for the last vial.

Zashou's hand closed on it first. "No. We'll use this one," she said, uncapping the vial and fitting it into the hypo.

"What?" said Vartra, his hand stopping in midair. He watched, mesmerized, as the Sholan female moved one of her skirt panels aside and, parting the fur on her thigh, applied the hypo, and pressed the trigger.

Rezac, sensitive as always to the mood of the group, swung his head around, sized up the potential situation, and unhurriedly moved to Vartra's side.

Zashou looked up at the doctor, rubbing her leg briefly. "That case you intend to carry contains the only Sholan samples of your enhanced gene. If anything happens to you or it, then all your work will be lost. We can't take that risk, Doctor. If the gene is carried in us as well, then we can ensure that enough of it reaches the monastery to infect all the telepaths on Shola."

"Zashou, my work is still experimental! I haven't finished correlating the data yet!"

"It's ready to test on Sholans now," she said. "The

animal trials were more than successful, we all know that from our work in the lab with you. And on the simulated tests you ran last night, the computer results were positive. The gene will enhance our telepathy, and breed true, as it did in the jeggets."

"We haven't time to discuss this now," said Tiernay, striding over to them, gun at the ready. "They've landed in the vehicle park. We must leave immediately!"

"Zashou's right," said Jaisa, leaving the doorway. "It's as near perfect as you're going to get it, Dr. Vartra. Too much depends on the contents of that case to leave it to chance. Zashou, I'll carry the gene, too." Propping her foot up on the rungs of a stool, she bared her thigh.

"No!" said Vartra, making a snatch for the hypoderm as Zashou held it against Jaisa's leg.

Rezec grasped hold of the doctor, pulling him back from the two females.

"This is utter madness, Zashou! Have you forgotten what the early side effects were in the jeggets? You could be risking epilepsy—insanity—perhaps even death by using it now!" He struggled in Rezac's grip.

"We haven't any choice," said Rezac. "It's going to spread whether we want it to or not now that the females are carriers. Anyway, Zashou's right. If we get out of here without a fight, we'll be damned lucky. The more of us carrying the gene the better."

"Go ahead, Zashou. I'll take it next." He inclined his head toward the female.

Zashou stepped around Vartra to Rezac's other side. A moment later it was done.

"Who's next?" she asked, looking challengingly round the room, the beaded braids in her hair chiming as they moved. "What about you, Shanka?" she asked her mate, heading toward him.

Shanka was keeping his eyes on the Valtegan craft coming in to land on the lawn at the side of the science building.

What the hell possessed you to do that? he sent. His tone was one of cold fury.

If we don't get out of here alive with the serum, then our one chance of beating the Valtegans is gone, she replied.

Vartra has the right of it, it's not ready yet! This whim of yours could cost us all our lives!

Our lives aren't worth much anyway, now that the Valtegans know we have telepaths. Are you going to take the serum or not?

What choice have I? He turned on her, his brows creased in anger, ears flicking backward. *Your actions will infect us all within the week. Whether I take it now or wait to catch it from you, I face the same risks. Do it and let's leave.*

His leg jerked slightly at the sting from the pressurized spray.

Vartra, meanwhile, had stopped struggling with Rezac. Defeated, he slumped down on the stool beside his bench. Rezac released him.

"Zashou, get over here and do me, then we can close Vartra's case and leave," said Tiernay. "Might as well stick together in this as in the rest," he grinned.

Moments later the hypo was packed into the briefcase and it was closed.

"Come on, Dr. Vartra. You can argue it out with us later," said Zashou, touching his hand with her fingertips.

"You're brave fools," growled Vartra, picking up the case and getting to his feet. "I just hope you're right and it *is* ready to use, otherwise it won't need the Valtegans to wipe us out."

Zashou picked up her box and followed the others out into the corridor.

Tiernay took the rear guard, ordering Rezac to the front. They were heading for the east wing where a small van waited for them in the internal delivery bay. Nyaz had remained with it.

We're on our way, Nyaz, sent Rezac, his feet moving silently over the tiled floor of the corridor as he scouted ahead.

Keeping his gun out of sight, he moved quickly past the busy labs to where the corridor branched left and right. On the wall beside him was the fire alarm, the button set into the wall behind a protective piece of glass. He glanced round the corner. All clear, good.

With a warning thought to the others, he raised his pistol butt and struck the glass.

The siren wailed out, building rapidly to an ear-splitting pitch. Around them doors were flung open and students began to stream out, jostling and shoving as they headed like a living tide to the nearest exit.

Keep together, warned Rezac, gun and hand stuffed inside the open front of his shirt.

They merged into the stream, going with them as far as the service elevator. Rezac stopped, standing back against the wall, visually checking that the others were still with him. Newer to his telepath skills than the rest of the group, he still preferred to double-check everything with what he still considered his normal senses.

The tide slowed until the last stragglers raced along the corridor, hardly glancing at them as they feigned the need to help an injured member of their small group.

Jaisa thumbed open the elevator door. With a loud mechanical grumble it slid back, revealing the dirty interior.

"Gods, don't they ever clean the goods areas?" muttered Shanka, leading the way in. "How long have we got before the building is empty?"

Rezac glanced at his wrist chronometer. "About another minute. Should be enough time."

Tiernay pressed the ground floor indicator. The door closed noisily, then the elevator lurched downward.

Machine pistols ready again, they formed a protective wedge in front of Zashou and Vartra. The elevator shuddered to a halt, five minds probing outside for any presences.

Nyaz? Tiernay sent a questing thought in his direction.

Clear for now.

Tiernay opened the door.

The chill air of the delivery bay hit them, bringing with it the smell of fuel and winter. Rezac shivered. Somehow this winter, the first of their occupation by the Valtegans, seemed colder than any other. For the first time, even his thick fur was not enough to keep him warm.

At last! they heard Nyaz send as he started up the engine. *There're people moving about outside, some of them Valtegans. I was afraid they'd find me first.*

The side of the van stood open, waiting for them. As they'd rehearsed, Rezac and Jaisa went first, bounding down from the loading level to the ground. Jaisa peeled off to face the back bay door, Rezac the front.

Vartra and Zashou followed, running quickly down the short ramp, flanked by Shanka and Tiernay. Again, one covered the rear, the other the front. Grasping the handle on the van's gaping side door, Vartra jumped in and headed for the back. Dumping her box in and off to one side, Zashou followed.

Valtegans! sent Jaisa.

And in front, added Rezac urgently. *Move, everyone!*

Jaisa backed toward the van, her guns still trained on the rear doors as they began to rattle.

Tiernay leaped in, colliding with Zashou and sending them both tumbling to the floor.

"Clear that bloody door!" hissed Rezac, glancing back to see what the commotion was.

They scrambled out of the way as Jaisa jumped in.

"Activate the outer doors, Nyaz," ordered Tiernay, leaning over the back of the front seat.

A loud bang echoed round the bay and the rear door began to slide ponderously back.

Rezac jumped in, holding his hand down to help Shanka. With a yowl of pain the other catapulted himself in, bringing with him the smell of singed fur.

Slamming the door shut, Rezac pushed through the group to the rear of the van as Nyaz began to edge it forward, engine revving loudly. The doors in front of them began slowly to slide apart.

"Get down!" yelled Rezac, throwing himself at the nearest body and pulling it to the floor with him.

One of the rear windows exploded in a shower of glass splinters as an energy bolt hit it.

"Go!" yelled Tiernay, crouching flat against the side wall. "Smash the doors, it doesn't matter any more!"

"I'm going, I'm going!" said Nyaz.

Tires squealed as the vehicle lurched forward. There was a jolt as one wing hit the doors, and then they were out in the open, Valtegan soldiers scattering in front of them as they hurtled away from the science building.

"Everyone stay flat," ordered Rezac, lifting his head slightly to look around the van.

"I'm as flat as I can be," wheezed a voice from under him. He looked down into Zashou's face. There was a distressed expression in her amber eyes, and her nose was wrinkled with pain.

"Sorry," he mumbled, sliding sideways off her, noticing as he did how soft her pelt felt. Smells good, too, he thought irrelevantly, then hurriedly blanked the thought lest she should pick it up. Just his luck to land on her.

"What held you up?" demanded Nyaz, glancing briefly round.

"We used the serum," said Tiernay, sticking his head over the top of the seat to look out the front.

"You what?" The van hit a curb and swerved as Nyaz looked over his shoulder again.

"Watch it! We used the serum," repeated Tiernay. "It was safer than risking it all to Dr. Vartra's case."

"Used the serum," echoed Nyaz, ears twitching once.

"Trouble ahead," warned Tiernay.

Rezac sat up, moving to look between the two.

"Slow down," he said. "Don't act suspiciously. They can't be after the van yet, and they won't see the back window till we pass them. Just be ready for trouble."

He turned his head briefly to those in the back. "Get the doctor under those sacks. They have his description but not ours."

Two Valtegan soldiers stood by the automatic barrier, energy rifles held ready as they saw the van approaching.

As Nyaz slowed down, one of them reached for a slim device at his side, holding it to his mouth. The other visibly tensed.

"Keep going, Nyaz! Heads down, everyone,"

growled Rezac, bobbing down and bracing himself between the two seats.

As the soldiers brought their rifles up to fire, the van accelerated straight for the barrier. Sparks exploded off the wing, followed by the shattering of the windshield. A gaping hole splattered with blood opened up to one side of Nyaz and the rest went suddenly opaque.

There was a jolt and a sharp crack as the barrier splintered. Then the van began to weave alarmingly down the narrow tree-lined avenue.

Rezac lurched between the seats, grasping the wheel with one hand as the unconscious youth slid sideways. With the other, he made a grab for Nyaz.

Tiernay scrambled over from the back. "No!" he cried, seizing the wounded youth's arm and trying to haul him free of the controls.

Rezac, tangled between the two of them, pushed Tiernay aside.

"Then get him out of my way, now, before we all die!" he snarled, climbing over Nyaz, ready to take his seat.

Grasping him round the chest, with a couple of tugs, Tiernay had him all but clear. Rezac swept Nyaz's legs out of the way and flung himself into the driver's seat.

With the back of his hand he punched at the windshield, enlarging the hole so he could see properly. He stamped down on the accelerator, tires spinning briefly in the slush before they caught and the van took off again.

From behind he heard the crack of the other rear window shattering. Jaisa gave a short yowl.

"Anyone hit?" he demanded.

"Missed me," said Jaisa, helping Vartra out from under the sacks. "How's Nyaz?"

"Bad," said Tiernay from where he squatted on the floor by the front passenger seat. He'd ripped off the youth's tunic and was making a wad out of it to press on what remained of Nyaz's shoulder.

Rezac glanced over as he threw the van round a sharp bend. "We can't risk a hospital, the Veltegans will pick him up. He knows too much."

"Take him to the monastery," said Vartra. "We've got all the facilities he needs there."

"He won't make it," said Rezac.

"He might," snapped the geneticist. "We've got to try!"

Rezac shrugged and concentrated on the road. *Get him in the back with the others, Tiernay. He's got more of a chance there. We need to change vehicles. The Valtegans will spot this one a mile away now,* he sent.

"Shanka, help me get Nyaz over the back."

Shanka scrambled forward and between them they managed to haul Nyaz through to the back of the van.

"Zashou," said Tiernay, getting her to take over keeping pressure on the wound, "see what you can do. You've had some success with your healing. Try and control the bleeding at least." He looked up at the others. "Jaisa, use the sacks to cover Nyaz. Keep him warm and try to stop him going into shock."

Tiernay left him with the others and climbed back into the front. As he did, his hand closed over a hole burned neatly through the top of the seat. He followed its path, finding an equally neat hole in the midst of the remains of the opaqued window. He shuddered.

Rezac glanced at him. "We were lucky. Nyaz wasn't. He's still alive."

Tiernay said nothing.

"They'll send a craft up looking for us," said Rezac, turning into the main street. "Keep your eyes open for any likely looking vehicles. We need to lose this one as soon as possible."

"Hadn't you better slow down? We don't want to be stopped for speeding."

Rezac gave a snort of amusement. "One look at us and they won't be pulling us up for speeding. I know what I'm doing," he said, weaving in and out between the vehicles to the accompaniment of a chorus of angry beeps.

Without warning, he turned sharply to the left, throwing the van round the corner and accelerating hard up the straight stretch.

"Watch out!" came Jaisa's voice from behind.

Rezac braked hard, turning again, this time to the

right, then he dog-legged the van across the next road, emerging in the back streets leading to the docks.

"Do you have to drive like a maniac?" yelled Shanka from the rear. "We'll none of us make it if you carry on like this!"

"You want to walk, just let me know," Rezac growled in reply, crossing the road and coming to an abrupt halt alongside a small general store. "I'm trying to keep us all alive."

He turned off the engine. "Wait here till I call you," he said, pulling out his gun. Looking at Tiernay, he nodded his head toward the door. "Come."

Behind them was a medium-sized white delivery van, back doors standing open. The cab was empty.

Rezac glanced up and down the street again, checking for traffic. Nothing for the moment. He gestured to the other to follow and cautiously they approached the store doorway.

What're you going to do? asked Tiernay.

Take the van. You get everyone loaded, I'll keep watch.

Dubiously Tiernay backed off, heading for the rear of their vehicle.

Standing to one side, Rezac could see into the shop. The delivery driver was a youngling, barely into adolescence. He'd be no problem. The storekeeper was another matter, but for the moment, the two were deep in conversation over a pile of papers.

Keeping his eyes on the store interior, he used his telepathy to check on how the others were doing.

Load Nyaz last, he sent to Tiernay.

It seemed to take forever. He risked a glance back at them, seeing Jaisa and Vartra lifting Nyaz out. They were the last.

He looked back into the store. The youth was heading toward the door. Stepping to one side, he waited till the youngling had emerged and shut the door.

Leaning forward, Rezac grabbed him by the arm and jerked him into the street.

"Hey!"

Pressing his gun into the hollow of the driver's back, Rezac pushed him toward his delivery van.

"Just keep your mouth shut, and nothing will happen to you," he said quietly, his mouth inches from the youth's ear. "We're borrowing your van."

"You can't do . . ."

"Quiet!" commanded Rezac, digging the gun in sharply. The youth subsided, ears flicking in distress as he stumbled toward the rear of his vehicle.

A car was approaching from the opposite direction, but Nyaz was inside now and Tiernay was closing the doors.

"Take it nice and easy," warned Rezac as the car drew level with them. "This gun has a very light trigger."

The youth glanced round, eyes wide with fear, then looked away as the car passed by. Rezac took the opportunity to hit him on the back of the head with the gun butt.

As Tiernay turned round, the youth collapsed against him. "What the hell?" he exclaimed, making a grab for him before he fell.

"Stick him in the back of our van," said Rezac, slinging his gun back over his shoulder.

What've you done to him? demanded Tiernay, his mental tone outraged.

I haven't shot him, sent Rezac dryly. *Just dump him and let's get out of here.* He headed for the front of the vehicle.

The engine was running by the time Tiernay joined him in the cab.

"That wasn't necessary," he said angrily as Rezac pulled away from the store.

"You want the law after us as well as the Valtegans? I thought not. Now we have a chance of getting out of Khalma alive. In a white van, we might even make it across country to the monastery. I reckon that's worth a lump on his head. You got a problem about what I do, we'll settle it later, not now," said Rezac coldly.

Once they'd left the city, Rezac pulled up in the first rest area they came to.

"I'm going to check on Nyaz. If you see anything that looks like trouble, call me," he said, opening the door.

"Rezac," said Tiernay, reaching out to stop him. "You were right back there. I just wanted you to know."

Rezac's ears flicked in acknowledgment before he got out. Maybe these younglings were beginning to realize there was a real world after all.

The snow underfoot was deeper here than in the city; it sent a chill through the pads of his feet. He stopped to sniff the air. More was on the way unless he was mistaken. Going round to the back, he pulled open one of the doors and climbed inside.

"How is he?" he asked, closing it behind him.

"I've done what I can," Zashou said, "but that's virtually nothing. How long till we reach the monastery?"

"About three hours' drive."

She shook her head. "I don't think he'll make it."

"We'll see. You and the others start rearranging the load so we can talk across the back seats, I'll have a look at his shoulder."

Found a first aid kit under the seat, sent Tiernay from the front.

Hang onto it. I've got this lot shifting the load. You should be able to hand it back to me in a few minutes, replied Rezac, flicking back Nyaz's eyelids and checking his pulse. His color was bad and his pulse weak. It didn't look hopeful.

He waited till the first aid kit was handed back before undoing the bloody makeshift dressing. Zashou had returned and was crouched at his side ready to help.

"I wouldn't look," he said. "Check through the kit and give me the largest dressing there is."

"I'm all right," she said, her tone slightly irritated.

Rezac raised an eye ridge at her, then turned back to Nyaz's shoulder. He lifted the pad exposing the wound. The shoulder was a mess. The joint was shattered, pieces of bone gleaming through the ruin of torn flesh and muscle. Blood was still oozing sluggishly from it. He heard Zashou gasp.

"The dressing?"

She handed him one.

He unwrapped it and placed it over the wound, securing it in place with the short strips of bandage attached to it.

"Pass me a couple of bandages," he said, holding his hand out to her.

He bound the dressing on more securely, using the remaining bandage to bind Nyaz's arm firmly across his chest.

"I thought the wound would have been cauterized by the energy bolt," said Zashou, her voice subdued.

"The glass probably did more damage," said Rezac, getting up. "Keep him warm and as still as possible. He might make it."

Vartra caught hold of him. "He'll lose his arm, won't he?" he asked quietly.

Rezac nodded then turned to look back at Zashou. *I don't suppose there's any analgesics in that kit?*

She shook her head.

Then pray he either doesn't make it or stays unconscious till we get to the monastery. He was aware of Zashou's gaze following him as he walked forward to the driver's seat.

You did well, he sent. As he climbed over the seat into the front, the last rays of daylight shone through the windscreen, dazzling him briefly.

At the other side of the room, Zashou moaned in her sleep. Already their minds were beginning to harmonize as their Leska Link began to strengthen for their Link day. Like Rezac, she was reliving those first days as a fugitive from the Valtegans—the days when she'd first become aware of Rezac as more than a fellow student.

You did well, he sent, his tone warmer than she had felt from him before.

He's a strange one, she thought. *Too much the loner, refusing to allow anyone to get close to him.* As he climbed over the seat into the front, the last of the daylight caught him, showing up the sleek brown fur that covered his muscular frame. He looked back at her briefly, almost as if he'd caught her thoughts.

She pulled back mentally and busied herself making sure Nyaz was as comfortable as possible.

*   *   *

The jolting of the van woke her. Her head felt thick and she ached all over. "Where are we?" she mumbled, pushing herself into a sitting position and peering around in the dark.

"On the forestry track," said Jaisa, who'd been watching Nyaz while she slept. "We're nearly there."

"How's Nyaz?"

"Still with us."

"Shanka," called Rezac from the front. "When we get there, I want you and Jaisa to go ahead and organize a work party of six to join us at the tunnel mouth. I'll need a couple of people to help conceal the van and cover its tracks, a couple for the stretcher, and the rest can help carry the provisions in the van up to the monastery. Tiernay and I will unload while we wait. Dr. Vartra, you go with them."

"Will do," called out Jaisa when Shanka didn't reply.

Zashou glanced at her mate. "What's wrong?" she asked quietly.

"Him."

"Who? Rezac?"

"Tiernay's supposed to be in charge, not him. Who does he think he is, ordering us all around?" he said, his voice low but angry.

"If Tiernay's not bothered, why are you? Rezac got us here safely."

"I'd have expected some support from you," he said.

"Not when you're wrong."

Shanka subsided into silence until the van drew to a stop.

"Let's move, people," said Tiernay from the front. "Dr. Vartra, will you tell Dr. Nyaam that Nyaz is seriously wounded and has lost a lot of blood, please?"

"Absolutely," said the doctor, getting to his feet. "I'll make sure the infirmary's ready for him."

Slinging her gun over her shoulder, Jaisa scrambled to the rear doors, pushed them open, and disappeared into the night.

Zashou made sure Nyaz was well covered by the

sacks, then put on her jacket. The air gusting into the van was freezing. She made her way to the opening and jumped out to land in thick snow. She gasped at the shock of it, wrapped her arms around her chest, and plowed through the snow to the front of the van. Flakes were landing on her eyelashes, making her blink as they melted.

Rezac was sprawled across the wheel, head resting on his forearms. He looked up as she tapped on the window, then reached over to open the door.

His tiredness hit her like a physical wave.

"I'm coming," he said, climbing down.

She followed him back to the rear where Tiernay joined them.

"Zashou, you get inside and push the boxes to the door. Rezac and I'll carry them," said Tiernay.

"Fine by me," she said, the relief at being able to get out of the cold evident in her voice. Tiernay gave her a hand up.

They'd barely finished unloading when Jaisa returned with the work party—and Dr. Nyaam, who immediately headed for Nyaz.

"Where's Shanka?" Tiernay asked Jaisa.

"He decided to stay," she replied, refusing eye contact.

They both picked up her unvoiced thought.

"You'll have to watch that one," Zashou heard Rezac say to Tiernay in a low voice. "He's a liability."

"He's my problem," said Tiernay, turning away.

"See that he doesn't become mine," Rezac growled, opening the cab door. Zashou was sitting on the passenger seat. He hesitated, then got in, closing the door behind him.

"I thought you'd want to get up to the monastery with the others," he said.

"I'm not much use at carrying weights, but I can help with the van," she said, looking over at him. "We each do what we can."

He nodded.

"Can't you leave this to someone else?" she asked. "You're dead on your feet."

"No. I want it done properly. Our lives depend on it." He turned to look into the interior. "How is he?"

"Touch and go," Dr. Nyaam answered. "Any idea how long he's been in shock?"

"None, I was driving. Zashou?"

She shook her head. "I slept through the last part of the journey. Jaisa might know."

"Did anyone give him food or drink after he sustained the injury?"

"No," said Zashou. "He's been unconscious since it happened."

"Let's get him up to the infirmary," said Nyaam, moving back to let the stretcher bearers load him. "Be careful," he warned, "he's on a drip."

When they were clear, a couple of youths climbed in.

"We're with you," said one as the other shut the rear doors.

Rezac drove back down the track until he came to a fork. Taking the left branch, he headed along it for a couple of kilometers before coming to a stop in front of a rocky outcrop. Ahead was a large tangle of thorny bushes still covered in thick green leaves. The few orange berries that the birds hadn't eaten made a splash of color against the layers of snow.

"This'll do." He turned round to the youths in the rear of the van. "Try to open the bushes out enough to let me drive into the center."

They nodded, drawing machetes out of their belts before they got down.

"You'd be better off getting out now," he said to Zashou. "There's no need for both of us to get ripped up by the thorns."

Nodding, she climbed out, aware that he was watching her. She walked ahead to stand in the shelter of the rock face. The headlights illuminated her, the light glinting off the beads in her hair and the silver bracelets that encircled her wrists.

Stamping her feet to keep them warm, she tucked her hands under her armpits. They seemed to be almost finished now. The bushes grew in long prickle-studded arches and the two younglings, both having had the sense to bring thick gloves, had been pulling these back and anchoring them under the shorter growths on the outside edges of the bushes. A large area near the heart of the bush was rapidly becoming a lot clearer.

As they began to hack at the ground growth with their machetes, Zashou looked back to the van, opening her mouth in a smile for Rezac. He glanced away, obviously unwilling to catch her eye.

She frowned, looking away quickly herself. Had she done something wrong? Surely not. She was only being friendly. Her thoughts were suddenly interrupted by one of the lads yelling "Ready!" and beckoning Rezac forward.

He started up the engine and slowly rolled the van into the heart of the bushes. It was a tight fit. Cutting the motor and lights, he opened the door and climbed down onto the relatively snow-free ground. She watched as, keeping his face to the van side, he inched his way out, the tiny sharp thorns catching on his tunic and legs. Just before he cleared the bush, a tenacious sucker wrapped itself around his calf, digging viciously into his flesh as he tried to pull loose. With a few choice words, he ripped his leg free and stumbled out into the clearing.

"Cover it up," he ordered, hopping on one leg as he rubbed the other, trying to get the tiny thorns out.

Zashou hid a grin behind her hand and tried to swallow her laughter.

"Are you all right?" she asked.

"I'm fine," he growled, refusing to look at her as he gave up on the leg.

The van concealed to his satisfaction, branches were cut for each of them to use as switches to erase the tire tracks and their footprints. The two younglings went ahead, Zashou and Rezac following a few meters behind them to make sure no traces of their passage remained.

The snow was falling faster now, adding another layer to conceal the marks of their passage.

Khuushoi is certainly smiling on us tonight, she sent to Rezac.

He grunted. *I don't hold much faith in Goddesses or Gods.*

Rezac glanced sideways at the female as every now and then she walked backward to check the effectiveness of her path-sweeping. Despite himself, he was beginning to be impressed by her tenacity. Intelligent, flamboyant in personality and image, it was natural to assume she was the same as her husband. Shanka didn't know what hard work was, but Zashou was a reliable and diligent member of the little research team headed by Dr. Vartra.

She played hard, too. Her main friends were the other members of their group, though to his knowledge she'd had a couple of lovers among the other students over the year they had all known each other.

Her mate did just enough work to manage to stay with the team and make it appear that he was doing more. He was frequently seen around campus with one if not two of his current half dozen females. He had money, and they enjoyed helping him spend it.

Rezac snorted in disgust. He despised people like Shanka, the socially advantaged who could buy their way out of any problem. He'd had dealings with too many of them in the past.

He felt a hand on his arm and realized Zashou was talking to him.

"Rezac, what is it? Gods, you're freezing!" she said.

"I'm fine," he said.

"No, you're not. Your fur is standing on end. You were exhausted when we arrived, never mind now. Your body can't cope with this cold. We've got to get you into the warm as soon as possible."

"I'm fine, I tell you," he snapped.

She grabbed hold of him, forcing him to stop. "Rezac, the snow has set in for the night. Even if we did nothing, our tracks would be gone by morning. Leave it to the younglings: They're dressed for it. One casualty today is enough! We don't need you becoming hypothermic."

He hesitated. There was sense in what she said and now that he'd stopped moving, he could feel himself trembling with fatigue and the cold.

"Come on, let's go ahead," she said, pulling him onward.

He nodded finally, throwing his branch into the nearest bush.

She did likewise and they increased their speed, overtaking the two youths.

"I'll leave it to you," said Rezac. "We're going on ahead."

They nodded, giving a brief wave as Zashou and Rezac passed them.

Gamely Zashou plodded through the snow in Rezac's wake. His longer legs took him farther ahead with each stride. Just as she thought she'd lost him, his hand grasped her.

"You're not in much better shape yourself," he said, "despite your jacket." He swung her up into his arms, refusing to put her down despite her protests. After a few minutes she stopped complaining, realizing they were actually making better speed.

"About time you shut up," he said. "Nearly deafened me with your moaning, yet you were the one that said we had to get back quickly! You need to learn your own limits, then you won't pick a job you aren't able to cope with."

"I didn't realize the snow was so deep," she said. "And you didn't realize it was so cold!"

He grunted and continued walking in silence, aware of the warmth of her body in his arms and her scent in his nostrils.

He woke suddenly, hypersensitive to her presence, only aware of their Link and his need for her. It had begun well enough, he was sure of it. So vivid had the dream been that he could still feel the pressure of her body against his chest.

In her bed, she moved restlessly and once again the pull of their Link surged through him—and her, calling them together. Throwing the blankets aside, he got to his feet. The fire had burned down to a faint glow. He shivered. He both dreaded and lived for their Link days because it was the only time he felt complete—when their minds spoke directly to each other without the ability to lie or hurt. Then they belonged together, bodies and souls as one, the way it was meant to be, deny it as they might the next day. Lifting the covers, he slipped into the bed beside her, reaching out to draw her closer. At his touch, she woke, her face creasing in a frown, ears flicking.

It's time, he sent, continuing to pull her closer despite her resistance.

You might be less demanding about it.

The words were sharper than the intent, he knew. Already she was relaxing against him, letting him wrap his arms around her.

Yesterday's over, Zashou. Let's leave it behind. This is our day now, he sent persuasively, his teeth gently catching hold of one of her ears.

Like a tide flowing up a river, their minds began to merge, becoming one. She sighed and reached a hand up to his neck. Her touch was like fire to his heightened senses, at once burning and relieving his need to hold her. He could feel the same need building in her as she pressed herself closer to him. The tension began to leave her body and within his arms, at last she began to relax.

*   *   *

Lijou greeted him in his private quarters, getting up as the door opened to admit him. "Thank you for accepting my invitation, Kaid," he said, reaching out to touch fingertips with him as he entered. "Well come to Stronghold. I intend to make sure your stay this time will be far more pleasant than your last one. Have you settled in? You're only a few doors away from me and from Kha'Qwa if you should need anything."

"I thought the suite was rather grand," Kaid murmured, returning the gesture and accepting the seat the priest indicated.

"One of our guest quarters," said Lijou, sitting down. "I sent for coffee and c'shar because I wasn't sure which you'd prefer."

"C'shar, please." It felt strange being here. Memories of years gone by came back to him as he looked round Lijou's personal office cum lounge. The last time he'd been in this room was when they'd come for Vanna. Before that, it had been Jyarti's, Lijou's predecessor as Head Priest.

"You must have spent a lot of time in this study," said Lijou as he poured him his drink.

"I divided it between here and the library," said Kaid.

"I was helping Jyarti with refining the religious aspects of the Brothers' training."

"And it's those skills we have need of again. I'm afraid you'll be something of a test case for us in our training of telepathic priests."

Kaid raised a questioning eye ridge as he picked up his mug.

"We've never had to initiate such a wide-scale training of telepaths before. You'll be our first, which is another reason why, with the help of Kha'Qwa, we'll be working with you. We need your feedback."

Kaid shrugged. "What help I can give is yours." He watched Lijou settle back into his chair, wondering what was coming next.

"We do have one expert here, one who'll surprise you. Tutor Sorli, from the Telepath Guild. He's requested some time here in retreat to meditate at the temple, but he's also agreed to help us."

"Sorli? What tears him away from Esken?" This was a surprise.

"You know as much as I do. He keeps his thoughts firmly to himself and will say nothing more on the subject. Naturally, I haven't pressed him about the matter."

"Naturally." Kaid hesitated, wondering if this was some plot of Esken's, then discarded the thought.

"Sorli may be an apologist for his Guild Master, but he's no one's puppet, Kaid. I have to admit, I considered the possibility, too."

"Sorli's as straight as a new blade. If he's here, then it's at his own request. Still, I wonder what goes on at their guild."

"We'll find out in time," said Lijou placidly. "We have one or two folk among the warriors guarding the Terran contingent. However, it wasn't about this I wanted to talk to you today, it was about Vartra. It's been nearly two weeks since you returned from the Margins, time for what you saw and heard there to sink in fully. We need to discuss it frankly now—need to decide what should become known only within the Order, and what can be made public."

"We need to ensure that no one else returns to the past," said Kaid grimly. "We know it can be altered. Now there is a balance; matters have come out best for us in this time. Should anyone else attempt to return and succeed, then the balance could be disrupted, maybe even allow the chance that the Valtegans still on Shola were not all killed in the Cataclysm. General Kezule had planned to weather the disaster out in the mountains with a few of his soldiers and some eggs in the hope of returning to take control of our world again once it was over. Had we not gone back, he might have succeeded."

He watched in satisfaction as the priest's face took on a look of profound shock, his ears lying flat against his skull in fear.

"It was that close?"

Kaid nodded. "You were right, Lijou. We had to return to the Margins for the good of Shola."

"Tell me it all."

Perhaps not all, thought Kaid. *Would it help prevent others even thinking of trying if they knew the only reason we survived was because I came from the past? Do I keep my life private, or make it public for the good of our world?*

CHAPTER 4

The cell door slid open with its usual clang. *You'd think in this day and age they could have made it silent,* Keeza thought, watching the two guards from her bunk bed.

"Get up. Face the rear wall," the nearer guard ordered. "Hands behind your back."

She stood, turning her back to them, and waited while he came across the narrow room. She was roughly grasped first by one hand then the other, as the metal wrist restraint was locked in place.

"What's it now?" she demanded. "You could at least leave me in peace tonight! Bother me all you want tomorrow."

"You should be so lucky," the guard snorted, grasping her by the upper arm and pulling her round to face him. "You got a visitor. Some official." He led her out of the cell.

"Don't get your hopes up," the other said, teeth prominent in his openmouthed grin as he locked the door behind him. "They don't grant pardons for the likes of you."

Used to the taunts over the last couple of days, she didn't bother answering them. This visitor, though, that intrigued her. What official would want to speak to her? What could they want from her? They'd gotten all they needed with their damned telepaths at the trial; they knew there was nothing left to tell.

Resisting slightly, she made them drag her along the corridors and through the successive check point gates till they came to the Chief Warden's office. A knock on the door, and she was thrust inside.

The figure at the window turned slowly to look at her. The first thing she noticed was the long gray robe.

"This is Keeza Lassah, Brother," said the Warden, getting to his feet. "I'll leave you alone while you talk to her."

L'Seuli nodded.

Narrowing her eyes against the last of the daylight, Keeza weighed him up. Of average height, he was stockily built, as far as she could tell with those robes. The sandy-colored pelt coupled with the rounded ears set low on his head suggested a desert dweller. The light behind him illuminated him from an angle, accentuating the planes of his face. A strong face, the jawline broad and firm, eyes set wide above his cheekbones, nose narrow, ending with pale flesh. He returned her gaze impassively. She gave an involuntary shudder. Like all of his kind, someone to reckon with.

Keeza waited till the warden had left before jerking her head backward to indicate her cuffs. "You going to let me go?"

He ignored her question. "I have a proposition for you, Keeza Lassah," he said. "A job that requires some of your skills."

She snorted derisively. "I thought you folk did your own killing! In case you haven't heard, I won't be around after dawn tomorrow."

"If you accept this task, your death sentence will be commuted—once certain safeguards have been taken."

Her eye ridges met in anger. "I won't have my mind messed with by those damned telepaths!"

He began to turn away. "As you wish. I'd have thought life and freedom were an acceptable payment for so simple an assignment."

She growled, tail flicking jerkily, ears flattening. Whatever it was, it was obviously dangerous, but it offered a chance of survival. "Tell me."

              *   *   *

"You want me to turn this into a Consortia?" There was frank disbelief in the female's voice as she surveyed L'Seuli's companion. "When I agreed to help you, I had no idea you'd provide me with such raw material!"

"Think of it as a challenge," said L'Seuli soothingly.

Khaimoe got to her feet and paced round Keeza, her silken robe rustling as she did. "She's got nothing to start with! No posture, no shape—and what do you call this?" With a lightning fast movement, she reached out to pluck a strand of Keeza's tabby brown hair, holding it out for him to inspect.

"Hey!" Keeza exclaimed, batting Khaimoe's hand away and pulling back from her. "I didn't ask to come here, just remember that!"

"She's been in a correction center, what do you expect?"

"A correction center?" Khaimoe's eyes narrowed as she returned to her chair. "What's she done?"

"Nothing that need worry you, Khaimoe, you have my word on that," said L'Seuli calmly, getting to his feet. "I think you're being unkind. Some decent food, oil treatments for her hair and she'll look the part. It isn't as if she's unattractive."

"What happens if she leaves here without permission? Who's responsible for her?"

"She won't leave, will you, Keeza?" he said, looking at her. "She's tagged. If she steps beyond the perimeter of this building, she won't be capable of continuing farther."

"And what turns this tag off?"

"Bringing her back inside, Khaimoe, that's all. I'll leave you to start your training. You have four weeks before we need her."

"Four weeks! Do you realize how long it takes for us to train a youngling properly?" exclaimed Khaimoe angrily. "And that's another thing! She's too old!"

"I think you'll find her a willing pupil. After all, she's got an incentive. We aren't expecting her to be perfect, just to have enough skills to deal with the target in the majority of situations that could occur."

"She's one of you, isn't she? You've foisted a Sister on me. A Consortia assassin, that's what you want, isn't it? Well, I won't do it!"

L'Seuli looked offended. "On the contrary, we want her to help keep someone alive. I assure you she's not of the Brotherhood. Her background is just as I've told you. If you feel you cannot rise to the challenge, then perhaps I should place her with another House."

"That won't be necessary," said Khaimoe, her tone now frosty. "We'll stick to our contract. You may return four weeks from today."

Inclining his head, L'Seuli turned and left the two females alone.

Khaimoe sat tapping her claws against the padded arm

of her chair, looking thoughtfully at the problem in front
of her. He was probably right, she admitted to herself.
What the female needed was feeding up and teaching how
to make the best of herself. If she read her right, though,
one like her wasn't interested in making herself attractive.

"Do you know what it is we do here?" she asked her
abruptly.

"Yeah. High class qwenes," Keeza replied with a sniff
of disdain.

"We do a damned sight more than cater to the sexual
side of Sholan nature, my girl," she said sharply. "Your
name?"

"Keeza Lassah."

"What did you do to land in a correction facility?"

"None of your damned business!"

"We operate on a basis of trust here, Keeza. I need to
know what your crime was."

"I killed a pack leader," she said, moving over to a
nearby chair and sitting down. Her body posture was simultaneously protective and aggressive.

"Ah." Enlightenment dawned. "I thought I recognized
the name. And you lived to tell the tale. Unusual."

Keeza laughed, a hard, humorless laugh. "Yeah, you
could call it alive. I'd only have lived until dawn unless I
agreed to do this job."

Strangely, the knowledge of her identity was comforting.
There might be some chance of success with her, after all.
Any female who could infiltrate one of the major Ranz
packs, and work her way close to the leader deserved a
second look. Not only that, but she'd successfully killed him
and lived to face trial. Oh, there had been a bloodbath
during her escape from the Pack den, and only Protector
involvement had ensured her survival, but nonetheless . . .

"Why? Why did you kill him?"

"That's my business," she replied sharply.

Khaimoe shrugged mentally. Her motive mattered not at
all. She looked over to the ornate timepiece on the wall
above the entrance and began to rise. "We have a break
at this time of evening. Come with me and I'll introduce
you to your tutors. You'll be sharing a room with one of
them."

"I don't share," Keeza growled as she got up.

"You will here. We find that sharing increases our students' awareness of the need to display oneself to the best advantage."

"I don't get on well with other females," she muttered, following her out the door into the corridor.

"Perfectly all right. You're sharing with a nice male called Mabu'h."

"A male!"

Khaimoe stopped and turned round to look at her. "Of course. There are two Sholan sexes after all. Our graduates go on to cater to the business and personal needs of males and females in every level of society."

"So what do you do?" Her surprise was obvious.

Khaimoe began to walk in step with her. "To put it simply, we're social entertainers and professional companions. Our graduates are well educated in all the fields of art, entertainment, and politics, making them acceptable at every level of society. You'd be surprised to know that many actually become contracted as life-mates to partners in important positions—people who haven't the time to develop the relationships necessary to gaining a mate and having a family."

"I hadn't realized."

"Those who need to know about us know these things, Keeza," she said not unkindly. "The rest see us only as Exotics." She laughed at Keeza's embarrassed ear flick. "Oh, yes, we do cater to that side as well, but not to the detriment of being whole, rounded people. Even in so short a time, if you apply yourself well, you'll have skills that will lift you above the ordinary once your mission is completed. A new start, Keeza." If she could motivate her now, it would be so much easier for them all.

Keeza made a noncommittal noise.

Later that night, after reading the files L'Seuli had provided, Khaimoe contacted Stronghold.

"What you're asking is beyond the bounds of good taste!" she fumed. "It's monstrous!"

"Don't tell me you don't cater to all types," said L'Seuli. "You have to. You wouldn't send your people out into the world unable to cope with the darker side."

"We deal with it, yes, but not like this!"

"She agreed to do it."

"She had no choice!"

"She originally chose death rather than submit to personality reprogramming. She has twice exercised her right to choose. That you don't agree with her choices is not my concern. Do you wish me to go elsewhere, Khaimoe? I thought your House would give her the best chance of survival. Was I wrong?" He raised a questioning eye ridge. "We've always come to you in the past. Should we now seek out a new ally?"

"You're all the same! So removed from our problems, aren't you? Above it all! You know damned well I'll do my best for her!"

"Information from our target is crucial, Khaimoe. This is more important than the life of one pack female. At least I've done what I can to help her. Now it's up to you."

Khaimoe broke the connection unceremoniously. Closing the folder, she shuddered with suppressed horror. Thank the good Gods that she wasn't the one faced with such a choice.

*   *   *

A full-throated yowl of fear rang through the village. At the same moment, every telepath saw the image of water and felt a mental surge of fear that was abruptly cut short.

Seated in the den with Carrie, Kusac started to his feet in shock. *Who—and where?* He sent on the widest band width he could.

Zhyaf! My brother! The mental cry echoed inside Kusac's head.

Dzaka and Meral came rushing into the room at Carrie's command. *See to Zhyaf,* she ordered.

I'm on my way, sent Vanna from the medical center. *Find Mara! She's the one that needs me!*

Dzaka, stay at the house. Where's Mara? Kusac demanded as Meral left at a run.

It was Carrie who replied as she began to run for the door. *Risho Bay! It's the sea! She's fallen from the Point!*

As he followed her, Kusac activated his wrist comm. "Ni-'Zulhu, get someone out to Risho Point immediately. Search for Mara."

"Over the site already, Liege. Our on-duty sensitive picked her up," came the faint reply.

"Do what you can. Help's on its way."

Kusac, Jack's seeing to Zhyaf, I'm heading for the Point now, sent Vanna.

When they arrived at the Point, Mara had already been loaded into the emergency vehicle. Rulla, dripping and shivering, was standing beside it wrapped in a blanket.

"What happened?" demanded Carrie, going instantly to his side.

"It was sheer luck," he said, rubbing a corner of the blanket across his forehead and ears. "She's been acting strangely these last few days." He looked obliquely at Kusac. "Stranger than usual," he amended. "Ever since her pregnancy was confirmed a couple of days ago. So I've been following her." He stopped again to wipe his face.

"How did she fall?" asked Kusac.

"She didn't fall, she jumped. I thought you realized that. The snow broke her fall, stopped her killing herself on the rocks on the way down. She'd have drowned, though, if I hadn't been there to pull her out." His shivers became more acute and his nose wrinkled prior to a loud sneeze.

The quiet hum of Vanna's craft rose in preparation for take-off and Kusac shepherded them all aside.

"She's alive, isn't she?" Carrie shouted above the noise of the engine as they headed over to their own vehicle.

Rulla nodded vigorously. "Was touch and go, but she'll live."

"Well done," said Kusac, sealing the aircar's door once they were all inside. "She owes her life to you. I'll get Garras to allocate a round-the-clock watch on her from now on. You shouldn't be trying to cope with this alone."

"I thought Zhyaf was told to sort out his relationship with her," said Carrie, frowning.

"He's tried, I'll grant him that," said Rulla. "He brought his sister to live with him as a role model for her. Teach her how to fit in, that sort of thing."

Carrie caught his grimace. "His older sister?" she hazarded.

"She's a very worthy Sholan matron," said Rulla hastily, trying not to sniff as he surreptitiously wiped his nose with the blanket.

"But Mara's Human, not Sholan! I could have told you that wouldn't work!" She looked at Kusac accusingly. "I taught kids her age back on Keiss, you know that, you were

with me often enough! Why didn't one of you tell me wha
was going on?"

Kusac felt his ears trying to lie back in embarrassmen
but refused to let them. "I considered it more importan
that you were kept free from any worries during your preg
nancy," he said. "Mara wasn't my concern, you were. Ther
were any number of people she could go to for help—
people who tried to approach her, but she wanted non
of them."

"They were all Sholan, Kusac. A girl that age, a teenager
needs someone of her own species to help her. She's stil
trying to become an adult Human female, never mind being
pushed into becoming a responsible Sholan matron! Didn'
that occur to any of you?" She looked from one to the
other of the two males.

"Liegena, the responsibility was mine," said Rulla quietly. "I was given the task of looking after her and her
Leska. Being male, I'm afraid I spent more of my efforts
on Zhyaf, assuming, wrongly it now seems, that Mara,
being about the same age as yourself, would take to our
ways as you did."

"She could have gone to Jack," Kusac said. "He's Human."
He flinched under his mate's withering glance.

"He's old enough to be her grandfather! And she's a
good few years younger than me, I'll have you know! What
she needs is a Human den mother, preferably one with
children of her own so she doesn't feel like she's being
watched."

They were approaching the village now, and Kusac used
that to turn his attention away from what was becoming an
embarrassing discussion.

Rulla was left to answer her. "My apologies, Liegena,"
he said, his ears flat against his skull. "It's not easy to judge
Human age. You're so small in comparison to an adult
Sholan . . ." He faltered to a stop under her glare.

"I think you'd better take a hot shower and get yourself
warmed up when you get back to your rooms," she said.
"You can report to me later. I'll have this matter sorted
out by then."

"Yes, Liegena," he said with a sigh.

Thankfully the fall hadn't affected Mara's pregnancy, and
beyond scrapes and bruising, the girl hadn't been seriously

jured, but it would be several days before she could be leased from the medical unit. Jack was sending to Vals-rth Telepath Guild for a Human psychiatrist to visit her. e wasn't the first Human to have problems integrating to the Sholan community, and likely wouldn't be the last. hyaf was suffering from shock and was being kept in over-ght for observation, but no problems were expected om him.

Kusac escaped to his office as soon as he could to search e Human telepath database for a suitable den mother r Mara, one who wouldn't object to coming to live on e estate.

"I want one without a mate," Carrie warned him. "I ant as little as possible to remind Mara of males."

He didn't want to know her reasoning right now; he just anted to get out of the line of fire.

Carrie, accompanied by Dzaka, headed off for Zhyaf and 1ara's home. She stood in the entrance hall and looked ound at the emptiness in disbelief. A rug of somber pat-rn, obviously well darned, lay across the length of the aneled floor. "It's as if he's made no effort to personalize he place."

Dzaka activated the lights as it was growing dark out-ide. "Zhyaf's family is from the northern end of the conti-ent," he said. "We, in the south, are a much more elaxed people."

She looked up at him with a grin. "We in the south is it 1ow, Dzaka? Do I detect a degree of proprietariness in our adoption of the estate?"

He smiled back, lifting his shoulders gently in a shrug. 'Life has regained pleasures I thought I'd lost, Liegena. I 1elong here now." He turned his attention to the door op-1osite. "That will be their lounge. The ones on either side vill be their bedrooms."

"I only want to see the public areas," she said, follow-ng him.

The lounge was as dark as the hallway had been. A ubiq-1itous desk, large and ungainly, squatted in a far corner. It vas obviously made of some cheap synthetic material that 1dded neither grace nor function to its appearance. With ts untidy clutter of papers and files, it dominated the room.

Seating was handled by three chairs set with their back to the door. The word easy could hardly be applied to them, Carrie thought as she walked slowly into the room. They were thinly padded and with only the barest suggestion of a dip in the center. Aligned in a neat row, they faced a long, low table. Shelving lined the opposite wall, the shelves a riot of cassettes laid on their sides or slumped against each other. To her left, a fire glowed feebly in the grate, obviously relying on the heating system to provide the warmth for the room.

Carrie shivered and pulled her cloak tighter. Through the window opposite she could see snow had begun to fall once more. "Is it me, or is it cold in here?"

"It could be warmer," admitted Dzaka, going across to pull the drapes. Once they'd been more brightly colored but like everything else she'd seen so far, there was an air of age and mustiness about them. "Zhyaf isn't one to pay much attention to his surroundings," he said, returning to her side. "Northerners are an abstemious lot, don't like unnecessary waste, tend to fight the cold with more clothing rather than more heat. They're cut off from the rest of us for most of the winter. In the days before air transport they had to make do till the thaws came."

"Yes, but just the same! It isn't like that now, and I know he's earning enough to have furnished the house far better than this!"

"It's probably the furniture from his last home. Zhyaf's more of a scholar than anything. At times he hardly seems to live in the same world as the rest of us."

"Poor Mara," said Carrie. "To have a Leska so unsuited to her personality. T'Chebbi told me that when they escorted her from Chagda, she immediately said she'd like to join the Brotherhood. Has she had any outlets that could bring her pleasure?"

Dzaka avoided looking at her. "Beyond chasing after any of the more presentable young males on the estate? Probably not. I know she's not been to any training sessions, and only visited Ghyan occasionally at the shrine for instruction."

"Is that all?" Carrie was aghast. "What's she done with her time?"

"Well, she's been over at the dig, but she's been incapable of settling to one area for any length of time, so no

ne's been able to rely on her. Rulla should know more
out that since they were in his charge."

"He said he spent most of his time with Zhyaf. What
out the Humans? Hasn't she made friends among them?"

"No, she's been told to stay away from them by their
ader, Ms. Southgate."

"What about off-duty time? There's the canteen up at
he dig."

He shook his head. "Not there either, nor at their
ccommodation."

"That's ridiculous!" She was furious now. "Mara's been
bandoned by everyone here! No one has looked out for
er at all! If only you'd not all been so afraid for me, this
aight never have happened! No wonder she tried to take
er life—she has no life here!"

"Her life is my brother," came the cold reply from be-
aind her. There was an underlying growl of anger present.
How dare you enter his house without permission?"

"Khartu Rakula, may I present the Liegena Clan Leader,
Carrie Aldatan?" said Dzaka, stepping smoothly between
Carrie and Zhyaf's sister. "We're here to collect some of
Mara's belongings."

"Clan Leader."

The tone was no warmer, Carrie noticed, as the female
urned and headed toward one of the doors in the hallway.

"That's his sister?"

"Yes." Dzaka's whisper was as quiet as hers had been.

"We've got to get her out of here!"

Dzaka touched her briefly on the arm. "We should return
o the hall now."

She followed him back out of the room and stood waiting
mpatiently. Khartu returned in a few minutes carrying a
small bag which she handed to Dzaka.

"I hope you will be doing something permanent to that
female. It's utterly preposterous that my brother's life
should depend on someone who is obviously as unbalanced
as she is. If you won't, then I'll appeal to the Guild."

Carrie looked up at this tall figure of Sholan righteous-
ness and wished for the millionth time she had a body as
readily able to convey her feelings as the Sholans. Instead
she allowed some of what she felt to leak beyond her barriers and watched Khartu's eyes widen as she stepped back
in shock.

"Tell me, Khartu, have you attended an orientation session at the shrine since you arrived?"

"What do you mean?"

"On this estate, we do things somewhat differently. All newcomers need to be told what our rules and regulation are. They have to fit into our community." She waited a moment to let this sink in. "We do not conform to outsid ers' ideas. How Mara will be treated is a matter for her physician, not for you. To my mind, it is utterly ridiculous for a female as young as Mara to be Leska-linked to a male as old as your brother! But that can't be helped. He's going to need a great deal of counseling to help him adjust, too." She turned and began to walk toward the door, then stopped.

"See the rest of Mara's belongings are sent to the villa, Khartu Rakula. You'll be pleased to know she will not be returning to this house. Good day."

Dzaka had to run to catch up with her. "Liegena . . ."

"Get Zhala to set up one of the guest rooms for Mara until we've found her a den mother," she said. "If only someone had told me something of what was going on! Never let this happen again, Dzaka," she said rounding on him. "No matter what Kusac says, tell me!"

"Yes, Liegena, but you have to realize we were all afraid that . . ."

"What?" she demanded, continuing down the snow cleared main street to the villa.

"That because of what had happened to you, her fear of having a Sholan cub would . . ."

"Would what, Dzaka?" She was losing patience with him now.

"That you'd become afraid of your own cub again."

She stopped dead and looked up at him in surprise. "You thought I'd be afraid of carrying my cub?" She reached out from the folds of her cloak to tweak his ear. "Never! Not this or any other cub, Dzaka. I know who and what I am now."

"What's that?"

"En'Shalla, Dzaka. The first En'Shalla Human," she said, taking him by the arm.

When Carrie returned home, she checked out the data files with Kusac. There was only one likely candidate and

was with little expectation of success that she contacted
e woman, inviting her out to the villa the next day for
i interview. Her fears, however, proved to be unfounded.
Ruth could have been the archetypal Mother. Of medium
ight, her figure could best be described as Junoesque.
avy fair hair with ginger highlights reached midway down
r back. Green eyes sparkled with amusement and interest
she glanced around the den. Arranging her long winter
iolan robes around herself, she sat down in one of the
isy chairs.

"Coffee?" Carrie asked.

"That would be nice," said Ruth, looking curiously at the
ightly patterned rugs and wall hangings. "Is this Sholan
ecoration? Or do I detect an Earth influence?"

"Sholan—southern Sholan," Carrie said, handing her a
iug. "There are apparently similarities, though. Being
eissian I wouldn't know."

Ruth accepted the mug. "Of course. I'd forgotten you
ere one of the original colonists. Be surprising if there
eren't similarities considering how well our species get on
igether. Your young male, Dzaka, wasn't very forthcom-
ig about the nature of this meeting. He was almost as
iysterious as you were yesterday! How about explaining
ie situation?"

"We have a young girl here, Mara Ryan, with a Sholan
.eska," began Carrie.

"Everyone at the Guild knows about Mara! What about
ie rest? What's the real problem with Mara?"

Carrie felt herself beginning to warm to the woman. "As
see it, it's twofold. First, she's not much more than a child
ierself. From what I can gather, her family were more than
iappy to see the back of her because of her Sholan Leska."
ihe stopped to take a sip of her coffee and collect her
houghts. "Secondly, everyone around her has been ex-
iecting her to fit into Sholan culture as easily as if she'd
ieen born to it."

"Because you did."

Carrie tilted her head to one side in a uniquely Sholan
;esture of embarrassed agreement. "I was the first. They
udged her by me, and I wasn't aware of what was happen-
ng then. Because of my injuries after the Challenge, no
ine wanted to involve me in her troubles." She sighed,
iicking up a spoon and stirring her coffee several times.

"Also, at that time, I was the only Human on the estate. Now Mara's pregnant, and her cub will look as Sholan as mine and Vanna's. Yesterday she tried to commit suicide."

Ruth made a noise of sympathy. "Was she badly hurt?"

"Thankfully, no, and the cub's all right, too, but she still wants to abort."

"What's the Sholan view? And yours, come to that."

"The Sholan attitude is colored by the fact that their females only become pregnant when they want to. To do so outside a contract with a partner, or your Leska, carries heavy social penalties. As for me, I can't afford to let my prejudices affect Mara." She smiled gently. "I've too newly become a mother. This is a Sholan estate, though, not Human, so Sholan attitudes tend to prevail."

"So what you want is to create a halfway house for Mara, a predominantly Human environment in which she can finish growing up," said Ruth thoughtfully.

"One without a male influence," added Carrie. "I want nothing to remind her of her life with Zhyaf."

"I do have a daughter," began Ruth.

"No problem. A younger girl she can show round the estate could be good for her. Provided you do realize that relationships—physical relationships—between Humans and Sholans are the norm and you don't mind your daughter growing up in our kind of environment."

"It's healthier than the one at the Guild," Ruth said frankly. "There's been no real effort to integrate us into the mainstream classes. A two-tier guild is already established with only the Humans needed in an official capacity getting adequate training. You know, the more I think about it, the more halfway houses—not only on this estate but elsewhere—seem like a good idea."

Ruth drained her mug and put it back on the low table in front of her. "She can't be the only young woman on Shola with cultural identity problems, and with more mixed Leska pairings happening, the problem is going to grow. Yes, I'd love to be involved."

"We're only concerned with those on our estate at the moment," said Carrie. "We occupy a unique position on Shola, an En'Shalla Clan, owing allegiance only to each other and the Head Priest of Vartra. Believe me, that's going to be a large enough responsibility for all of us." She leaned forward to refill her mug, gesturing to Ruth's at the me time. "I'm looking for someone to run our project, meone to be our den mother and set up pastoral care for ose not living with her. Are you interested?" Her instincts were usually right, and they were telling her Ruth as the person she needed.

"No disrespect intended, but before I commit myself to mething of this size, I'd like to know your chain of command. To whom would I be answerable?"

That was good, Carrie thought. Ruth's already looking t the consequences of her decision. "We'd have an advisory group until it was up and running. After that, you hould be pretty well autonomous. There's Jack Reynolds, ur physician, myself and my life-mate, Kusac, of course, nd Clan Leader Rhyasha up at the Aldatan estate."

"What about the Telepath Guild? What's their involvement?"

"None. We have established friendly relations with them, nd an exchange of medical and telepathic data, but hat's all."

Ruth nodded, obviously satisfied. "And my position? If leave the Telepath Guild to come here, I'll need some ecurity. I have my daughter to think of as well as myself."

"Once we know the project is working under your management, then, should you wish it, you'll become members of our clan. We can't do it before then because to accept someone into our clan is a serious matter for us. It involves a perpetual responsibility, and our clan is, as I've said, unique."

"Then I've only one more question. When do I move n?"

Carrie grinned. "Whenever you wish. We've a house ready for you—one of those large enough to accommodate a Sholan extended family." She paused. "There's just one other point. Would you mind keeping an eye on a nine-year-old kitling called Daira? It would only be during the days. He's an orphan and my bond-mother thought that having a young Sholan male around would be more balanced than putting her in a totally Human environment. He's about the same age as your daughter, isn't he?"

Ruth thought about it for a moment. "A couple of years younger. I'll give it a try, but if it doesn't work out . . ."

"Then we'll abandon the idea. Now, would you like to see your new home today?"

Leaving Ruth in the capable hands of Rulla, Carrie went to visit Mara. She found her weepy and depressed.

"Would you like to come and stay with us for a few days?" asked Carrie. "Unless you want to, there's no reason for you to live with Zhyaf, you know."

Mara blotted her eyes on the soggy tissue and looked at her hopefully. "I don't have to go back?"

"Not unless you want to. Do you?"

She shook her head. "Have you met his sister?" she asked tentatively.

"That one? Gods, what a dragon!"

Mara began to smile. "She is, isn't she?"

Carrie leaned forward conspiratorially. "How on earth did you stand her? I'd have been out of there like a shot I'll tell you!"

That started her giggling, then her face crumpled again and the tissue went back up to her eyes.

Carrie leaned forward and took it away from her, throwing it in the bin nearby and handing her a pile of fresh ones.

"But I'd nowhere to go," she sobbed. "I had to stay there!"

Taking Mara in her arms, Carrie hugged her close. "You have now. That silly mate of mine didn't let me know you were having problems. They all thought you should try and be Sholan, not stay Human. All that's going to change, Mara, I promise you. I've arranged for you to stay in the village with a woman called Ruth Brown."

Mara sat up, her sobs getting farther and farther apart as she looked at Carrie. "What's she like?"

"She laughs a lot, and she's got a daughter called Mandy who's twelve years old."

"I'd live in another house?"

"Yes, a new house. It'll take a bit of time for Ruth to get it the way she wants, but I'm sure you'd be glad to help her. She's grateful for the chance to leave the Telepath Guild and move out here onto the estate. She's also agreed to help us out by looking after a young Sholan orphan called Daira. His talent is more like ours, so he needs a home here. She could do with someone to help her, and I thought you'd be just the person."

"You want me to help her?"

"Why not? You can take Daira to the Warrior training sessions—and join in if you want to."

"But I'm pregnant!"

"I fought a Challenge when I was four months pregnant," Carrie reminded her quietly. "And before you say I lost my cub, it wasn't fighting that caused that, it was getting wounded. You'd only be training."

Tears welled up in her eyes again, spilling down over her cheeks. "You don't understand!"

"What don't I understand?"

"This child, it isn't human! Vanna showed me on the scanner yesterday!"

"I know it isn't, Mara. Our Links have changed us, you were told that. Our children will never be totally Human," she said gently.

"But it should be! It isn't Zhyaf's child! Its father is Human like me!" she wailed.

"What?" Carrie sat frozen. "What did you say?"

"The child isn't Zhyaf's! It should be Human!"

"My God." She was stunned, didn't know what to say. That a child conceived by two Human Leska partners would still be Sholan had never occurred to her.

"Zhyaf doesn't know yet!"

"I think you should assume he does," she said automatically. "It makes sense, though, Mara. We're not less than Human now, we're something more."

"I don't want the baby! I only got pregnant so that I wouldn't have a Sholan cub!" she wept, flinging herself back on the bed as her body shook convulsively.

"Vanna says you're only a few weeks pregnant, Mara." Carrie tried to sound as sympathetic as she could. "You've plenty of time to decide what to do. Wouldn't you rather just have the cub? You don't need to look after it. Clan members are fully entitled to have their cubs and leave them in the estate nursery to be brought up. A cub is a blessing to the whole Clan, and Vartra knows, we need all we can bear if our children are to have a choice of mates when they're older."

"Khartu said I would have to bring it up myself."

"Well, she was wrong," said Carrie firmly. "That might be the way up north, but not here. There's another option, too. Most mothers usually leave their children in the nursery during the day and take them home at night and on their days off. The choice is yours."

"I don't want it," she wailed, clutching her damp pillow.

"That's not something I can help you with," Carrie said gently, reaching out to stroke her hair. "Leave it for now. Let yourself get over this first. Meet Ruth and settle into your new home. Things may look different then."

"What about my Link days?" Despite herself, Mara was becoming a little calmer. The prospect of a new life was attractive.

"You'll have your own room. You can get Zhyaf to come to you rather than go back to that mausoleum of his," she said candidly.

"I can?"

"Of course! Ruth's a telepath. She knows what we are here, and the fact that she's happy to foster a Sholan cub shows she understands both our cultures. You'll find her very different from Zhyaf and Khartu, believe me!"

"When will they let me out?"

"In a day or two, depending when your next Link day is."

"Not for three days yet," she sniffed, dabbing her nose with the tissue and sitting up.

"Then Zhyaf can come to the villa," said Carrie getting up. "It's going to take at least that long for Ruth to move in and begin to get things straight. I have to go now," she said. "Kashini needs feeding, and I can feel her calling for me."

"How could you? How could you have a baby that looks so alien?"

Carrie frowned. "She looks nothing of the kind! She looks like both of us, part Human, part Sholan." Her face softened into a smile. "And wholly lovely! You'll find out for yourself when you come to stay. Now stop worrying and get some rest, then you'll be out of here all the sooner."

*   *   *

As Hanaz handed out the drinks to the guests, Governor Nesul returned to his seat.

"I called this informal meeting because I know we all share the same view of Guild Master Esken," he said. "And I think I've found a way to slow him down; we're all aware how busy it is at this time of year, but my office has been approached on several occasions over the last few days with complaints and petitions concerning that worthy male. I'm afraid, my colleagues," he glanced round the little assembly, "we can ignore it no longer."

"What are the nature of the complaints?" asked Lijou. "I presume they involve our various disciplines." He gestured toward Konis, Rhyasha, Kusac, and General Raiban.

"They do, but before I go into that, I'd prefer to have an update from each of you on the state of your current relations with the Telepath Guild. Father Lijou, would you start, please?"

"Were you aware Senior Tutor Sorli is on retreat with us at present? He's given me no reason, but has been helping us organize our college for training priests."

"I wasn't. That is interesting," said Nesul thoughtfully. "Tell me, what response are you getting from the various temples?"

"Mixed. Esken's influence extends beyond our own continent, I'm afraid. Fully half of the temples in the Western Isles and Nalgalan have replied that without orders from Esken they cannot accept our invitation to send their acolytes to us for instruction. The same, unfortunately, is true here."

"They need to be a guild, Nesul," said Raiban, raising her glass to her lips. "We need them free of Esken. Once the Priesthood is a guild, they'll flock to join it, you mark my words. Now we all know what the situation is, so for Vartra's sake, stop quartering the same scent and get on with why you called us out here tonight!"

"If you'll bear with me, Raiban," said Nesul calmly, "you'll see what I'm getting at. I don't think we're all aware of just how bad the situation is. What about you? How are you getting on with Esken?"

Raiban gave a snort of disgust, replacing her glass on the table forcefully. "Underfoot, more often than not. Insisting that if a mixed Leska pair is involved in the questioning of anyone, then a Telepath Guild member should be appointed too! His damned people are everywhere! And they're still turning up at ruins claiming that they must be blessed." She silenced their outraged murmurs with a wave of her hand. "Oh, they don't have access to explosives any more, they just want to mumble prayers, but that's not the point. They are prohibited from approaching the excavation sites and Esken knows it. All they're doing is continuing to make a damned nuisance of themselves, refusing to accep they're no longer involved."

Nesul nodded and looked over to Rhyasha Aldatan "How about the Terrans at the Telepath Guild?"

Rhyasha flicked her ears in a shrug. "He hasn't begur to integrate them into the mainstream of Guild education They're still working mainly from their own quarters with visiting teachers. They're being taught at the same pace as the Sholan students, which means it will take them something like fifteen years to graduate! If the student is dedicated, and very Talented, he or she can get access to advanced tuition because not all Esken's tutors agree with his methods. However, the whole situation is most unsatisfactory."

Nesul frowned, pushing himself more upright in his seat. "Why has this been allowed to continue?" he demanded.

"AlRel keeps a strict watch on him, Governor," Rhyasha said. "We repeatedly pull him up about it, but he manages to hold them back by other means. He refuses either to take their previous experience into consideration, or to condense their courses. As for those who also attend the Warrior Guild, they are kept even farther behind! We do what we can, but you know that each guild is autonomous."

"Then it's time all the guilds were reminded that this is an interspecies emergency we're dealing with," said Nesul grimly. "It's vital we have as many of the Humans as we can operating as fully trained telepaths as soon as possible, not only for the benefit of the Alliance but so that they can help their home world patrol their own sector of space!"

Raiban gave a grunt of surprise at his outburst, causing Nesul to look over at her. She shook her head in a negative and he turned instead to Konis.

"What's the feeling among the telepath clans?"

"Grumblings and complaints to me that only echo what's already been said. They won't complain officially on behalf of their clansfolk, but they will corner me when they can," he said. "I have a matter to bring to your attention tonight which may well have a bearing on this."

"I'm aware of it, Konis. Leave it for the moment, if you will." He looked at each of them in turn. "So the picture is uniform. Now Esken no longer holds the balance of power on the World Council, he's trying to take it at a lessser level—divert it before it reaches us. We can't act directly against him as it would take a vote of censure at an All-Guilds level to force him to resign in Sorli's favor, and I'd rather avoid the scandal that would cause. Esken does have some good qualities when all's said and done."

"So did Ghezu, but look what he became!" Raiban said in exasperation.

"Ghezu was another matter entirely. We were able to conceal his treasonable actions because of the news blockage regarding the whole of the Forces desert action," replied Nesul. "Thank the Gods Kaid did kill him and he wasn't returned for a public trial!"

Raiban growled. "We couldn't afford the scandal after so recently backing the Brotherhood's change to full guild status."

"Exactly Nesul's point," interrupted Konis. "We couldn't afford a scandal involving Esken at that last All-Guilds Council, and we still can't! We telepaths are so interwoven in the fabric of daily life that people can't afford to doubt us—we'd have a planet-wide panic! So what is it you're proposing, Nesul?"

"I've been looking into past precedents regarding similar circumstances, and if I can have the backing of those of you on the Council at tomorrow's meeting, some of our larger problems could well be solved."

"How?" demanded Raiban, lifting her glass again.

"We're on a planetary alert at the moment, so special powers can be used. One of those is the ability to elevate a group of people with vital skills to the status of a guild for the duration of the emergency."

"The priests," said Rhyasha. "But what skills have they got that would help a war effort?"

Lijou leaned forward to pick up his drink. "The Brotherhood lay-priests have pastoral duties on the starships that include helping the injured, talking to those who have lost friends or lovers in action, and rallying the troops if morale falls," he said. "Psychologically we have a measurably beneficial impact on the crew of any Forces craft, don't we, General Raiban?"

Raiban began to grin. "I like that, Nesul. Very nice, very nice indeed. Yes, Father Lijou, your work on our vessels in deep space is vital. I would certainly endorse any recommendation that your people be elevated to guild status on those grounds."

"Not quite guild status," corrected Nesul. "But it woul only require a rubber stamp at the next All-Guilds' meetin to ratify our appointment. How about you, Konis? Woul you cover our backs?"

"With pleasure, Governor. And I think I have a sugges tion for the problem with our Terran telepaths. It could b suggested by your office that unless the proper procedure for accelerating their education are implemented at the Te epath Guild, they will be advising them to enter one o more of Shola's temples as acolytes so that they can con tinue their training under the Brotherhood of Vartra."

Raiban laughed loudly at this. "By the Gods, if tha doesn't get Esken off that broad rear of his, nothing will He'll see his influence in the vanguard of the new telepathi skills disappearing completely from his grasp! Tell me Kusac, how are matters between you and Esken? You'r the only one Nesul hasn't asked for a report, and ther must be a reason for your presence."

"Things are quiet. We give him periodic reports on the research Vanna and Jack are doing, the same ones that g to AlRel, and he leaves us alone," said Kusac. "I mus admit to being baffled as to why I was included."

"For the insight and experiences you and your Leska have on the issue of the Terrans and Esken. And so I ca catch up on news of that young cub of yours at the end o the meeting," Nesul smiled. "You know what a family per son I am. Which brings me to your problem, Konis," he said, nodding in the direction of Kusac's father.

"Several of the telepaths in high office have used their positions to avoid settling down with a life-mate and pro ducing a family. The numbers involved are not large, but significant when you consider how many telepaths we've lost to mixed Leska pairings. I feel, Konis, although the situation isn't yet that serious, that no telepath of breeding age should be exempt. We need to ensure that the lines of pure Sholan telepaths don't die out because of a lack of cubs in this generation."

Around him, everyone but Konis began to grin as they realized what Nesul was suggesting.

"You knew the clans had approached me on this mat ter," he said. "It's all very well for the rest of you, but who the hell's going to tell Esken he's got to bond? Not me,

onsidering he views our family as taking a personal inter-
st in making his life as difficult as possible!"

"A family could slow him down even more, provided he
oesn't go to the Consortias for a bride," said Raiban.

"He can't go to the Consortias," snapped Konis, irritated
y the fact that it seemed they were all looking to him to
olve a problem he'd been hoping to avoid. "He has to
narry a telepath, and one chosen by me as Clan Lord!"

"Even if he married a female of your choice, he could
ack her off to his family estate as soon as she was preg-
ant," Raiban pointed out.

"What you need is a female who won't let herself be
ent to the provinces, and who would keep him so busy
lomestically that he'd have little time left for plotting,"
aid Rhyasha thoughtfully. "Not a young female, an older
one. Perhaps a widow? One with a couple of kitlings of
chool age, needing to attend the Guild. One who, on the
ace of it, should be quiet out of gratitude at being given
a new husband."

Konis' eye ridges met as he looked at his life-mate.
'What're you planning? You've got someone in mind,
aven't you?"

Rhyasha nodded, smiling broadly. "Someone on our estate who would enjoy running circles round Esken! Not of
our family, though her husband was, so Esken can't accuse
you of planting a spy in his den. She'd take to her change
of status like a kitling to the hunt! Before Esken knows
where he is, she'll be entertaining at the Guild. It's about
time that place saw some life! It's been getting progres-
sively more like a tomb over the years!"

"Konis," said Lijou, "may I suggest that you issue a letter to all Telepath Clan Leaders, and those in senior positions, saying something to the effect that because we are
losing telepaths from the breeding program to the mixed
Leska pairings, it's important that a positive and active approach be taken to encourage their Clan members to enter
into three-or-more-year contracts and have children, and
insist that Leska pairs do the same. Round it off by saying
you expect all senior telepaths to set an example by taking
life-mates if they haven't already. Accompany each letter
with a document detailing your choice of bride for that
specific person. That should solve the problem of Esken
feeling he's being singled out by you."

Lijou stopped for a moment before raising his hand in a negative gesture. "Before you say anything, yes, I do realize that includes myself." His tone this time was more somber.

Kusac stirred and looked from his father to Governor Nesul. "Could I say something here? I'd like to suggest that some of the Brothers on my estate—and possibly more at Stronghold—be considered as suitable mates." He glanced at his father, but there was no response.

"There are some now compatible genetically with us mixed Leskas, which means they have enough of a talent to form a Leska Link, but there are many others with gifts worth preserving and adding back into our gene pool. We can't ignore those gifts or talents that are common to us and the Humans. And it'll add much needed new blood into our families. It's worth trying, especially as it looks from the DNA tests on her that Taizia and Meral's cub is Talented."

"I can't authorize . . ."

"Yes, you can, Konis," interrupted Raiban. "All you do is inform several chosen people that they're part of a high security program. I think opening out the gene pool is a damned good idea. Might even breed back the fighting strain. Who're you going to pick for Kaid?"

"Ah," began Kusac.

"He's part of my son's Triad and as such is under no obligation to form a bond elsewhere," Konis interrupted smoothly.

"The Triad is temple registered," said Lijou. "Officially he's also a life-mate to Carrie."

"He's only genetically compatible with the mixed Leskas," said Kusac, finally finding his voice.

Raiban scowled. "Damned loss, if you ask me. Still, he's no telepath, so I suppose it doesn't really matter."

"I can't say this is part of a military research program when it isn't," Konis said, returning to the original discussion.

"It is as of now," said Raiban. "Nesul, I take it you have no objection?"

Nesul considered the options for a few moments. It was novel for Raiban to ask his opinion, and he was enjoying it. "Yes. I think it's worth a try, at least until the cubs born of such pairings are old enough to be tested for talents."

"Then that's decided, isn't it, Konis?" She grinned.

Going to be a few long faces in a day or two. Damn, but
d love to be a fly on the wall when some of the letters
ou're sending out arrive!"

As they made their way to their respective vehicles, Rai-
an fell into step beside Konis.

"Y'know, Nesul's been a lot easier to work with since
ur meeting on the *Rynara*. You brought him up to scratch
n the whole interstellar business, didn't you? Don't deny
," she said, grasping his shoulder briefly. "He couldn't
ave gotten his understanding any other way. What I want
o know is why it wasn't done sooner."

"I'm sure I've no idea what you're talking about, Raiban.
Only Master Esken can authorize a transfer of that magni-
ude, and there are very few of us capable of doing it. It's
ctually quite a dangerous procedure when a nontelepath
s involved."

"Been taking a page out of your son's book, eh?" chuck-
ed Raiban, eyes glowing with amusement in the light re-
lected from the palace. "Slippery slope, Konis. Once you
tart, it's never as easy to live by the rules our groundling
ousins swear by again! Good night to you."

"Good night," echoed Konis, watching her stride off
oward her official aircar.

"Konis," said Lijou. "A moment of your time, if you
lease."

He turned to face the priest. "Certainly. What can I do?"

"Be aware that Esken will go to the Consortias as soon
as the letter arrives," he said. "He has the right, he isn't a
Clan elder who needs to make a dynastic marriage, and
he's of the right age group."

"I know. It wasn't worth arguing the point with Raiban.
So just how do we make him marry the one we want?"

"It won't be the problem you think. We've had dealings
with Consortia Houses in the past, business dealings. I'll
have him watched. When we find out which House he's
gone to, I'll approach it with a proposition." He looked
over at Rhyasha. "If your female is willing, we can time it
so she's at the Guildhouse for a couple of days for her
official introduction to him and so on while she's in season.
Our Guild Master is far from sophisticated when it comes
to females. If she lays the right trail, she'll catch him."

Rhyasha laughed quietly. "Oh, she can do that!"

"What about the Consortia?" asked Konis.

Lijou flicked an ear. "For the right sum, when she visits she can ensure what she does makes him run to his intended bride."

"This is too well thought out for a spur of the moment plan, Lijou," said Konis.

"It's an old ploy, Clan Leader, ask your wife. Don't forget, since I went to Stronghold, I've had to train as one of the Brothers even though I couldn't fight. How could I help govern them if I understood nothing of the way they work?"

"Why are you helping me like this?" Konis demanded abruptly. "What will you gain from it?"

Lijou shrugged. "The same as you and all of Shola. The freedom to grow and evolve." He turned to leave.

"He wants Kha'Qwa," said Kusac, once Lijou was out of earshot, "but he'll never ask you. Let him bond with her, Father. She's Talented. We three owe him so much."

"Wait!" called Konis.

Lijou stopped and returned to face him again.

"You want Kha'Qwa?"

He hesitated before answering. "She'd be my choice Clan Lord. Like Esken, I have no need to make a life-bonding."

Konis' ears moved backward, then righted themselves as he watched the priest. "You may have her—at a price." Konis ignored the sharp intake of breath from his son. "I want you to take her as a life-mate in a temple wedding."

Lijou's mouth opened in a slow grin as he inclined his head to one side. "But of course, Clan Lord. I would have it no other way. I believe firmly that as Head Priest I should set an example to those entrusted to my care. Thank you— and good night to you and your family."

As the three of them watched Lijou enter the Brotherhood's vehicle, Konis sighed and began walking to their aircar.

"Why do I feel like I've been subtly manipulated?" he asked Rhyasha in a pained voice.

She linked her arm through his. "Perhaps because you have, but so very gently, and to such good purpose: that of making two people happy," she said, her voice holding a purring note of affection.

*   *   *

A couple of days later, when Carrie came down from the nursery, she found the house a hive of activity with Kitra residing over a large pile of greenery in the den. Pinelike needles and a scattering of red and purple berries lay on the floor around her.

"What's this all about?" she asked, stepping carefully round her before squatting down to her level to see what he was doing.

"Midwinter decorations," said Kitra, pausing. "Dzaka and I gathered them this morning on the way back from Mother's. He'll be back in a moment with a box of things he sent over for you."

"Things?"

"I forgot, this is your first festival, isn't it? Midwinter is one of our biggest festivals, when we celebrate the return of the sun and the start of the new year. Taizia says you call yours Christmas."

"Yes, we do," said Carrie reaching down to pick up a wreath that her bond-sister had already made. Kitra had woven several different thin evergreen branches into a large circle, crafting it so the various colored berries were distributed evenly throughout. "We even use similar colors, red and green."

Kitra nodded. "The sign of life in winter, and when I've put the white-leaved branches in, you'll have the newly spilled blood of the hunt on the snow, too."

"Yeuch," said Carrie. "Hardly a peaceful symbol!"

"Our festival isn't the same, Carrie," she reminded her quietly, returning to her weaving. "It's a time when Ghyakulla, the Green Goddess, must fight the frost and snow demons to get her son back from Khuushoi, Goddess of Winter."

"And the hunt?"

The door opened and Dzaka, carrying a large box, came in with Kusac.

"The hunt is when all the males go out to get food for Ghyakulla and her newly born son," said Kusac, bending down to touch her gently on the cheek as he passed her.

"Hang on a minute," said Carrie, turning round. "I thought Ghyakulla was getting her son back from Khuushoi! Where does this newborn come in?"

"It's a mixture of images and beliefs, like any religion," said Kusac, going down to the lounge level to get some mugs of coffee from the hot plate. "Everyone want some coffee?"

A chorus of affirmatives answered him.

"So what is it we're celebrating, exactly?" asked Carrie. A large cushion appeared beside her. She glanced up at Dzaka in thanks and arranged herself more comfortably on it.

"Dzaka, you're the real priest here, you tell her," said Kusac as he poured out the drinks.

"Both are true, Carrie," he said, squatting beside his box and Kitra. "Ghyakulla and Khuushoi are Sister goddesses. The land, as you know, is rich and fertile, full of the promise of life and good harvests. Winter is cold and sterile, nothing grows but the evergreens. So you see the natures of the two sisters. Ghyakulla had a son, a bright, loving child whom she cared for more than anything. Khuushoi was sterile, could bear no cubs, and in her winter fastness she became jealous."

"So she stole the child," nodded Carrie. "It's a familiar theme, but it's usually a daughter that the Mother Goddess of Earth has."

"It probably was originally, but now that child is Vartra," smiled Dzaka.

"Why am I not surprised?" murmured Carrie.

"As you say. A new religion blended onto an old one after the Cataclysm."

"Go on with the story."

"I'm no storyteller, Carrie," Dzaka excused himself. "The resident Storyteller will tell the tale properly on the first night of the festival."

"I'd like to hear your version of it, though."

"Khuushoi stole the child and took him down to her underground palace of snow and ice. Ghyakulla was beside herself with grief because she didn't know what had happened to him. She began to search frantically. It was the middle of winter, and no one had seen the child taken. All the animals and birds were huddled in their burrows and nests keeping warm or hibernating till the spring. All the trees were asleep, except those you see here—the evergreens. Ghyakulla asked each one in turn if they'd seen her on, but they were afraid of Khuushoi and lied, saying ney'd seen nothing. Save for one."

"This one," said Kitra, holding up a small twiglet covered 1 leaves that were a pale whitish green on one side and a arker green the other. "The snow tree."

Dzaka nodded. "It's really a bush," he said. "It told Ghykulla in a trembling voice what had happened and explained its fear that Winter and her frost demons would estroy it for telling her."

Kusac came up the steps with mugs of coffee for Kitra nd Carrie. "You tell it well, Dzaka. Better than I could."

Dzaka flicked his ears in mild embarrassment. "Teaching s one of our duties."

Kitra leaned against him. "A many-talented male, my Companion," she murmured. Though she said it teasingly, here was an undercurrent of pride and admiration in her voice. Dzaka's hand touched her neck affectionately.

Lijou may well have been right after all, Carrie sent privately to Kusac.

We'll see. Time enough for both of them yet, but I vouldn't be displeased, he replied, returning to fetch his nd Dzaka's drinks.

"What happened next?" asked Carrie.

"Ghyakulla promised the tree that it wouldn't suffer for helping her, and as a sign of her gratitude, she turned the underside of its leaves white and showed it how to hold the pale side up to the sky, so it would be unseen by Khuushoi and her demons."

"The tears of gratitude she shed on the bush also turned its green berries to the brightest red of any in winter," added Kitra. "That's why it's called the snow bush, and its berries, the Tears of Ghyakulla."

"Strange thing to do to a bush that wants to remain hidden," said Carrie, taking a drink of her coffee.

"Poetic license," said Kusac, nudging her in the ribs. "Don't be so literal! Carry on, Dzaka."

"Then she set off for her sister's palace. Khuushoi, alerted by her demons, tried to hide the way to her palace by covering the world in a blanket of snow. Every step of the way, her sister sent demons to hound Ghyakulla, but the power of the land is greater than that of winter and eventually, Ghyakulla reached the palace. There she confronted her sister."

Dzaka paused to take a drink before continuing. "Khuu shoi was prepared to fight it out, but not Ghyakulla. She understood the loneliness that had prompted her sister's act and offered a compromise."

"So Vartra visits Khuushoi for four months of the year," said Kitra.

"During that time, Winter, or Khuushoi, reigns and noth ing will grow till Vartra is returned to his mother," fin ished Dzaka.

"I like it," said Carrie. "But you still haven't explained the cub or the hunt."

"Better tell her that, too, or we'll never get any peace," said Kusac, stretching out beside her, half-leaning on her cushion.

"Besides, it's a nice way to spend some time together on such a cold day," said Kitra, moving even closer to her lover.

Dzaka draped his free arm over Kitra's shoulders. "We have to go for wood soon," he reminded her.

"Wood?" asked Carrie.

"Several large fires are needed over the three-day cele bration," said Kusac. "Dzaka and I are organizing a collec tion party from here to go and help my Mother's folk. This year the celebrations are being held at her estate for both Clans. We're also collecting our own New Year log. It's a section of one of the main trees cut for the central fire. Every home will get a piece to keep throughout the coming year. You and Kitra can come, too," he offered, "but we thought you'd prefer to stay in the warm and decorate the house."

"I'll show you how to make the garlands," said Kitra, "and weave your hopes and wishes for the New Year into them."

"Sounds like a good idea. How you can go out there without anything on your feet amazes me! It's too damned cold for me!"

"You get used to it," said Kusac amiably, reaching an arm round her waist. "We've never known anything else. Couldn't bear to not feel the ground beneath me. I like to know what I'm walking on."

Carrie gave a mock shudder. "Rather you than me at this time of year. Now the story, if you please, Dzaka."

"It's not really a story. At this time we celebrate the

rebirth of the sun, the lengthening of the days and the start of the new year. The festival is held over three days. On the first, we males do the final gathering of fuel for the fires, including the aromatic woods. We also collect piles of sweet grass to decorate the cavelike shelter for Ghyakulla that will sit just outside the large celebration hall that's being erected in the grounds of your bond-mother's home."

"What? You put up a portable banquet hall?"

"How else can we accommodate so many people?" asked Kusac. "The whole of both our Clans will be there. It's a time when everyone returns to their family for the celebrations."

"It must be vast," she murmured, trying to imagine just how large.

The size of one of the landing bays aboard the Khalossa, sent Kusac. *It's stored in panels and only used at midwinter and midsummer. We'll have one when the estate can afford it and we've a large enough Clan to warrant it.*

"It soon gets crowded," said Kitra. "You'll love it, Carrie. It's a wonderful time of year."

"While we're doing the gathering, the fastest younglings, males not above eighteen years of age, will be sent out as runners to every field on both estates to plant the Clan totems. They're posts carved with the faces of Ghyakulla's nature spirits and animals. There are especially large ones for the four compass points on the boundaries, particularly the north where Khuushoi lives."

"Then the young males over eighteen will start their passage into adulthood," said Kusac. "They will have spent the night before at the shrine with Ghyan purifying themselves and will build the symbolic cave and decorate it with the sweet grass when it arrives."

"That's where Ghyakulla is supposed to have had her child, right?"

"That's right. The first night is spent waiting for the new sun, or Ghyakulla's cub, to be born, so it's a time for the females of the tribe. All the newborns are blessed by the representative of the Green Goddess—we're being visited by the Priestess Tokui herself," said Kusac. "She wants to personally welcome our new cubs Kashini, Marak and Khayla, Taizia and Meral's daughter. She'll ask the Goddess to watch over them until they become adults."

"She'll also pass me over officially to Vartra's care at the ceremony," said Kitra. "As an adult female, until I have cubs, I'm in His protection."

"All the rites of adulthood are held on the second night," said Dzaka, "when young males dance to keep the frost and snow demons away from Ghyakulla's birth cave. It really is a wonderful time, Carrie. You'll see us as a people in a way you never have before. You'll understand our past, our origins."

"I'm really looking forward to it," she said, as memories of past festivals came to her from Kusac.

"Won't you miss your Christmas?" he asked, nuzzling her ear.

She considered it for a moment. "Not really. A good way to live is what matters, and nothing I've seen here really disagrees with what I learned as a child. What are our archaeologists doing?"

"Some have asked to join in, some are going to the Terran quarters at the Telepath Guild where they're celebrating their Christmas and watching the Guild festivities," said Kusac.

"What about Kaid?"

"My Father's remaining at Stronghold," said Dzaka quietly. "I wish he was returning, but he says he's so recently left .."

"He knows he's welcome which is what matters," said Kusac, reluctantly beginning to get to his feet. "We'd better be going, Dzaka."

"You didn't tell Carrie about the hunt," said Kitra as Dzaka began to move.

"The hunt is the second day," said Dzaka. "We males, plus those newly accepted into adulthood, go out to hunt. It's only a token one, but we do it to remember that the Goddess' consort, Vartra, hunted for her and the newborn cub."

"Hang on! Wasn't Vartra the cub? How can he be the consort, too?"

Dzaka shrugged, mouth open in a grin. "One of those things, Carrie. As his adult self, he is the Goddess' Consort; as the child, he is the newborn son just as the Goddess is a maiden and a mother at different times of year—and the mother hunting her stolen son, as well as the pregnant mother bearing her child. It's complicated and not a discussion for now. Ghyan is the one to really talk to about the theological side. He's the official Priest of Vartra after all. My work is of a different nature."

"Shall we look at what Mother's sent over?" asked Kitra after the two males had left.

"Sure."

Kitra pulled the box over and opened it, digging deeply in to pull out some brightly colored ridged paper shapes.

"Lanterns," she said with pleasure, taking one by either end and pulling it open. It unfolded to produce a rectangular lantern, its sides decorated by grinning animalistic faces.

"They're nature spirits," she explained. "We use them around the house to frighten Khuushoi's demons away. I wonder if Mother has included any lights for them?" She rummaged carefully in the box and came up with a smaller box which she opened. "Yes! We can have them lit, too!"

Carrie carefully reached into the bright, papery mass and pulled out another lantern. This was a round one, the face that of a hideous fish. "What's this? It's grotesque!"

Kitra laughed. "A demon-fish. Its ugliness frightens off Khuushoi's demons."

"If you've got things like that in the sea, I don't think I'll bother going swimming!"

"They're not that common, don't worry," she said. "They live off the north coast of the continent, in the colder waters. You'll see one at the front of the procession on the first night of the festival."

They felt Taizia's mental touch before she entered. "Hello, you two," she said, bending to greet them with a hug and a rub from her cheek. "It's too long since I saw my favorite bond-sister."

Carrie returned the hug. "It's lovely to see you. Where's Khayla? It's too long since I saw my favorite niece," she added, mocking Taizia.

"At home with Mother," she said, sitting down and settling her voluminous skirt around her. "Meral's gone with Kusac and Dzaka." She gave a gentle laugh, reaching out to put one hand on Carrie's knee, the other on her sister's. "Who'd have thought a year ago the three of us would be sitting here while our mates—all of them warriors, even Kusac!—went out to fulfill the traditional male role for the midwinter festival? And that two of us would have cubs!"

She shook her head, dispelling her moment of sentimentality. "You were talking about demon-fish. Did you know they're one of the most poisonous fish in our oceans? They live in cracks and crevices in the northerly cliffs and have to be hunted by divers. Each year several lives are lost in trying to catch them."

"What are they hunted for? Their taste?" asked Carrie.

"Goodness, no. They're poisonous, as I said. They're caught for their medicinal properties. They're rich in oils which are used to treat a variety of conditions including frostbite. You can't handle them safely until they've been dried and smoked, then you have to take the skins off carefully and scrape the oils from the inside. Now we can process the flesh to extract the oil from there too. Then we use the skin to make the ceremonial lamps."

Carrie dropped it with an exclamation of distaste.

"Not that one, silly! That's made of paper. They're far too valuable to use around the house. The ceremonial one is carried in at the start of the celebrations and suspended in the banquet hall for the duration of the festival."

"Would you like some c'shar, Taizia?" asked Kitra, suddenly remembering her self-imposed responsibilities as an assistant hostess to Carrie.

"Love one, youngling," she said.

"Can you ask for more coffee, too, please?" asked Carrie as the younger female scrambled to her feet.

"She's growing up fast," observed Taizia when she'd gone. "So many changes in our family in so short a time."

"I don't know how your parents have coped so well," said Carrie quietly. "First me and all the troubles I brought, including importing the Brotherhood onto your land, then you and Kitra both following in Kusac's footsteps and breaking from tradition."

"We're a robust family. Besides, because both of them work in AlRel, they have a more liberal outlook. They're dealing regularly with aliens and their very different cultures, so they realize the accepted way isn't necessarily right, or desirable. It's Father who's surprised me most. He's changed so much. We females are much more adaptable to start with. Now, while Kitra's not here, tell me how things are between her and Dzaka. We don't see her very often nowadays."

"Dzaka has a suite here, mainly because of Kitra. I worry in case she's staying here too often and it'll upset your parents, but Kusac says to leave them to it. They seem happy in each other's company, but they each have their own things to do as well."

"What about Dzaka? He was such an unknown quantity for so long. My parents didn't say anything, but they were concerned for Kitra."

"There's a lot of his father in him," said Carrie slowly, thinking of Kaid, wondering how he was faring at Stronghold, and despite herself, wishing he was returning for the festival. "His feelings go deep, and once he's begun to care, nothing will ever change that."

"Are you talking about Kaid, or Dzaka?"

Carrie looked up to see her friend's gentle smile. "Both, I suppose," she admitted. "Dzaka cared very deeply for the mate and cub he lost. Now he's beginning to care just as deeply for Kitra. As to what will come of it, your guess is as good as mine, but I would say it's up to Kitra to choose. He would never hurt her, I can tell you that."

Taizia sighed. "Then it looks like none of us will make a conventional marriage. Poor Father! I wonder what he'll do when Kitra tells him she wants Dzaka."

Carrie grinned. "You think so, too? Kusac's noncommittal at present. He says they've plenty of time."

"In a manner of speaking, yes they have, but Mother decided at not much older than Kitra that she was having Father, and did exactly what I did to get him!"

"You mean . . . she got herself pregnant? You're kidding!" laughed Carrie.

"No, honestly. Father let it slip when Kusac was trying to persuade them to endorse our bonding contract. I could hardly believe it either. Several Clan Leaders had approached the Clan Lord and asked that their sons be married to her—including, believe it or not, Father Lijou's. It looked like he'd be chosen until Mother made her announcement."

"Where did you find all this out?"

"From Mother," said Taizia serenely. "It wasn't difficult to pry it out of her in the dead of night when we were sitting up with Khayla. She really loves cubs, you know."

"Kitra's coming back," warned Carrie. She leaned forward, reaching out to touch Taizia's hand, covering it with hers and giving it a comforting squeeze. "Don't worry about yourself and Kitra. There are changes coming regarding eligible mates, and your father's agreed to them. You'll be able to work it out for yourself in a day or two, but I can't say any more at the moment."

Carrie could feel Taizia's joy. "Really? Vartra be praised!" she said, her face lighting up.

"Hush!" said Carrie, more aware than Taizia that Vartra indeed had a lot to do with the changes that were coming.

* * *

Esken sat and stared in disbelief at the letter he held in his hand. He had two immediate reactions. The first was to rip it to shreds, the other was to call for Sorli. Except Sorli had left. It was only to go on retreat, he'd said, but they both knew that unless the breach was healed by him, Sorli would not return.

He needed advice. Challa Kayal. He couldn't put a face to the name, but she was from the same clan as Nnadu, his head of the priests—ex-head, he corrected himself. He didn't know which news angered him most. That Lijou Kzaelan had been elevated to a virtual Guild Master in charge of all priests, or that he was expected to take a life-mate.

Tossing the letter onto his desk, he activated his personal comm. At least he could refuse Konis' suggestion of a mate, and it was no more than that. Technically he was free to choose whom he wished. First he'd talk to Nnadu.

"Challa, Master Esken?" repeated Nnadu. "Yes, I remember her. She took out a ten-year contract with one of the Aldatan Clan, but he died some years back. He was an interpreter serving on a starship, I believe. There was an accident, and he was killed. Why?"

"The Clan Lord wants all senior officials to take life-mates to set an example to the clans," growled Esken. "He says we can't take the risk of there not being enough pure Sholan telepaths in this generation to keep the breeding program going. It comes from the Governor's office, though."

"Seems a reasonable point," said Nnadu. "He's suggested Challa, has he? From what I remember, she's a good choice. Nice, quiet female. Has two kitlings already, so no problem of her not being able to give you cubs."

"Thank you, Nnadu," Esken said through clenched teeth.

'But I don't want cubs, either hers or my own!" He broke the connection abruptly.

Damn Konis and the Governor! They'd hatched this up between them! Well, he had another option. He'd see what the Consortias could offer in the way of an arranged marriage. At least a Consortia would leave him alone, and if they still insisted there should be telepathic cubs, then he'd find himself some willing Talented Companion. It shouldn't be too difficult to persuade her to let the Consortia raise them. No different from leaving them in the Clan nursery.

*   *   *

Sorli knocked on Lijou's office door, waiting till the Head Priest answered before opening it.

Lijou looked up at him. "You've come about the letter, haven't you?"

Sorli nodded affirmatively as he took the proffered seat in front of the desk. "You had one, too?"

"I did."

"Master Esken?"

"All senior officials, Tutor Sorli. You, I presume, were included because you're to be the next Telepath Guild Leader."

"I don't think so, Father Lijou," said Sorli with a sigh. "I'm considering tending my resignation as Senior Tutor to the Telepath Guild."

"May I ask why?"

Sorli looked at him calmly. "I'd prefer to say no more than that I have a serious difference of opinion with Master Esken regarding the course our Guild is presently taking. One that precludes my having any further involvement with him."

"Are you sure that matters between you are that serious?"

"I didn't make my decision to come to Stronghold on retreat lightly, Father."

Lijou could hear the note of reproach in the tutor's voice. If matters really were that bad, he had to do something now to prevent Sorli leaving the Telepath Guild. With him gone, their one hope for moderate leadership in the future was lost.

"Sorli, the World Council needs you at Valsgarth Guild-house. Without you there, Esken will do what he likes.

You've been able to influence him in the past—we need you to continue to do that."

"I'm tired, Father. Tired of fighting against the hurricane that's Esken," he said.

As Lijou watched, he seemed to slump down in the chair, looking worn and exhausted. "We're all fighting him, Sorli. He makes it so difficult for the rest of us, for Shola. He stifles change, has become so inflexible. We need to grow and evolve if we're not to be overtaken by these Terrans with their multiplicity of psychic Talents. They learn and innovate so quickly that in a matter of a decade or so, they could leave us standing."

"I know, but what can I do? I'm only one person. Since the arrival of the Humans, Esken listens more to Physician Khafsa than me. That's why there was the incident involving Physician Kyjishi and her Human Leska. I tried, Father Lijou, Vartra knows I tried!"

"And you succeeded, Sorli. They only used a hypnotic on them, nothing stronger, thanks to your intervention."

Sorli raised his head, a spark of interest coming into his eyes. "You're well informed."

Lijou reached for a piece of paper on his desk and pushed it across to him. "Read this."

Sorli took it and began to read. After a moment or two he handed it back. "All of this, the bondings, the priests, is because of Esken, isn't it?"

Lijou nodded. "You know as well as I that over the last few years Esken's assumed powers he has no right to, and misused some of those that were traditionally his. You might not be aware of how wide ranging an influence he's tried to have because you've not been in a position to see the larger picture. Did you know that he had half the members of the World Council intimidated to the point that they voted the way he wanted them to vote? That they were afraid all senior telepaths were in his claws?" Lijou sensed the shock the tutor felt at this disclosure.

"You can't be serious," said Sorli, his face creasing in concern.

"He even had Governor Nesul similarly intimidated. He refused him a mental transfer of knowledge concerning the state of affairs off-world in order to prevent him interfering in his plans for the mixed Leskas. He also intended that those Leskas would be in his palm, his private army to intimidate other guild masters and councillors by their very existence! We had to do something, Sorli!" He took a breath and lowered his voice, realizing that getting agitated wouldn't help him convince the other.

"We still need to stop him. He refuses to integrate the Terran telepaths and educate them properly, but I'm sure I don't need to tell you that. His way will fuel misunderstanding and prejudice between our species. We cannot treat Humans as secondary to us. If we do, they will become an even greater potential threat."

"He only reached an agreement over the mixed Leskas because of fear of the prophecy we found," said Sorli.

"He did it because you persuaded him," corrected Lijou. "For some time now, the Aldatans, AlRel, myself, and Governor Nesul have been working toward somehow curbing Esken yet still leaving him in charge of the Guild. We can't afford a scandal, Sorli, and if Esken's allowed to go unchecked any longer, we'll have no option but to act. You have to go back and help us. You're the best hope the telepaths have now, and in the future, as their Guild Master."

"You don't know what you're asking."

"Oh, yes, I do," said Lijou. "To leave as you did was taking a stand, showing Esken how seriously you disagreed with him, but you must return."

"*If* I went back, I'd need a good reason. To just return now would be to lose any vestiges of influence I have over him. You realize that, don't you?"

"I predict he'll contact you concerning this bonding. In fact, that's where we really could do with your help." He felt Sorli's surge of interest. He needed to fuel it, give the tutor a reason to go back to Esken.

"What makes you so sure? And what kind of help are you wanting?"

"The Clan Lord's suggested a bride for him, a certain Challa Kayal."

"I remember her. Intelligent female. Widowed now. She worked in the judiciary, didn't she?"

"I couldn't tell you, I'm afraid. Rhyasha Aldatan suggested her. What I think Esken will do is go to the Consortias for an arranged marriage. We want him to choose Challa."

Sorli looked puzzled. "I fail to see how he thinks a marriage with a nontelepathic Consortia could fulfill the instructions in that letter. The whole point of it is to produce more telepathic offspring."

"The Guild law states that if you are over a certain age, and not heir to a clan, you can marry outside the telepath clans. I assume Esken will then try to claim he can't have children or some such ploy to avoid making any other kind of arrangement."

"Why Challa?"

"Apparently she's his match. She's also got two kitlings of her own that she'll want to stay close to, so she won't allow him to send her away to his clan estate. As Rhyasha put it, he'll be too busy dealing with his domestic life to have time for plotting!"

Sorli's mouth twitched slightly. "It could be amusing," he admitted. "Unless a similar female has been chosen for me?"

"On that, I can reassure you, Sorli. You are highly thought of by everyone involved. The Clan Lord will have taken his usual care to suggest someone to suit you. If you have a preference, you could approach him. I'm sure he'd be amenable."

"If you don't mind me asking, who has he suggested for you?"

Lijou hesitated. Should he tell him? If he did, Sorli would realize it was a measure of their trust in him. It might just tip the balance. "Kha'Qwa. She's one of the Sisters here."

Sorli raised an eye ridge. "One of the Brotherhood? You were a contender for Clan Lord, weren't you? I'm surprised that a telepath wasn't insisted upon for you."

"It would have been but for one consideration," said Lijou. "This must not go beyond these walls, Sorli. Virtually since it was set up, Stronghold has been gathering those with lesser psychic talents. The Brothers are what they are because of their gifts—gifts that the Humans also have. It's been decided therefore to include certain Brothers and Sisters in the breeding program. It's a trial, to run until the cubs are old enough to be tested, then the matter will be reassesed. If it works, it may well bring back into the telepath gene pool all the talents that have been ignored for so long."

"I knew there would be changes the like of which we couldn't imagine," said Sorli, getting to his feet. "I tried to warn Esken, but he wouldn't listen. As you said, he feared t weakening his power base. Very well, Father Lijou, I will nd a reason to return if one does not arrive, but may I point out that if I'm to help you, I need to be kept informed as to what's going on."

Lijou rose and came out from behind his desk to escort Sorli to the door. "I will see to it personally, Tutor Sorli."

Sorli stopped by the door. "So Kaid's a telepath, is he? Bit of an anomaly, wouldn't you say? No wonder their Triad was able to return safely to the Margins."

Lijou's mouth opened in a slight smile. "That's not commonly known, Tutor, and I'd appreciate it staying that way. Kaid's a remarkable person in many ways."

"I'm sure he is."

CHAPTER 5

Master Rhyaz stood with General Raiban in front of the main viewing screen watching their prisoner. He was still lying motionless on the bed where he'd been deposited after his recent interrogation session.

"Is he all right?" Raiban demanded abruptly. "His eyes are open, but he looks like he's unconscious."

"Of course, General," Rhyaz answered. "He's resting, that's all—his way. He's constantly monitored, believe me."

Raiban nodded. "What have you managed to find out from him?"

"Very little," Rhyaz admitted. "Mainly a confirmation of what the Keissians working in Geshader and Tashkerra had already reported. That despite being warm-blooded, the Valtegans need a higher temperature than us or they become sluggish, and that they prefer lower light levels. They despise females of any species, and this particular Valtegan has shown no fear of us. Physiologically, the modern ones are only slightly different from Kezule."

"How about telepaths? Have you got one to read his mind yet?"

"We're moving slowly on that, General," said Rhyaz. "When a Sholan mind touched theirs, our modern captives went catatonic, then died. We don't want to risk that happening until we've got as much information as we can from him. I've had our resident telepath use his Talent in the same room as Kezule and he wasn't aware of it, but that's as far as I'm prepared to go at present."

Raiban flicked her ears in annoyance. "I've never known sleep deprivation not to reveal some information," she grumbled. "The resultant disorientation and exhaustion usually breaks down their resistance."

"Unless you're a Valtegan," Rhyaz said, trying not to

und irritated himself. He'd already discussed this with the
eneral several times before. He understood why she
und it difficult to believe, he had himself. "Or at least,
nless you're General Kezule," he amended. "The sensors
e implanted in him confirmed he was awake, as did our
iewers, but somehow he managed to get enough rest to
ombat that technique. And," he added, mindful of the
tate Kezule was currently in, "we did keep physically dis-
urbing him, too."

"I know, I know. I read the report," she said testily.
I've got the High Command breathing down my neck for
esults. I need to have something positive to tell them at
ur next meeting in a fortnight, and you don't seem to be
etting anywhere! What about drugs?"

"The medics don't understand his system well enough
et. Computer simulations are one thing, our only specimen
s another."

"Your more physical persuasion didn't seem to do much
ood." She indicated the still form of Kezule.

"In these circumstances, it rarely does," Rhyaz agreed,
'but it's less dangerous than drugs. We really need his co-
peration more than anything."

"So what's next?" Raiban faced away from the viewing
window. "More persuasion?"

"For a few days, combined with a more conciliatory approach and one or two luxuries added to his environment.
That's why I requested those items from Keiss."

"When are they due?"

"They're here now, General, being unloaded into our
depository area ready for use." As he turned from the window, a movement from his prisoner caught his eye. "He's
coming round," he said.

"Another time, Rhyaz. I've no wish to watch him lick
his wounds."

Her voice was gruff, and Rhyaz knew she disliked using
violence for questioning as much as he did. It was barbaric,
but when coupled with a softer approach, it occasionally
yielded results where other means had failed. Personally,
he didn't hold out much hope. If he'd read him right, Kezule was a line officer, as he had been. The General had
been out there in the mud, under fire with his troops—not
sitting dry and warm in the rear like some. This officer
wouldn't break easily.

*　　*　　*

Kezule stirred, feeling the energy coursing round his sys
tem, wakening his body now his mind was alert. Checkin
heart rate and breathing, he made sure they stayed at th
slow, steady rhythm he wanted them to believe was norma
If the opportunity came to escape, he didn't want them t
know how fast he could move, nor how much control h
had over his body functions.

He needed to keep his breathing shallow anyway—hi
ribs were somewhat bruised after his latest session with hi
tormentors. Surreptitiously he slid his hand between him
self and the wall and felt cautiously along his left side
trying not to register pain when he touched the lower ones
He knew they were watching him, and was sure there wa
nowhere in this sparsely furnished room that he wasn'
under full surveillance.

Sitting up slowly, he had to admit to himself that these
modern Sholans had gradually gone up in his esteem. They
were very different from their ancestors. It seemed his peo
ple had had a lasting effect on them after all. Theirs was
no technologically backward world now. He regretted they
hadn't met during the subduing of their planet: they'd have
been an enemy worth fighting. He'd hated waging war on
worlds of shocked and docile inhabitants. Oh, a few had
stood up to them, with their primitive weapons, but not
many—and not for long.

He eased himself off the hard, narrow bed and got care
fully to his feet. As he moved he became aware of the
swelling and bruising around his right arm and shoulder
and the left side of his face. It would pass. Physical pain
and privation he could tolerate, he was used to it. Granted,
it had been a few years since he had been exposed to them,
prior to the Emperor, *Praise be to Him,* promoting him to
guarding the royal hatchery on Shola. Thank the gods he
hadn't gone native and soft like some of the officers he
knew!

The sound of a hatch opening and shutting, combined
with a loud squeal drew his attention to the cage set in the
opposite wall. So they'd decided to feed him, had they? It
had been a long time since his last meal, two days at least.
A small hiss of amusement escaped him. Depriving him of
sleep hadn't worked. How were they to know he had a

nse of time to beat that of any manufactured device?
es, he'd eat, but he needed water first.

A few concessions had been made to his different physi-
ogy. One of them was the wide-topped bowl he needed
 drink from. The other was the one-piece coverall he
ore. Despite it having been laundered several times, he
uld still smell the stench of the Humans on it, but like
verything else in this room that was now his world, he'd
own accustomed to it.

He strolled over to the cage trying to gauge how bored
e was. At his approach, the inhabitant, a medium sized
rown mammal, set up a high-pitched screeching and tried
esperately to claw its way through the back corner of its
nclosure. Releasing it and chasing it round the room was
ut of the question today, but once he'd removed it from
1e cage, he could turn away and pretend to rip it limb
rom limb, devouring it a piece at a time while it still lived.
t wasn't something he'd ever actually done, but he'd seen
 used to intimidate Sholan prisoners in his time, and it
vas extremely effective. He hoped when he simulated it
hat it would have the same effect on his captors. However,
1e was too hungry for that.

Unlatching the cage door, he thrust his hand in, grasping
he terrified rodent and hauling it out. It squirmed and
hrieked frantically, trying to find a part of him into which
o fasten its long incisors. Grasping its head in his other
1and, with a sharp tug and twist, he dispatched it cleanly.
There were some animals that tasted better after a chase,
but these Sholan ones weren't in that category. Let them
get too terrified and it soured their blood and the flesh.

He took the carcass to the table and, putting it down,
proceeded to dismember it using the edges of his claws as
surrogate knives. He wasn't allowed such luxuries, so it was
as well he had his natural ones.

The smell of the still warm blood was making him even
hungrier. Licking his claws clean first, he'd just sat down
to eat when the door slid open. Two armed troopers came
into the room, guns trained on him. In their wake followed
an officer, one he hadn't seen before.

The Sholan approached the opposite edge of the table
before stopping. "We haven't met, General Kezule. I'm
Sub-Lieutenant Myak from Alien Relations. I'm here to

see you're being treated appropriately for a prisoner ⊂
your rank."

Kezule eyed him over the top of the piece of meat in h
hands. He grunted in reply and began to eat.

"I see I'm interrupting your meal. I must apologize fo
that, but my schedule is tight today, and this was the onl
time I could spare. I've brought one or two home comfort
for you."

The Sholan turned away so sharply that Kezule grinne
to himself. Yes, it still affected them to see a Valtegan ea
But what he'd said had caught his attention. Home com
forts? What did he mean by that? Continuing to eat, h
watched with interest as another trooper, carrying ∶
medium-sized box, was gestured in.

He brought the box to the lieutenant and stood there
while Myak reached inside. Bringing out a small cuboic
object, he placed it on the table a good arm's length away
from him.

"I believe it's some kind of puzzle belonging to you
people," said the officer, still keeping his eyes averted. He
reached in again, this time bringing out a small pile of fla
plastic squares covered in script, and a slim rectangular object with a viewing window on the front.

"We think these are books and a viewer."

Confused, Kezule stuffed the last of the meat he was
eating into his mouth and reached out for them. Turning
them over, he examined them from every angle. The writing was definitely that of his people, but subtly different,
as if in another dialect. He could only recognize a word
here and there.

"You put the cards into the slot," said Myak, pointing
to it. "There are several depressions on the front which
control the device."

Kezule chose one of the cards and inserted it, then
turned the unit over and placed a claw tip into one of the
small holes on the front. Nothing. He tried again and the
screen came to life, displaying what indeed was Valtegan
text, and recognizable at that.

"We don't know enough of your language to read it
properly, but our experts think it may be a story of some
kind."

"It's a book of holy sayings by the God-King, Emperor
Q'emgo'h," said Kezule. "May His memory be revered for

all time," he added reflexively. This brought home to him once and for all that his world was long gone. Q'emgo'h had been *his* Emperor, on the holy throne of the God-Kings when he'd been taken into captivity. For His sayings to be collected like this, He was dead. Distractedly, he fiddled with the other depressions till he got the text to scroll down. "Where did you get these?"

"Oh, they were found," Myak said offhandedly. "I knew you had nothing to do in your leisure time, so I brought these, and some paper and a writing stylus," he added, pulling the items from the box. "It must be bad enough being a captive, but to be without anything to do day after day . . . Now, is there anything else I can do for you? Have you any complaints about your treatment?"

Kezule hissed derisively, his crest raising up to its full height. "I survive," he said dryly.

Myak nodded. "Good. We have access to a few other odds and ends, but I may not be allowed to bring them to you unless you begin to cooperate with our personnel. It's not a lot they're asking, believe me. For a start," he said, his voice dropping persuasively, "if you would teach them your language, then we'd know what it is we're finding and whether it would be of interest to you, wouldn't we? You could even ask us to look for specific items."

Kezule held up the viewer. "This isn't from the past," he said. "We didn't have such devices as this then. And it's too new. Where did you get it?" His voice had taken on a hard edge, and he checked himself. He had to remember he was not the general here, he was the captive. "Where do they come from?" he asked again, moderating his tone.

Myak gestured to the trooper to leave and turned to go himself. "An exchange of information could perhaps be arranged," he said quietly. "Think about it. Oh, I almost forgot." He reached in his pocket and drew out a tall, slim container which he threw at Kezule.

Without thinking, Kezule was instantly alert, catching it almost as soon as it left the lieutenant's hand.

"I'm told it's a spice used for your food," Myak said.

Turning the container in his hand, Kezule realized it was a drum of powdered Iaalquoi—and it was relatively fresh! Where in the name of all the demons had they gotten this from? He tried to suppress the surge of relief that swept through him. the lack of the plant extract had already begun to affect him, and he'd been trying to avoid thinking of what would happen to him if none was available.

Two good reactions there, Lieutenant Myak, came the message from the telepath in the research viewing area. *His readings peaked when you threw him the tub, then when he saw what it was. I guess it's something he requires—a drug or some dietary supplement.*

Understood, Myak replied as he left. "Just think about my proposition," he repeated, stopping briefly at the door.

Myak joined the small group in the research area.

"If this herb is one he needs, or wants, it could be the lever we need to persuade him to cooperate," L'Seuli said. "Any idea what it is, Lieutenant?"

Mito shook her head. "None yet. I need to be fully updated on what you've found in the various ruins here. Anders and I can then continue where Jo left off with her catalog of the Keissian Valtegan bases."

Raguul grunted. "If you ask me, it's damned convenient that you've been working with Anders on this all along."

"It is rather, isn't it?" said Mito blandly as Nick Anders caught her eye conspiratorially. "Still, two get the work done faster than one, and speed is what we need. At least he can go in with this Kezule, if necessary. I can't."

"You have a point," Raguul conceded. "Well, I'm off home now. You know where I am if your people need me, Brother L'Seuli." With a brief nod in his direction, the commander left.

Mito heaved a sigh of relief when he'd gone. "What about you, Myak? Are you on leave, too?"

"Like the captain, I'm on call should they need me here." He looked over at the telepath who was sitting on one of the high-backed stools at the bench between them and the viewing window. "Zhyaf," he said, "the Clan Lord has asked me to accompany you back to the estate on a social visit. When do you go off duty?"

Zhyaf stirred, looking up at the lieutenant. "In about an hour."

"I'll take you for a tour of the facility," said L'Seuli. "When are you and Anders scheduled to start work, Mito?"

"Tomorrow," replied Anders as Mito wrinkled her nose in a grimace. "We don't rate any leave."

"Not true," said L'Seuli, shaking his head. "Your experience will be vital to our work here. We've scheduled you with shorter shifts than the others to compensate you for your lack of leave."

"You can't blame me for trying for a sympathy vote," grinned Anders, putting an arm around Mito's waist as they followed L'Seuli out into the open security area that fronted Kezule's prison.

*   *   *

"Good morning," said Vanna, putting her head around the kitchen door. "Can I come in? Today is Nylam's Day, the day of the Hunt, and of giving gifts. I've brought an early one for you."

"Please join us," said Kusac. "We've nearly finished, I'm afraid, but if you're hungry . . ."

"I've eaten, thanks," she said, putting her medikit on the table and slipping onto the seat near the door.

"Coffee or c'shar?" asked Carrie as Zhala hovered.

"Coffee, please."

"So what's this gift?" asked Carrie curiously.

"The trials are finished, and our contraceptive's ready to use. We can administer it in half-yearly or yearly doses, but I recommend that with the Jalna mission ahead of you, you ought to take the yearly one. I shouldn't think you'd want to bear another cub out in the field!"

Carrie grinned wryly with a sidelong glance at her mate. "I'll pass on that, thank you. Not that Kusac and Kaid weren't very good birthers, you understand."

"Of course," agreed Vanna, opening her kit and taking out the hypoderm.

"I'd prefer it if you didn't, too," said Kusac. "I was really very worried that something would go wrong."

"It all came right in the end, though," said Carrie, rolling up her sleeve ready for Vanna.

"I suggest you also offer this to the Sisters on the estate," said Kusac, "Just as a precaution. We need more cubs for our new clan, but they must be conceived voluntarily and not because of Leska links."

"I had just such a request from T'Chebbi last night." She glanced up at him. "I can't think why. I don't remember ever seeing her with any of the males around here."

Kusac exchanged a glance with Carrie. "She's gone to Stronghold for the next couple of days."

"Probably got a lover up there, then," said Vanna, packing her equipment away.

You don't think it's Kaid, do you? sent Carrie on their private link.

Pretty sure of it, cub. I remember how she reacted when we brought him back from Stronghold, and how she looked out for Dzaka.

They do go back a long way. Did I ever tell you that Kaid chose her as my guard not only because she's female, but because she's about my size? He wanted someone I could be comfortable with.

That was thoughtful of him. But I wonder . . .

Don't go matchmaking for him, she teased. *She's as much of a loner as he is.*

You merely prove my point, he replied placidly.

"Mara seems to be settling in well at Ruth's," said Vanna as Zhala arrived with her drink. "She was an excellent choice, Carrie, and a brilliant idea. Already a couple of the Human females from the dig have gone over to see her, and they were chatting happily to Mara as well."

"Thank you. I'm just glad there was someone like her to find. Zhyaf's been less morose, too, since we sent his sister back home and he was recruited for the Shanagi Project. Living at the center has opened his world out; he's having to become more involved in a real life now. He's even finding the work challenging."

"He'll be back sometime today," said Vanna. "It's their Link day tomorrow. And he's bringing Myak with him."

"Myak? Not Myak from the *Khalossa?*" asked Kusac, sitting up in surprise.

"The same. It turns out he's with AlRel."

"That crafty old bastard Raguul," muttered Kusac. "All along he's had a telepath acting undercover as his adjutant. No wonder he knew everything that was going on. That's tracking downwind of Guild regulations."

"It's a legitimate appointment, Garras says. Raguul requested him years ago because he's so involved with diplomacy missions. Your father obviously thought it an excellent idea."

"But what's Myak doing coming here?" asked Carrie.

"I'd have thought he'd want to go home like everyone else on leave. And if he's here, where's Commander Raguul?"

"Gone home, like you said. Why Myak's coming here, I've no idea, but we think it's connected with the Shanagi Project because you'll never guess who else is there. Mito and Anders!"

"What? They're still together?" Carrie could hardly believe it.

"Mm. Surprising, isn't it? She must have changed a lot. Rumor has it they've taken out a five-year bonding contract."

"Really? But why? I can't believe she'd be interested in having cubs, even if they could."

"I told you, with medical help, that's not such a remote possibility now," said Vanna. "The leaps forward we've made in understanding the genetics of both the Humans and ourselves are incredible. The samples from the latest ni'uzu epidemic alone have made all the difference. I'm still convinced it's something Kaid picked up in the Margins. Its ability to spread despite our quarantine restrictions convinced me. At least it was only in the form of a heavy cold."

"Who knows?" said Kusac. "Since we've all been exposed to it, we're stable now. That's what matters. The new Leska pair that arrived yesterday from the Guild proved that. I think it far more likely that Mito and Anders have bonded because of Human conventions. If they've been living together on Keiss, it's what the Humans around her would be doing, what Anders would want, and perhaps even herself. She was always insecure about herself as a female, though never as an officer."

"I've another piece of gossip," grinned Vanna.

"You're full of it today," said Carrie, sipping her drink. "With Kaid gone, we don't hear so much."

Vanna flicked an ear apologetically. "It comes to Garras now he's acting as your second."

"Well, don't keep us in suspense. Who does it involve this time?" chided Kusac.

"Rulla. Looks like he's lost his heart," she said with a chuckle. "I suggest you appoint another minder for Mara and Zhyaf, Rulla's too preoccupied right now. Although I don't think he was ever really right for the job."

"You're telling me," said Kusac ruefully. "We've already considered this and are looking for a replacement."

"Who is it?" demanded Carrie. "Who's he after?"

"Ruth! He's besotted with her!" Vanna laughed. "He fusses round her, gets underfoot by trying to help her all the time, and generally makes a nuisance of himself!"

"That could be a problem. I wanted Mara free of male influences for a while, and Rulla, being their main guardian, carries associations of the life I want her to forget."

"Oh, I wouldn't worry about Mara on that score," said Vanna. "She and Ruth's daughter, Mandy, are having a great time laughing at his antics! Nothing like seeing someone who was in charge of you brought down to the level of a youngling by love! Does wonders for the ego. Believe me, she'll not be harmed by having him around."

"What about Ruth? How does she feel about all this attention?" asked Kusac.

"Amused, but we'll see. It shouldn't be long before Rulla makes his invitation."

"What I want to know is why there's no gossip about Mara's Human lover—the one who fathered her child," said Carrie. "She refused to talk about it the night she spent with us."

"Have you checked with all the Human male Leskas?" asked Kusac.

Vanna nodded. "I have, and if it's one of them, they aren't admitting to it. Personally, I don't think it is. I'm sure she's just confused and it's Zhyaf's."

"No. She was so genuinely terrified at the thought of having a Sholan cub that I believe she really did make sure she didn't get pregnant by Zhyaf and did search out a Human partner," said Carrie, absently nibbling on a piece of rich fruit cake that Zhala had surreptitiously placed beside her.

"I thought there was no way for females in our Links to avoid becoming pregnant," said Kusac. "I thought that was the whole point of Vanna's search for a contraceptive."

"Oh, there are ways Human females can avoid pregnancy," said Carrie with a grin, "but the most common method wouldn't be practical for you Sholan males."

"It's not much use for Human males with Sholan female partners either," said Vanna. "At least, not according to Jack and Jiszoe."

"Oh," said Kusac, finally getting the drift of what they

neant. "Then this unknown Human must be a potential Triad member."

"Until you formed a Triad, there were none," said Vanna.

"That we know of," corrected Carrie. "You still don't like to admit you're part of a Triad yourself, even though Garras does."

Vanna sighed. "I'm not going through all that again with you, Carrie. For the sake of peace, I've let Garras persuade me to register us as a Triad with Ghyan at the temple. Let's leave it there."

"Not all Leska pairs attract a third," said Kusac. "I've been looking into details of the partners of the Sholan Leska pairs and only a small percentage of Leska-linked individuals seem to have a regular lover. Nowadays a Triad isn't so socially visible. There hasn't been the need to actively form them."

"And from which guilds do these partners come?" asked Vanna.

Kusac grinned. "You don't want to know, Vanna. It'll only confirm what Carrie said."

"Damn you both," she growled in mock anger.

"I've got a theory for you," said Kusac. "What if potential mixed Leskas are now being changed *before* they form a Link? I know," he said, forestalling Vanna. "It needs the gestalt, but maybe the gestalt isn't the only mechanism that triggers the change. What if there's another?"

Vanna groaned. "Don't do this to me, Kusac! We just got it all worked out! We don't need a loose gun out there changing all the rules."

"Why shouldn't it change again? It's an unstable gene. And since some of the Brothers and Sisters have been made genetically compatible with us by that new virus, why shouldn't it affect Humans the same way?" he argued. "Maybe that's a way to identify potential Leskas. We could bring them here and prepare them in advance for their Link. There'd be less shock to them both and it might even give them a choice of partners, avoiding mismatches like Zhyaf and Mara."

"You're dreaming, Kusac," said Vanna, finishing her drink and getting up. "I've got to go. Garras wants to join the hunt today. It's years since he's been on one."

A small mewl from the crib in the corner of the room

drew Vanna's attention. "Kashini's downstairs *and* awake," she said, her voice becoming instantly softer. "I haven't seen her for a week or two. Her eyes'll be open now."

"They are," said Carrie as Kusac got up and went over to the crib to pick up their cub. "She's a lively little thing, and she's grown."

She watched as her mate carefully lifted the child, cradling her back against his upper arm so she could see properly. What filled both of Carrie's arms, nestled happily in the crook of one of his.

I like your smallness, sent Kusac as he came back to them. *It's one of the things that makes you so very different from our females.*

"Flatterer," she smiled, admiring the picture they presented: their daughter with her blonde pelt so light against her dark-furred father.

Vanna reached out to touch the little one. "She's got your eyes, Kusac," she said as Kashini gazed up at her, both hands reaching out toward her. "And a look of you in her face, Carrie," she said with surprise. "I can't see Brynne at all in Marak."

Little squeaks of delight ensued as Vanna tickled her behind her ears. "Can I have a cuddle?"

"I don't know, Vanna," said Kusac with a straight face. "How do I know you won't drop her?"

"Oh, you . . . !" retorted Vanna, reaching out to take hold of her, but Kashini would have none of it and began to pull back and let out sounds of distress, ears now plastered flat to her skull.

"Don't tease her, Kusac," said Carrie, getting up and joining them. "He forgets she's too immature to understand a joke. She takes things literally."

Vanna looked on in a disbelief Carrie could feel as she took her daughter from Kusac. Holding her close against her chest, she began to make soothing noises, gently patting and stroking the cub until her distress faded.

"Sorry," said Kusac, ears flicking back and remaining there in apology. "She's a fully active telepath," he explained to Vanna. "She picked up the idea of you dropping her from me. I keep forgetting she can do that."

"I should have guessed," said Vanna wryly. "How could a child of yours be normal, even for a hybrid?"

"We're pretty sure it was the power of the Margin gateways

at wakened her Talent so early," said Carrie, passing the
ow quiet cub to her friend.

"She's so tiny, and so sweet," purred Vanna as she gath-
ed the cub into her arms. Kashini trilled with pleasure,
ad grabbing Vanna's finger, pulled it toward her mouth,
oceeding to chew on it.

"Ouch! You have sharp teeth, kit!" she said, removing
er finger from danger and playing pat with her instead.
How do you manage to feed her, Carrie?"

"I don't any more. Her nurse does for the moment, but
ot for much longer. We've had to give her solid food as
ell because she's so hungry."

"She's lovely, cub, and doing so well!" she sighed. "I
eally have to go now." She handed her back to Kusac.
We'll see you later tonight when we'll have your real
resents."

"See you then, Vanna," said Kusac, tucking Kashini over
is shoulder as she left.

Carrie moved to his side, lifting his free arm so she could
rap it around her shoulders. As she rested her head
gainst his chest, she felt the almost inaudible purr that
ibrated through him.

All I ever wanted, I now hold in my arms, he sent.

So do I, Kusac. She reached up to touch Kashini's foot
where it protruded from the bottom of the blanket. Cup-
ing her hand around it, she gently rubbed her fingers along
he webbing between her cub's toes, feeling them open
wider as Kashini began to purr with pleasure.

A discreet knock at the door and Yashui, the nurse, en-
ered. "Time for her to go upstairs, Liegena," she said
uietly.

Carrie sighed and let Kashini's foot go. "See you later,
little one," she said, moving aside so Kusac could hand
her over.

As she sat back down at the table, she watched her life-
mate lay his cheek alongside their daughter's, his tongue
flicking out to lick her gently behind the ear before he
handed her over to Yashui. The sight brought tears to her
eyes. She rubbed them away hurriedly, ashamed at being
still so emotional.

"Could Brynne have fathered Mara's child?" she asked
when they were alone.

"It's not him," said Kusac positively. "Vanna told me

he's been too busy with that Derwent person. Despite som
of his strange ideas, Brynne's been settling down, too. N
other females at all, and he's devoted to his son. H
wouldn't risk all that to be with Mara, knowing the troub
she caused for Dzaka and Kitra."

"Just a thought."

"I'm sure it isn't one of the Leska males."

"Well, with Jissoh and Nyash watching her, we shou
know soon."

"I've got to go and get ready for the hunt. Will you t
coming up to Mother's with me now?"

"Of course. Don't forget, you've to bring me somethin
back for the feast tonight."

He laughed. "Don't worry, I'll make sure I get the big
gest rhakla out there. I've got my reputation to live up t(
after all."

*   *   *

Lijou stood at his bedroom window looking down int
the main courtyard. Below, the younglings were still sweep
ing the night's fresh snowfall aside. Already the bones o
the central fire had been relaid in preparation for the festiv
ities later.

He felt Kha'Qwa's presence draw nearer, feeling the gen
tle touch of her mind, then her hand as she joined him.

"Good morning," she said, leaning against him, her tai
twining round his leg. "What holds your attention so closel
this morning?"

He hesitated. How to put it into words? "Have you eve
felt as if you're standing at the doorway to the future?
feel as if I'm there now, looking through it and wondering
what will happen. And although I'm part of it, although I
helped open the door, I'm afraid to go forward, Kha'Qwa.'

"Afraid of what?"

"The changes."

"I see none, Lijou. I see only the traditions of over a
thousand years as our people get ready for Nylam's Day,'
she said, looking out of the window.

"Look more closely and you'll see." He pointed to a
couple of black-robed figures hurrying across to the courtyard. "Already our tutors are wearing their new colors,
proclaiming them Priests, not lay-brothers. The old year
ends tonight, Kha'Qwa," he said, laying his arm across her

shoulders and continuing to look down into the courtyard. A new year, and new lives for all of us. Our right as a guild to choose those who possess lesser talents is being laid down in the new charter Rhyaz is drafting. In future, when we visit the guilds to recruit, we can openly take those we need. So much has happened this past year, and there is so much more still to come."

"Are you that afraid of change?"

"Some changes," he sighed. "But not others." His hand tightened briefly on her shoulder. "Not our new life together. I don't think Konis expected us to life-bond so soon!"

As he continued to watch the courtyard, he saw a small figure enter through the main gates. "I wonder what brings T'Chebbi here today. Who could she be coming to see?"

"It could only be Kaid."

"You think so?"

"I know so," she said with conviction. "I've never seen her so animated as she was when they were here to rescue him."

Lijou thought back over his last few meetings with T'Chebbi. "You could be right. I hope so. It worried me when he said he intended to stay here for Midwinter."

"If only for a short while, let the world take care of itself," she said, lowering her voice to the level of a soft purr and turning him away from the window. "You should be enjoying this morning with me. With all your talk of new years and new lives, tell me, how does it feel to be a newly mated male, and a father?"

"Believe me, it feels good, Kha'Qwa, and I don't mean to seem . . ." He stopped in mid-sentence, his attention suddenly completely focused on her. "What did you say?"

She laughed and began to move away from him. "I thought that would get your attention."

Reaching out, he grasped her by the arm, pulling her close again. "What did you say?" he asked her again. *Pregnant? It wasn't possible—was it? How could they possibly raise a cub at Stronghold!*

She stretched up to touch his neck. "You've never bothered to shield your thoughts from me, Lijou, and I've enough Talent to read you. You said the Clan Lord wanted us to set an example, so when I picked up what was in your mind last night, I decided it was time. I was right,

wasn't I? You do want us to share our cubs, don't you?
She tilted her head on one side, widening her eyes inno
cently as she looked into his.

"You never told me." *A father? He was going to be*
father at his age? And she could hear his thoughts?

"At your age?" she scoffed. "You're of an age with th
Clan Lord! As to being able to hear you, many of us ha
our gifts boosted by the new virus, Lijou, even you. I jus
never had the need to mention it till now."

"You're pregnant? Since last night?" He was finding i
difficult to take in her news.

She nodded. "Did I make the wrong decision?"

"No. No, of course not," he said. "Are you positive
How can you be so sure after only one night?" He suddenl
realized he didn't want her to be mistaken. She was right
this was their life. For too long he'd lived for his Guild
then the Brotherhood. Now, before it was too late, h
wanted a life that was his—his and Kha'Qwa's.

"I'm sure," she answered with a gentle laugh as his hand
touched her neck in an intimate gesture of affection. "We
females know these things."

"Perhaps we should make sure," he said, running his
fingers through her short flame-colored curls. He still hadn'
gotten over his relief at her acceptance of him as a life-
mate. Tall, and slim as any youngling, it had surprised many
of Stronghold when the lively fiery colored Kha'Qwa had
become his Companion several months earlier.

"It only takes once, honestly."

"I wouldn't want you to be disappointed if you found
you were mistaken." He began to nuzzle her cheek. "It
would be so upsetting for you."

"You're so thoughtful," she purred.

"Better to make absolutely sure."

"Mmm. What about your duties this morning?"

"Vriuzu's on his way to see to them," he mumbled,
catching the edge of her ear gently with his teeth.

"That's all right, then."

* * *

When the library door opened, Kaid knew it was
T'Chebbi. He looked up, eye ridges meeting in a frown.
"Is something wrong at the estate?" he asked.

"Nothing," she replied, approaching the desk where he

as working. "Needed to come. Have things in storage to collect. Meant I could see you, too. Not good to be without friends at this time of year."

"I'm used to being alone," he said, turning back to his work.

"Maybe we share our solitude for a short while."

He looked up sharply, catching her slight smile as she took the seat opposite him. He hadn't expected her to pay him another personal visit, especially after she'd avoided saying good-bye.

"Look tired, Tallinu. Still get bad nights? What does Father Lijou say?"

"I haven't mentioned it to him."

"Should. You need help."

He felt anger flare and repressed it, determined not to lose his temper with her. "Did you come here just to scold me, T'Chebbi? Or is there something else you want? I am capable of organizing my own life, you know." He switched off his comp pad. She was obviously determined to talk to him.

Her mouth opened in a deep grin. "I haven't eaten yet. Won't serve me as first meal's over, but they'll serve you. Always would."

"You're hungry? That's all?" Maybe it was no more than she said, a visit to collect the last of her belongings from the Guild.

She flicked her ears in agreement.

He gathered up the comp and book he'd been using and stuffed them into his robe pocket as he got to his feet. "I can't promise you that they'll cook for us," he began.

"Will," she interrupted him. "Said you hadn't eaten either, and if you came, they'd feed me, too."

Now she'd mentioned it, he realized he was hungry. "I prefer to go in at the end of the meal times," he said, opening the door. "Students never seem to keep quiet, even when they're eating."

T'Chebbi touched his arm, holding him back for a moment. "Tallinu, can't say good-byes—couldn't be there when you left. I do want to spend more time with you—if you want to."

Kaid grunted noncommittally as he stepped into the corridor—and the dark.

It was night. He stood at the head of a small group of warriors, waiting for the clouds to cover the moon once more. A sound to his right drew his attention, and he turned to see T'Chebbi. Her upper arm was bound with a bloodstained makeshift bandage.

"You shouldn't be here," he said, the sight of her throwing him into confusion. "You should be on Shola."

"Kaid!" The voice was as insistent as the hands that were shaking him by the shoulders. Gradually the dark receded and the corridor came back into focus, as did T'Chebbi. Leaning against the wall for support, he reached an unsteady hand out to touch her arm, an arm unblemished by any injury.

"Kaid, we *are* on Shola," she was saying. "Whatever you saw, it's not happening."

"I know. It was a vision. Jalna, I think, except you were there."

"Kusac's asked me to go," she said quietly. "What did you see?"

"Something and nothing," he said, pushing himself upright again as he tried to dispel the images. "It's unreliable T'Chebbi. Just flashes, nothing even worth seeing."

"You saw me with you on Jalna."

"That's all I saw. The visions are too short to be of any use." He was annoyed and frustrated. This was happening on average now once or twice a day. All his research over the last few days had turned up no probable cause for it.

"Perhaps have food sent up," said T'Chebbi. "You're overtired. Maybe that causes them."

He hesitated, then reluctantly nodded. Lack of sleep certainly didn't help.

Lijou shook Kha'Qwa gently. "We have to get up," he said. "Vriuzu sent that Kaid had another of those episodes."

"What was it?" she asked.

"Too short for him to pick it up. Why won't Kaid come and tell me what's happening? We'd have a chance of helping him sooner that way! I hate having to have him monitored like this. I feel like I'm spying on him."

"He won't blame you, Lijou."

"I still don't like it," he grumbled, throwing back the covers.

A full stomach made the world a friendlier place, Kaid decided. Their talk had been of changes on the estate since he'd left.

"Jissoh's a good choice for Mara. She's outgoing and doesn't easily take offense. With any luck, they might strike up a friendship. Nijou and Khy are fine for Zhyaf. Garras is handling things well. I knew he'd be a capable second for Kusac. This cub of Mara's, though." He shook his head thoughtfully. "Where did such a new element come from? How is it possible that we have an unknown compatible Human on the estate?"

"The new virus."

"Not possible. A lot of folk took colds, even the Human archaeologists had their own health problems, but they weren't necessarily connected. Unless Vanna's proved otherwise?"

"Her people still working on it," said T'Chebbi, leaning forward to replace her mug on the table between them. "She'll find out soon."

Memory tugged at him as he caught a trace of her scent. "Tell me," he said, "that perfume you wore . . .?"

Her ears twitched with embarrassment. "Was an aphrodisiac," she admitted. "Special one, though. Enhances any interest your partner has, doesn't create it."

"A fine distinction," he said dryly.

"Yes," she insisted. "One I learned of when was Consortia. Didn't make you want me, only made you lose inhibitions."

"Did you bring it with you?" He was curious to know.

She hesitated. "Maybe. Wouldn't use it again unless you ask. Wanted you once to see me as a female, one you might want. That was all. If you were interested, perfume helps, if not, nothing. You wouldn't notice it."

The meal had made him feel relaxed and slightly drowsy. Obviously the need to pick up her belongings had been at least partly an excuse. He held his hand out in an invitation to her. "You won't need it this time," he said as she accepted.

This pairing was gentler and slower as they took their time to see each other in a new way. There wasn't the

mental rapport he had with Carrie, but he could sense wha[t]
pleased T'Chebbi, and she certainly knew how to give
him pleasure.

Instinctively, as they began to climax, he reached men[-]
tally for her only to feel his mind explode into many piece[s]
as a memory that had been deliberately hidden from him
returned. With devastating clarity, he began to relive wha[t]
had happened to him during the night he'd spent in the
shrine before Kashini's Validation.

Along the corridor from Kaid's rooms, Lijou was alerted
and this time, he experienced it, too.

> *Tallinu!*
> *He needs to be focused on us.*
> *He's not listening! Tallinu! Tallinu!*
> *He calls himself Kaid now.*
> *Kaid, dammit! Kaid!*
>
> Confused, his chanting faltered as he tried to sense
> who was calling him.
>
> *He's not responding. We can't keep this up much
> longer.*
> *Get the doctor to do it. He's supposed to be the
> god, after all. Maybe he'll listen to him.*
>
> God? What talk was this of gods?
>
> *I can't!* The voice woke more memories.
> *You'd better, because we can't bring him back
> otherwise!*
>
> He heard the implicit threat. The litanies and chants
> all forgotten, he began to mentally back away. This
> didn't feel right. Whatever it was, he didn't want to
> know. Then his mind was grasped and held. Power-
> less, he now heard a voice he recognized only too
> well.
>
> *Kaid, we're not finished yet. There's work still to do.*
> *No! I've done enough for you! No more, Vartra, no
> more!* His mind shouted the refusal.
> *You will return once more. You're at the heart of
> matters both here and in the future. You have to
> return!*
> *NO!*
> *Got him!*
>
> As if from a great height, he saw his body slump
> forward onto the floor. A white rime of frost began to

form over his robe, then, as panic began to take hold, the image vanished as he was swept into a maelstrom of sound and heat and pain.

Fire licked along his limbs, burning and consuming him. The smell of seared fur and flesh filled his nostrils, and as he opened his mouth to scream, flames gushed out. Mercifully, he blacked out.

*   *   *

"You nearly lost him!" The voice was female, angry. "Until the good doctor believed us and lent his strength." Male. Then everything faded into blackness.

"He should be coming round any time now. I only gave him a light sedative."

A sharp prick against his arm almost made him flinch, but he suppressed it in time. He feigned unconsciousness, using his passive senses to see what he could learn first. No telepathy, they'd sense it immediately. The room they were in was small—no echoes—and smelled of antiseptic. Medical area then. So far, two voices, but there should be more.

"Are you sure it's necessary to wake him?" A third voice. "He's not going to appreciate being brought back, nor what you've done to him."

There was a familiarity about the voices, but he was still confused. He realized his limbs were bound to the surface on which he lay. That didn't please him.

A snort of laughter. "You don't know the meaning of anger! And he's awake, listening to all you've been saying." That voice he did recognize. Goran, Vartra's security chief.

Clenching his fists, he focused his mind on the bands surrounding them. Moments later, he'd snapped the left and was sitting up freeing his right hand as he scanned the room. Goran, Tiernay, Vartra, and one more he didn't know. Hiding at the back, he caught sight of Jaisa.

Without taking his eyes off them, he reached down to free his ankles. "You'd better have a damned good reason for this."

"We need you here, Tallinu," said Vartra.

Kaid swiveled his head to look at him, his blood running cold at the thought of remaining in the past. "Hear me well, Vartra, *I will not stay here!* Nothing you can do will keep me here. I don't care what it costs, I'm going home!"

"We don't intend to keep you here, Kaid. We'll return you to the future," said Jaisa, pushing Tiernay aside and stepping forward. "I wouldn't have helped them if I'd thought they didn't intend to do that."

He looked back to Vartra, unconsciously rubbing his upper arm. "How *do* you intend to get me back?" he demanded, swinging his legs off the treatment bed and jumping down to the floor. As he landed, he winced, putting his hand to his groin, feeling the tender muscles. A wave of nausea passed through him and he staggered back against the bed. "What the hell have you done to me?"

"We only needed you here for a short time, Tallinu," said Dr. Vartra apologetically. "I'm sorry, but we had no option."

Pushing himself upright again, Kaid lunged toward the doctor, but Goran was there first. "Hold on, lad," he said, knocking him aside and spinning him round. His arms snaked under Kaid's, grasping him across the shoulders and behind his neck.

Before he'd completed the move, Kaid was free. Constricting his chest muscles and pushing his arms up, he dropped down within Goran's grasp, landing him an elbow blow in the stomach. As he pivoted around and away, he followed it through with a blow from his knee under the jaw. Goran dropped like a stone.

"It wasn't Vartra, it was me." The voice was lazily arrogant. "He only did the research, I—applied it—to you."

Kaid looked across the room to where the speaker lounged against the countertop. A long face, topped by low-set ears and eyes of piercing blue stared back at him. Curling short hair of a rich dark brown contrasted with a lighter pelt: one of the Western Islanders. Like Dr. Vartra, he wore a white front-buttoning tunic. He was young, barely into his thirties.

"I don't suggest you try anything like that with me,"

the doctor continued. "All it would do is give you the rather dubious satisfaction of hitting an easy target."

"What did you do to me?" Kaid repeated, his voice dropping to a low growl. At his sides, his hands clenched briefly, then opened as his claws began to extend.

"Nothing drastic. Everything's still there and in working order, I assure you." Again the same confident arrogance. "My name's Rhioku by the way, Dr. Rhioku of Stronghold. Anything else, Dr. Vartra will tell you."

"There was no need for violence, Tallinu," said Vartra, breaking the tension as he stepped forward to help Goran to his feet.

Rhioku straightened up. "I suggest that those of us not involved any further should leave. The good Dr. Vartra wishes to talk privately to you."

"I can manage, Goran," Vartra reassured the security chief. "If we need you, I'll call."

Tail moving gently to show his lack of concern, Rhioku ambled past Kaid and waited for Tiernay to open the door.

"I'm staying," coughed Goran, pushing Vartra aside as he leaned on the end of the bed for support.

Kaid could feel Goran's anger and frustration. "Don't feel so bad about it," he said. "Fighting's my speciality."

"Mine, too," snapped Goran. "I was part of the military when we still had an army!"

Kaid shrugged. "That's the military for you. The Brotherhood of Vartra are the elite of my time."

"Your time! You belong here, in the past with us, dammit!"

"Enough, Goran!" snapped Vartra. "Leave. There's no reason now for you to stay."

"I'm staying," Goran snarled, straightening up and staring defiantly at the geneticist.

"You will leave us, Goran." Vartra's tone hit the command pitch and even Kaid felt himself straightening up in an instinctive response to it.

Vartra waited till the security chief had gone before indicating the chairs standing a few feet away. "Sit down, Tallinu. It's time for me to explain."

"Damned right it is." Angrily Kaid walked past him and sat down. "We only left three days ago! Why the hell did you need to call me back?"

"Three days for you, Tallinu, but seven months for us," Vartra said quietly.

"Seven months!" That shook him. He looked more closely at Vartra, then Jaisa. They had changed. Subliminally he'd noticed she had from the first but other events had been, and still were, more pressing. He turned back to Vartra.

"You owe me an explanation, not only for bringing me back, but for abusing my body while I was unconscious." The heat of the moment had passed, leaving him with an anger as cold as Khuushoi.

"When you left, I began working again on my gene enhancement program. I was trying to stabilize the changes I'd made, and take into account what I'd learned of the Humans from the female, Carrie."

Kaid made a dismissive gesture. "I know this. We worked that much out when we realized we'd left you with a sample of Carrie's blood."

Vartra glanced at Jaisa and back to him. "That's not all you left with us," he said. "As well as a sample of the mutated ni'uzu virus from Carrie, we had a sample from you. A sample of DNA that carried my enhancements but still included your ability to fight."

"Don't be ridiculous. You didn't take a blood sample from me!" As the silence lengthened, he looked over to Jaisa. "Not from me," he said, realizing the significance of the changes in her and the full enormity of her betrayal. His ears laid sideways in anger. "You used me, Jaisa!"

She reached out to touch his arm. "Only a little," she said. "I had to. The rest was real, Kaid."

"You've had my cub." He turned on Vartra. "You told her to do this! Is there nothing, no depths you won't sink to?"

"Sit down!" Once more Vartra's voice hit the command pitch, and automatically Kaid obeyed. "It had to be done. You are the only one we know of to have a natural immunity to the virus in our time. Which is why you, a telepath, can still fight. Yet you caught the modern equivalent and were enhanced by it without losing the ability to fight. Only your cub could carry through to the future the precise genes that will allow telepaths to fight again and contribute to them forming Leska links with the Humans." He stopped only long enough to sit down.

"Without this cub, everything you know could never have existed. Without her, telepaths might never fight again, whether or not they have a Human Leska. We need you to return to the future with the new gene that will stop the genetic drift. It'll also go a long way to ensuring that the hybrid children of mixed Leskas are less likely to suffer from birth defects. You're right," he leaned forward, "I will do *anything* I can to correct the damage done by my tampering. And *yes,* I do have the right to make those decisions."

He sat back, mouth opening slightly in a tired smile. "After all, aren't I destined to be a god in times yet to come? Believe me, Tallinu, I pay the price for those decisions on a daily basis. I can never forget what I've done, or the suffering that's been caused, but I also remember it freed us from the Valtegans."

"The fault isn't just yours. We played our part by using your serum too soon," said Jaisa quietly.

"No, the responsibility is mine alone," Vartra contradicted her. "Do you understand, Tallinu? It had to be you. But I can't leave it all to hang on the life of one cub. You are my backup, my second chance to get it right. Within you are the changes that must be spread among the Sholans of your day."

"The breeding program," Kaid muttered. "That's why it was started."

"You know?" Vartra sounded surprised.

"There is little we don't know. The Brotherhood's intelligence network is second to none," said Kaid. "How is this—fix—spread?" He was prepared to listen, no more.

"We've ensured it's passed on by two methods. A virus, like the ni'uzu but less deadly than it was originally for us."

"And?"

He hesitated. "We couldn't depend only on the virus in case your medics stopped it spreading before they realized its importance. So we designed it to be transmitted sexually as well."

Kaid began to growl deep in his throat, suddenly very aware of the tenderness in his groin. "You let that arrogant son of a tree-rhudda touch me . . . !"

"Enough, Tallinu! He's a doctor. It had to be done. Would you rather I'd asked Jaisa to do it?" Vartra demanded. "You'll never meet him again."

"I'll remember . . ."

"You'll forget." It was said with finality. "I won't. If what you say is true, I have an eternity of living with my actions ahead of me." There was a weariness in Vartra's voice this time. He stood up. "It's time to send you home."

"You're not messing with my mind, Vartra, nor is anyone else," he growled. "And just how do you intend to return me?"

"Crystals," said Jaisa. "Tiernay and I brought you back by locating your mind pattern."

"Seems you gained a lot from our time together," Kaid said bitterly. He could hardly bear to look at her; he felt used and betrayed by her on every level.

"Vartra didn't make me come to you that night. I came because I wanted to. There's no way he could have made me if I hadn't," she said, with a defiant look in Vartra's direction.

"She's my cub, Jaisa! Don't you understand? You stole her from me! It's my decision who I'll share them with—who I'll ask to carry them!"

"Mine, too."

"No! Not unless I ask you!" He looked at her puzzled expression. "You don't understand, do you?" He got up, turning away from her, affronted by her attitude. "Pairing with someone doesn't give you the right to share their cubs."

"Things are different here." She hesitated. "Would you like to see her?"

"No!"

"If you don't, you'll never have another chance. You may regret it."

He remained silent.

"Bring her in, Jaisa," said Vartra.

Jaisa looked uncertainly from one to the other.

"Do what the God says. Why change your habits for me? I'm nothing, not worthy of any consideration." He was angry beyond measure with both of them.

When she'd left the room, Vartra turned to him. "Stop getting this out of proportion, Tallinu. Many people have given their lives to save Shola from the Valtegans—your father for one. What you're being asked to do is nothing by comparison."

"You've played games with my mind since the beginning, Vartra. It would have been easier to die than to live with some of the things you've put me through! And my father's not dead," he said. "You can tell Zylisha that her sister and Rezac are still alive in our time. They survived in some kind of Valtegan cryogenic unit."

"They're alive?"

"I just said so," he snapped. "They're captives on a world called Jalna. In a few months we'll be heading out there to rescue them."

"By all the Gods!" It was Vartra's turn to be shocked.

"He sent a message for you. He said your plan worked."

"You see?" said Vartra, catching hold of his arm. "This *was* all necessary! Without my work they wouldn't have had the abilities to defeat the Valtegans! I just wish I'd gotten it right from the first."

"They left before we came here. Our visit didn't affect that outcome at all."

"I meant my initial work. What you carry now will set those first errors right, and what you gave to your daughter will save the lives of countless generations of unborn cubs!"

Kaid grunted in reply. Whatever the logic in Vartra's arguments, it didn't excuse his actions.

The door opened and Jaisa came in holding the child. "Come and see her," she said, walking into the center of the room where the light was brighter.

"A look won't hurt, Tallinu," said Vartra. "The cub has done nothing to earn your anger."

Reluctantly, Kaid got to his feet. He stood looking down at the sleeping infant.

"She's like you," she said. "Your eyes."

"Don't you mean Rezac's?" he asked. The words were said and regretted before he could stop them.

Startled, she looked up at him. "Not Rezac's, yours. His eyes were lighter."

"I didn't mean to say that," he mumbled, reaching a tentative finger down to touch the cub. An emotion he couldn't name flitted through him, then was gone. He'd never known Dzaka as an infant. Too late he heard the footsteps behind him and felt the hypoderm pressed to his neck.

As he began to crumple, Tiernay caught him. He felt himself being lifted and placed down on the treatment bed again. Gradually his consciousness began to fade.

The memory ended, spinning him back to his bedroom. He was lying on his back, looking up at the concerned faces of Lijou, T'Chebbi and Kha'Qwa. He barely saw them through the red mist of his rage. Like a coiled spring, he launched himself off the bed, landing beyond them.

"Kaid, calm down," began Lijou, keeping his voice even. "It happened weeks ago. You came back safely."

"He called me back to the Margins, Lijou! He used me— so did she!"

"Only to save lives, he made that clear. He sent you back with the corrected genes."

"I trusted him and he betrayed me! In Vartra's name, Lijou, they *stole* from my body, created a cub!" He stopped, realizing what he'd said. "In Vartra's name! He's no better than a criminal," he snarled, heading toward the door. "He's a sham, not a god! It's all lies and deceptions!"

"Stop him!" Kha'Qwa tried to reach the door before him.

Kaid flung her aside as he ran through the open doorway out into the lounge.

"He's heading for the temple," said Lijou, running over to where his mate had fallen. "I've alerted the guard. He's got to be stopped!"

"I'll stop him," said T'Chebbi, grabbing her belt from the chair by the door as she left. "Call off the guard, Lijou."

Thankfully, the building was nearly empty, most of the Brothers being involved in the hunt or preparations for the

evening. There was no sign of him, but she could track him
by his scent. As she raced along the corridor, she cursed
herself for not seeing this coming. She'd sensed danger,
that was what had made her head out to see him in the
first place. Judging by what had subsequently happened,
she'd triggered his memory and thereby created the danger
instead of averting it.

Reaching the top of the staircase, she saw the flick of his
tail as he rounded the corner to the temple doors. In the
distance, she could hear the approaching footfalls of the
guards and knew she was unlikely to reach him first. Dropping onto all fours, she leaped outward, beyond the stairs,
praying for a safe landing.

She cleared the flight of steps but landed awkwardly in
front of the guard, bringing them up short in confusion. As
she staggered to her feet, she drew her gun, baring her
teeth at them.

"He's mine! I'll take him," she snarled before she stumbled into the temple, slamming the door behind her.

T'Chebbi stood for a moment, looking and listening. He
could be anywhere. Then she saw him, standing a few meters from the statue, oblivious to anything but his own rage.

"You two-faced, tree climbing bastard of a jegget! You
lied to us! You used us for your own ends and pretended
it was for the good of Shola!" he roared as he took hold
of one of the heavy iron braziers and began rocking it.
"You're not a god! You never were! Just a male who decided to play god with innocent lives! How many did you
kill, Vartra? How many more will suffer just to see your
will done?"

As he paused for breath and to get a better grip on the
brazier's stand, T'Chebbi called out to him.

"Tallinu, step back from the brazier! I can't allow you
to damage the temple!"

Like one demented, he ignored her, continuing to pull at
it until it began to topple. Dancing back out of the way of
the burning coals, he headed for the other side.

"Tallinu, stop, or I'll shoot!" she yelled, watching in horrified fascination as the fire tumbled across the flagstones
to the floor-length seasonal tapestries that hung between
the pillars.

She looked back at Kaid. He was standing beyond the
right-hand brazier, pulling on the panels that hung there.

Taking careful aim, she sent a bolt of energy to hit the floor centimeters from his feet. Chips of stone flew into the air, and she saw him flinch as one hit him. He took no notice and continued to haul on the tapestry.

"Tallinu, stop!"

She heard a ripping sound as the panel came loose at one corner. Behind her, the door was pushed open. She had no time and no choice. Her shot hit him cleanly on the shoulder. He collapsed forward onto the tapestry, his weight finally dragging it and its retaining pole to the ground on top of him.

*   *   *

Killian hadn't been lying. The best part of a week had passed before the weather had cleared up enough for them to undertake the salvage trip into the mountains. Because of his specialized knowledge, Rezac, heavily cloaked and hooded in an effort to conceal his alienness, had accompanied Kris and Davies.

The trip had taken several days as the only device they'd had to cut the laser free from the ship's chassis was the energy gun Davies had brought with him. Thanks to it, other tools weren't in short supply: it made quick work of the Valtegan's locked toolbox.

The wagon they'd taken with them hadn't been large enough to transport all they thought they'd need back to Kaladar. A second pile of less essential items had been left stowed safely in the rear of the gutted vehicle. Once they'd delivered the first load, the cart and the guards would return for it.

The main room of their suite now looked more like a machine shop than a living area in a medieval castle. Carefully and painstakingly, they all helped to disassemble the boards and control panels they'd found, drawing detailed plans of where each component went. The days were short and no matter how many candles were lit in the chamber, there wasn't enough light for them to continue working after nightfall. This suited them as it delayed the work even more. They had to make this spin out long enough for help to reach them.

Killian visited them daily, usually before he sat in judgment in his main hall. He'd inspect their progress, asking questions of them in an effort to understand what they were doing. Their main problem was lack of tools and it wasn't uncommon for either Kris or Davies, in the company of a couple of guards, to go down to the blacksmith's forge to request either adjustments to tools the smith had already made, or to ask for new ones. Trying to carry out the precision high-tech work that they needed to do with the tools they had was rather like trying to tie a knot in sewing thread wearing thick mittens—nigh on impossible. At least, after he'd seen the small selection of tools they'd salvaged from the Valtegan scouter, Lord Killian appreciated their problems, and the delay.

The evenings they used for planning not only how their finished weapon would work, but also an escape. By common consensus, among themselves they spoke in Sholan, knowing it was a language that the Jalnians had never come across before. That evening, while Rezac and Davies tried to explain what they were trying to achieve to Kris, Jo sat by the fire talking to Zashou.

It was difficult for any of the Humans not to be aware that there was an armed truce between Zashou and her Leska. Like Jo, Zashou was nontechnical by education and though both of them could follow instructions when it came to helping assemble this monster of a weapon, they were unable to help the rest of the time.

Knowing how intolerable the couple had found their captivity with the Valtegans, Jo encouraged the other female to talk about her world. She was beginning to find herself fascinated by the Sholans and their culture.

"What was it like, living under the Valtegans?" she asked.

"On Shola? We saw very little of it," Zashou said, drawing her chair closer to the fire. "We were living in the monastery on my family's estate, guarded by Goran and his people."

"Goran?" asked Jo, leaning forward to throw some more wood on the fire. A shower of sparks fluttered up the chimney toward the night sky above.

"Chief of security. He protected us from discovery by the Valtegans and decided when we could go out to Nazule to get supplies, that sort of thing."

"Were you part of the monastery?"

Zashou laughed, making Rezac look instantly over in her direction. Jo watched him frown then look away hurriedly. Zashou had obviously disapproved of him taking an interest in their conversation, but why? It was innocent enough. She sighed inwardly before concentrating again on what the other female was saying.

"No. A group of students were acting the part of the acolytes. We—there were only the six of us, Nyaz, Tiernay, Jaisa, Rezac, Shanka and myself—were working with Dr. Vartra on his gene enhancement program. Until the Valtegans decided to round up all the telepaths, we lived in rooms on the ground floor. Goran had guards patrolling outside all night and if anything suspicious was spotted, he'd have us awakened and we'd hide down in the lab in the old mine. For about a month before we were captured, it was so unsafe that we were actually living down there as well."

"How long were you in hiding?"

"Nearly a year, but it wasn't all bad," she said. "There were one or two good times in the early days. We went on a shopping trip to Nazule that first winter, to get warmer clothing. It was freezing down in the labs despite the heating system they'd rigged up. It was on that trip that we saw them collaring telepaths for the first time."

"Collaring?" Jo asked.

"It's easier to tell you what happened," Zashou said. "Goran was leading our little expedition. As well as me, there was Rezac and Tiernay."

*   *   *

"You drive," said Goran, throwing the keys to Rezac.

The drive down to the plain had been uneventful, but things had been different once they reached the city.

As they drove through the streets to the center, Zashou realized that Goran hadn't been exaggerating about the number of Valtegans currently in Nazule. Every major street had armed soldiers at each junction carrying a device they assumed was a sensor of some kind because they were scanning the passersby.

The car stopped at traffic flow controls. Across the road, one of the scanners started beeping loudly. They watched as the Valtegran identified a Sholan who was then surrounded and dragged, none too gently, over to the scanner where the reading was checked.

"He's a telepath," said Tiernay, leaning across Goran to look out the window. "I can hear him broadcasting for help. We've got to do something, Goran!"

"Sit still," ordered Goran, hauling him back into his seat. "Keep your minds still, for the Gods' sake! Don't answer him, or we'll be caught, too."

"Dammit, we can't just sit here and . . ." began Tiernay angrily as the traffic signal changed.

As they drove on, they saw the Sholan telepath having a metallic collar placed around his neck.

"I want one of those scanners," muttered Goran, turning round in his seat to watch the tableau as they drove off. "I reckon that male up at Stronghold is working on a signal blocker. We've got a contact with someone at one of the major electronic labs in Khalma. She should be able to come up with something if we can get a sensor to her."

"We should have done something," muttered Tiernay, subsiding back into his seat.

"We will. We'll find a way to block their scanners," said Goran. "That way, we risk fewer lives. What did you want us to do? Attempt to rescue him in the middle of the city? Risk not only our own lives, but those of all the bystanders? I thought you were the one who didn't like violence!"

"We're here," said Rezac, effectively ending the conversation as he pulled into the parking lot for the store. He parked as near the entrance as he could, turning off the engine.

"If there's any trouble, those who can, get yourselves out of here and back to the shrine. No sense in us all getting caught," said Goran as they headed toward the entrance.

It was an in-and-out job. The items they wanted had been ordered in advance and all they had to do was collect them from the pickup point. As they stood waiting in the short line, Zashou caught sight of the armed Valtegan standing on the landing halfway up the stairs to the next level.

"Goran," she said, touching him on the elbow and nodding toward the stairs.

"Saw him, and the one by the rear exit," Goran said quietly. "Don't look at him, and he'll not notice us. We'll be out of here in a few minutes."

By the time they reached the main road from Nazule to Khalma, a roadblock was being set up. Three Valtegans accompanied by a Sholan Protector were supervising a group of Sholan workmen who were building a gatehouse and barrier across the road.

"Restricting civilian movements now," muttered Goran as Rezac slowed down. "Looks like this may be the last of your trips into town."

As they approached him, the Protector signaled for them to stop. Rezac lowered the side window.

"Play it real easy," muttered Goran. "We don't want any trouble."

"The Overlord has ordered that from today all vehicles entering or leaving the towns must have a pass," the Protector said to Rezac. "From tomorrow, if you want to travel out of Nazule, you'll have to apply to the Public Communications Office. If your journey is deemed necessary, you'll be issued with the relevant one. Where are you bound for?"

Goran leaned across Tiernay. "Officer, we come from the monastery. We get our supplies and mail in Nazule twice a week. We're returning there now."

The Protector pulled out a pad and scribbled on it. Tearing the leaf out, he handed it to Rezac. Goran took it from him.

"That temporary pass will get you into Nazule on your next trip. Apply then for your permanent one."

"What's this all about?" asked Goran, jerking an ear in the direction of the three Valtegans who stood with guns trained on them.

"Freedom fighters," he said shortly. "They're becoming a problem."

"How's this going to help?" asked Tiernay.

"Look youngling, I have my orders," growled the officer in a low voice. "I like it as much as you do. Now get going before that lot become curious. Never make them curious about you if you value your lives. Go." He stepped back and waved them on, leaving Tiernay with his ears flicking in acute annoyance.

"Got Sholan failings like the rest of us, after all?" said Rezac, mouth open in a slight grin as he drove off.

Tiernay growled, showing his teeth.

"Shut it!" snapped Goran. "Did any of you use your brains enough to try and pick up his thoughts?"

"Yes," said Rezac. "The Valtegans think that the restrictions will cut down the raids. The Protector's afraid it won't and that the Valtegans will start retributive action."

"It won't stop us," growled Goran, "and the lizards have already started revenge killings. Don't look at me like that," he snapped at Tiernay. "Either we let them grind us into the dust, or we die fighting to be free. You wouldn't be with us now if you were one of the rhakla! Harden yourself enough to face reality, boy. You don't have to stop caring, just don't let it touch you too much."

"Like you and him?" Tiernay asked angrily, jerking his head toward Rezac.

Goran and Rezac exchanged glances.

"Not like us," said Goran, his tone quieter. "Our type fights for the new world, yours and hers builds it."

The rest of the journey was made in silence. Goran headed off immediately for the caverns to contact his people on the outside to exchange the news on the upsurge of Valtegan activity in Nazule. Zashou, Tiernay, and Rezac were left to unload the parcels. Dusk had fallen, and it was beginning to freeze.

"If anyone complains they aren't warm enough after this," said Zashou darkly as she slipped yet again on the frozen path, "I'll have their hides!"

Rezac reached out a hand to steady her. "Come on. You'll feel better when you've got some hot food inside you. We missed second meal today, and I'm starving."

Zashou noticed that the dim hall of the shrine seemed somehow brighter than it had that morning. As they walked toward the curtain that concealed the door into the private area, the flames in the bowl held by the statue flickered slightly, casting moving shadows across its face, making it seem almost alive. She shivered and quickened her pace.

*   *   *

"I always found the temple an intimidating place," said Zashou. "I'm glad I wasn't one of the students."

"What did the collars do?"

"We were wearing them when you found us," she replied, shivering at the memory. "The green stone in the center lit up if we tried to use our telepathic abilities, letting everyone around know what we were doing. It also sent a signal to the control bracelets which the Valtegans wore. By pressing a few buttons, they were able to punish us from a distance of twenty meters."

"It must have been horrific."

"At first," she admitted. "When you have a talent, you use it automatically—it's like scratching when you have an itch, you don't even notice you're doing it. We had to train ourselves *not* to use it. It took some time but Rezac worked out how to disable it. Once he got mine off and adjusted it, then did the same to his, rather than alert them when we used our telepathy, it warned us when they were using their control bracelets near enough for us to be affected by it so we could fake our reaction."

"Clever."

"Oh, Rezac's got a way with electronics, and there's no one better when it comes to using our mental skills," she said.

Though Jo could hear the respect for his abilities in Zashou's voice, she could also feel the resentment behind it. She decided to probe a little further.

"What's he like?" she asked. "He seems pleasant enough, if a bit abrupt at times."

Zashou glanced over at her Leska, who looked up and locked eyes with her briefly. It was she who broke the contact.

"He is. It's his violent attitude to life in general that I can't stand," she said.

"I haven't noticed it," said Jo quietly.

"You don't have to live with him inside your head all the time. He views everything as a conflict."

"You were living on the front line of a war," said Jo. "I've been there, I know what it's like."

"You're a female, how could you know!"

"I fought in our war against the Valtegans. I had to go among them and spy on them. That's why I'm on this mission. I'm a soldier."

"You?" Zashou looked at her in frank disbelief.

"Tell us about your war on Keiss," said Rezac from the other side of the room.

The unexpectedness of his request, coupled with the touch of his mind against hers, threw Jo for a moment. Then Kris came to her rescue.

"You were on the First Contact team, weren't you, Jo? And you, too, Davies."

"Yeah, that was us," said Davies, looking up from his sketches and jottings. "I fought alongside Jo when we went into the Valtegan military base on Keiss to get Kusac and Carrie out."

"Tell us about it," repeated Rezac, getting up from the table and stretching. "I hadn't realized your females fought."

"They don't, generally, but Keiss was our first colony world and the resistance needed every fighter we could get," said Jo.

"This Kusac, he's the one you claim has a Human Leska, isn't he? Do they come into your story, too?" he asked, joining the two females by the fire.

"Carrie's his Leska," said Kris, pulling over another chair. "I know the official version, but I'd like to hear how it really was."

"You'd do better asking Gary," she said, trying to cover the confusion she felt at Rezac's sudden interest in her. His mental touch was so powerful and so different from any she'd felt before. Suddenly she was aware of just how bad the situation was between him and Zashou. He was hoping that her tale could make his Leska understand what it was like for another female to have to fight for her life and freedom.

"You start, I'll fill in here and there," said Davies, stopping at the table to pick up a piece of cheese left over from their meal.

An insistent noise dragged Kris from the depths of sleep. Still groggy, he lay there on his pallet listening till it came again.

"Kris! Are you awake?"

"Mmm," he grunted.

"Kris!"

"What?"

"Not so loud!" Jo hissed. "You'll wake Davies. Have you heard from Vyaka on the *Summer Bounty* yet?"

"No. Nothing."

"Aren't they overdue for contact? Wouldn't Carrie and Kusac have told the authorities about Rezac's message and gotten them to come back earlier?"

He pushed himself up, rubbing the sleep from his eyes, and peered up at the bed on which she lay. "It doesn't quite work that way, Jo," he mumbled sleepily. "They can't suddenly reappear here. They've got to wait for the right time. If they've no cargo, they've no justification for being in the port. I told you and Davies that the last time I contacted her, Vyaka said they'd be out of the system for a month."

"A month's almost up. They might be in range now. Couldn't you try?"

"I try every night before going to sleep, Jo," he said patiently. "Believe me, I'm as anxious as you to hear from her."

"Maybe if Rezac and Zashou helped?"

He was silent for a minute, unsure what to say to her. He disliked involving the two Sholans, didn't want them to know they had a contact, albeit one they couldn't reach at present. Rezac was just too damned impulsive. This was their mission, their call as to what they did, and he didn't want a battle for leadership developing between the Sholan and Jo. He was well aware that Rezac didn't like a female being in charge, nor was he very trusting of any of the Humans. At the moment, he was the one at a disadvantage, the outsider. If that changed, then they might well have problems.

"I'd rather keep Rezac in the dark about Vyaka for the time being," he said finally. "If you helped me, together we might be able to do it."

He sensed her shying away from his suggestion.

"Not unless we have to," she said.

He could feel her withdrawal from him. "Very well, but do take what I said seriously, Jo. Say nothing, at least for now, to Rezac. It's not good to trust too easily. We hardly know them yet."

"I'll keep it in mind," she replied. "Sorry I woke you. Good night."

"Good night," he said.

He lay down, listening to the bed creaking as she settled herself again. Against his chest, Scamp began to wriggle himself into a more comfortable position, scolding his Human friend gently all the while. Absentmindedly, Kris began to stroke the little creature's head and ears.

It's all right for you, he sent to his friend. *If she was a female jegget, you'd go rushing straight up to her and get stuck in! What's the presence of a few more people or jeggets to you? But it's just not that simple for us, Scamp,* he sighed.

CHAPTER 6

Running forward, she grasped the heavy pole, trying to pull it aside. Within moments, several of the guards, accompanied by Master Rhyaz and Vriuzu, were at her side; the pole was lifted and the tapestry pulled aside. Kaid lay there unconscious, on his shoulder a shallow, seared wound that oozed a colorless fluid.

T'Chebbi leaned forward to feel for his pulse. "He's alive," she said.

Vriuzu took hold of Kaid's wrist, turning it over to reset the psychic damper he wore to full strength. "His Triad partners mustn't know of this yet," he said. "Father Lijou requests that we join him in his office, Master Rhyaz."

Rhyaz nodded. "Take him up to the infirmary," he ordered. "I want him sedated until we've decided what's to be done about him. Vriuzu, this must be kept quiet. Organize a cleanup detail." He waved his hand in the direction of the tapestry. "Do what you can to repair it and get it rehung as quickly as possible."

"I understand what you're saying, Lijou," said Rhyaz, "but we can't have this happening again! He needs help that I don't think we can provide. He can't be allowed to go around cursing Vartra and telling everyone the truth of what happened to him. It's going to seriously jeopardize our new status, perhaps even give Esken the ammunition he needs to try and block your elevation to a guild at the next meeting."

"What are you suggesting, then?" asked Lijou quietly. "Remember, we're dealing with someone who's been tried by our Guild and our God beyond anything that's normal."

"Dammit, Lijou! I don't like this any more than you do! I was one of those who wanted him reinstated in the Brotherhood so he could be elected to the position I now hold! I'm sorry, but he'll have to be hospitalized. You'll know better than I whether or not he's got a rogue talent, but he's sure as hell not stable now! He went kzu-shu!"

"He didn't hurt anyone or do any irreparable damage."

"We were lucky this time," said Rhyaz.

Lijou's comm began to sound. He looked up at Kha'Qwa, indicating with a flick of his ear that she should answer the call.

"When—if—he's cured, then he can return," continued the Brotherhood's Warrior Master.

"Lijou," Kha'Qwa interrupted, setting the comm to privacy mode. "It's the infirmary. Noni's demanding to see Kaid, and they don't know what to do."

"Why weren't we informed she'd arrived?" demanded Rhyaz. "She not one of us. She's no right to even be on the premises without permission!"

"Who's going to stop her?" asked Kha'Qwa. "Be realistic, Master Rhyaz. You know most of our people prefer going to her than to the infirmary."

"Maybe she should open a surgery inside Stronghold," muttered the beleaguered warrior master.

"Don't be so pompous, Rhyaz," said Lijou, getting up. "Remember that not too long ago, you were one of those Brothers yourself. I'll answer the call, Kha'Qwa. Rhyaz, it might be wise if we requested a different physician and considered legitimizing Noni's treatment of our people. Obviously our infirmary and its staff are lacking something essential that she can provide. I'd had it in mind to do that for some time, had it not been for Ghezu."

He took his mate's place in front of the comm. "Let Noni see him," he said. "Does she know what's happened?"

"Of course I know," came the tart rejoinder from just out of screen range. "Who d'you think fetched me here? I'll need to see you, Master Lijou. Can't get all I need from Tallinu when he's under your damned drugs!"

"Let me know when you want me to join you, Noni," he said, trying not to smile. He didn't know what it was about her, but her presence made him feel that the problem wasn't so insurmountable after all.

"Now would be good," she said tartly.

"On my way." He closed the connection and looked at his co-guild master. "You were saying, Rhyaz?"

Rhyaz muttered under his breath as he got to his feet. "We'll see what Noni has to say before making a decision, but I'm having his room guarded. If he so much as stirs from his bed . . ."

"Thank you," said Lijou. "Half a dozen of my priests are down in the temple helping clear up, by the way. They send that they should be finished within the hour. The longest job will be securing the tapestry back to the pole. They suggest a temporary fix until the twenty-second hour, then we could close the temple for the night and effect a permanent repair."

Rhyaz nodded and turned to leave. He stopped at the door. "Lijou," he began, turning back.

"We're entering into a new era for the Brotherhood, Rhyaz," Lijou said, gently interrupting him. "It's never going to be the same again. Who knows what its final form will be? I don't, but until then, you and I will cope between us. I don't have the expertise you possess as a warrior, but I have organized important aspects of Stronghold for many years. A team, Rhyaz, that's what matters, with neither one more important than the other. I know we can achieve that. I'm looking forward to working with you, and I hope we'll become more than colleagues. I hope we'll become friends."

The slightly anxious look on Rhyaz's face went. "I would like that also, Master Lijou," he said, inclining his head. The gesture was marred only by his slightly sardonic smile.

Lijou laughed. "I'll let you know when I've news of Kaid."

"And I'll contact the medical guild for a replacement physician plus another medic. On the subject of Noni, d'you think she'd discuss with me the possibility of working in an official capacity as a healer at Stronghold?"

"Ask her and see," said Lijou.

Rhyaz smiled wryly. "She'll probably only see the youth who kept going to her for tinctures for cuts and bruises got in illegal fights."

"She did remind Garras of his wild days," said Lijou. "Thank goodness I didn't spend my adolescence here! I'll see you later."

Noni was waiting for him in the empty room next to Kaid's.

"So that's why he ran amok," Noni nodded as Lijou finished projecting what he remembered of Kaid's experience. "I'm not surprised! Perhaps I've been partly responsible for this," she admitted, looking down at the walking stick she held between her hands.

"How?"

"Tallinu was always one to keep himself to himself. He let nobody touch him till that time with Khemu, and I know now how badly that went for him. Then Carrie came along. I didn't want to see it happening to him again, so I pushed." She looked up at him from beneath lowered eye ridges. "You have to remember I know things, Lijou. I see 'em as clear as if they were happening now. I saw the life he could have, if he would, and tried to push him toward it." She sighed. "How was I to know what that damned Vartra had done! I told him there'd be cubs, his cubs. That's why he reacted so badly when he found out about the one this Jaisa female had."

"You weren't to know," said Lijou. "Their attitude is—was—so different! Almost alien to ours."

"That's as may be. Now we got to find out what else is wrong. T'Chebbi tells me he keeps having memories and visions without warning. What d'you know about this?"

"Very little. We were monitoring him because Kusac was afraid he was going to have a mental breakdown. When he has an episode, we pick it up, but they're so short we can't tell what they're about. He hasn't mentioned them to me at all. We've been looking for an excuse to confront him about it."

"When did these episodes begin? After he was taken back by Vartra, or before?"

"After, if what Kusac says is right. He became more distant to both of them from the day of the Validation. It happened the night before."

"The folk from the past, they made him forget this had happened, didn't they? That might be where the problem lies," she said thoughtfully. "For all I dislike your Guild, Lijou, they can at least erase and hide memories with reasonable skill."

She looked up at him again. "They still don't see the student for the class, though. These past folk didn't know as much, I'll be bound. If they made a mess of hiding this incident from his conscious mind, which is more than likely, and he was having memories from his past returning at the same time, then no wonder he thought he was going mad! Like a pot on the boil with the lid jammed down tight, that's what he's been! A pack of amateurs all, they are. It takes skill to hide a memory, even more to erase it without causing trauma to the patient."

Leaning heavily on her stick, she pushed herself up onto her feet. "Now we go and talk to Tallinu," she said.

The physician leaned forward to remove the small electrical device attached to Kaid's forehead. "Neat little gadget," he said, switching it off. "Chernarian origin. We're getting to test it. Uses brain waves or some such thing to keep the patient sedated. Much better for this kind of situation than drugs. He'll start coming to any moment now." He turned and walked to the door. "Press the buzzer if you need me. I'm only just down the corridor."

Kaid stirred, opening his eyes. He looked round, catching sight of T'Chebbi standing by the door beyond Lijou and Noni.

"Bad shot, T'Chebbi. I thought you at least would have finished it. Where'd you get me?" His voice was a lazy drawl.

"Left shoulder." Her reply was barely audible.

He nodded, winced, and slowly raised his other hand to his head, feeling the dressing there.

"The pole hit you," she added.

He turned his head to look at Noni. "It's all a sham, Noni. He played god with us, changed us because he thought he could. He betrayed and used me." He was tired of it all.

"Forget about that for now," said Noni, brushing the matter aside as if it were of no importance. "I need to know about these memories that keep coming without warning. Why didn't you tell me what was happening?"

"I'm telling you now, but you're not listening."

"The other ones. What were they, Tallinu?" she insisted. "Were they from the past?"

He started to frown but stopped as it pulled at the staples in his forehead. His head hurt abominably. "I had to remove the memory of meeting myself and the others before I could send myself—the cub—forward," he said. "I didn't know what to do. There was no time—the temple was exploding."

Noni grunted. "How did Vartra and his lot make you forget?"

"I don't know."

"Then I'll have to go look for it," she said. "I'd have thought you'd have learned by now how to stay out of trouble, boy. But no, you keep on getting into scrape after scrape," she grumbled. "I got better things to do than fix you up every few months, let me tell you!"

"Leave me be, Noni," he said, turning his head away from her. "I've had enough. You know damned well I never went looking for any of this. I told you, he's taken everything I had from me now. There's nothing left, not even my sanity. I can never be sure he won't do it again!"

Before anyone could even blink, Noni's hand shot out and grasped Kaid round the throat. Her talons extended and began to press into the flesh over his larynx.

"Tired of it, Tallinu? Really tired, or just fancy words?" she asked, her voice a low, menacing hiss.

His eyes flew open in shock, his hands reaching for her, but she increased the pressure and he let them fall back to the bed.

"I'll end it for you now, if you ask me. They won't," she said, jerking her ears backward at Lijou and T'Chebbi. "But I will. Just tighten my grip, that's all, till my claws meet in your throat." As she spoke, he could feel her hand doing just that. "Or should I start and wait for you to tell me to stop if you change your mind, eh? What's it to be, boy?" she asked as her clawtips began to press harder and his breath began to falter.

He tried to shift his hands again, to grasp hers, pull it away, but he couldn't move. She was suffocating him, and he couldn't stop her. Her face seemed to fade until he could see only her piercing brown eyes.

So this is how you die, Tallinu. Beaten by memories! A fine epitaph for a Brother—he died rather than face his fears!

Her mocking laugh echoed inside his head till finally he could stand it no more, and he broke free of her spell. "Enough!" he gasped, his hand hitting hers aside, then returning to massage his throat.

Noni turned to look at Lijou. "You get back to that new

life-mate of yours, Master Lijou. She wants to make plans with you for that nursery you'll need in a few months. As for you," she said, fixing her eyes on T'Chebbi. "Go fetch us some c'shar, my girl. A person could die of thirst in this rambling bird's nest of a place! I'll see to Tallinu."

Lijou got to his feet, his confusion evident in the set of his ears. "I'm not going to even think about how you knew," he said. "I'll be in my office on the first floor. There's a guard outside . . ."

"Guard?" she interrupted. "Why would I be needing a guard, pray tell me, Master Lijou? You stop fretting, we'll be fine."

She waited till they'd gone before turning on Kaid. "I've never met a greater fool than you, Tallinu! By the Gods, I don't know who gifted you their brains when you were conceived, but I have my doubts that they had any themselves! Have you any idea just how lucky you are?" she demanded. "You lie here moaning and whining about what Vartra's taken from you, yet you possess some of the greatest gifts He could bestow and you don't even realize it!"

"Gifts? What gifts?" he demanded, pushing himself up against the pillows so he could see her more easily. "When he knew I came from their time, he used me, Noni! He cared nothing for me as a person! He had one of the females—Jaisa—conceive a cub without asking me! I have a daughter I'll never know living in the past!"

Noni snorted in disgust. "Listen to yourself, will you? A daughter living in the past? You have *nothing* living in the past! They're dead, not even dust now, Tallinu! Long gone. He did what I'd have done in His place. Used the tools at hand, namely you. You had what none of them possessed, boy. You'd been touched by the Humans, and you were of their people, a Sholan from their time, not modern like Kusac. So Vartra got you to sire a daughter. With her they could breed any number of the new strain of telepaths. You were the father to her, she became their mother. Your Triad, not Vartra, is responsible for the mixed Leskas! Stop whining for one cub when you'll have more than enough to delight you!"

"I've told you I don't want cubs, Noni," he snarled.

"Then why such a fuss over this one?" she retorted. "If she means nothing to you, let her go."

"You're doing it again, tying me up in your own brand of logic," he growled angrily.

"You wanted to know His other gifts," she continued, ignoring him. "Because of Him, you live here and now. Had you stayed in their world, you'd have been in constant danger from those trying to kill the telepaths for causing the Cataclysm. Instead you got a fresh start. You have Dzaka, as fine a son as anyone could wish, now he's gotten over his stupidity with Ghezu. You're part of a family that cares deeply for you; you have not only as a lover, but as a third, the female you wanted so much it robbed you of common sense! In fact, by registering the Triad at the temple, you're as legitimately her husband as Kusac is under the old laws. Then there's Kashini. If not for you, she could never have existed. And what has all this cost you? A few nightmares and a lost cub! If that's a ruined life, then the Gods take pity on you, Tallinu, because I, for one, won't!"

"It's not that simple, and you know it! What he's done has cost me my faith! I can't believe in him any more!"

Noni sighed, reaching out to touch his hand where it lay on the covers. "You're confusing the person with the God, Tallinu. Vartra the person made you his carrier, *he* told the female to conceive that night, not Vartra the God. When you have time, think it through carefully. Look at what Vartra the God has said to you, not Vartra the person."

He didn't want to listen to her, didn't want excuses for Vartra's behavior to be found—but some of what she was saying made sense. The hand holding his tightened slightly in a gesture of affection.

"Good. Just look at the differences, that's all I'm saying. Then come to me with your questions. He speaks to me, too," she said with a small grin. "Now comes the hard part. I need you to let me into your mind."

He would have pulled away from her in shock, but her hand held his in a grip of steel.

"No," she said firmly. "I think I know what's happening. When will you learn to bring your problems to me? You make them worse by waiting. I could have solved all this weeks ago had you only told me."

"You can't do anything, Noni. My Talent's unstable, I know it is. That's why I came here, because I was afraid that I'd cause harm to Carrie or the cub."

"You're not unstable, boy," she retorted sharply, "you're

unhinged! I never heard such rubbish in my life! Did it ever occur to you that your very existence as a member of the Brotherhood is a testament to the strength and stability of your mind and Talent? You're the only telepath on Shola without a Human Leska that's capable of fighting. You survived childhood with that damned M'Zushi family, survived the pack wars in Ranz, and were finally picked up by a recruitment team from Stronghold. How the hell did you do that with an unstable Talent, eh?"

He remembered Kusac asking him the same question and now, as then, he had no answer.

"Trust me, Tallinu. I need to know what Vartra's people did to you to lock the memory of your return to the Margins away until now. That's what damaged your mind. I'll look nowhere else, believe me."

He studied her face, feeling her sending him the truth of what she was saying.

"Sometime, Tallinu, you've got to start trusting people," she said softly.

Slowly he nodded his head.

"That's my lad," she said, her voice dropping till it was almost a whisper. "Always had time for you, though never knew why, but you've repaid me over and over lately as you've traveled the path I knew you had to take. You've done well, Tallinu, better than many predicted you would."

He could barely hear her voice now, and once more her eyes dominated him. Tiredness swept through him and gratefully, he shut his eyes and let go.

When T'Chebbi returned, Noni had finished and Kaid was still sleeping.

"It's done, child," she said in response to her mute appeal. She took the mug from her, taking a sip to taste it. "It'll do," she said. "Not fresh c'shar, but then I didn't expect it from the kitchens here. Tallinu won't be wanting his for a while yet. You might as well have it."

"What was it?" T'Chebbi asked, taking the other vacant seat. "What caused all his memories and visions?"

"Mainly those mental butchers from the past," Noni said. "They were afraid he'd be so angry at what they'd done that he'd try to sabotage Vartra's work. They blocked the memory, hoping he'd pair several times before it returned. It was done in such a way that it interfered with the memories of his meeting with Carrie that were trying to resurface." She took a large mouthful of her drink and sat back in her chair, closing her eyes.

"Would you do me a favor, child? Ask Father Lijou if he could find me somewhere to rest for an hour or two before I go home. Mental healings aren't easy, and I'm getting old."

"Of course, Noni," she said, putting her mug down and heading for the door.

"And child," she said, opening her eyes and pinning her with a look. "Keep the next cub."

*   *   *

Carrie had spent the morning with the female members of her family, helping to prepare for the evening's feast. Root vegetables, specially set aside earlier in the autumn, had been scrubbed by the army of clansfolk working inside the feasting hall. Above the roasting pits, the meat that would form the main dish was already cooking. At midday, the plaintive sound of a horn caused everyone to stop.

Rhyasha dried her hands on a towel and passed it to Carrie. "Time for Nylam's Dance," she said. "All our young males eligible to become adults will take their place in the dance for the first time."

"Does that include Kusac?" she asked, joining the throng of people filing outside.

"Good gracious, no, he's far too old for that! This ceremony is for those who've reached their eighteenth year. Although not fully adult, they're considered legally old enough to ask a female for a bonding contract. There will be one or two of the older males dancing with them today, but you'll not be able to recognize anyone as they all wear masks."

At one edge of the circle, the drummers were already settled at their instruments and had begun to beat out a low, steady rhythm. The drums were of all shapes and sizes, ranging from small ones held between the knees to large ones made from hollowed out logs. The range of sounds they were producing was unlike anything Carrie had heard before.

"We'll stand opposite," said her bond-mother, drawing her to the edge of the circle painted on the ground. She pointed to a group of older males waiting on one side.

"See, not everyone dances. For one thing, there wouldn't be enough room."

"Will there be enough game?"

"Oh, yes. I make sure there's enough livestock to release for the festival. Each hunter is allowed to bring back only two kills, and only the senior clansmales are allowed to hunt the rhakla. The hunt is more symbolic than anything else these days."

As Carrie watched, the dancers began to gather. A group, shepherded by Ghyan, were first to enter, and she knew these were the younglings that by the end of a successful hunt would have entered early adulthood.

"There's quite a few with dark pelts like Kusac," she said.

"He has cousins who share the same coloring," agreed Rhyasha. "Any one of them could be Kusac if he were dancing, but that's part of the fun and the mystery of it! Those who've been successful will dance again tonight, approaching the females of their choice and inviting them to spend the night with them. Kitra was trying to persuade Dzaka to dance, but he was concerned that some other male would try to claim her and she'd not be able to tell the difference. It's the first time she's watched the hunt as an adult female, after all, and she wants to join in the fun."

"Surely no one would do that to her!"

"It's not unknown for the males to pretend to be someone else when after a popular female." Rhyasha looked down at her with a twinkle in her eyes. "The music at the evening dance is very different from what they'll play now. If Dzaka does decide to take part, I'll stay with her till he comes to claim her."

Their conversation ended as the drummers began to beat a louder rhythm. Almost magically, the circle was filled with dancers. Dressed in costumes made from decorated animal pelts, their faces hidden behind masks, they began to move in time to the beat of the drums. Their movements, she realized, mimicked those of the animals depicted on the masks they wore.

They're playing the parts of the creatures they hope to catch, sent Rhyasha, linking her arm through Carrie's. *Dancing to please Nylam, Liege of the Hunt. It's also one of the few chances the young males get to show off for us females! I'll wager quite a few bonding contracts will be made in a few days' time. Ghyan will find himself quite busy, as will the estate birthers in six months!*

The clouds began to part, allowing the sunlight to shine through for the first time that day. Now Carrie could see the light glinting off the ornaments worked into the costumes.

Mirrors and bells to ward off Khuushoi's demons, sent Rhyasha, tugging gently at Carrie's arm to draw her attention to the ring of smaller fires that encircled them. *Look, there's Konis and Kusac. Over there by the fires, upwind of us. You'll hear the music change in a minute, then they'll throw a special incense on the flames. It heightens the dancers' senses, making it easier for them to commune with the God and follow the trails of His creatures.*

Carrie watched as father and son waited till the tone of the drums became a deep, booming sound that seemed to echo through the very ground. Then the two males began throwing handfuls of powder into the fire. Sparks flew into the air and, gradually, wisps of scented smoke began to rise and drift across the circle toward them. Kusac and his father moved on to the next fire to repeat the process.

As she returned to watching the dancers, she felt a pang of regret that Kusac wasn't in the circle. She sensed her Leska's gentle amusement.

You'd have me play the hunter now, would you?

They look so . . . she searched for an appropriate word . . . *primitive and wild in their costumes. They remind me of you after the Challenge you fought on Keiss.*

In that case, I'll not risk dancing tonight! Who knows whose invitation you might accept before I reached you! was his teasing reply.

Dusk had fallen by the time the hunters returned. A stir at the entrance to the banqueting hall drew their attention. One of the runners burst through the doors into the warmly lit interior and stopped, looking around till he located their little group. At a hurried walking pace, he threaded his way between the tables till he reached the one where Carrie sat with her family and Myak.

Crossing his forearms over his chest, the youth bowed his head to Rhyasha. "Clan Leader, the Liegen has returned. He asks that the Liegena meets him outside to accept his kill."

Startled, Carrie looked over to Rhyasha.

With a smile, she held out her arms. "I'll watch Kashini for you. He's honoring you before our Clans. Hunters who make good kills may award them to the female of their choice, even if they're bonded to another."

"There's more, Clan Leader," said the youngling hesitantly. "The Liegen asks that Liegenas Taizia and Kitra, and the Human Ruth, also come as there are those who'd award their kills to them."

"Now this I must see!" said Rhyasha, getting to her feet, Kashini now tucked firmly against her shoulder. "Give me Kashini's blanket, cub, we'll come with you." She turned to her bond-mate. "Konis? Myak?"

"Of course. All our daughters being honored this way is worth seeing."

On the way out, they stopped to collect Ruth.

"Me?" she asked in frank amazement. "Who'd do that for me?"

"I'll give you one guess," laughed Carrie.

She groaned as she got up. "Rulla! What on Earth am I going to do about him?"

"Whatever you want," said Carrie. "Your life is your own. All I ask is that you don't let it interfere with what we're trying to achieve with Mara at the moment."

"Accept his kill," said Taizia, drawing her cloak around herself as they neared the entrance. "To refuse it would be a public humiliation he doesn't deserve. If you're not interested in him, wait till he asks you to be with him, then tell him. He'll ask you tonight, that's for sure. This is his chance as an older male to show you what a good provider he could be."

Kitra pressed herself close between Carrie and her mother. "Tell me it's Dzaka," she said, a worried look on her young face. "I don't want it to be anyone else."

"Haven't you sent to him to find out?" teased Rhyasha.

"I daren't!"

"Kusac wouldn't allow it to be anyone else," Carrie said comfortingly, taking her young bond-sister's hand in hers.

"Are you sure?"

"We're sure," said her mother, caressing Kitra's cheek with her free hand. "Hush, my kitling—it's Dzaka. Just enjoy accepting your first kill offering."

Outside, in front of the huge cooking fire, a group of hunters stood waiting to be joined by the females the runners had been dispatched to fetch. Beyond them were the tables where the meat would be butchered before being put to roast at the fire. Ghyan, accompanied by a priest from the temple of Nylam, stood waiting to bless the kills. Farther off stood the runners who would take the animals' heads out to place on the ceremonial posts in the fields of the two estates.

Kusac was accompanied by Meral, Dzaka, and Rulla. They'd been hunting together and had each managed to catch one of the deerlike creatures that formed the main herd animal on the Aldatan lands.

With due solemnity, their catches were shown to their respective mates—or in Rulla's case, the object of his passion—and equally solemnly examined by the recipient.

"It's a little bigger than the last one," said Kusac quietly, grinning at Carrie.

She leaned forward, looking critically at the carcass. "The wild animals on Keiss hardly count as rhakla," she said. "But it is as clean a kill. Won't it affect the herds when so many bucks are being slaughtered?"

"No. We use the festival to cull them. Only the ones we want to be hunted are released from their winter pens," he said, hefting the carcass over his shoulder again and beginning to walk over to Ghyan and the visiting acolyte.

Ghyan waited till all their little group were gathered before murmuring the ritual thanks and blessing. That done, they went to the tables where the heads were removed and given to the runners who then disappeared into the night with them.

As they walked back to the hall, Carrie asked, "Are the heads used to frighten the demons again?"

"Not this time. We put them on the stakes to ensure the herds and the land are fruitful in this new year."

Carrie gently nudged him, drawing his attention to Kitra and Dzaka who were walking in front of them. "He's so serious, isn't he? The last time he did this must have been for Nnya, his dead mate."

"This means a lot to him," said Kusac. "Like most of the Brothers, he's not publicly demonstrative, but he is genuinely fond of my sister, though."

"I get the feeling that it means more to him than just making her first hunt something special."

Kusac laughed gently. "Still building a life for them? We'll see. I don't know that either of them is ready for a deep commitment yet."

Later that night, Kashini safely abed with her nurse, Carrie was able to enjoy herself. After they'd all eaten, in the company of Taizia and Rhyasha, she wandered through the hall meeting and talking to the various community leaders on the main estate. They stopped to exchange greetings with the Human archaeologists, deciding to remain when they realized Pam Southgate, their leader, was absent, having gone to the Terran enclave at the Telepath Guild for the duration of the festival.

Through the babble of chatter, gradually Carrie realized she could hear the sounds of the drums again. Looking round, she saw the hall was beginning to empty.

Taizia leaned forward to pat her hand. "Come on, you must see this," she said. "It's the dance of thanks for a successful hunt. Now we'll see all the newly promoted males falling over themselves to attract the females! It's fun seeing who pairs off with whom."

"It's cold outside, Taizia. I'd rather stay here," Carrie said.

"Come on," said her bond-sister, getting to her feet. "You're going to see this. You'll enjoy it once you're out there. It isn't as cold as you think."

As she allowed herself to be dragged outside to the circle, Carrie reached mentally for Kusac. Finding him preoccupied, she turned her attention back to what Tazia was saying.

"We'll stand by the fire, so you'll stay warm, never fear," she said, drawing her close to one of the smaller fires.

The night was illuminated by the glow not only from the main fire ahead of them, but from the dozen smaller fires that ringed the dancing circle.

The music, as Rhyasha had said, was subtly different. So were the dancers. The tempo was deep and fast, making not only the ground but the very air seem to vibrate to its sound. Firelight flickered off the dancers, casting their bodies and costumes into an ever-changing swirling pattern of dark and light. Around them all, like a mantle of black

elvet, the night seemed to enclose watchers and dancers
like in a world dominated by the rhythmic beat of the
drums.

Sparks from the fires flickering up into the night air were
counterpointed by the flash of the mirrors in the costumes.
Beneath the swirling beat could be heard the sharp, clear
sound of the tiny decorative bells as the dancers leaped
and twirled among each other, somehow managing to
avoid collisions.

Carrie could feel the night come alive with the sexual
tension generated by the minds of the young males in the
circle. Now was their time, their chance, to impress and
attract the females. The beat changed, becoming softer,
more seductive, drawing a response from the audience of
females. She could feel it touch her, make her heart beat
faster, and realized that like everyone present, she was beginning to sway in time with the music.

Can you feel it? sent Taizia, holding onto her arm, face
aglow with pleasure. *You must be able to!*

What? asked Carrie, wrapping her arms around her body
as she felt this new awareness slowly building in her mind.
Then it began to spill throughout her body, awakening all
her senses, leaving her tingling with anticipation.

*That! Our collective response to the males! Look how they
show off!*

She was right. Those nearest the edge of the circle were
leaping as high as they could, the fur on their bodies bushed
out till they looked twice their normal size.

They look terrifying, sent Carrie, a shiver of fear—and
more—running through her. *I've never seen them like this
before, not even in a Challenge!*

*Wonderful, isn't it? From the feel of it, I'd say it's going
to be a fruitful year for the Clans, too!*

Suddenly, in response to some unspoken signal, the dancers broke out from the circle and began to pace toward the
watchers as the drumbeat died down to a low throbbing
sound. There was a collective sigh from the females as the
males seemed to melt into the crowd.

Look, one's approaching Ruth! Taizia pointed to where
the Human female was hastily trying to back away from a
dancer. *It's Rulla, it has to be!*

Then the dancer removed his mask, catching hold of the
woman by the arm.

*There you are! I knew he'd approach her! Do you think
she'll have him?*

It looks like he's insisting too much, replied Carrie, concerned for her.

*Don't worry, we have marshals. They'll pick up anyone
who's genuinely distressed. The males know this and
wouldn't risk the dishonor they'd face.*

So engrossed was she in watching Ruth, who was now
standing listening to Rulla pleading his cause, that when a
hand touched her shoulder and she turned to face a dancer,
she gave a gasp of fear. She began to back away but found
Taizia standing behind her, holding her firmly.

What are you doing? You must at least listen to him.

The thought came into her mind that this male wanted
only an embrace from her.

*See? He isn't compromising you, he only wants to hold
you for a moment.*

I'm not interested! she sent, trying to twist her arm free
from Taizia's grip. *Where's Kusac?*

An embrace, Carrie! Let him have one, then he'll go, Taizia sent persuasively. *I'm here, no harm can come to you.*

*Why's he doing this? He must know who I am! Let me
go, Taizia! I told you, I'm not interested!*

The dancer held out his hands and stepped forward,
cocking his head questioningly on one side.

Carrie looked into the mask of one of Shola's feral fe-
lines. *That isn't a hunt mask.*

*They wear different ones for this dance. Come on, Carrie,
what's an embrace going to cost you?*

She couldn't look away now—she felt drawn to him. He
had to be familiar to her, yet there was nothing she could
actually recognize about him. No one who didn't know her
personally would dare to approach her, the new co-Leader
of the En'Shalla Clan—especially with her life-mate's sister
beside her. She could hear his breathing begin to slow after
his exertions, see his pelt begin to lie flat again, but his
body lost none of its tension as he waited for her response.

He was tall, and dark pelted, but in the flickering glow
cast by the fires, that meant nothing. His scent was hidden
beneath the smell of wood smoke, damp fur, and the animal
skins he wore. Around his waist was a belt from which
hung strips of soft leather decorated with beads and tiny
mirrored circles. Interspersed between them were strips of

ir into which tiny bells had been fixed. His wrists wore
road bands with similar decorations. Without realizing it,
ne found her hands were within his.

Good for you! sent Taizia, her mental tone an amused
urr as she stepped back from them.

As if in a daze, she felt herself being drawn closer till
he rested against his damp pelt, then her hands were re-
ased as his arms folded around her and he bent to rest
is chin on her shoulder. She felt him lift one arm to re-
1ove his mask, then her head was cupped in his hand and
is face was against hers as he began to gently nuzzle her
heek.

At his touch, memories from the past began to rise, and
he remembered the first time Kusac had held her back on
keiss. His fur had been damp then. Her body stirred, senses
hat had been asleep since she'd had her cub awakening
gain. A wave of desire swept through her as the male's
eeth gently closed on her cheek and his tonguetip touched
er skin.

Involuntarily, her hands went to his waist and as she held
im, a familiar magic returned.

It is *you!* she sent, her hands tightening in his pelt. *That
vas a mean trick to play on me!*

Not so, Kusac replied, his mouth now finding hers. *You
dmired the dancers this morning. I wanted to surprise you,
hat's all.*

You certainly did. She relaxed against him, too swept up
n their shared sensations to argue. She could feel his heart
eating faster now, feel a desire as strong as her own rising
n him. *We shouldn't be here. Our Link's started.*

I know. Slowly they parted, then he bent to lift her in
is arms. "Are you wearing the new damper Vanna and
Garras gifted to us this evening?"

"Yes."

"Then we can try them out tonight." He looked over to
vhere his sister now stood with her mate. "Taizia, Meral,
hank you for watching her for me," he said.

"Go," she said. "I can feel you both from here! And
witch on those dampers now!" she called after them.

From the doorway to the banquet hall, Konis, Rhyasha
nd Sub-Lieutenant Myak stood watching.

"Who'd have thought they'd both be so constant after

all they've been through?" said Konis. "And we have a granddaughter as well. Harvests ripen in the strangest of fields."

"I knew it would work out," said Rhyasha, linking arms with him. "I know our son, and I had faith in the Gods."

"Hmm. What about you, Myak?" asked Konis as they threaded their way through the tables back to the inner hearth. "Or will you give me more of the bland platitudes you used back when they turned up on the *Khalossa?*"

"I felt there was more at work than just the whim of an adolescent male," said Myak. "They needed to be given a chance. As for the rest, I merely followed orders, Master Konis."

"Aye, but whose orders? You have as many links as the Brotherhood!"

Myak looked reproachfully at him. "You appointed me to be an aide to Commander Raguul. I merely do that to the best of my ability, Clan Lord."

"Don't tease him, Konis," said Rhyasha, taking hold of Myak with her other arm. "The past is gone now. We all played the parts we had to, and all has come out well. Let's leave it at that. More wine, Myak?" she asked as they reached their seats.

"Where d'you think you're taking me?" Carrie asked, sitting up in his arms. "I'm not going to some cave tonight!"

"Absolutely not," he agreed. "There's a small garden shelter nearby—you'd call it a summer house—which I made ready for tonight. With these new dampers on, we don't need to change our plans. And," he said, stepping over a low hedge, "if there's anyone near enough to be affected, they'll enjoy tonight even more!"

"What's with this carrying me everywhere?" she asked. "I can walk, you know. In fact, Vanna says I can join you at the Warriors Guild in a couple of weeks."

He stopped dead and set her down on her feet—in snow almost a foot deep.

She shrieked as the damp coldness instantly soaked the lightweight shoes she was wearing. "Kusac!"

"What? You wanted to walk."

"You know I can't walk in snow dressed like this!"

"Would you like me to carry you?" he asked, grinning.

"Yes, please," she said between gritted teeth, determined not to let him hear them chattering with the cold.

He lifted her up and began walking again.

"You're getting too sure of yourself," she said as he stopped in front of the summer house.

"Will you open the door, or shall I put you down again and do it myself?"

She leaned forward, pressing her hand on the palm lock. The door slid open, spilling warm air out around them. As they stepped inside, it shut behind them, leaving them standing in the gentle glow cast by the heating unit. On the floor, a wide sleeping pallet covered with cushions and rugs almost filled the main room.

As Kusac set her down, she looked around. "I thought from what you said we were roughing it."

"Time enough for that on Jalna. This is Nylam's night, let's enjoy it," he said, helping her off with her cloak. "Sit down, and I'll see to your shoes."

Carrie lowered herself onto the cushions, making sure she kept her wet feet off the bedding. While she adjusted the setting on her personal damper, Kusac knelt beside her and began to pull off her shoes.

"What about you?" she asked as he began to rub her feet gently with his hands. "Your feet are bare and you walked all the way here."

"I'm used to it. Wearing shoes like you would seem stranger. Better?" Lifting her foot, he began to gently lick her instep with the smooth tip of his tongue.

"Hey! That tickles," she said indignantly, trying to pull free.

"I decided to start with your feet tonight," he said, his voice a velvet purr.

"Idiot," she murmured, relaxing back against the cushions as he began to lick her ankle. She could feel their Link drawing them closer again, bringing them shared sensations. Already the distinction between *her* and *him* was beginning to blur.

Her skin was soft and cool, tasting faintly of honey. He pushed her robe farther up, letting his teeth and tongue gently find the softness and warmth of her calves then her thighs, feeling her begin to tremble as her body came alive under his touch. He stretched out beside her, finding her arms waiting to hold him close. She'd already undone her robe and he pushed it aside, his mouth covering her throat in a reaffirmation of his love for her. He felt her need for him flare deep in her belly, the fire leaping out from her to surge through him too. In one almost painful spasm, he was ready for her.

He tugged the rest of her robe open, lifting her free of it and tossing it aside. *I want to hold you,* he sent, covering her face in flicks of his tongue and tiny bites as her arms closed round him, pulling his body close.

Wherever he touched her, it was as if an electric current passed between them, focusing all her awareness there. His hand caressed her neck, his tongue and teeth following, drawing a river of fire through her. Moments after his mouth closed on her breast, for the space of a heartbeat, he stilled.

I forgot, he sent, lifting his head, but she drew him down again.

It feels good. She could feel his response, the shock of possibly breaking an unknown taboo of hers, if not his peoples'. *No. Tonight is ours,* she sent, arching her body against his as her hand clenched in his hair. *You know I'm no longer feeding our cub.* She felt herself begin to fragment, to merge with him.

This is like the first time, they thought as their joined minds spiraled upward taking their bodies with them until they were one.

Afterward, Kusac reached for the edge of the blanket and pulled it across them both, drawing Carrie back against the curve of his body. Lazily he licked the back of her ear as she pressed herself closer to him.

"Welcome back," he murmured.

"Welcome back yourself," she said sleepily. "Was that us or the dance?"

"Probably a bit of both," he said. "It's more intense for our Clan because we're telepaths."

"I can see why you pack all the younglings off under supervision before the dancing starts."

"Tonight was particularly strong. I don't remember it being so compulsive before," he murmured. "But then, last time I didn't have a Leska who was my life-mate." His teeth closed briefly on her ear lobe. "I think we should sleep, unless . . ."

His only answer was her gentle breathing.

The next morning, Jissoh came to their villa to speak to Carrie. Only because it touched on Mara did she agree to speak to her on their Link day.

"Last night, Mara was with one of the Humans from the digging," said Jissoh. "I followed them, but I didn't get a close enough look to identify him. They didn't stay talking for long."

"You're sure it was one of the archaeologists?"

She nodded. "Yes, Clan Leader. One of the males."

Carrie tapped her fingers on her chair arm in an unconscious Sholan gesture. "Continue watching her. Ask Garras to appoint someone to keep an eye on the Human males. Let's see if she meets up with him today. It's the last day of the festival, their last chance to meet inconspicuously."

"Yes, Clan Leader."

* * *

Sorli sighed to himself as he began packing the last of his possession into his bag. This was not going as he'd hoped. He'd been here for nearly two hours now, and not a word, not a mental touch from the Guild Master. He'd gone to the library first to collect his books, thinking that perhaps Master Esken might prefer a more public meeting. Finished there, he went to the classroom, then his study. Now here he was in his living quarters with his packing almost complete.

He didn't want to initiate a meeting himself because to do so would be backing down from his stance that Esken should accept the changes gracefully since the alternative was unthinkable. But what was he to do if Esken didn't come to him? Then he felt it; the Master's presence. Collecting his thoughts behind his shielding, he waited.

A tap on the open door, then Esken stood inside. "Thank the Gods you're back, Sorli! I've need of your counsel," he said, coming into the room. "Did you enjoy the festivals? We had the Terrans visiting ours on the last two days. The first they spent celebrating the birth of their own God."

"I spent it at the Chekoi estate, with my betrothed's family," said Sorli, continuing to fold his clothes and place them in the bag.

"You, too, eh? I hope she's a better choice than mine. They tried to foist a widow with two kitlings on me. Me! A Guild Master, with all the work it takes to run this place and oversee all the other telepath guildhouses on Shola!" He snorted his disgust before seeming to take in what Sorli was actually doing.

"Packing? What are you doing, Sorli? I thought you'd returned to your post."

Sorli hesitated. "It depends, Master Esken."

Esken frowned, coming round to sit on the chair opposite him. "Depends? What kind of talk is this? You've had a break. Surely it's time for you to resume your duties now."

"I made my position clear the last time we spoke, Master Esken," said Sorli, looking across the bed at him. "This hasn't been a break."

"Oh, that," said Esken, waving his hand dismissively. "That's dealt with, Sorli. You made some good points, ones that Khafsa echoed when I had to see him later that day. I need to take it easier now, my health's not up to all the recent stressful events. It's time for you to take on some of my duties, help me run things around here, move up in the world. Having a mate will make it easier for you, I'm sure." His mouth opened in a large smile as he positively beamed at Sorli. "Now, start unpacking while I tell you what I'd like you to do."

Sorli stood dumbfounded. He hadn't expected this at all. Was it genuine though, or was Esken hoping to bribe him into staying?

"What duties would I be taking over?" he asked, finding his tongue at last.

"The mixed Leskas for one. You get on far better with the Aldatans than I ever did," Esken said frankly. "The less I have to deal with them, the better it will be for my blood pressure. If Governor Nesul is agreeable, you can replace me on the World Council. I'll brief you fully, and you'll keep me informed as to what's going on, of course. I'm going to handle the business of overseeing all our guildhouses and the Terrans. You can see to the day to day running of this guildhouse. You've been involved in it anyway for several years now. It'll mean giving up most of your teaching duties, but you'll still have your Leska pairs to work with."

Sorli found his legs didn't want to support him, and as a consequence, he sat down rather more heavily than usual on the bed. "Your health must indeed be bad, Master Esken," he heard himself murmur.

"It's nothing that taking it easy and the right treatment won't cure," said Esken. "Now, Mentor Sorli, are you going to unpack?"

He pulled his thoughts together hastily. The promotion seemed genuine, even down to him now being recognized officially as the next Guild Master. While he hesitated, Esken began to speak again.

"There are a few people I can afford to lose, Sorli," he said quietly. "You, however, are not one of them." He sighed. "You want the cold truth? My only way out is through you; I cannot back down. All that's left to me is to retire from the fight gracefully. Now will you stay?"

"Your health?" Sorli asked.

"That's genuine. Anger will be my undoing if I let it, Sorli, and I won't."

"If your offer is genuine," said Sorli, "then I accept, but should it happen that you . . ."

Esken waved his hand again. "There's enough to keep me busy in the areas I intend to pursue. I was spread too thin anyway. If I concentrate my efforts, I can still make my mark on this new society we're building." He leaned forward. "Now to what I want you to help me with. I need you to find out which of the Consortia Houses would be the best for me to contact regarding finding a wife."

Sorli began to frown.

"I have the right, Sorli," said Esken hastily. "My age alone qualifies me to choose a Consortia. Even Konis Aldatan has admitted that. Can you honestly see me with a young wife and two kitlings?"

"The purpose of these marriages is to have cubs," Sorli felt obliged to point out. "Telepathic cubs."

"I'm not a clan heir, the law doesn't force me to accept the Clan Leader's choice, nor to father cubs, you know that as well as I do."

Sorli sighed. "Very well, I'll do what I can, Master Esken."

"Thank you, Sorli," said Esken. "If you wish to leave

your unpacking, one of the younglings could do it for you later. You're entitled now to appoint an assistant." The Guild Master got to his feet. "Why not come and have some c'shar with me?"

"You know," said Sorli, getting up and turning his back on the packing, "I think I will do just that. Thank you, Master Esken."

As he followed Esken from the room, he resolved that from now on, he would take full advantage of his new position. In the past he'd been too readily available for the Guild Master to call on, to the extent that he'd ended up replacing any assistant Esken might have appointed to do his day to day running about. Not any more: never again would he contribute to his own servitude. Esken would find him a changed person indeed.

*   *   *

It was two days since the incident in the temple, and Kaid had been released from the infirmary back to his own room. For the time being, there was a guard outside his suite, and Vriuzu and a couple of the Brothers who also had enough telepathic ability were keeping him under constant surveillance. So far, there had been no more episodes.

Noni had located every memory from his childhood in the Margins, and from the time when Vartra had called him back. She'd made him relive each one and had tried to help him understand it before finally pronouncing that nothing was left to resurface unexpectedly. What did remain, however, was his sense of betrayal and outrage at what Vartra had done.

He felt empty, without a purpose. Now he saw everything to do with the Margins—including the Triad—as a plot on the part of Vartra to fill him with a need to return to the past. Turning over on his side, he winced. His shoulder and head were healing, but slowly. Noni's ointments worked, he'd say that for them, but he'd have preferred fastheal.

Noni had argued with him for hours, trying to get him to admit that the Triad was genuine, nothing to do with Vartra, but he wouldn't accept it.

"You were pulled to her by the bond you share," she insisted.

"No. It was nothing but an obsession."

"It works the same as a Leska Link, only slightly weaker, Tallinu!"

"If that's true, then it's because of Vartra's tampering with our genes."

"It is not!"

"The Triads came after the Cataclysm, after the enhanced telepaths."

"It didn't enhance the warriors, it couldn't! Why won't you listen to me, boy!"

"They had minor talents, like the Brotherhood today. It enhanced that as it's enhanced the Brothers today."

"Dammit, boy! Does it matter? You have the female you wanted, and legally, not just as a lover! You belong with each other, all three of you! Would you now break the oaths you made with them?"

He refused to answer, and in a rage, she left.

*   *   *

"What is it, Noni?" asked Kusac as her attendant opened the door to him.

"Come in, young Aldatan, come in! How's that cub of yours, eh? She'll be beginning to get lively now, I'll be bound. You'll have some c'shar with me?"

Realizing she didn't want to talk in front of anyone else, Kusac said no more. As he joined her at the table he handed her a large package.

"I brought some more coffee for you," he said, sitting down.

Noni accepted the package and sniffed at the wrapping. "So this is the instant stuff. Then we'll try it now. Teusi, you can go for the next hour. We've business to discuss."

Teusi nodded. "I'll get the supplies from the village for you now," he said, collecting his coat from the hook near the door.

Noni pushed the tray of dried herbs she was mixing aside, waiting till they were alone.

"What's all the mystery?" asked Kusac, getting up and going over to the stove to heat some water. "You said you'd tell me when I got here."

"Rhyaz asked me to go up to his bird's nest once a week to hold a clinic, as he calls it," she said.

"That's good, isn't it? You usually treat the Brothers and Sisters anyway."

"Don't know that I want to do it," she grumbled, watching him spoon the brown granules into the mugs.

He turned to look at her, leaning against the cold portion of the hob. "You're flattered, but it would mean there'd be fewer of them coming here to see you. I expect you see their visits as social occasions. If you had a clinic, you'd have less time with them."

She opened her mouth in a grin. "Not bad."

"So why did you send for me?"

"Tallinu. He needs you here with him."

Kusac frowned. "What's happened?"

He listened while she told him, only turning aside to make the drinks when the water boiled. Picking up the mugs, he returned to the table.

"You say the incident's been contained? Only those involved know about it?"

"And you," she said, sipping her drink. "It's got almost as strong a taste," she observed, taking a larger, second sip. "Still makes our c'shar taste bland by comparison."

"What? Oh. Yes, it does," he said, momentarily thrown. "What is it you want me to do?"

"Did you bring your things like I said?"

"Yes. They're out in the aircar."

"I want you living with him four days out of five," said Noni. "On your Link days, that T'Chebbi female can come over. He's not to be left alone. He's seeing the world aslant at present and needs you there to keep putting him right."

"Has he asked for me to do this?"

"Don't be foolish! He won't even admit he needs help, let alone ask for it! And before you suggest physicians and hospitals, that'll only make him worse. He'll lose all touch with reality and become completely isolated."

"What about Carrie and our cub? They need me too, especially at this time. And just how am I supposed to force my presence on him?"

"She'll be going to that Warriors Guild shortly. Won't do her any harm to do it without you. Remind her how strong she can be on her own. She'll do fine. Get T'Chebbi to keep her company. When she isn't with Tallinu."

"What're you scheming at now, Noni? Are you trying to match Kaid and T'Chebbi? At this time, surely you'd do well to leave that alone."

"You were telepath reared, weren't you? I keep forgetting," she muttered. "It's different for the rest of us. You isolate yourselves."

"We don't. Far from it, in fact."

"Compared to the rest of us, you do. You go to the Warriors Guild. How do they live? They don't shut themselves up alone in one room unless they're with a lover, do they? They have dormitories. They sleep several to a room, share beds. That's the normal Sholan way."

"We did as cubs at the Guild."

"But not when you all got older and your Talents got stronger."

"We need the mental privacy, Noni," he said, irritated. "What's your point?"

"That's my point!" she snapped. "You're different. Tallinu, now, he was brought up sharing quarters—and more in his case," she muttered darkly.

Kusac's ears flicked forward and unconsciously his mind reached out to learn more. Not too subtly, it was thrust aside.

"None of your business. Brothers, especially those like Tallinu and Garras—and Dzaka—did you know he worked as a team with Nnya, his dead mate? No? Thought not. Lijou told me. Anyway, those who become sword-brothers depend on each other for their lives. They trust each other, know each other. And how do they do this?" she demanded. "They live together: they share a relationship closer than family, or lovers. That's what you've got to build with him."

"You're asking a lot, Noni," he said, shifting uncomfortably under her gaze. "He may not want such a relationship with me, especially if I have to force it on him."

"You'll find a way," said Noni, raising her mug. "Drink up, or I'll start thinking this brew of yours is poisoned. Go talk to Lijou and Rhyaz. They'll tell you how it is at Stronghold. Vriuzu, now, he'll probably have most experience of it, and the Talent to give you a sending so you *really* know."

Kusac took a drink, thinking through what she was saying. "When you said Dzaka and Nnya were sword brothers, does that mean . . ." he began.

"You'll have to see for yourself where it leads," she said. "Everyone makes their own rules, young Aldatan. Depends what you want—what he wants. Garras certainly had his fair share of female lovers, so did Tallinu before Khemu."

"Have you spoken to T'Chebbi about this? Is she . . . are they . . . ?" He stopped, unsure what to ask.

"Comrades in arms," she said. "The rest is their business. Yes, I spoke to her, and she'll be looking out for Carrie personally—as Tallinu intended she should if the Triad hadn't gotten in the way. Now you finish your drink and get over there. Speak to the folk I've mentioned, then start helping Tallinu."

"Are you going to take Rhyaz up on his offer?" he asked.

"Impudent youngling!" she snorted, banging her mug down on the table. The glint of amusement in her eyes belied the words. "You'll have to wait and see like the rest of them, won't you?"

*   *   *

Kusac realized that the last time he'd been this anxious about a confrontation had been when he'd asked his father to dissolve his betrothal contract to Rala Vailkoi. Nodding to the guard on duty, he hesitated outside Kaid's suite, glad he'd decided to leave his bag with Lijou for the time being.

"You can go now," he said.

He waited till he was alone in the corridor, tugging nervously at the belt on his robe, trying to settle it less awkwardly round his waist. It was the first time he'd worn a priest's robe, and it sat uncomfortably on him, psychologically as well as physically.

He'd followed Noni's advice to the word, speaking to the two Guild Masters, explaining what it was he hoped to achieve. Then he'd seen Vriuzu. He now knew as much as it was possible to know about life at Stronghold without actually having experienced it. All that was left for him to do now was open the door.

From Master Rhyaz' office, the palm lock had been activated to accept his print and, taking a deep breath, he placed his hand on it. From now on, he had to remain confident of what he was doing, for if he had doubts, Kaid would pick them up.

The lounge was empty. As he walked through it to the bedroom, he felt the touch of Kaid's mind at the edges of his own.

"How's the shoulder?" he asked, stopping just inside the doorway.

Kaid was lying on the bed watching a vidcast. Using the remote to switch it off, he looked up.

"They shouldn't have sent for you," he said. "I'm not going back to the estate yet."

"They didn't send for me, I came on my own. I realized the Warrior Guild isn't enough. I need the specialized training I can only get here. It was bunk in with you, or Vriuzu. So here I am."

Kaid looked at him blankly. "You're joking."

"No. They haven't made any other rooms over for telepaths yet. Is there a problem? You shared with Garras, didn't you?"

"Yes . . ." The *but* was unspoken. "What about Carrie? Does she know?" he asked, sitting up.

"That I'm coming here to train with you?" asked Kusac, going over to the dispenser. "Of course. She'll be fine. She's got T'Chebbi and Dzaka to watch over her. Do you want a drink?"

"No. Look, Kusac, you can't come here. I can't teach you," he said.

"Are you refusing?" Kusac asked quietly, punching his choice of drink into the dispenser keypad.

"It's not that simple. You don't understand what . . ." Kaid began, getting to his feet.

"I understand that on Jalna our lives will depend on each other," Kusac interrupted. "I've only just started to get to know you, Kaid." He turned, holding his drink in front of him. "We've begun to be friends, but we've a lot more to learn about each other, haven't we? I want to know the person who's guarding my back. You can't deny me that. It's part of the Brotherhood Creed, and we've both sworn to Father Lijou to uphold it."

Kaid stopped in front of him. "It's all an empty sham, Kusac, you know it is! The god Vartra doesn't exist! The rituals are meaningless, invented to feed the ego of one male—one who's used us and lied to us!"

"I'm not here to argue with you, Kaid. You know well enough that the Creed's a way of life that's worked for the Brothers since the Order was founded. Whether Vartra was a person or a god doesn't affect that." Kusac walked past him to sit on the end of the bed. Kaid's impotent rage was only too tangible on every level. Sitting down, he presented less of a potential threat.

"And just when did you swear the Creed?" Kaid demanded.

"Today, when I saw Father Lijou," Kusac replied more calmly than he felt.

"Did he tell you what happened to me? That Vartra pulled me back to the past? How he told Jaisa to bear my cub?" The bed bounced as Kaid flung himself back down on it, letting out a low grunt of pain as he jarred his shoulder.

Kusac put the glass down on the floor, shaking the spilled liquid off his hand. "He told me. Damned foolish thing to do, trying to set fire to the temple, don't you think?"

"I was angry. I still am," Kaid snarled. "He used me! Messed with my mind and stole a cub from me! All because he wanted to play god some more!"

"We were the ones who went back and told him he'd be a god," said Kusac. "And you name me any god that isn't mean, devious, and downright nasty according to the legends!"

"You think you've got all the bloody answers, don't you? What if I do refuse to train you? What then, Kusac Aldatan?"

"Then," said Kusac, picking up his glass again and taking a mouthful of ale, "you're forsworn to me by oaths that don't involve Vartra." He locked eyes with Kaid. "But you're not going to refuse, are you?" he said quietly. "I know what I'm asking you to do, and I know you're going to delight in making my life hell because I've asked, but we'll be doing this together."

"You damned Aldatans are all the same. Never know when to give in. Stay, then, if that's what you choose to do," Kaid sighed, lying back on the bed. "But be damned sure it *is* what you want!"

If the first day had been hard work, the second was worse. Kaid drove him relentlessly till every muscle ached and he could hardly move. The training he'd done with him before was nothing compared to this.

"You've got a lot to learn yet," said Kaid, walking alongside him as they made their way to the gymnasium showers. "Before, I was teaching you how to protect yourself. Now

'm training you to be a Brother. It doesn't just involve the
dvanced combat, you've got the paramedic training, too.
:very Brother has to be able to treat his own and other
>eople's wounds and administer the necessary drugs under
1eld combat conditions."

"Can't we use knowledge transfers?" asked Kusac, limp-
ng into the nearest shower stall and reaching for a tap.
'It'd save some time. I used it with you for the telepathy
kills."

"We could, with the medical knowledge," Kaid con-
:eded, "but don't think it means you'll have an easier time,
·ou won't. Take a quick shower, no more. I'll wait in the
nassage area for you. I want those muscles loosened up so
_/ou can work tomorrow."

Kusac groaned.

As he pushed open the door to the massage room, Kusac
:ealized there was a small group of students gathered round
ɔne of the tables. Kaid moved away from it as he came in.

"You've volunteered to be their victim," he said with
what Kusac recognized as the first attempt at humor he'd
heard from him in the last two days. "Up you get," he said,
indicating the table that the students had backed away
from. He turned his attention to the younglings. "Here's
your chance to see what it's like to work on someone with
sore muscles, someone who's going to wriggle and moan
wherever you touch him!"

Nervous laughter greeted his remark as Kusac climbed
reluctantly onto the table.

Kaid, I don't know that I can tolerate their touch!

Then learn to block it. You'll need to out in the field, was
the short reply.

With gritted teeth, Kusa submitted to their inexpert
ministrations.

Use the litanies. That's what they're for, Kaid reminded
him as he flinched when one youth pressed too hard on a
nerve in his back.

I am!

Later, as Kusac soaked the last of the stiffness away in
a hot bath in their suite, Kaid came in. He squatted down
at the side of the tub.

"You won't make me quit, you know," said Kusac. "I
don't give up that easily."

"This is only the beginning," said Kaid. "Tomorrow the real work starts."

Kusac was aware of Kaid gauging and assessing him with both mind and eyes. It was the first time he'd felt Kaid using his abilities: his mental touch was hard and uncompromising. He tensed, unsure what was coming next.

"You've done better than I thought you would—so far," he said. "It can't be easy for you with your telepath's background. I was sure you wouldn't last out that massage. The students were more than a little clumsy." The mental contact faded, then was gone.

"Almost didn't," he admitted, relaxing a little.

"Why are you here, Kusac? What do you want?"

Kusac frowned, surprised at the question. "I told you. I want to get to know you as a person and a warrior. I want to work with you."

"Do you understand what you're asking? Did someone explain it to you?"

"Yes. I asked Master Rhyaz."

Kaid nodded, beginning to stand up. "Noni sent you, didn't she?"

"No one sent me," said Kusac, suddenly feeling vulnerable. He sat upright, making the water surge around him as he did. He kept a wary eye on Kaid. "I chose to come."

Kaid lunged forward, his hand closing round Kusac's throat in a crushing grip. His face was only inches away, teeth bared as he began to growl ominously.

Fear flared inside Kusac, but he didn't dare move. His hands clutched convulsively at the sides of the bath, knuckles whitening, claws extending till they hurt. If this attack was real, there was nothing he could do to defend himself. Had Kaid gone mad? Was he out of control?

"Release me from my oath to you!" Kaid snarled, his hand tightening. "Give me back my freedom. No more Liege and liegeman. Then ask me!"

Slowly Kusac tilted his head back, mind working furiously as he looked up into Kaid's eyes. There was no color in them, only large circles of black. No Sholan easily tolerated being touched on the neck; it was too vulnerable to teeth and claws. Why had no one had warned him of this? That he had to ask, yes, but not this! What the hell was the response? Was there one? And his oath—was Kaid testing how strong his faith in him was?

"I release you from your oath of allegiance, and I want ɔ be paired with you," he said, not knowing how else to ut it, praying he'd got it right.

"I think not." The growl deepened and the claws began ɔ prick his flesh.

Kusac let out a single curse. "*Goddammit!* I want to be *vinned* with you! A sword-brother, like Garras was!"

The grip lessened. "You think you know the cost, but ou don't," Kaid growled. "No one ever does at first."

"I felt what it meant." His throat was stretched too taut. I'll pay it."

Suddenly the pressure was gone, but as he let his head lrop, he realized Kaid's hand had remained where it was. Iis eyes, though, were still dark.

"We'll see. Maybe you won't stay on the trail. Maybe t'll be me that can't pay the cost of any of it, including the ɔath to Vartra." His hand gently kneaded the muscles on Kusac's neck for a moment before he released him and urned away. "Don't stay in too long. It's almost time for hird meal," he said as he left the room.

As the door slid closed behind him, Kusac gradually let ;o his grip on the bath. The encounter had left him badly ;haken. He realized there was a lot about Kaid he didn't <now.

Later that night, Kusac woke suddenly. He lay there try-ing to work out what had disturbed him, then he sensed what it was. It was the silence. Mentally, he checked the room. Nothing. He was alone. Activating the night light, he threw back the covers and leaped to his feet. A quick touch on Kaid's side of the bed confirmed it was cold: he'd been gone for some time.

Cursing, he ran for the door, grabbing his robe as he went, hastily pulling it on while trying to sense where his friend had gone. Despite Kaid's psychic damper, he found the faint mental pattern, but reaching him physically was another matter since he couldn't yet find his way through the maze of corridors on his own. He had to find him and find him fast before someone, or something, got hurt. Switching off his own damper, in desperation he reached for Carrie, waiting impatiently for her to wake enough to answer him.

I need to find Kaid. Join with me, he sent as soon as he felt their link strengthen.

He's on the lower levels, where Ghezu held him prisoner, she replied. *The Gods help him! He's reliving some of the memories, Kusac!*

Keep your distance, cub. Don't let his crystal draw you in. Guide me there. Going over to a set of drawers, he scrabbled in the top one for the flashlight he'd seen there earlier in the day.

Her directions led him past Lijou's quarters to the other side of the main building to what had once been Ghezu's office, and was now Rhyaz's. A crack of light at the edge of the door showed it was slightly ajar. He pushed it open. At the far end was a small alcove that Carrie told him led down to the lower corridors.

I'll manage from here. Better that he doesn't sense you around, cub.

I want to know how he is. Her mental tone was determined.

Tomorrow. I'll be home early.

Not soon enough. I'll go if you promise to contact me later.

I will. Now go before he senses you! he replied, switching on his flashlight as he pushed open the door and stepped into the dark opening.

Cautiously he edged his way down the steep stairs. Beneath his feet, he could feel the uneven wear on the stone treads. This route was old and well used. At the bottom, the corridor opened out and, in the distance, he could see a pool of light spilling out from one of the rooms. Switching off the flashlight, he pushed it into his pocket and headed swiftly toward it.

As he approached the door, he could feel the atmosphere around him darkening. He could sense Kaid's presence. From within the room came the sound of faint voices. Kaid stood just inside, his back toward him. Beyond him stood three ghostly figures, the central of which was also Kaid. He was being held at the table by Zhaya while Ghezu forced his head up with a knife held to his throat.

Instantly Kusac realized that Carrie had been right. What he was seeing was a projection of Kaid's memories from his captivity and torture in these rooms.

"I want those codes, Kaid, and I want them now."

The voice was faint and he had to strain to hear it.

"You've had my answer. Go rot in hell, Ghezu."

Kaid's voice seemed to come simultaneously from the person in front of him and the hazy image he was projecting. The anger and hate in the air, Kusac could have cut with a knife. He shuddered, unable to look away as he watched Kaid reliving the memory.

Ghezu's moves were almost too quick for his eye to follow. A flash of silver followed by the sound of the knife thudding into wood, then the room reeked of the metallic scent of freshly spilled blood. The ghostly Kaid yowled and began to collapse, but Ghezu reached out to grab him by the hair, hauling him upright again.

"I told you it was real this time, Kaid. I will have those codes from you if I have to destroy you an inch at a time. Now, are you ready to talk yet, or shall I start on the next finger?"

Kusac felt his friend's fear fill the room, his soul-deep terror of being maimed seeping out to touch even him. Death was nothing compared to this, it was life Kaid feared. Transfixed, Kusac could do nothing as he experienced the other's agony, and his fierce determination not to betray his friends. In front of him, Kaid's shoulders began to slump and his ears disappeared from sight.

"Hold him up," the ghost-Ghezu ordered, pulling the knife out of the wood and flicking the severed finger to the floor.

Zhaya obeyed, wrapping one arm around Kaid's chest while continuing to hold his wrists down on the table with his other hand.

"The codes," Ghazu repeated. "I want the codes, Kaid."

Kaid's chin was still lolling against his chest. Ghezu leaned forward. "I can't hear you, Kaid. You aren't going to lose your voice because of a little pain, are you?"

"Go screw yourself," came the faint reply.

Ghezu pulled back and once more his knife flashed down, this time landing on Kaid's hand with a dull cracking sound.

Instinctively, Kusac winced as the ghostly Kaid jerked violently in Zhaya's grasp, letting out another but weaker yowl of pain before collapsing against his captor. Gods, he knew what Ghezu had done to Kaid, but to actually see it! The scene wavered slightly, then steadied. As it did, Kusac realized that the miasma of fear was being pushed slowly back. He knew then what Kaid was doing.

Ghezu grasped Kaid by the hair again, pulling his head back so he could see him. "What are the codes, Kaid? All you have to do is give them to me and all this will stop. Tell me the codes."

His face furrowed with pain, ears invisible against his skull, Kaid's voice was barely audible. "Never." Then his eyes flickered, and he began to slump lower within Zhaya's grasp.

In front of him, his friend staggered slightly as the images finally began to fade. As Kusac ran forward to help him, he caught a last glimpse of Ghezu angrily landing two more blows with his knife pommel on the unconscious Kaid's hand.

"Kaid, in the God's name, let me help you," he said, grabbing him firmly round the waist. Kaid resisted when Kusac tried to turn him toward the door.

"No," he said. "I need to sit for a moment." He began walking toward the wooden chair that stood facing the desk. "I should have known it was impossible to keep you away," he said. "I felt the crystal warming. You shouldn't have come. I didn't mean for you to see this."

"It wasn't Carrie," said Kusac, fetching the other chair and sitting down opposite him. "It was me. I woke and found you gone."

"You contacted her, though." The tone was resigned.

"I needed to find you before you did anything . . ." He stopped.

Kaid's mouth opened in a slow smile. "Don't worry, I'm

ot going to try and destroy the temple again. You were
ght. It was a stupid thing to do."

"Being a telepath leaves you exposed to emotions, both
our own and those of the people around you. You're
:arning to cope with your feelings again," said Kusac. "I
now how difficult it is because after Carrie and I Linked,
had to learn a different way of coping with the violence
ithin me."

"Uh huh."

"Did you know you were projecting that memory?"
Kusac asked.

"I had to see it from outside of myself, to understand
vhat happened to me. I needed to face the fear again, and
ontrol it." The last was said quietly.

"You did." Again Kusac shuddered. "Anyone would
ave been afraid of that, Kaid. I don't think I could have
eld out as long as you did."

Tiredly, Kaid stood up. "If you want to be a sword-
rother, you'll have to be that strong. It's part of the price.
Anyway, I found out what I needed to know. That memory
von't trouble me again." He turned away and walked
lowly toward the door, stopping to look back at Kusac.
'Are you coming? I don't know about you, but I want
ome coffee and something to eat."

"What did you need to find out?" asked Kusac, hurriedly
getting to his feet.

Kaid gave him an amused look before he switched out
he light. "Work it out for yourself. It's good training.
When you know, come and tell me."

CHAPTER 7

L'Seuli sat on the edge of the work counter, watching her as she looked through the viewing window at the Valtegan. There was a rapt look on her face as she followed his every movement.

"They're about to feed him," he said, breaking the silence. "You don't have to watch."

She turned to look at him, her gray eyes giving nothing away. "I need to know the worst, don't I? How bad can it be? He's got lousy table manners, so what?"

L'Seuli pulled a pack of stim twigs from the pocket of his robe and offered her one. She hesitated, then, as he nodded and held it out closer to her, she accepted. As she turned back to the window, he said quietly, "He kills his own food—eats it raw, Keeza, for the fresh blood."

Her head flicked back to face him, a flash of fear in her eyes, then she turned away again. The feeding cage was opened from behind and a chiddoe thrust into it. It squeaked frantically, trying to claw its way back into the other room away from the scent of the alien predator.

Kezule walked over to the cage, standing in front of it, blocking their view. As he reached into the cage and pulled it out, the terrified squeals of the chiddoe rose in volume to be cut off abruptly as he snapped its neck. L'Seuli noticed her flinch.

Turning, the Valtegan made his way to the table and began meticulously to skin and gut the carcass. He took care to ensure that no blood was spilled before dismembering it.

She watched it all with a terrible fascination—he could feel it, disgusting and attracting her at the same time.

"Tell me about him."

"He's a general, was in charge of a hatchery, guarding some of the wives of his Emperor."

"Why?"

"Apparently the Emperor's young need to be hatched in the world on which they'll live. After laying their clutch, the females were to be shipped home and Kezule was to remain here with the young males and a small group of new females to start a new hatchery for them."

"What kind of general is he?"

"Ground Forces as far as we can gather."

"From that Human world, Keiss, was he?"

"Yes. Keiss," he said. There was no need for her to know more than was necessary.

"What else?"

"We don't know that much about him, Keeza," he said. That's why I picked you for this mission. You've gotten close to a pack leader, you can get close to him."

Her laugh sent a shiver down his spine. "Yeah, sure. He's likely to be really interested in me as a female."

"Several Human females have done what you're about to do, Keeza—spied on the Valtegans by getting close to them sexually. It's up to you how you achieve that closeness, but they are sexually compatible with both the Humans and us."

"You mean up to him," she muttered, watching as Kezule's forked tongue flicked across his claws and fingers, licking off the blood that was seeping onto them from the piece of raw chiddoe in his hands.

"Khaimoe said you did very well at her House," he said gently. "You learned many things with her, not all of them of a sexual nature. If you wish to avoid a physical relationship with him, then use what you've learned."

Abruptly she turned away from the window. "I've seen enough. Let's get this over with. Take me to your mindwarpers. The sooner I'm done with this place, the better."

L'Seuli stood up and went over to the door, waiting for her to join him. "You haven't forgotten that we have to erase all memory of this from your mind before we send you in with him?"

"I haven't forgotten. Just you make damned sure that when it's over, I get my memories back!"

He reached out to take her by the chin, looking into her eyes as he spoke. "You have my word on it, Keeza Lassah. Your memories will be returned to you when this is over." He let her go and palmed the lock.

"I don't want any memories of this," she said hurriedly, indicating the cell on the other side of the viewing screen. "That I want to forget. And the pack time. Can they do that?"

"Yes, if that's what you wish," he said, accompanying her out into the corridor. He took her by the elbow and steered her toward the room opposite. "The telepath who will do this is no ordinary one, no state-provided reprogrammer like you would have faced at the correction facility."

"I'm glad to hear it," she said.

As they entered the medical examination room, the two figures silhouetted against the window broke off their conversation and turned toward them.

"We're ready now, Master Konis, Master Lijou," said L'Seuli, taking Keeza over to the easy chairs.

*   *   *

The room felt empty now that he'd had left for the estate. He'd been angry that someone had persuaded Kusac to ask to become his sword-brother. Whoever it was knew him too well: he couldn't have turned him down flat, not Kusac. He remembered when he'd first seen him. All fierce determination to defend his Leska, yet terrified to the core of his being of what they were, what they might become. Now, he held his estate, and his Clan, on his own merit.

But could a telepath, even if he could fight, make a sword-brother? He stopped the thought there with a self-derisory smile. What was he when it came down to it? Had he made a good sword-brother to Garras? He must have, else Garras wouldn't have stayed with him all those years. Only the need for him to run the family business till his nephew came of age had broken their partnership. Their oath still existed, after a fashion: it was what Garras had used to get him to come out to the *Khalossa*.

There had been no repercussions regarding the damage he'd caused in the temple—no disciplinary action beyond being confined to his quarters under guard until Kusac had arrived. His constant presence, except on his Link days with Carrie, was Lijou and Rhyaz's guarantee that nothing of the sort would happen again.

Now that he was alone again, however fleetingly, he'd

ad time to reflect. He realized now what his fear and anger ad almost cost him. It was time he made amends.

Sighing, he got up and padded over to the drawer unit o fetch a clean robe. As he put it on, he realized that the purple banding of the Priesthood had been added to it by housekeeping. The law required him to always wear purple now that he was a recognized telepath, but at least this way he could follow its spirit if not its letter and keep his identity as a full telepath hidden. Fastening the belt, he left his room and made his way to Lijou's office.

Knocking on the door, he waited. After a moment or two, Yaszho, Lijou's aide, answered, joining him in the corridor.

"It's Brother Tallinu, Master Lijou."

"Five minutes, Yaszho," came Lijou's voice. "I need this finished first."

Yaszho looked apologetically at him before closing the door and heading off on some errand.

"Just remember what you've always said about Kaid. You don't control someone like him; you point him in the right direction and let go," said Kha'Qwa.

"I know, but he has to realize that he's no longer responsible only to himself. He's been outcast for nearly eleven years now."

"Not so. He's been liegeman to Kusac for going on a year."

Lijou made an exasperated noise.

"He has, and now he's training Kusac as a sword-brother," said Kha'Qwa. "If they take the oath, then they're answerable to each other in a way that transcends other oaths."

"Is it enough? What he tried to do to the temple was . . ."

"Utterly reprehensible, but understandable, given the circumstances. I'd say the fact he's here to see you means he recognizes your authority," said Kha'Qwa, getting to her feet.

"We'll see."

"I'm going. Don't keep him waiting any longer," she said, leaning over to rub her cheek against his in an affectionate gesture.

*   *   *

Their Link day over, Kusac had only just left for Stronghold as T'Chebbi arrived home. "Kaid says to start training now," she said, accompanying Carrie into the villa.

"Now? But I've two weeks yet before I go to the Warriors Guild!"

"Plenty time. You be where you were before Challenge by then. Physician Vanna says all right. Told me what you mustn't do."

Carrie stopped to eye her consideringly. "And what if I prefer to wait?"

T'Chebbi shrugged. "Your decision, but Human males at Warrior Guild will get what they expect."

"Just what d'you mean by that?" Carrie demanded, stung by her words.

"They expect a *Terran* female," said T'Chebbi, eyes widening slightly. "Kaid said you go there as you were, you get respect quickly. If not, have to earn it. Take longer."

"Kaid's saying a helluva lot for someone who isn't here," she muttered, angry that he'd chosen an incentive he knew she'd respond to. "Did he happen to say anything else?" She hoped he'd sent her a personal message.

"No, Clan Leader," murmured T'Chebbi, looking away.

Carrie started walking toward the stairs, annoyed that her question had been so obvious to the Sister. "You can cut that out for a start," she replied sharply. "Call me Carrie like everyone else does. What're we practicing?"

"Three things. Sword skills, firearms, and beginning to build stamina. Last one we go more slowly with," said T'Chebbi, remaining at the bottom of the stairs. "You change into practice clothes, then we go to training hall where Garras working with younglings."

It was back to basics, with the mind-numbing but necessary patterns of defense and attack moves using the heavy wooden practice swords. That night, a soak in a hot herbal bath went a long way to easing her aches and pains. Every movement, no matter how small, hurt, and she discovered muscles she'd forgotten existed.

She groaned as she hobbled down to the lower level of the den. "I'd no idea I was so unfit."

"Not unfit. Your body being a mother, not a warrior, is all," T'Chebbi contradicted her.

As she collapsed carefully onto the larger settee, Carrie grimaced up at her. "I hope you aren't just saying that to make me feel better."

"Is true," the Sholan female confirmed, clasping her hands behind her back. "Joints loosen off, muscles become less firm—needs to for you to give birth."

"Hmm. Well, I'm not moving till after third meal when I go up to see Kashini," Carrie said, making herself comfortable with the cushions. Then she sensed T'Chebbi's diffidence and sighed. "What is it you don't want to tell me? What have you got planned for this evening?"

"Brought comp program back from Stronghold. Teaches tactics by simulating battles. You see consequences of decisions. Garras coming over to help us."

"And just when am I going to have time with my daughter?" she demanded. "It's bad enough her father not being here without her seeing very little of me as well!"

T'Chebbi's ears flicked back in embarrassment, then righted themselves. "You must be able to cope alone in field if you get separated from rest of us. Kusac learning same things."

"If I'm separated from Kusac for too long, then we'll both be too ill to do anything!" she countered. "Three days, including our Link day, that's all the safety margin we have, T'Chebbi, then nothing but getting us together will save our lives."

"These skills may help you rejoin him before that happens. Even more important for you than others." Her tone was determined.

Carrie sighed. She was right, but it seemed so unfair that all her time was being taken up this way when she wanted to be with her cub. Yes, she'd been getting a little bored with the inactivity, but to go from that to this so suddenly!

"Very well, but I want half an hour with my daughter after we've eaten."

"Is fine," agreed T'Chebbi, turning to leave.

"T'Chebbi, aren't you staying to eat with me? I thought the idea was you'd be a companion for me as well as a teacher." As the other female hesitated, obviously undecided, Carrie realized what she'd done wrong. "I'd like your company, T'Chebbi. Please join me."

T'Chebbi's mouth opened slightly in a faint smile and, lifting a fold of her heavy woolen robe, she stepped down to the lower level to join her.

* * *

The Sholan officers stood between Kezule and the light, unconsciously shielding him from its glare while they talked quietly. He let his head drop and forced his muscles to relax: the pain induced by tensing them was almost as severe as that caused by their beating. He strained to hear what they were saying, but it proved useless as the language they were speaking was one he didn't know.

His eyes were sore and rimed with matter from exposure to the light they used when questioning him. He flicked his tongue across parched and swollen lips, tasting and smelling his own dried blood. A shudder ran through him. This session had been longer than the others, and he didn't know how much more he could take. It was time to allow them some of the answers he'd prepared against this moment.

Twisting his wrists against the straps that held him to the chair, he tried to ease the pressure of the bands. It achieved nothing. His own struggles notwithstanding, the heat generated by the four of them combined with the brightness of the light in the airless room had made his body swell.

The door opened, drawing his attention from their conversation to the new arrival.

"Refreshments, sirs," said a female voice.

Kezule lifted his head, instantly aware of the presence of the female and the carafe of water. His tongue flicked out, tasting the air to make sure.

"Bring it over to the table," said his inquisitor.

He watched her crossing from the door to the group in front of him. She stopped, waiting till they held out their mugs, then began to pour the liquid into them. He sniffed, tongue flicking out again in the hope of picking up some moisture from the air, but all he tasted was the sweat of the Sholan males and the fear of the female.

"Pity you won't cooperate, General," said his tormentor, turning to look at him as he raised his mug to his mouth. "You could have had some water with us."

Kezule blinked as the light briefly hit his eyes. He missed what caused the commotion, only aware of it as he was suddenly drenched. Splatters of water hit him in the face and across the chest making him gasp at its coldness. Collecting his wits, he flicked his tongue out to capture the rivulets running down his face. The relief was instant, but so was the craving for more. Only after he'd licked up every available drop did he turn his attention to the Sholans.

"You damned clumsy she-jegget!" yelled one of the others as the female scrambled across the floor for the jug.

"Your pardon," she stammered. "It was so dark . . . I couldn't see after outside. I'm sorry."

Her voice ended on a wail as the inquisitor casually drew back his arm and sent her reeling across the room to collide with the wall. Kezule watched her slide, stunned, to the floor.

"Do that again and I'll feed you to the lizard," he said, his voice cold with anger. "Now get out of here. You can clean up later." He turned to look at Kezule. "Would you like that, Kezule? You could vent your anger with me on her. I know how much you like females, and that's the Valtegan way, isn't it?"

Kezule looked back at him, saying nothing. Something wasn't quite right, but he was in no state to make full sense of it now. Later, when this was over, when there were no distractions. He tensed as the male drained his mug, replaced it on the table and advanced on him, tail swaying lazily. As if at a distance, he heard the door closing as the female left.

"Time for us to start again, Kezule," purred his inquisitor.

His head was abruptly hauled against the solid back of the chair by one of the other Sholans. Once more the bright light hit him full in the face. Instinctively, he shut his eyes, trying to blot it out. The suddenness of it sent a shock rushing through his system. He'd let his attention slip and hadn't noticed what the other two were doing.

"Where is your home world?"

He said nothing, tensing in expectation of the blow, not knowing where it would fall. It landed on his right side, over his already bruised ribs. As he doubled over in pain, he clenched his hands, pulling against the restraints, claws gouging the wood as his breath was forced out in a grunt of pain.

"We can keep this up for hours, Kezule," said the officer. "Can you hold out that long? Where's your home world?"

"I don't know," he hissed, trying not to cause himself more pain by gasping for the air he needed. "I was not the commander of starships, only of soldiers on the battlefield. I read land maps, not star maps!" It was true. He'd traveled in state quarters, not on the bridge with the crew. His work had come later, subduing the inhabitants.

A few terse words were exchanged, again in a language he didn't understand.

"Its name, then. If you don't know its location, you surely know its name."

"Kiju'iz," he spat, "for what good it'll do you! Even if it were on your charts, why should you call it that?" Again the truth, but coupled with a lie. It was the name of the world on which he'd hatched, but it was not one of the Four.

"Now we're making some progress," the officer drawled. "Give him a drink."

His head was released and a mug brought to him by the third male—and relief from the light as he stood in front of him. Peering through eyes that were beginning to water again, he stretched his head toward the wide-mouthed cup. It was moved just out of his reach.

He hissed in frustration, his need for water increasing because of its presence. Against reason, he attempted to lean forward, pulling at his restraints in an effort to reach it.

"The location of Kiju'iz, Kezule, or no drink."

He was coming to hate that voice despite his efforts to remain distanced from them. "You want an answer? I give you a lie, then. It's all I got. I didn't command the ships!"

The cup came closer, but only close enough for his tongue to touch the water. Cursing, he began to lap as fast as he could, waiting for it to be snatched away at any moment. It wasn't. When he'd finished, he sat back. "Your name," he said, his voice low with anger as he pulled at the bands. "I want to know the name of my enemy."

"I know your name, Kezule," said the officer, leaning closer for a moment. "That's all that's necessary. Why did you come to Shola?"

It was the same questions time after time, not just today, but all the other times he'd been brought here. He knew them almost by rote now. He'd had plenty of leisure to work out the answers, and now he must give them a few at a time, to prevent them getting tired of his lack of cooperation and resorting to drugs. If they did, he'd have no control over what he said. By appearing to cooperate, he bought himself time.

"You made a start, Kezule, don't stop now. Be a realist and make it easier on yourself. You could earn a few more luxuries, like that book for the reader. Let's face it, you know by the end of the hunt we'll have everything we want from you. It's just a question of time, and we've plenty of that."

Anger raged through him. Not if he could help it! He'd begun assessing his chances for escape from the first. Security was tight now, but if he cooperated, they might grow lax, giving him his opportunity.

Through streaming eyes, he saw the arm raise again. "We need land," he said through clenched teeth. "An empire such as ours has need of resources."

The arm lowered, and the officer moved just enough to block the light a fraction. "What resources?"

"Slaves. Your world will be no loss to us," Kezule hissed, twisting his head to avoid even more of the light's glare. "Your telepaths may have driven us off Shola, but when we return, we'll annihilate you!" He saw the look that passed between his interrogator and the other two. Then he realized. "They've been back, maybe not here, but close." He began to laugh, until the pain in his ribs turned it to a groan of agony. "That's where the reader came from, and the herb!"

"I don't think they'll be back after so long, Kezule. I'll wager they've forgotten all about us."

He heard, for the first time, the note of doubt in the officer's voice. "Our memories don't fade," he wheezed contemptuously, trying not to breathe too deeply. "They're passed down from generation to generation. We can't forget."

There was a short silence during which he managed to recover enough to sit upright again. Every time he took a breath, it felt like his lungs were laced with fire.

"You say a vast empire. How vast would that be? Two worlds?"

Kezule was amused and let it show. It would do no harm for these inferior beings to realize just what they were trying to pit themselves against. "Too many for you and those puny Humans to take on. In my time, there were twelve,

not counting this backwater lump of dirt you call home."
Not strictly true, they'd only had six or seven subjugated
worlds. He'd lost count; it mattered not at all to him. The
chaos the telepaths' treachery had caused might have rendered this world unusable, but it couldn't possibly have
touched the four worlds at the heart of their empire.

"All supported by a slave economy, eh? What did these
slaves do?"

"What they were fit for—menial work," sneered Kezule,
aware that the level of pain he was suffering was rising
beyond his ability to cope—and it was making him incau-
tious. He was tired, deadly tired. He blinked repeatedly,
trying to work the grit from his eyes. The room was beginning to take on a surreal glow.

"We were born to rule. The God chose to be incarnated
in His Emperor—praise be to Him. We are His chosen
kind, all others are dust beneath the throne of the God-
King," he mumbled.

"Get that damned servant. I want more water. I won't
have him passing out on us now!"

There was a minute or two's respite. Then he heard the
door open and close, smelled the Sholan female approaching with the water.

His head was pulled back, and this time the cup was put
to his mouth. He was so exhausted he could barely drink,
so much of it dribbled down his chin onto his already
soaked coverall.

"Enough," said the officer, but the cup remained for a
few moments more. "I said enough! Gods, they don't
choose you for intelligence, do they?"

Through partly open eyes, Kezule watched him thrust
the female aside. "You don't have much time for females
either, Kezule, do you? What are they like, your females?
Do you keep them in their place? If you ask me, letting
them out of the home was the biggest mistake we made."

Confused, Kezule blinked owlishly at the interrogator as
he moved in front of the light again. He didn't understand
this. The Sholan commander was a female. What mind
games was he now playing?

"Do yours try to run things if you don't keep then under
control? Is that why you dislike them? Pity we need them
at all, if you ask me. Don't you agree?"

"I guarded several of the Emperor's wives on Shola,"

zule said, trying to keep his thoughts straight. "My sa-
d trust, to see all the female young were killed. Only
les were to live."

'You killed the daughters, eh? Why was that? He got
ough females, then, this God-King of yours?"

'Daughters could be taken, impregnated by other males
set up rivals," he mumbled. Why the interest in females
of a sudden? "Daughters given only to those worthy.
y wife is one."

"Your wife?" He could hear the surprise in the officer's
ice. "There was no mention of a wife when you came
us."

"Sent her off with the other wives."

"To look after your family. Commendable, General."

Kezule found this strangely amusing. A laugh escaped
n, quickly turned to a prolonged hiss of agony. "Ours
ly lay eggs and eat—anything that moves. That's why
tchery needs guards, to save the young." Talking was
coming an effort that he couldn't sustain much longer.

"That's why you use the females of other species, is it?
ey aren't as—hungry?"

This wasn't going as he'd planned, he thought through
e haze of pain. How had he gotten sidetracked into this?
e wanted to feed them false information, make them be-
ve what he said, so he'd make them vulnerable by trust-
g him. He peered through half-open eyes at the male in
ont of him. His outline was vague and indistinct now.

"Is that why you use other females? Because only the
osen ones get mates?"

"Yes. No. Soldiers don't have females, they get drones.
emale slaves are given as rewards."

"Why didn't your kind come back to Shola, Kezule? You
emed to like our people, you took some as hostages."

"Pets. Could mind-read the other slaves. Helped control
em. Females useless—they fight too much for amusing
oops. Used others."

"I didn't ask that, I asked why you thought they didn't
ome back."

He sat there, his silence lengthening until his head was
ocked with an open-handed blow. Fresh pain burned his
eek, and as his head hit the back of the chair, it began to
ound. He closed his eyes, tasting blood in his mouth again.

"Too much trouble with telepaths," he mumbled. "W
grow laalquoi other worlds, don't need this one."

"Laalquoi. What's that?"

"Herb. Use it to honor Emperor." Something solid no
A question he had anticipated. "When eat, use it."

"We must stop now, Brother." A new voice, one of t
other officers. An expletive from the interrogator.

"Take him back to his room. She can clean him up.
he snapped.

He passed out as he felt the restraints round his wris
and ankles tighten before they were released.

*   *   *

Until yesterday, Brynne had managed to avoid the co
that had affected most of the estate. Now, however, he w
beginning to feel decidedly under the weather. A call
warn Ross Derwent had not put him off as he'd hope
Instead, he'd insisted he come over.

"I'm incredibly resistant to colds and flu," he'd said. "M
lessons are important if you want to progress. You los
enough time as it is."

Brynne sighed. "I'll be over within an hour, Ross."

So, an hour later, he was waiting to be admitted to Ros
rooms at the Accommodation Guildhouse in Valsgarth.

"You must have smelled the coffee," Ross said, openin
the door to him.

Nodding a brief greeting, Brynne followed him into th
small lounge, sitting down in his accustomed seat on th
settee.

While Ross fetched him a drink from the kitchen, Brynn
looked round the room. Nearly every time he visited, Ros
had acquired some new knickknack from his wandering
around the Sholan countryside. Often he accompanied hin
but he hadn't been over during the midwinter festivals, s
Ross had been left to his own devices.

Apart from Jack's quarters in the medical unit, Ross
rooms had the least Sholan influence of any he'd seer
among the Human settlers. It was like a slice of transporte
Earth culture. Jack's apartment had become more Shola
since his Companion had moved in to live with him, bu
Ross had remained true to his own heritage, whateve
that was.

Partially completed projects covered the desk and the

fee table in front of him, a mute testament not only to
ss' inquiring mind, but his butterfly disposition. He'd
it on one idea for a month or two, then when something
ghter came along, he'd be off on that trail. It made him
erson full of information—but only to a certain level.

Today, maps lay scattered everywhere. Brynne pulled the
rest across to him. Turning it, he recognized the Dzahai
untains and the surrounding area. Ross had highlighted
onghold and Vartra's Retreat, and from both of them
l ruled lines down to the Kysubi Plains.

"Ley lines," said Ross, returning with a mug which he
ded to Brynne. "See how they connect Stronghold and
Retreat?"

"Yes," he said dubiously. "You know my opinion on ley
es, Ross. Just because they exist on Earth doesn't mean
y exist here."

"Oh, ye of little faith," he chided gently. "I found them,
erefore they must exist. That's what the other lines are.
ey meet in the Kysubi Plains, and unless I'm mistaken,
where the archaeologists are uncovering an ancient city.
hat do you bet that they find a temple there?"

"Bit of a foregone conclusion," said Brynne, wrapping
hands around the mug. It was cold outside, but he
dn't realized how cold. His fingers felt stiff and frozen.
least the heat from the mug was helping. "Most major
es have at least one temple in them."

"You're right," Ross nodded, "but I fully expect this to
a temple to Vartra." His tone was one of pride.

Brynne frowned as he looked at his self-appointed tutor.
inning, shoulder-length hair framed a face past its middle
ars, one wrinkled and browned by sun and wind alike.
le blue eyes set on either side of a long, aristocratic nose
garded him expectantly.

"It must be this cold fogging my brain," Brynne said,
ut if all this earth energy you keep on talking about is
ere, how come it's linked to Vartra and not Ghyakulla,
eir Green Goddess? Surely Vartra's an improbable
anet deity."

"On the face of it, perhaps, but He is Ghyakulla's Con-
rt. What should be more natural than that here the planet
ould be masculine instead of feminine?"

"I think you're using a reverse logic. You've found a
nnection, so you want it to work. Vartra, whatever leg-

ends He may have been blended into, is credited with cre
ing the Shola that exists now, saving His world from t
ravages of the Cataclysm. Hardly the equivalent of Eart
Mother Goddess, the source of all life and energy. He
did you—find—the ley lines anyway?" He took a sip of
drink, wishing that he'd stayed at home on the estate. I
wasn't up to this type of discussion. He needed all his w
about him when talking to Ross, otherwise he found hi
self being railroaded into a variety of mad schemes a
expeditions.

"I dowsed for them on the map."

"Dowsed? Using what?" He knew about dowsin
They'd used it on Earth in the Cassandra Project.

"My dowsing crystal of course."

"Ross, I hardly think using a piece of Earth quartz on
Sholan map is going to give you any kind of accurate r
sult." Was it him, or was Ross becoming more fanatical
his outlook these days?

"You'll see, Brynne. I intend that we should go out the
today. I want you to take me to Stronghold. I know it's
source of natural power, and I want to have the opportuni
to feel it for myself. If it keeps you happy, I can use n
dowsing crystal there to prove that it works on Shola."

"Not today, Ross," said Brynne, shaking his head ar
holding his mug closer. "In fact, not at all. I really shouldn
have come out. I just hope you don't catch this bug I'v
got."

He saw Ross' eyes narrow briefly in anger, then h
reached out and put his hand to Brynne's forehea
"You're burning up," he said. "Today is definitely of
you've got a fever." He got to his feet. "Let me go and ge
you something for it. In an hour or two, you'll be feeling
lot better. You can stay here till you're over it."

As shivers began to shake through him, Brynne looke
up. The room was becoming a little blurred. "I can't sta
Ross. I need to go back to the estate. If I'm down with
fever, then Vanna will be suffering my symptoms."

"She'll be fine, Brynne," said Ross from the doorwa
into his kitchen. "You told me there's Dr. Reynolds ov
there. If she does take ill, and I doubt she will, he can se
to her."

"You don't understand," he said, putting the mug dow
and pushing himself up to his feet. "It isn't what you think

real. We *are* linked. What affects me, affects her. She
n't actually be ill, just suffering my symptoms, but they
:d to know that!" He staggered slightly as the room
am around him, then Ross' hand was there to steady
n. "At least call her."

'You aren't going anywhere, my lad," he said, "except
1."

Despite what he'd been told, Ross did not call Vanna
1 was totally unprepared for the arrival on his doorstep
ortly afterward, of a Sholan female obviously on the
int of collapse.

'Brynne" she said succinctly. "I want Brynne." Her legs
gan to buckle under her, and she fell forward against
n.

Despite his surprise, Ross managed to catch hold of her
d help her into the apartment. He tried to steer her
ward a chair, but she would have none of it.

"Brynne," she insisted with a ferocity that almost
unted even him.

"Brynne's not well, my dear," he said gently, trying again
lead her to the chair. "And if I may say so, you're none
o well either. You should have stayed at home. He's in
fe hands here."

Her hand gripped his arm, claws penetrating through his
eater to dig into his flesh. "Take me to him," she or-
red, ears lying sideways in anger at being ignored.

She watched Derwent wince as he began to lead her to
e bedroom. "This really isn't necessary," he began, but
e cut him short with a gesture as he opened the door.

Brynne lay in the bed, his face flushed with fever, tossing
d turning in a tangle of sheets and blankets.

Vanna let go of Derwent and stumbled over to her
:ska, sitting down beside him and grasping one of his
nds. Despite his attempts to pull away from her, she hung
1. Gradually he began to grow less restless and as he
lled, his eyes flickered. Blinking away the sweat, he
oked up at her.

"Vanna," he said, his hand tightening briefly on hers. "It
ime on suddenly, I didn't have time to get home. Did
oss send for you? I told him you needed to know. Sorry.
tried to block it."

"You shouldn't have, it only made it worse for us both,"

she said, reaching out to push the damp curly hair ba
from his face. "Let the block go, I can cope. If you'd spe
more time at the estate learning how to use your Tale
instead of spending it here, you'd have picked up a fe
tricks, too."

"Don't scold, Vanna," Brynne said, letting his ey
close again.

"I'm not," she said gently, touching his neck. "You'
just not too good at blocking. You've caused us Link dep
vation. How d'you feel now?"

"Better without the nausea and stomach pains," he a
mitted, "but apart from that, like death warmed over."

"You've caught that cold we all had a few weeks ag
Because you came out, you've probably got a seconda
infection on top of it. You should have stayed home whe
you knew you were ill."

"I'm afraid it was I who suggested he come," said Ros
coming into the room and sitting in the easy chair. "
thought it was just a cold. You're his Leska, aren't you?

Vanna stared at him angrily. "Why didn't you conta
me as Brynne asked, Mr. Derwent?"

"I would have, had he grown worse, but I'm quite cap
ble of nursing someone with a mild fever, Dr. Vanna."

"Physician Kyjishi." Her voice was cold. "Since he
here, I'd prefer not to move him till the fever's broken
As she spoke, she gently probed round the edges of Ros
mind. That he resented not only her presence but her in
fluence over someone he considered his pupil, was obviou
but beneath that was a shield as strong as any that Kusa
and Carrie could use. Reluctantly, she gave up.

"Of course. Stay as long as you need," said Ross. "It
obvious your presence is helping him. It seems I underest
mated your dependency on each other."

"Kept trying to tell you," muttered Brynne, beginning t
move fretfully again.

Hush, sent Vanna. It was strange seeing him as the vu
nerable one for the first time.

Brynne tried to laugh, ending on a coughing fit. *Rathe
a reversal of roles, don't you think? Ironic.*

I said hush, she repeated, tightening her hand roun
his again.

"I'm glad you came, actually," said Ross abruptly, un
aware of their mental conversation. "The fever I can dea

with, as I said, but the other symptoms . . . I thought it was some kind of allergy."

"Nothing but our being together would have helped," said Vanna, gently releasing Brynne and getting up. "It's part of the price of being Leskas. I have to ask one more favor. I didn't have a chance to collect my medikit before I left. Can I use your comm to ask someone from the estate to bring it over to me?"

"By all means. It's in the lounge on the desk."

"Thank you," she said stiffly. She didn't like the male, never had, and it was mutual.

"You shouldn't be so concerned. It's only a fever," said Ross.

"You're applying Human rules to him," she said tersely. "He's altered. He's part Sholan now, no longer just Human. Human medical facts don't apply, only our own mixed Leska ones matter."

"I don't see how . . ."

"That's your problem, not mine," she said with finality. "I'm a fully qualified medical doctor. What's your field of expertise? Not medicine, that's for sure. I don't need amateurs telling me what to do!" With that, she stalked past him into the lounge.

When Carrie arrived, Vanna had bullied Ross into helping her strip all the blankets off Brynne and change the bed. Though she couldn't gauge his temperature accurately without her equipment, she knew it was high enough to cause concern. He was also steadfastly refusing to drink, becoming more agitated as she tried to persuade him. She gave up after the mug was batted across the room, spilling the water onto the carpet.

Ross left her sponging Brynne down with cold water while he went to open the door. His surprise at finding a Human standing there was evident.

"Mr. Derwent? I'm Carrie Aldatan, Vanna's friend." She saw his eyes flick behind her to where T'Chebbi stood in her black Brotherhood robe. "This is Sister T'Chebbi Kymai."

"Come in," he said, standing back and holding the door open for them.

"I'll remain in the main room, Clan Leader," said T'Chebbi, handing her the medikit.

Carrie nodded and followed Ross through to the bedroom.

"You shouldn't have brought it by yourself," Vanna said, relief nonetheless evident in the set of her ears. She took the proffered case.

"I didn't, I brought T'Chebbi with me. It's time I started going out and about again, Vanna."

Vanna took out the sampling unit and fitted it on Brynne's forearm, latching it closed again.

"I suppose so, but Kusac will kill me if anything happens to you."

"What could happen? I've T'Chebbi with me. Well, what's it say?" she asked impatiently.

"Give me a moment," Vanna said, punching the keypad on the side of the unit. "Ah, here we are. Surprise, surprise, it's the same infection we all had. Nothing else, thankfully, so Brynne must just have caught a chill on top of it. His electrolyte balance is off, but I expected that. He won't drink. I'm going to need a drip to rehydrate him."

"He looks very feverish. He's not going to be as ill as Kaid was, is he?" Carrie asked, eyeing Brynne, who was muttering in his sleep.

"I shouldn't think so. I am reading a foreign substance in his bloodstream, though. It's only a trace. I'll take a sample to analyze later."

"How about you?"

"Surviving. I've got a splitting headache with the effort of blocking his symptoms. I should have brought my own damper," she said with an embarrassed grin as she took the blood sample vial out of the diagnostic unit.

"I can lend you mine," said Carrie, reaching for the small device attached to her wrist unit.

"No," said Vanna, putting her hand out to stop her friend. "It's set for you and Kusac, not us. Thank you for the thought, though. If T'Chebbi wouldn't mind, I need a rehydration unit from the center. Jack can give it to her, and if she could pick up my damper from the house . . .?"

"Sure. Just tell T'Chebbi what you want."

"I think the substance you're detecting could be the tea I gave Brynne," interrupted Ross. "It contains herbs from Earth. You'll find it pretty near impossible to analyze, I'm afraid."

"You'd be surprised what we can analyze," said Vanna, going past him into the lounge to speak to T'Chebbi.

Carrie looked over at where Ross stood by the door. "You've been teaching Brynne, haven't you? What's your field?"

Ross smiled. "I cover a lot of fields, my dear," he said gently. "My skills go back to the earliest times."

"You work alone, then."

"Most of what I do is listen to people with troubles and try to guide them back onto the right path. My work is most unglamorous."

Carrie gave him a long look. "It'll be interesting to see what Brynne has learned."

"I only take one pupil at a time, I'm afraid," he said, his tone mildly apologetic.

"Not when you take on one of a Leska pair," she said. "Our minds exist together. Whether or not you like it, because of her shared consciousness with Brynne, Vanna is also your pupil."

Carrie saw from Ross' face that he hadn't considered that possibility. It pleased her to be able to wrong-foot him: He was so damned smug! "You should have lived on Shola for a while before deciding to take on one of the Leska telepaths as a pupil."

"Brynne approached me," he murmured.

"Common sense should have told you to wait. I've a pretty shrewd idea of what you are, so I'll only warn you once. Study Vanna's report on the mixed Leska pairings, because she's the leading medical expert on us. What one experiences, so does the other. When one is in pain, so is the other: when one dies, we both die. It's the price we pay for what we share. Tread carefully, Ross Derwent, and make sure no harm comes to Brynne, or through him to Vanna, lest you have me to answer to. She's very dear to me—and my life-mate."

"Strong words, young lady, but on whose authority do you issue them?" he asked with frozen politeness.

"My own, as their Clan Leader, and as an En'Shalla Priest," she said. "Don't make the mistake of thinking of me as just a Terran woman. I'm not."

T'Chebbi made her presence felt with a polite cough. Her robe was open, displaying the short sword she always wore. At her left hip, her hand rested negligently on the butt of her energy pistol.

"Clan Leader, are you sure you can spare me? Maylgu is downstairs in the lobby. She could go."

Carrie hesitated. This was a time for gestures, ones that wouldn't be lost on Ross. "Yes, ask Maylgu to go. You remain with me, T'Chebbi."

The Sister nodded once, then turned and walked crisply from the room as Vanna returned.

Carrie caught Ross Derwent's gaze with hers, narrowing them to accentuate the vertical pupil which she alone of the Human mixed Leskas had.

"T'Chebbi is one of my Clan, too, Mr. Derwent," she said, her English suddenly accentuated by a low, Sholan accent. "We have a great many of the Brotherhood of Vartra among our number."

Brynne broke the tension by beginning to mutter and thrash around in the bed. Vanna bent over him, crooning gently and murmuring soothing words as she stroked his cheeks, pushing the dark sweat-soaked tendrils of long hair back from his face. Slowly he began to settle again.

"Carrie, you should go home now," said her friend. "I know you've got other things to see to. Brynne will be fine as soon as I get the right medication."

Are you sure? I don't like leaving you here without a guard.

I'll be fine. You made your point about us not being folk to take lightly, replied Vanna.

Did I lean too hard?

No, I don't think so. He's made no effort to understand us at all. It's time he realized there is a higher authority than his own judgment to answer to. Now, go home. We'll be fine, honestly.

Where is your guard? How did you come to be here without Nyash or Lasad?

I didn't tell them I was coming.

I'll send one of them out to you when I get back. Carrie got to her feet. "Keep in touch, Vanna. Send if you need anything."

"I will."

"Good-bye, Mr. Derwent," she said.

When she'd gone, Ross disappeared, returning a few minutes later with a cup of coffee.

"Why don't you sit in the chair and take a break for a few minutes? Brynne is sleeping for now," he said solicitously. "I'll watch him till your attendant returns."

"That's kind of you," she said, pushing herself up from the bed. "I was up late with our cub last night."

"Your cub?" he asked as she moved over to the chair and settled herself.

"Brynne's and mine. He must have told you. If he didn't, it was on all the vidcasts; so was Carrie's." She took a large mouthful of her drink.

"I remember something about a half-Sholan child," he said, handing her the mug. "So the young lady who was here chose to give up her humanity just to bear her Sholan lover's children? I find it hard to understand the reasoning behind such a sacrifice."

"But it's all right for me to give up my Sholanness to bear a Human's cub, is it?" she asked with a low growl. "I'd be careful what you say, Mr. Derwent. You might find yourself accused of prejudice. And by the way, Carrie's married to Kusac Aldatan."

"If my words caused offense, do forgive me," he said, sitting down beside Brynne. "It wasn't intended that way."

Vanna gave a low, warning growl.

"If you were up all night then you definitely need a rest," Ross said, his voice now soothing, almost hypnotic. "It'll refresh you. I'll wake you if there's any change in Brynne."

Vanna felt herself beginning to relax at last.

When Maylgu returned, she buzzed the door to Derwent's apartment. Getting no reply, she tried again. After another two minutes, she headed downstairs for the public comm and contacted Carrie at the villa. Within fifteen minutes, she was standing outside the door with Garras, Carrie, and the Accommodation supervisor.

"This is most irregular," the supervisor was saying as she took the master key to the locking mechanism. "He's a good tenant, never any bother, not like some."

"Just open the door," said Carrie impatiently as she reached mentally for her friend. There was no change. It felt as if Vanna were deeply asleep. She needed to touch her to find out more. As for Brynne, his mind was protected by a barrier like the one she'd felt Derwent using.

Then the door was open, and she was pushing the supervisor aside.

"Carrie, let me go first," said Garras, taking hold of her arm and pulling her back.

The lounge was empty, and she headed straight for the bedroom, Garras lunged after her again but this time she pulled free. Vanna was sprawled, deeply asleep, in the easy chair. Stopping only long enough to confirm that she was neither harmed nor bound, Carrie turned her attention to Brynne, and to Derwent, who was sitting beyond him.

"Check Vanna thoroughly," Carrie said to Maylgu. "Garras, keep an eye on Derwent."

The latter, sitting at the other side of the bed, was just beginning to stir from the trancelike state he'd been in when they'd entered.

"I'll see to Brynne," said Carrie. A touch to his forehead confirmed what his color had already told her; his skin was cool and he was sleeping quietly.

"I should have expected you to come back," Derwent said ruefully, as he scrubbed at his face with his hands.

She watched as his color gradually returned and the lines of tiredness began to ease. Probing at the edges of the Terran's mind, Carrie hoped that while he was in this condition, she could read something of what he'd been doing. The barrier was still there, and as firm as ever despite his exhaustion.

"Vanna's asleep, Garras," said Maylgu, "but it's not natural. I'd say drug induced."

Garras began to growl deep in his throat.

"Wait," said Carrie, turning round to look at the two males. "I want to know what the hell you've been doing, Ross. I thought I made it clear you were to leave them alone."

"They're both fine," he said. "The herbs I gave Brynne earlier were only part of the treatment. I needed to finish it with a little healing of my own before your friend's drugs came. As for Vanna, I gave her a mild sleeping draught, that's all. She'll wake shortly. She needed the rest anyway."

"How dare you use your homemade medicines on my friends! You had no right to deny Brynne proper medical attention, especially when it was at the hands of his Leska! And as for drugging Vanna . . ."

"You're no healer," said Garras, his voice deep and

ngry. "If you were, the Telepath Guild wouldn't have al-
owed you off their premises."

"No, I'm not a healer," he admitted. "At least, not of
ving people. I deal more with the world of nature and the
ouls of the departed."

Garras let out an exclamation of disbelief.

"Brynne wasn't about to die," Derwent added hastily.
However, I do have an extensive knowledge of herbal
medicines. As I said, I'd given him something to break the
ever, and I couldn't allow your physician's drugs to inter-
ere with it. There could have been complications."

"And the healing?" demanded Carrie.

Derwent shrugged. "I linked to his mind and boosted his
wn natural healing ability, that's all. It's worked, as you
an see."

"That has nothing to do with the matter," Garras
rowled. "It's an offense for you to do what you've done.
The unlicensed use of telepathy is strictly against all Guild
aws. I'm personally reporting you not only to the Telepath
Guild, but to the All-Guilds Council."

"I think you're overreacting. Brynne is on the mend, and
us he's my pupil, I have the right to treat him when he
consents to it. What can your authorities do to me anyway?
'm a Terran, not subject to your laws. I'm sure the head
of the Terran contingent will support me."

"You live in Valsgarth, outside the Guild where the Terrans operate, refusing to have anything to do with either
group," said Carrie. "They won't protect you, especially
against us. No one has the right to teach skills except
through the Guild system. You're in direct violation of the
treaty that brought you here. You could be imprisoned or
deported back to Earth."

"I don't think so, no matter what your connections are,"
said Ross. "My basic rights of freedom are the same here
as on Earth, even under Sholan laws. All I did was give
him a traditional herbal tea. Hardly a hanging offense, my
dear," he smiled.

"Don't act the innocent with me. We both know you've
done more than that. You've altered Brynne's mind," said
Carrie. "Although he's asleep, there's too much brain activity in an area not usually used by us. It's like extra connections have been made."

"Brynne is fine, my dear," said Ross, his voice full of

calm confidence. "You don't need to concern yourse
with that."

"Don't," she said coldly, pushing his mind away from
hers. "I'm not susceptible to hypnotic or psychic suggestion
You've got no ethics at all, have you? Nothing matters bu
achieving what you want."

Ross blinked, a surprised look coming over his face. "I'n
sure I don't know what you mean," he murmured.

"You're so damned confident and arrogant, aren't you'
You think you can do what you want, ride roughshod ove
other peoples' rights and beliefs, then claim you were onl
exercising your own civil rights! I've read about you peopl
and your New Era movement. You don't respect the Sho
lan culture or any other, so why should you assume it wi
protect you? It only protects its own citizens, and, Mr. Ros
Derwent, you aren't an Alliance citizen!"

"Are you?" he countered. "Will they listen to you? A
Human woman? I don't think so."

"Yes, Mr. Derwent, they will," said Garras, activating hi
wrist comm. "Keiss is a junior member of the Alliance, and
that gives Carrie citizenship. However, she's also the life-
mate of a Sholan, and co-leader of a Sholan clan in he
own right."

Ross dived forward in an effort to stop Garras using his
comm, but was easily pushed aside by the larger male.

"Ni'Zulhu, I want that backup now," Garras said into
the unit, grabbing Ross by the neck of his sweater with his
free hand.

"Affirmed," came the quiet response.

Ross stumbled against the edge of the bed and as he
righted himself, turned angrily on Garras, trying to pull free.

"You've no right to . . ." he began, stopping only when
he found Maylgu grasping him from behind by both arms
and drawing him into the center of the room.

"Keep a hold on him, Maylgu," Garras ordered. "We're
taking him back with us. Master Konis can decide what to
do with him; it's his department. Get him out of my sight
before I'm tempted to make this personal," he added.

"What's all the row?" asked a sleepy voice as Vanna
yawned and stretched.

"Are you all right?" asked Garras, going instantly to her
side. "Derwent drugged you so he could work on Brynne."

"What?" Instantly awake, she sat up, peering past him

t her sleeping Leska. "He feels all right," she said. "His
ever—has it gone?"

"It has. You know that corner of his mind that you were
omplaining about before?" asked Carrie. "Well, I can
ense what you meant now. Derwent's been messing with
is mind in some way."

"I knew he'd done something to him! Just wait till I get
my hands on . . ." She launched herself out of the chair
but was brought up short by Garras wrapping both arms
round her waist and hanging onto her.

"No. We're taking him to the Clan Lord. He'll be dealt
with, Vanna, and in such a way that he'll wish he'd never
come to Shola. We're waiting for Ni'Zulhu's folk to arrive,
and then we're going home. Why don't you search that
kitchen of his for the herbs he used?"

She nodded reluctantly and Garras released her. As she
walked past Derwent, he was treated to a full display of an
enraged hissing and growling Sholan, pelt bushed out till
even she looked enormous.

Carrie sat back after straining forward to watch her display and grinned at Garras. "Impressive, isn't she?"

"Always. How's Brynne, really?" His nose creased in
concern.

"Superficially, it's as I said. The fever's broken, so he's
past the worst. As for what's happened to his mind, I can't
tell. Vanna's all right, that's the main thing, so whatever it
is can't be too dangerous yet. We'll need a medical telepath
to figure out what, I'm afraid, unless Derwent can be made
to tell us. The penalty for what he's done is to have the
areas of his brain that control his psychic abilities
destroyed."

Garras' eyes widened in surprise.

"That's why Kusac had to face the hearing on the *Khalossa* because of me."

"No wonder you were both so concerned," he murmured. "Well, it's no more than Derwent deserves from
what Vanna's told me. As well as what he's done to
Brynne, he was trying to convince the younglings at the
Guild that using their Talent involved a religious
commitment."

"Fool," said Carrie as the door chime went. "Ni'Zulhu
already?"

"They were waiting in the commercial vehicle park. You

get the door while I get Brynne," he said, waiting for her
to move aside before pulling back the covers and carefull
scooping the still sleeping Human up into his arms.

Carrie snatched a blanket from the end of the bed and
spread it over Brynne's still form.

* * *

Spring had come suddenly to this mountain region of
Jalna. One night they lay trying to sleep as the wind howled
and gusted round their tower, the next day, blue skies and
sunlight heralded the beginning of the thaw.

Jo and Zashou threw the shutters wide open, letting in
the warm air to freshen all three of their chambers. From
the courtyard down below, the voices of the townsfolk setting up their weekly market were happier and lighter, antic-
ipating the arrival in a few days of the first of the spring
caravans from the valley.

Rezac paced in front of the window, tail swaying angrily
from side to side. Not for him the woolen robes that the
Human males wore; they restricted his movements, making
him even more irritated than his continued captivity was
doing. He preferred to use a shirt as a tunic. Zashou, too,
had refused the female clothing sent for her, wearing instead the robe that Rezac refused.

Through the window came the sound of angry, raised
voices and the clash of metal on metal. Rezac was first to
the window, Kris and Davies jostling with him to see what
was happening below.

"What is it?" demanded Jo, hovering just behind the
males. "What's going on?"

"Looks like one of the soldiers has turned on some stall
holders," said Kris. "Three guards have gone to help, and
they're trying to subdue him."

There was a dull thump, audible even as high up as they
were, then more angry, raised voices.

"One of the villagers just clocked the soldier from behind
with a cooking pot," said Davies. "He's being trussed up
like a Sunday turkey now. That's a hell of a lot of rope for
one man. Killian's there," he added as the Lord's voice
drifted up to them.

"What's he saying? I can't hear him properly," she demanded, trying to push them aside in an effort to see.

"He's doubling the guard, that's all."

"Will you look at him!" said Kris, pointing. "What the hell kind of outfit is that?"

Jo managed to push Davies aside and clung to the stone window ledge, peering over it to see what was happening.

The person Kris had been alluding to was, indeed, a sight to see. Dressed in a hooded robe of the deepest blue, he was bent over the prone body of the bound guard.

"He's not one of their priests," she said. "Dye that color's expensive, so he's someone of major importance. Look at the people around him, how they're reacting to his presence."

"There isn't anyone near him," said Rezac.

"Precisely," she said. "They're terrified of him. What's he doing to the captive? Oh, I see. He's made a mark on his forehead. Is he a senior priest?"

"I thought all their priests dressed in brown," said Kris. "The one that came with Killian the other day did."

"Perhaps a higher rank, or a different order," she said thoughtfully, watching as the man stepped back and the unconscious soldier was hauled off into the castle.

"I get the feeling they were expecting this."

"Don't be ridiculous," said Rezac. "How could they anticipate something like this?"

"We were told the Jalnians were a violent people, so violent that none of the species who trade here want them allowed into space," said Jo. "We've never witnessed anything to substantiate this allegation—till now. Perhaps this is what they were talking about."

"One incident isn't enough to base an assumption like that on," said Kris, turning away.

"I agree, but could their violence be seasonal? We arrived at the end of a late winter. Now it's spring."

"Why should it be seasonal?" asked Rezac, leaving the window to take a seat at the worktable.

"Spring is the mating season on most worlds," said Jo. "Maybe it's something to do with that."

"Do your people become violent in the mating season?" asked Rezac curiously. "Ours don't. Our females have personal seasons, but they aren't tied into the weather cycles of Shola."

Jo flushed slightly. Rezac had been taking an interest in Human customs lately and had been making a point of asking her for information.

"No," was her short reply.

"They have a cycle that matches that of the Earth's moon," said Davies, taking sole control of the window now that the others were gone. "But I don't know how that's affected them either on Shola or here, given the moon doesn't have a twenty-eight-day orbit on either world."

"This is getting a little too personal, fellas," said Jo in a tone that effectively stopped the conversation. "We were talking about the Jalnians. Could they have violent episodes caused by a reaction to wind-borne pollen?"

"It hasn't been thawing long enough for that," said Kris, picking up the cables he was working on. "I'd say we have to wait and see if it happens again. I'd like to know who the chap in that blue robe was, though."

Jo settled herself at the main table where she continued sorting and dismantling components from damaged boards.

The sound of footsteps on the stairs a few minutes later made them all look toward the door.

"Killian and one other," said Rezac.

Jo found his abilities uncanny. He had a knack for correctly telling them how many people were approaching their door before they arrived. He said he didn't fully trust his psychic senses, but for all that, he was seldom wrong and his mind was always on the alert.

The guard on duty outside opened the door and stepped inside, checking the room before confirming it was safe for his Lord to enter. A younger man, somewhere in his early twenties, followed Killian inside.

"How goes the work today?" demanded the Lord, striding over to the table to examine what they were doing. "What're these?" He gestured at several panels connected to each other by thick wires.

"Don't touch," said Kris hurriedly, putting a hand out to block Killian's inquisitive finger. "These'll be the units that will enable us to control the weapon. This laser wasn't designed to be used independently, it was supposed to be an integral part of a scouter. We have to adapt everything, including the power it uses."

"What powers these?"

"The same battery that'll power the laser," said Davies, pointing to a large cylindrical container stored under their worktable.

Killian shook his head, obviously no wiser. "These are

matters for the priests," he said, "not for the likes of me. I'm a soldier, fighting's been my life. You told me that his . . . laser . . . is downstairs in the guarded chamber. When will you be working on that?"

"Until we get these units made, we can't begin to work on the actual laser," said Rezac, looking up from where he was painstakingly attempting to mount some of the smaller components onto a board. "We've told you there are many weeks of work to be done before we can give you your weapon. We're just grateful their tech level is so primitive."

The younger man, meanwhile, had edged closer to the other table until he was standing beside Jo, looking at what she was doing.

"You're taking this apart," he said, his tone one of suspicion.

She looked up at him. Dark, penetrating eyes bored into hers, demanding without words to know what she was doing. Instinctively she glanced over to Killian, then back to him. There was a resemblance in the square shape of the jawline and the set of the eyes.

"Yes, I am," she said, putting down the tweezerlike tool she'd been using. "These panels are too damaged to use, so I'm taking off the sound components. They'll be checked to see they're working, then we can use them to build the control panels we need."

He leaned closer, his plaited scalp lock falling forward across his face. He brushed it behind his ear, then reached out to pick up one of the small gray components.

"They have script on them," he said, turning it round to examine it from every angle. "Symbols such as priests and mages use."

"It identifies what the piece does."

"It looks like a stone. How can this do anything?" he asked, turning the component over between his fingers. Light glinted off the tiny locating pegs on its base.

"We pass an electrical current through it."

He placed it back on the table. "Our priests and mages know of electricity," he said. "The power of the Storm God, they say."

"Um. Yes. Well, I wouldn't know," she said, at a loss for a reply.

This time he reached for a panel that was splintered and

broken. "How do you get the pieces off? They look to be one with this plate."

"They just pull out."

"Taradain," called Killian.

"Coming, Father," he replied, putting the panel back down. "I'll return tomorrow so you can tell me more about this," he said before turning to leave. "They should dine with us tonight, Father," he said. "Belamor wanted to speak with them: he could do so at dinner."

"I told you, I don't want word getting around that we have off-worlders here," said Killian, his tone one of censure.

"All but the furred one could pass as Jalnians," said Taradain, joining him at the doorway.

Killian looked round the room. "Where is the other?" he demanded.

"She's feeling unwell," said Kris. "She's lying down."

Killian gestured to his son to go and check. As he made for the bedroom door, Rezac rose to his feet with a growl of anger.

Jo watched Kris clamp his hand firmly on the Sholan's arm. *No! He's only checking that she's there. He won't touch her.*

She could feel him primed for an explosion if he picked up the slightest distress from his Leska. His tail was rigid and beginning to bush out as his low, ominous growl continued.

Taradain did no more than open the door and glance within before shutting it again. "She's there," he confirmed.

Slowly Rezac began to relax and as he did, Jo sensed what Zashou had been talking about when she said his attitude to life was confrontational. To be prepared for trouble was one thing, to expect it all the time was to live on a razor's edge. The sooner they escaped from here and returned Rezac and Zashou to Shola, the better. They'd lived for too long without the normal securities of life.

"Is she sick?" demanded Killian. "If she needs medicines, I can send my apothecary to you."

"She'll be fine," said Jo. "It's the lack of fresh air, that's all. We need to get out now the thaw's begun." She looked hopefully at Killian, trying not to push her suggestion mentally. "The Sholans particularly. They aren't used to remaining indoors for long periods of time."

"If you'd made more progress, then you'd be working

from the chamber where this *laser* is stored," Killian replied, waiting for his son to precede him from the room. "There is plenty of fresh air there."

As the door closed behind them, Kris let out a sigh of relief.

"Good try," said Davies. "It might work, you never know. Getting him to let Rezac and Zashou out into the fresh air will be difficult, they're too obviously alien. Looks like you've got an admirer, Jo. Killian's son seemed quite taken with you."

"Don't be ridiculous."

"He's right, Jo," said Kris. "I was definitely picking up an interest in you from him. Be careful. If we end up going down to eat with them, don't let Taradain take you off alone."

"Lay off it, you two," she said scornfully. "Why should he be interested in me?"

"It's not you I'm concerned about," said Kris, looking back at his work. "Just remember how the Jalnians view women. We're outside whatever codes of conduct their polite circle has because we're only alien captives."

"It's been a long winter. He's probably bored with the women of the keep," said Davies.

"He's not going to jeopardize our work here by making a pass at me."

"He's right," growled Rezac. "You shouldn't go. Stay here with us, let the males eat with them. I won't be there to protect you."

Jo felt Kris' quick flash of annoyance. "I'll protect her if need be, Rezac," he said stiffly.

"I'm quite capable of protecting myself," Jo snapped, annoyed with both of them. "Don't either of you confuse me with the Jalnian females." She got up and headed for her room, wanting a break from the intensity of emotions that were filling her mind. She still hadn't mastered shielding enough to cut out strong sending, but a few yards and a wooden door added to the barriers she could erect.

As she stormed across the room, she heard the sound of tiny claws accompanying her. When she opened the bedroom door, Scamp darted in before she could stop him. Annoyed as she was with the two men, she didn't have the patience to chase the jegget and evict him. She shut the door firmly behind her and flung herself down on the bed.

Moments later, she felt a thump beside her and a small, wet nose pushed its way through her hair to nuzzle her cheek.

Rezac huffed and got to his feet. "I'll talk to her," he growled.

"No," said Kris, pushing his chair back so fast it screeched across the floorboards. "I don't think so, Rezac. She's our concern, not yours."

He knocked on the door, waiting for a reply. When none came, he opened it and entered.

"Look, Jo, unlike Rezac, I didn't mean to suggest you couldn't defend yourself," he said awkwardly, closing the door behind him. "I was only trying to alert you to the possibility of a situation developing."

"I know exactly what you and Rezac meant. I told you, it isn't going to happen," she said, dislodging Scamp and sitting up. "He's got no chance of getting me on my own and neither has anyone else, so you can both forget it!"

"I didn't mean that. I can't vouch for Rezac, but I certainly didn't."

"If I didn't know better, I'd think you were jealous of him!"

"It's not jealousy. He's Sholan, for God's sake. Why should I be jealous of a Sholan? I know how you feel about aliens after your experiences with the Valtegans. It's just that recently he's been trying to get too involved with you and what you're doing."

Jo had noticed Rezac's changed attitude toward herself and put it down to a desire on his part to understand the Humans more. However, if it was making Kris jealous, then perhaps there was more to it.

"Don't think I'm not aware of your interest in me, Kris, but I'm not about to jeopardize this mission by getting involved with anyone. Grant me at least some modicum of professionalism," she said coldly.

"What mission, Jo?" he asked quietly. "It's done, finished. We found out about the cube—and we're captives, marooned here on Jalna for God knows how long!" He moved closer, his tone becoming persuasive. "Who'd blame us for taking comfort in a closer relationship if that was what we both wanted? Davies won't, and Rezac's got his Leska."

Jo slid off the bed and stood up, eyeing him warily. Scamp began chittering loudly and angrily at both of them.

"You'd better see to your pet. He's a giveaway, Kris. He's too tied into your mind not to let me know how you feel."

His face took on a slightly stricken look. "How did you find out?"

"You and Rezac constantly mind-speaking to me has increased my awareness. Now I'd prefer you to leave. As you said, I shouldn't let myself be alone with men. I might come to harm." She laced her voice with heavy sarcasm.

Stopping only long enough to call Scamp to his side, Kris turned abruptly on his heel and stalked out. Left alone, Jo sat back down on the bed feeling decidedly shaky.

The invitation to dine came later that day via Durvan, who arrived complete with a change of clothing for all the Humans, including a more revealing dress for Jo.

"Now tell me he isn't interested," muttered Kris as he headed for the bedroom to wash and change.

Left alone with Davies, Jo sighed.

"You're going to have to decide," he said, getting up.

"Decide what?" she asked tiredly. The day had been depressing, with her speaking to neither Rezac nor Kris, and both males avoiding her as much as was possible in their cramped environment.

"Which one you want."

She sat up, shocked by what he'd said. "Which one?" she echoed.

"Come on, Jo. You must be the only one who hasn't noticed. Why d'you think Zashou's been so touchy the last couple of days?"

"You're mistaken! You must be! I've done nothing to make either of them think . . . How could they think that!"

"In a way it's really got nothing to do with you," he said, leaning forward to touch her cheek gently. "They're interested in you, I didn't say you were interested in them. Something you might want to consider, given Rezac's lack of trust of us, I have a suspicion his interest has something to do with the fact you're a telepath. He wants you for your mind," he said with a grin.

"Not funny, Gary. He's got a Leska. He can't have more than one . . ." she faltered, looking up at him. "Can he?"

"He's one of the first telepaths altered by Vartra. Who's to say what he's capable of? I don't know, you'd have to ask Kris. Maybe Rezac can have a Human Leska as well as a Sholan one."

"I can't ask Kris that!"

"Make up your mind as soon as you can, Jo, and put them both out of their misery. This atmosphere isn't good for any of us."

"I don't want either of them! I made that clear to Kris. I can't speak to Rezac because he hasn't said anything to me yet!"

"He will," said Davies, moving off to change. "If I'm right, he won't have any option, and maybe neither will you."

Rezac sat in the chair by the fire after they'd left, half-dozing in the warmth. Zashou was still lying down. It was nothing much, only that her cycle had restarted. After so long in stasis, it wasn't surprising her first should make her feel poorly.

Zashou was aware of his interest in the Human female, but, he hoped, not the nature of it. Unfortunately, she couldn't have cared less. It had begun innocently enough, with him hoping through Jo's stories, and that of the other Humans, that Zashou could see that when you live in brutal times, you often had to be equally brutal yourself to combat it.

The relief of having other telepaths to talk to after so long meant that he'd frequently touched Jo's mind, grown accustomed to the feel of it. She hadn't shrunk away from him because he'd been a fighter. She didn't like conflict, but then who in their right mind did? She would be prepared to do what was necessary to win.

Now, though, what had been a meeting of similar minds, was more. Almost against his will, he felt drawn to her, as he'd been further drawn to Zashou by the forming of their Link. There was a difference in the degree of the pull, however. It had nothing like the intensity of the Leska Link.

It had come as a shock to him, to find himself attracted to an alien female. He'd despised the Valtegans for just such behavior, and the one time the Emperor had decided to see what a Sholan female was like, he'd gone into a

ed fury—until they'd used their control bracelets on him.
Zashou had instantly reacted to not only his anger but also
his punishment, and the experiment was never repeated. It
had nearly cost them their lives, happening as it did, early
in their captivity. Emperor Q'emgo'h, however, hadn't been
prepared to lose his pets quite so quickly.

From Jo's mind, he knew about the reality of the mixed
Leskas, and though he was convinced it was to do with
Vartra's gene enhancement, he was at a loss to know why
he, a Sholan male, should find her attractive, unless it was
another form of psychic link. Without realizing it, his
thoughts began to drift back to the past.

Rezac sat watching the screen, waiting for the
weekly report from the Laasoi Peninsula to come up.
Out of the corner of his eye he saw Zashou padding
over in his direction, clipboard in hand. She stopped
beside him.

"How's it going?" she asked. "Any info for me yet?"

"Not finished loading," he said shortly, pulling down
his sweater sleeves again. The erratic heating in the
underground labs was worse than usual today. He'd
been alternately chilly then overly warm all morning,
and it was making him uncomfortable and edgy. On
top of that, against his will, he'd kept finding himself
looking over to where she was working. Now, all he
could think of was her scent and his overwhelming
desire to take hold of her.

"Will it be much longer? Vartra needs this urgently."

"S'cuse me," said Jaisa as she squeezed round
behind them.

With an exclamation of surprise, Zashou stumbled
against him, her free hand going out to clutch at him
in an effort to break her fall.

Instinctively, his hands went out to catch her. As
they touched, his mind exploded in a myriad of flickering images. Where her hand lay within his, his skin
felt seared, burned by the intensity of her touch.

"Oh, sorry," he heard Jaisa say. He *knew* she was
reaching out to help Zashou. She mustn't touch them,
he realized as he fought the mental confusion of the
images in an effort to communicate his alarm to her.

The lab suddenly came into focus once more, but

everything began to slow down. He had to stop Jaisa. He opened his mouth to yell 'No!'—but for the first time his reactions weren't fast enough, and desperately afraid, he watched Jaisa's hand inching toward Zashou's arm. Then the two females touched.

Rezac felt the backlash of the shock that flung Jaisa a good ten feet. Pain lanced through Zashou's mind to be instantly echoed in his. Her body suddenly went limp, her eyes rolling back till only the whites showed.

He grabbed her, staggering himself as he came off his stool and found his legs unable to support him. He fell, managing to twist to one side so he didn't land on her. Pain exploded in his skull as he struck it on the edge of a crate behind him.

Faces swam into view, then receded. He blinked, trying to concentrate. With a sickening lurch, his vision righted itself.

"What's happened? Is she all right?" asked an angry voice he recognized as belonging to her husband Shanka.

He discovered that he was lying on the floor, his arms clasping Zashou close against his chest. A new face pushed the others away. Mentor Viaz. Irrelevantly he wondered what Viaz was doing in the lab. Trying to move, he found he couldn't because of the way Zashou was lying across him.

Viaz reached out to move Zashou aside.

"No, she's all right," Rezac said sharply, pushing his hand away. "I can feel her coming round." He stopped, realizing what he'd said. She was there, in his mind with him, and he could *feel* her surfacing to consciousness.

She stirred, moaning softly because of the pain in her head, then sat bolt upright, her panic filling everyone's minds.

You're in my mind! What are you doing there? Get out! she sent, fear on her face as she pulled free of him and scrambled backward, waves of nausea threatening to make her throw up. She fetched up against Vartra's legs, looking round in panic.

Viaz's hand moved closer to Rezac.

"Let me help," he said.

Zashou's nausea was affecting him, too. This time Rezac gratefully accepted the help, letting Viaz pull him into a sitting position. He put his hand to his head, bringing it away covered in blood.

"I think we should go up to the infirmary and dress that cut," said Viaz calmly. "Dr. Vartra, perhaps you would be so kind as to bring Zashou."

"Certainly," said Vartra, bending down to help her.

Rezac looked round. "Jaisa?"

"She's fine," said Viaz. "Just winded, that's all."

He could feel Zashou's panic still filling his mind. "For the Gods' sake, stop it, Zashou," he snapped. "I haven't done anything to you, nor am I about to." His head was throbbing fit to burst, as was hers.

"What the hell is going on?" demanded Shanka, trying to push past Vartra to his mate.

"Tiernay, see to Shanka, please. He's to remain here," said Vartra.

"A Leska Link?" Zashou said in horror, trying to pull away from the doctor. "No, it can't be! Not Rezac, for pity's sake! He killed Jaisa's mother!"

Rezac staggered to his feet while Vartra made soothing noises to Zashou, holding onto her to prevent her from running away. Grasping the edge of the workbench, he took a couple of unsteady steps till he reached her. With Zashou's mind wide open to everyone's thoughts, his felt unbearably raw and exposed. He pushed Viaz aside and took hold of her by the upper arms, beginning to shake her.

"Stop it!" he said. "Get your mind under control now, Zashou. I won't put up with your hysteria."

His anger penetrated through her fear in a way reason couldn't. Every mental barrier she had learned went up and she retreated behind them, fear in her eyes as she watched him. He tried to withdraw his thoughts from hers but couldn't. He was forced to remain at the edges of her mind, a presence over which he had no control.

"Good," he said, letting her go. "This Link isn't my choice either, Zashou."

"Liar!"

"Enough," said Vartra. "Let's go upstairs and discuss this in private."

"I'm her husband, I've a right to go with her," Shanka called angrily after them as they left the lab.

The discussion had solved nothing. Zashou made her feelings perfectly clear. The flashing images had been their exchange of memories as their minds had begun to Link for the first time. Now she knew everything about his past in Ranz and hated him for it. He'd stormed out in anger, heading out of the monastery to run through the woods until he was exhausted.

When he'd returned, he felt Zashou wake. Someone was at her bedroom door. Slowly he made his way along the corridor until he was standing just out of sight of her open door. He could hear the conversation in his mind as well as with his ears.

Shanka had finally been let out of the lab. He'd made straight for their room and had stormed in on her. "Where is he?" he demanded.

"Who?"

"Rezac! He's here, or he's been here," he said striding over to the curtains and pulling them back.

"What are you talking about?" she asked, confused as she rubbed her hands across her eyes.

"Why was the door locked if you didn't have him in here?"

"I was resting, I didn't want to see anyone," she said.

"I'm not anyone," he snapped, prowling round the room, tail lashing, hackles up. "I'm your mate! It's my room, too! Why did you have to choose him of all people? Why not me if you had to have a Leska?"

"You can't choose your Leska, Shanka," she said, and Rezac could sense her trying to keep her temper. "I didn't choose him; it happened."

"Don't give me that! You've no right to have a Leska, you're married."

"I have as much right to have a Leska—or lovers—as you."

"You know I don't have one," he said, his voice becoming deceptively calm.

"No," she said coldly, "you have lovers, in fives at a time!" She turned away from him.

He grunted contemptuously. "You've had lovers, too."

"So what? Ours was never a love match, only an arrangement between our families. You're not denying me the rights of any Sholan are you?"

"Damned right I am! You're my mate, you'll not take any more lovers!"

"Don't be ridiculous, Shanka," she said, rounding on him. "You've no right to tell me what to do. I'll do as I choose."

"Not Rezac. You'll not have Rezac," he snarled, advancing on her.

"I haven't said I want him! Just leave me alone, Shanka. Get out of here and leave me alone!" She began to back off as he got closer, his hand outstretched to grab her.

Rezac waited no longer. "She told you to leave," he said.

Zashou's eyes widened as she saw him standing in the open doorway.

Shanka turned round. "This is none of your business," he snarled, ears lying sideways in anger.

"You want him out?" Rezac asked, looking at Zashou over Shanka's head.

She hesitated.

You want him to leave? he sent.

She nodded slowly, backing farther into the room.

Rezac stepped in. "Out, now," he said, jerking his head toward the door in case the other was in any doubt.

"Get the hell out, Rezac, you've no right to interfere!"

Reaching forward, Rezac grabbed Shanka by the tunic. "I said out! You want to argue in the corridor, fine, but not in here," he said, hauling him out through the open doorway.

Zashou followed them. A portion of his mind heard the sound of running feet. An image of Tiernay and Goran flashed into his mind as Zashou turned to look at them. They skidded to a stop beside him and Shanka.

"We'll take it from here, Rezac," said Tiernay as Goran grasped Shanka firmly by the arm and began dragging the protesting youth down the corridor.

Rezac let him go and shrugged, feigning indifference. "I'll settle it with him later."

"We picked up what happened. We'll see to it," repeated Tiernay, laying a restraining hand on Rezac's arm.

Shaking himself free, Rezac moved aside and locked eyes with the group's leader. "He's my problem now, Tiernay. Keep him away from her. She's *my* Leska."

Tiernay looked away first. "Violence isn't an answer."

"Tell him that. He was about to strike her."

"He'll be dealt with. Your attitude could endanger our work, Rezac. We'll see he doesn't threaten Zashou again. Leave him alone," Tiernay ordered before turning to follow Goran and Shanka.

Aware of her mounting fear of him, Rezac looked over to Zashou.

She took a step back into the room, standing partly behind the door frame.

He shook his head. "I'm not going to touch you," he said. "I only came because I felt your fear. They'll see to Shanka this time. He won't bother you again. If he does, send to me. I'll deal with him. All right?" He waited, but she said nothing, only looked at him with eyes enlarged by fear.

"All right?" he repeated.

She nodded.

"Good," he said, then left.

Mental barriers up, he ran through every curse he knew on his way back to his room. That damned Leska Link! He thought he'd left his past behind him, but now she knew everything, just as he knew everything about her, and she was terrified of him. She was too scared to see why he'd had to join the pack or how he'd been trapped in it with no way out until the University scouts had picked him up. They'd understood how he'd been trapped and had wiped the slate clean, given him and his family a fresh start. She wouldn't. All she'd ever seen was her fear of him.

His legs twitched, waking him from what was becoming an increasingly distressing memory. His first waking awareness was of the little Human. The meal was over and they were returning to their quarters in the tower. That Taradain was interested in Jo had become obvious. However, nothing he'd said or done had smacked of any impropriety. He knew this was true because he realized he was there, at the edges of her mind—and she'd felt him.

What the . . . ! Rezac, get the hell out of my mind!

He tried to back away but found it nigh on impossible. Redoubling his efforts, he succeeded and instantly retreated behind his shields. His face creased in worry. What was happening to him? He knew he hadn't consciously reached for her, so how had he managed to wake up linked to her? Hearing them outside the door, he hastily pushed the worries aside and tried to compose himself. He hoped she wouldn't ask him for an explanation because he didn't have one.

CHAPTER 8

The door opened, admitting Jo first. She stormed over to Rezac and stood squarely in front of him.

"Just what the hell was that all about?" she demanded in a low voice. "You were in my mind, and you *took* what happened at dinner with Taradain from me! You invaded the privacy of my mind, Rezac!"

He sat up instantly, aware of the two Human males standing by the worktable, keeping a watchful eye—and ear—on their interchange.

"I was concerned," he said, aware it was a lame comment to make.

"You had no right to pry into my mind! What I do is none of your concern!"

"You're right, I have no excuse," he said, desperately trying to keep his eyes on her face. This was the first time he'd seen her displayed in female clothing, and he found it unnerving. She was breathing rapidly in her distress and anger, and it was causing a fascinating effect on what he could see of her breasts above the low front of her dress. It was the first time he'd been aware of that part of Human femininity.

He forced himself to look away. "It was just concern," he said in a rush, standing up. "I'll try to see it doesn't happen again. It was instinctive—to protect a female." He knew he was babbling, but he couldn't help it, not when he could see her smooth, curved flesh and smell her scent so strongly. She gave out all the signals of motherhood, yet he knew for a certainty that she was not pregnant, nor ever had been.

Stepping past her, he fled for the room he shared with Zashou, angry, confused, and ashamed at the emotions that were coursing through him.

As he entered, Zashou regarded him from the bed. "I

didn't think you'd be that attracted to her," she said.
"There must be something to what they've been saying
about these mixed Leska pairings after all. Thank the Gods
I'm not interested in either of the males!"

"Leave me alone, Zashou," he said, heading for his pallet
by the fire and lowering himself down onto it. "You know
I can't help it."

"Maybe now that you have someone else to bother,
you'll leave me alone more often," she continued, her
tone waspish.

He looked over to the bed. In the firelight, he could see
her only dimly. "What I feel for you," he said quietly, "that
can never change. I don't know what this—emotion—I
have for her is, but it can't alter that."

"Pity. It would take the pressure off me. Just don't assume because she's got you aroused that you're coming
anywhere near me, because you aren't! Go take a cold
shower!"

He began to growl softly in anger. "Damn you, Zashou!
I've never done anything to harm you! Why do you have
to treat me like this? It wasn't my fault we Linked!"

"You wanted me! That's why the Link happened," she
hissed angrily. "I had a husband, a life, before that! And as
for never hurting me, you almost raped me the first time!"

His growl rose in pitch. "You can lie to yourself, Zashou,
but that night, you were as eager to pair with me as I was
with you! Now leave me alone!" He flung himself down on
his bed, wrapping the blankets around himself, cutting off
her voice. Raising his shields, he did his best to block her,
but memories of their first night began to surface. Memories helped sometimes, and of course he had both hers and
his of that night.

She'd wakened confused, not sure what had
brought her out of her uneasy sleep.

Rezac crouched in a patch of deep shadow, watching her, keeping his mind still lest she sense his presence. Each minute that passed was forcing them
together whether they wished it or not. His presence
here in her room was evidence of that. It had been
utter madness on his part to creep in while she was

asleep, but being close by her had, at least, eased the ache, the longing to hold her.

He shook his head slowly, trying to stop thinking about it, but like his tongue would probe at a sore tooth, he couldn't stop. The Link was amplifying the attraction he already felt for her. He knew he was probably making it worse for himself by coming in to look at her, but it didn't matter. When she fell asleep again, he'd leave. He shut his eyes as another bout of nausea hit him.

Zashou lay still. There was someone else in the room. Rezac. It had to be him. She recognized his presence. Despite herself, she felt her body responding to his nearness. She pushed herself up on one elbow, catching the glint of his eyes as he looked over at her.

Outside, the clouds parted and a shaft of moonlight stabbed through the window beside her, dazzling her briefly.

He stood by the bed looking down at her with no memory of having crossed the room.

Zashou blinked up at him. Putting her hand up to her eyes to shade them, she sat up.

The beads in her hair chimed softly against each other, arousing him to fever pitch. He caught hold of her wrist, feeling their Link flare into thought-sharing despite his block.

Rezac?

"I don't like this any more than you," he said. "I don't want a mate. Females weaken your will, tie you to one place—make you vulnerable." He knelt on the bed, ears flicking as he watched her. Why did it have to be her of all females, the only one who mattered to him?

Stretching out for her, he let his anger build, let it overwhelm her presence. He didn't want to feel her thoughts, not now, not ever. He knew she feared and hated him; that was enough. He slipped his free hand behind her head, pulling her face close, nipping at

her cheek, then her jaw. Releasing her wrist, his other
hand went behind her back as he pushed her down
onto the bed again. His hand slid down to the looser
skin at the base of her neck and grasped her tightly
by the scruff, his mouth closing over her throat.

She froze under him, then slowly tipped her head
back, making no move to escape.

Mentally he pushed aside the surprise he felt. He
didn't care why she had surrendered, nor even if she
did. This Leska Link left them no choice. The need to
have her was dominating him and despite his anger
and the block, he could now sense the same urgency
in her, not only from her mind, but from her body.

Light-headed, he released her. Sitting up again, he
ran his hands slowly through her silky fur, feeling the
suppleness of her body beneath. She felt even softer
than he'd imagined. The bed cover stopped him and
impatiently he pulled it aside as his body responded
to her proximity.

"Rezac, not like this, please," she said urgently,
keeping her voice low so as not to carry.

He stopped to strip his tunic off. While he did, she
tried to move away but he grasped her round the hips
and pulled her back.

"You've got Shanka for the polish, I'm as you find
me." His voice was low and rough as he leaned
over her.

"Rezac, no!" She struggled in his grip, one hand
trying to prise his hand away, the other hitting at his
face. "I submitted, don't just take me!"

He snarled at her, his hands going to catch hers,
pinioning them against the pillow in one of his.

Not like this! Please, Rezac! she sent frantically as
he guided himself into her. In that first moment of
contact, his mind exploded, then she was clinging to
him, as caught up as he in the maelstrom of their
emotions and desires.

Where they touched, a current seemed to flow between them, sweeping their minds together in a whirl-
pool of sensuality till they were one. Time seemed to
stretch as they shared each other's every sensation.
His mouth found her ear as his hands closed over
her shoulders. She felt so warm and soft pressed

against him, smelled so good. It was all he'd dreamed of, and more.

Mental barriers fell before the sheer onslaught of physical sensations. He knew instantly what pleased her and responded to it.

Her hands cupped his face, teeth nipping his cheek, her tongue taking turns with the bites, then her hands moved down his back and across his hips, her claws tracing patterns of fire, making him shudder with pleasure. Anger and bitterness were gone, all that mattered for both of them was now.

Sensations merged till it was impossible to tell where one ended and the other began. This was a pairing such as neither of them had experienced before. Deep inside, Rezac knew that this night Zashou had bound him to her in a way no female had ever managed—and that it had very little to do with their Link.

The moment of unity shattered into a thousand shards as their bodies climaxed, their minds fragmenting and separating yet still Linked—till death.

As his surroundings came back into focus, he found himself lying on his side, Zashou cradled against his chest. He lifted his hand to her face, running hypersensitive fingertips across her cheek, wanting the moment to last yet only too aware of its bitter sweetness. She was everything he'd ever dreamed of in a mate.

For the first time, her eyes were gentle as they looked at him, and he sensed what he'd never thought to find within her—an equal attraction to him that she could no longer conceal. Then footsteps sounded outside.

"Zashou?" a voice called quietly. "Are you awake?"

Rezac pulled away from her, the moment utterly lost. Rolling soundlessly off the bed to the floor, he let out an oath and a low growl, ears flattening, tail beginning to lash from side to side.

He won't come in, sent Zashou.

He's your mate. I haven't the right to be here.

We're Leskas, she replied. *He won't come in. We were given this room for us, Shanka knows this.*

The floor outside creaked as Shanka waited for a moment before leaving.

"This whole situation is impossible," growled Rezac, turning away from her to look out of the window. "I refuse to hide in the shadows from him!"

"You've antagonized him enough, Rezac. Don't cause any more trouble between him and me."

He turned back to look at her. "Why don't you leave him?" he asked abruptly. "You don't love him."

"That's not true!"

Rezac made a sound of disgust. "Have you forgotten what we just shared? I know exactly what you think of him."

She looked away for a moment. "At least Shanka has never treated me like you did," was her angry retort. "What you just did to me was tantamount to rape!"

Rezac growled deep in his throat, ears flattening sideways in anger. "Is that what you intend to tell Shanka? That I raped you? You'll say nothing about how much *you* wanted me, and enjoyed our pairing?"

"I didn't enjoy it, I merely tolerated it, and you must be mad if you think I would tell Shanka about tonight! I told you, you've caused enough trouble between us already!"

Angrily, Rezac reached across the bed for her and pulled her toward him. Taking her firmly by the arms, he shook her. "There's nothing that can sever our Link, short of a mutual suicide pact," he growled, "and I've no intention of dying! As for your husband, I gave up living in shadows when I left Ranz for Khalma. You're mine now, not his!"

"I don't belong to you or anyone," she hissed, trying to pull away from him.

"Don't you?" he said, drawing her close and covering her face and neck with tiny bites and licks, ignoring her efforts to escape him. He felt the pull of their Link flare again and her struggles grew less frantic before finally they stopped.

A shudder ran through her body as her hands clutched his arms, and she lifted her face to his.

Relaxing his grip on her, he nuzzled her ear.

"See?" he whispered. "You can no more fight the Link than I can."

"Shanka will have to accept it," she said, putting a tentative hand up to his face.

"Will he also accept that I can't keep my hands off you, whether or not I want to?" he demanded. "Only when I touch you does the pain inside stop." His claws flexed out, pricking her flesh despite her long fur. Instantly aware he had hurt her, he nevertheless didn't retract them.

He pulled her close again, once more covering her face and neck with sharp bites and licks, ignoring her small cries of pleasure as he breathed in her scent, surrounded his senses with all that made her Zashou.

Breathless, she wrapped her arms round him. *It's the same for me,* she sent, a soft moan escaping her. *This Link isn't fair to either of us.*

"What's *fair?*" he asked with a harsh laugh. "I've never known fair!" He let her go and turned away, the anger building up inside him again. He picked up his tunic and quickly pulled it on. "Good night."

Ignoring her mental distress and confusion, he yanked open the door and stepped into the corridor to the common room. Zashou's room was almost opposite the open doorway. He could see Vartra there, taking a rare break, sitting talking to Jaisa. Beyond him Shanka sat with Tiernay. They all looked up as he banged the door behind him. Rezac felt the fur around his face and across his shoulders begin to rise.

Shanka flinched, looking away from him. He knew Rezac had been with Zashou but wasn't prepared to take up the other's silent challenge.

With an effort, Rezac contained his rage, pushing back the incipient tunnel vision that would have made him target Shanka. Ignoring them all, he crossed the lounge, going out through the other door and heading for his room.

He slammed his door shut, locking it behind him. If he had his way, he'd share Zashou with no one. If he'd a mate like her, he'd not want any other lovers. He knew he could satisfy her to the point where she wouldn't notice anyone but him.

He flung himself into the chair, annoyed that he'd left her, and that he'd hurt her. Even now, through their Link, he could feel her distress. There had been no need to leave, he could have stayed all night had he wished, she'd not have turned him away. That was the problem; what she felt for him was only because of the Link. Why in all the hells did it have to be her? Why not a female he cared nothing for? Why couldn't he accept what he now had with her? *Because you want her to care for you,* came the answer.

His anger was abating now into despair. He got up and went over to the drawer unit, pulling open the top one. His hand closed round the bottle of sleeping pills Vartra had given them all. So many telepaths in one building would make sleep impossible at times, he'd said, and insisted they all take some in case. The sooner they got that shielding device mass-produced, the better. Then at least they could all get some peace in their own rooms.

He swallowed two pills before thinking to read the label. Only one at night. He shrugged, throwing the bottle back in the drawer and shutting it. Why hadn't he stayed with her? Why had he let his damned pride stand in the way? What they'd just shared only made him want her more and though the urgency born of their Link had diminished some, it was still not satisfied. *He* wasn't satisfied.

Lying down on the bed, he put the light out, realizing that unless she was always there, he would never be content. He tried to convince himself that what he'd said earlier was true. He didn't want a mate, she'd only make him vulnerable, but it sounded hollow now. He tried to comfort himself with the thought that at least he had memories, but that wasn't enough either when her constant presence in his mind only exacerbated his need to hold her, to touch her. The tablets began to make him drowsy, and gradually he drifted into sleep.

The next morning, he woke before anyone. Silently he padded out into the main chamber, poking at the night fire, stirring up the glowing embers until they blazed high again.

Throwing some more logs on it, he turned his attention to the dining table.

Breakfast had already been left for them. When he unwrapped one of the loaves from its cloth, it was warm to the touch. He broke it open and, reaching for the knife, began spreading the butter over it, noticing as he did that there was a slightly more pronounced greenish tint to it this morning. He'd just placed some cold meat and cheese on it when Davies emerged from the other bedroom.

"Morning," he said, coming over to join Rezac at the table. "What kind of stunt did you pull on Jo last night? She was as mad as hell."

Caught with his mouth full, Rezac could do nothing but lower his ears in mute apology.

"Look," said Davies, helping himself to another lump of bread, "we're going to be shut up here for God knows how long. It makes sense to get on with each other. The last thing we need is us falling out."

Swallowing the last piece, Rezac glared at him. "I did nothing to her!"

"Keep your voice down! You must have done something or she wouldn't have gone ballistic," he said, grasping him by the arm. "I'm not your enemy, I'm actually trying to help. Now, what happened?"

Rezac resisted the urge to pull away: he was telling the truth, his touch was friendly, and the Gods knew he needed a friend. "I was sleeping while you were at dinner. When I woke, I was linked to Jo's mind," he muttered. "I did nothing, honestly. I wouldn't invade her privacy, but she thinks I did."

Davies let him go and turned his attention to the plate of sliced meat. "How d'you manage that?"

"I don't know. It's never happened before—and I can't be sure it won't happen again. My Talent's never been uncontrollable like this."

Davies took a bite from his sandwich, looking thoughtfully at him. "Linked, you said. Like the Link you have with Zashou?"

"No," he said automatically, then stopped, thinking for a moment. "Similar, but nowhere near as strong. The involuntary part is the same. I found it more difficult than I expected to disengage my mind from hers," he admitted.

As Davies continued to eat his sandwich, Rezac felt some

f his defensiveness begin to dissolve. Relaxing the tensed
uscles around his neck, he reached out for some more
read and meat.

"Are you attracted to her?" Davies asked abruptly.

The suddenness of the question made him jump. "No, of
ourse not! She's not my kind. How could I find her attrac-
ve?" he said, unable to prevent his ears lying backward
acute embarrassment. "You told me that only Vartra's
hanges attracted us to each other as a species," he said.

"That's true," Davies nodded, "but I've been thinking.
Ve've all been exposed to those changes of Vartra's. It
ouldn't affect me, though, not being telepathic."

"How?"

"That virus, it affected out people as I said. The Sholan
elepath who was our contact had just gotten over it, and
o went down with a mild cold or something on our trip
ut here. I reckon she's had it. Kris certainly has. When
ou came out of stasis, both of you were, to put it mildly,
un down and weak. You probably picked it up from them
hen. It's a bloody miracle you even survived that long,"
e said candidly, reaching for the jug of weak ale that was
heir main drink. He pulled over a tankard and poured
imself a drink. "If you ask me, you're the same as the
holan telepaths back home. You're as turned on to our
eople as they are to you. The telepaths, that is," he
mended, taking a swig.

Rezac watched him in frozen shock. It made sense; it
made a chillingly obvious sense.

"I can see you agree," said Davies, putting his tankard
down. "I've never heard of Leskas that are more than two,
ut it doesn't mean it can't happen. As you said, you were
he first to use Vartra's virus. The changes in you haven't
een diluted by breeding, so who knows what could be?
'm no authority on all this, but I seriously think you should
onsider talking to Kris about it."

"No!" growled Rezac, breaking free of his daze. "He
ees me as a rival for her now."

"Aren't you?" said Davies quietly. "From just watching
the way you follow her with your eyes, I'd say you were
interested. Whatever else he is, Kris is a damned good telepath. He's got to know how you feel. If your mind is reaching for hers and linking, and you want her, you've got to
talk to Kris before this gets out of hand. We can't afford

to be divided among ourselves. What about Zashou? How is she taking this?"

"She couldn't give a damn," Rezac muttered, pulling the jug over and pouring himself a drink. "She's the only one I really want. Dammit, if I could stop this . . . attraction to Jo, don't you think I would? I can feel the trouble it's causing, too! I just can't stop it!"

"Then talk to Kris before it's too late and he sees you as an enemy, not a friend in trouble."

His thoughts in turmoil, only one fact registered fully on his confused mind. "Why didn't you tell me before about this telepath on the ship that brought you?" Rezac demanded. "Are you still in contact with her?"

"No," said Davies. "We decided not to tell you about her. It's irrelevant now, in my opinion. We should have heard from her weeks ago, but Kris can't sense her at all. He can't even pick up the two Sholan telepaths who were brought here by the Valtegans."

Rezac began to growl. "Another piece hidden from me! It seems the lack of trust is already there."

"Look at it from our point of view," said Davies reasonably. "Jo's our leader, in charge of this mission. You have a problem with females in positions of authority, and we want to avoid any leadership wrangles. You do tend to try to take matters into your own hands."

Rezac winced inwardly, aware of the truth of the Human's words. "Females are weaker, they let emotions cloud their judgment," he said defensively.

Davies raised an eyebrow. "And you don't? For a telepath, you have to be the most impulsive one I've met, and I've met a few. I suppose it's your age and background."

"What's that supposed to mean? You know nothing about me or my background!" he said angrily, beginning to rise from his seat.

"Sit down, and stop being such a damned fool," said Davies equably, taking another mouthful of ale. "You're not an adult yet, are you? Around twenty-five or so? All males from eighteen to thirty are now sent off-world with the Forces to train their natural aggression. The only ones exempt are Telepaths, Warriors, and the Brotherhood, and they undergo such a rigorous disciplinary program that they aren't about to go berserk at the drop of a hat—like you're about to do," he added.

This made Rezac pause. He'd been told none of this. His world had obviously changed drastically. Slowly he sat own again.

"Females run a lot more of life on Shola than anyone ares to admit," Davies continued. "I can see it, being on he outside. On balance, I'd say it was a matriarchy with a igh degree of meritocracy and equal opportunity—once he males are old enough to come home. You're going to ave to get your head round that before you get back, therwise you're just not going to fit in. You've got a problem with Jo running things, and you reckon it's up to you o step in and make the hard decisions because we won't. 'orget that, Rezac. We chose Jo because she *can* make hem. She had to out in the field on Keiss. She made some eal hard decisions there, ones she still lives with today, so lon't write her off as *just a female*. Fit in with us, Rezac, nake an effort, then you'll find it easier to go to Kris and ;et his help with Jo. He's more likely to be able to reach her than any of us. Now, do you want to know what we ound out last night at dinner?"

"Yes," said Rezac, between clenched teeth. No matter how badly he'd been insulted by this hairless individual beside him, he needed to know what had happened. Damnit, he could break him in half with one hand! What justification had he for talking to him like this? *Because he's ight,* came the little voice again. He was growing to hate his conscience!

From the start, it had been obvious that Taradain was interested in Jo. He'd had her seated beside him, on his father's right hand, whereas the men had been consigned to Killian's left. All evening he'd leaned over her solicitously, seeing she had plenty to eat and drink, though she drank sparingly. Both food and wine had been a pleasant change from their normal fare of ale and fatty meat. Even the bread had appeared almost white by comparison with the gritty gray-green flat loaves they were usually given.

"Belamor! I see you've managed to join us after all!" Killian said, his voice carrying effortlessly across the hall. "Join us at the high table."

Davies had looked up to see who it was.

Neither the light of the twenty torches lining the

great hall, nor that of the hundreds of candles in their sconces, could dismiss the shadows that seemed to cling to the hooded figure in the lapis-colored robe that slowly approached them. All that could be heard of his progress across the wooden floor was the regular tapping of his staff as it touched the ground with every other step.

Davies felt a shiver course through him as he recognized the person they'd seen from the window earlier that day.

He stopped in front of Killian, his face still concealed within the shadow of his hood. Davies was glad the broad table separated them.

"These are my visitors," said Killian, indicating the three of them with a wave of his hand. "Take that damned hood off, Belamor," he added, returning to picking his way through the plates of meat in front of him. "I know it pleases you to wear it, but not at my table."

Davies watched as the hand that held the staff tightened, gnarled fingers whitening briefly. His eyes followed the other hand as it went up to pull back the hood. It was almost with relief that he saw the man was human after all. Gaunt almost to the point of emaciation, the faintly olive tint to his skin did nothing to dispel the image of a walking corpse that sprang into his mind.

From beneath a black skullcap, wispy gray hair framed the hollow-cheeked face. It was enlivened only by the piercingly dark blue eyes that looked straight into his own. It was a brief glance, but Davies felt as if his mind had been invaded and stripped of anything that might be useful to the man in front of him. On Belamor's forehead sat a thin circlet of silver, bearing in the center a single round green stone, twin in color to the larger one set atop his staff—

"Green stones? Describe them to me," said Rezac.

"A deep emerald color, like that of plants in the early spring," said Davies.

"You said rounded. Not cut and polished? More like a pebble that's been tumbled in a stream?"

Davies frowned. "Yes, exactly like that, but how did ou know?"

Rezac shook his head mutely, gesturing for him to continue.

"Sit and eat," said Killian. "Belamor is my mage. While the priests pray for our souls, Belamor fights the demons that plague us—or so he claims. That's right, isn't it, Belamor? How's the one you wrestled with this morning? Properly subdued yet?"

"It will be several days before that one is subdued, Lord Killian," said the mage. For one so frail in appearance, his voice was deep and full of power. "He is only the first. There will be more. I trust you are wearing the amulets I prepared for your family?" He turned, and leaning on his staff, walked down the table to the far end to take the place left empty for him.

"Do I look like a fool, Belamor? Of course we wear them. We've been wearing them all winter!" replied Killian testily.

"What does Belamor do?" Kris asked the young man seated next to him.

"Diabolical things, Father Narwen says," he replied in an undertone. "He uses dark powers to aid him in his spell casting and the reading of portents so he can predict the future for our Lord."

"He uses magic?"

The youth looked sharply at him. "Did I not just say so? The most offensive odors and smells, to say nothing of explosions, come from his workroom at all times of day and night. There was one just this afternoon. Surely even you must have heard it!"

Kris shook his head. "No. We heard nothing. Tell me, does he make . . ." he searched for an appropriate word. "Does he make devices? Weapons? Powder that explodes?"

His companion looked fearfully down the table to where the mage was accepting a goblet of wine.

"I have to pass his room every day," he said quietly, turning back to Kris. "There are times when the very air makes my hair stand on end. What he does is unnatural, against the Gods' order. He even has a

pole atop his window that calls the lightning down
when he commands it! Take my warning seriously: if
you value your life, do not cross Belamor."

"Certainly a man to be wary of," murmured Kris.
"The guard today in the courtyard, I saw Belamor
treating him. Is he also the apothecary?"

"Our apothecary is a gentle man, a priest, not one
such as Belamor!" Even the youth's tone of voice
was shocked.

"Then why did he treat the guard?"

"Demons," he said shortly, turning away. "No one
else would dare go near him."

"Demons? D'you believe he was possessed or
something?"

The youth ignored him, beginning to talk to the
woman on his left instead, making it clear he refused
to be drawn into further discussion.

"Demonic possession?" asked Rezac. "Magic and spells?
What kind of world is this?"

"A very young one, culturally," said Davies through a
mouthful of his sandwich. "Magic is how psychic talents
were seen, and still are by some, on Earth. Keiss, too, to a
degree. That's why the villagers where Carrie lived were
afraid of her. Kris said that the young man truly believed
what he said about the mage, but that doesn't help us
much. On Earth he would probably have been called an
alchemist, someone who mixed magic with primitive science
in an effort to understand the physical world."

"Are you saying the magic he uses is actually the same
as the Talents we have?"

"So Kris thinks," agreed Davies. A noise from one of
the bedrooms drew their attention. "We'd best leave this
for now," he said quietly. "Just try not to make things any
worse than they are with Jo and Kris, okay?"

Rezac grunted and continued eating.

*   *   *

Kezule could smell her almost before he was fully awake.
He fought down the revulsion her scent caused him and
lay still, waiting till he could orient himself properly. She
was touching him. He felt the coolness of a damp cloth
against his throbbing wrists. Another scent, one he recog-

ized from last time; a salve. It drew the heat out of the
wounds almost as soon as it was applied.

He hadn't been unconscious long, no more than fifteen
minutes. Long enough for them to move him back to his
prison. Stirring, he turned his head away from her, flicking
his tongue out to taste the air. The scents were familiar.
As he moved, he'd heard a sharp intake of breath from the
female and her touch had gone. Her fear-smell got
stronger.

A wave of nausea and dizziness swept through him, a
reaction to the pain he'd suffered. His stomach began to
convulse and he sat up abruptly, making his pounding head
throb even more. Something cold and hard was thrust into
his hands. Opening his eyes, he saw it was a bowl.

For several minutes, his gut spasmed, each time stopping
just short of throwing up its meager contents. Gradually
the seizures stopped, and as he leaned against the wall
gasping, he looked at the female properly for the first time.

She was of medium height compared to the males he'd
met so far, and her fur was comprised of every shade he'd
seen on Sholans. A shapeless gray tunic was her only garment. Fearfully, in an outstretched hand, she held a cup
of water.

He took it from her and drank greedily, never taking his
eyes off her. She'd instantly backed away from him till she
bumped into the table. Her fear-scent became terror.
Swinging his legs onto the floor, he attempted to stand but
he was too weak.

"Need medic," he said clutching the bed for support.
Damn, but he was too old for this! He could have taken it
in his stride ten years ago—five even, but now . . .

"One's coming," she stammered, her Sholan almost in-
comprehensible to him. She began to edge herself along
the table till she had put it between them. Scuttling for the
door, she crouched there, tail almost touching the floor,
ears flat against her skull.

Why was she, an unprotected female, here? He'd never
seen one since he'd been brought here, so why now? Surely
they realized they'd handed him a hostage? He put the
thought aside as pain stabbed through him, and he was
forced to lie down again.

The door slid open. He saw the female try to rush past

the male, only to be thrust back inside by the accompanying officer—one he knew too well.

"Let me out! You can't keep me in here!" she yowled. "You didn't say anything about . . ."

The officer backhanded her, sending her spinning against the now closed door. "You'll do as you're ordered," he said coldly. Ignoring her, he followed the medic over to where Kezule lay watching the byplay with vague interest.

Not a potential hostage, then. She appeared to have no value to them.

The officer stood over him, listening while the medic reported on the condition of his various cuts and bruises, including his injured ribs. The examination was brisk and efficient, but left him in worse pain.

"Lucky you decided to be cooperative today, General," said his interrogator as the medic began bandaging his wrists. "I'm prepared to allow you some analgesics this time."

"He's not going to be mobile for a few hours after they're administered," warned the medic. "He needs plenty of fluids, and food, if he can eat. He'll need nursing. Leave the female to see to him."

A whimper of terror from the entrance accompanied the remark. Then he felt a sharp sting on his neck and the pain began to recede. A warm lethargy started to spread through his body. Even his headache was no longer troubling him.

"Try not to eat the help, Kezule," the officer drawled as he turned to leave. "The only one to lose will be you. Replacing her would be too inconvenient."

Then he was alone with the whimpering female.

"So this is your grand plan, Rhyaz," said Raiban, as the Brother and the medic entered the control room. "One terrified female."

"She's more, General," said Rhyaz, joining her at the viewing area. "She's been trained by one of the leading Consortia houses. We had hoped to place her inside his room several days ago, but she wasn't quite ready."

"To do what? Whimper? How much training does that take, Rhyaz? Did she know she'd be dealing with a Valtegan?" Her voice was heavy with sarcasm.

"She was fully apprised of the situation, General, and agreed to take part in this experiment," said Rhyaz. "

wouldn't feel sorry for her. She's a convicted murderer, facing the death penalty. This is her chance for a pardon."

"You'd release a murderer back into society? Or do you expect her to die during the course of her mission? Who is she anyway?"

"Keeza Lassah. Of course we hope she won't die. We've invested a lot of time and effort in training her."

"What's the rationale behind this?"

"Simple. Kezule and his ilk used Sholans as slaves. Putting someone else in with him who is as much a prisoner as he is, someone seen to have far less value to us than he has, may make Kezule react to her as he would to the Sholan slaves he had. He's had no one to talk to but me for the last five weeks. The isolation doesn't seem to be affecting him the way it does us, but it must be getting to him. Perhaps the company will at last make his tongue grow loose."

Raiban gave a reluctant grunt of assent. "And how do you propose to communicate with her?"

"That's my job, General," said Zhyaf. "Her mind's been programmed to be receptive to mental suggestions. I've already established a link with her and am constantly monitoring her emotions and surface thoughts. When necessary I can go deeper."

"She's had all memories of her programming suppressed," said Rhyaz. "Kezule must have no reason to suspect she's been placed with him as a spy."

"And if her life's endangered? What then?" asked Raiban.

Rhyaz shrugged. "This is a war, General. There are always casualties. We're already grooming a replacement in case we need her. As I said, hopefully we won't. If we had to go in to rescue Keeza, he'd know she was our agent."

Raiban nodded and turned away from the window, beginning to walk toward the door. "What information do you hope to get?"

"If we can start a dialogue going between the two of them, any stray comment from Kezule could be useful. A reference to his sun being brighter or dimmer than ours could help us pinpoint his solar system. We intend Zhyaf to mentally guide her toward the questions we want her to ask him."

"Isn't that dangerous for her? I presume she isn't a telepath."

"She's not. It could be dangerous," replied Zhyaf, "if she didn't have some degree of sensitivity. There's not much, but enough. When this is over, she'll need training to learn to live with her heightened senses."

"Don't you feel her terror, Zhyaf? I thought you damned telepaths were squeamish about this sort of thing."

"Yes, General Raiban, I do! But I have to put it aside if I'm to help Keeza," he snapped. "I find it totally morally reprehensible!"

Raiban grunted as she waited for the door to slide open. "Good to know someone's looking out for her."

When Raiban had gone, Rhyaz turned to Zhyaf. "I'd prefer you to moderate your emotional outbursts in future, Interpreter Zhyaf," he said quietly. "How's she doing?"

"How do you think she feels, alone with an alien like that? A species that's known to be violent?" asked Zhyaf angrily.

"She's been taught how to placate a violent male, Zhyaf," said Rhyaz. "And with more than her body. She'll grovel as well as any Chemerian merchant does when discovered in an illegal transaction. She's been as well trained as possible in the time available to us. We've given her every chance to survive. Now it's up to her—and you."

"I'll do my job, Master Rhyaz," he said coldly, entering his new data into his comm. "You do realize he said that our females were useless for pairing with because they were too violent, don't you?"

"We didn't know that until now. Just remember, she should already be dead, Zhyaf," said Rhyaz sharply. The damned telepath kept taking this morally superior attitude with them! It was getting to be annoying.

"And Kezule has never been imprisoned with one of our females before. It may be that the isolation *has* gotten to him, and we just can't tell. We know they have a high sex drive, and he may just turn to her for some kind of relief or companionship. *That's* what we're hoping for! Dammit, I don't care if he rapes her in revenge for what I've done to him if it helps us get the bastards that murdered the millions of Sholans on our two colony worlds! She's a weapon, Zhyaf, like all of us are at Stronghold. Every day there's a chance that one of my Brothers or Sisters may be killed during the course of a mission, but they take that risk. This experiment is vital. I can't afford to care for one criminal!"

Zhyaf's ears lowered till they were flat against his skull, showing he was suitably chastened. "Your pardon, Guild Master," he said quietly. "I'd forgotten our two colonies. Are you really training a replacement?"

"No, we're not. This is a one-shot experiment, Zhyaf. It must succeed." He watched the tension leave Zhyaf's face as the telepath's ears rose.

"Do you want me to help her overcome her terror, Master Rhyaz?"

"No. She has to react to him naturally, or he'll never trust her."

"What if she doesn't lose her fear?" he asked. "What if she becomes so terrified she can't do what we want? It's against Guild laws to manipulate her mind."

"You're En'Shalla now, not subject to the Telepath Guild," Rhyaz growled, "and you're under contract to us. You'll do as you're ordered, Zhyaf. Don't lose sight of our objective. We might not know where they are, but those damned Valtegans are out there somewhere, and we're at war with them!" Angrily, he turned and stalked from the room, leaving the two males behind. He liked what he was having to do as little as Raiban and Zhyaf, but dammit, they didn't have to rub it in!

*   *   *

"Mentor Sorli, how pleasant to hear from you," said Lijou. "First of all, let me personally congratulate you on your promotion."

"Thank you, Master Lijou. May I return the compliment? It's good to know our priests will have their own Guild from now on. I would have been in touch sooner, had it not been for my promotion." His left ear moved fractionally, indicating mild embarrassment as he lowered his voice. "I must admit I didn't expect Master Esken to hand over the reins quite so suddenly. If I didn't know better, I'd say he'd set me here to divert the hunt from his own door! Father Ghyan and I have been busy implementing the Terran education program. An update will be on its way to you in the next day or two."

"Thank you, Sorli. I must admit that the last three weeks

have been novel. To have such mutual cooperation between our Guilds was unheard of till now. We were hard-pressed to know what to do with the sheer number of acolytes arriving at the Retreat! From famine to feast, as they say."

"Indeed," smiled Sorli. "They've been one burden less for me, I have to admit. The Terrans are a headache on their own. There's a lot of hard work ahead for both of us, but I'd rather that than relive the last few years." Briefly his smile faded, then reasserted itself. "I'm actually contacting you on official business. Master Esken has requested an escort to bring his future Consortia bride from Ranz to our Guildhouse."

Lijou raised an eye ridge.

"Oh, he didn't specify a Brotherhood escort, but since I have heard there's trouble brewing in Ranz, I thought the Brotherhood would be more appropriate than the Warriors. After all," he said, his eyes widening guilelessly, "it would be terrible indeed if anything should happen to her on her way here."

"Quite," murmured Lijou, the corner of his mouth twitching slightly as he repressed a smile. "We'd be happy to provide an escort from the House of Khaimoe to your Guild. When is it for, and what is the name of the lucky female?"

"There's not many of a standing that would satisfy our Master," said Sorli. "I'm sure you could hazard a guess."

"I'm afraid I don't keep up to date with social politics," said Lijou, dipping his ear apologetically. "I couldn't begin to speculate."

"Juilmi Rraoud."

Lijou feigned surprise. "I have heard of her. A talented hostess and an intellectual. Esken has set his sights high."

"She accepted," murmured Sorli, "against all wagers to the contrary, and quite suddenly, too. She's to be escorted here for the sixth hour tomorrow for her first meeting with Master Esken."

"I'll see all is in order, Mentor Sorli," said Lijou, adopting a formal tone for the moment. "And yourself? Ghyan told me you'd life-bonded with Mayoi Kyusha some three weeks ago. How do you find married life?"

Sorli's expression softened perceptibly. "To have someone to share the good and the bad with for the first time—it makes life so much more enjoyable, Master Lijou. Did you know she was at the Guildhouse all along? I'd even worked with her once or twice."

"Fancy that," murmured Lijou. "I take it that everything has worked out well for you and her?"

"Without doubt. She's been working in the medical section recently, on the case the Clan Lord sent to us. In fact, that was my next piece of news. It seems like we've had the best of the people the Terrans intend to send us. The last arrivals had abilities that were considered on the fringes of belief by even those Humans who do believe in telepathy as a science. We've had to invent new definitions for them. This Derwent, for instance, he's a prime example. He says he's a healer of souls, a guider of the dead, but a large number of the Terrans say he can't be because he's from the wrong culture! If you listen to one group, he's even the wrong sex, it being a female's skill, one that a male is mentally incapable of doing! It's like a pasture full of holes made by those damned jumping rodents—you know the ones, the farmers hate 'em. What're they called?"

"Chiddoes," Lijou supplied, again hiding a smile.

"Yes, them. You know what I mean. You catch your foot in one of their burrows and you break your ankle. We need to have them more thoroughly screened on Earth before they come here, Master Lijou."

"I agree, Sorli. I'll add my petition to yours at AlRel. But back to Derwent. What did you find out about him?"

"It's very inconclusive," said Sorli, with a sigh. "Brynne Stevens refuses to allow a medical telepath to examine his mind, and all we can get out of Derwent is that he did nothing to him, that any changes are due to his training methods and come directly from Brynne himself."

"What do you think?"

"I'm afraid he may be right. We had Brynne's mind covertly scanned while he was ill, and there's nothing there that isn't basically the same as any other Human, certainly nothing like the difference that Physician Kyjishi and Clan Leader Carrie have been talking about. It is possible that Derwent's training methods produce different results in a mixed Leska than they would in either species. We're unlikely to find out since Derwent flatly refuses to teach anyone else, or even talk about what he was teaching Brynne."

"An impasse, unless Mr. Stevens decides to tell us himself, which, I take it, he doesn't. How is he?"

"He's fine. It was just the virus that we all caught," said Sorli. "I apologize that there isn't better news, but Derwent's still being detained here under observation."

"What's AlRel ultimately going to do with him?"

"Deport him unless he cooperates. He's got a week left to make up his mind. Personally, I think we'd be better off without him, but it isn't my decision. He's still trying to preach his belief that Shola is a living planet, the body of Vartra, and that every Talent is a gift from the God to whom we owe devotion and worship." He gave a snort of amusement. "I can just see our Master Builder ordering his Guild to pray to the Gods as they lay each stone for a new civic building!"

"It would certainly extend the time it takes to build anything," agreed Lijou. "And I am in complete agreement with you on the danger he poses to the younglings at our Guilds. Thank Vartra he can get nowhere near my colleges! I hate to think what someone like that would say to the acolytes."

"Well, I'd best be going now, Master Lijou. Thank you for your time, and tomorrow's escort. Did I mention that Challa Kayal also arrives at the Guildhouse to see Master Esken tomorrow?"

"No, you didn't," said Lijou with a smile. "Let's hope he chooses the right partner tomorrow."

"I hope so, too," said Sorli.

*   *   *

Cautiously, Mara emerged from the tunnel into the lower chamber of the dig, glancing around to see who was there. Most of the Terran team worked upstairs in the ancient lab, but there was usually someone on duty here. Around her, the rusting remains of the vehicles that had once been hidden within the hillside were being exposed from their resting places in the dust and debris. So, too, were the corpses of the Sholans and Valtegans whose final battle this had been.

On the other side of the chamber, the three trestle tables that were the archaeologists' field lab were butted against one another, forming an open-sided square. Sitting in their midst was Josh Lewis. With a gesture she knew well, he brushed his sandy hair back from his face. There was a harassed look on his face as he passed an artifact back to one of the Sholan diggers.

"I've dozens of these damned things," he said. "All in the same condition—rusty, empty, and full of muck. Tell the others to clean 'em out first and only bring ones that have bullets in them to me. Otherwise, just pick a box and throw them in with the rest!"

The youth lowered his ears disappointedly and, with a nod, slouched back to the face of the excavation.

Looking quickly behind her to make sure her faithful shadow was still missing, Mara headed over to him at what she hoped was a casual pace.

Josh glanced up as her shadow fell across him. "I'm really rather busy just now, Mara, unless you fancy helping me."

"I can't stay long. I'm followed wherever I go these days," she said quietly, leaning on the tabletop in front of him. She liked Josh, and wasn't looking forward to what she had to tell him. Of all her brief liaisons, for some reason she couldn't explain, the few hours they'd spent together had meant the most to her.

He frowned, dark brows meeting in concern. "Why should they follow you? Surely you're in no danger here on the estate."

"Nothing like that," she assured him, wishing she could tell what he was thinking. His mind, unlike those of most of the unTalented she knew, remained a closed book to her. "I need to warn you, to tell you something important."

She let her voice tail off, unsure how to continue. How could she tell him that she'd used him to get pregnant with a Human child, only to discover it was as much a hybrid as Vanna's and Carrie's cubs? The look on his face, perhaps even the feel of his mind, would be full of revulsion for her. She realized now that she deserved it. Somehow, she'd passed this damned virus on to him, contaminated him in some way so that his children would never be Human. She'd stolen from him the one thing she'd resented losing herself, her Humanity.

"What is it?" he asked, putting his hand up again to brush back his unruly long hair.

There was no putting it off if she was going to tell him before Jissoh finally caught up with her. "The night we spent together, I let you make me pregnant," she said quietly, looking away from him.

She counted two hundred heartbeats before he broke the silence. "Why?"

"It was only a matter of time before Zhyaf made me pregnant, and I couldn't bear the thought of having a child that wasn't Human." She found the rough surface of the table fascinating and absently picked at a loose sliver of wood. "Except it isn't Human. It's a cub, like theirs."

"Pardon?"

She looked up as she sensed his disbelief and astonishment. "You fathered a Sholan cub on me, Josh."

He looked round the cavern, desperately making sure no one was within earshot. "Are you trying to tell me that your child—*my* child—isn't Human? You've got to be kidding, Mara!" he said, his voice angry despite its quietness. "If this is your idea of a joke, it isn't funny! I knew I should have stayed away from you, everyone warned me!"

"I'm not joking, it's the truth. They're following me because I won't tell them who the father is." She stopped abruptly, looking over to the cave mouth. "I've got to go, Jissoh's found me," she said, moving away.

He stood up, lunging across the table to catch hold of her arm. "Just wait a minute. You can't come in here and drop a bombshell like that on me and then walk off without explaining it!"

Frantically she tried to pull away, but his fingers tightened their grip. Reaching up, she tried to pry herself loose. "You don't understand," she said. "It's *you* they want! They want to find out how a nontelepath could father a hybrid cub!"

"I didn't," he said bluntly. "They can run tests on me to prove I didn't. You're lying, Mara, and I'm going to expose your lies!"

She stopped struggling and watched as Jissoh broke into a run. From behind her, she could sense Rulla approaching from the upper level opening. "It isn't a lie, Josh. I'm sorry."

Carrie was contacted at the range where she and T'Chebbi were practicing their marksmanship. They left immediately, telling Jissoh to rendezvous with them at Vanna's lab.

As she made her way there, she reached for Josh's mind, finding it easy to penetrate the few rudimentary mental barriers that shock had not removed. She found what she expected.

"He's one of us," she said as she entered Vanna's office, leaving T'Chebbi outside with Jissoh and Rulla. The two young Humans sat at opposite sides of the room, in various stages of unhappiness. "A minor Talent, but there."

"Looks like Kusac was right after all," Vanna sighed, swinging round on her desk seat to face Carrie. "This is probably another Triad." She turned back to Josh and Mara. "Thanks to you two, I'm going to have to rewrite all my neat little theories," she said with a half-grin, trying to keep her tone light.

"There's got to be some mistake here," said Josh, nervously scratching his bearded chin. "Okay, I'll admit I might have a Talent, a small one as you say, but as for being one of you, that's a hell of a long way from second guessing who's on the phone or at the door!"

"As you say, you have a lesser Talent, but that could be because it's underdeveloped," said Carrie, moving toward one of the empty chairs. "We don't know how sensitive the thirds will become in time and with association with us, but we do all share the same altered genes, and that's easily checked."

"That doesn't make me the father of Mara's child."

"No, it doesn't," Vanna agreed, "but it does mean you could be, and that coupled with the fact that Mara claims you are .."

"Come on!" he exclaimed, half-rising from the chair, "she's lying! You don't believe her, do you?"

"Why should she lie?" asked Carrie. "You have paired with her, haven't you?"

"Only once! She's trying to make me responsible for it, that's all! It must be Zhyaf's!"

"Well, we'll know when the cub's born," said Vanna equably. "We're only interested in taking a few blood samples and the like from you so we can establish that you are one of us. You have no responsibility to Mara or the cub, as far as we're concerned. That's a private matter between the two of you. Although I should tell you that Mara has no *need* to make any male responsible for her cub, so she's no reason to lie about it. You're not on Earth, you know!"

"I don't want the cub. I want to abort," said Mara quietly.

Carrie watched Vanna's eye ridges meet in a frown as she studied the Human girl through narrowed eyes. "You've decided, then," she said. It was sad, but not unexpected.

"I didn't want it for the right reasons. I only wanted to avoid having Zhyaf's cub. Ruth thinks I'm right."

Mara's voice was quiet and controlled, with none of the self-justification Carrie would have expected from one her age. It looked like Ruth's influence was beginning to have a positive effect.

"I don't think that's your decision to make," said Josh.

Carrie leaned forward to touch Josh's arm before Vanna could speak. "It is her decision, and only hers," she said gently. "You claim you can't possibly be the father, so why should you be entitled to an opinion? Children, and cubs, should only be brought into the world when they are wanted. Sholan females can choose whether or not to conceive at the time, we can't."

"She just said she chose to get pregnant," objected Josh. "Look, I'm not saying she *should* have the kid, just that it isn't only her decision."

"I've decided," said Mara flatly. "I'll live with that decision. The cub shouldn't have to. When can I come in?"

"Leave it till tomorrow at seventh hour. Give yourself till then to be sure," said Vanna. "Josh, would you mind going down to the lab and giving M'Zio a blood sample? We keep a database on our people, and we need to add you to it. We'll also be asking Father Ghyan to contact you to test your Talent."

"Look, no offense, Physician, but I'm not interested. I enjoy my work, and something like this is going to bring my boss down on me like a landslide. Anyway, I've no intention of becoming a telepath, even if I was one of you. Which I'm not," he added.

"Don't worry, Josh, we'll take up as little time as possible," Carrie reassured him. "Your place here at the dig isn't dependent on Pam Southgate; she hasn't got the power to dismiss you. We need to know what your abilities are, so we can get a clearer picture of what's happening to the Talented in both our species. When we know what your strengths are, we can tell you, and then you can decide whether or not you want to develop them."

Josh stood there looking stunned. "It's true, then."

"Your blood tests will confirm it," said Vanna, getting up to call Rulla in to escort him down the corridor to the medic. "This will only take a few minutes. We'll make sure you're taken back to the dig."

Carrie waited till he'd gone before speaking to Mara again. "Why didn't you tell us who it was?" she asked. "Did you think you'd be in trouble? You shouldn't have, Mara. What you do is up to you so long as you don't hurt anyone else. You're an adult, you know, not a child."

Mara's eyes began to flood with tears. "I thought I wanted a baby, but I don't. I just didn't want to have Zhyaf's. I couldn't do what my Mom did. She had too many kids, she never wanted me. She was glad when your people took me away." She wrapped her arms around herself and began gently swaying back and forth as the tears spilled down her face. "I should have listened to you when you said I could only have Sholan cubs. You were right."

Carrie went to comfort her, sending to Vanna as she did. *Get Ruth.*

Already on her way.

Kneeling in front of her, Carrie folded the girl in her arms, holding her tight and murmuring reassuring words while pushing aside her anger at what was coming to light about the girl's past. "It's all right, Mara. You're with us now. You have a family, people who care."

Though Mara rested her head on Carrie's shoulder, she couldn't relax and remained a small, tight knot of misery, her distress barely held in check.

A minute or two later, the door opened and Ruth looked into the room. "I thought I'd find you here," she said, coming in and going over to Mara. She placed a gentle hand against the girl's cheek, then caressed her shoulder. "Come with me, my pet. I think it's time we went home." She looked at Carrie as she let Mara go and began to move back from her.

"She's told you what she wants to do, I see. Her decision didn't come easy, I hope you realize that."

"I know it didn't," said Carrie, helping Mara up from the chair. "It's taken a lot of courage for her to make this decision."

Ruth wrapped her arm around the girl's shoulders, drawing her close against her side. Vanna handed her a tissue.

"Dry your eyes, Mara," said Ruth gently, pressing it against one of the girl's tightly clenched fists. "You don't want the world to know you've been crying, do you?"

Automatically her hand opened as she responded to Ruth's adult presence. She dabbed at her eyes, the tears already beginning to dry up.

"That's the girl. Now we'd best get back. I'm going to need your help with Vrada. That young male's been up at the Shrine again, playing in the mud field they call a garden! You should see him! He's like a walking mud ball— it's caked into his pelt. I've told him it's the scrubbing brush for him!"

Mara began to smile. "Not really," she said. "You wouldn't do that to him, would you?"

As they walked towards the door, Ruth made a noise very like a growl. "You haven't seen the brushes they use to get that kind of dirt out, my girl! I'd call them scrubbing brushes. I'm going to need you to hold him under the shower while I scrub! I'm not having that muddy little wriggler running all over our clean house!"

Carrie laughed as they left. "She's not far wrong," she said, returning to her seat. "I remember when Kusac was working on the villa. He used to come home covered in plaster and concrete."

"I suppose it must be easier to wash dirt off if you don't have fur," said Vanna absently. "Well, looks like we're going to have to run those checks Kusac suggested after all. Thank Vartra we've got Mentor Sorli to deal with rather than Esken!"

"The Gods have been kind to us," Carrie agreed. "I leave for the Warrior Guild tomorrow, so I won't be here to help you, but Dzaka and Garras will. Once you've identified all those with our particular genetic signature, try and persuade them to come to the estate. We want to see if it's possible for them to have some degree of choice in a Leska partner."

"That's if they are Leska material."

"They're at least capable of being the third in a Triad if they haven't the Talent to find a Leska," said Carrie confidently.

"What about the gestalt? What's it for if not to trigger the changes?"

"We've yet to find out, but we do know one of us can use it to harness the power of the other in moments of crisis. It doesn't just double what you have. When we've triggered it, the energy we have access to is unbelievable. It's far more than the sum of what we individually possess."

Vanna made a small noise of disbelief as she began to turn back to her work. "I'll believe there's another Leska rigger when I see it happening," she said.

"You will," said Carrie, getting up. "I'll wager you a meal in one of the best restaurants in Valsgarth."

"You're on," said Vanna.

*   *   *

Kaid headed out of the main gates and down the snow-lined road to the village of Dzahai. Overhead, the sun shone in a sky that was the sharp, deep blue of winter. The air was fresh, a breeze bringing with it the scent of the winter conifers on the slopes that sheltered Stronghold. Kaid breathed deeply, closing his eyes for a moment and enjoying the freedom of the morning. He'd been caged for too long, he needed a break. For nearly a month now, he'd had either Kusac or T'Chebbi constantly with him.

He shook his head, sending his hair flying in every direction, then raked it back between his ears, imposing a little order on it. For the first time in weeks, it felt good to be alive, even if the coolness that had grown between him and T'Chebbi hadn't yet been resolved. He'd purposely headed out early so as to avoid her. A group of youngling students passed him, mouths gaping in awe as they recognized him. He flicked an ear at them, instantly regretting it as the still tender scar on his forehead ached. Hurrying by, he took the righthand junction that led not to the center of the village, but to Noni's.

The bushes, hidden beneath their blanket of snow, and the bare limbs of the trees still clad with the previous night's frost gave the cottage an unearthly quality. He pushed the gate open just as Teusi, Noni's attendant, opened the door.

"Well come, Brother Tallinu," he said. "I'm on my way to the stores. Again," he added with a wry smile as he stepped aside for Kaid to pass him.

"Don't you get tired of this?" Kaid murmured, stopping for a moment.

Teusi grinned. "Yes, but the opportunity to learn he craft is worth the minor inconveniences. Have a pleasan visit."

"What brings you here, then?" demanded Noni as Kaid closed the outer door behind him.

"It was you, wasn't it, Noni? You sent Kusac, told him to ask to be my sword-brother, didn't you?"

"Who said I did?" she demanded, continuing to stir the peppery smelling concoction on the stove.

"I do. Who else would have suggested it?" He moved over to the sink unit, leaning against it while he watched her.

"Like old times, Tallinu," she said, glancing sideways at him. "You standing there in your priest's robe, watching me prepare my bruise and cut ointment."

"I'm only wearing the robe because . . ."

"It's warm, it's all you got with you, people expect it of you—and it's got nothing to do with how you feel about Vartra," she supplied for him, her face creasing in a scowl. "I know, I heard it all before—when you were a youngling and just started training here."

It was Kaid's turn to frown. "I wasn't a youngling."

"You were barely more than a cub!" she retorted, turning back to her potion. "Still had crib marks on your ass!"

"I'm not going to let you make me angry, Noni," he said, folding his arms in front of him.

She nodded. "Better. You've got some of your self-control back. You needed it, Tallinu. Fill the kettle and put it on to boil, lad. I'm almost done here."

Unfolding his arms, he pushed himself away from the sink and approached her.

"When they brought you in from Ranz, you were hard and brittle," she said as he returned to the sink to fill the kettle. She waited till he'd finished and brought it back to her, setting it down on the hob.

"Everything was an excuse for a fight. You trusted no one and believed nothing. We were worried we'd lost you. Then, from one week to the next, you changed. Never did tell me what caused it."

He shrugged, looking down at where his feet protruded

rom the edge of his robe. "Everything suddenly fitted to-
ether and made sense—in those days."

"Then you left. Put them into a real panic, that did."
he laughed at the memory. "Thought you'd run away.
ent scouts after you to bring you back."

Kaid shifted uncomfortably, clenching the claws on his
oes. "I'd only gone to get T'Chebbi."

"Why? One as hard as you'd become, who'd killed so
many in pack fights, why'd you go after her, Tallinu?" she
sked, moving the pan away from the open hob and replac-
ng it with the kettle.

"I said I'd get her out. Then the Brothers picked me up,
nd I couldn't. I had to go back for her," he said
defensively.

"Why? She was nothing, only a low-life pack qwene. I'll
grant she was in a sad state when you brought her to me,
out she meant nothing to you. You weren't interested in
her. Then later, when you and Garras became sword-brothers and were told to go after your first rogue telepath,
what then?"

"We brought him in for training," he said, adding
sharply, "and T'Chebbi wasn't a qwene! Where is all this
leading? What's your point, Noni?"

"Just that for all that hardness you had, you took on
work that needed compassion," she said, taking hold of the
strings round the neck of the small ceramic pot within the
larger pan of boiling water. Carefully she lifted it out, setting it down on the hob. She gestured for Kaid to take it
over to the sink to cool down, a job he'd done many times
for her in the past.

While he did, she took hold of her walking stick and
made her way over to her easy chair.

"Compassion?" he said, joining her at the table. "I think
not, unless you mean those we couldn't save we killed
quickly and cleanly."

"There are easier ways of saving lives, Tallinu, and you
knew it. Protection contracts . . ."

"Stop it, Noni. You're seeing what you want to see, not
what was. I chose that work because in Ranz I found I was
good at it. I'll ask again, where's this all leading?"

"Yes, I sent Kusac to you. You needed to go back to
what you knew, the skills you had always relied on. You
needed to know you have a place in Kusac's life that has

nothing to do with either Vartra or the Triad. Now yo
know that."

"A Noni-manufactured one," he growled.

"D'you think for a moment that the Aldatan cub woul
put himself in your hands at my asking without wanting t
do it himself?" she demanded. "A fine opinion you hav
of your Liege!"

"He's no longer my Liege. I made him release me fron
my oath."

"You what?" She was outraged. "Sometimes I despai
of you, boy!"

"You don't understand, Noni," he began.

"Damned right I don't! To force your Liege to releas
you is beyond . . ."

"Wait! Neither of us could take the sword-brother oatl
if he was my Liege!"

"Huh," she said, only a little mollified. "I bet you didn'
tell him that, did you? You made some test of it for him
I'll be bound."

Kaid said nothing, refusing to meet her eyes.

Noni growled. "You ask too much of others, Tallinu."

"Only what I expect of myself," he replied quickly.

"Not everyone can meet your high standards. They're
unrealistic, and the sooner you admit it to yourself, the
easier you'll find life. Kettle's boiled," she said pointedly
as on the hob, its low whistle was becoming a high-pitched
shriek of urgency.

He muttered angrily under his breath as he got to his
feet.

"What you've got to do, Tallinu," she said gently as he
moved the kettle then went about collecting mugs and the
makings of a brew of c'shar, "is find a base from which to
build your new life."

He stopped dead and turned round to look at her.

"Yes, your new life. Your past is gone, as surely as the
ashes of those that lived in the time of the Margins. You've
to learn to live as a telepath, with new skills, new aware-
nesses, and new responsibilities. You don't have to change
the person you were much, just enough so you can accept
what you now realize you've been all along. Since you
didn't know which way to turn, I reckoned building on your
relationship with Kusac and Carrie would be good. In them
you have two people who genuinely care about you, people

ou'd already let yourself be tied to. Unless you plan to
rce them to release you from those oaths as well?"

"I'm no oath breaker and you know it! I told you why
needed to be released from that oath!"

"Yes, so you did," she nodded. "Now prove to me that
y trust and faith in you hasn't been misplaced."

"Why should I?" he demanded. "Why should I have to
rove anything to anyone?"

"Because I'm Noni, Grandmother—and it's easier than
roving it to yourself, which is what you're trying to do."
Her voice was very quiet.

He looked at her for a full minute before turning back
o his brewing. Slowly, almost ritually, he spooned the dried
eaves into the brew pot, then poured the boiling water
ver them.

"The sword-brother oath is sworn in Vartra's name," he
aid when the silence grew too long. "As all our other ones
re. I can't swear by him, Noni. At him, yes, but not by
im. And I haven't decided if I want Kusac—or anyone—
s a sword-brother yet. It takes time."

"And your other oaths, to them, and to Lijou?"

He gave her a scornful look over his shoulder and began
o pour the drinks. "I gave them at a time when I did
believe."

"What did you believe in? You didn't know Vartra as a
person existed then."

"The God, of course," he said, irritated, stirring in whitener and sweetener.

"So what changed?"

She was probing, pushing him in directions he didn't
want to go. "I'd prefer to drop this," he said, picking up
the mugs and taking them over to her.

"I'd rather you didn't," she said, accepting hers from
him.

He resumed his seat at the table, sipping cautiously at
the hot drink.

"What changed?"

He sighed. He didn't want to do this, it wasn't why he'd
come. "You know very well. You saw my memories. He
used me, Noni."

"The person did, not the God," she corrected him.

"It's the same."

"No. The God came after. Don't confuse the two, Tal-

linu. Vartra the person is dust, probably not even that aft
so long."

Somewhere in the back of his mind a memory began
niggle. The night he'd gone down with the fever. Had
had a vision, or had it been nothing but a fever dream? H
frowned, prodding at the thought, trying to make it surfac

"Put yourself in his place," Noni continued. "You'
working to increase the numbers of telepaths. Along com
the Valtegans. They find out about telepaths and sudden
your research is vital to Shola, and threatening to then
They've been unstoppable so far, and all that might tur
this herd of aliens is your enhanced telepaths. What woul
you have done?"

He realized she was talking to him and pulled himse
back from his own thoughts. "What do you mean?
wouldn't have been trying to alter what the Gods gave u
in the first place!"

"Did you stop long enough to think that what Vartra di
when he took you back had already been done, becaus
you were here, and Kashini and Marak? He was merel
playing out the role the older Gods gave him."

"Gods? What Gods, Noni?" he asked angrily. "Ther
are no Gods, only the voices of our ancestors speaking t
us down through time!"

Noni caught his eye. "And just what is a God? Isn't it
being with supernatural powers, who has the ability to ap
pear to us in visions, to foretell the future? Don't they exis
outside the normal lines of time itself? All Gods probabl
began as people once, but their worshipers molded then
into something more, kept their spirits alive rather tha
letting them seek the afterlife they probably craved
Haven't you said many times that Vartra the God seeme
to be expiating a great wrong He'd done? An ancestor tha
has to live on beyond death, who is controlled by his wor
shipers, doesn't *he* fit the description of a God?"

Remember this meeting, remember what I told you. The
memory of Vartra's voice was so strong he shivered, spilling
his c'shar. It was as if the God was whispering in his ear.

"What is it?" Noni demanded sharply. "Have you re
membered something?"

"A vision—or a fever dream," he said, putting the mug
down with a hand that was still far from steady. "He said

I helped create Him by praying to Him and believing in Him. He can't rest because of us." He lowered his head.

"That's what I just said," agreed Noni. "His spirit, trapped for eternity, trying to make amends for what He did. Why did He come to you? What was His message?"

Ears laid back, Kaid shook his head, unwilling to speak.

"I'll guess, shall I? Trust, and that He needed you. Am I right?" she asked softly. "He knew what was coming, didn't He? He, the God, knew His efforts to make you forget when He was alive, had failed. That's why He asked you to trust him."

Mutely, Kaid nodded. He remembered it all now.

"And will you? Though the male He was might have used you, the God has never played you false. Whatever He did, He's paid for it this last fifteen hundred years, Tallinu. Snared, neither alive nor dead, unable to rest for all that time. It beggars belief." Her voice was hushed at the thought of it. "We have some responsibility for keeping Him trapped, Tallinu."

"Yes," he said, his voice hardly audible. "We do."

CHAPTER 9

The hands that touched her face were gentle, yet she was aware of the strength within them that was being held in check. With a touch as light as a feather, the fingers trailed down her cheek, brushing her neck only hesitantly, before coming to rest on her shoulders. His body pressed against hers, his warmth gradually dispelling the chill that seemed to hold her in its thrall. She felt his breath against her cheek, then the touch of his face against hers. His pelt felt silky-soft against her skin. He said her name as if it were a caress. "Jo."

With a stifled cry, she sat bolt upright in bed, shaking and sweating. Her first thought was for the two men sleeping by the fire. Straining her senses, she could detect nothing but the even sound of their breathing. The last thing she wanted was them knowing she'd been woken by the nightmare yet again.

The sound of him saying her name still echoed inside her mind as she pulled the covers around herself. Dawn lit the sky; it was nearly morning. She didn't have to go back to sleep again, she thought with relief. He had to be dreaming about her, there just wasn't any other rational explanation. But why? And why was she finding herself, against all reason, drawn to him, an alien? It just wasn't logical! Equally irrational was why he was interested in her when he had enough troubles dealing with his Leska, Zashou. They were a couple. You just didn't go around breaking up couples as if it were of no importance, no matter what his people's morals were.

Then there was Kris—and Taradain! Both of them hovering round her like predatory animals, waiting for the slightest sign of interest from her so they could stake their claim. She groaned. Why couldn't they all realize that she didn't want any of them! Her life was pretty well complete without the need for a man, thank you very much. Why did they think it wasn't? Probably their biological hard wiring, she thought glumly. They couldn't help it.

A movement from the fireside drew her attention.

"Can't help what?" asked Davies sleepily.

Damn! She hadn't realized she'd vocalized the thought.

Davies sat up. "Nightmare?" he asked quietly. "Want to talk about it?"

She opened her mouth to say no, then changed her mind and nodded.

Davies carefully pushed back his blankets and clambered to his feet. Clad only in the breech clout that was all the underwear this culture possessed, he was shivering as he picked up his robe and began to pull it on.

"Give me a moment, and we can go into the other room," he whispered.

Again Jo nodded, straightening her legs out so she could lean forward to pull the drapes round the end of her bed for privacy.

A couple of minutes later, she joined him by the fire in the lounge. "I know it's spring, but it's still bloody freezing," Davies said as he energetically poked the fire to coax a blaze out of it. "Now, what's up?" he asked, sitting down in one of the chairs that still ringed the hearth from the night before.

Jo sat down beside him. "I don't know, Gary, that's the problem."

"Try starting with the nightmare. You haven't told me what it's about yet."

She rubbed her hands over her face, trying to rid herself of the lingering images, wondering how best to describe them. "It's like having a phantom lover," she said at last. "I'm there, in the dark, with someone. He's touching my face, then he takes me in his arms and holds me close. That's when I wake up."

"That doesn't sound like a nightmare," he said gently.

"It wouldn't be if it wasn't who I think it is."

"Let me guess. Rezac."

She looked sharply at him. "How did you know?"

"Rezac and I had a talk the other morning," he said. "You're having the same effect on him, Jo, and he can't help it either. Kris is the only one who might know what's happening, but neither of you will talk to him."

"How can I? He's interested in me, too. I can't exactly ask him why I'm having erotic dreams about Rezac, if that's what they are!"

Davies frowned. "What d'you mean? Do you think they aren't dreams?"

"They're so real, Gary. I can actually feel his touch! When I wake up, I can still hear him saying my name."

"You've got to talk to Kris, Jo. You can't let this situation go on any longer. It's bad for all of us."

"I know. I've got to choose one of them. You said that before, but I can't." She got to her feet and began to pace round the semicircle of chairs. "I can't choose Rezac. He's not human and, anyway, he's got a partner. But why does it have to be anyone? This isn't my problem, it's theirs!"

"I don't think so. I've a feeling that this business with Rezac is more. It seems to me it has all the signs of a Leska Link, but I'm no expert. That's why you need to talk to Kris."

"I don't believe it does. Rezac was one of the first enhanced telepaths, wasn't he?" She came to a stop in front of him. "It's far more likely that he's subconsciously reaching out to me in his sleep, sublimating his desires, if you like, and I don't want either them or him!"

"If you're right, then by choosing Kris, you'll be letting him know in no uncertain terms that you're not interested," said Davies reasonably. "I know it's their problem, but it's also yours because only you have the solution. Unless, of course, you prefer Taradain?"

"Don't be ridiculous," she snapped, angry with him for even suggesting the young lordling. "He's no more than a boy!"

"Then tell the poor little sod that you're with one of the men here! If he gets the impression you're stringing him along, we don't know how he'll react—or Killian, come to that."

"He hasn't said or done anything yet beyond general pleasantries," she said, sitting down again. She was sick of it all. This was coming between them and their work. None of them needed distractions like this. As leader, what would she want done if it didn't involve herself? She had to admit she'd be giving this hypothetical woman the same advice

Gary was giving her. It had to be Kris. She couldn't bear the thought of being with another alien after what she'd gone through with the Valtegans. She shuddered as the memories began to surface. Hurriedly she pushed them back down where they belonged.

"You're right, I have to choose," she sighed. "Kris. I'll have Kris, but I'm not speaking to him till tonight."

"In that case, I'll spend the night in here," he said. "Let you have some privacy."

The day passed slowly. She kept finding herself drawn over to the table where the men were working, to Rezac in particular. The need to be close to him was stronger than it had been the day before. Resolutely she tried to resist it—when she noticed it. Several times she found herself standing at his side, watching what he was doing, without remembering how she got there. Once he reached up to touch her arm. She jumped back as if stung. His touch felt charged in some way, as if he were transmitting static electricity to her.

He had been just as taken aback as she, and as they both mumbled apologies, she hastily retreated, returning to her own work beside Zashou.

The Sholan female thought the whole situation amusing. Still not fully recovered, she sat listlessly sorting through the components Jo handed her.

"You like Rezac, then?" she asked, mouth open in a slight grin. It was the first sign of animation she'd shown for several days.

Jo was caught with nothing safe to say. If she said she didn't, she was insulting them both. If she said she did, she was treading on Zashou's territory.

"You should approach him," Zashou said. "He's certainly attracted to you. Don't worry, he had lovers on Shola before we were captured," she reassured her. "If it weren't for our Link, I wouldn't be with him. He's not my choice for a mate, or a lover."

"He seems very nice," she said, desperately trying to think of something acceptable to say.

"You'd probably find him so, being a soldier yourself," she said dryly. "Not me. We have nothing in common at all. You'd be good for him."

"I'm sorry, but much as I like Rezac, I don't want to

become his lover," she said, getting to her feet. "Will you excuse me? I have a terrible headache coming on. Perhaps if I lie down . . ." She let her voice trail off and beat a retreat to the bedroom.

With mixed feelings, Jo waited for Kris to come to bed. Finally the door opened, and he stood silhouetted as he said good night to the others. The fire cast enough light for her to see him as he moved around, undressing for bed.

Since the liberation of Keiss, she'd slept alone. After her experiences at Geshader and Tashkerra, the domed pleasure cities of the invaders, she hadn't been able to face intimacy with anyone. Even now, as the memories began to return, she shuddered: skin so cool it was clammy, and the hard hands with sharp, nonretracting claws that lacerated her flesh wherever they groped her, despite the fact that she was one of their favored "pets." The ones she'd been sent to had been no more than rutting animals.

From his bed by the fire, Kris raised himself on his elbow, looking over at her. She could hear Scamp chirring in quiet distress. "Jo? Are you all right?"

She had to go to him now, before she lost her nerve. Whatever was causing this attraction to Rezac was sexual in nature, and as the day had progressed, so had her frustration till she was now at the point where she needed a man, any man. It was so unlike her! All she could think was that maybe it was the eve of Rezac's Link day and he was projecting.

Clambering out of bed, she padded across the wooden floor till she was standing over him. "Kris, I don't know what's happening to me, but I have to choose one of you, and I want it to be you." The words came out in a rush and sounded clumsy even to her, but she was beyond caring now, driven only by her need and her equal determination that it would be Kris, not Rezac, that she lay with.

"Jo," he began.

"For God's sake, shut up Kris! I know you want me, I can feel it!" she hissed. "Look at Scamp!" The jegget had come out from under the covers when Kris had and was now twining himself round Jo's ankles, purring madly, winding his tail round her. "Even he knows!"

"Jo, I can sense what you're going through, but it isn't

e you need, it's Rezac. I wish to God it weren't, believe
e, but it is."

She hunkered down beside him. "I won't have him! I
ant to lie with one of my own kind, feel human flesh next
me! There've been too many aliens, Kris," She knew
e was almost pleading with him, but she couldn't help it.
When I came back from a tour in one of the Valtegan
ties, my own people looked at me as if I was unclean,
id I wasn't. Do you understand? I *can't* go to him!"

He reached out to touch her check gently with the back
f his hand. "From what I've sensed, I think you're Linked
Rezac in some way, and a Sholan mind link involves
airing at least once so your minds can merge. Sleeping
ith me now will only make it worse, honestly. His people
re gentle; they're nothing like the Valtegans."

"How would you know?" she demanded, pulling away
om him. "You've never lain with an alien!"

"I've been with a couple of Sholan females," he admit-
d, letting his hand drop. "They're like us, Jo, inside,
here it really matters. They're a very sensual species. He
on't harm you in any way. Quite a few men and women
n Shola have Sholan lovers."

This shocked her. "You *chose* to sleep with them?
liens?" She could hardly believe him.

He winced visibly. "You slept with Valtegans."

"That wasn't my choice! I was working for the under-
round, gathering information!"

"Aren't you doing to me what you just said was done to
ou at your base? Am I more unclean because I chose to
nake love to them?" he asked.

She hesitated, realizing his accusation was justified.
"What you did is your business," she said, kneeling down.
Reaching out, she touched the base of his throat, drawing
er fingers lightly down his bare flesh, stopping only when
he came to the blankets. She could feel him shudder, re-
ponding to her arousal. Telepathy made it difficult to hide
uch feelings, and for once, she blessed her gift.

His lips touched hers, their softness a balm to her in-
lamed senses. She reached for his face, her hands holding
is cheeks as she returned his kiss. Suddenly Rezac was
here, in her mind, dominating it.

No, he sent, *not him! It's me you need!*

Where she touched Kris, she felt not his flesh, but fur,

and as she looked at his face, it altered subtly until it w
Rezac she saw.

With a cry of horror and anger, she flung Kris aside an
leaped to her feet, backing away from him to crouch, ter
fied, against the end of her bed.

"What the hell's happening?" Kris demanded, pickin
himself up.

"You changed," she stammered. "You became him—
Rezac."

He sighed. "I tried to tell you," he said. "I've heard o
this happening before. Once you've paired with him, it'
be over, none of this desire—lust—call it what you wan
It's only this intense the first time."

"But I wanted you, not him," she whispered through th
confusion that filled her.

"I want that, too," he said gently. "And it can be, afte
tonight."

She shook her head. "No. He's in my mind. I'll never b
free of him." Anger raged through her again. "Damn him
Why did he have to do this to me? He's got his ow
woman!"

"It isn't Rezac, it's the Link calling you together, Jc
Don't blame him."

She barely heard him as she began to run to the doo
Shift swirling round her, she exploded into the lounge
looking around wildly for Rezac.

"I thought it would be tonight," said Zashou from he
seat by the fire. "He's in the bedroom."

Jo ran to their door, flinging it open. Rezac stood in fron
of the fire, his back to her.

"What have you done to me?" she demanded. "Get ou
of my mind and my life, damn you! I don't want you
Rezac! I won't have you! It's Kris I want!"

He turned to face her, ears flattened to invisibility. "
knew you'd come," he said. "You can't ignore it any more
than I can." He came toward her, and she backed away
into the lounge.

"Don't you dare touch me! You're doing it, making me
feel like this! There isn't any Link!"

He followed her, suddenly lunging out with terrifying
speed to catch hold of her. "It's time we finished this," he
said, drawing her with him back into the bedroom.

"Gary, stop him!" she said, struggling against his grip.

Davies half rose to his feet, but Zashou shook her head. Leave them. It's better seen to now. You'll be doing her o favors if you interfere."

"Gary!" she shrieked, trying to hang onto the doorpost Rezac pulled her firmly into the bedroom. "Stop him, ammit!"

Shutting the door, Rezac released her and leaned against to prevent her escaping.

She whimpered, backing away from him, watching for te slightest move in her direction. She was terrified at the ower of the emotions rushing through her. The sense of eing drawn to him was stronger than ever now.

Don't be afraid, he sent. *I won't touch you against your ill.*

"Stop it! You know I'm no good at mind-speaking!"

"You're a fighter, like me," he said. "We've both fought his as best we could, but it's stronger than either of us. nstead of defeat, look on it as a mission. I've never been ith a Human before, just as you've never paired with a holan. It's unknown territory for both of us, and the only ay out is through it."

She shuddered as a wave of lust spread through her.

"That's the Link," he agreed. "They're right, it is like a eska Link, only not as strong." He moved away from the oor. "I'm not causing it, or adding to it in any way. Everyhing you feel, I'm feeling, too. It would have been better or both of us if it had never happened, but that's not the ase, I'm afraid." He was desperate not to scare her. He new if he did, he'd have another problem like the one ith Zashou on his hands, and he couldn't bear that.

Knowing her fear of aliens, he'd had plenty of time to hink it through, to work out the best way to approach her vhen the time came. Slowly he began to undo his belt, hrowing it aside before pulling off his tunic.

Her eyes were becoming heavy as a warm lassitude pread through her. She tried to blink it away, aware with part of her mind that she was falling deep into some kind of enthrallment where what he was saying actually made ense.

As he moved to put his tunic on the nearest chair, he ensed what was happening to her and thanked all the

Gods. It had to be female-oriented because he wasn't exp
riencing anything. It was akin to the effect jeggets had
their prey—hypnotic. At least it was damping her terro
making it easier for him to approach her.

Holding his arms out to the side, he turned arour
slowly. "See? I'm not so different from your males,"
said. "We know we're compatible because you say yo
friend has a Sholan Leska. I believe that now," he adde
wryly. "There really is nothing to be afraid of." His voi
was a low, persuasive purr.

She frowned, narrowing her eyes. Was it her imaginatio
or had he moved closer to her? And there was somethir
very different about him.

"We might even enjoy it," he said, taking a slow ste
toward her.

She stood her ground. "You're sexless," she sai
shocked. "How can you possibly . . ."

He laughed gently. "I'd be at a loss if I was. No, I'm mal
Let me show you." *Slowly, slowly,* he told himself. This wa
so difficult for him. Patience was not one of his strong point
but he was determined to get it right this time.

As he came closer, she wrapped her arms protectivel
across her chest, suddenly realizing just how thin and re
vealing her night shift was. Her dismay drew his attentio
to its deficiencies. Though her legs, unlike his people's
were straight, the glimpses he got of them hinted at a lengt
and muscular firmness that only fueled his own mountin
desire.

"I don't want to know." She backed off again, but hi
hand reached out to catch her. "You said you wouldn'
force me," she said, suddenly afraid.

"And I won't," he said, adjusting his grip to make sur
his claws remained sheathed. With his other hand, he
reached out to touch her short cap of hair.

She flinched instinctively, then stood still. His touch wa
like fire, a cool fire that flared brightly through her body
leaving her leaning against him, trembling.

The hands that now held her face were gentle, yet she
was aware of the strength within them that was being kep

check. With a touch as light as a feather, his fingers
iled down her cheek, brushing her neck only hesitantly
fore coming to rest on her shoulders. His body pressed
ainst hers and she felt his breath warm against her cheek.
en he laid his face against hers. It felt silky-soft against
r skin. He said her name as if it were a caress. "Jo."

It was the dream! Oh, God, this was what she'd seen!
He turned his face to hers, his nose feeling cool as it
iefly touched her. Once more her inner fire flared, this
ne starting low down in her belly. Against her will, a soft
oan escaped her as she clutched him by the arm.
"Doesn't it feel good?" His voice was barely a whisper,
en his lips touched hers.

She leaned into the kiss, flicking her tongue across his
os, anxious to have more of the strange, cool fire coursing
rough her. Surprised, he nevertheless responded, tasting
r himself the heat.
Hesitantly he touched her neck, not sure if she'd allow
ch an intimate gesture yet. Again, she responded with a
ftly muffled sound.
Taking one of her hands in his, he placed it so her palm
as touching his side. He encouraged her to move it across
s ribs then down his flank, following the lie of his pelt,
cross to his thigh.

She felt him tense, his muscles briefly tightening. Clutch-
g her hand, he drew it across to his lower belly. One
oment she was touching the smoothness of his groin, the
ext she was holding his genitals, well aware he was a com-
lete male. Before shock made her instinctively release
im, he'd begun to swell.

Reluctantly he pulled himself away from her. "No more
et," he said with a small shudder. "I want to see you."
is voice had deepened now that he was fully aroused.
He reached for the neck of her shift which she was still
lutching. Gently he opened her fingers; she didn't resist
im. Putting his hands to her shoulders, he pushed her gar-
ent back, letting it fall to where she still held her arms
cross her chest.

"Tomorrow," he said. "Tomorrow you can share t
with your Kris if you want, and nothing will disturb you
promise, but this night is ours."

His voice is so gentle, she thought as the heavy langu
rolled through her again. As if in a dream, she moved I
arms, letting the shift fall to her waist.

Rezac gently tried to force it lower, but the opening w
too narrow to pass over her hips. Dropping his head,
pulled the seam toward him, carefully biting through t
stitching for another inch or two, his eyes all the wh
still on her face. He let it go and straightened up. Nothi
prevented it from falling to the ground now.

She watched as he took a step back, his eyes traveli
over her nakedness. Strangely, she found she wasn't emb;
rassed. His reaction would have been satisfying enough f
any woman.

Tentatively he reached out to stroke her breast. ";
beautiful," he murmured. "So different from our females

There was no going back now, no stopping for either
them, she realized. Part of her mind was totally bemus
by all that was happening, unable to understand how
male so different from her own kind could engender su
feelings and responses from her. He was beautiful, thoug
Firelight flickered across his pelt, highlighting his muscl
making the dark brown fur gleam. His hair, almost bla
in this light, was long, framing his face almost like a man
In the dim light, his eyes glowed. She looked lower, seeir
the well-muscled chest that tapered only slightly in to th
hips, then the immensely powerful thighs and lower leg
the joints in all the wrong places to her eyes. His tail flicke
into view as it swept lazily from side to side. She'd forgo
ten his tail.

Looking back up to his face, she realized he was waitin
for a signal from her. Reaching out, she took hold of h
hand, placing it over her left breast. He didn't need a se
ond invitation. Leaning forward, he teased her nipples wit
the tip of his tongue, fascinated by her response.

She remained leaning against him, supported by his le
arm, her head lolling back against his shoulder. The sens;
tions he was creating entranced her—as did those she fe
from him. His other hand was exploring her body, strokin

gently across her back, moving lower over her buttocks and across her hips to her belly. By the time he ran his fingertips up the inside of her thighs, she was trembling on the edge of orgasm.

Where? he sent. *Where do I enter you? You're as different from our females as I am from your males.*

She showed him, body arching with pleasure as he briefly touched her before scooping her into his arms and carrying her over to his pallet by the fire. He knelt, placing her down amid the rugs. Pulling him close, she felt her body thrill to the silky touch of his belly fur against her bare skin. Her hands curved round his hips, stroking down to his thighs, then curling round between his legs before returning to his lower back where the root of his tail lay.

As she touched him there, he moaned, reaching behind to stop her. *Not yet,* he sent, rearing up. He grasped her round the waist and eased her into a position he hoped would be right for both of them. He couldn't wait any longer; her scent, the sight of her nakedness, was driving him wild, and he had to stay in control. The Gods had given him a second chance, why, he had no idea, but this time, he *had* to get it right!

She realized what he was doing, but before her fear had time to take hold, he'd entered her. Instantly their minds merged in an explosion of sensations and images. She could feel not only his movements within her, but also how tightly her body gripped him.

"Dear God," she whispered as he came down on top of her again, his long fur stroking her belly as he began to move more urgently. His mouth closed on her cheek, alternately licking and nipping her till he reached her mouth. She held him there with a kiss as wild as he could wish for. They climaxed as one, bound now into a Triad.

Images continued to flicker through her mind, images of his life, until she knew him as intimately as she knew herself. As the Link faded, leaving them once more separate, she felt Rezac begin to move away from her, both mentally and physically, tensing himself as he did.

Her Talent now fully awakened, she sent to him, wanting to know why. Even before he responded, she knew what it was, that it touched the very heart of his trouble with Zashou: her inability from that first knowledge of him, to accept him not only for what he was, but for what he'd been. He was expecting an outburst of anger from her similar to Zashou's when she'd discovered they'd formed a Leska Link. She remembered then how Zashou had yelled at him, what she'd said and felt about having a Link to him, and realized with shame that she'd behaved no better than his Leska.

He withdrew from her, sitting back among the rumpled covers.

"I'm sorry, Rezac," she said, reaching out to touch him. An echo of the fire they'd felt was still there, sending a tingle through her. This time, she didn't let go. "I was only thinking of myself. I forgot that you have feelings, too. I had no right to say what I did."

He looked up, ears hidden by his hair, and shrugged. "It's all right, Jo. You weren't to know, especially considering what you went through with the Valtegans."

"It's not all right," she insisted, sitting up and moving closer to him. "I am sorry, and you were right, we did enjoy ourselves."

His ears lifted slightly. "We did, didn't we? I made a mess of it with Zashou. She's never forgiven me for that—or for being what I am."

For a moment she saw the unsure young male who hid behind the battle-hardened warrior. She smiled, taking him by the chin, drawing him close enough to kiss. *The magic's still there,* she sent as she felt them once more sharing sensations.

I know.

Do we have Link days?

Perhaps. There were no Links like this when we left Shola. She felt his hesitation. *Will you stay with me till it passes?*

She moved closer. "Hold me, make me want to stay," she whispered, her mouth catching hold of his ear. "I would like to."

He began to purr, a sound she'd never heard a Sholan make before. "Let me speak to Zashou, tell her what we're doing."

"Will she mind?"

His laugh had a bitter edge to it as he scrambled to his feet. "No, she'll be pleased." He took a couple of steps away from her, then returned to her side, kneeling down again. "What about Kris?"

"I want to be with you, Rezac," she said gently. "You said tonight was ours."

"You really do mean it," he said, surprised. "But how can you, when you know what I've done?"

"We're the same, Rezac. We've paid a price for freedom that others can't understand. You were forced to join the packs because of your family, to pay a debt they owed. That's not your fault. The authorities pardoned you when you were recruited for the Telepath Program. It's not what you were that matters, it's what you are now." Again she kissed him.

"How can you see it the way you do?" he asked, between kisses.

"Because we're alike, you and I."

He stood up reluctantly, letting his fingers trail off her cheek till he was no longer touching her. "I'll not be long," he said.

Taking his tunic from the chair, he hastily pulled it on before going into the lounge. It was empty apart from Kris, who sat there waiting for him. He slowed to a stop as the Human looked up at him.

"I figured she'd be staying the night with you," Kris said, indicating a small bundle on the table. "Her things. Washcloth, towel, clothes, you know the stuff."

"Thank you," said Rezac, stepping over to pick them up. "Zashou?"

"She's in with us." He got to his feet. "She says you can use the bed."

"I'm sorry, Kris. I wouldn't have come between you if I could have helped it."

"Leave it for tonight, Rezac," Kris said tiredly. "I found out what I wanted to know. Go on back to her. She'll be worrying about you because I'm here."

Rezac picked up the bundle and turned to leave. "Kris. The only person who won tonight was Jo. She's beginning to heal now. I can promise you that the Valtegans won't bother her dreams again."

"I'm glad. Now go back to her, Rezac. I'm fine."

Jo, draped in a blanket, was returning from the chest where the wash basin stood.

Rezac put the bundle down on the chair. "Kris gave me some clothes for you," he said.

"Kris?"

He nodded, going over to his pallet and sitting down. "He cares a great deal for you," he said quietly as she came over to join him.

"I know. I like him a lot, too." She stepped past him, sitting next to the fire.

"Are you sure you wouldn't rather be with him?"

"I'm sure, Rezac."

She edged closer to him until he grasped her at the waist with both hands and lifted her up beside him, tucking her against his side. She let out a small cry of surprise, never having felt his full strength before.

"What happens now?" she asked, relaxing against him.

"Anything we want. I suggest sleep, unless you're hungry. I always bring some food into the room at night."

"Sleep sounds fine," she murmured. "But take off your tunic first. I like the feel of your body next to mine—your fur feels so good."

He began to purr, a gentle, rumbling sound that came from deep within him. "You are just so unbelievable," he said, his hand caressing her neck. "If we don't have Link days, will you still want to spend a night with me when we can?"

"When we want," she corrected him. "Tell me, though, why do we need to stay together for a whole day? We don't need to exchange memories, do we?"

"It's safest to be alone when we're this highly sexually charged. It can affect those around us with rather embarrassing consequences. As to not having to exchange memories, look into your mind and you'll find I'm there. I've been sensing your presence within mine for several days now. Not intrusive, just there."

"I've felt the same," she agreed, mouth opening in an enormous yawn.

"Sleep time, I think. We can use the bed if you wish."

"Is this where you sleep?"

He nodded.

"Then here is fine. This will be our space. Now take off your tunic!" she said, sitting up and tugging the hem of it upward, much to his amusement.

As they settled down in the warm glow of the fire, Rezac knew that in this alien female, he'd at last found a soul mate.

*   *   *

T'Chebbi was leaning against a fence where the path to Noni's joined the main road.

"Am I not even allowed to leave Stronghold alone?" he asked quietly as she fell in step beside him.

"Want you kept from hurting yourself," she said shortly. "Not my idea." Her breath formed small clouds in the crisp air.

"Do they expect me to climb a mountain and throw myself off?" he asked, turning to look at her, eye ridges raised in mock surprise. "They don't know me very well."

"Who does, these days?" she retorted.

They walked in silence for some time, Kaid trying to fathom what was wrong with her. "Is that you speaking, or them?"

She stopped abruptly, turning to face him. "You want truth, or polite answer?" Her ears were pricked forward.

He winced and looked away for a moment. "Truth."

"You drive Kusac too hard; you forget his upbringing. Why put yourselves down on duty roster? No need. Could pick and choose missions—achieve same! No need to do execution detail!" She turned away from him and started walking again.

He felt her anger like a physical blow and by the time he'd collected his wits again, he had to run to catch up with her. "Did Kusac complain?"

"No. Carrie did. Loudly, to me, after he'd left. Why take him on that detail?"

"Because of the U'Churians that trade on Jalna. He's never really fought our own kind, never had to kill Sholans. I don't want him freezing up on me if we have to shoot U'Churians."

She stopped again. "That's fighting. This was legalized murder."

"They chose their death," he said reasonably. "They had the choice of a lethal injection or mental reprogramming. It was their decision."

"Even we aren't given that duty till near graduation, and you take him after only a month!" She made a noise of disgust.

"He coped, didn't he? We don't have long until it's time to leave for Jalna."

"Carrie didn't. I had to calm her!"

"She has to learn, too. The world's still too bright, too soft for her now she's a new mother. That has to be left behind. At least she only experienced it secondhand."

T'Chebbi snorted. "What you trying to prove, Kaid? That you have no feelings even though you are a telepath? Were never this hard before."

He grasped her arm, angry with what she was saying, angry because it echoed what Noni had said.

"Is that what you think?" he demanded. "That I don't care about them? Why d'you think I'm pushing so hard? I'm to take two complete novices out into the field on an alien world to rescue nine people, that's why! If it was up to me, I'd take more than six months, maybe as much as a year, to get them properly trained!"

"May be true, but you expect too much! Don't need to teach them everything. You're trying to show that you're the same, that nothing's changed—that's what this about! It has—you have. Only you won't admit it."

Angrily he pushed her aside, heading back to Stronghold at a pace that wasn't far short of a run.

Once inside, he hesitated at the temple doors. A month and a half ago, he'd have gone there, but not surprisingly, he was now barred. He continued up the stairs to his suite, going into the bedroom and closing the door. His head hurt, and he massaged his throbbing forehead as he sat down on the bed.

Maybe she was right and he was pushing Kusac too hard, but he couldn't risk taking them to Jalna untrained. The duty officer had offered to reassign the execution detail to another team, but he'd refused for the very reasons he'd told her—they might have to fight U'Churians, and they were remarkably like Sholans if the Chemerian vids were accurate. T'Chebbi was right that it had been too soon, though, even if Kusac had coped with it.

Kusac had balked when he'd realized why they were there, and had seemed about to object, then, jaws clenched, ears back, he'd stood in line with the rest of the detail. Afterward, he'd refused to talk about it.

Lying down on his bed, Kaid wondered if he should see the physician about the headache but decided against it. He'd only say it was due to his Talent developing and there was nothing he could do.

Were Noni and T'Chebbi right? Was he sinking himself so deeply into his work that he was losing sight of the people involved? For T'Chebbi to openly criticize him like that was unprecedented. Tiredness and pain claimed him, and he was drifting into sleep by the time he heard T'Chebbi enter the lounge next door.

It was dark when he woke. Someone had drawn the drapes and thrown a rug over him—T'Chebbi. Reaching out, he passed his hand over the light sensor till a gentle glow filled the room. He pushed aside the rug, got up, and went to the door, activating it. The lounge was empty.

Instinctively he reached for her mental pattern, then headed downstairs to the refectory. As he got nearer, the smell of hot food made him realize how hungry he was.

Looking around, he located T'Chebbi before going up to the counter to collect a meal, then he joined her.

She acknowledged his presence with a flick of her ear.

"Thank you for looking after me," he said quietly.

She afforded him only a grunt and continued eating.

Sighing inwardly, he attacked his roast fowl with his knife and fingers.

She waited till he'd finished, then, picking up her plates, got to her feet. He followed her over to the trolley, stacking his dish on top of hers.

"I'm taking a shower," she said as they left the refectory and headed back toward the entrance hall.

"Use mine," he said. "Unless you particularly want to use the communal one."

Again she grunted, but chose to accompany him back to his rooms.

After she'd gone into the bathroom, he sat in the lounge thinking over what she'd said earlier, trying to understand why it had angered him so much. His thoughts kept returning to the few times they'd been intimate and it wasn't long before he was forced to admit to himself that he'd enjoyed her company. The female side of her he hardly knew at all, and he had been fascinated by it. Almost immediately came the realization that he wanted and valued that side of her.

His decision made, he got up and entered the bedroom. Taking off his robe, he flung it aside and went into the bathroom. Going over to the shower unit, he reached out to touch T'Chebbi's shoulder, drawing her attention to his presence.

"Would you like some help?" he asked, ears folding back despite his efforts. "It's easier for me to scrub your back."

Suspiciously she eyed him over her shoulder, then, picking up the bottle of soap, she handed it to him and moved over to allow him into the shower.

Stepping under the cascading water, he gasped briefly at the suddenness of its heat. T'Chebbi stood with her back to him, tail hanging down till it almost touched the ground, her unbound hair lying forward over her chest.

Pouring some soap onto his hand, he put the bottle back on the rack and began to gently massage it into her pelt, quickly working it into a lather. As he rubbed it into her sides, he watched the soapy waves trickling down to the small of her back, parting on either side of her tail before running down her legs.

He let his mind become still, just enjoying the firmness of her body beneath his hands, letting his massage gradually become a caress. Crouching down, he worked his way lower, smoothing the suds over her flanks, feeling her muscles clench under his hands as he stroked her lower back just around the base of her tail. She turned her head and looked down at him, blinking away the water that clung to her eyelashes.

He let his hands trail around her thighs and as she began to sway, he felt the tension leave her body. Standing up, his hands circled her waist, steadying her, letting his cheek rest against the side of her head.

"Easy there. You should have left it a little longer before showering. The heat's making you light-headed."

"Perhaps."

He slid one hand slowly across her chest, encouraging her to lean against him. "Perhaps you were right," he said. "Perhaps I care too much and don't know the way to show it."

She started to purr, a low sound of pleasure, as his tongue began to lick her ear.

"It's not lack of caring," he murmured.

"*I* know." She turned round, arms outstretched to hold him. "You needed to."

Afterward, he lay curled around her, enjoying her body warmth and the quiet contentment that flowed from her to him.

"Will you have him?" she asked.

"Mmm?"

"As sword-brother."

"Maybe. Why?"

"Does he know what it entails?"

Kaid snorted gently with amusement. "He thinks he does! He's full of fears and uncertainties now." He reached out to run his hand through her hair.

"Why? He trusted you before."

"He didn't know me before."

She turned her face till she was looking up at him. "Did either you or Garras ask . . ." She let her voice trail off into silence.

"No. The situation never arose."

He sounded unconcerned by her question. She could afford to push the issue. "Would you have?"

"I took the oath with him," he said. "It wasn't part of our pact, but had the need been there and he asked, then in those days, yes. You're very curious all of a sudden."

"Never had a sword-brother, so don't know. About Kusac, would you ask him, if the need arose?"

Kaid stretched his body to its full length, tail flicking against her leg. "He's afraid I might ask," he yawned. "Afraid of what he'd say."

"Would you?" she insisted.

"Who knows? He could be the one to need me. Why is it so important for you to know this?"

"Tell him if it's not part of the ritual. Don't keep him afraid."

"He needs to decide what he wants to bring to this relationship. If I tell him that, then he doesn't need to look inside himself for the answers."

"Did you do this to Garras?"

He began to laugh softly. "You've got it wrong, kitling. Garras did this to *me*!"

She hadn't expected that. Somehow she'd always thought Kaid had been the senior.

Kaid reached out for the brush that lay on his night table and began to run it through the long hank of hair that lay in his other hand. "You know, you do have beautiful hair," he said in the voice of someone to whom it had just come as a revelation.

"Every time I return, she hopes for a message from you,' T'Chebbi said quietly.

The brush strokes stopped and she felt his body tense. "She?"

"Carrie. Your mate. I'd take a message."

He didn't know how to answer her.

"There's no danger to her or cub now. Visions and memories both stopped."

He began brushing her hair again, but it was more automatic now. How had she known? He didn't remember telling anyone of that fear. "I'm not ready to see her yet. I have to get used to the changes in my life—know who I am first."

She flicked her ears in assent and he sensed that she did understand. "Would it help if I went to him so you could be together?"

"You'd do that?" Her offer shocked him. He saw her frown, concerned at his reaction.

"Is there reason why not?"

"None," he said hastily, breaking eye contact with her, the hair grooming forgotten. He laid the brush aside. "Would you really go to him for me?"

"Not just, but yes."

A sudden thought hit him. "Not out of gratitude—you owe me nothing, T'Chebbi, now or in the past."

Her hand touched his arm. "Not that. Because I want to. Couldn't approach him any other way—he's Clan Leader after all. Knowing he'll have company might make it easier for you both."

"And fun for you," he murmured, giving voice to her unspoken thought.

She batted at him, making him start back in surprise. "Stop reading me!" she said, but there was no anger in her voice. "Why not? I have much to offer."

"Heart failure for one," he said, rolling over and getting to his feet. "Just don't use that perfume on him!"

Still lying on her back, she looked over at him as he picked up his robe and began to put it on. "Would you rather I didn't?"

Kneeling on the bed, he leaned over her and flicked her ear gently with a finger. "You do what feels right for you," he said. "No, I don't mind."

She caught his hand. "Tallinu," she began, but he stopped her with a shake of his head.

"No. Not now," he said with finality, carefully releasing himself. "Maybe some day, but not yet." He stood up again. "Take me to the temple, T'Chebbi. They won't let me in alone and I need to meditate."

"At this time of night?" she asked, sitting up, her hair falling in a tawny gray curtain around her face and shoulders.

"Yes, now. Please."

*   *   *

From his bed, Kezule watched Keeza through half-closed eyes. Her presence puzzled him. Originally she'd been left to nurse him, and, he surmised, as a punishment for clumsiness. However, she was still here. Since the visit from the medic, no one had been near him. Food had arrived at the usual times, for him, but there had been none of the cooked carrion her people ate. Did they expect him to feed her out of his rations? Evidently. He'd tested the theory by starving her for several days and sleeping only for short intervals. Nothing. No food was slipped in while they supposed him to be asleep.

She'd found a corner in the room that she considered the most defendable and had kept to it, dragging a couple of spare dining chairs over to make a primitive barricade. It was totally useless, she knew that as well as he did, but it made her feel more secure. He was prepared to let her keep it—for now.

Like him, she'd attempted to stay awake but had soon succumbed to exhaustion. She sat there now, her head slowly drooping toward her knees until, with a sudden jerk, she pulled herself upright again.

A noise from the feeding cage drew his attention. He decided to remain "asleep" and see what she'd do. Hunger and sheer desperation had to drive her to some action soon. A frantic scrabbling heralded the arrival of his meal. He remained still, watching, waiting.

Keeza's ears pricked up as she heard the noise. Her nose picked up the new scent immediately and she lifted her head to look over to the wall mounted cage. Two chiddoes. She was so hungry she could feel the walls of her stomach touching each other. The thought of eating raw meat didn't bother her now, what bothered her was not eating. At least she'd managed to get some water while he slept. Picking up her bowl, she took a sip of the stale, lukewarm liquid. To her, it tasted as good as the most expensive off-world wine.

There were two options. Steal a chiddoe now, and face the consequences later, or wait and ask him. If she waited, and he said no, as she fully expected him to do, then he'd be watching her in future and she wouldn't get an opportunity to steal. Taking it now also meant he'd watch her in future, but at least she'd have eaten one meal. What the hell were they playing at? Why had they left her here without even feeding her? And why wouldn't they communicate with her? She'd asked herself these questions every day and still had only one logical answer. This had been intended from the first. What were they trying to find out? How a Valtegan killed a Sholan using only his bare hands, or was there more to it?

He was still asleep. She risked moving slightly. No reaction. Slowly she stood up, waited a few moments, then carefully began to move one of her chairs, trying not to let it scrape against the floor. She sidled out. Her legs felt unsteady, but that wasn't surprising considering how hungry she was and how long it had been since last she'd actually used them. Sitting crushed up inside her barricade hadn't been easy or comfortable.

Slowly she edged her way over to the cage where the two chiddoes were now small bundles of terrified fur cowering shaking in the corner. Not unlike her own situation, she thought. If they stopped feeding him, would he see her as food? She shuddered and pushed the thought from her mind.

Carefully she lifted the catch, opening the door. Reaching inside, she grabbed hold of one of the creatures, pulling it out and firmly shutting the cage again. She could feel its heartbeat as she held the terrified creature in her hand. Kill it, how could she kill it? It squirmed, trying to get free, and let out one small shriek. She grabbed it in both hands, squeezing them over it and holding it close to her chest in an effort to stifle the sounds it was making. Moving more quickly, she headed back for her fortress. Suddenly its struggles stopped, and it lay still within her grasp. Stopping, she opened her hands. Its head lolled at an impossible angle, sightless eyes staring up at her. Horrified, she would have dropped it but for the fact the Valtegan was looming over her, his large hand closing over hers and the dead chiddoe.

He backhanded her, sending her reeling before he pulled her back and dealt her another blow to the other side of her head.

"Steal my food, would you?" he demanded. "Let your own people feed you, they left you here. Next time, I kill you," he said, opening his hand to remove the creature from her limp grasp. His next blow sent her staggering against her barricade. She landed awkwardly on top of it, sliding down to the floor in an unconscious heap. Blood seeped slowly from a cut over one rapidly swelling eye.

Turning his back on her, he went to the table and sat down to begin preparing the carcass.

"He'll kill her," said Mito anxiously from her post at the other side of the room.

Anders looked questioningly at Zhyaf.

"She's still with us, unconscious but alive," he said.

"Why d'you think he did that?" Anders asked the telepath.

"Protecting his territory, reminding her who's in charge," he said shortly, turning away from the viewing window to his desk comm.

"Mito?"

"Testing us," she said, getting up to join him. "Seeing if we'll react. He knows he's being watched, his body language tells us that loud and clear."

"He must still be considering the possibility that she's a spy for us."

"I would say so," she agreed. "He's not beating her up for his own amusement, or he'd have done it before now. I think he's waiting to see if we'll intervene on her behalf. He's letting us know he isn't prepared to feed her out of his own rations."

"What's he likely to do next?"

She shrugged. "Eat."

"Well, at least he's finally communicating with her," Anders sighed.

They watched him prepare the carcass, sprinkling the

herb on it before beginning to eat. He repeated the proce
dure with the second, then returned to his bed.

"Take a break now, Zhyaf," said Anders. "Get your
lunch. Nothing much is likely to happen for a while."

Zhyaf got up from the bench. "Can I bring you back
anything?"

"A selection of sandwiches," said Mito, "and a jug of
coffee. I reckon this is going to be a long shift."

Pain was the first thing she was aware of when she came
to. She tried to open her eyes, panicking until she remembered he'd hit her. Putting a hand experimentally up to
her face, she gently probed the blood-encrusted cut on her
forehead and the puffy eye beneath it. No wonder she
couldn't open it. Licking her fingers, she gently eased the
eyelashes apart and attempted to open her eyes again. Only
a crack, but it was enough. She could still see, the Gods
be praised!

She tried moving then, unable to stop a groan escaping
her as she pulled herself free from the tangle of chairs.
Landing on hands and knees, she collapsed to the floor,
every muscle and joint a jangle of pain.

"Bring them here," a harsh, sibilant voice ordered her.

She froze, then lifting her head, looked toward the table
where Kezule was finishing his last meal of the day.

"I've humored you long enough. It's over."

Getting stiffly to her feet, she picked up one of the utili-
tarian metal chairs and limped over to the table. Keeping
her distance, she pushed it toward him then, as swiftly as
she could, headed back for the other. When she'd done,
she retreated to her corner, head throbbing, body aching.

She watched him eating, the smell of raw meat and fresh
blood making her stomach growl with hunger. When he
looked in her direction, she drew her legs up, wrapped her
arms around them, and buried her face against her knees.
She did not want him noticing her.

Ignoring her completely, he finished his food, licked his
hands clean, and got up. He was tired, but until he knew
he could trust her not to try and murder him in his sleep,
he couldn't afford the luxury of more than a series of naps.

He lay facing the room, head turned toward her corner,
and shut his eyes. He'd purposely left the remains of his
meal out as a temptation for her. If they wouldn't feed her,

he'd have to, once she realized he was the master. They'd taught him that lesson, now he'd teach her; she would eat only at his pleasure.

He'd dozed and wakened several times before he sensed her moving. She'd done well to last this long, he thought grudgingly. He'd not have been so patient. Waiting till her hand was reaching out for his plate of scraps, he leaped from the bed, landing beside her. One hand flattened hers to the table, the other grasped her by the throat.

Her cry of terror was strangled before she'd made it. "A born thief," he said with contempt, tongue flicking toward her face till it almost touched her. "I told you next time you'd die."

Her free hand scrabbled at his as she squirmed, trying to break loose. Her mouth opened as she tried desperately to speak. He relaxed his hold a fraction, just enough for her to catch her breath.

"Please, I have to eat! I've had nothing for days!"

"The dead don't eat." He let her see his needle-sharp teeth. "Maybe I use you as food." He let his tongue flick out to touch her face this time. She tasted vile, but it was necessary.

"I'm not food," she wept. "You can't eat me! I'm a person, for Vartra's sake!"

"You're nothing. Your own people don't want you. They let you starve, not me," he said, releasing her other hand.

"Please, don't kill me." She was whimpering in earnest now, tears coursing down her face, mingling with the dried blood. "I'll do anything, anything you want, only don't kill me."

With a noise of disgust, he let her go, watching as she collapsed in a small, sobbing heap on the floor. "You aren't worth killing, certainly not worth eating." He turned his back on her, returning to sit on his bed. "Clean yourself up," he ordered. "Your stench is offensive."

He watched her push herself upright and make her way painfully to the basin. Filling it with water, she splashed it over her face, trying to rinse the blood from her pelt. Finished, she turned and looked around for something to dry herself on. Seeing the towel, she looked over to him. He stared unblinkingly at her. She hesitated, then lifted the hem of her tunic, patting her face dry on that.

Stretching out on his bed, he ignored her, waiting to see

what she'd do next. It was a good fifteen minutes before she spoke.

"I need to eat," she said in a small voice.

"No. Your feeding is not my concern."

She began to weep. "Please, your scraps . . . If you don't want them . . . I'm so hungry!"

He considered it for a moment. She was desperate now. If he didn't let her have them, she might do something reckless. After all, she had nothing to lose.

"Bring them to me."

With pathetic eagerness, she scurried over to the table, retrieved the plate, and approached him, holding it out at arm's length.

He took it from her, picking over the scraps, watching her as he did so. Her ears, which had risen, began to fall backward till he could no longer see them amid her hair. Picking up a morsel, he put it in his mouth. A tiny whimper escaped her.

Abruptly he handed the plate back to her. "You eat when I say you can eat," he said. "Take it and go back to your corner."

Clutching the plate tightly to her chest, she limped back to her barren sanctuary, hunkered down on her heels and waited.

Disgusted, he snarled, "Eat it!" and shut his eyes. He couldn't stand to see her eagerness to eat what he considered carrion. He'd owned a pet before, all leading members of the military had a pet telepath, but he'd treated him well, for a slave. This went against the grain. Even inferior species deserved some dignity, but his captors had placed him in this position. The score was mounting, and one day, he'd exact a proper price for the indignities and injuries to his person. Meanwhile, he had to make sure this female didn't dare pose a threat to him.

"Thank Vartra!" Mito sighed. "I thought he'd let her starve to death."

"I didn't think that," said Rhyaz, "but I think it was close. I was depending on his sense of what was right and proper to save her. He considers it our dereliction of duty that she's starving, but we've made it his responsibility, and he isn't one to shirk those, however unpleasant. How is she coping?" he asked Zhyaf. "How much of that was acting on Keeza's part?"

"None," said the telepath shortly. "She made use of what she'd learned with the Consortias, but that was real."

"In a day or two, I think Myak will pay him a visit. A few goodies now would go down well."

"What about the food?" asked Anders. "Does he get more to account for feeding her?"

"Not yet. She can survive for a couple of days on the scraps that Kezule will let her have."

"What reason are you going to give him for leaving Keeza there?" asked Mito.

"Whim. Remember, I'm the one who enjoys inflicting pain and humiliation on both of them," he said with a wry smile. "I don't need reasons. You needn't stay any longer. We've seen what we needed to for tonight. The next shift's been waiting for the last hour. Go and get some rest."

"Don't you find it difficult to play a part like this?" asked Mito, gathering her personal belongings.

Rhyaz afforded her a curious look. "You get used to it. Reminding myself what's at stake makes it easier."

When breakfast arrived, Kezule strolled over to the cage, taking the first chiddoe out and releasing it.

"You want to eat, you catch it," he said. "Kill it and bring it to me, then you can have some."

She looked at him in horror. "I can't kill it!"

The blow was light by Valtegan standards, but it still sent her reeling across into the table. The chiddoe squeaked and dashed under the bed.

"Address me as General," he hissed, "and don't ever tell me what you can't do! You will obey me in everything, instantly, and without argument. Understood?"

"Yes, General," she mumbled, regaining her balance.

His hand grasped her by the throat again, and squeezed. This time, he let her feel the sharpness of his claws. "Maybe I eat you after all, for being so clumsy." His face was almost touching hers, and he made sure she got a close look at his teeth.

"Yes, General," she said, her good eye wide with terror.

He released her. "Now catch it!"

Her chase did afford him some small amount of amusement as he sat and prepared the other chiddoe. Her bruises and hunger had slowed her down, and she was hard pushed to corner the little rodent. Finally she trapped it under one of the blankets he'd given her permission to use. Had he not, she'd still have been chasing it by the time his last meal of the day arrived.

She stood with the squirming creature held in front of her for him to see.

"Now kill it," he said.

She tried to strangle it, but only got herself bitten in the process.

"Surely you know how to kill!" he said in exasperation.

She shook her head.

He showed her, then demonstrated how to skin and gut it. Slicing off a haunch, he threw it to her. Snatching it up, she retreated to her corner and sat waiting. For a moment he was baffled, knowing how hungry she was, then he remembered. "You may eat," he said.

Over the next couple of days, he found tasks for her to perform, simple ones that he could well have done himself, but he'd decided she should earn her right to eat. When there was nothing to do, he made her sit in her corner.

For each meal, he made her fetch a chiddoe and watched as she killed and prepared it, dealing her a blow each time she didn't do it the way he'd shown her. Then he'd eat it before getting the second one himself. Sometimes he left her only the scraps, others, a piece of raw meat.

On the third day, shortly before the last meal was due, the door slid open, admitting two troopers who immediately took up positions covering him with their rifles.

"General Kezule. It's nice to see you again," said Sub-Lieutenant Myak, strolling in behind them. "I've been authorized to let you have another item or two." He gestured toward the still open door through which two more troopers entered. Going straight to the bed, they lifted it up. Staggering slightly under its weight, they carried it from the room, tilting it on its side to get it through the doorway.

Kezule was extremely curious, but he kept his gaze on Myak. He saw the female raise her head and move slightly as if to get up, then, as she caught sight of his eyes flicking in her direction, she subsided again.

A few minutes later, the males reentered, carrying a different bed, one that began look more familiar as it was righted to carry it across the room.

"I think you'll find this more suited to you than the beds we use," Myak said. "The rewards of cooperation. Have you had any thoughts on items you would like us to find for you?"

"I need little," Kezule replied shortly.

"Very well. Remember, cooperation will make your life more comfortable." He turned to leave, then stopped to look over his shoulder. "We have more books, and more of that herb. I hope I have the opportunity to give them to you soon."

"Take her," said Kezule abruptly. "Take the female with you. Her presence offends me."

Again Myak stopped. "I'm afraid I can't do that." His tone was regretful. "It's not in my authority to remove her. I can have them bring a blanket for her, though."

"She's your responsibility, not mine. Do as you wish," said Kezule dismissively.

Before the door closed, a trooper returned with a blanket which he threw at the female. She reached out to pick it up, then froze.

"Leave it," Kezule snapped, getting up and going over to the new bed. Pulling back the covers, he felt the mattress. It gave beneath his hand. He tugged it free of the retaining frame to examine it more closely. It was filled with some type of yielding substance that gave slightly when pressed, yet when released, sprang back into shape. He let it fall back into its frame. Like the books and the reader, similar yet just different enough.

He strode over to the female, catching hold of her by the hair and yanking her to her feet. "Where did they get this?" he demanded. "This wasn't left behind from the past, was it? Where did it come from?"

"I don't know," she said, hands grasping hold of his arm as she tried to find her footing. "What past? I know nothing about the past!"

He shook her like a small animal, her weight meaning nothing to him. "Don't lie! You know where it came from! Tell me!"

"I don't," she wailed, tears of pain beginning to spill from her eyes. "How should I know? I'm not one of them! I don't work for them!"

"My people, where are they?" he demanded, shaking he
again. "Here, or on another world?"

"They were on the Humans' world, but we drove then
off!"

He dropped her, striding back to the table. Sitting down
he began to think furiously. His people had returned bu
had been driven off—by these misbegotten fur-covered
mammals! He began to hiss, a low sound of anger and rage
This distorted the natural order of things! They'd neve
been defeated before! How had this species gotten to the
level where they could drive them off so easily? Could the
events on Shola have been repeated throughout thei
Empire?

He had only a vague notion of where the home worlds
of his people were in relation to Shola, though he knew
the distances involved were immense. But whatever had
happened, if they could get to the Humans' world, why
hadn't they returned here? Was there something he'd
missed by remaining on Shola during the fall of the meteor-
ite—by being taken captive? Whatever it was, the answer
was devastating for his kind, and he was sure it lay in the
past, not here. If he could only return to his own time, then
none of this need happen! The appearance of the items this
Myak brought now made sense. They came from the
Human world. He had to escape, and soon. No, he corrected himself, not soon. He had all the time he needed, if
he could find those who'd brought him here and force them
to return him to his own time.

The Human female had been pregnant. She'd have
birthed her young by now. All to the good. The child could
be the lever he needed to force them to take him back.
From now on, he'd watch for any opportunities to escape,
for any clue as to what went on outside those opaque doors
and walls. They wanted him to request items they could
find, did they? The tech level of his modern counterparts
might be different, but he knew from what they'd given
him already that there were strong similarities between
what they had then and now. There were one or two things
that might just give him the edge, items whose purpose
might not be easily divined by these Sholans.

He got to his feet and went over to the bed. Carefully
he lowered himself to its surface, feeling it give slowly beneath him. There had been improvements. In his time, they

hadn't developed such a versatile filling. Stretching out full length, he allowed himself to experience the pleasure of feeling the mattress adjust itself to his shape, supporting yet relaxing his back at the same time. Even the riser for his head was made of the same substance. He closed his eyes, enjoying the comfort.

He came awake with a shock, quickly realizing that several hours had passed. Sitting up, he immediately looked over at the female. She was lying slumped on the floor, obviously asleep, the blanket still lying where it had been left. A glance at the table told him she hadn't touched the leavings of his meal either.

Either this was a very subtle move on their part to place a spy with him, or she was actually of no value to them. Information was what they wanted, and now he knew exactly why. His people might have been driven off, but they wouldn't have led the Sholans to their home worlds!

Did they really think he'd talk to this pitiful wretch? He, a General, one of the Chosen of the God-King—*May His memory be revered for all time*—would he be likely to befriend one of their females, one of breeding age who was allowed to run free? Worse, one who had been thrown into his prison, obviously for him to use? They didn't know him! And if they did, they could gauge the rest of his people accordingly, he realized. Had they been unable to secure captives, then? The Sholan telepaths wouldn't have been forgotten, they would have their place in his people's racial memory. When next they came across the Sholans, they'd recognize their species immediately. But what response would be programmed in with the memory?

He began to think it through logically. The telepaths had been trusted, taken by the highest of his people as pets, their talents used to help control the other slave races, let their masters know when they were thinking forbidden thoughts, planning escape. And they had betrayed those who'd shown them trust and favor. The natural response would be fear, and a desire to destroy them. What if they had managed to touch their masters' minds after all? His pet couldn't; he said the Valtegan mind was too different for him to read. He wasn't lying, of that Kezule was sure. But what if some of them *were* able to touch his people's minds? Highly talented ones? He seemed to remember that they sometimes formed pairs. Yes, pairs of them might

prove powerful enough to reach a mind so superior t
theirs. Then the response would be to keep away from suc
people, to kill them on sight lest they touch their mind:
And if these Sholan pairs had had such abilities, the firs
to be affected would be the highest within the Empire
those who had the highly prized pairs . . . perhaps the God
King Himself!

He shivered, his blood running cold as he grasped th
enormity of what might have happened the day that th
Sholans had struck back. Their mental attack could have
been repeated throughout the colonized worlds, causing the
same devastation that Shola had suffered, completely wip
ing out the top layers of Valtegan society in one blow. N
wonder they had never returned to this world! No wonde
they had been driven off the Human planet! So much sud
denly became clear. This was why they were so desperate
for information! Then he remembered the Human female
again. She'd touched his mind, stolen his unspoken words
He began to sweat, smelled his own rising fear. Why hadn'
they used her again? Taken from him that which they
wanted? She'd been breeding, though. Maybe only the
pregnant females could do it. It would explain why they'd
needed Sholan help to defeat his species. Whatever the
reason, they hadn't used her against him . . . yet. He had
to get out before they loosed another pregnant Human
on him.

He heard a sound from the corner where the female
slept. Looking in her direction, he saw her stirring. Perhaps
her presence was not such an imposition after all. Perhaps
he could turn it to his advantage.

* * *

When Kusac emerged from the shower, Carrie was lying
on the bed playing with Kashini. As the door opened, the
cub turned, ears pricked toward it, body tense with anticipation, small tail pointing upward to the ceiling, quivering.

He entered, and with a mewl of pleasure, she bounded
across the bed, launching herself into space at her father.
Carrie, heart leaping into her mouth with fear, dived after
her, but Kusac was already there.

"Hey, what's all this about?" he asked her, holding her
close to his chest as her small hands twined themselves
deep into his long fur. "You mustn't jump off the bed like

that! You gave your mother an awful scare," he scolded as he sat down beside a rather pale Carrie. "She's gotten very active," he added.

"Far too active," said Carrie, pushing herself back into a sitting position.

"And larger."

Kashini had grown a lot in the last few weeks. She was now nearly the size of a plump four-month-old Human baby. She was mobile now, though still very unsteady on her legs. At times it looked as if her belly barely cleared the ground. Already the differences between her and a pure Sholan cub were beginning to show. Her straighter lower limbs made four-legged locomotion less easy, as had been the case with Marak, and Vanna's opinion was that it would help them to stand and walk upright earlier.

"I know. I only see her in the evenings now that I'm at the Warrior Guild." Carrie moved back to allow her mate to stretch out on the bed.

Kashini, totally unaware of the anxiety her leap of faith had caused, was now crawling up her father's chest till she reached his face. Once there, she began licking him furiously.

"Yes, I'm pleased to see you, too," he said, running an affectionate hand through the cub's downy hair before tickling her behind the ears. "I've only been having a shower, you know!"

A loud buzzing purr greeted his attentions and, rolling onto her back, she reached up to grasp his hand with both of hers. The furious licks continued for a short while, then turned into attempts to chew his fingers.

"She's teething," said Carrie, holding out a hand covered in bright pink scratches. Kusac winced in sympathy. "Her teeth are sharp, aren't they?" she commented. "Human children don't cause their parents these problems."

"Would you rather have had a Human child?" he asked, flicking Kashini's nose with his fingertips in an effort to remove them from her mouth.

"Don't be silly. You know that's not important to me," said Carrie, reaching out to tickle his ribs, well aware of his thoughts, even at the end of their Link day.

He moved away, letting Kashini roll onto the bed between them. "You're ganging up on me," he complained in fun. "Not fair!"

"That's what you get for teasing me," she said, watching in amusement as Kashini, now out of Kusac's sight upon the pillows, began to stalk his ear. An experimental swipe went wide, missing him by inches.

The cub hunkered down, rear end raised, a frown on her face as she tracked the targeted ear.

"How were things at Stronghold?" she asked just an instant before the cub pounced, claws and teeth closing sharply on her father's ear.

Kusac yowled, reaching up to grab her and save his ear from further savagery. "That's enough, cub," he said firmly, holding her round the ribs, suspended in midair above his face. He tried hard to ignore Carrie who was by now rolling around on the bed, laughing.

"Not to bite me. That's naughty. I think it's time you went back to the nursery. It's well past your bedtime." Sitting up, he transferred her to the crook of his arm and got up.

"Let me say good night first," said Carrie, coming closer to the edge of the bed.

Kusac knelt down till Kashini was level with her. She leaned forward to caress her daughter's cheek and plant a kiss on her brow.

"Good night, Kashini," she whispered, rubbing her cheek against her child's. "Sleep well."

"I hadn't realized how much of a handful she'd become. I should have been here to help you," said Kusac apologetically when he returned. "How do you cope?"

"You're doing what you have to," she said. "I have lots of help, as well as the nurse. Dzaka's been wonderful, and, strangely enough, Kitra. She's kept me company and played with Kashini a lot."

"Dzaka?" He sounded surprised.

"He said since you were away because of his father, it was his responsibility to help me. He still considers himself her personal guard and has even asked for a permanent bed to be made up in the nursery lounge! He and Kitra sleep there when she's staying overnight. You'd say he's taken to looking after her *like a kitling to the hunt*."

Kusac grunted as he stretched out beside her. "Not surprising considering he was a father once. It's Kitra's sudden liking for domesticity that worries me."

"Don't," said Carrie, reaching out to take his hand. "It's a novelty for now. Once her new term begins at the Guild, she'll be back with friends and interests appropriate to her own age. You'll see."

"I hope so," he said. "Now tell me what you've been doing."

"The same old routine training," she said, pulling a face. "Tell me what you've been up to. You feel more relaxed this time."

Though their Link meant that each was constantly aware of what the other was thinking and doing, they preferred to discuss the more memorable events, both good and bad. It made coping with the sudden influx of information every five days easier.

"I am," he admitted, turning on his side so he was facing her. "No doubt you heard the tale of Master Esken's wife."

"We all did, but go on," she said, aware there was better to come.

"Kaid and I were given the job of picking her up from the Consortia House."

She sat up in astonishment. "With the way Esken feels about our family, they actually sent you?"

He nodded. "Kaid checked, but apparently Master Lijou himself asked for us to be given the detail. So yesterday, we headed out to Ranz to pick her up from the House. She was heavily wrapped up against the cold, but we didn't think anything of it at the time. We'd no sooner taken off than she asked us to stop at a house on the outskirts of the city. They were obviously expecting her, and as soon as we'd landed, she went inside. She couldn't have been gone more than fifteen minutes, but when she came back, there was something different about her. I couldn't put my finger on it, though. Even Kaid sensed it. Once we were underway, she took her coat off and settled down to chat with us. She was very nice, insisted on getting *us* drinks from the dispenser, that sort of thing. Not at all what I'd expected."

"What were you expecting?"

"Some high-class intellectual, too good to talk to the likes of us. You should have seen Esken's instructions on how we were to treat her, Carrie." A low purr of amusement accompanied his grin. "We were not to initiate conversation with her unless she expressly asked for it. We were to see she was offered drinks and snacks on the jour ney, and anything else she might request. She couldn't have been more different! As I said, she fetched drinks for us and when it came time for us to eat, she scrounged sand wiches from us rather than eat the fancy delicacies Esken had sent along! She's got a healthy appetite, I'll say that for her. She also spent quite a bit of time asking questions about our good Guild Master."

"I'll bet she did! What happened when you arrived?"

"Esken was waiting, all smiles and politeness till he saw us. Then he commandeered the nearest aircar and, stuffing her into it, headed off to the temple. We were trying to work out what was going on when Sorli strolled up, asking us why we'd brought Mother's friend rather than the Consortia. That's when we realized what had happened."

"The Consortia and Challa must have been in league from the first," said Carrie. "Your mother said at the time that Juilmi Rraoud had accepted too easily and she intended to find out why. Now we know."

"Lijou at least was aware of what was happening. Esken must have assumed, as we were obviously supposed to, that we'd brought the Consortia. Our presence was probably calculated to make him decide to take no chances on being persuaded out of this marriage. That's why he took her to the temple to have the life-bonding ceremony performed immediately."

"I wonder when he figured out that he was marrying the wrong female. I'd have loved to have been a fly on the wall at that moment," Carrie laughed.

"I think during the ceremony. She must have had him make his vows first because they're binding from the time he makes them. When he came back, his face was like a thundercloud! We left as quickly as we could."

A gentle beeping from the comm unit in the other room drew their attention. "I wonder who it is," said Kusac, frowning as he got up to answer it.

She switched off her damper, allowing their minds to completely share, sensing Kusac doing the same as he went into the other room.

"Father Lijou," he said in surprise. "What can we do for you?"

"I apologize for the lateness of the call, but I wanted to

let you know there was no need for you to return to Stronghold for the next couple of days," the head priest said.

"Is Kaid all right?"

"Kaid's fine," Lijou reassured him. "He's requested a few days at the Retreat, that's all. Take some time off, Kusac, be with your family. You've both been working hard, you deserve a break. In fact, make that an order," he said with a slow smile. "Leave it with me, I'll let Rhyaz know."

"Is he all right?" Kusac insisted.

Lijou's ears flicked to emphasize his affirmative. "He really is fine. He needs to see to matters of a spiritual nature, nothing more, I assure you. T'Chebbi will contact you when it's time to return."

The call over, Kusac returned to the bedroom.

"So Noni was right," said Carrie. "Kaid is finally healing. Now, what shall we do with this extra time together?"

Kusac began to kiss her, sliding his hands down her sides till he was holding her bottom. *I know what I want to do now.*

Tomorrow?

See our friends, and the rest of my family, he replied, tipping her down onto her back, his tail snaking round her leg.

CHAPTER 10

It had been five weeks since he'd last visited the temple and he had no idea what had prompted him to come now. Curiosity? A desire to see if Vartra the God would speak to him again? He pulled open the door and waited for T'Chebbi to precede him. He'd rushed her so much that she only had enough time to dress, nothing more, so her hair remained an unbound cloud of browns, golds, and grays that reached down almost to her waist. As she passed him, he reached out to touch it. She stopped to look up at him, puzzled by the gesture.

He shrugged and followed her inside. Stopping, he inhaled the aromatic air, taking comfort from the familiar scent of the incense. Torches cast flickering shadows that were almost old friends to him. It was good to be back in the environment that had once been a home to him. He must be getting old if such things suddenly meant so much.

"Not old, just in need of comfort as we all are at certain times in our lives." Father Lijou's voice came from the shadows at the far end of the main aisle. "It's good to see you back again, Tallinu."

As the Guild Master stepped out from behind a pillar, Kaid began to walk toward him. The glow from the braziers flanking the statue of Vartra turned the streaks of white on the priest's face and ear tips golden. *The color of Kashini's pelt, and her mother's hair,* he thought, realizing as he did that his mind was straying into irrelevancies.

"Not irrelevancies," said Lijou as he stopped in front of him. "Sometimes, during the hours of darkness, we can see what truly matters. The light of day often blinds us to what is in front of our noses all along. What brings you here this late, Tallinu?"

"A visit, nothing more, Father Lijou," Kaid said. "Don't read more into it than there is."

"I would never do that, Tallinu." He reached out to take Kaid by the arm, drawing him away from the central area. 'Let's go somewhere quieter."

They walked between the pillars, toward the side wall where the entrance to the largest of the shrines was housed.

"Ghyakulla," said Kaid, blinking as he followed Lijou through the narrow doorway. The light in the Goddess' shrine was blinding after the dimness of the main temple.

Lijou led him to a small wooden seat, its back set against the raw rock face. "Did Father Jyarti ever bring you here? This is one of my favorite places for meditating."

"A few times," Kaid admitted, sitting down and looking round the chamber. Concealed lamps that duplicated sunlight illuminated the shrine, nourishing the plants and allowing them to thrive within their rocky womb. "He said it wasn't time for me to know the Goddess yet."

Beneath his feet, the carpet of grass that covered the cavern floor felt warm. Around him, bushes and rare plants bloomed, their flowers a delight to the senses. A movement of air brought the subtle scent of the nung blossom to his nostrils. He turned his head till he could see the gnarled tree standing in pride of place on a small grass-covered rise. Memories of the day he'd gone to Noni for help for Carrie came back sharply to him. The nung tree had been in bloom then, too.

"We're lucky to have a shrine such as this," said Lijou. "Only Ghyakulla's own temple has one better. The rest are merely painted rooms or chambers. I never could understand how one could worship the Goddess of Shola in a place that was not full of Her living creations. How do the Humans worship their Goddess?"

"Their Goddess doesn't have a formal cult," said Kaid absently as he looked around for the source of the running water. It hadn't been there when he'd last visited. "Just people like Derwent."

"Surely not. No Goddess could be so impoverished, I'm sure."

"Carrie left Earth when she was but a kitling, Father Lijou," said Kaid, finally catching sight of the small stream that issued from under a rocky overhang to his right. "According to Derwent, their planet has lost touch with the world of the Green Goddess."

"Ah, that explains how someone like him came about.

Perhaps, when they are ready, we have more to teach ther than they think. I come here often. The sound of wate soothes my soul like nothing else can. As I said, we'r fortunate indeed to be able to enjoy a taste of summer a the year round in our windswept mountains."

"It reminds me of the Wilderness on board th *Khalossa*."

"The Wilderness? I suppose it does, in a way. Just don' let illusion become confused with reality, Tallinu."

Kaid swung his head round to look at the priest, frown ing. "Illusion?"

"The Wilderness exists to entertain; this does not. I teaches us many things about life if we can but sit and listen and watch."

A flash of light caught his eye. Kaid turned his head to see what it was, but all he could see was the rock face He looked back at Lijou. "What lessons are you speaking of, Father?"

Lijou raised an eye ridge. "You ask me that when you've learned so many of them? You disappoint me, Tallinu."

Again the flash of light, and again, when he turned to look, he could see nothing.

"What do you see?"

"Something shining," said Kaid, forcing his attention back to the Head Priest.

"Then go and see what it is."

Their eyes met. "It's an illusion," said Kaid. "A flicker of light, nothing more."

"As you say," agreed Lijou, beginning to get to his feet. "The restrictions on you entering the temple are lifted, Tal-linu. You may come and go whenever you wish."

Kaid hardly heard what he said. Something in the rock face was catching his attention and he needed to know what it was. He felt a hand on his shoulder and started in surprise.

"You've been looking at the same piece of rock face for the last five minutes," said Lijou gently. "Why not go over and see what it is?"

Kaid hesitated, then, getting to his feet, he began to walk toward it. The grass was slightly damp and as he moved across it, the scent of the warm, rich earth rose around him. Reaching the chamber wall, he stooped to look down at the rock face.

"Nothing," he said, fingers going to probe at it in disbelief. "It was nothing!"

"Look again, Tallinu," said Lijou from the doorway.

Extending his claws, Kaid scraped away at the lichen and
loose debris. Within moments, he'd exposed a small, blue-
white crystal, still embedded in the living wall of the Dzahai
Mountains. "A crystal! How could I possibly have seen it
from where we sat?" he asked, gently rubbing his fingertips
over the planes as he looked over at Lijou.

"Yet you knew it was there, hidden within the rock,"
said the priest. "I think it's time you visited Guardian
Dhaika at the Retreat, Tallinu."

Kaid straightened up. "Why?"

"The Guardian will tell you, my friend. Come to me
tomorrow morning and I'll arrange for you to visit him.
You needn't take Sister T'Chebbi with you unless you wish
to," he added as he left the chamber.

Thoughtfully Kaid turned back to the crystal, giving it
one last rub before he, too, left the shrine.

T'Chebbi was waiting for him by the main doors. "Father
Lijou said my job is over."

Kaid nodded. "I go to the Retreat tomorrow. I'm to see
Guardian Dhaika." He watched her, wanting to see what
her reaction would be. Even so, he almost missed the slight
relaxing of her ears and their immediate recovery. She
didn't want to leave.

"You may come if you wish," he said.

She shrugged and began to turn away. "When do we
leave?"

Lijou headed straight for the night desk, requesting that
the duty messenger meet him in his office immediately.
He'd no sooner sat down than the Brother was scratching
at his door.

"Take this to Noni," Lijou said, handing him a portable
comm unit. "Apologize for disturbing her at this hour, then
give her the note. If she doesn't let you in, suggest it. Set
this up on her table, dial into Stronghold, then leave.
Understand?"

The Brother nodded once, picked up the comm unit,
and left.

"Damned cloak-and-dagger stuff," Lijou muttered.

"What is?" asked Kha'Qwa as she pushed his office door

open. "What's happening that's so important it can't wait till morning?"

"Kaid. Noni wanted to know immediately he was ready to go to the Retreat."

"Ready to go? To do what?" she asked, going over to his less formal seats and curling up in one of them.

"It's one of our rituals. Not everyone is suitable. In fact very few are, but Tallinu is."

"What ritual?"

"Ghyakulla's."

"Ghyakulla? I know she's both mother and consort to Vartra, but I've never heard of anyone doing a ritual of hers here at Stronghold. Which ritual do you mean?"

"Some rituals are known only to senior members of the Brotherhood, Kha'Qwa. It's a dream time one. When I heard that Tallinu had actually escaped from his body during his captivity, I knew that one day he'd need to take the ritual. It'll help center him, give him the strength he now needs to complete his healing."

"If he's still feeling betrayed by Vartra, then how will a ritual involving Ghyakulla help?"

"I met him in the temple not an hour ago. He chose to go there. Trust me, Kha'Qwa, this is my field. He's ready to meet Ghyakulla."

"Meet? How can he meet Her?" Her voice was high-pitched with surprise.

"Ah, well, I suppose you ought not to know," he mumbled, avoiding her gaze. "But I need someone to share these burdens with! Yes, there are such rituals, and yes, I've taken some of them in my time. Who can say who it is you meet on these dream walks. I choose to believe it is Ghyakulla."

"How many have taken this particular ritual?"

"Not many," he admitted. "I have. It does involve some danger. People have been lost in the dream worlds and been unable to return, just like those we lost in the Margins rituals."

"Is it wise for him to try this so soon after his trip to the Margins?"

"He must. He's been called by Ghyakulla Herself."

"How do you know?"

"I was there, Kha'Qwa," he said gently, getting up and going to join her. "He saw the light in Ghyakulla's shrine

hining off a crystal set in the rock face. I saw nothing till
we'd scraped off the lichen and muck that covered it."

"Good grief. I'm sorry, Lijou. I shouldn't have doubted
you, but we seem to be suddenly living in such active times!
There were always one or two who heard the Gods, and if
you looked, you could sometimes see their hands at work
in your life, but now . . . They're so active!"

"Think of them as the spirits of our ancestors, and remember that we went back in time to disturb them. Doesn't
their intervention seem less fantastic?"

"I suppose," she agreed dubiously.

The comm beeped, calling him back to his desk.

"He was fast," said Kha'Qwa with a sigh, pulling her
robe more firmly about herself.

"Aircar," said Lijou shortly, turning the unit on.

"You'd better have a damned good reason for hauling
me out of my bed in the middle of the night," Noni said,
ears lying sideways in anger.

"You wanted to know immediately when the Goddess
called him, Noni," said Lijou. "You were most specific.
Immediately, you said."

Her ears lifted. "Already? By Vartra, when I get it right,
I really get it right," she muttered. "What'd you do?
What'd you tell him?"

"I'm sending him to the Retreat for a few days to see
the Guardian. I hope that fits in with what you wanted,
because that's what he's doing."

"Fine, fine. You did well, Master Lijou," she said. "And
you were right to disturb me. Now tell that lad of yours to
get back in here and take this contraption away with him."

"It stays, Noni. Please do me the courtesy of keeping it
there. It makes communications between us much easier."

"I told you, I hate these damned . . ." She stopped in
mid-flow and regarded him for a moment. "It can stay,"
she said abruptly. "You and that young mate of yours get
back to bed and let an old woman get some sleep.
Goodnight."

Taken aback by the suddenness of her capitulation, Lijou
stared at the blank screen for a moment before turning
it off.

"That's it?" asked Kha'Qwa. "Nothing more? No explanation?"

He shook his head. "We won't get one either. Not til
it's over, and then only if we're lucky."

Within an hour, Noni, accompanied by her assistan
Teusi, was waiting in Guardian Dhaika's private lounge.

"Noni, what in the God's name are you doing here a
this hour?" Dhaika demanded, then stopped, catching sigh
of Teusi. "By your leave, Noni. Teusi, fetch some hot c'sha
for us, please." He waited till the youth had left befor
continuing. "When does he arrive?"

"Tomorrow morning. Lijou dragged me from my bed, s
I didn't see why you should get to sleep on undisturbed."
She grinned an evil grin. "Remember, don't teach him hov
to dream walk alone."

Dhaika sat down. "I have to if the Goddess has callec
him, Noni, no matter what's been decided."

"You'd turn your back on the Council? Knowing wha
it could cost us—could cost Shola?" she demanded.

"You tread your own path all the time, Noni," he re
torted angrily. "You ignored the ruling on noninvolvemen
with the Human female! Don't talk to me about my duty
My duty is also to this Retreat, to the God, and Goddess!"

"I'm not saying neglect the Goddess!" she snapped
"Take him there, let him meet Her! Just don't let him take
the ritual! It's too soon. We need them all, not just him
Dhaika. Shola needs an En'Shalla Triad as Guardians!"

He remained silent, glowering across the space that sepa
rated them.

"Let Ghyakulla decide, if you prefer it put that way,"
she sighed. "The rituals are ours, our way of understanding
the entities. All you are being asked to do is not to teach
him how to dream walk."

"All, Noni? When did the Council ask for a small mat
ter? Believe me, this is nothing small they are demanding!
This touches on the heart of my faith, what I believe in
and stand for!"

"Then trust Her to know what She wants to do! If She
wants him taught to walk, She'll do it, right? His mind is
beginning to heal. A shock like this could unhinge him. He
needs to bind himself more tightly to his Triad first. This
is not the time for leaps of faith. One step at a time,
Dhaika. Let him meet Her, feel Her power, understand
Her Link to Vartra first."

"If he needs to be more tightly bound to them, why haven't you seen to it? You're always meddling in other people's affairs!"

"Because last time, I leaned too hard, I admit it," she said, her voice suddenly quiet and tired. "This time, he needs to do it himself. He went to the temple for the first time tonight. If you push him into this too soon, we could lose him altogether. He could turn his back on us all. Do what the Council asks, Dhaika."

"Demands, more like," he snorted. "You know the Council usually does what you want, and the odd time it doesn't, you do it anyway!"

"No one is ordering you. You're the one in charge here."

"There are Guardians and Guardians, as you well know, Noni!"

"Yes. There are, aren't there?" Her voice was like ice. "It is well within the purview of our Council to ask you to do a lesser ritual and let the Goddess decide, and you know that."

"I wasn't even at the meeting when this was decided!"

"It wasn't our fault you were at your granddaughter's Validation. Your protests have all been recorded, don't worry. If not for the Council, do it because at the end of the day, the Goddess can look after Herself, and Kaid Tallinu can't. He'd be out of his depth in this."

"Don't tell me that finally someone has come along who matters more than all your plottings and schemings," he said, the incredulity obvious in his voice. "I don't believe it!"

"Stop gloating," she snapped, leaning forward on her stick. "Whatever you do or don't think you know, you know nothing!"

"I'll do it, Noni. Not for you or the Council, for him. For Kaid Tallinu, the cub who appeared out of nowhere on my doorstep forty-odd years ago!"

"Do it for whatever reasons you like," she said, leaning back in the chair and closing her eyes, "just say you'll do it, then we can all get back to bed."

*   *   *

Rezac heard footsteps in the corridor outside. Turning his head, he saw Goran enter. "We've got a job on tonight, and I need your people to help," Goran said, taking his stim twig out of his mouth. "I'm taking the outdoor patrol with me, so your security will be down to the people inside the monastery until we get back."

"Job?" said Vartra, his brows meeting in a frown. "What job? My people are here to be protected, not risked in guerrilla fights."

"That Jaisa girl of yours. Got a message that her family's back and the Valtegans are doing a raid on their area tonight. We need to get in first and pull them out, but we need more people. I haven't enough, and there's no time to wait for another cell to arrive."

"It's nearly mealtime!" said Vartra.

"Better that way. Less to go wrong if you get hit on an empty stomach," said Rezac.

"What's going on?" demanded Zashou as she and Jaisa came in. "Wh . . ."

"Sit down and listen and you might find out," said Rezac.

With an angry glare at him, Zashou sat.

"Jaisa," said Goran, turning to the girl, "your folks have shown up back at home. There's a roundup scheduled for your village later tonight. We're the nearest unit. Idea is to go and get them before the Valtegans do. Can you draw us a plan of the area immediately around your house?"

Jaisa looked dazedly around the room as she lowered herself into a chair. "Yes, but . . ."

Goran reached in his pocket and pulled out a notepad and stylus and handed it to her. "You just do that drawing and leave the worrying to us."

"I'm coming," said Rezac, picking up the gun that lay on the small table beside him. Slipping it into his side holster, he folded away his cleaning kit.

Goran looked at him and nodded. "Glad to have you. Pity you're part of this program. I'd have you on my team any day."

"Count me in," said Tiernay. "I won't ask others to do something for my people that I'm not prepared to do myself."

"Shanka and I'll come," said Zashou, glaring at Rezac.

"You're not a fighter," said Rezac. "Don't come just

to make an impression. You'll be more liability than
help."

"Who elected you leader?" demanded Shanka.
"And stop insulting my wife! We're coming, Goran."

"I'll need folk to stay with the van, give us covering
fire if needed once we've got them. You can do that,"
said Goran, his eyes still on Rezac.

Two hours later, they were crouched against the
hedges lining the street where Jaisa's family home
stood. The night was bitterly cold: An icy wind gusted
the scudding clouds across a jet-black sky. From behind them, the twin moons cast an intermittent, pallid
glow. Though the snow had been cleared from the
pedestrian paths, it still lay deep in the gardens and
surrounding fields.

"I don't like this," Rezac muttered to Goran. "It feels
wrong. Like a trap."

Goran nodded. "Can you sense any Valtegans?"

"Can't tell. I'm picking up the usual static, but too
much to be able to make sense of it. It isn't what I'd
expect so close to telepaths, though."

"Suppressed?"

"Could be. Jaisa, what d'you get?" He turned to
the female behind him. "Don't try to reach them. If
they've been collared, it could warn the Valtegans."

"It doesn't feel like them at all," she said, her nose
creasing with concern as she mentally scanned the
house opposite for the thought patterns of her family.
"Are you sure they're here?"

"They were seen earlier today," confirmed Goran.
"Come up here with me. I'll get us closer."

Rezac let her pass him. Then, as Goran and Jaisa
moved nearer to the end of the lane, he and Lamas
got ready to give covering fire if necessary.

While Lamas checked the hedge for any openings,
Rezac began checking the houses opposite. His gentle probe brought him a contact and, without warning,
he suddenly found himself sucked into the other's
mind.

The Valtegan towered over them, energy rifle
trained at their heads in case they made the slightest

sound. Three more stood at the window, watching the street.

Shock catapulted him back to his own mind. Dazed, he reeled against Goran.

"What the hell . . . !" exclaimed the other, grabbing hold of him to prevent him crashing through the hedge.

"Trap," Rezac managed to gasp.

Even as he steadied Rezac, Goran issued the animal call that was their alarm signal. Jaisa sent to the others but it was too late; one of Tiernay's group had already vaulted into the garden alongside them. They'd disclosed their presence.

Across the street and beside them, doors were flung wide, the lights within briefly silhouetting the Valtegan soldiers as they rushed out.

"Over the hedge!" yelled Goran, diving into the bushes for cover as energy beams lanced through the night.

Adrenaline hit Rezac's system like a shock wave, and grabbing the nearest person, he flung her over the hedge then followed himself. He rolled as he landed. Leaping to his feet, he grabbed his companion, dragging her across the garden to the far side of the house. Vaulting the ornamental brick wall at the rear of the building, he ran, keeping his head low, till he reached Goran and deposited Jaisa at his feet.

"Lamas?"

A quick mental check of their group confirmed his fears. Rezac shook his head. "Didn't make it. Rest are fine." As he unslung his gun, he noted that Jaisa had managed to keep hold of hers.

"Tiernay?" demanded Goran as he began returning fire to the garden opposite.

"They're working around behind us," Rezac replied, waiting for a lull before standing up to send off a spray of bullets in the same direction. "Got one," he muttered, ducking down again as a reptilian scream rent the air and Valtegan fire increased.

Fragments of brick from the wall splattered down on them as a shot came too close for comfort. In front of them, sections of the hedge burst into flames, sending clouds of acrid smoke drifting across the road.

"All to our good," muttered Goran. "We need to even the odds a little. On my signal."

The barrage began to diminish as the Valtegans realized there was no return fire. Rezac could now sense a group of them to his right.

"Now!" said Goran, springing to his feet and sending a hail of bullets into the hedge opposite.

Rezac faced the other way, shooting across the junction, barely aware of Jaisa's dogged supporting fire. A few seconds' burst, and he ducked down again. Realizing she hadn't, he reached out and grabbed her leg. *Down!*

More screams, none of them Sholan. Sharp, sibilant voices called to each other, then silence fell save for the sound of running feet. Rezac risked a look. Three Valtegans were heading for more substantial cover. He raised his gun, managing to clip one as the other two dived for shelter behind a low wall.

"This lot are as useless as the last," Goran said with satisfaction. "They can slaughter us from the safety of their aircars, but on the ground, they're worthless."

Coming up behind you, sent Tiernay as the group he led cleared the back gate and began crawling through the snow on their bellies to join them. *What now?*

"Tiernay," Rezac warned Goran verbally, as the other, hearing their movements, swung round, weapon pointed at them.

"The door's opening!" said Jaisa, beginning to stand up as she saw a pool of light from her parents' front door spill onto the pathway. The gun in her hand hung loosely by her side. "They're coming out!"

"Get down!" hissed Rezac, grabbing her by the arm and hauling her back beside him. She collapsed on her knees in the snow, the gun falling unnoticed from her grasp. Rezac grabbed it up and thrust it through his belt. She was in no fit state to be carrying a weapon now.

Into the night stumbled three Sholans, held firmly by their Valtegan captors.

"Stop shooting! Surrender, or we kill!" came the shout from the lead soldier. "No escape! We many." Though his Sholan words were mangled, his message was clear.

"I want that van fired up and ready to go," Goran said quietly. "Get the rest, especially Jaisa, down the lane to cover our escape. You stay with me."

Automatically Rezac reached for Tiernay, passing the message on. As he did, he quickly checked on Zashou. She was safe.

"Done," he said, peering through the brick latticework at the prisoners opposite them. He knew their options had just run out. "Jaisa, go back with the others."

"I'm staying," she said, her voice unsteady as she pushed herself up onto her haunches.

As the van's engine burst into life, Jaisa leaped to her feet. "You're leaving without them! If you won't save them, then I will!"

Rezac lunged after her, grabbing her by the belt to prevent her from clambering over the wall. She struggled, trying to pull free, but he held on. "Jaisa, stop it, damn you!" he hissed. "You'll get us all killed!"

"Get a grip on her, dammit," Goran snarled, glancing briefly at them.

Desperately she flailed at him with her fists, knocking his gun to the ground. With a growl of anger, he cuffed her hard enough to stun. Grasping her by the scruff, he bent to retrieve his weapon. She sprawled in the snow beside him, a crumpled, sobbing heap.

Goran caught his eye. He twitched first one ear, then the other, toward the hostages.

Standing up, Rezac hauled Jaisa with him. Pinning her against his side with his free arm, he flicked his gun onto single shots. He watched the hostages, waiting for a clear shot as Jaisa's young brother, kicking and yowling for all he was worth, tried to break free. For a moment, the tussle drew the attention of the other two soldiers.

As Rezac bought his gun up, Jaisa's mother looked directly at him. Their minds touched, then her eyes closed in quiet acceptance. He fired.

She fell instantly, the sudden weight of her body

making her captor stagger. Goran's first shot reached
the father at the same moment; his second missed
the cub, hitting the guard instead as the Valtegan continued to twist and turn, trying to shake off the biting
and clawing fury attached to his arm.

Jaisa's body arched against him, her keen of anguish almost deafening. Then shock hit her and she
slumped in defeat, unable to accept what she'd just
seen.

"Go!" hissed Goran, waiting for a second shot at
the child. "Get back to the van!"

Lifting Jaisa free of the ground, Rezac backed
down the garden. He got as far as the gate before
she started to fight him again.

"You killed them!" Her voice was a high-pitched
scream of agony. She struggled to free her arms, lifting her feet and trying to rake his legs with her claws.
"You killed them, Rezac!" she howled.

Stop it, Jaisa, he sent. *We couldn't save them. Better we killed them than the Valtegans. At least it was
quick.* Inwardly he began to curse. Of all the lousy
breaks, hers had to be the worst.

He tightened his grip, trying to keep her struggles
under control. "Shut up, damn it, Jaisa! You'll draw
the Valtegans to us!" He had to drag her now as her
feet sought for purchase in the snow-covered grass.

"Let me go!" she howled, baring her teeth as she
turned her head toward his unprotected face and
neck. "Let me go, Rezac! I'll kill you for this!" She
snapped at him, her head darting for his throat as she
tried to deliver a mortal wound.

Swearing, he pulled back just in time. Ahead of
them, Tiernay was standing at the open gate.

"What the hell's up with her?" he demanded, stepping forward.

"Cover me," Rezac ordered, stuffing his gun in its
holster as he struggled with Jaisa. Scooping her up,
he threw her over his shoulder and ran down the
alleyway, stopping only when he reached the side
door of the van. Willing hands pulled him inside.

"Let me go!" Jaisa snarled, kicking and struggling

as he tried to swing her down to the floor. "Let me go, damn you! My brother's still out there!"

Rezac's head spun as she landed a crack across his forehead with her fist. He lost his footing and tripped, crashing down to the floor of the van on top of her. Stunned, they lay there as the rest of the team tumbled in. Goran was last. The van accelerated violently, throwing them all backward.

"Get that bloody door shut!" ordered Goran. "Any pursuit, Maro?" he yelled at the driver.

"None yet! They expected us to shoot it out!" he yelled over his shoulder.

Rezac rolled off Jaisa and scrambled up onto his hands and knees. "You all right?" he asked. When he got no reply, he touched her shoulder. "Jaisa, are you all right?"

Muted sobs came from her as she jerked away from him.

Goran pushed himself up off the van floor, helping the figure beside him to sit up. "Jaisa, we got your brother," he said. "Somehow he got away and ran in the right direction."

Jaisa raised her head and peered at the small shape crawling toward her.

"Jaisa?" His voice was small and very unsteady.

"Oh, Tal!" she wept as the cub flung himself into her arms.

The van took a corner at speed, spinning violently on the icy road, pitching them from side to side until it finally recovered and righted itself.

"Watch it!" yelled Goran, scrambling his way up front to join his own people. Tiernay followed close behind.

On all fours, Rezac crawled forward to join them.

"What happened back there?" asked Tiernay. "Where are Jaisa's parents? Did the Valtegans kill them?"

Rezac glanced at Goran.

"We had to do it," Goran said, keeping his voice low. "We walked into a trap. There were just too many of them."

"You *killed* them?"

"Would you rather leave them for the Valtegans to torture?" asked Rezac.

"It was quick and clean," said Goran. "We couldn't leave them alive. They knew too much."

"In the name of the Gods, we came to rescue them, not kill them!"

Goran shrugged. "Rescue if we could, kill if we couldn't."

"Dammit, Goran, you had no right to do that!"

"How'd you manage to get the cub?" asked Rezac, ignoring Tiernay's outburst.

"He got real lucky," said Goran, staring at Tiernay with narrowed eyes. "I'm in charge out here, not you. We might not have rescued her parents, but we saved lives tonight, boy, the cub's for one. Told you, you got to be hard to lead. Now you know just how hard."

"You'd have killed her brother, too?" Tiernay asked in disbelief.

"You're nothing but murderers," said Zashou angrily. "Hired killers!"

"You got it," said Goran. "Hired to protect you with our own lives." He turned his head to look at her. "We're at war, girl. Those lizards'll turn you into just so much dead meat as quick as look at you. Wouldn't put it past them to eat you, too! Killing them was the kindest thing we could do for her folks. Hope if ever I'm caught, you'll do the same for me."

"You make me sick, both of you," she said disgustedly, turning her back on them and moving closer to Jaisa and her brother.

Shanka opened his mouth in a grin. "You've tarnished your reputation again, Rezac," he said, putting a protective arm around his mate. "Not doing too well, are you?"

Rezac looked away, trying to keep his hackles from rising. That male had a knack for getting under his skin. He stretched his fingers, claws extending until they were fully flexed.

He felt Goran touch his arm. Forcing his hands to relax, he looked up. The older male was holding out a stim twig. He shook his head.

Goran offered it again. "Go on," he said. "Won't

hurt once in a while. That was a good shot back there. You got a steady hand when it counts."

Rezac acknowledged the compliment with a slight movement of his head. Hesitating, he changed his mind about the twig and took it from the older male. Putting it in his mouth, he crushed the end with his back teeth. The slightly bitter taste made him swallow convulsively. Moments later, a feeling of light-headedness swept through him. He spat the twig out into his hand.

"Nice looker, that one," Goran said quietly, ear flicking briefly in Zashou's direction. "Got some strange ideas, but she'll learn. She'll come round to you, don't worry. Females like her prefer strong males." Goran grinned conspiratorially at him.

Rezac looked sideways at him and blinked, trying to focus on his face. "Don't know what you mean," he mumbled, taking several deep breaths in an effort to clear his head.

Goran grinned again. "It only makes your head swim like that the first few times. Try it again now."

Rezac stuck the twig in his pocket. "Maybe later," he said, taking hold of one of the grab ropes as the van swept round another corner.

Within minutes of the van hitting the back roads, snow began to fall, a blizzard so thick there was no chance of them being followed. Tiernay sat up front to help navigate, mentally checking the road ahead for any other vehicles.

When they finally reached the monastery, Dr. Kimin and her nurse Layul were waiting for them at the tunnel entrance. While Kimin took immediate charge of Jaisa, Layul saw to her brother.

"So you've come to live with us, have you?" he said, taking the cub by the arm and drawing him into the shelter of the tunnel. "I think you'll like it here. I'm taking you up to the surgery to check you out first. Then while they sort out a bed for you, you can have something to eat. You hungry? Of course you are. Cubs your age are always hungry!"

Rezac followed them, listening with half an ear to Layul's steady stream of chatter. It seemed to be working. Already Tal's mind had begun to relax and lose its brittleness.

He stopped in their lounge to grab a bowl of stew and a mug of c'shar from the hot plates before heading for his room. He didn't feel like company, and after being dropped in the snow, his gun needed cleaning as soon as possible. Wiser not to do it in front of the others tonight. Besides, he was tired.

A knock on the door roused him from sleep. Sitting up, he rubbed his eyes and looked at the timepiece on the wall. It was the twenty-first hour! Who could want him at this time of night?

Before he even reached the door, he knew it was Jaisa. He could sense the drug-induced calmness that almost kept the grief and terror at bay. Opening the door, he tensed himself for her anger and accusations.

She stood in the dim hallway, ears flicking uncontrollably. "Can I come in?" she asked, looking up and down the hall, obviously hoping not to be noticed.

Rezac stood aside to let her enter. "How's your brother?"

"They didn't hurt him," she said, moving over to the bed and perching on the end of it. "He's still upstairs. Dr. Kimin sedated him and put him up in her room for tonight."

"That's good," he said, closing the door. He waited, knowing she'd tell him why she was here when she was ready.

"Goran told me what the Valtegans do when they're interrogating our people," she said, pulling her toweling robe tighter. She shivered and looked up at him, her eye ridges meeting. "I hadn't realized they were so brutal."

"We're not people to them," he said, returning to his bed and making himself comfortable at the opposite end from her. "We're possessions, and there are plenty of us. What do the deaths of two or three, or even a hundred of us mean to them? Nothing."

"Thank you for saving my mother from that," she said abruptly. "I didn't mean what I said. If I'm ever caught by them, will you do the same for me?"

"We'd all do it for each other," he said. "You've no need to worry."

"Don't leave it to anyone else," she said, tears beginning to roll down her face. "You do it. For me and Tal. I trust you; I know it'll be quick."

Rezac nodded, aware of her distress. He knew he should be doing more to comfort her, but he was at a complete loss as to what to do or say.

She sniffed and scrubbed at her face with the back of her hand as she got up. At the door she stopped, her back still to him. "I just came to say I was sorry."

Rezac sat up. "There's no need. I wish we could have rescued them."

"I know."

"Look, you don't have to leave. You can stay if you want," he said awkwardly.

"I'd like to," she said, turning round. "For the company. There's no one else I can go to."

"Then stay," said Rezac, moving so he could pull the covers back.

She crossed the room and stood beside the bed, hesitating.

He held his hand out. "Come on," he said. "You need to get some sleep."

Taking his hand, she climbed into the bed, curling up at his side as he pulled the covers over them both.

Reaching across her, he turned the light out, gently easing his arm under her head as he lay down. He heard her sigh and felt her relax. A few minutes later, her breathing was slow and regular. It was his turn to sigh. He knew he'd get little sleep that night. He didn't like sharing his bed for more than a few hours, but he felt that he owed her his company for at least tonight.

He woke with a start, mentally checking the room to see what had wakened him. Nothing. They were alone. The pale light of dawn filtered through the curtains. Then he felt Jaisa's hand traveling slowly across his chest toward his neck. As he took hold of it, she moved her leg, sliding it between his as her tail flicked across him. Where her face lay against his chest, she began to bite him gently.

He reached down, the need to move her leg suddenly becoming urgent. Obligingly, she moved, only to replace her leg with her hand.

With a noise halfway between a growl and a groan of pleasure, Rezac grasped her by the waist and tipped her onto her back. Her robe was pushed unceremoniously aside, and as he lowered himself onto her, she grasped him just as demandingly. Her hands clasped his hips, claw tips pricking his flesh as she pulled him inside her.

"Not so fast!" he gasped, his claws flexing against her back as he tried to slow her down.

Their minds touched, each a little aware of what the other felt. Jaisa returned to biting his chest, her teeth this time not so gentle. He lowered his head, tongue rasping against her jaw then he began to nip her, too. Slowly he let the sensations build. As she began to climax, he could hold back no longer.

Afterward, she fell asleep, emotionally and physically drained. Making sure she was covered by the blankets, Rezac left her there and headed for the refectory. Collecting his food from the counter, he joined the others at their table.

Tiernay looked up as he sat down. "I don't suppose you've seen Jaisa? She wasn't in her room when I stopped by."

"She's in mine," he said, concentrating on his food. "I left her sleeping."

"I don't believe it!" said Zashou. "She saw you kill her mother! She'd never spend the night with you!"

"Leave him alone, Zashou," said Tiernay. "Neither of them needs to justify their actions to you."

Goran leaned forward and slid a couple of photos from his pocket across the table to her. "You want to know why she went to Rezac? Look at these, girl."

Curious despite herself, Zashou picked them up and turned them over. With an exclamation of horror, she threw them back at Goran. Her chair fell over as she stumbled to her feet, ears plastered back in distress.

"I showed these to Jaisa last night," Goran said, picking them up again. "That's what they do to hostages, that's what we saved them from. Now you know why she went to Rezac last night."

"What you did was despicable!" Zashou said. "Hadn't she suffered enough without you showing her those . . . horror pictures?"

"She needed to know we're different from the Valtegans," said Goran. "Now leave her alone to get her comfort where she wants. Just because you're too prissy to take up with a real male, don't expect her to be the same!"

"How dare you infer that . . . Ooh!" Beside herself with rage, Zashou turned and ran from the room.

"Just what do you mean by that?" Shanka growled, pushing his chair back and getting to his feet.

"He meant nothing, Shanka," said Tiernay, fixing Goran with a meaningful stare.

Shanka's tail flicked. "He'd better not," he said, before stalking after his mate.

Tiernay sighed. "Did you have to set them off like that?" he asked Goran. "Whatever you think of her, Goran, Zashou's all right, and we're trying to get Shanka to pull his weight. If we keep baiting each other like this, we'll split the team apart. Leave us to sort out our own internal politics, if you please."

Goran shrugged. "She wanted to know why Jaisa spent the night with Rezac. I told her."

"Well, I'd prefer you not involve yourself like that again. I can handle my own people."

"Whatever you say," said Goran, getting up. "But I've done you a favor. At least now it's me she hates, not Rezac or Jaisa."

Rezac's jerky movements brought Jo instantly awake. As she tried to move away from him, he clutched her closer, beginning to make small noises of distress. She was groggy herself, but she'd picked up enough of his dream to understand what was wrong. His mind had returned to the time before he and Zashou were Leskas, when he'd had to kill Jaisa's mother.

She knew exactly what he'd gone through. She'd had to make a similar decision herself during a raid on one of the Valtegan guard posts on Keiss.

Pulling an arm free, she reached out to touch his face,

trying to wake him. She wasted a good couple of minutes till she remembered seeing Carrie grab Kusac by the ear to get his attention. She knew from last night just how sensitive to the touch Sholan ears could be, and Rezac's were no exception. Taking hold of one, she tugged. Nothing. She tried again, then gave up and sank her teeth into the thin flesh near the tip. That produced the desired result.

With a grunt of pain, the ear was flicked from her mouth and his hand came up instinctively to brush her away. Instead, he touched her cheek and froze, eyes flicking open. Face to face, they lay looking at each other.

Jo broke the silence. "You were having a nightmare."

"I know," he said, his voice quiet. She felt him try to block their contact as he tensed, waiting for her to say more.

"It was a brave thing you did, killing Jaisa's mother," she said, letting her hand touch his cheek, replaying her memory of that day on Keiss. "I've had to do it too. She was a friend, and the fear of not killing her outright was the worst part of it."

Rezac let his breath out in a long sigh. "What do you know about our customs?" he asked, his voice barely above a whisper. He could hardly credit what he was doing. Had he lost his senses? He shouldn't even be thinking of this, let along doing it! He ignored that side of his mind, sure beyond doubt that this was what he wanted.

"I know what you know, I just don't know where to find the memory yet."

"Then I'll ask you," he said, lowering his face till his mouth was touching her throat. He began to lick her gently with the tip of his tongue, great long sweeps that sent fire racing through her, the fire that she'd experienced for the first time the night before.

She tilted her head up, lost in a world of shared senses, bounded by the circle of his arms and the covers wrapped around them. His scent filled her nostrils and at this moment, Linked as they were, her sense of smell was as sharp as his. The warmth of his body was like a fire before which the cold that the Valtegans had put within her finally began to melt.

She could feel the texture of his tongue change as he used a different part of it. Now it was rougher, sending even stronger shivers of pleasure coursing through her.

Then his teeth closed over her larynx. Her eyes flew open, but with her throat held like this, she could do nothing, see nothing but the ceiling above her.

To be like this is to be at the mercy of the person whose jaws hold you, he sent. *It's either a death grip—or one of love, when you accept your partner as your lover. I want you as my lover, Jo. Will you have me?* He let her go and raised his head to look at her.

He'd never seemed more alien than he did now. She looked at his face—so nearly human despite its covering of short fur—and wondered what the hell she was doing here, in bed with a member of another species. It was utter madness, an act of pure insanity! Moving her hands, she touched him, letting her fingers push through his pelt and twine themselves in his long belly fur.

She remembered how it had felt when they'd joined, their minds so bound together there had only been *us*. The sensible portion of her mind cut in, asking her if she was prepared to throw herself away on a pair of velvet-brown eyes and a dark, soft pelt. She was shocked to hear herself say, *Yes*.

He began to purr, the sound fuller and slower than the one she'd heard the night before. It seemed to come from deep within the heart of him.

His jaws tightened until she could feel his canines pressing into her flesh, then suddenly, they were gone, and he was covering her face with a multitude of tiny bites and licks. It was erotic yet ticklish. She began to giggle, trying futilely to fend him off.

"Rezac, please, let me catch my breath," she gasped at last.

He moved back, giving her the space she needed to make herself comfortable again. While she did, he propped himself up on one arm, watching her, still purring. "Would you believe you're the first female I've ever asked to be my lover?"

"I'd believe it," she said. "How on earth did you manage to survive so long? So much hurt and anger in you, it's a wonder you didn't try to end it all."

"I couldn't, because of Zashou," he said, looking away for a moment. "To do that would be to kill her as well."

"I hope I haven't complicated your life," she said quietly.

"What if you have?" he countered, moving closer again.

"You've brought me the first taste of happiness in a relationship that I've ever known. From you I sense none of the hatred and criticism that Zashou feels for me. You really understand what it was like. The Gods know, I didn't choose my life!"

"I know," she said soothingly, stroking his cheek, loving its velvety texture. Her eyes were becoming heavy as the now familiar lassitude stole through her. "Stop talking and make love to me."

"Make love?" he purred, beginning to kiss her. "What a lovely way to say it. I've never made love before."

* * *

As soon as he'd recovered enough to escape from Vanna's and Garras' home, Brynne had returned to his room at the Terran house on the estate. It seemed as if everyone with a vested interest in either the Humans, or the mixed Leska pairs, had been to visit him as soon as he was well enough to be questioned. From Clan Lord Aldatan down, they wanted either information on Derwent's teaching, or permission to do brain scans to find out for themselves what, if anything, was different.

He'd refused to cooperate out of embarrassment. He wanted to drop the whole issue. His experiences with Derwent when he fell ill had made him face what he'd really known all along. Derwent's gifts were minor in comparison to those of the Sholans; his knowledge was a self-acquired, crazy mixture of annexed traditions he considered useful from the many different Earth cultures. However, as far as he was concerned, the Sholans had nothing of value to teach him as his knowledge was the only truth. That had been why he'd refused to accept the reality of Brynne's Link with Vanna.

Brynne realized his own ignorance had contributed to Derwent's ability to convince him he was a great teacher. In that, Vanna had been right. It was time for him to face reality and catch up with his own long neglected studies. So here he was, at the Shrine, with Father Ghyan.

Ghyan's voice broke into his wandering thoughts. "One of my advanced students is taking the acolytes for their meditation this morning," he said, standing up. "Normally I don't go to these sessions until they're ready to sit their final tests. However, I'm finding it hard to concentrate today. A little meditation might help me focus. Would you like to accompany me?"

"A break would be good," Brynne agreed, stretching his arms and rotating his shoulders to free them of tightness. He hadn't realized how much writing was involved in learning to use his mental abilities.

As they walked down the corridor to the Shrine room, Ghyan began to tell him about the statue of Vartra and its dedication. He barely listened, managing to make appropriate responses when he felt one was expected of him.

"You're not really interested, are you?" Ghyan asked gently, touching him on the arm to insure that he had his attention. "Perhaps you've not allowed yourself enough time to recover from your illness."

"I'm sorry, Father Ghyan," he apologized. "I'm fine, just a little tired."

"It takes a while to build up your strength after a fever like that. I think we should find you something less demanding to do for a few days. The Litanies would be good as, in fact, would meditation. It's part of your course anyway. Leave it with me," he said, opening the door into the Shrine and waiting for Brynne to enter. "When we finish here, I'll get someone to accompany you to the training hall. Have a long, hot bath, and then go home and rest. Tomorrow's another day."

"I really am fine, Father," he tried to protest, but Ghyan cut him short.

"Half-day sessions are more than enough for this week, Brynne. There's no rush, you know. No one standing over you demanding you finish the course in a finite time. Here on the Valsgarth Estate, the teaching is tailored to the individual: It takes as long as it takes. Were you under pressure from your Mr. Derwent? I assure you that's not the case here."

Brynne eyed him carefully as they approached the braziers flanking the God. What was he up to? Was this just a more subtle approach to find out what Derwent had been doing?

"No, Brynne, it isn't," replied Ghyan, stopping to pick up a piece of incense to crumble over the flames. "I want to know only what you wish to freely tell me. Anything we discuss will stay within our Order."

Brynne grunted and picked up a piece of incense, copying what the priest had done. "Ross was like a man driven or possessed. He was never still, always on the go testing one or another of his theories. Yes, he pushed me. Said I was wasting time when I was with Vanna, or went to see our son."

"Someone like him, with no ties, no loved ones, would think like that," Ghyan murmured, approaching the God. He crossed his forearms over his chest, bowing in respect before passing the statue. He stopped, obviously waiting for Brynne.

As he made the same bow of respect to the statue before joining his teacher, Brynne remembered his visit to the Retreat with Derwent. He must go back there some day. On his own, though. He owed it to Guardian Dhaika.

Walking along the side of the curtain, Ghyan stopped and pulled back a section to reveal a door. He laughed as he opened it. "No, not some secret place, Brynne! Merely the storage for the prayer mats! Come, help me set them out. They're light enough that shifting them won't tire you unduly."

The last mat had just been laid as a group of ten younglings scampered into the hall, their plain black robes flapping around their bare feel. They ground to an ignominious halt as they saw who was there.

"Father Ghyan," the foremost one stammered. "We hadn't expected anyone."

Brynne watched Ghyan frown at the youths. "Running within the building is strictly forbidden, let alone within the Shrine! Have you no respect for the God? Dzio, I had expected better of you! Chya, have you learned nothing in your time with Rulla? You will both report to me when you finish your studies today! Now attend to your chores! The rest of you, snow clearing detail after lessons until it's too dark to see!"

The group dispersed to their various jobs, faces sullen, ears almost invisible. A couple of minutes later, Rulla arrived.

"Take a mat, Brynne," said Gyan. "The lesson will begin shortly."

Brynne watched him go over to the Brother and exchange a few, terse words with him before he returned.

Rulla, meanwhile, began organizing those fetching the meditation lamp, oil, and incense from its cupboard.

Not knowing the words for the Litany of Preparation, Brynne couldn't join in, but he found the cadence soothing and relaxing. Under the watchful eye of Father Ghyan, he let himself go, let his mind gently join with those of the students. Without a senior telepath present, this would not normally happen, but since he was here now, Ghyan had decided to work them harder and stretch their abilities.

As instructed, Brynne focused his attention on the meditation lamp, watching the flame's gentle glow, letting it fill his vision. Ghyan was providing the instructions mentally, and gradually the glow grew and filled his mind till nothing else remained.

He felt light, as if his body were floating. Relaxing into it, he found an inner peace start to build. Images began to form, images of snow-covered hills. Trees, their green-needled branches coated with frost, swayed slightly in the wind that came down from the high lands above. High overhead, he heard the cry of a hunting bird and looked up, watching it soar against the sharp, blue sky. The throaty yowl of a catlike predator drew his eyes back to the land, and he scanned the tree line, looking for a movement against the carpet of white that covered everything.

As he watched, the wind changed direction and the snow began to melt, sliding from the trees to the ground below. Throughout the landscape, patches of green started to emerge, and beneath his feet he could now feel grass. Color flooded the land as flowers rose from the soil, opening their petals to the warmth of the sun. He could smell the spring.

Khuushoi's time will not last for long, then I will rule again.

It was the last thing he remembered, as with a start and a cry of fear, he found himself suddenly sprawled across his mat, his face pressed against the wooden floorboards.

Later, Ghyan called Father Lijou, who listened attentively to him.

"He's the second," said Lijou. "I think the Gods have decided we've been too complaisant. They are creating work for us, Ghyan."

"What should I do, Master Lijou?"

"Nothing. Continue with his training as if he were one

of us. Report to me if this, or anything else unusual happens. It's possible it was just an isolated vision rather than a calling. He is a Human, after all. We need to be sure."

"If it is Ghyakulla, then she's showing her acceptance of the Humans among us."

"I'm sure She is. That may even be why She's spoken to him. They are a force in our lives, and on our worlds. We cannot ignore them, so why should She? Better to have them bound to Her than against her, especially with the likes of Derwent around."

"There's bad news concerning him," said Ghyan. "He managed to escape from the medical center and they haven't yet been able to locate him."

Lijou frowned. "When did that happen?"

"Yesterday."

"They haven't requested any of our personnel."

"They will," said Ghyan. "The memory of Fyak is too fresh for the authorities to allow another religious fanatic to run loose."

"Let's hope they find him before Khuushoi does the job for them. The weather here has been bitter. How is it with you?"

"The same. You'd hardly think that spring begins in a couple of weeks."

"That soon? Well, our calendar never did reflect the weather accurately. Keep me posted on this, Ghyan, but I wouldn't worry unduly."

* * *

Mara hung around the upper cavern of the dig, waiting for Josh. It was coming up to second meal, time for everyone to take a break. He'd been working with Bob and Meral, and as the three males came level with her, Josh stopped.

"Catch you over there," he said to the other two. He waited till they'd gone. "You shouldn't be here. Pam's on the warpath this morning."

"I've every right to be here," she said mildly. "It is my Clan's land, after all."

"It's not worth arguing over it with her, believe me. Look, I'm still in deep shit because of last time. I'd appreciate it if you didn't come here to see me."

"I'm actually here for a valid reason," she said. "I've

come to ask you to share third meal with us. It's my thank you for coming to visit me when I was in the medical unit."

"It was the least I could do," he mumbled, looking away from her. "I wasn't exactly responsible, but I was involved."

"I really am sorry for what I did, Josh, but it would have been even worse to have gone on with . . ." she faltered, unsure what word to use.

He looked up, a slight smile on his face. "I understand, Mara. Hell, I'm not ready to be a father yet, so why should it be different for you? Look, are you all right? With your Leska, I mean? To put yourself through what you did, the suicide attempt and the pregnancy, just because of him, you must have a pretty terrible relationship."

"It hasn't been good," she admitted, stuffing her hands in the pockets of her long overcoat. "Zhyaf's a good person, just so reserved and staid. We get along a lot better now he's working in the capital."

"What's he doing?" Josh asked, slowly beginning to walk toward the upper level.

Mara fell in step beside him. "Government work. I'm sorry, I can't discuss it. I better not go any farther," she said, reaching out to stop him. "Don't want to get you into trouble. Will you come over tonight?" Anxiously she searched his face, hoping he'd accept. She gave a small laugh. "You know, if you were a Sholan male, I'd know exactly what to say and do, but . . ."

"If it makes it easier, why not pretend I am?" he said gently.

Frowning, she turned her head sideways in the Sholan gesture of embarrassed questioning. "You're serious," she said, beginning to smile as she picked up his tentative sending. "All right. I have cooked a meal for tonight and would like you to come and share it with me. I would like us to spend some time together—a lot of it, in fact." The words came out in a rush and she could feel her face turning crimson as she said them.

"I'd be delighted to come," he replied, taking hold of her hand. "And if your invitation means you'd like us to get to know each other better, I'd like that, too. There's something about you, Mara Ryan, a wildness in your soul, that appeals to me."

She felt his hand tighten on hers briefly as he moved closer, leaning forward to kiss her.

"And just what do you think you're doing?" demanded the sharp voice of Pam Southgate.

"Wonderful timing, hasn't she?" murmured Josh, his lips brushing hers before they separated.

"I made it quite clear that you were not to set foot in these excavations again, Mara Ryan. Leave immediately." She turned her back on the girl, letting her know in no uncertain terms that she considered the matter closed.

"As for you, I warned you last time what would happen if I had reason to speak to you again about fraternizing with the natives. Obviously that piece of trash is more important to you than our work here. Pack your bags, Mr. Lewis, you're on the first shuttle back to Shanagi!"

"Now just a minute," began Josh.

"Who are you calling a piece of trash?" demanded Mara, grabbing the woman by the arm and swinging her back to face her.

"Take your hand off me," Pam said angrily, shaking her arm free. "Now get off this site before I call one of the men to have you thrown off!"

"Excuse me," said a deep, feminine voice from behind them all. "Did I hear you making a specist remark about my fosterling?"

Mara turned round. "Ruth!"

"Don't be ridiculous!" Pam snapped. "I'm not a specist!"

Ruth smiled lazily. "I beg to disagree. Calling Mara a native and a piece of trash tells me exactly what you think of the Sholans."

"I beg your pardon, but I have a high regard for the Sholan people! And I don't care whether she's your fosterling or not, she's a piece of trash! She'd slept with just about every Sholan male here before she started on my team! That's trash in *my* book!"

Mara cringed back, moving out of the line of fire. "I did not! Josh is the only one!" As she did, she realized a small crowd had begun to gather round them. The fluting trill of Touiban voices caught her attention and moments later, they'd pushed their way into the center of the group and were milling round the four of them.

"You've upset the Touibans," Josh accused Pam.

"I've upset the Touibans?" Pam demanded, rounding on him. "If you hadn't encouraged this . . . person . . . to visit you, none of this would have happened!"

Mara tugged at Ruth's sleeve, ready to die with embarrassment. "Ruth, can we leave it? Please, let's just go."

"No, my pet. There's more at stake here than just you," Ruth said, patting Mara's hand reassuringly. "This is harassment and specism and I'm not standing for it."

One of the Touibans darted between them, his trill a high-pitched riff of sound as he reached up to pat Mara's face. The air became scented with a gentle perfume unlike any she'd smelled before. He turned then to Pam, grimacing and shaking his head, his voice now deep and staccato.

From behind and above her, a second voice answered the Touiban notes sounding slightly mechanical and stilted in comparison to the fluidity of the first speaker's voice.

Pandemonium broke out, with excited Touibans darting from place to place. Mara closed her eyes, feeling suddenly nauseous. Strong hands grasped her, holding her upright.

"You're fine," Josh's voice said reassuringly in her ear. "It happens when you try to watch the Touibans move. Took us ages to get the knack of it. And don't worry about what Pam said, I know all I need to about your past."

The voices had moved, their focus now just behind her. Cautiously she opened her eyes again.

"What happened?"

"Carrie and Kusac are here," he said. "They've got Kashini with them. I don't think the Touibans have ever seen a Sholan cub before, judging by their reactions."

Their rapid movements had stopped and now they stood rooted to the spot, pointing at the cub in wonder. She was equally taken with them, emitting small mewls of pleasure as she reached out toward them and their glittering jewelry with eager hands.

One valiant soul gingerly extended his hand. It was grasped and immediately hauled toward the cub's mouth.

"Not a good idea," said Carrie, shaking her head in a negative as she reached forward quickly to stop her daughter. "Sharp teeth."

"All tiny ones have sharp teeth with which they try their mothers' tempers. It is a fact of life with which we parents have to exist. She is so like her father, yet she is also like you, truly a harmonious blending of both your people."

"Thank you, Speaker. You honor us," said Kusac. "Would you excuse me while I see what is troubling my people?"

"Ah, it is the thin, angry female again, she who knows no gentleness of nature. She says disparaging things about your people and mine, and causes upset. She tries to exclude the fine young Human male from this diggings where his help is most useful and his presence near us a pleasure. Why do you let her remain? For harmoniousness to be achieved it is necessary to tune voices till the harsh notes are gone. She is such a harsh note, and it were better she went than any other Humans."

Kusac looked from the Touiban Speaker to Pam, then back. "Is that a request, Speaker?"

The Speaker hesitated and turned his face to Mara and Josh. "Yes."

Mara could feel Kusac's surprise. For a Touiban to limit himself to one short word was unheard of. They'd not only followed what had been said, but had interfered and taken her side against the head of this team. She could hardly believe what was happening.

Before she had time for that to sink in, she heard another trill of sound, then she and Josh were surrounded by eleven Touibans and being escorted toward the far end of the chamber. As they left, she heard Kusac say, "I will see what I can do, Speaker. Thank you for supporting my people."

Hands gripped the edges of her coat, gently tugging her and Josh forward until they had reached the refectory tables. Their trills blended, forming a gentle melody of sound that was accompanied by the same, strange scent. Then the glittering, brightly colored folk were gone, their bodies interweaving with each other as if performing some exotic dance as they made their way back to rejoin their Speaker.

Handing Kashini to Carrie, Kusac remained talking to Ruth and Pam while the mother and cub came over to join them.

"I've got to hand it to you, Mara," said Carrie, sitting down beside them, "I've never known the Touibans do that before, neither has Kusac! They've certainly taken a fancy to you. Josh, you've made an impression on them, too, and they don't impress easily!"

"I don't know how," he murmured. "I haven't had much to do with them. Mostly I just get on with my work."

"They value dedication to the job in hand, in case you hadn't noticed. I take it they broke up an unpleasant scene."

"She'd just ordered me off the site, and fired Josh," said Mara. "Can she do that? Can she send him back to Shanagi?"

"No, she can't. She doesn't have the power to do that," Carrie reassured her, turning Kashini so she could sit her daughter more comfortably on her lap. She looked from one to the other and smiled. "I take it you've patched up your differences?"

"You could say that," said Josh with a slow grin, moving his hand across the table to take Mara's. "Despite Pam's inopportune arrival."

Mara felt her heart leap as his hand squeezed hers comfortingly.

"I'm pleased for you. I suggest you forget about Pam Southgate. Kusac intends to have her returned to Shanagi. I'm sure we won't have a problem, considering the Speaker has officially requested it. Greg's next in command, isn't he? Will he cope? Has he led a team before? If we can avoid bringing in someone new, we'd prefer it."

"Greg can cope," said Josh confidently. "He'd have been team leader had it not been for Pam pulling strings to get the post."

"Hi, kids," said Ruth, settling herself into the seat opposite them. "All settled. She'll not bother you again." She held her arms out across the table for Kashini. "Do I get a cuddle, then, young lady?"

"She'll either sleep like a log or keep the whole house awake tonight," said Carrie ruefully, lifting her daughter up and trying to pass her across the table to Ruth.

Kashini had ideas of her own. As soon as she felt the table top beneath her feet, she scrabbled for a purchase, twisting and turning till her weight meant that Carrie had to rest her on the surface. That was it. With a bound she flung herself at Ruth, knocking the breath out of her as she landed, arms and legs splayed, claws out, against her chest.

It was difficult to tell who yowled louder. Ruth from the insertion of twenty small needle-sharp claws or Kashini at the shock of Ruth's reaction. Nonetheless, Ruth grabbed the squirming bundle firmly.

"You are a handful, madam," she admonished, disengaging the claws and arranging the cub's weight to make them both comfortable. "Thank God my Mandy was nowhere near this big—or active—at two months! Sholan females have my sympathy!"

Rulla appeared at her side, his hand going to touch her shoulder. "Clan Leader," he said, flicking an ear in deference to Carrie. "Is everything all right?" he asked Ruth. "I heard you from the other side of the cavern." His eye ridges were creased with concern.

"I'm fine," she said, gently bouncing Kashini up and down on her lap. "It was this little rascal here. She launched herself at me and drew blood when she landed! It takes a strong woman to handle you Sholans, Rulla," she said, looking up at him. "All teeth and claws, you are."

Wide-eyed with embarrassment, Rulla glanced at Carrie, begging silently for help, and tried to ignore Mara and Josh's grins. "We have our gentler side, too, Ruth," he mumbled. "You know that."

"I suppose you have your moments," she said, wagging a finger in front of Kashini for the cub to catch.

He leaned down till his head was level with hers, his hand stealing round her shoulder till it began to caress her neck. "Ruth, Dzinea, you'll have them thinking I treat you like one of those scratching posts you talk of," he said, trying to keep his voice low. "You know that isn't so!"

Mara suddenly discovered a need to cough and found herself being thumped on the back by a grinning Carrie.

Nice to see him less than his usual pompous self, isn't it? Ruth winds him round her finger beautifully! sent Carrie.

It's even better at home, Mara replied, gesturing to show Carrie she was fine.

Josh had turned to look at Kusac and Pam and had missed the byplay. "Is it that easy? He can send her away just like that?"

Mara looked round, too. Kusac had called Dzaka over, and Pam was now being firmly escorted toward the tunnel down to the lower level.

"Not quite, but his father will support his decision," said Carrie. "We can't afford to have prejudice here. We're working to help people like yourself who are trying to come to terms with the fact that they've just acquired a Leska from another species. It's hard enough for them to deal with their own emotions and fears without having to cope with the Pam Southgates of the world. I'm just glad we were here when it happened."

"What if you hadn't been?" The words were out before Mara could stop them.

"Garras would have been informed and the matter put on hold till I'd returned in the evening. And I'd have made exactly the same decision. This is our home, Mara, and Josh's, before it's anything else."

"Mine?" asked Josh.

"Yours, too," she confirmed, rescuing the spoon that Kashini had picked up from the table. "You know your test was positive. That makes you one of us, and a member of our Clan—if that's what you want. The choice is yours. If you decide to join us, then nothing and no one but Kusac has the power to make you leave here."

"So when the team pulls out, I can stay?"

"We can demand that you stay," she grinned. "Not even the Terran Ambassador could order you to leave if you chose not to. It goes with being a member of our En'Shalla Clan. However, we would ask you to start training your Talent so as to give the claim some basis in fact. It could help you in your work anyway. When I pick up items, I sometimes have a feel for their previous owners, who they were and what they used the item for, that kind of thing. It should strengthen those intuitive hunches of yours."

"Psychometry," mumbled Josh, obviously embarrassed. "How'd you guess? And what about my work? I'm an archeologist, not a telepath. That's what I want to do."

Carrie shrugged. "Every Human's Talent seems to include hunches. As to your work, quite a few Terrans only train part-time. You could join their classes. Kusac's coming over now. Would you mind helping him fetch some drinks for us, please, Josh?"

"Sure," he said, getting up.

As they came down into the lower cavern, Kusac grasped Carrie briefly by the arm, holding her back. He nodded toward where his sister and Dzaka were working on something buried in the cavern floor.

"Look at them," he said. "I've never seen or felt Dzaka so relaxed, and as for Kitra! Is that really my little sister? There's an air about her that Mother has. A sort of . . ." He stopped, searching for the word. "A quiet contentment, a glow."

"I tried to warn you," Carrie said softly, holding onto his arm. "She'll choose Dzaka as her life-mate, Kusac."

"I think you're right," he said, reaching up to stroke Kashini's back as the cub began to squirm and mewl at the interruption of their walk.

Kitra looked up and waved happily at them.

"You know," said Carrie, beginning to move again, "in years to come, I can tease Dzaka about that evening when Rhyasha and I railroaded him into becoming Kitra's first lover. I think we knew even then that they were right for each other."

"Female's intuition?" asked Kusac. "Pity it didn't work for you! I remember my first attempts at persuading you to accept me!"

"That was different," she said primly as they walked down the tunnel and out into the winter sunshine. "We were the first, and you were a different species."

"But you loved me, right from the earliest days, you loved me."

"Did I? I suppose I must have."

"Yes, you did. I know you did," he insisted, catching her arm again and stopping. "I felt it."

"Then I suppose you must be right," she said, maintaining her unconcerned air.

"You, cub, are a tease," he said, pulling her into an embrace.

Kashini immediately began to purr with delight, and leaning down, wrapped her tiny arms round her mother's neck.

Carrie laughed, kissing both of them before slipping quickly out of their embraces. She skipped a few paces down the path, still laughing at them. "A female's got to have her secrets!" She turned and headed for the waiting aircar. "Come on, Jack and Jiszoe are holding second meal for us and Jiszoe says he's starving!"

* * *

Ghyakulla's shrine at the Retreat was, as Lijou said, very different, yet it had its own beauty. Like its sister, it lay within the heart of the mountain.

The air in the cavern was warm, heated by nearby underground streams of hot water that, their warmth lost to the mountain, finally emerged in the plain below. Lighting had

been installed, but it was sparing and diffuse, in keeping
with the ambience of the shrine.

Columns of naturally shaped rock, their surfaces covered
with growths of subterranean molds and fungii, stretched
upward for thirty meters. As he walked beside Guardian
Dhaika, Kaid found himself wondering why both Stronghold and Vartra's Retreat should have shrines to the Goddess that cast the one in Her own temple into the shade.

"These existed before it was possible to rebuild the
plainslands," said Dhaika. "When the floods subsided, it
was decided it would be better to move the Goddess' temple to the lowlands to make her accessible to more of her
people. And, of course, the buildings you mention already
belonged to Vartra."

Kaid stopped short, a little startled at the Guardian's
ability to pick him up.

Resting his hand on Kaid's forearm, Dhaika drew him
on toward the altar. Though aware of the paintings that
covered the sides, Kaid saw only the statue of the Goddess
that adorned the top. In Her arms She held a male cub
scarcely older than Kashini. A kitling, feet within the protective curl of the Goddess' tail, leaned against Her, looking up into Her face. In front of Her crouched an older
child, its attention wholly captivated by a small animal.

Kaid walked up to the montage, reaching out to touch
the carving of the cub. The bodies of the Goddess and Her
children were of natural stone, but touches of color had
been added so that the eyes seemed about to blink, the
hair, ruffled by an unseen breeze, about to lie flat again.
He let his hand slide away from the cub, looking at the
creature the youngling was trying to attract. It was a jegget,
its sable-tipped cream pelt rendered in vibrant, living colors
which contrasted with the cool warmth of the stone people.

"I had no idea this place existed," said Kaid, turning
away from the sculpture. "Why? Why this, here?"

"It's said this is Vartra's Shrine to His Mother, and in
light of recent events, who can deny the possibility of it
being the truth? It's never been a public part of the Retreat, more a place where those who feel they've been
called by the Goddess come to talk to Her. Only the older
acolytes—they're priests now, of course—of Ghyakulla
come here regularly. And myself."

Kaid raised a quizzical eye ridge.

"Ghyakulla is the Mother of all living things," said Dhaika enigmatically. "Shall we begin?"

Prayer mats had been set out for them, and as Kaid arranged himself comfortably on one, Dhaika began to send to him.

This is similar to a meditation session. Focus on the brazier to the left of the altar, then recite your litanies as usual. When you're in a light trance, I'll guide you to the realm of the Goddess.

Kaid found it took longer than usual for him to relax. When finally he was floating within the familiar gray mist, he didn't at first realize that he was listening to the Guardian's instructions. Almost imperceptibly, the haze was parting, leaving him suspended in a darkness as black as night. Curiously he looked about him, gradually realizing that the darkness wasn't complete and that around him he could see ribbons of light flickering and shimmering as they streaked past him. As he concentrated on them, the colors brightened till he could pick out a gold one here, a blue one there. *If the trails left by shuttles could be seen, then surely they would look like this,* he thought. Then he realized that one of them was approaching him.

Like a river in spate, it rushed toward him, growing larger and larger. A green light shot through with coruscating silver filaments engulfed him, sweeping him up and bearing him irresistibly onward. Strangely, he felt no fear, only intense curiosity. Within his mind, he could hear the Guardian telling him that all was as it should be.

Ahead of him, as if at the end of a tunnel, he could see a brilliant white light. He knew that it was toward this he was being taken. The sensation of movement slowed until, without warning, he found himself deposited before a gateway. A wooden door, flanked by the boles of two enormous trees, barred his way. Abruptly, the presence that was Guardian Dhaika was gone, and he was alone.

This isn't real, it's a hallucination, he told himself. *A trip to the realms of the spirit.* He reached out to touch the door.

"It's damned solid for an illusion," he murmured as he looked for some handle or catch with which to open it.

There was nothing, save for a carving in the center which looked hauntingly familiar. He passed his hand over it, letting his fingers trace their way across the triple spirals within which was set a blue-white crystal.

As he touched the stone, the door swung slowly open to reveal a forest within. He hesitated, knowing he was expected to enter, but reluctant to commit himself.

Pushing his fears aside, he stepped through, instantly turning back to check on the door. There was nothing, only the forest. He sniffed, breathing in the rich, humid air of summer. He knew immediately which way to go; someone had left a trail. It was nothing he could identify, but it was different, it demanded to be followed. Within a few paces, he found himself on a narrow track heading in the same direction.

At a steady lope, he followed the trail, noticing that as the forest began to thin, the path widened. Suddenly the cool greenness was behind him and ahead lay an open clearing. Overhead, the sun blazed down from a summer sky. Dazzled, he put his hands to his forehead, shielding his eyes from the glare. The tang of wood smoke hung in the air, and up ahead, he could hear the sound of a grindstone.

Slowly the scene in front of him began to resolve itself. At the far edge of the clearing stood a rustic house, smoke coiling lazily upward from the single chimney. Against one side was an open lean-to. Within it a figure, back turned to him, was working. The sound of metal being drawn across stone filled the air and every now and then a shower of sparks would light up the dim interior.

Kaid frowned. This was unlike anything he could imagine being associated with the Green Goddess. Curious, he began to cross the clearing.

As he drew close, the noise stopped, and the figure turned to meet him. "I knew you could make the journey."

"You!" said Kaid angrily, fists clenching at his sides as he stopped. "You dared to use the Goddess to bring me here!"

A voice was calling him, he realized. He ought to answer. Concentrating, he focused on the brightness of the distant flame, making it come closer until all he could see was its golden glow. Beyond it, he knew, lay the other side of reality, and Guardian Dhaika. It was only a small step, then he was blinking and pushing himself up stiffly into a sitting position.

"I was concerned," said the Guardian, sitting back on his haunches. "You were gone for some time."

"It was Vartra, not the Green Goddess, who called me." He felt tired, and still not wholly of this world.

"Vartra?" Dhaika was shocked.

Kaid got to his feet, rearranging his robe before slipping his hands within the opposite sleeves. "I must return to Stronghold, Guardian Dhaika. Vartra has work for me."

*   *   *

Gary Davies was eating breakfast in the lounge with Kris and Zashou when they heard the guards outside their chambers thump their spears on the ground in a salute to their Lord.

"A bit early for them," murmured Davies, setting down his tankard of ale. "Wonder what they want."

The door opened to admit Lord Killian accompanied by Belamor and an irate Taradain.

"My son has reminded me that your continued safety is my concern," said Killian, moving further into the room. "With the coming of spring, those of us foolish enough not to wear our talismans all year round bring them to Belamor to have their protective spell renewed. You can't, therefore Belamor has brought them to you." He beckoned his mage forward. "Get on with it, Belamor. Do your magic, then we can all carry on with our work."

As the mage came toward their table, Davies watched Taradain's eyes search the chamber for Jo.

"They're not all here," the youth said abruptly. "I have a special talisman for Jo."

Belamor paused in opening the silk-wrapped parcel he had laid on the table. "A special one? And where did you get that?" he asked, his voice sharp with sarcasm. "From some hedge wizard in the town? Some drunken sot who peddles his skills in the inns for ale?"

Killian looked at his son, who began to flush an unbecoming color. "Give it to me," he commanded, holding out his hand. "Special, eh? Let me guess. You've had it made into a love charm. Lust would be more like it!"

"Do you think I'd risk her life for that?" countered the youth.

"You risk it by giving her a Demon talisman made by an amateur," said Belamor, returning to his parcel. He drew back the final wrapping to reveal five metal disks on leather thongs. Set within the center of each was a green stone.

"Give me the talisman." There was a hard edge to Killian's voice this time. "We'll let her choose which one she wants. Where is the wench anyway?" he asked Kris.

"Sleeping," he replied shortly.

"I need them all here," said Belamor. "Each talisman must be keyed to the wearer."

Davies wished for the millionth time that he had enough telepathic abilities to be able to mind-speak on even the most basic level—hell, to even be aware of the gist of what his friends were saying!

"Your furry friend, where's he?" demanded Killian, looking at Zashou.

"Sleeping," she replied.

Killian began to chuckle as he turned to his son. "Seems like she's made her choice, lad! She prefers the male creature to a boy like you!"

Taradain stiffened, his face contorted with anger. "That's a lie! She'd have nothing to do with him!" He ran to the table, grabbing Kris by the arm. "Tell him it's a lie!"

Kris looked away from him, his eyes catching Davies'. "I'm sorry," was all he could say.

"Our people, we depend on each other," said Davies, thinking rapidly. He had to defuse the situation now before it got out of hand. "There's a physical need for each other—males to females, females to males. Without it we die."

"You're lying! She couldn't! It's not true!"

"It's true," said Zashou, reaching out to touch him. "We're different, alien . . . not from your world. She only looks like your people."

Taradain pulled away from them, looking toward the two bedroom doors. "Where is she?" he demanded. "Which room?"

"Leave it, boy. You're making an even bigger fool of yourself than you already have," laughed Killian. "I told you to leave her alone from the first! Maybe next time you'll listen to me!"

"Don't disturb them," began Kris, getting to his feet as Taradain headed toward one of the bedrooms. "There's no need. We aren't lying."

"Shut up!" snarled the youth, breaking into a run.

Reaching the door, he flung it wide open, standing there a moment before heading toward the other room.

Davies got up, looking toward Killian. "Is this necessary?"

"He won't believe you till he's seen for himself," said the Lord, wiping tears of laughter from his eyes. "Maybe this'll rid him once and for all of his damned fool romantic notions!"

Taradain wrenched the door open. For a moment he stood there, then, as an enraged snarl came from within, he spun on his heel and ran from the chamber.

Killian pulled a chair out from the worktable and sat down, his ample bulk shaking with mirth.

Moments later, Rezac, his tunic held around himself, came into the room. He closed the door behind him. "Dammit, why the hell didn't one of you stop him? We're entitled to privacy! Jo's as twitchy as hell as it is without this!"

Killian's laughter didn't diminish, in fact it increased. He waved a limp hand in Belamor's direction. "Get on with it," he managed to say at last. "I owe you a favor," he said to Rezac. "You can have your fresh air. My son has needed something like this for some time now. Maybe this'll finally make a man of him!"

"Leave it, Rezac," said Davies in Sholan, making a warning gesture.

Belamor threw Killian an angry look. "I can't work in these conditions," he snapped. "Either curtail your mirth or leave!"

As the Lord began to cough, Davies decided it would be a good move to take him a drink. Picking up his own tankard, he stepped over and handed it to him. Gratefully Killian accepted it, downing the contents in one gulp.

"So you have a dependence on each other," he said, handing him the empty tankard. "It's as well I housed you all together, isn't it?"

"It is indeed," said Davies, aware of the implied threat. "However, if you hadn't, we would have told you."

"I need the woman as well," said Belamor, picking up the first of the pendants.

As he returned to his seat, Davies saw Zashou stiffen, a look of fear frozen on her face. At the same moment, he heard a small sound of anger, quickly stifled, from Rezac.

"You," Belamor commanded, beckoning to Kris.

Davies watched as Kris got up and came round the table. Belamor fastened the pendant round his neck, then placed his hand over where it lay against the Human's chest. Closing his eyes, Belamor began to chant in a low, monotonous voice. After a few moments, he removed his hand and sketched a few symbols in the air. They were too fast for Davies to follow, but he comforted himself with the knowledge that they probably wouldn't have made sense to him anyway. They might be able speak the local language, but they'd never seen it written.

Belamor dismissed Kris and beckoned to Zashou. With stiff, jerky movements, the Sholan female came to the mage's side.

"I want the other female," he reminded Killian before repeating the procedure with Zashou.

"Fetch her," Killian ordered Rezac.

The Sholan turned angrily and left the room, returning a couple of minutes later with Jo, now fully clothed. Davies was surprised when, eyes to the floor, she headed straight for him. He moved over, leaving her enough room to sit beside him. Putting his arm around her waist, he leaned toward her.

"When this bloke's done his stuff, go back to Rezac," he said quietly in Sholan.

"I can't," she whispered, turning a panic-stricken face to him.

"Do it," he ordered. "If you don't, you'll only be hurting yourselves. Give this Link a chance, Jo. You both deserve that. If you won't go, I'll take you!" He put on a grim face hoping to make her smile.

It did. "You wouldn't."

"Watch me," he said, in a fair imitation of a Sholan growl.

"I said you," said Belamor, tapping him sharply on the shoulder.

When Belamor and Killian left, Rezac tore off his pendant and flung it the length of the room, then turned and grasped hold of Jo's, about to do the same.

She put her hand over it to stop him. "Why? It's time you told us what these are."

"The Valtegans used these stones to control their slaves," he said. "When you found us, the collars we were wearing were slave collars."

"They were part of a device that let them know if we used r telepathic abilities," said Zashou, reaching up to untie rs. "Then they'd punish us with pain." She shuddered as e put it on the table and pushed it away from her.

"They aren't part of a device now," Davies pointed out. Vhy would the Jalnians have Valtegan stones? What are ey using them for?"

"Talismans," said Kris, picking up Zashou's to examine "Did the rest of you feel Belamor touch your minds?"

A chorus of assents—except from Gary—answered him.

"Psi powers on a world that believes in magic," he said oughtfully, holding it up to the window to look through "Where do the stones come from?"

"A plant. It's the hardened sap, kind of like a resinous ubstance," replied Rezac, hovering near Jo. "They called laalquoi. They grow it on all their worlds. They were rming it on Shola in our time."

"Then they might have been here?" asked Kris, putting back on the table. "Did you ever hear the name Jalna entioned?"

Rezac shook his head. "Never. And there were no Hu-uanoid slaves either. If they were here, then they left be-pre our time."

"But why use the stones as a talisman against demons? hey must have some effect on the violent ones, but hat?" asked Jo.

"Calming them," said Zashou, leaning back in her chair. The Valtegan females wore them all the time, otherwise he males would never have gotten near enough either to nate with them or to take the eggs out before they atched."

Rezac leaned forward to touch Jo's cheek. "We have to o," he said, with an embarrassed glance at Zashou. "Our ime isn't over."

"Go," said Zashou. "You're affecting me with your eeds. I can do without adding sexual frustration to my list of ailments. And," she added more prosaically, "if I can ense it, so can Kris and Davies. Go."

Jo flushed, hesitating, then she caught sight of Davies getting to his feet. Hurriedly she rose and went with Rezac.

CHAPTER 11

Kezule had been given extra food that morning: a fowl
some kind. It had made a welcome change to his die
though he knew that wasn't why it had been included.
had been his captors' way of not feeding the female. The
an hour later, fresh linen had been put in the feeding cag
He'd sent the female for it, telling her to put it in a ne:
pile on the bed before she ate.

She sat in her corner, chewing on the bones of th
chiddoe, her newly acquired blanket clutched tightly roun
her. She was watching him intently, no fear on her fac
now. She'd learned he didn't lash out without reason.
she obeyed him, there were no beatings.

Clean linen meant they'd open the shower unit. It wa
long overdue. Despite the air-conditioning, her smell wa
becoming overpowering. He rose from the table and wer
over to the bed, sitting down to examine the pile of clothin
and bedding. Apart from clean coveralls for himself, ther
were two fresh tunics for her, plus an extra towel. Pickin
them up, he threw them onto the nearest chair.

"When they open the shower, you go first. Scrub tha
hide of yours till it's clean. Your stench is offensive to me
Take only the towel, come back for the tunic whe:
you've washed."

As he spoke, a section of wall by the basin slid back t
reveal his cell's shower cubicle. Immediately she was or
her feet, the plate returned to the table as she snatched u;
the towel.

To be clean again! She'd lost track of how long she's
been trapped in the cell with the Valtegan—days, weeks—
she had no way of knowing.

She pressed open the front seal of her tunic, pulling i
off and throwing it distastefully onto the floor. Her smel:
might disgust him, but it appalled her. She hadn't even had

means to groom herself and remove the loose fur and ed blood from her pelt. Leaning forward into the cubicle, reached for the controls, selecting the temperature be-e turning on the water. Flattening her ears, she stepped letting the warm stream cascade over her head and wn her shoulders. She felt a pleasure akin to rapture as pressurized needles of water pounded her limbs, mas-zing the aches and pains, washing away the accumulated me. Reaching for the soap, she began with her hair. She pt her eyes shut; she didn't even want to think about at color the water would be.

In the observation room, Zhyaf began to murmur into e recording device.

"He's getting her thoughts now," said Mito quietly to r bond-mate. "You know, he's handling her very sensi-ely. She isn't even aware that she's being monitored, let one being fed suggestions. His isn't an easy job."

Anders grunted, keeping his eyes on Kezule. "Just as ell. I swear Kezule would sense it. This general of ours is ie wily old bird. Apart from his outburst yesterday, he's een so controlled, so self-assured. Do you realize, we don't en know what age he is? We assume he's past his prime, it we've no idea of the length of their natural life span."

"Talking of physiology, any news on the drug tests?"

"Not hopeful. The comp sims predict disastrous results we use any of the drugs common to most Alliance citi-ens. They're testing Touiban specific pharmaceuticals at e moment. Looks like all we can do is use up those found n Keiss, and they're for medical purposes, not interroga-on."

"I'd have thought that they could have extrapolated mething useful from them by now."

"They're working on it as well. It all takes time, Mito."

"So what's next?" she asked, fiddling with the controls n the telemetry monitor.

"Leave things as they are for a few days, see what he oes now he's realized we've rewarded him for interacting ith Keeza. If he starts talking to her, conversations I iean, not just commands, then we can leave it to run its ourse. If not, Rhyaz wants to start the heavy interroga-ions again."

"I hate them. It's so barbaric."

Anders looked briefly in her direction, reaching out
caress her cheek. "None of us like it, Mito. Just rememb
that in there sits a predator more powerful than any spec
you've yet encountered. His people have a weapon capab
of destroying all life on a planet. They destroyed two
your worlds already—millions of people died. And they
still out there somewhere. We need to know where."

"Then what? If you're right, we've very little chance
beating them. Apart from those on Keiss, we've not fou
a trace of them. I think we'd do better leaving them w
alone."

"And live in fear that they'll return?" He shook his hea
turning back to the viewing panel. "No, we have to fi
out where they come from. It's our only chance of surviv
The Sholans beat them once. Together, the Alliance c
do it again, I know we can."

A deep sigh from behind them made them turn roun
Zhyaf was switching off his recorder. As he sat back in h
chair, he rubbed his hands across his face.

"How'd it go?" asked Mito.

"We don't know till we see how he responds to her im
plementation of my suggestions," he said tiredly. "I ha
to probe her mind carefully, make suggestions and see ho
she reacts. I can't force her to do something she's afraid
doing, not without her realizing she's being used."

"How's she coping?" asked Anders.

Zhyaf's face registered his surprise at the question. "Yc
do care! Better. Regular food, even if it isn't nearly enoug
and that blanket last night, have helped stabilize her. Sh
now has a measure of security within the constant fear."

"Of course I care. I'd have to be damned insensitive n
to! What about Kezule's outburst last night?"

"It had a logical reason. She knew it was an isolate
incident. You have to see it from her point of view," h
said, getting up and going over to the drink dispenser. "H
hasn't abused her in any way, he's . . ."

"I'd call it abuse," interrupted Mito.

"It's not," Zhyaf insisted, picking up his mug of c'sha
and returning to his seat. "Not in her mind. He's bee
training her, showing her what he considers appropriat
behavior. Now she understands, she can do what he want:
keep out of his way. She can survive." He took a sip of hi
drink. "By Vartra, she deserves her freedom after this!"

* * *

Kezule had stretched out on his bed. He was thinking. It
ruck him as interesting that the reward the day before
ad come not after he'd decided to give them some infor-
ation for the first time, but after he'd made it obvious he
as taking responsibility for the female. They were study-
ig how he treated her, using it to further their understand-
ig of his people. Well, there was little he could do about
iat, and little they could discover about his people beyond
ie reality of their natural supremacy.

The sound of water stopped, and he heard her moving
round. He realized he could hear a new sound, a strange
ne: a low, almost inaudible rumbling. Getting up, he went
o the doorway.

Startled, she jumped back, clutching the towel. Her ears
ad vanished in the mass of fuzzy hair that topped her
ead. Beneath it, her enormous gray eyes peered out, con-
tantly scanning him. He could smell her terror, and he
ealized the noise had stopped.

"Pleasure. You make sounds of pleasure." He was
tunned. Never had his pet made such noises. "But why?"

"Why, my General?" she stammered.

"Why pleasure noises?"

He watched understanding dawn. "The shower . . . to be
:lean again." She retreated till her back was touching the
vall. "I'm sorry. I won't do it again, my General."

"Dry yourself outside," he ordered, gesturing to the
loor. "I want to shower."

Hugging the wall, she sidled past him, fleeing into the
main room. He watched her retreating figure, understanding for the first time what the attraction to a female from
a different species could be. Lonely, isolated, with no hope
of returning to his own world, he realized that the presence
of another living being was more important to him than he
cared to admit.

The smell of her damp fur still lingered in the air. Snort-
ing, he began to strip. He'd seen them, those in higher
offices, with their *special* pets! They made a mockery of
their class. So much for dignity and self-control! He hissed
in anger, threw his coverall to the floor and stepped into
the shower cubicle. He expected the common soldiers to
behave that way when they were given female slaves as a
reward—after all, they weren't allowed to breed and their

access to the drones was restricted. Of course they'd g
into rut! It was part of what they all were, part of the
competitive nature! But he was neither a common soldie
nor a depraved elite. He would not sink to their depths b
taking an alien female!

The hot water was soothing and relaxing. He found h
mood began to improve as he stood there letting it ru
down his body in rivulets. He turned his face up to the je
closing his eyes and momentarily raising his crest. At lea
her scent was so alien there was no chance of him bein
attracted to her. She didn't even smell like a real female!

*   *   *

"Kaid said what?" demanded Carrie, hardly creditin
what T'Chebbi was saying. "He said you weren't needed?"

T'Chebbi nodded. "Also, wants us ready to leave Shol
in one month."

"But he actually sat there and told you that yo
weren't needed?"

T'Chebbi sighed. "Stood, actually."

"The bastard! What's happening to him, T'Chebbi?
thought he was getting better, then this."

"Is better," she said, pulling a stim twig pack from he
pocket. Taking one out, she put the pack on the table ir
front of her.

Carrie reached out and picked it up, examining the wrap
per before putting it back. "When did you start using
them?" She'd been so sure there was something betweer
T'Chebbi and Kaid.

"Nights can be long up in Dzahai."

Carrie made an exasperated noise. Privacy be damned.
she needed to know what was going on. "Look, I thought
you and he had some sort of understanding. What happened to that?"

T'Chebbi nibbled delicately at the end of the twig, visibly
considering her answer before she replied. "Friends, Clan
Leader, who sometimes share bed like Kusac does, sometimes more."

"Don't *Clan Leader* me, T'Chebbi!" she said, exasperated. "Just what's going on with Kaid?"

She looked up, meeting Carrie's eyes for the first time
that evening. "Don't know. Told you, he said Vartra had
called him, not Green Goddess, and there was much to do

short time. You should go to him, call him. Maybe he
ls you."

"I have," she said shortly. "Twice. Kusac persuaded me
do it. Father Lijou answered, gave me some plausible
cuse from Kaid to save embarrassing me, but he refuses
speak to me. Besides, it's been weeks since Kaid was at
e Retreat." She picked up her mug, looked into it unhap-
ly, and swirled the contents around. "Kusac says very
tle about his time with Kaid at Stronghold. He keeps it
ore or less private even during our Link time. He's as
cretive about it as you are." She looked up at the other
male. "What's this sword-brother ritual all about? All
ve managed to find out is that most of them are single
x pairs, and many of them are lovers." She didn't dare
k the question.

"I think nothing happens, Carrie," said T'Chebbi, obvi-
sly unbending. "He didn't look for sword-brother, Kusac
d the asking."

"What about Garras?"

"Garras asked Kaid. Sword-brothers have complex rela-
onship. Much of it is for in field, when fighting. Those you
e at Warrior Guild take that oath because already
vers."

Carrie breathed a sigh of relief. Common sense said it
as unlikely, but she still knew so little about this complex
ciety that was now hers. "Does Kaid ever ask about me?"
She made a negative gesture. "I tell him when I arrive."

"Then he doesn't." She drained her mug and sat back in
er seat. "Why? What happened? Did I do or say some-
ing to upset him?"

"Don't know, Carrie. Must be resolved before we leave
r Jalna. Go and see him."

"I can't. I have my pride, too, T'Chebbi. He even refused
o come to our birthday celebrations, and he knew it was
usac's coming of age."

T'Chebbi flattened her ears briefly in sympathy as she
egan to chew the twig properly. She leaned forward and,
icking up the pack, held it out to Carrie. "Try one."

Carrie looked at her in surprise, then grinned. "Does it
elp? Is that why Kaid uses them?"

T'Chebbi purred with amusement. "Who knows with
im? Is late. Share a shower with me. Will relax us both.
eave foolish males to sort themselves out."

* * *

Garras lay awake, his body cupped around Vanna's, h
left hand resting on her belly, feeling its gentle rise and f
as she breathed. They'd know today, Jack had said. He w
scared, part of him wanting to know, part not. He wante
these few minutes before she woke to stretch endlessly.

The rhythm of her breathing changed, became deeper
she began to surface to wakefulness. He sighed, his han
automatically caressing her, stroking the breasts that we
already beginning to form.

She mumbled in her sleep, turning toward him, her fac
instinctively seeking his, her hands touching his neck.

"Good morning," he said, gently licking her cheek.

She mumbled something indistinct in reply and he ha
to laugh. "You're not awake yet, are you?"

A negative grunt was his only answer.

From beyond the door, he heard voices but before h
could do more than begin to disentangle himself, a seri
of sharp raps on the door preceded its opening. Jack, fo
lowed by Jiszoe, strode in.

"Rise and shine!" said Jack, heading for the drapes an
pulling them back to let the winter sunshine stream int
the room.

Garras tried to shield his eyes. "What's going on?" h
asked.

"Come on, you two slugabeds!" he boomed, striding ove
to them. "Wake up that pretty little wife of yours, Garra
We've brought breakfast—and something else!"

Vanna groaned, finally pushing herself up from th
covers.

"Good morning, Vanna," said Jiszoe brightly, coming t
sit on her side of the bed. "May the sun shine on yo
this morning."

"It already is," she grumbled, rubbing the sleep from he
eyes and blinking in the bright spring sunlight.

Behind them hovered three of the estate younglings wh
were doing some work experience among the Leska house
holds. Two carried trays groaning with food and hot drinks
the third carried a folding table.

"Don't stand there gawping," said Jack, "get the tabl
set up, the food on it, and leave!"

"Yes, Physician!" they chorused, and within two minute

flat, they were gone, leaving first meal set out on the table which had been placed at Vanna's side.

"Good morning, Jiszoe," said Vanna, taking the robe the other female was holding out to her.

"What's going on, Jack?" demanded Garras, unsure whether to be offended or amused by their intrusion.

Jack hauled the nearest chair over and sat down beside him. "Well, it's like this," he said. "I remember what it was like when I was in a similar situation to yours, so, to save you worrying, we've brought the news to you."

"The news?" Vanna's ears swiveled round to catch every word.

Jack nodded to Jiszoe. "My Companion has a gift for you," he said. Even as he spoke, Vanna turned back to Jiszoe. Jack handed Garras a piece of paper. "And this is for you," he added.

Garras took it from him, somewhat stunned. He couldn't look at it.

"This is for you," he heard Jiszoe say. "I searched the archives with the help of Brother Ghyan. It's how the ancient Triads recorded their family history. They needed to keep a record of which male fathered which child."

"Thank you," said Vanna, her voice faint as she took the decorated hide-bound book from Jiszoe.

"Aren't you going to read it?" Jack prompted Garras.

Vanna placed the book on the bed between them. "Read it," she said.

"I can't," he said. His heart had leaped into his mouth and was pounding fit to burst.

"Would they be here if the news was bad?" she demanded. "Read it before I do!"

He snatched the paper away just in case and forced himself to read it.

"Well?" she asked. "In Vartra's name, tell me!"

"This cub's mine—ours," he said, hardly able to believe what he had read. "A daughter."

"Let me see!"

The hand that passed it to her was shaking. "Is it definite?" he asked Jack.

"Not a shred of doubt, Garras," said Jack, patting his arm. "You have the child you both wanted."

Vanna let out a whoop of pleasure and flung her arms around him. "They were right," she said, covering his face in tiny licks. "And we were wrong, thank Vartra! A cub of our own, Garras! Ours!"

"So we have." He was still somewhat stunned as he returned the embrace. He'd had such hopes for so long, and it had hurt more than he could ever let her guess to sit back and watch them disappear one by one as she had formed her Leska Link with the Human and borne his cub. It would take a while for him to get used to this.

No, it won't! she sent, letting him go and bouncing out of bed to put on her robe. *You'll get used to it! And this time, you* will *stay and help me move the furniture!*

He began to laugh. "I'll do it with pleasure," he said. "Now eat! We can't let the food our friends have brought go to waste, nor their company! You've picked at your meals too long, Vanna. I want our daughter to be healthy when she joins us, not some poor, half-starved wraith!"

Vanna picked up a piece of fruit and began eating it as she bounced back onto the bed beside him. "Yes, Garras," she said meekly.

Later that day, the new arrivals filed into the training center to join those already there from the estates. These were the people—fifty in all—from all over the continent who had the particular genes that would probably lead to them forming a Leska Link. As Vanna began the introductory talk, Garras watched his life-mate with pride. There was a new confidence about her, a glow that she'd not had when she'd carried Marak. He loved his foster son as if he were his own, but this cub, this was his first. She would be the first of several, he hoped. It was what they had both wanted before there had ever been a Brynne Stevens in their lives: to share their cubs with each other.

He looked at the sea of faces, both Human and Sholan, male and female. There was enough work for a lifetime here, helping these young adults learn to live with each other, to accept their Leska partners if Links formed, and to train them to defend themselves and their families. With Vanna and their cubs—and Brynne's—at his side, he could call himself content.

Scanning them not just with his eyes, but with his other senses, he could already pick out the potential troublemakers. There would always be those, but what would life be without a Challenge here and there?

* * *

T'Chebbi's wrist comm buzzed. She looked at Carrie and, getting a nod in reply, quietly slipped from the back of the hall. Outside, she took the call. It was Kaid.

"I've decided," he said shortly. "Bring Carrie to the Retreat for the eleventh hour. I'll have a room set aside for you as we discussed."

"What I tell her?"

"Tell her you need to visit. Or whatever you like, but bring her. And get her to put her damper on full power."

* * *

The Retreat came into view as they crested the rise. "When are you going to tell me why we've come here?" asked Kusac, flicking an ear in the building's direction.

Kaid kept on walking, heading down the slope to the side entrance. He knew Kusac would follow him.

"Kaid!"

He could hear him slithering down the icy snow-dusted trail behind him. The trick was not to walk too fast as the slope was steeper than it appeared. Kusac would either figure it out for himself, or reach the door well ahead of him. The next few seconds should tell him which. There was a muffled curse that included his name, then apart from the odd skidding noise, nothing. Until he reached the door.

"You might have waited," said Kusac, following him into the Retreat. "Why are we here?"

"I want to visit a shrine," he said, heading down the left-hand corridor till he came to the only door on his right. Stopping, he looked at Kusac. "So do you." He slapped his hand on the palm lock.

"I do?" He followed Kaid into the small chapel.

Kaid closed the door behind them. "You asked me to bring you to the Warriors' Tomb."

The room was bare save for the ubiquitous glowing brazier and a large rectangular catafalque that stood on raised steps just beyond it.

"This is the tomb."

Kusac moved closer to the stone monolith, mounting the first shallow step. Reaching out, he ran his fingertips over the carvings on the side. The battle scenes had been worked in deeply cut relief panels. As he studied them, he could see the same two warriors, fighting either side by side or covering each other's backs, present in each.

"I don't remember asking you about this," he murmured, taking the second, higher step as he moved to the longer side.

Kaid watched as he leaned across the lid to see the portraits.

"It's certainly a work of great beauty. Who were they, these warriors?"

Kaid climbed the steps in front of him, leaning across the corner to see the carved faces. "No one knows. Their names weren't recorded, but they stand for all sword brothers."

He felt Kusac's start of surprise and when he spoke, the younger male's voice sounded a little strained.

"It's good they were buried together. Friends who shared their lives shouldn't be parted in death."

"They were more than friends. They were lovers."

He would have stepped back then, but Kaid reached out swiftly, clamping his hand over the other's arm, anchoring him to the tomb.

Kusac raised his face to Kaid's. "Surely not all sword brothers are lovers."

"Some are, some aren't, but those who are were lovers before they swore the oath. When death runs close behind you, Kusac, the need to know you're alive can be overwhelming. If your sword-brother had risked everything for you, and needed that reassurance, what would you do?" He locked eyes with the younger male.

Kusac hesitated before answering. "I don't know, Kaid. I'd offer what I could," he said quietly.

Kaid nodded slowly. "It's enough. You had to consider it, Kusac. You needed to know *your* limits within our relationship. No one knows what can happen after the heat of battle. So swear the sword-brother's oath with me, in the name of Vartra the God, over this tomb."

The arm within his grip moved as Kusac now tried to pull free. His ears were beginning to fold back and his pupils were dilating. Caught on the edge like this, he was unprepared, and Kaid couldn't help but be aware of his thoughts. He felt trapped and once more vulnerable at the hands of this male he felt hardly knew despite their weeks of living together.

"Will you swear it with me?" Kaid demanded, tightening his grip till his claws began to penetrate. Would Kusac swear, or would he break and run?

The movements stopped. "I will," Kusac said, his voice tense.

"Then swear that from this day onward, my fight will be your fight, in battle you'll never be more than a sword's reach from my side, and that my honor you'll hold as dear as your own."

As he repeated the oath, Kusac's voice grew firmer.

"Swear also that if I'm killed, you'll not risk your lives in seeking revenge." Kaid watched a look of puzzlement cross Kusac's face. "Swear it!"

"I swear!"

"Swear it in Vartra's name!" Kaid said, pulling him closer till their faces were only inches apart.

"I swear it in Vartra's name, dammit!" There was anger creeping into Kusac's voice now, and Kaid saw his free hand begin to clench into a fist. "What will you swear in return, Kaid? What do *you* offer *me*?"

At last he'd understood that it must be an equal relationship. "I swear the same, and give myself," he said simply, opening his mind and reaching out to him with it.

The contact was immediate and totally overwhelming. Kaid realized immediately he'd made a mistake, but it was too late to pull back. As Kusac's mind merged with his, so, too, did Carrie's. Surrounded and absorbed by them both, Kaid tried to pull free.

Taken totally unaware not only by Kaid, but by his Leska's sudden presence, Kusac wasn't prepared for their Link to explode within their conjoined minds. It surged through all three of them, awakening sexual responses identical to those he and Carrie experienced on their Link days. Then images and memories began to flash through his mind at such speed he'd no chance to make sense of them. They slowed, ceasing abruptly, leaving both him and Kaid focused on Carrie. Because of the heightened sensuality, he/Kaid ached to touch her, to hold her; she felt so close that they *knew* they could touch her! The need was so strong that he/Kaid reached out for her. Moments later, the gestalt flared into being, magnifying their Talents more than threefold. Before there was time to react, Carrie had instinctively

grasped control, but the energies were too much for her—
and her control begin to slip.

In the small staff dining room at the Retreat, Carrie gave
a cry of shock as she was suddenly swept into the Link
between Kusac and Kaid. Her physical senses dulled, she
staggered and would have fallen had T'Chebbi not caught
her. Clinging to the female as though she was a lifeline,
she couldn't move as the images from Kaid flashed through
her mind, images she already had. The strength left her
body and shuddering, she sagged against the Sholan female.

T'Chebbi swung Carrie up into her arms and strode over
to the small settee, placing her down on it. As she tried to
stand, the arms round her neck tightened, holding her
there.

"Carrie," T'Chebbi said anxiously, kneeling on the floor
beside her. She touched her face.

Carrie gasped at the touch, one hand instantly reaching
for T'Chebbi's to remove it. "We're Linked," she moaned.
"All three of us together! Oh, Gods, no!" She shuddered
again. "They *both* want me!"

T'Chebbi froze. Carrie's breath was warm on her face as
the Human turned her head, laying her cheek against hers.

"You smell different, feel softer," Carrie said, her voice
a whisper as she began to caress T'Chebbi's fingertips and
palm. "Your hand's smaller than theirs."

At her neck, Carrie's own hand was now moving slowly
and sensually among the tiny braids. Drawn into the fringes
of their Link, T'Chebbi could sense a little of what was
happening. Kaid had been right to anticipate trouble. The
normal light mental rapport that he'd said was the most
the Brothers and Sisters of Vartra could achieve, had become far more—it was a total three-way Link.

They'd talked about the sword-brother's oath the last
time she'd seen Kaid, discussed what she should do if anything went wrong. Her mind, though, was blank: She could
remember nothing. Then she felt Carrie touch her scruff.

Hurriedly she reached up, removing her hand, trapping it
firmly within her own. "Not there, Carrie," she said gently.

"T'Chebbi—I can feel them touching me," she moaned.
"As if I were there with them!"

What in the names of all the devils had he said? Then

he remembered. *If a Link forms, and it shouldn't, bring
er to us at the shrine of the Warriors' Tomb*. But neither
f them had anticipated this.

She gathered Carrie closer, holding her like a child as
he Human female tried to reach her face. "Hush. It's all
ight, Carrie. It'll pass. Try to relax, don't fight it." She
egan to stand up.

"I can't! Both of them inside my mind . . . It's too much,
"Chebbi!" Suddenly Carrie's body stiffened and with a cry
f pain, she passed out.

Hastily T'Chebbi laid her down, checking her pulse. Out
old. Leaving the room at a run, she headed for the shrine.
he stopped briefly at the door. When Carrie had passed
ut, her awareness of the two males had gone. Now she
vas unsure what she'd find, uncertain whether she should
disturb them. Taking a breath, she activated the palm lock.

They lay unmoving, several feet apart, at the foot of the
atafalque steps. She checked Kusac first, then Kaid. Same
s Carrie, unconscious, both of them. Taking Kaid by the
houlders, she shook him. Nothing. Pulling her arm back,
he slapped his face hard.

He stirred then, moaning as he put his hand to his cheek.
he helped him sit up, noticing as she did that he flinched
vhen her hand touched his uncovered pelt.

"Carrie joined the Link," she said. "Like you, she
assed out."

He tried to stand and she moved back, offering him her
arm to lean on. He accepted but once again let her go
vhen he was upright.

"You all right?"

"I will be," he said, staggering over to Kusac. "Help me
nove him into the other room."

"What room?" She was puzzled. She'd never heard of a
room within the shrine.

"Room for those who take their oath as lovers," he said,
crouching down by Kusac's prone form. "He'll need her."
He began to turn him over onto his back, straightening his
limbs, wincing when his hands touched the other's pelt.

"What happened?"

He ignored her, carefully checking Kusac's eyes. "We've
time. Help me lift him."

She reached out to touch his hand. He flinched away and
glanced briefly up at her. "Sorry. I'm still tuned in to

them." He was angry with himself. He should have realize
this could happen. "I want to get them together befor
either of them comes around."

Between them, they got Kusac to his feet and across t
the concealed door at the far end.

"Go and get Carrie," he said, activating the door. "I ca
manage the rest."

When she returned, Kusac was already lying on the bed
Kaid had stripped his robe from him and was putting it o
the chair that stood against one wall.

"I'll take her," he said.

Silently T'Chebbi let him take the unconscious femal
from her arms, watching how the strain left his face a
he did.

He placed her next to Kusac, turning her slightly till he
was sure their bodies were touching. Pulling the cover ove
them, he turned away and began walking back toward her

She watched him wince slightly as, from the corner o
her eye, she saw Kusac's arm curl instinctively over Carrie
Was he *that* closely Linked to them?

As the door shut behind them, Kaid leaned against th
wall for a moment, closing his eyes.

"Still Linked, aren't you?" she asked, taking hold of th
covered part of his arm. "Come. We'll go to the room Car
rie and I used."

He nodded and let himself be guided there.

The small dining room boasted a couple of settees and
a drinks dispenser as well as a table and chairs. It was for
the larger settee he headed. Sitting down, he leaned his
elbows on his knees, rubbing his hands tiredly over his face.

"I should sleep," he mumbled. "It'll help isolate me from
their Link."

T'Chebbi squatted in front of him, taking his hands away
from his face. "Not their Link, Kaid. Belongs to all three
of you. What happened?"

He pulled his hands free, leaning against the back of the
settee. "I miscalculated," he said. "Their gestalt happened.
I think Carrie triggered it with her fear." He glanced up at
her, a puzzled look on his face. "It was the damnedest
thing, T'Chebbi—a three-way Leska Link! Or what I'd
imagine one would be," he amended. "When Carrie's mind
joined us, she was our natural focus, we both turned to

er. How did she react?" he asked cautiously, watching her
through half-closed eyes.

"Said she felt you both touching her." A small silence,
then, "She initiated love play with me. It distressed her."

"Damn," he said, closing his eyes briefly. "I keep forget-
ng that because of their age and sheltered upbringing,
they're not as sophisticated as the rest of us. Particularly
Carrie. What did you do?"

"I tried to bring her to you, but she passed out. What
he did was nothing, no problem for me. Been down that
trail before, Kaid, but only when training at Consortia
House. Is problem for Carrie, though. She's where I was
ill not so long ago."

He tilted his head questioningly at her, finding himself
ntrigued.

"Afraid of appropriateness of her pleasure in the touch
of others. Noticed it when we showered first time. Have
been working on it with her. Should be no guilt in enjoying
closeness with friends, male or female."

He nodded. "Sensual means sexual to her. That would
it in with what I know of Human attitudes. They're so
much more insular than us. However," he added with a
wry smile, "being a telepath adds its own restrictions, I've
discovered. I understand now why I've always kept people
at a distance. It's worse now that my sense of touch is so
much more heightened than it was before."

T'Chebbi stood up and began unbuckling her weapons
belt. "Then since you allow me close, must be attracted to
me," she purred, letting it drop to the ground with a thud.
She began unfastening her robe.

Kaid frowned. "What're you doing?"

"Only on edges of your Link, but left me unsatisfied.
Since they're together now, must be worse for you," she
said, letting her robe fall. Leaning forward, she rested one
knee on the settee, her hand going to his shoulder to steady
herself. "Don't intend to stay like this. Do you?" Her
mouth touched his before moving to his cheek where she
fastened her teeth into him, giving him a sharp nip.

He hissed at the momentary pain even as he reached for
her. "The door," he said a few minutes later as they lay
entangled on his robe.

"Put privacy lock on when we came in," she said, hoping
that whatever had awakened the wildness in him stayed.

"Were you really afraid of your sensuality? I though
that was part of your training."

"Was. Something precious, to be enjoyed," she mur
mured as he nibbled and licked at her ear. "Pack tim
destroyed that. You gave it back."

He could sense a terrible darkness hovering within he
mind and immediately began to distract her. "Forget thos
times," he said. "You're here with me now, that's wha
counts."

"You use my words against me," she said, her voice trail
ing off.

Their lovemaking had been equally wild, but with its ful
fillment came their mental release. Lying in Carrie's arms
Kusac began to talk.

"It wasn't Kaid's fault, Carrie. You mustn't blame him
He had no way of knowing what would happen. Even
couldn't have predicted it."

"I'm not blaming him," she said, laying her head agains
his shoulder. "It was just too much, Kusac! To have bot!
of you wanting me like that . . . He must have guessed
something like this might happen, though. Why else have
T'Chebbi bring me here?"

"Thank the Gods he did!"

"But why? Why Link with you at all?"

"He only followed tradition, Carrie, except traditior
doesn't take into account Triads where all three are grade
one telepaths."

"But what I did to T'Chebbi! What will she think of
me?"

He held her close. "What did you do? Nothing terrible,
surely. Touch her, like a lover would? Kaid and I did the
same. Did you feel any revulsion from her?"

"No, but . . ."

"There was no harm in it, Carrie. She'll not think anything of it, she knows why it happened. You've shared
showers with her, she'll see it in the same light as that,
honestly."

"What about Kaid? Will he see it the same way?"

He could laugh now, but it had bothered him, too. "Kaid
isn't interested in me, it's you he's in love with. Neither of
us could pair with someone we weren't attracted to."

"You shared a bed. You were worried about him."

"Only telepaths tend to sleep alone unless they have a over or mate. Noni reminded me of that. As for being orried about what he'd ask of me in our oath, it's never asy to tell someone you care about that you don't find em sexually attractive. I was more concerned about the any mental games he's played on me lately. I haven't nown what to make of him. To be honest, I'm glad he pened his mind to me. I understand him a lot better now."

"In that case, you can explain his behavior to me over he past weeks!"

"That's not for me to do, cub, and you know it. Before ve leave, you need to speak to him, Carrie."

"No. He can come to me. He's taken great pains to avoid ne since he left the villa."

"We'll go to him, then."

"No." She was adamant. "The first move is his. If it's oo much effort to speak to me when we're in the same ouilding, then we've really nothing to say to each other."

"There shouldn't be something like this between us, Carrie."

She stopped him by putting her hand over his mouth. "I lidn't start it, Kusac. He did. He promised to speak to me and hasn't. If he has a problem with our Triad, then it's even more important he talks to one of us. The first move will be his, or not at all."

He had to accept what she was saying. There was no point in them falling out over it. He could always speak to Kaid later.

"You will not interfere," she said, removing her hand to kiss him. *This is between him and me. He has to learn to deal with relationships, learn that his actions can hurt and if they do, he must be the one to make amends. He's full of good advice for others, but until he realizes it applies to him, too, he'll have learned nothing.*

Kusac decided the only sensible course was to keep his nose out of the matter. It was clearly fraught with chiddoe holes for the unwary.

T'Chebbi came for them, telling Kusac that Kaid would see him back at Stronghold, and she would give him a lift there. He glanced hopefully at Carrie, but she stared ahead in stony silence as they walked to the parking area where the aircar waited.

*   *   *

Kaid arrived at his room an hour or so after Kusac. When he came in, he was carrying a long package which he placed on his desk. "Well, you succeeded," he said. "Despite the worst I could throw at you, you proved yourself a capable warrior."

"I thought you were leaning heavily on me," said Kusac from his chair by the window.

"You didn't complain."

"Would it have mattered?" he asked, raising an eye ridge. "I know now why you were doing it."

Kaid grinned. "Not in the least."

"Tell me something, Kaid. I know the ritual involves mental rapport, but why did you open your mind to me like that? Why did you give yourself in the oath?"

Kaid's grin faded. "It wasn't that that caused the problem," he began.

"I know," Kusac interrupted. "You did it right. It just wasn't meant to cope with telepaths. I only want to know why you opened your mind to me."

"Do you need to ask?"

"Yes, because I can't believe what I sensed unless you tell me." He was still stunned.

Kaid turned away and began to unwrap the parcel. "Come and see these," he said quietly.

Kusac got up from his chair and went over to join him. Kaid was stalling. Why? He decided to go along with it for now, but he was determined he'd have his answer.

"Swords!" he exclaimed, looking at the two identical blades each lying on their oil-soaked woolen wrapping. A third shape remained concealed within its cloth.

"It's customary for the senior of the sword-brothers to gift a sword once the oath is taken," said Kaid, lifting one of the blades by its wrapper. He held it out to Kusac. "This one is yours. The third is for Carrie. We'll need them on Jalna."

Kusac took it from him. It was plain, but its very lack of ornamentation was its beauty. Slightly curved, the actual blade was some thirty inches long. Quillons and pommel were made of undecorated bronze, the grip, a soft, crisscrossed leather binding in black. It was the blade, though, that held his eyes. As the light fell on it, it appeared to ripple and move in his hands.

"This is . . ."

"Made by Mijushu Rhayfso," he nodded. "The son of e Warrior Guild Master."

"But you can't just walk in and buy swords like this from m, Kaid! He only sells to those he chooses!" He couldn't :lieve what he was holding. "A warrior would almost die r the privilege of owning one of these! And they take :ars to make!"

"Not necessarily," said Kaid. "You like it?"

"Like it?" He threw the wrapping to the table and took e sword in both hands, swinging it experimentally to get e feel of it.

"They're individually balanced. Rhayfso had all the nec- sary details at the Guild."

"It's so light it seems to almost dance in my hands," he aid, his tone one of awe as he stepped back and swung e blade through a couple of classic movements. "How id you manage to persuade him to make them?"

"I've made a few friends in my time, done a few favors. Ie said he was honored to be asked to make us blades. He ad the steel already set aside for just such a special task." Kusac brought the blade to rest and reverently replaced : in its wrapping.

"You asked why I gave you myself," Kaid said quietly. Because we are three. Because we needed to be equals, nd we weren't. I had no knowledge of my mental Talents, nd you lacked the Brotherhood skills. You still have a lot o learn, Kusac, but you're no longer the novice you were. Neither am I. As for Carrie," he stopped. "Letting you ave the same knowledge of me that she has was the only vay to give you parity with her." He turned away and)egan wrapping up his own sword. "Besides, you already ad the rest of me."

Kusac reached out and took hold of him by the shoulder, urning him round to face him. "Kaid."

"Enough. You earned my loyalty and my love long ago,)oth of you. Now go home to your wife and cub. Your ime here is over for now. We leave in a month. I'll join ou at the estate as soon as I can."

Kusac pulled him into an embrace. "You know how we feel about you," he said. "You know why I had to ask. I :ouldn't trust what I sensed, I had to hear you say it to believe it."

Kaid patted him affectionately before releasing him.
know. This has been a strange time for all of us, but i
over now, thank Vartra. Now go home!"

*   *   *

Zashou did not feel well. Her stomach ached in a sc
of not-quite-there way, her hands and feet felt swoll
when she woke, and she itched. Not just in a place or tw
but all over. She tried not to scratch but there were tim
that she was hard-pressed not to claw herself till she dre
blood. And she could think of absolutely no reason wl
she should be like this.

It wasn't some rapacious insect form on Jalna, she'd ha
the female Jo help check her pelt in all the usual places—
behind the ears, her scruff and so on. Nothing. If she we
to sum it up, she felt uncomfortable within her own bod
as if it suddenly didn't want her living in it. If all that wasn
enough, there were the mood swings. She knew when sl
was being less than her sunny self, but she couldn't help i
couldn't stop it. Hell, she thought candidly, as far as tl
Humans were concerned, they'd never seen her any othe
way than this. How were they to know this wasn't the rea
her? All they had to go by was Rezac's opinion of her, an
she knew what that was.

She picked disconsolately at her first meal. She wasn
even hungry today.

"Eat something, Zashou," said Rezac from the other sid
of the table. "You're beginning to lose weight. You'll neve
feel better if you don't eat."

With an effort, she bit back a snappy retort. His ton
had been concerned. "I can't. It makes me feel nauseous.

He got up and left her to it, returning to his work at th
other table—beside Jo. That sent a sharp pang of jealous
through her. They got on so well together, she could fee
it even though they both tried to hide it from her. Who'
have guessed that one like him, another soldier, coul
awaken the gentleness in him that she'd failed to see? An
why did it worry her?

Pushing aside her plate, she took the green pendant fron
the pocket of her robe and began to examine it. The scrip
round the edge of the disk meant nothing to her, they wer
merely the superstitious symbols of this backward culture
The stone, though, was another matter. She rubbed it gen

y with her thumb, feeling it begin to warm to her touch.
certainly looked and felt the same as those they'd worn
the Valtegan collars, but why should those be here on
lna?

A shadow fell across her and she looked up to find Kris
tting down opposite. "Tell me more about the stones, Za-
ou," he said.

"What's to tell?" she asked, putting down the talisman.
had taken on an unpleasant texture now, become slightly
icky to the touch, and she was beginning to feel even
ore queasy. "We told you everything the other morning."

He reached out to pick it up, but her hand was there
rst, claws extended, making a cage over the pendant.

"It's mine!" she hissed, baring her teeth. "Leave it! Play
ith your own!" She felt suddenly clammy. Scooping up
e pendant, she saw her hand had left a wet imprint on
he table. Frightened, she found herself shaking as her
orge began to rise. Pushing herself away from the table,
he got to her feet and ran for her room.

"Rezac!" Kris called, getting hastily to his feet. He
eedn't have bothered, the Sholan was already following
er.

"What's wrong?" asked Davies, obviously concerned.

"I think we've got a problem," said Kris.

"What kind of problem?" asked Jo.

"I want to examine her first," said Kris as angry voices,
ollowed by a short yowl of pain came from the bedroom.

"Rezac!" said Jo, starting forward.

Kris grabbed her, holding her back. "No. Not you, Jo.
Leave this to us."

"Dammit, Kris! He's been hurt!" She rounded angrily
on him, trying to pry his hand off. She stopped abruptly as
she saw Rezac back out of the room clutching his forearm,
pelt bushed out, tail lashing angrily from side to side. The
door slammed shut and silence fell.

Jo pulled free and ran over to him, Kris and Davies
close behind.

"Let me see your arm," she demanded.

Shock had set in and he was shaking as Kris took him
by the elbow and steered him to the dining table. Jo hauled
out a chair for him to sit on.

"Get some water and towels," she ordered, grabbing a
chair for herself.

"Jo, let me see to him," said Kris. "You're too involve
to treat him. Come on, move over."

Reluctantly she moved.

"Let me see your arm," he said to Rezac, but the Shola
was sitting staring into space. Kris reached up and took hi
by the chin, shaking his face slightly to get his attentio

Gradually his eyes lost their glazed look and he focuse
on Kris. "She's pregnant," he blurted out, then caught sig
of Jo. "Oh, Gods," he groaned, shutting his eyes. Fro
under his hand, blood was slowly oozing, soaking into h
pelt and staining his fingers red.

"Keep your hand on it for now, Rezac," Kris sai
crouching down beside him. "Jo, find something to use a
a tourniquet."

She ran to their room, colliding with Davies on his wa
back. When she returned, she handed him a ribbon.

Kris raised an eyebrow as he accepted it.

"Something Taradain gave me," she muttere
embarrassed.

The tourniquet in place, Kris got Rezac to release h
arm. He sighed with relief when he saw the extent of th
damage. "You'll be fine," he said, taking the towel fro
Davies and dipping it in the bowl of water. "Only a fles
wound. Not as bad as it looks. It won't even need stitche
Get him a drink, Jo, he's gone pale around the nose. I'
rather he didn't pass out on us."

Quickly and efficiently, he cleaned the wound as best h
could and began to bind it with portions torn from one c
Jo's clean shifts.

"So Zashou's pregnant," he said as he worked. "Hov
far on?"

"She didn't say." Rezac's voice was quiet as he looke
past him to Jo.

"I take it she isn't exactly thrilled with the news."

"Neither of us are. It's more than that. She didn't choose
to be pregnant. That just can't happen, Kris. And she'
sick, too."

"I know. The pregnancy, it's part of the new Links, Rezac,
said Kris, tying off the last knot and sitting back. "Your fe
males lose the ability to choose to become pregnant."

He looked at the Human, brows meeting in puzzlement
"What do you mean?"

"The virus we told you about, it changes us. Your females become like ours, unable to control their fertility. Males, too. They change." He stopped, realizing that Jo had had no idea of the implications of her new relationship with Rezac either. He watched understanding dawn on Rezac's face.

"You're saying I could be pregnant, too." Jo's voice filled the silence.

"A slight chance," agreed Kris quietly.

"It's not possible!" Rezac's voice held panic and anger in equal measure.

"It's possible," said Jo, her voice quiet and even. "I told you, we were infected on the trip out. We passed it on to you. I've got a standard Human contraceptive implant, but if the virus changed me, it may not be effective any longer."

Kris was surprised at how well she was taking the news. Even her mind felt calm.

"We can't sit here and wait to be rescued any longer," said Davies. "We've got a snowball's chance in hell of escaping here with a heavily pregnant female who's sick. I'm not being callous," he added hastily as all eyes turned on him. "I'm being practical. Someone has to be. It's going to be difficult enough as it is."

"He's right," said Rezac, keeping his face turned away from Jo. Experimentally he flexed his arm. "We can start by trying to contact that ship of yours again, and the two telepaths on Jalna."

"Kris has tried the ship every night for the past two weeks and gotten nothing," said Jo. "As for the two captive telepaths, forget it. You, of all people, should realize the danger in giving away the fact we're telepaths. What if they're being used for their talents? We could lead the wrong people right to the gates of the castle and be worse off than we are now."

"She's right," said Kris. "Besides, your sending when we awakened you was so powerful that they should have picked it up and tried to contact us. The fact that they didn't suggests they're dead."

"We should try nonetheless. You can't be sure."

"I said no. The risks are too great."

"You could help me try to contact the ship again tonight," Kris suggested to Rezac.

"Now that's a good idea," said Davies. "You and Rezac combined ought to be able to raise them."

"If we're going to try to escape, we need to decide where we're heading," said Jo. "Getting out of here isn't enough."

"The spaceport," said Rezac immediately. "Steal a ship and get off this godsforsaken world!"

"You haven't seen the spaceport," said Davies.

"Interstellar ships don't land here, only the cargo pods do, or at best, shuttles. None of them is capable of deep space flight."

"Let's work on that one when we get there," said Rezac. "Getting out is the first part. To do that, we have to start working on the laser downstairs."

"We need outside help. I wish there was some way we could get a message to Railin," said Jo quietly.

"Railin? You'd trust him after what he did?"

"He didn't betray us, Gary."

"I'm with Jo on that," said Kris. "Yes, we were expected, but I don't think it was our storyteller. It could have been the mapmaker, even the girl at the tavern—what was her name?"

"Jainie," supplied Jo. "I don't think it was her either."

"Okay, I bow to superior mind power," sighed Davies. "I can't fight against the two of you. However, he'll be down in the plains now, collecting more stories for this winter. We have to do this one on our own."

Kris stood up. "I'd better go and see to Zashou. Gary, you clean up. Rezac, you stay put. You're still in shock. I don't want you moving about for a while. I think we'll have to call in Killian's apothecary. I need dressings for your arm, and I've a feeling we'll need his skills in treating Zashou."

Left alone with Jo, Rezac sat wondering what the hell he could say to her.

"There isn't much to say," said Jo, making him start in surprise. "If it's anyone's fault Zashou is pregnant, it's ours because we infected you."

"It's no one's fault," sighed Rezac, ears flattening. "En'-Shalla. The will of the Gods. My relationship with Zashou was doomed from the start. I let my anger stand between us, force us apart, because I couldn't believe she'd want someone like me."

"But you love her."

He reached out to touch her hand where it lay in her

lap. "I love you, too." He hesitated when she didn't respond, then he took hold of her hand anyway. "How likely is it you're pregnant, too?"

"Likely. I'll know in a few weeks."

He searched her face, reached carefully for her mind, strengthening the Link till he could sense her mood. She was calm, far too calm. None of this was touching her at all. "You're wearing the pendant."

She stirred, looking over at him. "Yes. I thought it a wise precaution. The people here obviously think it works, otherwise Killian wouldn't go to the bother of having his mage make them specially for us. Until we have a good reason for not wearing them, I think we should."

"Jo, if you are carrying my cub, I'm sorry . . . I mean, if we were home, on Shola, I wouldn't mind, but here . . . Damn! I'm making a mess of this, aren't I?"

"Rather," she agreed, a strange smile coming over her face.

"If you are, how would you feel about it?"

"Pregnant. I'd feel pregnant, Rezac."

"I didn't know . . . I wouldn't have done it if I had known." He was floundering now. Two females, both pregnant by him, and he couldn't talk to either of them coherently. He didn't even know how *he* felt about it!

"We would have. We had no option, remember?"

He knew how she should be reacting, knew that it was the stone that was calming her, but he was glad for it. He was clutching at grass, but he had to try to salvage what he could. He couldn't bear to lose her the way it looked as if he was losing Zashou.

"I'm sorry, Jo. I know you won't believe me, but I do love you. If it were any time but now, I'd want you to carry my cub, if that's what you wanted. I want us to be together."

"And Zashou?"

"I love her, too. She wasn't always this bad. It got worse after you awakened us, I don't know why. I want you both! Don't turn away from me because of this."

Again the strange smile. "I believe you."

"But . . ." He couldn't understand her reaction even with the influence of the pendant. "You could be carrying my cub, an alien cub, Jo."

"This is different. If I am pregnant, the cub's different,

Rezac. Not alien, ours. Would you undo the time we shared? Make it something less than it was by calling us alien to each other?"

"You know I wouldn't," he whispered.

Her hand turned within his, clasping it hard, almost triggering his claws. "Then we concentrate on getting out of here, and leave the rest to your gods."

He leaned forward, placing his lips against her throat.

"And, Rezac. Don't fight me over leadership of the group. Pregnant or not, I'm leader."

* * *

"No refreshments," said Mrowbay sadly, his ears drooping in disappointment. "Never have the Chemerians neglected to offer us nibbles and drinks before."

Sheeowl clapped his broad back in a friendly manner. "Abstinence is good for you," she said. "Your rear is spreading so fast these days, I swear it's distorting your comms seat!"

"They were indecently fast by their standards," said Manesh thoughtfully as they made their way down the corridor to the docking bays. "I think they want us to leave."

"Perhaps we leave more slowly, eh?" said Tirak, mouth widening in a humorless grin as he slowed down. "Maybe we'll . . ."

"Pardon, Captain. Trouble ahead," interrupted Mrowbay, his manner suddenly businesslike. He pointed to the bend ahead.

Tirak came to an immediate stop. Mrowbay's hearing was proverbial. His hand went to his side, resting on the butt of his pistol. "Maybe we find out now."

Round the corner came a group of Sumaan mercenaries wearing the badge of one of the leading Chemerian Houses. In their midst, in his powered chair, was their employer. And something—some*one*—else.

"Kathan's beard!" swore Sheeowl. "He's one of us! What the hell's going on?"

"Easy," said Tirak as his crew's hands went to their guns. "Let's take it by the rules."

The figure saw them and shouted, reaching its hand up in the air to attract their attention.

"Mrowbay?" demanded Tirak.

The comm officer shook his head. "Couldn't understand him."

"He's not one of us," said Sheeowl abruptly as the figure tried to push its way through the Sumaan. "That's not clothing, that's his color!"

"Recommend we don't interfere, Captain. Against the Sumaan, we're outnumbered."

Manesh's words faded till they were barely audible as the world around him took on a distant quality. It was as if he were sitting back as an observer within his own skull. He realized he was running toward the group of Sumaan with the intention of freeing the captives with his bare hands if need be. That part of him prayed his crew were not far behind.

Shock at his audacity gave him the element of surprise as he flung himself between the two leading mercenaries. He plucked up not the one they'd all seen, but the other— a pale, hairless alien. He kept going, ramming his way through them and on down the corridor.

The passive part, now numb with fear, realized that she— it was female?—was lying quiet in his grasp. She wasn't afraid. In fact, he got the impression she was trying to calm him! As he ran up the ramp into his craft, suddenly, with a lurch that almost caused him to fall, his mind was his own again.

Caroming off the bulkhead, he stopped by the comm unit. Dumping her on the ground, he kept hold of her arm. He thumbed the alarm. "Nayash, seal the ship!" he yelled into the speaker seconds before the klaxon blared its in-ship warning. The clack of claws hitting the metal ramp sounded behind him as Mrowbay and Sheeowl followed him, each clutching the other alien firmly by a wrist.

Sheeowl stopped and released him to Mrowbay. "I'll take it, Captain," she said, nodding toward the female.

Tirak handed her over and turned to look behind him.

"No sign of them, Captain," said Manesh, backing up the ramp, gun leveled outward to cover them.

Tirak headed for the bridge at a run. Flinging himself into his seat, he began scanning the array in front of him. He couldn't think properly with the damned alarm blaring in his ears like this! Folding them down, he opened his mouth just as the sound died.

"Ramps retracting," said Sayuk from her nav post.

"Loading hatch closed," said Nayash. "What now, Captain?"

"Open a channel to station command. No doubt they're anxious to share their thoughts with us," he said dryly, rubbing his aching temples. Damn, but his head hurt!

"No need, Captain," said Mrowbay. "They're on line to us. Patching it to your console now."

The screen flickered briefly, then displayed the station commander, his large saucer-shaped ears trembling with barely concealed rage.

"Lioksu. Had not thought to speak to you so soon," he said. "What is your pleasure?"

"You have prisoners belonging to Ambassador Taira Khebo. Return immediately," the Chemerian snapped.

"He's mad," muttered Sheeowl on his left.

"Prisoners, Lioksu? No prisoners on my ship. Are mistaken."

"You lie! Return them or suffer consequences!"

Tirak sat back in his seat, obviously relaxed and at ease. "Strong words, Lioksu. Hope you can prove them. U'Churian Traders Council will not like these allegations."

With a visible effort, the Chemerian stilled his ears. He blinked, once. "You attacked guards of Ambassador Taira Khebo. You took prisoners from them. They are on your ship now."

"Sumaan were in our way, Lioksu. I admit I pushed through them. But assure you, only U'Churians here. Think well before you accuse me of kidnapping."

Lioksu stared silently out of the screen at him. "You took them. Were thieves. Stealing from Free Trade area. Return them now, and we talk no more on this matter."

"Are you accusing U'Churians of theft, Lioksu? Serious matter, that. You know the law." He sat forward, hardening his voice, allowing a growl of menace to creep into it. "They must be given over to a captain of same species for trial. Send them to me, send me charge sheets. If crimes committed, they stand trial—on U'Chur. If allegations false, you pay large compensation fee."

Once more the Chemerian regarded him in silence, large eyes blinking slowly. Tirak knew he had him rattled now. With any luck he wouldn't push it. The U'Churians were a force to be reckoned with, even at the main Chemerian trading station.

"Perhaps Taira Khebo will drop charges," Lioksu said at last.

"Perhaps? We leave in two minutes, Lioksu. Either send people and charge sheets or stop delaying my departure!"

The screen blacked, the connection severed at source.

Sheeowl let out her breath in a huff of relief.

"Take us out, Nayash," said Tirak, getting to his feet. "I'll be in the rec, with our visitors." They didn't need him here, but he needed to see his two unwanted guests.

Holding onto the grab rail, he made his way back down the corridor to the recreation room. Sitting huddled together at one side of the dining table were the two aliens. Manesh sat opposite them, covering them with her pistol. One was as hairless as a newborn, the other—was he U'Churian? Apart from the color, the similarity was startling. A half empty tumbler of water sat in front of them.

A series of loud clangs and bumps reverberated through the hull. They were disengaging from the station.

"Stow that away," said Tirak, taking a seat.

Holstering her gun, Manesh reached for the glass. "They speak our language, Captain. Not well, but they speak it." She got up and went over to the kitchen area, stowing the tumbler under the restraining net in the cleansing unit. "The lad's not one of us."

He could smell them now. Their scents were mingled, but he could detect the underlying sharpness that was hers. Manesh returned to her seat.

"Sholan," said the young male. He pointed to the female. "She is Human."

"You made me attack the Sumaan. Risk my life and that of my crew," he said, his voice deepening to an angry rumble. "You did something inside my head."

The lad looked at the female who stirred, sitting up straighter. "Needed help." She spoke slowly, sounding each word as if for the first time.

"You could have asked!"

She shook her head. "No time. No . . ." She stopped, a frown creasing her smooth brow. "Not enough speech to tell you."

He growled. "You're doing fine now!"

"Then, not . . . touched your mind." She looked at the male, her gesture translating as one of helplessness.

He spoke a word, then a phrase in what Tirak assumed

was his own language. "We mind-speak others. Learn your words. Slowly. Using take time." His speech was equally faltering. "Learn now."

"Seems they understand more than they can speak," said Manesh in a low voice, leaning close to him. "Mind-speaking. Just before you rushed them, you looked like you'd swallowed a whole pachuv."

"Huh. Felt like it," he muttered. Then louder. "So you little bastards controlled my mind, did you?"

"Yes."

The lad grabbed her arm and began to talk rapidly, ears folding as he gestured frantically.

She turned away from him. "Yes," she said firmly. "I did, not Taynar." He subsided unhappily, leaning back against the seat.

Tirak had seen the look before on his sister's children's faces. Sulking. "By Kathan, you're kids!" he swore, leaning forward. "What the hell were you doing to get captured by the Chemerians? Stealing in the market?"

"No! Not steal," she said emphatically. "We stolen! From home! Chemerian friends. Help us, then decide keep us. Need escape."

"*You* were stolen!" exclaimed Manesh, her calm exterior fractured by their tale. "Who stole you? From where?"

"My world," she said. "Traveling to his. Valtegan stole us, took ship to escape. Captain die trying to kill him."

"Drifted," said Taynar, showing interest now that the tale had progressed from the issue of who had done what to Tirak. "Chemerians rescue us. We think friends, treaties with Shola they have, but not. Hold us prisoner."

"So the Chemerians are Sholan allies," said Tirak. The ship gave a tiny lurch, and he wound his feet round the chair legs for anchorage as the gravity system adjusted itself. It was so much second nature that he was surprised when the two young ones yowled and clutched at the table for support.

Mrowbay's voice came over the ship's system. "Leaving station orbit, Captain. What heading?"

"Stay with our original course," said Tirak, never taking his eyes from them. "So the Chemerians turned out to be not quite so friendly. Why? What did they want with you?"

They fell silent, glancing sideways at each other. "Don't know," the female said finally.

Tirak banged the table with the side of his fist, making
em jump. "Don't give me that!" he roared, his voice fill-
g the room, mane bristling with rage. "You know damned
ell what they wanted, and I want to know now!"

He watched a mutinous look come over the female's
ce, and when the lad moved to open his mouth, a sur-
ised look crossed his face and he subsided.

"Mind readers!" he muttered disgustedly. "Sheeowl, to
e rec! Lock them up, Manesh. One in each of the passen-
r cabins. When they're ready to talk, then . . . we'll see."

He waited till Manesh and Sheeowl had deposited their
nwanted visitors in the cabins and rejoined him. "Sugges-
ons, Manesh. How do we secure these . . ." He ground
 a halt, unsure what to call them.

"Frightened children, Captain," supplied Sheeowl, taking
ree drinks from the locker by the heating unit. Going to
e table, she slipped onto the bench seat and passed them
ut. Snapping the tab on hers, she waited for it to heat up.

"Dangerous aliens," he said firmly. "Don't be fooled by
eir age. You didn't have them pushing your mind aside,
aking your body run at the Sumaan like that!"

"I did wonder what you were doing," she said, taking a
ip of her drink. "It seemed insane at the time, but it
orked. They were as taken aback by your attack as we
ere!"

"It *was* insane! I don't even want to think of what should
ave happened."

"It occurs to me that the Sumaan guards were slower
han usual, Captain," said Manesh. "Much slower."

"Mmm. He's right," said Sheeowl, reaching across to
pen Tirak's drink for him. "Much slower."

"Have you seen the political implications of this, Cap-
ain? Two new species, at least one allied to the Chemeri-
ns, both able to bend others with the power of their
inds . . ."

"We don't know that for sure," Tirak interrupted Ma-
esh, taking a sip of his drink. "The female certainly has
trange mental abilities."

"Kate," said Sheeowl.

"Our most pressing problem for the moment is how to
keep them from doing that mind trick again!"

"We can't," said Manesh.

"You could try putting them on their honor," su[g]
gested Sheeowl.

The other two looked at her. "You aren't serious
suggesting . . . ?" Tirak let the sentence hang unfinished[.]

"Think about it, Captain. To have allies, they must [be]
trustworthy and be capable of trusting others. They mu[st]
have an honor system. I say put them on their honor [to]
not interfere with our minds again."

Tirak looked at his security officer.

Manesh shrugged her head to one side, nose wrinklin[g].
"It's all we have."

A deep rumble of anger built within him. "When they'[ve]
been alone for a few hours, maybe they'll be more cooper[a]tive," he muttered.

Sheeowl looked guilty, dipping her ears in apology. "[I]
left the connecting door open. Taynar became distressed [at]
the thought of being separated from Kate."

Tirak opened his mouth to reprimand her, then stoppe[d].
The error was his. He hadn't actually said he wanted the[m]
kept apart.

"In fact," she continued, toying with her drink, "he sai[d]
they were dependent on each other. Like mates."

"What? Mates? Them? Impossible!" The idea offende[d]
his sensibilities. There were strict rules governing the con[-]
duct of minors, never mind the fact they were of differen[t]
species.

"Improbable," corrected Manesh. "And therefore likel[y]
true. Far simpler to say they are lovers. Do you want the[m]
separated, Captain?"

"No," he sighed. "Dependency on each other like mates[?]
What the hell is he talking about?"

"At a wild guess, a sexual dependency?" suggeste[d]
Sheeowl. "Maybe their species evolved together? They ma[y]
be old enough to be a legitimate couple among thei[r]
species."

"Nothing about them would surprise me!" he muttered[.]
"More likely he's just afraid of being alone. Keep 'e[m]
under surveillance for now, feed them when we eat. On[e]
way or another, I intend to find out what's going on be[-]
tween their species and the Chemerians."

CHAPTER 12

"I'm doing what I can, Strick!" said Jeran, keeping his voice low as he checked the container off on his cargo manifest. "I can't afford to get caught any more than you! I've seen what they do to slaves involved in the rebellion!" He shuddered at the memory. "It takes me weeks to get the components together, then I have to build the damned thing! I'm totally dependent on what goods are arriving. If no one's shipping what I need, I can't make your communicators!"

"If you made the range greater, we wouldn't need so many!"

Jeran growled, throwing his clipboard on the counter and stalking off down the aisles of containers. He made no effort to keep his tail from betraying his anger. Stopping, he scanned the shelves for the goods Strick needed for his caravan. Reaching up, he snagged a small box with his claw tips and pulled it down, catching it as it fell.

Returning to his desk, he placed it in front of the Jalnian. "It's in this box," he said, pushing it over to him. "Packed in with the dried fungii. Now go! Before they get suspicious!"

Strick took the container. "You wanted to know if another Valtegan ship came. There's one in now. Landed two hours ago."

His ears pricked forward. "What do they want? Any more of my people on board?"

"I told you, the ship that brought you was different. This is one of the usual ones."

"I thought you said they didn't come often."

"They don't. I checked. The last one was some fifty years ago. They take a collection of foodstuffs—grain, vegetables, fruit, and meat. Soil too, this time."

"A science ship! What the hell's a science ship doi here?"

Strick frowned. "Science ship?"

"One taking samples to run tests," he said absently, mi working as he tried to figure out what the Valtegans want with bio samples. "How long have they been comi here?"

Strick shrugged. "Didn't bother checking any farth back."

"Not interested in conquest, then. Why the hell are th testing the soil and crops?"

"I'll leave you to it. Like you said, Jeran, I got to go."

The Jalnian's words cut through his thoughts. "Right He hesitated. "I don't suppose . . ."

"I'm sorry. U'Churian craft in plenty, a couple of Cal barans, and that Chemerian ship, but none like you."

Jeran nodded, watching as the other left the warehous stopping briefly to exchange pleasantries with the Jalnia guards on duty at the door.

*　　*　　*

"Well?" demanded Rezac as the apothecary came ou "What is it?"

The little man peered across the room to where Killia sat, obviously waiting for his command before speakin "I've seen it before, but not often," he said, responding t the gesture to approach the Lord. "It wasn't easy, yo know, her not being one of us, but that's what made simpler. If you see what I mean."

"Get on with it, man! Stop dithering," snapped Killia shifting his bulk restlessly in the chair. "What's wron with her?"

"I usually see it in young children. Then, being young they've got a chance. But when it's an adult," he shook hi head, making tiny, concerned sounds.

Rezac was far more disturbed than he cared to admi One of the worrying factors was that he was experiencin very little of what Zashou was feeling. Normally he fe everything to some degree, but with Zashou's advancin pregnancy, their Link had dimmed.

He wanted to shout and rage, to pick this little whit slug of a male up and shake him till the solution droppe out of him. Luckily, Jo's firm presence was helping him

st, contain his impotent fury. Now she was urging him to
ep his mouth shut and leave this to the rest of them.

Killian was making sounds of his own by this time, and
ey were far from tiny. "Arnor, if you don't get on with
. . ."

The apothecary looked at him in surprise. "The food,"
said. "It's the food. Didn't I say that? The lady being
alien makes it quite definite."

"The food?" echoed Jo.

"Her stomach just can't cope with our food."

"So what's the cure?" Killian demanded.

"Oh, that's the really simple part," said Arnor, adjusting
s cap, a large smile on his face. "Take her home. Or to
e Port to her own kind. Once she's able to eat the food
e's used to . . ." He faltered to a halt, the smile dying.
Not an option?" He sighed. "Then beyond giving your
tchen a special diet for her, there's little I can do." He
ook his head sadly. "It's really just a matter of time,
n afraid."

"You have to let us go, Killian," said Jo. "You're killing
er if you keep us here."

Anger like a red mist swept through Rezac, then sud-
enly he felt his mind grasped and held firmly. Rage as he
ight, he could do nothing; his body refused to respond.
ammit, Jo! he sent, but Kris answered him.

Not Jo, me. Violence now will achieve nothing, so be still!

Killian turned a cold stare on her as he dismissed Arnor
ith a wave of his hand. "Do what is needed," he said.

"Wait! There must be more you can do!" exclaimed Jo,
sing from the table.

Arnor hesitated, his kindly face creased in concern. "I
an ease the symptoms, give you an oil to rub in the sores,
tisane for the irritation and the pain."

"Do it, I said," repeated Killian. "She'll get what help I
an give her, and when you've finished your work for me,
ll see to it personally that you're escorted to the Port and
ut aboard a ship that will take you home." He pushed
imself up from his seat. "Now you have an incentive to
nish the weapon. You are responsible for her life, not
e." He turned and followed the apothecary from the
oom.

"He's lying," said Jo once the door closed behind him.

"He has no intention of letting us go. This son-of-a-bi[?] is empire building and he's using us to help him."

"Let me guess," said Davies. "Control of the spacepor[?]"

"Got it in one," she agreed.

The hold on Rezac's mind was released, and he slump[?] to the table. "You bastard," he said to Kris. "You did th[?] before, when they brought the talismans, didn't you?"

Kris reached forward, touching his fingertips to Reza[?] hand, but the other pulled back. "I had to. We're captiv[?] Rezac. If we do anything to upset the balance we have [?] the moment, it could jeopardize any escape plans."

"What escape plans?" he asked, not bothering to ke[?] the withering contempt from his voice. "We have nor[?] Just be careful, Kris, that you don't consign Jo to dea[?] with Zashou and me! The Gods know what will happen [?] her if we die!"

"I know what's at risk, Rezac. I've lived with yo[?] people."

"Enough, Kris," said Jo, cutting him short. "How so[?] till we can start working downstairs on the laser?"

"Really? Or for effect?"

"Either, dammit! We need to get out of here and asse[?] the potential for escape! Sitting here on our butts h[?] achieved damned little. There's not going to be a rescue [?] time for us!"

"Today. We can get the power source taken down to th[?] laser now. Apart from a cursory check to see it arriv[?] here intact, we've not given it a good going over."

"What about the controls we're working on? Can we c[?] anything to hurry that along?"

"Not without power, and we need that downstairs [?] check the laser," said Kris.

"You and Rezac check over all the control connection[?] make sure they're sound, then check them against th[?] plans," said Davies. "We were about ready to test [?] anyway."

"We can't afford to blow this, Gary," warned Kris. "W[?] damage any of the components for the controls, and we'[?] had it."

"Then, godammit, we fake it!" Davies snapped. "Wha[?] d'you suggest? I'm not sitting here watching my frienc[?] die!"

Jo reached out and put her hand on Davies' shoulde[?]

ueezing it gently. "Easy. No point in falling out with each
her. We all want the same thing, right, Kris? Now let's
t moving. Rezac, you make a start on the controls, I'm
ing in to see Zashou," she said, getting to her feet.

Rezac looked up at her. "Not a good idea. She's not in
e most receptive frame of mind."

"She shouldn't be alone now either. If she won't speak
you, then she'll speak to me! She can't deny that I'm
volved, too. See if you can get some boiled water for me,
d when you do, Gary, you bring it in, please, before you
down to check the laser. Bring it in a tankard or some-
ing. I think Zashou will be able to drink that more easily
an cold water."

Jo went to her own room and picked up a hairbrush
fore going to see Zashou. As the days had passed, she
d begun to understand this unlikely pair and the culture
om which they'd come. They were gregarious, a tribal
eople, needing the company of their own kind far more
an Humans did. One thing Zashou had lacked for a long
me was the feminine side of life. Well, she could at least
ve her some female company. If Rezac was right and
ashou saw her as taking the pressure out of her Leska
ink with him, then it shouldn't be too difficult to establish
common ground of friendship with her.

Zashou was lying on her side, facing the door. She
pened her eyes as Jo approached.

"What do you want?" she asked tiredly. "I'd rather be
lone."

"I've come to talk to you," Jo said, finding a place to
erch beside her. "The apothecary, Arnor, is sending up
ome oil for your skin. I think we should ask for a tub of
ot water, put some of the oil in it and let you soak for
while."

"What's the point? I'm dying, aren't I?"

"You will if that's your attitude," said Jo sharply. "Arn-
r's getting a special diet prepared for you, one low in
whatever it is in the food that's upsetting you. And we're
vorking on the laser now. Killian's said he'll release us
vhen it's finished."

"And you believe him?"

"Maybe, but we're also working on an escape plan. Actu-
lly, I've come in for a selfish reason. I want some female

company. You think I don't get tired of those males? The constant bickering, the need to be one up on each other it's tiring, Zashou. I can't remember when I last did som thing for myself as a female."

Zashou opened her eyes again, looking curiously at he "You like being female? I thought you wished to be o of them."

"Just because I'm in the military doesn't mean I'm le of a female than you." She pulled the brush from whe she'd tucked it in her belt and toyed idly with it. "M mother and I used to brush each other's hair every nig before we left Earth for Keiss," she said reminiscentl "We were the only two females in a household of men. was good to get away from my dad and my brothers for while each evening."

Zashou pushed herself up till she was able to see without craning her neck. "Jaisa and I did that, at the mo astery, before . . ." She faltered and Jo knew she didn want to say anything controversial. She waited.

"Before they tried to rescue her family," she continue finally. "Our friendship was never quite the same after tha Where is your mother now? Didn't she mind you joinir the military, fighting the Valtegans?"

"My mother died in the journey to Keiss," she sai "Many people did. There was an accident during the cros ing. We all traveled in cryo units, so we didn't find out t we arrived."

Zashou's hand touched hers, and she felt the other fe male's concern. "I'm sorry. I didn't intend to poke at ol wounds."

Jo smiled. "It was a long time ago, Zashou. But I though perhaps we could take some time together, leave the male to their own devices for a while, and just be females! Ho long is it since you had your hair unbraided and brushed?

"Too long," she said candidly. "It takes so long to do i myself, and I don't want Rezac . . ." She stopped, fac taking on a cautious look.

"Rezac isn't one for female company," said Jo diplomat cally. "I think he's never had the chance to develop th gentler side of his nature."

"Gentler side?"

She sensed the disbelief in the Sholan's voice. "It's there

Zashou, but at the moment he'd rather cut off his right hand than admit it!"

Zashou laughed—only a small one, but it was the first Jo had heard.

"He would, wouldn't he? Why? Why does he have to see me—us—as something to weaken him?"

"I didn't come to talk about Rezac, but you know the answer, Zashou. He gave it to you as he did to me, when we Linked," she said quietly.

Zashou reached out and took the brush from her. "Maybe we'll talk about Rezac another time," she said, equally quietly. Leaning forward, she ran her hand across Jo's short hair. "So soft. It makes mine feel harsh by comparison. You should grow it, Jo." She began to pull the brush through Jo's hair.

"I came to brush yours," said Jo.

"I know, but yours will take only a little time to do."

Jo relaxed. She was seeing a very different individual from the petulant female she'd thought Zashou to be. And she liked this person.

Rezac brings out the worst in me, she admitted. *Then this—illness hasn't made it easier.*

Again Jo sensed this was a taboo subject for now. No matter. The situation was clear-cut, they all knew that. They must escape or Zashou, and Rezac, and possibly even herself, would die.

"My hair used to be long," said Jo. "I cut it when I joined the guerrillas on Keiss. Less work to keep it clean and tidy when you're living rough."

"Males are lucky. It is in their natures to fight. When it involves us, we lose our female side."

Jo put her hand up to cover Zashou's and the brush. "Then let's reclaim it," she said.

By late afternoon, the heavy cylindrical container that had been the shuttle's backup power source had been moved down to the barn where the laser and the larger parts of the craft had been stored. Upstairs, Rezac had checked out their cannibalized control unit, and Jo had done wonders for both her own and Zashou's morale.

The oil and tisanes had arrived, along with the where-withal for them to boil water when they needed it. It was only an iron tripod with a swinging arm and a pot to hang from the hook, but it gave them a little more independence.

Jo got Davies to request the bath, and a succession of guards had brought buckets of hot water to fill it. They had not been amused by the demeaning work, and their sour faces had afforded both Jo and Zashou some amusement.

Hair unbound and forming a mass of tightly curled ringlets, Zashou had taken the first of her baths with the oil. Afterward, she'd agreed to allow Davies to come in and massage more oil into her pelt on the understanding that Jo remained, too. It wasn't that she didn't trust the Human male, she hastened to say, but she was nervous of being touched quite so intimately.

How did you manage with Rezac? How could you let him touch you? Zashou sent as Davies, now working on her back, massaged the oil deep into the roots of her dense pelt.

He was very gentle with me. He was aware of how afraid I was and tried to show me there was no reason for my fears.

Pity he didn't do the same with me.

Jo detected the note of bitterness, the first that day. She stopped plaiting and reached out to touch the other's cheek. *You frightened him, Zashou. Still do. You know he loves you, and he wanted to win you himself. He resents your Link as much as you do because it gave neither of you the choice. I'm sorry that you both had to suffer so much for it to be easier for me.*

"Y'know, back home on Keiss, I'd be the envy of everyone," said Davies, his hands gently easing the muscles over the top of Zashou's shoulders. "Here I am, massaging one of the most beautiful Sholan females I've seen, and there's nothing in it!"

"Nothing in it?" asked Zashou.

"Watch her neck, Gary," warned Jo. "The loose skin at the back's her scruff. Grasping it triggers a freeze response."

"Okay. I mean, there's nothing sexual in it," he explained, carefully circling her neck.

"Sensual," said Jo, fastening off the end of the braid on which she was working.

"Plenty of that," agreed Davies, with an old-fashioned glance at her. "I hadn't realized just how soft your fur could be."

"You've never had a Sholan partner, Gary? You're slipping!"

"That was never me, Jo, you should know that. Things are different now that our lives aren't always on the line."

Jo looked up at him. She didn't need to speak.

"Anyway," he continued, "you Sholan females can look quite intimidating to a male like me. After all, get the approach wrong and there you are facing some six feet of powerfully built teeth and claws."

"Is that how you see us?" There was a purr of amusement in Zashou's voice.

"Yes, ma'am!" he said cheerfully, moving off her and getting down to the floor. "So this is the first chance I've had to meet one of you ladies up close and personal."

As Jo sat back, too, Zashou rolled over and looked up at him. "So what do you think now?"

Davies grinned, glancing briefly at Jo. "You're nowhere near as intimidating lying down."

Zashou's purr deepened. "I see you have charmers among your own males, Jo. I'm surprised no one has approached him!"

"Oh, I don't live on Shola like Kris," he said, going over to the washbasin to clean his hands. "I live on Keiss. Jo and I, we're local experts on the Valtegans, so we've been kept busy back home."

"Then why haven't you visited Shola?"

"Who'd invite us? We need an official invitation to go to your world, Zashou."

"I'll invite you, for the amusement I'll get watching the females cope with your charming nature. Where will they take us when we get home, Jo?"

Jo continued with her braiding. This was the last one. Her arms ached, but the change in Zashou had been worth it. "To Carrie's and Kusac's, I assume. The Aldatan Estate."

Zashou was quiet for a moment. "I really will be going home," she said quietly. "You knew Carrie, didn't you? Would she invite you for a visit?"

"She might. We got on well when we met, but I only knew her for a couple of weeks."

There was a knock at the door, and Kris stuck his head in. "Durvan says our presence is requested for dinner," he said.

Jo nodded. "You're done," she said to Zashou, slipping the last bead onto the end of the braid. "If you get up, I'll give your pelt a quick brush."

Zashou got slowly to her feet, standing patiently while Jo ran the brush quickly over her. The soft amber fur gleamed in the last rays of the sun. Kris coughed and backed out hurriedly as Davies turned round and let out a whistle of approval.

"Gary," said Jo warningly as she picked up Zashou's robe and held it out to her.

"I'm going," he said, and headed for the door.

"What?" asked Zashou, taking it from her.

"He saw you as a female," said Jo.

The Sholan was obviously confused. "But he knows . . . Oh." She touched her belly. "I start to resemble you more because of this cub."

"Zashou . . ." she began.

"It's all right," sighed Zashou, slipping the robe on. "Your males are not that much different from ours. Your shape is part of what draws Rezac to you. To be able to persuade a female to carry his cub makes a male feel important. Rezac's thoughts are full of it. He could at least keep them to himself!"

The bitterness had returned. Jo swung Zashou to face her. "So what?" she demanded. "I could be pregnant by him, too! If we are, it isn't his fault, d'you hear me? It's the damned virus! At least your cub is fathered by one of your own kind! If I'm pregnant, mine isn't, mine is alien, but you don't hear me bitching about it."

Zashou tried to back off, intimidated by Jo's anger and aggression. "I only meant . . ."

"I know what you mean, Zashou! Just accept it, like I have to. There's nothing else we can do. Not accepting it just makes life more difficult for everyone than it already is. We have more important things to worry about."

"But you're his lover!"

Jo let her go, her anger suddenly evaporating. "Yes, I am." She could feel Rezac hovering at the edges of her mind, worried for her. Since he'd realized she could also be pregnant, his presence within her mind had intensified. For all his protestations that females were a tie he didn't want, she knew them for the facade they were. Worry, guilt, and pride fought within him, and he didn't know which he should feel.

Against all reason, he'd touched her in a way she couldn't explain, a way no Human man had. She'd suddenly become part of a world that defied logic, a world where an officer in charge of a mission had no option but to start an affair with an alien, and risk becoming pregnant. She shuddered, and pushed it to the back of her mind. When she had the time, she'd worry about it. Not now. She felt guilty for taking her anger out on Zashou.

She felt a hand touch her cheek and blinked, looking into Zashou's amber eyes.

"You're right. We must escape before anything else. I will try to make my peace with Rezac over this cub."

"I'm sorry, Zashou. I should never have yelled at you like that. This is all so confusing for me. I don't know what to think or feel right now."

She found herself enveloped in a hug, felt the gentle vibration of Zashou's chest against hers as the Sholan purred gently in amusement. "We're not so different, you and I," she said. "After all this time, I still don't know what to think about Rezac! He's so . . . confusing!"

The meal was a nightmare. Killian had been the life and soul of the party, full of unsubtle humor regarding women, obviously aimed at Taradain, who sat through it all in a silent but furious rage. Jo wondered why Killian had bothered to insist she come, too; the level of conversation was more suitable for male-only company. Then, toward the end of the meal, the storyteller was announced. She sensed both Kris and Gary suddenly become alert.

It was, indeed, Railin. He proceeded to regale the company with two winter tales of encounters with beasts and monsters in the high pass. The latter she finally began to recognize as the tale of the crashing of the shuttle, the one he'd told them in the Inn. He'd refined it to a work of art that praised Lord Killian's bravery for protecting the good people of Kaladar from the evil that fell from the sky.

As he took a break, Jo sent to Kris. *Ask him why he's here.*

Is it wise? Killian doesn't realize we're telepaths. If we let Railin know . . .

Send to him!

She watched Railin carefully, seeing the usual glazed look come over his face. It affected everyone like that at first, telepaths just learned to conceal it better.

The full news had to wait till they returned upstairs. Zashou had taken over a chair as a makeshift bed and was settled there wrapped in her blankets. Jo looked curiously at her, then at Rezac, but all felt well—in fact, very peaceful. The remains of Zashou's special meal was on the table nearby and, for a wonder, she'd managed to eat most of it.

"Railin's here to find out why Killian has kept us. Apparently he should have informed the rebellion leaders that we were here. He didn't," said Kris, sitting at the table.

Davies joined him. "So Killian really is building his own little power base."

"It appears so," said Jo, taking one of the easy chairs. "In return for this information, Railin is willing to help us escape."

"Is he, now?" Davies' tone was thoughtful.

"We could be leaping from one cage to another," said Rezac. "We should try to escape on our own."

"If it were possible, yes, but it isn't," said Jo. "We've accepted his help."

"You should not have made that decision without a discussion." Rezac's voice was a low growl of disapproval.

Jo turned to look at him, but Davies answered first.

"Jo's the leader, Rezac. She calls the shots. I agree with you about Railin, but it's still her call. Besides, he needed an answer there and then. We couldn't be sure of reaching him later. He's not a telepath."

With an effort, Rezac flattened his ears in a gesture of apology. "I led for too long," he muttered. "I'm not accustomed to having others making the decisions."

"Railin is acting for the leader of the rebellion, Lord Tarolyn," continued Jo. "He's Lord of the state of Galrayin, Bradogan's neighbor, and the least suspect state because he considers he's bought Tarolyn with off-world goods."

"Why upset a good deal? What's in it for Tarolyn?" asked Davies.

"He will take over the Port, but . . ."

"No altruist, then," said Rezac.

"I'd suspect him if he were," said Jo frankly. "He's a

nore enlightened landowner. Believes his serfs will work
harder if they have a stake in the land, so all his people
are free. He wants true off-world trade available to all on
Jalna at a fair price. And he wants to control it."

"My bet is that Killian plans to use this gun against Tarolyn, then Bradogan."

"Killian isn't exactly a despot," said Davies. "Fair
enough, he's doing what he is to us, but his people seem
content enough."

"People are rarely black or white," said Jo. "Killian's no
exception. However, it isn't up to us to back one leader
against the other. In helping us escape, Tarolyn will achieve
what he wants, which is to prevent Killian risking the whole
rebellion in a preemptive strike on him."

"And the creation of a weapon too dangerous to be let
loose on Jalna," added Kris. "There's been no mention
made of bringing it with us."

"There will be," said Rezac. "You wait and see. So how
does he plan to get us out of here?"

"He doesn't know yet. There isn't enough time to help
us this trip, but he'll be back in six weeks with help. This
caravan is one of merchants. The next will include
soldiers."

"Six weeks," said Rezac, looking at Jo bleakly. "Have
we got six weeks?"

"Railin is going to see some of the food his caravan
carries is handed to the cook for Zashou," said Jo. "He's
from Galrayin himself. They know of the problem, and
have more or less eradicated it from their land. They provide the bulk of the food sold in the Port to the spacers and
Bradogan. That's another reason why the rebellion chose
Tarolyn to lead them. What his father and he have done
with their land can be done by all the landowners. He plans
to negotiate with the aliens for the appropriate technology
to speed up the process."

"Terraforming on a massive scale. But why? Arnor in-
ferred this allergy to the food is rare. And who has
achieved that level of eco-engineering?" asked Davies.

Jo turned to look at Gary. "There is a species that can,
and they trade at the Port. It'll cost, of course . . ."

"And then some!"

". . . but in return, Tarolyn will open Jalna up for trade.
It'd mean a bigger local market for everyone."

"You still haven't said why this land issue is so important."

"That's the interesting part," said Kris. "Tarolyn believes there's a correlation between the episodic violence and what's poisoning the land."

"How could the food be responsible for the violence?" asked Zashou, taking an interest in the discussion for the first time.

"Not the food, something in the soil," corrected Jo. "Everything in the food chain is dependent on the soil. The plants, the cattle that eat them, and the people."

"Not to mention the water that runs through it," added Kris. "Tarolyn's father had an epidemic of his people getting sick and dying from this allergy. He systematically began cleansing the land and replanting with crops and cattle from areas that had a low incidence of related deaths. It worked, and as a side effect, he realized they also had far fewer incidences of violence during the winter and early spring."

"The time when the people live off food stored for the winter," said Davies. "It makes sense."

Jo had noticed Rezac reaching out for the remains of his meal. He'd picked up a piece of bread and was looking intently at it. "I know what it is," he said quietly. "I know what's poisoning us."

"You do?" asked Jo. "What?"

"The Valtegan plant that makes the stones. Laalquoi."

"It can't be that," said Kris. "You said the stones were used to control telepaths, to subdue them. And how could a plant contaminate the food chain on such a vast scale?"

Rezac turned round and held the bread out to him. "Look at it! Have you noticed how much greener it's become over the weeks we've been here?" he demanded.

Kris took it from him and examined it. "He's right. It has."

"Old grain," said Rezac. "They're reaching the last of their reserves now. We *know* it's in the food. Zashou's allergy is proof of that. We don't need to know how, dammit!"

"They've been here before," said Jo. "That's where the plants came from."

"That's how they know the stones control the violence," said Zashou.

"I'll buy some of it," said Kris, handing the bread back to Rezac. "But I still don't see the relationship between the plant and the violence if the stone subdues people."

"Maybe it mutated on Jalna. What the hell does it matter anyway?" asked Davies. "I agree with Rezac on that. But have you folks considered that perhaps the reason you can't reach our ship, or any other telepaths on Jalna, is because we're eating that damned plant and it's blocking you?"

Kris sat down suddenly. "Right under our noses," he said quietly, "and we missed it."

"It's my bet that Vyaka thinks we're dead, along with the two missing Sholan telepaths," Davies continued. "I think we can forget any help, people. We're on our own for sure now."

"No," said Jo, rousing herself. "No, we're not. Rezac's sending was answered by Carrie and Kusac. They know we're alive. They'll come, I know they will. But you're right, Gary, we have to act as if they won't, because when they arrive, they still won't be able to reach us! Tarolyn's help is even more important now."

Silence greeted her remark for a few minutes as they each absorbed the implications of what they'd discovered.

Rezac turned to Zashou. "Six weeks," he said. "Can you cope?"

"I'll have to," she said, leaning back against her pillows. "The meal tonight didn't make me feel sick. If this Railin's food is better, then I should be all right. We don't have an option. If we try to escape on our own, we risk everything."

"I suggest we develop our own plan," said Jo, rousing herself. "Keep it in reserve in case we can't wait the six weeks. In which case, we head for Galrayin and Tarolyn's help anyway."

"Sounds the wisest course all round," said Kris. "However, you've overlooked one thing, Jo. We can mind-speak to each other. Why isn't this laalquoi affecting us? We don't know for sure that when help comes, they won't be able to contact us."

"No, we don't, and I've no idea why our Talents aren't affected, just damned glad that they aren't! Keep checking for other telepaths, Kris, but carefully. Try not to draw attention to us. The same with you, Rezac. I don't know enough about my Talent to use it properly yet."

Rezac and I will teach you, sent Kris. *It's important that you learn. We can do a lot with knowledge transfers. I'm not good at them, but it's better than nothing.*

Jo nodded her agreement. "We should cut back on the food we eat during the day. The meals with Killian are safe because he uses Tarolyn's produce. We don't know what harm we've done ourselves already, all we know for sure is that Zashou is more susceptible to it than we are."

"I suggest we turn in now," said Kris, yawning and stretching. "Someone's coming for us early in the morning to escort us down to the barn."

"Don't forget to try contacting the ship again, Kris, please," reminded Jo.

"I never forget, Jo."

She made an apologetic gesture. "I have to say it."

He nodded understandingly as he left.

As Davies began to move off to the bedroom, Rezac came over to sit with Jo.

Will you come with me? Zashou says you need my company tonight.

Jo looked from him to Zashou in surprise.

Go with him. You need his company more than I do. I will stay here.

We could talk. His hand touched hers hesitantly.

She knew what would happen if she went with him. Already she could feel her resolve not to get too involved with him emotionally beginning to weaken.

Talk and sleep only, he sent, his tone firm. *To do anything else at this time would be to risk too much.*

His fingers were interlaced with hers, and she didn't even remember taking his hand. "It's magic," she muttered, as she let him help her to her feet. "This damned world's finally getting to me."

*   *   *

"The sword is beautiful, Kusac," she admitted, wrapping it up again. "but it's no substitute for Kaid."

"He didn't send it for that reason. They were also birthday gifts, he said."

"I'd rather have talked to him than this."

"I understand your anger. But if you won't contact him, and you won't let me talk to him about it, what's left, Carrie?"

"Don't ask me. You know him as well as I do now!"

He did, and he'd been trying to figure it out for himself during the trip home. What made the most sense was one of the last things Kaid had said before he'd left. "I think it has something to do with his need to feel he'd earned the right to be our third, rather than just had it given to him by fate."

"In that case, he should be in touch now. Look," she'd said, coming over to sit beside him, "let's just leave it. This is just getting me more annoyed, and you know it. I contacted Conrad and Quin. They're due over in an hour or two for third meal. I thought it better that you met them socially rather than at the Warriors Guild tomorrow. T'Chebbi's coming, too."

"T'Chebbi?" he'd asked.

"We've gotten close," Carrie had said, with a flash of wry humor, "especially after this afternoon."

Now they waited for the two Humans to arrive. A knock on the door, and they were ushered in by Dzaka.

Dzaka? sent Kusac as he rose to greet them.

Everyone's curious about them, Carrie replied. *After all, they assume they're taking over our protection on this mission.*

The two men were very different. Conrad was tall, his brown curly hair now reaching almost to his shoulders. He sported a small mustache that outlined his upper lip, adding a maturity to his youthful appearance. Quin was a good six inches shorter, and appeared some dozen or so years older. His hairline might be receding, but his round, mobile face and stocky build belied the age one would automatically attach to him. Both now wore Sholan winter robes in preference to the usual Human attire.

"You must be Kusac," said Conrad, coming down the den steps toward them. He held his hand out, palm upward, in the Sholan telepath greeting. "I'm Conrad and this is Quin. It's a pleasure to meet you at last."

Kusac touched fingertips with him, then turned to do the same to Quin.

"Believe you've been up at Stronghold," said Quin as Kusac gestured to them to sit down.

"As you say, at last we meet. Yes, I've been up at Stronghold. I'm sorry my own training has prevented us from meeting till now." As he'd touched each of them, he'd liked what he'd felt. Kaid had chosen well.

"Love to see the place some day," Quin continued, taking one of the easy chairs. "I'm interested in different combat styles, and I've heard those used by the Brotherhood aren't taught outside."

"I'm afraid so," said Kusac, sitting down. "Each of our guilds possesses a unique skill, and to learn the discipline, you have to belong to the appropriate guild. However, when Kaid joins us, I'm sure he'll be passing on some of his techniques. Can I offer you some coffee? We've a little time before we eat."

T'Chebbi arrived as Kusac was pouring the drinks. As she moved past him to find a seat, Kusac realized that she'd dressed for the occasion. Naturally longer furred than was common, she'd decided to wear something lighter in weight than winter clothing. The paneled tunic of soft gray accentuated her tabby coloring, and tonight, she'd left her hair unbound.

You're about to spill the coffee, came Carrie's gentle thought, and he looked back quickly to the brimming mug. Realizing that the Human males were also busy looking at T'Chebbi, hastily Kusac tipped a little into his own mug and continued pouring the drinks and handing them round. *I hadn't realized she could look so attractive,* he sent by way of explanation.

Oh, T'Chebbi's been changing a lot recently. I think she's rediscovered herself. I'm glad she took my advice. We've become good friends while you two have been playing warriors up in the mountains.

He gave her a long look as he passed her mug over to her. "Coffee or c'shar, T'Chebbi?" he asked, turning his attention to the Sister.

The following day, they had a few hours to themselves while they waited for Conrad and Quin to move their belongings from the Warriors Guild to one of the dormitory houses in the estate village. They'd decided that they could make better use of the time left to them there.

The estate boasted two villages. The main one centered around Carrie's and Kusac's home, the other, primarily a farming community, was set deeper among the cultivated fields. The latter was still in a state of upheaval as existing houses were being renovated and new ones built. However, the construction halted by the winter hadn't yet restarted.

Scattered here and there were isolated cottages, and it was these Kusac planned to make use of. They were the ideal place to mount mock rescue and attack missions. Using Garras and Dzaka as leaders, opposition troops could be made up from the Brothers and Sisters on the estate. There was even the opportunity for the older younglings under Garras' tuition to get some realistic combat experience. Rulla had been given the task of organizing all the younglings into clearing the snow around the chosen locations. They'd taken pity on them, though, and were augmenting the traditional shovels with snow-clearing vehicles from the main estate.

This morning Kusac wanted to catch up on what was happening with the new arrivals at the training center. They'd had a week now to settle in, and he wanted to know what progress had been made. Carrie had told him the day before that out of the fifty people—Sholans and Humans—already two Leska Links had formed. Both were mixed Links, but there the comparison ended. One had gone badly wrong, leaving the Sholan female, Nikuu, completely bereft of her Talent beyond her Link to her Leska. The other pair, Tamghi and his Human partner, Kora, were fine.

Ruth had instantly offered to take Nikuu and Dillan under her care and Carrie had thankfully agreed. It was there that they were going now.

"She's the ideal person to help them," she said as they walked down the street to Ruth's home. "She's got this capacity for really caring about all those under her roof, and they can sense it. She's worked wonders with Mara, you know, and as for Josh . . . Let's just say that after he got over the shock of being one of us, he went to see Ruth. Since then, he's been completely stable. Confused now and then, but that's natural. She even persuaded him to start training his Talent with Ghyan. He's been sharing classes with Brynne actually."

"How's he getting on? You haven't mentioned him lately, so I presume all is going well."

"Fine. He's really gotten interested in the religious side. Ghyan says that he should go to the Retreat soon if he wants to take his studies further in that direction."

"A Human priest of Vartra," said Kusac, his hand reaching for hers. "Sometimes the changes seem to happen over-

night. We really are becoming an integrated species here.
And to think it all started because of you."

"You had some involvement as I recall," she said with
a laugh as they reached Ruth's door.

"Just a little. About five feet of it." he agreed, tugging
her closer and wrapping his arm around her back as the
door opened. "Good morning, Mara," he said. "May the
sun shine on you all. We've come to see Ruth."

"She's expecting you," said Mara, standing aside and
opening the door wide for them. "Is it about Dillan and
Nikuu? She's better today."

"We thought we'd see how they are," said Carrie as they
followed the young woman into the large communal lounge.

"Ruth's in the kitchen," she said, pointing to the door
at the far end. "I won't come with you. There isn't enough
room for us all in there."

"Is Josh up at the dig?"

She nodded. "I'm going up later. Dr. Michaels is here
today. I thought it best to stay away till he's left."

Who? asked Kusac.

*Head of the Human archaeology project on Shola. He's
visiting from Shanagi. He's here to see how Greg is handling
the team.*

And how's he doing?

*Fine. They're making a lot more headway since that Pam
character was sent packing.*

Like those in the other dormitory houses, Ruth's kitchen
was huge. It had to be to cater for the number of people
the house could accommodate. This house, however, was
purposely not full. Ruth would add to or subtract from her
residents when and as she pleased. Quite a few people had
visited her, among them several of the archaeologists hungry for a taste of the familiar atmosphere of home.

At one end of the table sat a female Kusac took to be
Nikuu. She was stirring a bowl of something. Ruth stood
beside her, adding some herbs from the jar in her hand.
She started to rise, but Kusac waved her down.

"Don't disturb yourself, please."

He knew she was from his clan, but he didn't recognize
her. It was her eyes that held him. Though they were out-
wardly calm, he could sense the terror that lurked behind
them.

"Hello there!" Ruth said, smiling up at them. "Wondered when you'd get around to calling on us. We're making a traditional dumpling stew. Will you stay for lunch? We've also got rhubarb crumble."

"Rhubarb? Here, on Shola?" asked Carrie, stepping over the bench seat and sitting down. "Where'd you get rhubarb from here, and at this time of year?"

Ruth pulled a face. "It's only canned, I'm afraid, but I got Jack to request some as an agricultural experiment—and one or two other essential kitchen garden plants."

"Rhubarb?" asked Kusac, taking a seat.

"Just try it," said Carrie. "It's one of my favorite cooked fruits. A real taste of home!"

"It's mine, too," said Dillan, coming in from the smaller kitchen. "We haven't met yet." He held his hand out toward Carrie. "I'm Dillan Powell, and this is Nikuu Aldatan, my Leska. She's from your bond-mother's estate."

"Clan Leaders," said Nikuu, putting the bowl aside to hold out her hand in greeting.

Ruth snagged the bowl, moving farther down the table with it.

"I'm so sorry to hear of your misfortune," said Kusac, holding onto her hand for a long moment. "Do you know yet how it happened?"

She shrugged her shoulders, ears lying back slightly before righting themselves. "Gestalt backlash, the doctors from the medical center said. I'm lucky, though." She looked up at Dillan who had moved to stand beside her, his hand resting on her shoulder. "He's my other senses. He mind-speaks for me. Without our Link, I would be deaf and blind."

Firmly suppressing the thought that had it not been for their Link, the tragedy could never have happened at all, Kusac reached mentally for the young male. *How is she really?*

Just this side of hysteria. I daren't leave her sight for more than a few minutes. You should have known her before this happened. She was such a happy person. This just isn't fair.

I know, but at least she has you. Can you cope? It can't be easy giving her the amount of mental attention that you are.

You noticed? There was a slight smile on his face. *I have help. Ruth and Mara take it in turns to mentally support her so that I can have a break—you know, just maintain a normal link.*

She's lucky to have Linked with someone like you.

We chose each other, Dillan replied with the same slight smile. *I know I'm lucky to have her.*

"It's good to know you have such a loving Leska," Carrie said to Nikuu. "How are you feeling? Is there anything we can do for you? Anything you need?"

She shook her head, dark curls falling across her face to be flicked back by a slightly trembling hand. "I'm fine. It'll take some getting used to, but everyone here is so helpful. I'll have to give up my work, though. I was training in the judiciary to be a truthsayer. I'll miss that."

"There'll be work here for you, never fear," said Carrie. "We'll need people with a knowledge of the law. What was your profession, Dillan?"

"I worked in business, with computers," he said, moving to sit down beside Nikuu. "Nothing particularly useful here on Shola."

"You'd be surprised," said Kusac. "First things first, though. Nikuu is our main concern. Ruth, I am going to arrange for someone to tutor them daily. Would you mind them working here? We need to make sure Dillan is brought up to Nikuu's level as quickly as possible."

"If Nikuu is ready for that," said Ruth, "she can help him. You'd be surprised what they're learning to do between them."

"I'd rather be busy," said Nikuu.

"Then I'll make arrangements today," said Kusac.

"You're staying for lunch, though," said Ruth. "You must. Nikuu made the dumplings." She pointed to the bowl.

"We'd love to," said Carrie. "Dumplings and rhubarb crumble! I can't remember when I last tasted either!"

* * *

Rhyaz settled in the easy chair opposite Lijou and took one of the sweet pastries from the plate his colleague indicated. "Kha'Qwa's, you say? Don't remember her being much of a one for home baking." His mouth opened in a small grin.

"My bond-mate has developed a great many homely skills lately. I think perhaps it's because there's a cub on the way," said Lijou with a quiet pleasure he couldn't keep out of his voice.

"Congratulations to you both! I had heard as much. It's good that you have a life of your own, Lijou, one apart from the demands of the Guilds. Maybe one day I'll be able to do the same." He took a bite of the pastry.

Lijou set a mug of c'shar down in front of him. "I think you'll find it won't be long before the Brotherhood is drawn into the Clan Leader's program, especially if the cubs of our unions are Talented. You may have the excuse to take a mate sooner than you think."

"We'll see. One step at a time, Lijou. We've still got to get used to being recognized as priests."

"Thank you for coming to see me, Rhyaz, especially when I know you're so busy, but I'm very concerned about the female, Keeza."

"Even I need to take a break now and then. In fact, I'm glad of the excuse—and the pastries!" He helped himself to another one. "This has been a heavy week. You've been getting the reports, haven't you? I gave instructions you were to be sent our confidential ones, not those that Raiban gets."

Lijou nodded. "And I thank you for that. It helps to be kept fully informed. It's the reports that are disturbing me. How is Keeza coping? You say very little about her state of mind or health."

Rhyaz sighed. "Mixed, Lijou. Keeza's found out a great deal for us. We know Kezule was given the job of guarding the hatchery as a reward for long service, courage under fire, that sort of thing, so it's no retirement post. He told her he was given one of the Emperor's daughters as a wife. So our General was thought highly of. Short of the planetary governor of Shola at the time, I don't think we could have gotten our hands on a more important prisoner. Unfortunately for us, his position has never been such that he had access to military information of the kind Raiban wants. Keeza's role is necessary."

"This is all new information? I don't remember reading about it."

"Yes, culled over the last week. As for Keeza, her reactions to her captivity have been interesting. It's the first opportunity we've had to study someone in a controlled hostage-type situation. She's been personalizing Kezule, making him hers as if trying to give herself an illusion of having some control over what's happening. She's been copying him too, using the herb on her own food."

"This spice or herb that he uses. You don't make any mention of lab results yet."

"Still analyzing it. It's a complex chemical. I'm no scientist, but as I understand it, it gives him dietary supplements he needs. His general health and his mental state have both improved since he started taking it. Look at the way he's prepared to interact with Keeza now. My gut reaction is that it makes them more sociable, able to cooperate with each other." He shrugged, putting down the mug. "Of course, I have nothing to back up this feeling, and recent events have called the hypothesis into question. It could be a drug that is specific only to Valtegans of his age, or only to males. The list of possibilities is endless, and until we have something conclusive from the labs, it's all speculation."

"Hunches are valid, Rhyaz, that's one thing I've learned as a telepath. Your people are so close to us in talents that you'd do well to listen to them, too. Even certain Humans set a lot of store by them. What effect is it having on her?"

"No idea. We need blood samples, and to get those . . ." He left the sentence hanging.

"Yours is a task I don't envy, my friend," sighed Lijou. "But you said something about recent events. Has something happened?"

"We had an incident yesterday. She got overconfident, made a sexual approach to him. The control team thought they'd have to terminate."

Lijou took a sharp breath. "How is she?"

"She's all right, luckily. He stopped as they were about to go in. He gave systematic beating a new meaning, Lijou. With his extra strength . . . And he used it more effectively than we do." He looked up at the priest. "This ancient breed of Valtegans is totally different from the ones we've met on Keiss. I pray that we never meet the likes of him."

Lijou shut his eyes briefly. He'd visited the center at Shanagi where Kezule was being held. Only once, but it had been enough for him. "This is what I was afraid of. May the Gods forgive us for what we're doing to Keeza Laasah. We should never have decided to put her in with him, Rhyaz. The cost to her physically and emotionally surely isn't worth it."

"I dislike what's happening as much as you, Lijou, but

you mustn't lose sight of the fact that she entered willingly into this contract. She knew exactly what was expected of her, even observed Kezule before she agreed to being processed by you and Konis. When it's over, she'll remember nothing of this, and she'll be given a new start in life. She can return to the Consortia House to finish training there if she wishes, or choose a cash settlement to do with what she wants. Remember she's a convicted murderer. If it weren't for this experiment, she'd be dead by now. She is being well recompensed for this."

"I know, Rhyaz. But what she's suffered at his hands! And it could still cost her her life! She hasn't deserved such treatment, even if she did consent to it!"

"We have the greater good to consider," reminded the Brotherhood Warrior Master gently. "I don't need to remind you of the destruction of Szurtha and Khyaal, do I? Millions of lives lost to the Valtegans. The information we have already gathered because of her is invaluable. We are all tools, Lijou, used by someone or something. Even you and I. Who's to say that the idea to use her didn't come from Vartra Himself? Through Kaid and the Aldatans, we know that His later work with the telepaths was to find a solution to the problem of the Valtegan invasion. He could be influencing this matter in ways that we can't yet recognize."

"I thought philosophy was supposed to be my provenance," sighed Lijou. "I know you're probably right, and I know that one life—particularly that of a convicted murderer—is very little when put in the balance against so many, but someone has to care for her, Rhyaz. How long will you let this go on?"

"I haven't decided yet. For the foreseeable future. He may experience remorse, start opening up to her. If not, we begin beating Kezule again as soon as she's healed."

"I can even feel sorry for him," said Lijou quietly. "The fact he's kept his sanity for so long when he knows there's no possibility of escape is incredible."

"He's a strong person in many ways, Lijou. We take no chances with him. One Valtegan at large is enough," Rhyaz said grimly.

"Then it's been confirmed that it was a Valtegan? What actually happened to the missing Leska pair? I was never fully briefed on that."

"We've good reason to believe that at least one Valtegan was involved because of the nature of the wounds on the bodies. The Leska couple were due to be picked up by a deep space shuttle at the Human female's home, a settlement called Hillfort. We know their shuttle left Keiss as their departure from the planet was logged, but nothing is known of their whereabouts from then on. The dead bodies of the female's relatives were found later that day at the landing site. They'd been shot by a Valtegan energy weapon. It's being kept quiet because Governor Hamilton doesn't want to start a panic. We do have a potential problem with the young male's family, however. He's Taynar Arrazo, the youngest son of the Arrazo Clan Leader. They'll have to be told soon that he's missing."

"What about Keiss? They can't risk the lives of the people there by not starting a search for any more Valtegan survivors."

"The *Khalossa* is still based there. Her troops are on training maneuvers on the planet's surface at present, with the help of the Keissian military. Commander Raguul has been recalled, of course. Given the identity of the captain of the missing shuttle, though, it's a forgone conclusion that there was some conflict and the ship was damaged. They could be drifting anywhere between Keiss and Vartra knows where. We have very little chance of finding them at all."

"Surely there's a homing signal or something you could track them by?"

"We've looked, but that presupposes the ship is still functioning and that they are still in this sector of space. I imagine that the Valtegan was headed for his home world, wherever that is. If we find that craft, I believe we'll have found at least one of the four Valtegan worlds. It's an impossible task, Lijou. I'm afraid that young couple and their captain are as good as dead."

"It grieves me to say so, but let's pray that they are. It's preferable to being held captive by the Valtegans."

"I agree with you on that, Father."

* * *

Kusac turned away from his comm and looked down into the lower level of the den where Carrie sat on the floor fletching arrows to take to Jalna. Normally it was a job she enjoyed doing, but today nothing seemed to be going right for her.

With an exclamation of disgust, she threw the offending arrow across the room. "I loathe binding! I've got glue all over the flights again!" she muttered angrily.

Kusac knew exactly what was wrong with her. It had been two weeks since they'd been at the Retreat and they'd still had no word from Kaid. He pushed himself away from the desk and went to join her. Crouching down beside her, he gently turned her to face him.

"Leave the arrows," he said. "You'll only ruin more of them. It's time you dealt with what's really bothering you."

"I'm trying to," she said, refusing to look at him as she picked up another. "It's just that I keep getting the glue over everything!"

He took it from her, laying it back on the low table. "Go and see Kaid."

"I don't want to see Kaid, I want to finish these damned arrows!" she said, trying to move away from him.

"Carrie, do you think I can't sense what's happening to you?" he asked, holding her tighter. "You need to spend time with him. I can feel that bond you have calling you together. You've both tried to ignore it for too long. Go to him. You need some time together."

She sat back on her heels, looking up at him. "No, Kusac. If he can ignore it, then so can I."

"This could jeopardize our mission, Carrie. Nine people are depending on us. Will you let this stand between them and their rescue?"

"Kaid is."

"One of you has to have some sense! Why not you? Go to him, Carrie. Have it out with him if you will, but resolve it. For my sake if nothing else."

"For your sake?"

He could feel her questioning thought. "We're a Triad, and he's my sword-brother. There is no male dearer to me save my father, and it hurts me to see this barrier between the two of you."

"I'm angry with him, Kusac. He has no right to ignore me like this."

"I don't understand it either, but there must be a reason. Ask him."

"I'll do more than ask him," she muttered. "I'll give him a piece of my mind!"

"Then go and do it now, get it over with," he said, getting to his feet and helping her up. "Before you lose your nerve," he added.

"Nerve? I don't need any nerve to do this!"

He could feel her outrage and grinned quietly to himself as they began to walk toward the stairs. "Take what time you need, we'll be fine, Kashini and I. I've plenty to do to keep me busy."

She stopped. "Like what?"

"Like going over the inventory with Conrad and Quin. Remember, we leave for Jalna in two weeks. It's time to start checking through the things we've put aside to take."

Pulling a face, she resumed walking. "I'll leave you to it, then."

He walked with her to the garage, helping her into the aircar and running his own quick check that all was in order before she took off. As he turned around to walk back to the house, he saw T'Chebbi waiting for him.

"Can you fetch Conrad and Quin, please, T'Chebbi? It's time we went through that inventory."

Nodding, she headed off to fetch the two Humans.

Boring though the task was, by midafternoon, they had amassed a large pile of equipment in the den.

It was T'Chebbi who called a halt. "Need to pack in crates and label this. One crate for each category," she said. "Add any more and we lose things in wrong crates."

"You're right," Kusac said, sitting back on his haunches. "There should be some crates in the storehouse next to where you're staying," he said to Conrad.

"Tomorrow," said T'Chebbi firmly, getting up and surveying the three males. "Go home now. Make own list for tomorrow, things you each want. Done enough for today."

Conrad got to his feet. "We'll bring the crates over tomorrow morning," he said.

Slightly surprised at her taking charge of the situation, Kusac murmured good-bye as she saw them out. Getting to his feet, he stretched, suddenly realizing how stiff he was. He went over to the hotplate and poured himself a coffee. He hadn't thought it would be such a tiring job. He heard the door open then close.

"Coffee, T'Chebbi?" he asked, looking over at her as she came back down to join him.

"Please."

He handed her his mug, getting a second one for himself. As he did, the restlessness he'd been feeling for the last few minutes began to resolve itself. He turned to find her still standing behind him.

"Your timing is impeccable," he said. "You knew she'd reached Stronghold, didn't you? That's why you sent them away. Thank you."

T'Chebbi nodded and slowly stepped aside for him to pass.

"I don't need company, T'Chebbi," he said as he settled himself in his favorite chair. "You're welcome to stay, but I'm fine on my own." He watched her come round his side of the table, then sit on the edge of it opposite him. She began sipping her drink. He could feel her nervousness as she gathered the courage to speak.

"Why be alone?" she asked quietly. "I would stay with you. Kaid and I spend time together now and then. When they are together, would be nice for us share some time, too."

Echoes of Carrie and Kaid's bond were getting stronger now. It was no more than an attraction, a pull that he felt, but he was sure what the outcome would be. That was enough to make him susceptible to an attractive female making an approach to him. And T'Chebbi was attractive. Not the least of it was the air of the competent warrior about her.

He leaned forward, holding his hand out to her. "That could be, T'Chebbi. But I don't really know much about you," he said as she took hold of his hand. "Talk to me. Tell me about yourself." He sensed her surprise, then a quiet amusement as she began to purr gently.

"Knew you were different. What you want to know?" she asked.

"How did you and Kaid meet?"

*   *   *

Carrie braced herself as she got out of the aircar at Stronghold. She wasn't looking forward to this. Already alerted by security to her arrival, a small reception committee stood on the main steps waiting for her.

"Clan Leader, well come," said L'Seuli, inclining his head. "We don't get many visits from the En'Shalla Brothers and Sisters."

With a bare nod of acknowledgment she continued past him, heart thumping. Kusac had been right about losing her nerve. She was very afraid she was about to do just that. In the main hallway, she stopped, trying to get her bearings. It looked very different from when she'd last been here. Fifteen hundred years had wrought a great many changes.

Her eyes were drawn to the top of the main staircase where Father Lijou stood. A gesture from him and her reception committee suddenly had pressing business elsewhere.

"Where is he?" she asked as he descended the steps toward her.

In the Temple, through the doors on your right. He used mind-speech, a tight sending that none but she would receive. *When he's not at classes, he's to be found there. I'm glad you came. He's become too solitary. I've told him he can't solve this alone, that he needs to speak to you.*

It'll be solved before I leave, she replied, turning toward the temple doors.

If you need me . . .

Thank you.

The door was heavy, but as she leaned into it, it opened smoothly. Stepping inside, she saw him immediately. He was sitting, his back to a pillar, at the side of the temple near the statue of Vartra. Some half a dozen other Sholans were also there.

She took a deep breath. "Out. Leave us," she ordered, her voice louder than she'd intended in the silence of the temple.

Every head but his turned to look at her, then they scrambled to their feet, leaving in a hurried flurry of black robes, bowing sketchily to her as they passed.

Her footsteps echoed hollowly as she walked down the central aisle to where he was sitting on his prayer mat. She stopped beside him.

"We need to talk, Kaid. Now."

He stirred, slowly increasing his breathing as he came

t of the light trance he'd been in. Now she could hear
e litany he was reciting.

"I'm sure that for once, Vartra won't mind you short-
anging Him," she said. If he was trying to annoy her, he
as succeeding.

He finished, and with an inclination of his head to the
od, turned to look up at her. "Vartra is always due proper
spect," he said, his tone mild as he clasped his hands on
s lap.

"And I'm due none?"

The bitterness in her voice startled him and he looked
her properly. She wore Terran style trousers and a long-
eeved military jacket. The colors, red edged with black
d purple, showed her Sholan Clan and the fact that she
as an En'Shalla Brotherhood Priest. Oddly, it accentuated
er alienness.

"Am I due no respect?" she repeated. "Why have you
fused to speak to me, Kaid? You're treating me as if I
ere no better than a qwene! We're friends, and a Triad,
had you forgotten that?"

He looked down at his hands. "No, I haven't forgotten.
told you I needed some time to myself, Carrie. You
ouldn't have come," he said quietly.

"You've had weeks of it. We're running out of time now.
ust when did you intend to return to the estate?"

When he remained silent, she spoke again. "I've missed
ou," she said, her voice as quiet as his had been. She
eached down to touch his hair, her fingers twining among
he uneven lengths that reached just below his shoulders.
You look different."

He lifted his head, eyes glowing in the dim light of the
emple. "I am. The person who was brought out from these
ungeons and who walked the Fire Margins with you
vasn't me. Kaid Tallinu was destroyed."

"You weren't destroyed, Kaid. You survived the worst
hey could do to you."

"They only began it."

He got to his feet, black robe swirling round his feet as
he turned to lean against the pillar, feeling the welcome
coolness of the stone against his hands. Just being in her
presence had brought to the surface all that he'd fought so
long to subdue and try to understand.

"I started having visions, flashes of the future—memo-

ries. They came at any time of day or night. I couldn't st
them. I was confused, couldn't tell what was real a
longer, so I came here. I was afraid I was losing my mi
that I'd harm you or the cub."

"Why didn't you tell us? We would have tried to he
you at home. There was no need for you to leave, Kaic
She reached out, but he backed away, moving farth
around the pillar.

"Dammit, Carrie, you don't understand! I had to g
away from you! I thought I'd come to terms with it, bu
hadn't. Finding out that I belonged to the past, and yo
kindness to the cub I was then—our night at Noni's—
left me with this . . ." He searched for the word, unable
find it at first. ". . . this *dependence* on you that try as
might, I cannot erase! All I thought about while I was i
prisoned here by Ghezu was you! You dominated n
thoughts so much that I was physically pulled to where yo
were." He stopped, turning his face away from her, h
ears invisible.

"I don't know if what I feel for you is real, Carrie. I'
afraid that it isn't. I would have told you myself tomorro
at the estate."

There was a small silence before she spoke. "I didn
realize I'd caused you so much pain, or that you needed t
forget me," she said. "You're right, I shouldn't have in
truded on you." Though she tried to hide it, he could hea
the hurt in her voice. "The mission's more important tha
me, Kaid. Come to the estate tomorrow. I won't add t
your troubles, that I promise. Good-bye."

He listened to her footsteps receding. When she'd gone
the lonely silence in the temple settled on him like a weigh
She'd said good-bye—and meant it. He hadn't been pre
pared for her to walk out of his life. He remembered wha
she'd said when he'd told her he was coming here. *Promis
you'll talk to me before you make a final decision.* What sh
wanted, what she felt, was also important, and he hadn't le
her say anything.

He turned and began to run toward the entrance. *Wait
I need to ask you something!* he sent.

She was standing at the top of the steps outside the mai
doors. Around her, curious students were making their way
to and from classes.

He stopped in front of her. "Carrie, why did you come?" he had to know.

"It's not important now, Kaid." She turned away and began walking down the steps.

He lunged after her, catching her by the arm, using the contact to touch her mind with his before she could reject him. He could hardly believe what he sensed. "You came to spend time with me!"

Her anger surged through him as she tried to pull away. "Stop it, Kaid! You have no right to pry!"

He grasped her by the other arm. "Why did you pair with me at Noni's?" he demanded.

"You know why! You're the one trying to forget, remember?" Her voice was low and intense. "Leave me some pride, Kaid!"

"Tell me why! I need to hear it from you!" He tightened his grip on her arms.

"How could you ask me that in front of all these people! Let me go at once!" she hissed, trying again to pull free.

"You mustn't leave," he said, his mouth touching hers as he pulled her close. "I've been a fool. Thinking about is isn't the answer." His kiss was deep and full of the passion he felt for her.

She went rigid with shock.

Reluctantly he stopped, drawing back a little from her, aware for the first time of their audience of now highly interested students. "You're right, it's far too public here." He looked beyond her into the courtyard. "Your aircar? Please, come with me." Taking her by the hand, he urged her toward the vehicle.

She hesitated, now totally confused by him. "Kaid . . ."

"I want to take you somewhere. Please. Trust me."

She let him lead her to her craft, handing him the card when he stopped at the door. "You might as well drive. I've no idea what's going on," she said.

Touching her cheek briefly, he took it from her and made for the pilot's seat.

As she fastened herself in beside him, the small craft rose gently into the air until it was above Stronghold, then headed out toward the Retreat.

"Where are we going?"

"You'll see."

She knew for herself how Kusac had felt with Kaid now.

This was not the person she'd known before. Suddenly s
felt nervous. A sidelong look told her that much about h
had changed. He'd regained the weight he'd lost, and af
the training he and Kusac had been doing, was obviou
at the peak of physical health. But he had been ill. Ev
he'd been worried about his sanity.

"This isn't some test or mind game, is it, Kaid?"

He glanced at her, seeing the worried look on her fa
His ears dipped and remained there. "No. No games wi
you, Carrie. They weren't games with Kusac either. I knc
how to help other people face their fears and overcor
them, that's what I was doing. I'm just not very good
handling my own," he added quietly.

Carrie looked out at the scenery. It was breathtakin
and in watching it unfold beneath her, she forgot some
her worries about him. The harsh savagery of the land w
softened by a deep blanket of snow. Scattered here ar
there, the winter trees were oases of deep green in the s
of white. A small herd of mountain rhaklas, frightened l
the sound of their vehicle, bolted toward a small copse.

"We're flying over one of the wildest parts of the Dzah
Range," he said. "Good hunting land."

"It's beautiful."

He banked the craft, heading upward toward the peal
ahead of them. "We're going to the town just beyond th
Retreat. It's not far."

Within a few minutes she could see the distant rooftop
Once more Kaid veered away, heading now for a nearb
hillside, its lower slope dotted with trees. As they cam
closer, gradually she made out the shape of a house nestlin
amid the trees at the lee of the rock face. This must b
their destination.

Kaid slowed the aircar, keeping it hovering in front c
the house for a moment while he activated the comm un
and transmitted a harmonic pulse of sound at the stubl
antenna on the domed roof. That done, he let the craf
sink gently to the ground and began to power it down. H
turned to face her. "Well come to my home."

"You were next door to us when we moved quarters th
first time on the *Khalossa*, weren't you?" she asked as sh
watched him key the palm lock on the door at the side o
the house.

He looked surprised for a moment. "Yes, I was. Funny
at you should remember it now. If you give . . ."

"Not really," she said, holding her hand out to him.

". . . me your hand, I'll key the door . . ." He ground
a halt and took her hand instead, nose wrinkling in a
int grin.

"Happens now and then," she added as he placed it on
e lock plate.

"You can come here when you wish," he said, standing
ack to let her enter.

Before her, a long, narrow hall, its walls lined with dark
aneled wood, stretched the length of the building. She
ollowed him down till they reached the entrance to the
ounge. It was the picture window she saw first. Going over
o it, she looked out across the clearing in front of the
ouse to the craggy peaks beyond. The setting sun was
taining their snowy heights a deep orange. "It's beautiful,
ut so isolated, Kaid!"

"It's what I would have chosen," he said. "The only way
1 is by air."

She heard the faint hum as around her, the house came
o life.

"It'll warm up quickly. I was out here last week to check
hat everything was all right. I haven't lived here since I
vas called to the *Khalossa*."

"How did you find a place like this?" she asked, turning
way from the window. It was so unlike any Sholan home
he'd ever seen. She'd thought everybody lived in houses
on large clan estates.

Kaid stood by his desk, setting the environmental con-
rols. "Jyarti, Father Lijou's predecessor, left it to me. I've
spent a lot of time working on it over the past ten or so
years. I didn't have much else to do."

A faint noise from behind startled her. Turning quickly,
she saw a blind descending, closing off the view. As the
lighting came on, she looked back to Kaid, watching as
he crossed the room to the kitchen area on her left. Her
uneasiness returned.

"I brought some coffee over with the supplies last week.
Would you like some?" he asked, looking at her across
the counter.

"If I do, are you going to tell me that it's too late to
take me back and we'll have to stay the night?"

He smiled sadly. "No, Carrie. We can leave any tim you wish."

"Then, yes." She could trust him. He was a person his word. For a moment, she watched him set about findi mugs and the coffee, and then turned her attention to th rest of the room.

It was built on two levels. The one they were in, th lower, was the lounge. The decor was simple and unclu tered. Walls and ceiling were a warm off-white, and th floor was covered with a practical brown-and-gray marle carpet. A low, round table, a couple of easy chairs, and pile of floor cushions completed the main furnishings.

His work desk was set against the wall by the entranc Opposite was a niche in which sat a small statue of Vartr with the traditional blue glass candle holder in front of i A recessed shelf unit below it looked intriguing, and sh moved away from the window to look at it.

On her way, she glanced over to the higher level. Fror floor to ceiling, narrow vertical blinds, open at this time acted as a room divider. Beyond them she could make ou his bed. Unconsciously, she quickened her pace.

Kaid sighed. Gods, she was as skittish as a virgin! The he smiled wryly to himself. He was no better right now Why was she afraid of him? He'd done nothing he coulc think of to cause her to be like this. Still concerned, h began to pour the coffee.

There wasn't much on the unit. A comp pad, a reade and half a dozen cartridges for it, and a piece of the carvec blue-white crystal in the form of a crouching chiddoe. She picked it up, feeling the smoothness of the workmanship He might have a home, but Kaid hadn't set down roots nc matter how many years he'd lived there. There were none of the knickknacks that most people accumulated over a lifetime.

Then help me grow some roots. The thought was faint. so faint she couldn't be sure she'd heard it. She frowned, looking round. Had it been him or her imagination? He was carrying the drinks into the lounge now.

She sighed, wanting this to be over, wishing she'd never agreed to come with him in the first place. When they'd been together at Noni's, she hadn't felt this nervous with him. He'd been ill then, weakened by the injuries inflicted on him by Fyak and Ghezu. Now he felt and looked totally

fferent—just as he'd said he was in the temple. Replacing
.e ornament, she moved over to the table where he was
tting down her mug. She sat opposite him, her mind sud-
:nly made up.

"Look, maybe you were right. Maybe we should just let
hat was between us die, especially if you're that
nhappy . . ."

"No!" Then quieter, as he leaned toward her. "No, I
on't want that, Carrie. I was wrong. What I said was
rong."

"I don't think you know *what* you want!"

"I know what I don't want. When you left me in the
:mple . . ." He stopped, remembering vividly how he'd
:lt.

"I can't go through this again, Kaid!"

"It won't happen again. How could it?"

"I didn't expect it to happen at all after what we shared
t Noni's, what we said to each other in the Margins!"

She was slipping away from him, he could feel it, and he
idn't know what to do or say. "I want you to stay, Carrie.
/ou want me, too, or you wouldn't have come out to
;tronghold. I'm not going to let you go."

His intensity suddenly frightened her. This was no youth
)f Kusac's age, this was a mature male, someone used to
;etting what he wanted.

She stood up, praying he wouldn't see how badly her
egs were trembling. "You said you'd take me back when
I wanted. I want to leave now, Kaid."

Time slowed, crystallizing around him. "If that's what
you really want," he heard himself saying as he rose.
"There's nothing I can say to change your mind?"

"Nothing," she said, shutting herself off from her emotions. She didn't want to think or feel anything right now.
She'd let herself care for him only to have it thrown back
at her: his choice, not hers. She had to leave.

He followed her across to the door. Before they reached
it, she felt herself grasped by the arm and spun round. *Then
I have no choice but to show you,* he sent, gripping her
tightly as his mouth found hers, his teeth nipping her in
his urgency.

He sent again, letting her experience how he'd felt when
she left him alone in the temple, and how he felt now at
the prospect of being without her.

She pushed against him, fear in her eyes and mind as h
feelings flooded through her. She tried to block them, b
he forced the mental contact, all his loneliness and emp
ness rushing in on her. It overwhelmed her, and as h
struggles slowed, she began to taste blood in her mouth.

He tightened his grip on her arms. *What is it I need
say or do to make you stay? I, Kaid Tallinu, love you, Ca
rie! Not the cub I was in the past, but me, whoever the he
I am!* He broke the kiss, eyes searching her face. "I don
want to live without you, can't you feel it? Don't leav
me, Carrie."

Because of her struggles, his robe was gaping at the neck
Something glinted, catching the light, and her eye. Sh
reached for it, and found herself holding his Triad pendan
Startled, she looked up at him.

"I thought you'd taken it off."

"I put it on after you left the Retreat. I told you, I mean
to come back. I hoped you'd let me have the time to thin
through whether what I felt for you was real. Vartra know
I wanted it so much that I couldn't trust what I felt!"

"And now?"

"Now I don't care It's what I *feel* that matters." He
pulled her close, kissing her again, his tongue parting he
lips, tasting her blood for the first time.

Gods, I'm sorry. I didn't mean to hurt you. He licked a
the graze, frantic to make it better, stop it hurting. Sud
denly the rigidity left her, and as she let go the pendant
her body molded itself to his.

It's all right. It doesn't hurt much. Hesitantly her arm
came up to hold him.

He had to tell her now, before they went any further. "
have another fear, Carrie. I had a vision. One that I'm
afraid was about us."

"What was it? Was it about Jalna?"

"No." He tightened his grip momentarily, unable to look
her in the eyes. "Noni said I'd father cubs. I don't want
to make you pregnant, and Vartra's changes have a habit
of working."

She said nothing for a moment, even her mind was still.
"Not now that we have a contraceptive," she said quietly.

"I held my cub in the vision, Carrie." He looked at her
now. "There will be one."

"You didn't see the mother? Perhaps it's not me."

"It was someone I cared deeply for."

This was not the time for either of them to mention 'Chebbi.

"Not even Vartra's changes could make me fertile at the rong time, Kaid."

Then he realized what she could be thinking. "I don't ıean that . . . We couldn't . . . I don't know if I want cubs, 'arrie, but if I did . . . if you did . . ." He was floundering gain, making a mess of it.

She couldn't help but smile at his confusion. "It can't appen, believe me."

Relieved now that he'd told her everything, he pressed er closer still, letting her know that he wanted her, was ;ady for her, all the while kissing her as fiercely as if he'd ιever have another chance. Now there was nothing to keep ıem apart. He could hear her thoughts, feel the new fears ıse as she began to tremble within his grasp.

He's as unlike Kusac as anyone could be! A fighter, a riest—he's a killer for God's sake—he's never lived any- here but on the edge! Why do I love him?

Her eyes looked at him steadily despite the quickened ıeart beat he could feel even through the thickness of ıer jacket.

Gods, he's so strong! My hand can't circle his forearm! Ie could crush me and I couldn't stop him!

He cupped her face with his hands, remembering that ıer only physical knowledge of him had been when he'd een weak from the fever of his wounds. Not now, now he vas able to love her properly.

Don't be afraid. I couldn't hurt you any more than Kusac ould. Slowly, almost reluctantly, he backed away from her, hen scooped her up in his arms. *How long do we have?* he ısked as he stepped through the blinds into his bedroom.

As long as we want. Kusac said it was time we had the pportunity to be together again. He asks when you're com- ng home. He's missed you, too.

He felt the truth of her sending. *Tomorrow. We'll return ogether.* He set her down gently on her feet. Reaching out, he pressed the seal on her jacket, helping her take it off.

She stood there, still trembling. She needed more time. Their disagreement was too recent.

"Sit. I'll get our coffee," he said.

He didn't hurry, knowing events were moving just a little

too fast for her. He was surprised at how she'd reacted
his vision. He recalled it, reliving the emotions he'd felt
the time. He'd helped birth Kashini, was legally her guar-
ian, too, but to share a cub with Carrie? For a moment th
idea didn't seem so remote, so unbelievable. Their Tria
was registered at the temple, which gave him equal statu
with Kusac as her life-mate. It had been no idle gesture c
Kusac's part either, nor done without Carrie's fu
agreement. They all knew that each member of a Tria
took equal responsibility for any cubs. Then he dismisse
the idea. A nice dream, but not what his life was made c

When he returned, he almost stopped dead in surpris
Clad only in her undertunic, Carrie sat in the center of h
bed. Stepping over her discarded clothes, he put the mug
on the night table. From behind him he heard the so
sounds of her getting to her feet.

She stood there, looking at him. "Tallinu. Please, be sur
this time," she began.

He placed a finger against her lips. "I am very sure." H
unfastened the cord of his robe, letting it fall open as h
reached for the seal on the front of her tunic. A touch an
it parted. As her warm body-scent filled his nostrils, he sli
his hands inside her tunic, puling her nakedness against hi
When her flesh touched him, he was the one trembling.

He kissed her, long and slowly this time, then, droppin
his robe to the floor, he knelt on the bed, urging her to si
beside him. Bending his head, he let his teeth and tongu
travel across her face and neck as his hands began to strok
the smooth curves of her body.

Memories of their first pairing came to his mind, an
these he shared with her. As she reached for him, tryin
to pull him down onto the bed, he felt her need burnin
deep within him, felt the crystal he always wore start t
warm.

"No, not yet," he said, his voice so low it was barely
more than a purr.

Again he felt a flash of apprehension from her as she
realized what Kusac had meant all those weeks before
Kaid Tallinu was totally Sholan, with no Human side.

Tallinu laughed gently, caressing her throat with his fin
gertips. "You've no need to fear me, Carrie. Our Links
have brought me enough knowledge."

I'm not afraid of you.

Her breasts enticed him and he reached down to cup one
his hand. "Only a little," he murmured, bending down
flick the rough surface of his tongue across it.

A soft moan of pleasure escaped her and she ran her
ands across his chest till she touched the leather pouch.
Our crystal."

"That I could never remove," he said, feeling it begin to
ulse in time to her heart beat.

With a deep purr, he sat back on his haunches, turning
er slightly so her back was to him. Taking her by the
aist, he lifted her up till she was kneeling astride him.
upporting her there, he began to tease her with his teeth
nd tongue. First the lobes of her ear, then her neck, her
oulder, and on down her side to her flank.

With gentle cries of pleasure, she twisted and turned,
ying to reach him, but he kept her held where she was.
hen he reached the softness of her thighs. The strength
uddenly left her legs and she collapsed against him. Al-
hough he'd barely touched her, she was already on the
dge of her climax.

Slowly he lowered her, letting her sink down, gasping as
he surrounded him. Their crystal flared as his heartbeat
ow echoed hers, but he scarcely noticed it so intense were
he sensations they were sharing. Small moans escaped her
nd her hands clutched at his thighs, nails digging through
is pelt into his flesh. His purr deepened and leaning for-
ard slightly, he slid his hands upward, closing them over
er breasts.

"I dreamed of you," he whispered, his voice barely audi-
le as she turned her head to look at him. "When I was
lone, when I needed to work, you kept coming to me,
istracting me. Dzinae." He supported her again, beginning
o move within her. He saw a flash of fear in her eyes and
new she'd never paired like this before.

"Sholan-style, my Dzinae. Like me." He purred, his
ongue flicking out to lick her cheek just as their minds
oined.

Upward they spiraled, becoming one, reaching outward
ill at the edges of their bond they could sense Kusac and
'Chebbi beginning their own journey.

En'Shalla, little Human. There is *a balance.*

With a cry she arched away from Kaid, collapsing forward on her forearms, pulling him down with her.

Quick reflexes meant he landed on his hands, pois
above her. Almost instantly he swelled to full arousal a
as one, they began to climax.

Afterward, with a deep, shuddering breath, he collapse
with her onto his side. His tail flicked round her upper le
holding her with as much urgency as did his arms. Grad
ally the sharing of memories of their time apart began
slow, then stopped, leaving their minds once more the
own.

*Vartra's bones, Carrie, you're not real—are you a dzina
I don't remember it being like this before!*

You were ill, and it was our first time together, she se
as they parted and she turned to face him. *I hear
someone . . .* she began

*I heard Him too, and felt them. It was Vartra. He's a forc
in my life that I can't escape, but we have reached son
compromises.* He smiled wryly.

In her gentle laugh, he could hear the underlying pur
"Compromises with a God. Why doesn't that surprise me
So, is Kusac now aware of us when we're together?"

"He was the first time. It was us who weren't aware
him. I think that ritual at the Retreat strengthened ou
mutual bond."

"That's why T'Chebbi went to him."

"Her choice, Carrie, but I swear he'll be glad she did,
he said with a chuckle. "She's not my lover, and even
she were, she'd be free to do as she wished."

"She *should* be your lover," she said, rubbing her fac
against the long fur on his chest. "You obviously care fo
each other, but that's between you."

He began to trace her features with a fingertip. *Wher
I said how Sholan you were, I had no idea you were s
like us.*

What's a dzinae? she asked, taking his hand in hers t
caress the sensitive areas on his palm.

He grinned. *A heavenly reward for those who've don
Vartra's will. Males and females whose only wish is to pleas
your senses. They're said to visit the overly pious and teas
them unmercifully.*

And did I do that to you?

Oh, yes, my dzinae, you certainly did! His thoughts wer
warm and loving as he stroked her face. "You were all th
distraction Vartra could hope for!"

She laughed, stretching out against him. "I'm hungry. Have you anything we can eat?"

He looked embarrassed. "I brought some food with me last week."

Arching an eyebrow at him, she sat up and began fastening her tunic. "You were expecting company?"

"I hoped you'd come here with me one day, yes," he admitted. "You're the only female I've ever brought here."

"Thank you for bringing me," she said, kissing him before getting to her feet. She looked down at where he still lay watching her. "Well, are you going to feed me, then?"

CHAPTER 13

A gentle glow penetrated her eyelids. Morning. But thi morning was different. Kusac didn't lie with his arm restin on her hip like this, and it was definitely not his scent sh could smell. Then she remembered and opened her eyes.

In front of her, the polarized window had brightenec allowing her a clear view of the grounds outside. Sunligh glinted off the snow, sending sparkles of light dancing int the bedroom. A chiddoe still in its winter coat hopped int view, stopping every now and then to scrabble for som edible greenery.

She turned her head to look at Tallinu. He was stil asleep, lying on his stomach beside her, his breath gentl huffing against her neck.

He had changed, she thought with lazy contentment as careful not to wake him, she turned to lie on her back And she liked the changes. Last night there had been n holding back from him, either physically or mentally. He' finally accepted how he felt and made his commitment t her.

She looked around, interested to see what this inner re treat was like. They'd been a little too involved with eacl other the night before for her to take much interest i her surroundings, she remembered with a small grin. She' noticed that the walls were dark, but now she saw they were a blue as deep as the sky at dusk. On the wall beyonc him, a sword hanging by its decorative scabbard caught he eye. It had a vaguely familiar look to it, but she couldn' remember where she'd seen it before. Beneath it was a dresser of drawers on which a collection of small figures was arranged. Curious, she pushed herself up on one elbow to get a better look.

"I paint them for relaxation." His voice was low and still hazy with sleep. "The sword is the one Garras gave me

hen we became sword-brothers. You'll have seen its twin
t Vanna's."

"You're awake," she said, reaching out to run her hand
cross his back, stopping as she felt the knots of the scars
.ill there.

He flinched and began to turn over.

"I'm sorry. I thought they'd healed."

"All but one or two, and they'll go in time," he said.
Does the room meet with your approval?"

"I love the whole house. It's like you, complex in its
implicity."

He laughed, looping his arm round her waist to draw her
own beside him. Before he could, her hand slid up to the
ack of his neck and closed over his scruff. With an effort
f will, he lay still, waiting to see what she'd do next. He'd
ever submitted to a female before.

She leaned over him, her kisses gentle, first on one lip,
hen the other, then her tongue flicked across them both
s she laughingly teased him.

He tried to capture her with his teeth, but she deftly
avoided him, choosing instead to close hers on the lower
dge of his ear. With a small growl, he reached up to take
old of her chin when suddenly she released his ear and
ightened her grip on his scruff, pulling his head back till
is neck was arched toward her.

Now he froze, unable to move, caught between his re-
ponse as a warrior and a lover, feeling suddenly exposed
nd vulnerable.

"I'm not letting you go this time," she said, her voice a
ow purr before she closed her teeth over his larynx, press-
ng them hard into his flesh.

Her teeth might be small and blunt compared to his, but
here was no doubt in his mind that they possessed an equal
ability to kill. A momentary panic rushed through him, then
suddenly, as she released him, he found himself wanting
her more than ever. Confused, his hands clutched her close,
finding her as willing as he was. As their bodies joined,
once more their minds began to share.

*   *   *

Dzaka was waiting for them when they arrived home,
and his father's warmth of greeting surprised him.

"Tomorrow, early, we have business to attend to at the

Arrazo estate," Kaid said, his arm still around Dzaka
shoulders. "Where is everyone?"

"In the garage, packing equipment," said Dzaka.

"You walk with Carrie, I want to go on ahead."

Dzaka slowed down, looking at Carrie, who merel
shrugged and linked her arm in his.

"We keep getting left like this, don't we, Dzaka?" sh
said with a smile. "So it's time to confront your grandpa
ents, is it? I think Kusac will want to go, possibly even m
bond-father. It'll be quite a meeting."

"It's not necessary, Clan Leader," he murmured, begin
ning to walk again. "I have what I wanted—my father. An
I know he and Khemu cared for me. It's all I need."

"Stop the titles, Dzaka. I keep telling you, and you stil
keep doing it!" she said, giving his arm a shake. "You'r
already my bond-son through Tallinu, and will be my bond
brother as well when you and Kitra become life-mates."

"I've no aspirations in that direction, Carrie," he sai
hastily.

"No, but Kitra has, I'll warrant, and you'd not object
now would you? Truth," she said as he hesitated.

Dzaka grinned down at her. "No, I wouldn't," he sai
candidly. "Question for question, Carrie. How is my fa
ther really?"

"He's fine, Dzaka," she said. "It takes time to get ove
what he went through, but it truly is behind him now."

"Thank Vartra," he sighed as they walked into the
garage.

You heard Him, too? Kaid was asking Kusac.

Even T'Chebbi heard it, but only through me, Kusac re
plied, looking up at him from where he was squatting on
the floor amid a pile of crates and various goods. *We sense*
little more, though.

Nor us. The message was meant for Carrie, obviously, bu
I think it was also intended to reassure us.

Having you back with us, and seeing Carrie content, is al
the reassurance I need, Tallinu. "Well come home, Kaid,"
Kusac said, holding out his hand.

The call came during third meal as they sat round the
table in the kitchen with T'Chebbi, Kitra, and Dzaka.
Kusac took it on his wrist com.

"General Raiban from Shanagi," said Ni'Zulhu's voice.

Kusac looked at Kaid as he rose to his feet. "They're bringing the mission forward."

Kaid nodded. "Wouldn't surprise me. It's been three months since they heard from Jo Edwards and her party. Take the call. I'll alert Quin and Conrad," he said getting up.

When Kusac returned, he looked round the small group. "We leave for Chagda Station at dusk tomorrow," he said. "Once there, we meet Captain Kishasayzar and the crew of the *Hkariyash*. They'll be taking us to Jalna."

"We're undercover from the moment we leave the estate," warned Kaid, glancing from T'Chebbi to Carrie and Kusac. "Conrad and Quin will be smuggled aboard with our trade goods. From that point on, we're a delegation of U'Churian merchants escorting a Solnian representative on her first trip to Jalna."

T'Chebbi rose. "I get this dye from Vanna for us."

Kaid grasped her gently by the arm. "Eat first. We have time enough. Conrad and Quin will join us after their meal. Kusac, you have estate business to discuss with Garras. You deal with that. Carrie, you have Jack and Jiszoe to see. Kashini's welfare is all you need worry about. We four can see to the rest till you're free."

As he was speaking, Kusac rejoined his mate at the table, well aware of her numbed reaction to the news.

I'm not ready. Jack and Jiszoe were going to move in here to look after Kashini. It's too soon!

Perhaps it's better this way, less time to dread our parting from her, he sent, wrapping an arm round her shoulders. *Nothing can be as bad as the Margins.*

Kaid leaned across the table, reaching out to touch her hand briefly. "We're ready, Carrie. Don't worry. I watched you all training today. We'll be fine. It won't be long before you're back with your cub, I promise."

"Don't make promises, Kaid," she said, letting him hold her fingertips for a moment. "We don't know what will happen out there. I have to find my own way of coping." She smiled briefly at him then picked up her fork again. "I don't know about you, but I'm not prepared to face Zhala's wrath if we let her meal spoil!"

"Most of the work is done," said Kaid, reaching for a piece of bread. "Your early start has put us ahead of schedule, Kusac. We'll need to work through much of the night, but we can be ready."

"I'll call in the other Brothers to help us. If we do the organization and they do the packing, we should be finished soon enough."

Later that night, Konis arrived. As Dzaka ushered him into the den, he stopped to survey Kaid. "Now you and Kusac could be brothers." he said. "Vanna's dye works well. How long will it last? I'm not sure I like the longer pelts, though."

"It's augmented by slow release drugs, like the longer fur," said Kusac, getting up to greet him. "My pelt's been growing for some time now. You never mentioned it before."

"I see you fairly regularly, Kusac," Konis said, coming down to join them. "Kaid I haven't seen for some time. The change in him seems greater. You're well, I take it?" he asked Kaid, clasping his arm in passing.

"Fine now, Clan Lord."

"Konis will do," he said, lowering himself onto the settee. "Try and find a moment to go and say good-bye to your mother and Taizia, Kusac. They're both fretting themselves into a real state."

"Is that why you're here?" Kusac grinned, heading over to the dresser that held their collection of spirits. "Nezzu?"

"I'd prefer that Keissian brandy, if you have any," he said hopefully. "Don't let me hold you back, by the way. Can I do anything to help?"

"Yes," said Kaid before Kusac could speak. "There is something you could do for me."

Kusac looked at him in surprise as he pulled a bottle of brandy from the cupboard. "You, Kaid?" he asked, picking up several glasses.

"Neul Arrazo," said Konis. "Am I right?"

Kaid's mouth opened in a smile. "Well guessed, Konis. I intended to see him tomorrow, but we'll not have time now. I don't want to leave the matter of Dzaka's legitimacy unfinished."

Konis nodded. "I understand, but it's better left to me. My office has been preparing the case against him, and Neul will be told about Dzaka, believe me. Your son has been registered by me on the Clan records; that's what matters most. However, right now we have a complication with the Arrazo Clan."

Kusac's ears swiveled forward to catch every word as he handed small glasses of the liquor to his father and Kaid. "What complication?" he asked.

"His youngest son, Taynar, is missing, and with him, his Leska, a Human called Kate Harvey."

"A mixed pair? Why weren't we told?" asked Kusac.

"Where did they go missing?"

"The information's been restricted because of the circumstances surrounding their disappearance," said Konis. "I'm now at liberty to tell you, though."

At dusk the following day, they left for Chagda Station on a routine military flight. Carrie was inconsolable, sitting silently for the duration, refusing to talk. Leaving Kashini had been as big a wrench as she'd feared, and nothing Kusac or Kaid could do or say lessened it.

As they docked, Conrad and Quin were concealed in their containers for immediate transportation to the hold of the *Hkariyash*. Once there, they'd be released. The Sholan contingent and Carrie made their way in a more orthodox fashion to the bar where they were to meet with Captain Kishasayzar. The formalities of their cover observed, they accompanied the Sumaan back to his ship where loading had been completed. Within the hour, they had undocked and were heading out of the Sholan system for Jalna.

* * *

"He's unconscious, Master Rhyaz," said the physician, stepping back from where Kezule lay slumped on the table. "I strongly recommend that you let him recover fully before any more of this kind of questioning. He's told you all he's going to for now. This is his third day of it."

Rhyaz wondered if he could hear a slight note of censure in the other's voice. "Can he manage without treatment?" he asked tiredly, massaging his right hand. He'd managed to hit it on the side of the chair and it hurt like hell right now. These sessions took their toll on him also, in more ways than one.

"The female's got enough knowledge to doctor him in there, if that's what you mean," Fazzu said. "He's got no serious injuries."

"Send in basic first aid, nothing more."

"Master Rhyaz," said L'Seuli, touching him on the arm to get his attention. "We should leave. You also need attention."

He nodded and followed his aide outside. "In the control room, L'Seuli. I want to observe his return." He didn't, but he needed to.

As they entered, he noted that there were two new faces on duty.

"Mito and Anders are on leave, Master Rhyaz," said Zhyaf, looking round. "This is Dzyash," he said, indicating the male, "and Nayla, our linguist."

"Your medikit please, Dzyash," said L'Seuli, grabbing a vacant chair.

Rhyaz nodded a greeting to them and took the chair L'Seuli had procured.

"Master Rhyaz, your hand, if you please," he said, placing the kit on the counter and opening it.

Rhyaz held his hand out and turned his attention to the window, watching Keeza. She was pacing the room, her tail flicking angrily from side to side.

"She's been like that for the last half hour," said Zhyaf.

"Angry, is she?" he asked, wincing as L'Seuli wiped the cut with antiseptic.

"Rage would be a more appropriate description. He may be a captive, but she feels we're treating him as if he were also a criminal."

"We don't treat criminals like this," said Rhyaz.

"Don't expect logic from her, Master Rhyaz," warned Zhyaf. "Psychologically she's in her own world, one she shares with him. Her current state is such that you should alert the guards to be careful of her when they take him back."

"Do it," snapped Rhyaz, trying not to hiss as L'Seuli sprayed his knuckles with the standard anti-inflammatory and antibiotic spray. It hurt, but he'd rather it did; he didn't want to go the way of Ghezu.

"I think you've chipped or cracked the bone," said L'Seuli. "It's going to be painful for a good few days, I'm afraid."

"It's painful now, dammit," he said, snatching his hand back. "What's she planning to do?" he demanded of Zhyaf.

"Her thoughts are jumbled . . . Too confused," apologized the telepath. "All I can say is her mood's unstable."

"Order the guards to shoot her if necessary." He heard Zhyaf's sharp intake of breath followed by L'Seuli's quiet answer as he turned his attention to what was about to happen on the other side of the viewing screen.

"They use stunners, Zhyaf. We don't risk more powerful weapons around Kezule."

Her senses stretched to the utmost, Keeza heard the faint sound as the door began to open. Swinging round from her position by the table, she watched two guards come into the room. Rifles trained on her, they took up positions that covered her but left the doorway clear.

They brought Kezule in next, his limp form supported by two more troopers. She began to growl deep in her throat as she saw the condition he was in. Never taking her eyes off them, she watched as they deposited him on the bed and backed away. One of Fazzu's assistants followed, carrying a tray of first aid equipment. Nervously he edged past her, put down the tray, and was about to leave when she attacked him.

Kezule had begun to stir as they laid him down, and the sound of her enraged roar was enough to make him painfully turn his head to see what was happening.

"Vartra's bones!" swore Dzyash, watching as she knocked the medic to the ground and pulled her arm back, claws fully extended, ready to strike him.

The beams from two stunners hit her simultaneously in the back and, yowling in agony, Keeza collapsed to the floor.

Rhyaz stood up. He'd seen enough. "L'Seuli," he said in an undervoice as they left the control room, "I'm going to make damned sure Raiban pays everything that Keeza Lassah is due, and then some!"

"Yes, sir," his aide murmured, following him along the corridor.

Kezule drifted in and out of consciousness for the next few hours. When he finally surfaced, the female was still lying where she'd fallen. Every breath sent fire across his chest, causing him to gasp. They'd concentrated on his ribs again. He found slowing his breathing was of little help this time, it barely touched the pain he was suffering. He needed to exert some control, and that would take him dangerously close to a laalgo level, but he needed to be able to concentrate if he was to assess the damage they'd done.

He slowed his heart rate to the point where he began to feel light-headed, then, increasing it a fraction, waited. Gradually the pain of breathing began to recede. Now he could turn his mind inward. The God-King be praised that they knew nothing of his abilities to control his body functions.

What he found left him shaken. This time, the fact that they knew so little about his physiology had worked against him. Damage, serious damage, had been done to those parts of his internal system that allowed him to boost his ability to repair himself. And his reserves were too low to rely on time alone. Though they didn't know it, this last session of questioning could cost him his life.

"I can't tell what the hell's going on here, Zhyaf," said Dzyash, turning to look at him. "The readings are all over the place. First his blood pressure drops like a stone, then it's up! Now, from the looks of it, he's about to go into shock. I want a physician on standby. I'm not prepared to be responsible for him."

"Call one, then," said Zhyaf. "Don't look to me to make your decisions, Dzyash. You're in charge of the bio-readings. If you think he needs a medic, call one." He saw the other's look, felt his purposely unconcealed anger, and decided he'd better explain. "Send for the medic now," he said, turning to give the youth his full attention.

"I apologize for sounding brusque, Dzyash, but I'm constantly monitoring Keeza, and I'm concerned about her. You have to use your own judgment here. Situations can develop in seconds, giving us no time to confer. You wouldn't have been picked for the project if you didn't have the necessary skills."

Dzyash nodded. Turning his gaze back to the bio-readings, he asked, "How is she? Will she come around soon?"

"She's moving toward consciousness now. Just coming out of a state akin to a very powerful dream, but I can't make sense of it. Her thoughts are even more confused than they were before. I get wisps of memories of her experiences before she was processed, but not enough to cause real problems. I am concerned as to her mental well-being, though. She is seriously disturbed, but then, going through this, what can I expect? It's utterly barbaric!"

"We're getting results, though," said Nayla. "In this case, surely the end justifies the means?"

The door opened and Fazzu, still on call, entered. "What's up?" he asked, going over to Dzyash's work station to look at the traces. "Looks reasonably stable to me."

"He is now, but the readings suggested he was about to go into shock a few minutes ago. I'd prefer it if you stayed until he's really stable."

"Very well," said Fazzu, putting his medikit on the counter and pulling a chair up beside Dzyash. "I've no other patients tonight."

As she came round, Keeza's muscles spasmed involuntarily, making her moan with pain. Her limbs were a mass of prickling tingles as the circulation began to return to them. She remembered Kezule and raised her head, looking over to where he lay on the bed.

He was facing her, and she could see the angry swelling around the blood-encrusted cut on his cheek. "Come," he hissed, gesturing her over with an unsteady hand. "Need help."

She got to her feet, unable to stop herself mewling in pain as she forced herself upright. Stopping at the table, she picked up the tray of antiseptics and bandages.

"Later," he said, pushing it aside as she stood beside him. "Get food. Need food now. Must eat to heal." His words were punctuated by small hisses of pain.

"How? How can I get food?" she asked.

"Ask. They monitor us. Ask!" The word was a long, drawn out hiss.

She looked round, wondering where the listening device was, where she should direct her words.

"Just ask!"

"He needs food!" she said, turning round as she spoke. "D'you hear me, you bastards? He needs food, or he can't heal!"

"What now?" asked Dzyash.

"She believes him," added Zhyaf, looking at Fazzu.

The medic frowned. "Food, to help him heal? It's possible, I suppose. When's his next meal due?"

Nayla checked her wrist comm. "Not for two hours."

"We need someone to go in and talk to them, and it isn't going to be me," he said. "Is Brother L'Seuli still here? Send for him."

The food finally arrived. Keeza dispatched and prepared it quickly and efficiently, covering it liberally, as he'd asked, with the ground laalquoi powder. Supporting him, she fed it to him a piece at a time till it was all gone. When he was finished, she fetched him water.

"More food," he said, pushing himself up on his elbow. "Need more."

This time, when L'Seuli came, two guards backed a growling and spitting Keeza into a corner while a third covered Kezule at close range.

"Why the need for extra food, Kezule?" L'Seuli asked, pulling a chair over and sitting near his bed.

Kezule hissed a sentence in Valtegan, baring his needle-sharp teeth. He was caught this time, didn't have an option. He needed the food, his life depended on it.

"You want extra food, you need to cooperate with me," L'Seuli said, leaning back and folding his arms. "I don't intend to wait long, either." His tail swayed lazily.

What would be the least damaging piece of information to give him? He'd not anticipated having to discuss his physiology, hadn't any half-truths prepared, and he was too ill to think coherently. "I can speed my healing, but need food. Laalgo uses body reserves. I have none."

L'Seuli raised an eye ridge. "You can speed up your ability to heal? Useful, but hardly necessary, Kezule. You and I both know you're not that badly hurt." He got to his feet and turned to go.

From her corner, Keeza let forth a flood of invectives that contained a few even he hadn't heard before.

"You want I die?" Kezule asked, lying down. "Is fine. No future for me here anyway." He had to tell them or die. He began to cough, each intake of breath convulsing him with pain.

"You're not dying, dammit!" said L'Seuli, striding over to the bedside. "Stop the acting!"

Kezule reached out and grasped L'Seuli by the jacket,

ulling his face level with his. "You damage me this time
a ways you not know!"

The guard stepped forward as L'Seuli's fingers grasped
ezule's palm, twisting it back against the wrist, but the
'altegan had already released him and the hold was unnec-
ssary. Both pulled away, Kezule to fall back on his bed,
oughing again.

"When you recover, you will explain how we managed
o hurt you, and how you speed up your healing processes,"
narled L'Seuli. "Give him what he wants!" With that, he
urned and strode out of the room, the guards following in
is wake.

"Don't go that close to him again," said Rhyaz, his voice
uiet as L'Seuli joined him in the control room.

"I'm sorry, Guild Master," said L'Seuli, ears dipping in
pology. He knew he'd acted foolishly, and Rhyaz's quiet
ensure was worse than the chewing out he knew he
eserved.

"Fazzu, once he's had enough to eat, and when they're
ettled, use the sedative gas," said Rhyaz. "I want a full
ange of tests run on them, including body scans for him.
want to know exactly what damage he's suffered. Com-
are them with the originals. There must be some obvious
ifferences, swellings, internal bleeding, anything to let us
now what's happening."

Fazzu nodded. "Any treatment? What do you want done
vith them when we've finished?"

Rhyaz looked surprised. "Return them exactly as they
vere. No treatment, I don't want them knowing they've
een disturbed. Keeza is showing signs of violence that I
lon't like. I want to know why. On second thought, better
can her as well. She might have sustained a head injury
rom that beating a fortnight ago."

"Yes, Master Rhyaz."

Once Kezule had gorged himself into a stupor, Keeza
egan bathing his cheek. He stopped her, grasping her by
he wrist and pulling her arm in front of his mouth. Slowly,
ie sank his teeth into her, making sure that those that
arried the serum penetrated deeply enough to inject it.
she mewled in shock, unable to pull free of his grasp. When

he was done, he opened his mouth, taking care not to te:
her flesh.

As she looked at the dozens of tiny oozing punctu
wounds in utter shock, he pulled her closer, till he cou
speak into her ear and not be overheard.

"The bite is nothing, but it is poisoned. I need to go in
laalgo to heal. There is no Sholan word for it. You watc
me; watch me well. When I waken, then I take the poisc
from you."

He released her. "Now, help me out of the clothes, the
see to the wounds," he said, lying back tiredly. It wasn't
poison exactly, but he needed her to think it was. For him
it was as drastic a step as going into the laalgo state. H
couldn't remember if he'd seen any of the Sholan pets wit
bite marks, but he knew it worked on the females of som
of the slave species. She needed to be focused on him
protective of him to a greater degree than she already wa
because while in laalgo, he'd be utterly defenseless.

The cut on his face and the visible bruising treated wit
antiseptic and salve, he had her cover him with the bla
kets, telling her to press them close against his naked bod

"Your blanket, too," he ordered. "Stay close, lie on th
bed against me. I need the warmth. I'll be in laalgo fo
several days. When I wake, you give me water, then foo
Let no one touch me or try to wake me. You understand?

She nodded, standing there holding her blanket clutche
in front of her.

Again he reached out and pulled her close. "They try t
wake me too soon, it could kill me. If I die, so do yo
Only when I wake will I stop the poison."

"But what if it kills me first?"

"Won't kill you quickly," he grinned humorlessly. "Mak
you feel sick, maybe, but I'll wake in time." One day, th
tables would be reversed. This new indignity was alread
added to his list.

"What's taking so long?" fretted Fazzu, pacing the con
trol room. "Is he performing some damned ritual o
something?"

"I don't believe it! She's lying down with him!" ex
claimed Nayla. "I saw the tape of what happened last tim
she approached him! You'd think she'd have learned he
lesson."

"He's asked her to join him," said L'Seuli from his perch
n the edge of the counter. "Her body language is too
onfident for it to be her idea. Zhyaf? What do you say?"

"Her fear's abated, certainly but she's still nervous. I'd
ave to agree with you, though. This looks like something
e's told her to do."

"Why?" asked Dzyash. "We know he hates the thought
f any intimacy with alien females, so why is he inviting
t now?"

"Why do people lie close, apart from for paring?" asked
'Seuli. "Warmth. He's had her add her blanket to those
n his bed, now he wants her lying on the top beside him.
Not for sexual reasons. Some desert tribes males allow their
avored herding beasts on their beds at night in the winter,
specially the pregnant females. Remember, he sees her as
pet."

"His readings are falling," said Dzyash suddenly. "Falling
apidly. Heartbeat, respiration, temperature, the lot!"

L'Seuli leaped down to get a better view of the screen over
Dzyash's shoulder. "What's happening?" he demanded.

"I think we're about to see him go into a hibernation
tate," said Fazzu. "It's a theory we've been discussing,
jiven that he's got similarities to our reptiles, but I didn't
xpect it to actually happen." He pointed to the screen.
"Look, increased brain activity. He's certainly doing some-
hing to himself."

"What about the sedative gas?" asked Nayla.

"Leave it till he's stabilized. If we interfere in what's
obviously a natural process for him, it could be fatal. For
now, we watch and wait."

*   *   *

Mentor Sorli had been allocated an office on the ground
loor: one of the reception rooms which would be converted
or him. He'd refused, deciding instead to have one of the
Leska suites.

It was his favorite part of the building, reached by a
narrow spiral stone staircase. Dubbed the bird run, the corridor that connected the half dozen or so suites was wooden
loored—not stained, highly treated wood, but rough,
scarred by generations of clawed Sholan feet and bleached
almost white by scrubbing and sanding. It was where the
newly Linked Leska pairs lived while learning how to cope

with their partner and combined abilities. It was also where established pairs would stay while visiting Valsgarth. The were isolated to a degree from the bustle and hubbub of the daily life of the Guildhouse.

He'd chosen the suite at the end of the corridor. Coincidentally it had what he considered the best views of the grounds. His office looked out across the plain to the woodland, beyond which the ornate white-domed roof of the temple was visible.

As he stood by his desk, the door burst open, admitting Esken. Sorli's aide, Maeshou, trailed unhappily behind him trying to apologize for the disturbance.

"Tell this assistant of yours not to try and keep me out of your office again, Sorli," snapped Esken. "I've had bad enough day without her adding to it."

Sorli gestured to Maeshou, letting her know there was nothing more she could do.

"Master Esken, won't you take a seat? What brings you here?" he asked, indicating the comfortable chairs just beyond his desk.

Esken was already on his way there, grumbling. "D'you know what Challa's doing now? Redecorating *my* apartments! First she moves in—despite my direct orders not to mark you—then her damned cubs join her! They could board downstairs like the others, but no, that's not good enough for her! Now this! I can't move for painters and carpenters hammering and sawing everywhere." He stopped as Sorli sat down opposite him.

"Why the hell did you have to have your office up in this Gods' forsaken bit of building?" he demanded. "Must have climbed at least a hundred steps. Damned inconvenient of you, Sorli."

"Not a hundred, Master Esken," Sorli murmured. "About thirty-nine in all. I'm sorry to hear of your troubles but to what do I owe this visit?"

"This is no call to exchange pleasantries, Sorli. I'm disappointed in you, damned disappointed. I expected a report from you concerning the latest happenings with the mixed Leskas. Instead I have to hear the news from Khafsa when the female's brought into the medical center because she's lost her Talent! And I knew nothing about the Aldatans testing all the telepaths! They've taken some thirty from all over the continent to live at their estate! Just what d'you

hink you're doing, Sorli? Do I have to remind you that
'm still the Guild Master here? You've let your promotion
o to your head!"

Sorli's temper had been rising during Esken's tirade.
Now it had reached its zenith. "Master Esken, I am in
harge of the mixed Leskas. You yourself appointed me
o the position, and to oversee the daily running of this
Guildhouse. I am doing this. The testing of the telepaths
was not my concern. It was requested at a higher level, by
he military, I believe. It's no longer my job to keep you
nformed of gossip! You have aides in plenty to do that,
and your legions of whispering jeggets like Khafsa!"

"You forget yourself, Sorli." Esken's tone was arctic.
'An appointment can be reversed as easily as it is made."

Sorli got to his feet. He hated confrontations, and prayed
hat Esken couldn't tell how badly this was upsetting him.
'You forget, Master Esken, that I returned on the clear
understanding that I would be independent of you. Do you
ealize just what damage you've done to our Guild? You
efused Governor Nesul a legitimate request for a knowledge transfer to bring him up to date on the off-world polit-
cal situation. You blackmailed and frightened members of
he ruling council into voting your way at meetings; you
antagonized the Aldatan Clan, and the Clan Lord, to the
point where he removed his daughters from their training
here and none of his family will visit this Guildhouse without bodyguards! You kidnapped and drugged Physician
Kyjishi and her Leska, Brynne Stevens . . . Do I need to
continue, Master Esken? Don't threaten me with demotion,
because before you can do that, I will very publicly leave
here and join the Brotherhood of Vartra as a priest!"

He stopped, taking a deep breath, then turned and
walked slowly to the door. Pressing his hand to the lock,
he stood back. "Good day, Master Esken. I've nothing
more to say to you."

Esken got silently to his feet and walked to the door. He
stopped as he drew level with Sorli and opened his mouth.

"Good day," repeated Sorli, looking past him into his
outer office and the bird run beyond.

Esken left, and Sorli thumbed the door closed. Letting
out a sigh of relief, he leaned against the wall for a moment, shaking.

In the adjoining room, his mate, Mayoi, looked across to

where Lijou and Kha'Qwa sat. Their door had been ope
and they'd heard everything. "Would you excuse me a mo
ment," she murmured, getting to her feet.

Kha'Qwa reached out a comforting hand. "Tell him w
wish to take him out for a meal. I think you both need
change of scene right now."

Mayoi smiled. "That should help, but give us a few min
utes first." As she left, she made sure to close the doo
behind her.

"We must do something, Lijou, else Sorli will leave an
we'll be back where we started. It's time for the Brother
hood to get involved."

"Involved?" Then he realized what she meant. "Oh, no
We're not going to start intimidating . . ."

"Esken's proved himself to be untrustworthy, Lijou. Shoul
we lose Sorli because of him? I don't think so. I'll speak t
Rhyaz when we get home. Now hush, I can hear them. Hel
me get up. I've been sitting in this position long enough."

Instantly Lijou was at her side, helping her out of th
chair. More than halfway through her pregnancy, she wa
beginning to find herself less agile than usual.

Events took their own turn as, a couple of days later
Master Esken was struck down with a heart seizure in th
middle of one of his rages. While he was recovering i
the medical unit next to the Guildhouse, he requested a
truthsayer and notary and tendered his resignation as Mas
ter of the Telepath Guild. A week later, Mentor Sorli wa
confirmed in his new post as Guild Master.

"Was the Brotherhood involved?" Lijou asked Kha'Qwa
when he heard the news.

She shrugged prettily and reached for another rainbow
fruit. "How could they be? Master Esken had a heart sei
zure, Infonet just said so."

He looked at her suspiciously for a moment, but when
she winced and tried to make herself more comfortable as
the cub inside her kicked, he decided there were other
things he'd rather think about.

*　　　*　　　*

Left to her own devices, Keeza had quickly developed a
rhythm of resting, eating, and sleeping. The resting drifted

into trancelike states where more of the strange dreams came to her. Most importantly, though, the food and the enforced rest were returning her to full health.

The dreams were troubled, all about a time she had no memory of, a time of conflict and fighting, the night around her laced with the glow of energy weapon beams and the screams of the injured and dying. There were others, more peaceful ones, of gardens and flowers, and an old female who spoke kindly words. These she liked and when she could, returned to them, enjoying the quiet of the garden and the scent of the blossoms there.

Kezule had wakened once to drink and gorge again. She'd fed him as before, piece by piece till he was done. When he got her to help him to the bathroom to wash the strips of dead skin from his body she could almost see the shape of the undigested food pressing against his distended belly.

Strangely, it didn't disgust her. Perhaps she'd gotten as used to the coolness of his smooth, hairless skin as she was to his musty scent.

"You felt the sickness?" he asked as she wrapped him once more in the blankets.

"A little," she said, glancing involuntarily at the bite on her forearm.

"Show me."

She held it out for his inspection. The dozens of tiny puncture wounds were healing, but the scabs over them had a greenish tint.

He grunted. It had worked. "No one has disturbed us?"

"No one."

"They feed you?"

"They send your food, and I eat it." Her nose wrinkled in concern, ears flicking back worriedly. "Do I do right, my General?" she asked, risking a touch to his face.

"Yes," he said shortly, turning away from her. Anger began to build within him and he tried to suppress it. His body responded slowly, but it responded: he was healing. He needed to be calm to go back into laalgo, but his anger was justified. They had made it impossible for him to do without her attentions; they were responsible for the indignity of what he'd had to do—what he still had to do. He hissed, then closed his eyes and began to compose himself once more, feeling the laalquoi begin reacting within his stomach. This was a long healing. His ability to cope had been badly lessened by his treatment and injuries.

She watched as he grew still and cool. The chill of his body had frightened her at first, but she'd realized this was part of his laalgo state. Lying back, she settled down, cuddling herself close against the mound of blankets that was him. He needed *her* to protect him. Well, he'd learn his trust wasn't misplaced. She pushed herself up on an elbow and looked down into his still face. He was just different, not ugly as she'd first thought.

His crest lay folded, almost invisible against the central ridge of his skull. Beneath closed eyelids, the bulbous eyes were still: no eyelashes to quiver, no eyebrows above them either. Forehead and cheeks curved upward till they met in a nose that wasn't quite what a nose should be; his nostrils were just two slits which dilated almost imperceptibly as he breathed. Below them, his deadly sharp teeth were concealed behind a wide, almost V-shaped mouth.

She risked touching his cheek, her fingers gently checking the still swollen cut and the yellowing flesh surrounding it. He was healing very slowly for him, but he was healing. Sighing, she lay back down, drawing comfort from the fact that her body warmth was helping him.

"I want those test results," said Fazzu from the bio-scanner console. "Why haven't they come up with them yet?"

"Takes time," said Dzyash, hovering behind him. He disliked it when the physician took over his station like this, and he'd been doing it a little too frequently of late. "Now they know he can manufacture chemicals almost at will, they've been working on the cadavers as well. They'll have the findings soon. I'm sure they've told you that already."

"No need to be snippy with me, boy," growled Fazzu, pushing the chair away from the work counter and getting to his feet. "Get on with your job and leave me to mine!" With that he stalked out of the room.

Dzyash resumed his seat, his frown changing to a slow smile as Nayla reached out a comforting hand to pat him.

"Don't take it personally, Dzyash. He's as concerned as the rest of us," said Zhyaf, glancing over to him. "It makes him irritable."

"We're all worried for her, Zhyaf," said Nayla, "but we don't all behave like Fazzu."

Zhyaf shrugged and turned back to his work. "I'll be a damned sight happier when I know what Kezule pumped into her," he growled. "She's focusing too much on him, unheathily so. I'm afraid she's going to try approaching him again, and next time, she might not be so lucky."

"Not a lot we can do," murmured Nayla.

"Don't be too sure about that," muttered Zhyaf.

Dzyash turned to look at him. "Don't do anything unorthodox, Zhyaf," he warned. "That could cost her her life. We don't know how she's supposed to be reacting to that bite. It could be this is what he's intended. She's sure as hell as protective of him as a mother with a cub!"

Zhyaf snorted contemptuously. "This is no mothering response, believe me! I take your point, though," he sighed. "I'll leave her alone."

Keeza lay in the dark, looking at the ceiling. It had been over a week now since he'd last woken. It couldn't take much longer, surely. Faintly, as if at a distance, she sensed an alarm go off.

A buzzer began to sound in the control room. Everyone froze, looking up at the alarm light set into the wall above Dzyash's station. Dzyash was the first to react. Dropping the mug of c'shar he'd been fetching from the dispenser, he ran to his monitors.

"Vartra's bones, we're losing him! His readings are dropping off the monitor!"

"Checking for system failure," said Nayla quietly, patching through to his console.

"I'll call for the physician," said Zhyaf, reaching for his comm.

"No time. He's flatlined," said Dzyash, activating the cell lights then spinning round for the medikit. "I'm going in. You two, cover me!"

"Don't be so damned foolish!" said Nayla, trying to grab him as he went past. "Help's coming! It isn't our job to . . ."

He pulled away angrily, slapping his palm on the door mechanism. "If he dies, so could she! We don't know what that bite did yet! Come on!" Grasping her by the arm, he hauled her out into the corridor and down to the entrance to Kezule's cell.

"This is madness! He's dangerous—he could escape!" Nayla said angrily.

Dzyash slammed Nayla's hand against the lock, holding it there long enough for it to be scanned, then released her. "He's dying, dammit! He's not capable of hurting anyone!" he snarled, putting his own palm on the plate. Seconds later, the door began to slide open.

As light flooded the room, Keeza sat up, blinking in the sudden glare. What was happening? It wasn't time for the lights to go on. Then the door opened, and two Sholans rushed in.

She rose, spanning Kezule in a four-legged stance, pelt bristling and rising around her face and neck, teeth bared, watching them as they skidded to a stop.

"It's all right, Keeza," said the male, holding out a placating hand. "I'm a medic, here to help him. He's dying, Keeza."

"You lie!" she snarled. "He's in laalgo!"

"No. His heart's stopped. He needs medical attention now," said Dzyash, edging slowly closer.

Bunching her thigh muscles, she leaped across the still form, landing on the floor in front of the bed. "You're not touching him!"

"Watch her," said Zhyaf's voice from the doorway. "She's prepared to kill."

"Then do something, dammit! Mind-zap her or whatever the hell it is you do!" said Dzyash angrily.

Keeza crouched lower, tail lashing from side to side in warning. "Leave him alone! You caused his injuries, you've done him enough harm!"

Guards pushed Zhyaf aside, training their guns on Keeza. "Move away," ordered the lead one, waving his rifle at Keeza. "Let the medic through."

She remembered the pain of the last time and glanced over her shoulder at Kezule. Did he need help? He said not to let them wake him, but if he was dying, surely that was different? Confused, she backed up till she felt the bed behind her then turned to touch his face. Cold, icy cold. She heard a movement and looked up at them again, growling warningly.

"Keeza, we've got no time! Let me examine him, please," said the medic.

He was right, she should let him check Kezule. He mustn't die because of her. She'd be failing in her trust if she allowed that to happen. Still growling, she moved aside, not taking her eyes off the guards and their guns.

Dzyash was at the bedside in an instant, pulling back the covers, feeling at Kezule's throat for a pulse.

Nayla joined him, opening the medikit he'd placed on the bed. Searching through it, she drew out a vial and began loading the hypo.

"Epinephrin compound," he snapped, holding out his hand for it.

"Loaded," she said, passing it. "Standard dose for resuss. You could kill him . . ." she began.

"He's dead if I don't," he said, putting the hypo to Kezule's neck. As he did, the Valtegan's clawed hand closed round his throat.

With a full-throated roar, Kezule surged from the bed, shaking Dzyash once as he took in his surroundings. Turning, he saw Keeza's eyes widen briefly before she flung herself at the Sholan opposite her. Feeling blood trickling down his hand, he remembered the one he was holding. As if he weighed no more than a chiddoe, he lifted him and threw him at the guards.

Hearing the mewl of fear from beside him, he reached out and pulled the female in front of him as a shield. Keeza, he saw, had hold of the other, and his gun.

"Bring him here," he ordered, moving toward the fallen guard. With his foot, he snagged one of the rifles, pulling it closer. Shifting his grip on her, he took her by the throat and carefully leaned down to pick up the gun.

Dragging her captive with her, Keeza raced across to join him, landing a vicious kick to the head of the guard who was scrabbling for the one remaining weapon. He collapsed and seconds later, she had the rifle.

"We're leaving," Kezule said, aiming at the two guards blocking the doorway. "Move, or die."

Beside him, Keeza fired. One of the guards collapsed, screaming in agony. She fired again, and his screams were silenced. The other dropped his weapon, and arms held high, backed away from the door.

"Better safe," she said, looking at him. "They want you too much."

She was right. He'd been out of the field for too long. "Do you know this place?"

She nodded, and taking her captive in a similar neck hold, began to move forward. "I know the way out."

"They'll have exits covered. Need a different way," he said following her.

As they emerged into the corridor, they could see the guards at the far end, alerted by the noise, coming toward them.

"Main exit's through them," said Keeza, making sure to keep her prisoner in front of her.

"Behind?"

"More rooms, an elevator, no exits."

"Windows. We need a room with windows." He shook the female, careful of his strength and claws. He needed her alive. "Take us to one."

Nayla pointed down the corridor. "Down there," she croaked.

"We go this way," he said to Keeza, heading down the corridor, keeping his back to the wall. "Which one?" he hissed in his captive's ear. "Trick us, and you'll die like your friend. Help us, you'll go free."

Keeza hit the door lock on the cell before following him.

The guards at the far end were approaching slowly. Hearing a familiar faint whine, she flattened herself and her hostage to the wall, reaching out to press Kezule back as an energy bolt hissed past them.

"Tell them not to shoot," said Keeza, twisting the male so he was facing the advancing troopers.

"Don't shoot!" he said, his voice shaking as he clutched at the hand gripping his neck.

"Louder!" She jabbed the gun into his side.

"Don't shoot! They'll kill us!" he yelled, dropping his arms and trying to steady himself against the wall.

At Stronghold, L'Seuli charged unceremoniously into the Guild Master's bedroom, activating the light as he entered.

"Kezule's broken out," he said, picking up Rhyaz's clothes and handing them to him. "An aircar's being readied for us now."

"What?" Rhyaz rubbed the sleep from his eyes and reached automatically for what his aide was holding out to him.

"Kezule's escaped," repeated L'Seuli. "He and Keeza have Zhyaf Rakula and Nayla Kiolma as hostages."

Rhyaz was up in an instant. "Inform the Aldatan Estate," he ordered, pulling on his robe. "And get an . . ."

"The estate's been informed and a speeder is waiting in the courtyard. I've also told Father Lijou."

"Any casualties? In Vartra's name, how'd he get out?" he asked, buckling on his weapons belt and moving toward the door.

"Three casualties. Dzyash Liosoe, the medic on duty with Zhyaf and Nayla, and two of the guards. The medical alarm was triggered by Kezule's bio-sensor, and they went in. We don't know any more yet because he's taken the surviving team members," said L'Seuli, running to keep up with him.

Garras reached for his wrist comm and, picking it up, stumbled from the bedroom into the lounge. Activating it, he slumped down in the nearest chair.

"Whatizzit?" he mumbled.

"Garras, Ruth here. It's Mara. Something's happened to Zhyaf! I need Vanna's help now!"

"What?" he demanded, instantly awake. "Mara? And Zhyaf? He's at . . ."

"Shanagi, I know! Can you get Vanna here as quickly as possible?"

"On our way," he said, already heading back to the bedroom. He'd scarcely entered the room when L'Seuli called from Stronghold.

"Kezule's escaped and taken Zhyaf as a hostage," the Brother said.

"I know. Just had Ruth call about it. Hold on, I need to wake Vanna."

Vanna was already sitting up. "I heard. Mara?"

"Ruth needs help. You head over there, I'll arrange a sitter for Marak and join you."

She nodded. "Wake Jack, I'll need him, too," she said, scrambling out of bed and grabbing her clothes. "Get the center alerted. I'll be taking Mara there."

Garras nodded and returned to his call. "What happened?"

"No real details at present. All we know is he and Keeza are at large in the building and Zhyaf is one of two hostages. Neither of them know he's a telepath, which could be to the good or not. I need you to keep a line of communication open to us. You'll probably know more about what's going on than we do."

"Vanna's taking Mara to the medical center here. Patch through to them and we'll pick you up there. Keep me posted, L'Seuli."

The line cleared, Garras grabbed his robe, slipped it on, and fastened it quickly. That done, he headed back for the lounge and started his calls.

For a wonder, Mara had seemed quite calm and had readily agreed to accompany Vanna to the center. Clutching tightly to Ruth's arm, she now sat on the edge of the bed in one of the private rooms.

"It's Keeza that's got Zhyaf," she said, "not Kezule. He's got the other one, Nayla." Her eyes were wide and she was shivering.

"What is Zhyaf seeing or feeling at the moment?" asked Vanna from her chair opposite the young Human girl.

"Keeza's using him as a shield. He's worried about the guards. He's afraid they'll shoot him by accident."

Garras, entering the room quietly, heard her last remark. "They've been told," he said. "They will do nothing to endanger his life, believe me. They're going to try to negotiate with them."

Mara turned to look at him. "Negotiate? What can you offer him?" she asked, the first real note of panic in her voice. "He's alone, a captive on a hostile alien world, stranded in time, for God's sake! What can you possibly offer him?"

Garras said nothing as he looked at his mate.

"Let's see what happens, Mara," said Vanna, leaning forward to hold her hand. "He might want to negotiate, you don't know. Is Zhyaf capable of speaking to them?"

"He's too frightened, Vanna! All I'm getting is coming through our Link—he won't communicate with me. They're using Nayla to lead them to a room with a window." She stopped suddenly, looking over to Garras again. "If you tell them what's happening, they'll know! They'll kill him!" she said, her voice rising in fear. "Zhyaf told me weeks ago that Keeza's become sensitive because of him. She'll know, Vanna! She'll feel him if he sends to me!"

Vanna looked at Garras. "She's right," she said. "If they

find out he's spying on them, telling us what they're planning . . ."

"Knowledge that could also help save their lives," said Garras. "We have to tell them at Shanagi, Mara. Let them decide. They're the ones on the spot after all."

"No!" There was a note of hysteria now as she clung tighter to Ruth. "Zhyaf isn't risking it, I won't!"

Vanna patted her hand again and got to her feet. "All right, Mara. We won't push you. I'm going to leave you here with Ruth for a moment. I'll just be next door if you need me."

Mara nodded, and Vanna could feel her eyes boring into her back as she left the room. She sent to Garras, asking him to join her. Once outside, she drew him over to the nursing station opposite, where Jack was sitting with the on-duty medic.

"You will not press her for details of what's happening," she said firmly to her mate. "Both of them are frightened enough without that! She's no more than a youngling, and she's staring her own death in the jaws here, amid what should be the safety of her friends!" A shudder ran through her at the horror of the situation and she reached out to touch Garras for comfort.

"We need the information, Vanna," he said, drawing her close. "Rhyaz and L'Seuli are on their way there now. We can't afford to let him get free, nor Keeza in her present state!"

"Two lives are at risk, Garras," she said, then stopped. "Gods, I forgot Josh! He's Linked to her, too!"

"Only a minor one," said Garras, "but we should have him here in case." He looked over to the medic. "Call him, get him over here, but leave the explanations to us." He turned back to Vanna. "Three lives have already been lost. If they escape, many more will be at risk, perhaps even ours. They must be stopped, Vanna."

"Let me go in and speak to the lass, Vanna," said Jack. "I know Ruth's with her, but I've been involved in similar situations on Keis. Ruth, bless her, hasn't."

"I have to look out for the welfare of my patients, Jack. I don't feel it's in *her* best interests to push her! If she gets hysterical, what do we do? Sedate her and risk Zhyaf collapsing, too? And what if they do kill Zhyaf?"

"We unfortunately get the chance to try out that tech nique we were discussing," said Jack.

Garras looked at him with interest.

"Sholans expect to die if their Leska dies, but Humans haven't been brought up with that belief," the doctor said "It might be possible to keep her alive if Zhyaf is killed."

"How?" Garras looked skeptically from one to the other.

"The Triads are the key. We're hoping that the third partner can replace the missing Leska," said Vanna.

Garras' expression softened. "I can understand why you'd like to think it possible, but I really don't believe it is. Mixed Leska pairs are much more strongly Linked than the Sholan ones. Look at the pair we lost. The lad died and so did the Human female. And Josh isn't even a fully Talented telepath."

"They hadn't been allowed to pair even once, and they weren't a Triad," objected Vanna. "As far as we can tell, it's the shock of the other's death that kills the partner. If we were able to cushion her, support her mentally, have Josh there, too, it might work."

"Would she want to live with Zhyaf dead? Prolonging life for the sake of it isn't right, Vanna."

"Mara? Yes, she'd want to live. She gets on with Zhyaf now they don't have to live together, but it's Josh who's the love of her young life."

"Shall I go in, then?" asked Jack.

"Yes, you go in, Jack. I'll wait for Josh with Garras."

"I need to be there to relay what we find," objected her mate.

Vanna looked at him. "Give Jack a chance to talk to her without her fearing her every word is being passed to the troops at Shanagi."

Garras sighed. "Very well."

"The next room," whimpered Nayla, her voice trembling with fear.

"Check this one," said Kezule as they stopped by a bend in the corridor. "I'll remain here." He turned to look at Keeza, staring at her with unblinking eyes. "Do not harm him. We'll take him with us."

Keeza nodded and moved toward the door. The corridor was short, only two rooms on one side, on the other, the elevator as the female had said. Activating the first door, he peered cautiously in as it began to slide open. It was a small staff lounge, empty at this time of night, and there was a window.

Hauling Zhyaf with her, she made for the far wall and peered carefully out into the night. A deserted quadrangle, bounded by lawns and three low brick walls. To one side she could make out an aircar. She let out a low chuckle as she started back to Kezule.

"So it's your car," she said. "Fitting that we should use it."

"Keeza," said Zhyaf, keeping his voice low as he stumbled along in her grip, "think what you're doing. You should be helping us, not him."

From outside, they could hear an exchange of shots and the low, terrified yowling of Nayla.

"Shut up!" she hissed, shaking him, her claws just puncturing the flesh on the sides of his neck. "Why should I help you? You've done nothing for me! He fed me, gave me a purpose when you abandoned me!"

"We never beat you! He did!"

"I deserved it. You beat him for no reason," she snarled, hauling him back to the door. "Now shut up! It's thanks to him you're still alive!"

Looking out, she saw Kezule standing on her side of the bend. "General!" she called quietly, pitching her voice so he would hear her. When he looked at her, she gestured with her gun.

"For Vartra's sake, think, Keeza," Zhyaf hissed. "He'll kill you when he's free! He won't need you then! You have no future with him!"

She leaned forward, biting his ear sharply, making him yowl in pain, a sound cut off abruptly as she tightened her grip on the back of his neck. "I have no future with you! I killed two guards, you want I should kill you, too?"

Kezule took in the hostage's bleeding ear as he ran toward her. He'd forgotten she'd be aggressively violent toward males other than him. "Remember who's in charge," he said icily, pushing her back inside. "Do not hurt him again!"

"Yes, General," she said, forcing her ears down in apology. "There is a window, and an aircar."

Kezule sealed the door and slung his rifle over his shoulder. "The pistol," he ordered, holding out his hand. She

gave it to him and he fired at the locking plate, destroyir
it. "See to the window," he said, handing it back and glan
ing around the room for something with which to bind th
captives. An overall lying across the back of a chair caugh
his eye.

Pushing Nayla onto the chair, he took hold of the overa
and began ripping lengths from it. Swiftly he bound he
then joined Keeza.

"The window's sealed. I'll need to break it."

"Do so. Give him to me," he ordered, taking hold c
Zhyaf's wrists and tying them together. "Hurry. They ar
close behind."

Keeza backed off from the window, aimed her rifle at i
and fired. Nothing happened. She spat curses. "Stun guns,'
she said with disgust as she pulled the pistol from he
pocket again. Standing to one side, she leveled the pistc
at the window and fired. The glass exploded in a showe
of shards. Using the rifle butt, she swept the frame clear o
shards. She hesitated, remembering what the male had saic
and looked at Kezule. "The poison in my arm . . ."

"Will be seen to. Now go." He pushed her forward anc
a moment later she was standing in the courtyard holdin,
her hands up to take Zhyaf from him.

She staggered slightly under his weight, letting him fal
with her support to land on his feet. Grabbing him by the
arm, she hustled him over to the aircar. Stopping, she rifled
in his pockets for his card. Pushing it into the reader set
on the vehicle's wing, she waited impatiently for the door
to slide open. A worried glance behind told her Kezule was
following, bringing the female with him.

"Please, you said you'd spare me," Nayla whimpered
when he stopped. "I told you where the window was."

Keeza shoved Zhyaf inside and followed him, making
sure he was secured in the rear seat by the safety strap.
Then, she clambered into the pilot's seat and shoved the
card into the slot. Hearing a thump, she glanced over to
see Nayla drop bonelessly to the ground.

"Go," he said, climbing in behind her and closing the
door.

"They've killed her!" said Mara, leaping to her feet.
"Oh, God! They've killed Nayla!" She began pacing the

om, wringing her hands, a look of terror on her face.
They've taken him with them!"

"Mara, if they've taken him, they want him alive," said
uth soothingly, getting up to take hold of her fosterling.

Mara avoided her and darted round the other side of her
ed. "You don't understand," she said, leaning forward on
. "He killed Nayla! He promised he would let her go!
hyaf's next, and that means me!" Her voice ended on a
igh-pitched wail.

Jack eased himself out of his chair. "Vanna, m'dear, I
nink we have to sedate Mara now. She's obviously becom-
ng too hysterical for Zhyaf's good. Would you mind hand-
ng me your hypo?"

"Don't you come near me," said Mara angrily, pulling
erself upright again. "How dare you suggest that! You
now that it'll affect Zhyaf!"

"And so will your hysterics!" Jack snapped, his mustache
airly bristling with an anger equal to hers. "Pull yourself
ogether, girl! He's the one facing that damned Valtegan,
ot you, he needs his wits about him! Give the man a
hance, Mara," he said, softening his tone as he saw tears
egin to spill down her cheeks. "Kezule and that Keeza
woman are only two people. Through you, Zhyaf has all of
is to help him and give him advice. Now send to him, lass.
Tell him to keep calm, we're doing everything we can."

She covered her face with her hands and began to sob
gently as Jack eased his way toward her and enfolded her
in his bear hug. "Come on, lass," he said, patting her back
gently as he brought her back into the center of the room.
"You have to be brave for both of you."

There was something he'd noticed while in laalgo, something alien about himself, he remembered. What was it?
He thought back, trying to recall it.

"Where to, General?" Keeza asked as she headed out
of the grounds of the installation, then upward to lose
themselves in the traffic that passed overhead.

Irritated at the interruption, Kezule turned in his seat to
look at the captive Sholan behind him. "I want countryside—woodland in which to lose us. Which direction?" he
demanded.

Zhyaf heard the question but couldn't make his brain
work. He was numb with fear. He knew just how deadly

Kezule was. The Valtegan reached out for him, nonretra
tile claws coming closer to his face. He shrank back in h
seat, opened his mouth—and found it too dry to speak. H
swallowed furiously, managing to get enough spit togethe
to croak an answer.

"West. Taykui Forest."

"Hey, this thing's got onboard mapping!" said Keez
fiddling with the multitude of recessed switches. "We'v
got ourselves an important hostage here, General. Hol
on, I'm finding Shanagi. Yes. He's right. The forest's t
the west."

"Head for there. Can this craft be tracked?"

Zhyaf shook his head. "Only if you use satellite link."

Keeza made an impressed noise. "Real important, th
male. Who are you?" she demanded, looking back briefl
His face was vaguely familiar, but from where? She turne
her attention to the aircar's comm where the airway route
were being displayed. They were coming up to a westerl
turnoff point.

Kezule turned back to look out the front of the craft. A
he did, he realized that the windshield afforded a clear viev
of the occupants. "I can be seen," he said, sliding down o
the seat.

"No," croaked Zhyaf. "'Screen's opaque from outside
Can't see in."

He looked to Keeza for confirmation.

"On the upmarket models, yes, and this is definitely one
of those. It feels like he's telling the truth."

Kezule kept his gaze on her. Feels like the truth? Wha
was she saying? Could she be aware of the male's thoughts?
If she was one of the mind readers, he'd have known by
now, surely. The ones who'd brought him to this time had
touched his mind, stolen his words. If she could do that,
she'd have done it before now, if only to have avoided
his beatings.

"Feels like the truth?"

She shrugged, keeping her eyes on the other traffic as
she banked the vehicle to the left, joining the flow of traffic
heading west. "I had strange dreams while you were in
laalgo. I heard the alarm before they came in for you this
evening."

He turned so he could see them both. "The alarm. What
caused it?" he demanded.

"He should know, he was one of the three that came in
st," she said.

"Thought you were dying. Came to help you," Zhyaf
id. "Please, a drink. Can't talk. Mouth too dry."

Kezule hissed in annoyance.

"Where?" asked Keeza.

"The button on your door. In there."

Keeza pressed a claw tip into the recess. A hatch slid
ack revealing a collection of drink and food containers.
he took two drinks at random and handed them to Kezule.

"I will fly this craft," he hissed. "I will not feed him!"

"I think I'd be better piloting, General," she said care-
ully. "I know these vehicles, know the traffic regulations."

The hiss turned to a snarl. Again she was right. He glared
t Zhyaf. "First tell me what set the alarm off."

The captive's eyes widened in fear as he tried to look
way from him. "I . . . don't know."

Kezule's hand lashed out with a blow that rocked his
ead, bouncing it off the interior wall. "What set it off!"
e demanded.

"I don't know," moaned Zhyaf, tears of pain clouding
is sight as he tried to sit up.

Grasping him by the throat, Kezule pulled him forward
ntil the safety strap stopped him. "Tell me!"

"Bio-sensors!" he whimpered. "Under your skin."

Shoving him back into his seat, Kezule began to curse in
is own language while hastily pressing along the inside of
is right thigh. That was what he'd been trying to remem-
er! Oh, they were cunning, these furred vermin, but not
as cunning as he would be! He found it: a tiny, regular
lump, unnoticeable until he'd known it was there. Clenching the muscle, he scored the taut flesh with his claw tip,
then applied pressure on either side of the wound. Blood
oozed out, bringing with it the tiny sensor. Picking it up,
he put it between his teeth and bit down sharply on it.

"Now we cannot be tracked. Unless . . ." He looked back
at Zhyaf.

"No more I know of," he stammered.

"Beside you, General," Keeza said, nodding toward him.
"First aid kit in the door unit."

Inside he found a medical case with adhesive dressings.
He took one and placed it over the small cut. That seen
to, he opened the first drink container, and leaning back,

held it to Zhyaf's lips, letting him quench his thirst. Wh
he'd done, he opened the other for himself.

"They thought you'd died?" Keeza asked.

He glanced consideringly at her. She had no need
know the details. "Part of laalgo," was all he said.

"There's food as well. Can you eat anything other th:
raw meat?"

"No," he said shortly. "In the forest I can hunt. Mu
eat soon." Already the rush of energy from his awakenir
was beginning to dissipate. He needed answers from th
male, answers he already knew Keeza didn't have. Handi
the empty containers to her, he turned once more to h
hostage.

"What the hell have you done to her?" Josh demande
as soon as he saw Mara. One side of her face was swolle
and already beginning to turn a livid purple. He was :
her side instantly, his arms protectively around her, glarin
at them.

Ghyan shut the door and reached mentally for Rut!
Vanna had her hands full at the moment explaining to Jos
what had happened. The exchange only took seconds, bu
by the end of it, he knew all that had gone before. Th
situation was indeed grim. He glanced at Garras, noting th
ear piece and throat microphone he was using.

"The bio-feed's dead," Garras said quietly. "We've n
way of tracking them now."

Mara heard him anyway. She pulled herself away fron
Josh and faced him. "It wasn't Zhyaf," she said defensively
"He didn't say where it was. Kezule knew, he didn't ever
need to ask him!"

"Mara, no one's criticizing Zhyaf. He's the one there,'
said Garras. "He must do what he has to do to survive. Nc
one will blame him for telling Kezule about the bio-feed.''

She nodded, wrapping her arms tight around her chest,
and began to pace the room again.

She's hardly sat still since we brought her here, sent
Vanna.

*We'd do the same. When she can do nothing to help,
movement is her only palliative,* Ghyan replied, deftly moving their thoughts to a private level where there was no
possibility of Mara or anyone else overhearing them.

Zhyaf will allow her to tell us nothing about where they *e.* *He says Keeza has been sensitized, could pick him up.* *Understandable. Now tell me, how may I help?*

She indicated the group gathered in the room. *We're* *ne of us really experienced telepaths, Ghyan. Is it possible* *r you to reach Zhyaf without . . .*

He cut her short. *No. I hope no one has tried.* There was *a* anger in his mental tone. *Zhyaf is experienced. If he says* *e's in danger, then his judgment must be accepted.*

Vanna sighed. *I thought as much. No, no one has tried.* *he Brotherhood are leaving this to us. Zhyaf is an En'-* *halla, after all. In that case, I need your help in a different* *irection, Ghyan. If the worst should happen, I need your* *elp to try and save Mara's life.*

As she outlined her plan, Ghyan listened in disbelief, *aking his head. Impossible!*

Try, Ghyan. That's all I ask. Support me. If the gestalt *iggers, I need Josh's mind there to answer it, to take hold* *f it and use it to bind him to Mara.*

Vanna, what you're asking is . . .

You've never experienced a gestalt. Believe me, it can *nove mountains! Carrie used it to shape-change—it left her* *ith eyes like ours!*

I have often wondered about that.

Just try, Ghyan! It could save her life!

I'll do what I can, of course . . .

Jack leaned toward Garras. "What's happening at *hanagi?"*

"Rhyaz has alerted the Protectorate to try and track *lown Zhyaf's aircar. They don't hold out much hope,* *hough.* The spaceport's on alert, as is the seaport and all *najor aircar hire firms. The Brotherhood is starting sweeps* *of the surrounding countryside on the assumption that he* *sn't likely to go to ground in the city. For one thing, there's* *he food problem. Where could he get fresh raw meat with-* *out attracting attention?"*

"What the hell does he intend to do? Just hide?"

Garras shrugged. "He could try and steal a suitable craft *and head home, except, does he know where it is, and* *would he be welcome on a world fifteen hundred years* *older than he is? This wasn't a planned escape, Jack, it was* *one of opportunity. My bet is he has no plan at present."*

* * *

"We've left the city limits now, General," said Keez "There's very little traffic here at this time. We'll stick o like a sore tail."

Kezule considered the options. Stay in the air and dra attention to themselves, or land and be vulnerable to searc parties because they weren't far enough away from the cit On balance, he'd rather take his chances on land. "Fin somewhere to set us down. Somewhere we can conce: the craft."

"There's what looks like a clearing up ahead."

"Take it."

Josh, placated now, was sitting on the bed trying to per suade Mara to stop pacing. "You'll only wear yourself ou make him tired, too," he said.

She stopped. "He was due home later tonight. Our Lin day is due," she whispered.

Thank Vartra! Vanna sent to Ghyan. *Our first piece o hope!*

The priest turned to her in surprise.

Don't you see? It could make strengthening her Link wit Josh easier!

Keeza taxied the craft under the overhanging branche: of the nearest trees, bringing it slowly to a stop. She turnec to look at Kezule, face creasing in concern when she saw the state of him. His skin had paled to the point where i seemed blanched of color. It accentuated his thinness. Like the last time he'd woken, he'd burned off a lot of his body fat.

"Gods, you're freezing as well as starving!" she said. "I forgot you need clothing for warmth!" Reaching for the console, she switched on the heating unit. "You, come here," she ordered, reaching back for Zhyaf. "I want your clothing!"

"There are clothes on board," he said quietly. "I was due to return home tonight."

"Huh! Your unlucky night, wasn't it? Where are they?"

"In the locker beside me," he said, nodding to the stor-age unit that took up the space next to him.

Reaching over her seat, she pressed the release for the locker. The door swung open to reveal a carry bag. Grasp-ing hold of it, she pulled it forward onto her lap and began going through the contents. Her rummaging revealed a pale gray tunic and a woolen robe of purple edged with black. Keeping them, she flung the bag behind her.

"This first, General, then the robe," she said, passing them to Kezule.

Forcing his frozen limbs to move, Kezule took the clothes from her and began to put them on. Already the cabin was warmer and he was beginning to thaw out. He began to see the advantages of a fur pelt.

Accompanied by L'Seuli, Rhyaz strode into the military building where Kezule had been housed. "Where's Nayla Kiolma?" he demanded of the guards on duty.

"In the medical bay, sir, along with the injured guards," said the senior trooper. He turned to one of his men. "Take the Guild Master to the . . ."

Rhyaz was already on his way. "Damned incompetent . . ."

"Us or them, sir?" murmured L'Seuli, trying to keep pace with him.

Rhyaz glanced at him as they reached the open doors of the control room and, next to it, Kezule's cell. "What's that supposed to mean?"

"That it was our team who broke security regulations."

He stepped into the cell. Blood had sprayed everywhere, decorating the walls and ceiling with arcs of crimson that had run in myriad tiny rivulets toward the floor. The metallic scent of it filled the air. *Like a slaughterhouse,* thought Rhyaz. *Kezule would have been right at home here.* On his right he saw the body of a guard, his face convulsed in agony.

"That would be the one Keeza killed with the stunner. The other," L'Seuli nodded to the left. "She broke his neck with a kick to the head."

"Feisty," Rhyaz murmured, looking. "I can see how she survived the packs."

Beyond the second guard, lying in a pool of blood, was the medic from the control room.

"Dzyash Liosoe," supplied L'Seuli as he followed Rhyaz across the room to look down at the body. Seeing something glittering under the table, he went to retrieve it. "Hypoderm, loaded with a Valtegan stimulant," he said, examining it. "They must have reacted to a medical emergency."

"This was not our team, L'Seuli," said Rhyaz, bending down to look at the corpse. He gently moved the head to one side to get a closer look at the wounds. "We had no medic because of the danger of this happening. Recording should have taken precedence, not medical intervention." Five puncture wounds, one through the carotid. He'd seen enough. Turning, he left the room, heading for the medical bay next door.

Nayla lay on an examination bed with the physician tending her. On nearby chairs sat the two surviving guards, one covered in blood that was obviously not his own. They were being questioned by the senior officer on duty. Seeing Rhyaz enter, he snapped to attention, arms crossed over his chest, head bowing briefly in salute. "Guild Master Rhyaz, I am just debriefing these . . ."

"L'Seuli, see to it," Rhyaz said, going over the injured female. "You, Lieutenant, get the security vid set up for me. I want to see for myself what happened."

"Yes, sir!"

The physician turned round and dipped his head in lieu of a salute. "Slight concussion and bruising to the head, nothing more, Master Rhyaz," he said. "She's been severely traumatized, though, and I suggest that questioning her . . ."

"I need the information now," said Rhyaz, cutting him short. "Kezule is at large with an En'Shalla Leska telepath as hostage. That takes precedence, I'm afraid."

"The guards can tell you as much . . ." He ground to a halt and stepped back as Rhyaz continued to look at him.

She was already beginning to sit up as he stepped closer to the bed. "Nayla, why did you go into Kezule's cell?"

"He died, Guild Master," she said, running a trembling hand across her ears. "The alarm went off as he flatlined. Dzyash said we had to save him because of Keeza. I swear by Vartra, Master Rhyaz, he *was* dead!"

"Where were the guards on duty outside the cell?"

"There were none," she said.

"Carry on."

"Dzyash was about to give him the stimulant when suddenly he . . . he . . . just sprang at him!" She was shaking, eyes wide with fear, obviously reliving the moment.

"Continue your report, Sub-Lieutenant Kiolma!" he ordered sharply.

She drew a shaking breath and her trembling began to lessen. "Kezule caught Dzyash by the throat and leaped up from the bed, then he threw him at the guards and grabbed hold of me."

"Did you see what Keeza was doing?"

"Some. When Kezule grabbed Dzyash, she went for Zhyaf, then attacked the guards, kicking one and shooting the other. Then they dragged us out into the corridor. The exit was blocked by troopers, so he wanted to leave by a window. They forced me to tell them where the nearest room with one was." She looked up at him, her eyes and her voice asking for compassion.

He nodded. From the amount of dried blood on her clothing, she could only have been a few feet away from Kezule when he'd killed Dzyash. "You did the right thing, Lieutenant. Continue, if you please."

"I . . . I took them there—it was the small mess room on this floor, the one looking out on the eastern quadrangle. There was an aircar. They used that to escape. I thought he was going to kill me at the end," she said, rubbing at her eyes as they began to overflow with tears. "When he raised his arm . . . Then I woke up in here."

"At any point did they discuss where they intended to go, what they intended to do?"

"No, sir. They had no time. I'm sure this wasn't a planned escape. Kezule—he moved so *fast,* sir!"

Rhyaz patted her briefly on the shoulder. "Your actions, from the time you were taken hostage, were acceptable, Sub-Lieutenant Kiolma. You did nothing to put either yourself or Zhyaf at risk. I'll leave you with the physician for now. In the morning, see that your report reaches me by fifth hour. If you aren't fit to do it yourself, ask for a Recorder to transcribe it. Put down every detail you remember, no matter how trivial it seems."

He rejoined L'Seuli, drawing him away from the guards. "Well?"

"The guards on duty outside the cell had left their post. They decided to stroll down to those guarding the corridor leading to the elevator," said L'Seuli, his tone one of anger and disgust. "We have one of each pair here."

Rhyaz nodded, catching sight of the Lieutenant standing in the doorway. "The vid's ready. This I want to see," he

said, his tone grim. "Any news from the Aldatan Estate?
Or if they've got a fix on Kezule using the bio-monitor?"

L'Seuli flicked his ears in denial, adjusting the earpiece
through which he was being constantly updated. "The bio-
monitor went dead a few minutes ago. He must have found
it, though how, I've no idea. As for Mara, she's still only
getting information through their passive link—wait!" He
stopped dead, putting his hand up to his ear and listening
intently. "Zhyaf's sent to Mara. Kezule's been questioning
him about the Aldatans—where they live, how far it is, has
the female had her cub. Zhyaf's asking what to tell him."

"He's lying," said Keeza, frowning as she looked at the
map over his shoulder. "They don't live in the mountains,
or even on that side of the continent." She pushed her
hand past Zhyaf and ran a finger across the map, waiting
for his reaction. The flash of fear was as strong as she'd
hoped. "Here."

"I can smell him," grunted Kezule. "You're right."

She looked at the name of the nearest town. "Valsgarth!" she said, grasping Zhyaf by the shoulder and turning him round to face her. "The telepath town! I remember
you now!" She frowned, trying to concentrate. The memory
was there if only she could find it, but everything about the
past was so hazy, and thinking about it made her head hurt.

"He's a mind reader?" hissed Kezule. "They talk to each
other, steal thoughts!"

Keeza's claws tightened on Zhyaf's shoulder, digging
through to his flesh, making him mewl with pain. The pain
in her head grew worse, a pounding throbbing that
wouldn't stop. She shook her head. "Off-world? They're
gone, not here?"

"Who?" Kezule demanded, reaching out for her. "Who's
gone off-world?"

'Them. The ones you want, the Aldatans." She was beginning to sway as the pain threatened to engulf her. Her
grasp on Zhyaf loosened, and she slumped back in her seat.
"You did things to my mind," she moaned, putting her
hands up to massage her aching temples. Then Kezule's
clawed hand gripped her shoulder and she was pulled
toward him and shaken violently.

"They are the Aldatans? All three of them?"

Her concentration broken, she found the mist of pain

efore her eyes begin to lift. "Yes. He lied," she said, glaring at Zhyaf. "They live at Valsgarth, on the estate where ll the mixed Leskas live, him, too. He has a Human partner like her—like Carrie."

Kezule released her, turning to Zhyaf. "A telepath like hem. Is that true?"

Zhyaf said nothing, just shrank back in his seat.

Anger raged through him. "They talk to each other without words," he said. "They can tell where we are!"

"No! I haven't told them!"

Kezule lunged forward, and Keeza heard a sickening rack. More slowly, the Valtegan sat back in his seat and ooked at Keeza.

She knew that cold, unblinking stare. "No. Not me, my General," she whimpered, setting her ears flat against her ead and trying to make herself as small as possible. "He sed my mind! I'm not a telepath!" Her words ended on wail of fear as she cringed away from him, crossing her orearms in front of her face. But nothing happened.

After a moment or two, she risked looking between her aised arms. He was still staring at her.

"You, I need," he said. "Gather food and drink. We eave now."

Slowly she lowered her arms. "The aircar?"

"We leave it here. As you said, there's not enough traffic. Easier to kill us in the air, not so easy on the ground where we can hide." He picked up the map and began to fold t. "Hurry!"

CHAPTER 14

"Keeza's asking him where Carrie and Kusac live. He's told them in the mountains, by Ranz, but she's sensed he's lying." Hands clasped in front of herself, Mara kept walking back and forth over the same piece of carpet.

"She's dragging her finger across the map, making him look." The tremor in her voice was increasing and she was rubbing her thumbs across each other in a small, repetitive gesture. "He's afraid she'll sense his fear and know which town . . . She's picked him up! She knows—knows it's Valsgarth and he's a telepath—and she remembers him!" Mara stopped dead, her face draining of all color, and began to whimper in fear. "Keeza's telling Kezule what Zhyaf is and that he did things to her mind. Oh, God! He's so *afraid* Kezule's coming for him!" Her voice rose in pitch as her fear increased.

Vanna moved toward her. "Mara," she began, but the girl crouched down in an unconscious imitation of her Leska's position, trying to back away. Suddenly her hands flew protectively to her neck, and with a shriek of pure terror, she collapsed.

"Ghyan, do it!" ordered Vanna, leaping across the room to the girl's side. "Stop her from dying!" The hypoderm was against Mara's neck and the stimulant administered before she'd finished speaking.

For some time, the priest had been gently touching the edges of Mara's mind without her being aware of his passive presence. Now, at the moment of Zhyaf's death, Ghyan flinched. Too much was at stake, though, and he pushed himself to overcome not only his own fears but hers. As she collapsed, screaming her disbelief, he reached out mentally and grasped hold of her consciousness.

"Josh, get over here," snapped Vanna, sitting back and handing the hypo to Jack to reload. "Get her up on the

ed, and hold onto her. Let her know you're there. Reach
ut with your mind and touch hers! Ghyan will be there to
elp you."

Mara wanted to live, but the Link still bound her to
Zhyaf. Inexorably she was being drawn down with him.
Then she felt Ghyan's presence trapping her, preventing
her from following.

She fought against it, her fists batting weakly at the arms
that held her. Why was he trying to stop her? He must
know she had to follow her Leska. Another mind flared
beside hers. She looked eagerly. Zhyaf! It had to be,
couldn't be anyone else! Then she realized the touch was
Josh's.

"No," she mumbled. "Lemme go." Talking hurt. Her
throat, it ached so! She felt the sting of the hypo against
her neck again, the rush as the stimulant surged through
her body. Gasping for breath, she sensed the room growing
darker and colder around her.

Stay with us, Mara, she heard Ghyan saying. *You don't
need to leave. Stay with us.* But the thoughts and voices
around her were fading as she was pulled farther and farther from them.

She'd thought herself beyond additional terror, but suddenly, with a stark clarity, she realized what was happening
to her: She was dying. She tried to scream but was unable
to make her bruised and crushed throat work. *No!* she
shrieked silently. *I wasn't killed!* The darkness and the coldness were closing round her inexorably, like the waters of
Risho Bay.

As she silently shrieked her denial again, a power she'd
only felt once before exploded within her. Grasping it, she
held on. The other presence in her mind—Josh—was suddenly catapulted into its heart and she could sense him
floundering, trying desperately to understand the nature of
the gestalt.

Mara, help me. She could sense his confusion, the beginnings of fear; he was totally out of his depth. Nothing he'd
learned from Ghyan had prepared him for this—nothing
could. *Mara!*

His voice was growing fainter as she was swept toward
what remained of Zhyaf. Josh's presence was disrupting the
forces and already the gestalt was beginning to falter and

weaken. *I don't know how to control it! It only happene*
once before! she heard herself whimpering.

Josh tried desperately to fight back the nausea caused b
the swirling, sickening maelstrom of mental energies int
which he'd been thrust by Ghyan. Both their lives wer
now in the balance. It had been assumed Mara knew ho
to control this, but she didn't—she was almost as much c
a novice as he was! He had no instincts, nothing to guid
him; this was Sholan through and through, not Human
Then he remembered what she'd said. Control. She didn'
know how to control it.

He could feel them both slipping away from reality
nearer the yawning emptiness that terrified Mara. Th
voices of the others in the room were very faint, as was hi
perception of where he was. *Control,* and *where.* Was tha
it? Was it enough to be utterly determined they would re
main where they were, among the living? It was all he had

While he was still aware of his physical self, he graspe
Mara tightly, concentrating on seeing her mentally, pushing
aside the swirling colors as if parting his way through ar
impenetrable jungle. Faintly at first, the image of Mara'
face and body formed. As it did, he could feel her become
more solid in his arms, but it was a still puppet he held
not a living, breathing woman. He needed her mind. Reach
ing out with his, he searched, as he'd been taught, for hers
Finding it, he clung onto it as firmly as he was clinging onto
her physical body.

He could see it now, the black center of the whirlpoo
to which Mara was being drawn. There was still a sense of
Zhyaf there, but so faint now as to be almost imperceptible

No. You're not following him, he sent to her. *Stay with*
me, Mara. I need you. He's beyond that now. Let him gc
on in peace and stay with me.

On the brink of the darkness, she hesitated.

Taking advantage of this, he forced her to retreat, draw
ing her back with him. As he did, suddenly his awareness
expanded, encompassing Mara as well. Images flickered be
fore his eyes—images of Mara's life—moving faster and
faster till they became a continuous blur.

With a sickening jolt, suddenly it was over and he was
lying on the bed, Mara clasped tightly within his arms. He

felt her hand move. Confused and shocked as he was, this one fact penetrated. *She'd moved!*

I'm here. Her thought was faint, but it was enough as he took her face in his hands and began to kiss her. She *was* there, in his arms and in his mind, a constant presence, her thoughts flowing to him just as his were flowing to her.

Leskas, Mara sent.

He raised his head, looking around the now empty room, wondering why they were alone.

You shouldn't have come after me. You've bound us to each other. We're one now, Leskas.

He looked down at her. A single tear was rolling down her cheek. Pushing himself up on one elbow, he gently wiped it away. Now he felt her fears as if they were his own and realized that from now on, they were.

"I'm sorry Zhyaf's gone," he said, keeping his voice low. "He was a good person, but you were mismatched, Mara. There was nothing either of you could have done to make your relationship work."

"He died alone and in terror."

"Not alone, you were there, we all were. He knew that, Mara. He wouldn't have wanted you to die with him." He felt protective of her, something he'd never experienced toward any woman before. "You've no need to feel any guilt, ask Vanna." He looked round for the Physician, then remembered they were alone.

"They left because we're Leskas now," Mara said quietly.

"Huh?" He looked back at her. "Yes, I know, but why would they leave because of that?" Reaching out, he smoothed the hair back from her face, noticing for the first time just how blue her eyes were. The first stirrings of desire began, and he tried to push them aside.

"That's why. Leskas have to pair to complete their Link."

"We're already lovers," he said, stroking her cheek before realizing that wasn't doing a lot to help him deny his need to make love to her. He remembered just how close to death they'd come and shuddered.

"Not Leska lovers." She turned her face away from him. "It's too soon for me, Josh, but we'll have no choice now the Link's started to pull us together."

"How different can it be? Don't worry, it's too soon for

me, too, Mara." He began to let her go and move back,
but as he did, he felt a compulsion to return to her side.

She gave a shaky laugh and turned her head round again.
"Oh, it's different, and you're just starting to find out
how different."

He frowned. "You aren't making sense." He remained
by her side, wanting to leave, wanting to stay and hold her
close. Her scent drifted up to him., warm and feminine,
reminding him of honeysuckle on a summer's evening.

"You've never been able to smell my scent before."

Her words jerked his mind back from the daydream. "It's
your perfume," he said uneasily.

She shook her head. "Sholan senses. You took over my
Link with Zhyaf. You share those senses with me now."

"That's not possible. You know we've got less sensitive
noses than the Sholans," he objected as once more the
honeysuckle scent teased his nostrils. She touched his hand,
and it was as if fire spread to him through her fingertips.

"The Link's no respecter of feelings," she said quietly,
her fingers curling round his.

Suddenly he was aware of her desire, a twin flame to his
own. It rushed through him shattering his self-control. He
reached for her, pulling her close as he slipped back down
on the bed beside her. As his mouth closed on hers, it was
as if it was for the first time. She was so soft and warm,
her skin tasting like honey. He fumbled at the fastening of
her robe, his hands suddenly clumsy. Forcing himself to
slow down, he pushed it aside to find her naked beneath it.

With a groan, he suddenly became aware of his own
physical discomfort and began to haul at his belt buckle.
She helped him, her hands trembling in their combined
urgency. Finally he pulled her naked body against his, gasping at the strength of the compulsion to mate that now
surged through him.

Not yet, she sent, guiding his head down to her breasts.
It gets better.

Greedily he fastened his mouth over her nipple, catching
it between his teeth, feeling it harden, hearing her moan in
pleasure as she pressed herself closer, her fingers tightening
almost painfully in his hair. Her sensations coursed through
him, merging with his, increasing his desire.

She drew her fingernails down his back, making him
shudder. Then, cupping his face with one hand, she drew

him up and began to kiss him as her other hand trailed down his side to his hip.

Reluctantly he pulled back from her. "What are you doing to me?" he whispered, moving until he was kneeling between her legs. "It was never like this before."

For answer, she pulled him down on top of her, lifting herself up to meet him. As they joined, their minds merged once more, this time so absolutely that he lost all sense of his identity: there was only *them*, their hearts beating as one, their bodies moving in time as they climbed higher and higher to the climax that sealed them together.

As they lay catching their breath afterward, their minds began to part.

Leska Link. We're the only Human Leskas, he heard Mara say.

* * *

Dawn's light began to filter down through the canopy of trees, illuminating the gloom around them. They'd been walking for hours, it seemed to Keeza. They'd had two brief stops. On both occasions, Kezule had her startle the wildlife. Both times he'd managed to make a kill with the pistol. The first had been a large catlike predator distantly related to the Sholans. She'd had to run and fetch the body. Touching it made her gorge rise. Though offered some of the flesh, Keeza had refused, unable to stomach eating a creature that so closely resembled her own kind.

Kezule had shrugged and begun to eat.

The second kill had been a rhakla, and this she had shared with him. That stop had been shorter as the general had swiftly skinned and butchered the carcass then wrapped it in its pelt to take with them.

"The Aldatans, how long are they expected to be off-world, and where have they gone?" he asked.

"On a rescue mission," she said without thinking as he mindlessly put one foot in front of the other, praying that he'd call another halt before she collapsed. She was feeling decidedly unwell.

"How long?"

"Month to get there, same back, and however long it takes in between," she muttered. "They've been gone three weeks already." Her foot snagged in a chiddoe hole, jerking her out of her daze as she stumbled.

His hand caught her, the fingers firm yet gentle on her arm as, taking care his claws didn't hurt her, he pulled her upright again.

She stammered her thanks, feeling her body become slick with sweat and her temperature start to rise as he continued to hold her.

"You're hot," he observed, tongue flicking out toward her.

"The poison—your bite," she began. "I'm dying, aren't I? That's why you didn't bother killing me." Her vision was beginning to blur now, and she had to blink to keep the sweat from her eyes.

"Not dying, no." There was a grim look on his face as his hand tightened. Stooping, he set down his bundle of raw meat.

His unblinking eyes held her as if paralyzed; the thought of struggling didn't occur to her. Raising a shaking arm to her face, she wiped away the sweat. His skin had darkened, was now a deeper green, more like the vegetation around them. Suddenly she was frightened.

He pulled her closer, moving his grip till he held her by the wrist.

"You promised to neutralize the poison," she said, her disorientation making her reckless.

"Is what I'm doing," he said, his tongue flicking out to touch the hairless palm of her hand.

Seeing the anger on his face, she cringed back.

He pulled her close again. "I need what your body produced to combat my bite," he hissed angrily, claws tightening round her flesh. "Blame your people, Keeza. I have never used a pet this way!"

She fought against him as he reached for her other arm, her claws extending as she tried to hit him.

"Fool of a female!" he snarled, raising his hand instead. "Have it your way, then!"

Her last memory of him was of that hand, armed with razor-sharp claws, descending toward her face.

It had taken Kezule two days to reach the Ferraki Hills and bypass the Taykui Estate, but now he was as far northeast as was practicable for the time being. He'd also found a suitable place to literally go to earth. A narrow fissure in the rock face, just wide enough for him to squeeze through, provided a place for him to bed down and sleep some of the waiting time away. First he'd need to gather the local undergrowth to form bedding, then hunt and eat. Three months in all, but they'd been gone several weeks already. In a month, he'd start making his way to their estate. Time enough for him to observe their security and slip in unnoticed. He'd be able to locate their home at leisure, then settle down to wait and watch for the Aldatans to return. Then, by the spirit of the God-King, Emperor Q'emgo'h— *may His memory be revered for all time*—debts would be settled!

*   *   *

"So you think Kezule and Keeza are headed for the estate?" Garras asked Rhyaz.

"It's a strong probability, given the questions he asked Zhyaf," said Rhyaz. "He specifically asked about the people who brought him forward to our time. It's my bet that he wants to be returned so he can change the course of history, make sure he and the eggs escape."

Garras unconsciously drummed his fingers on Rhyaz's table. "Even though he knows they're off-world?"

"What other course of action is available to him?" asked the Guild Master.

"He could try and reach one of those home worlds," said Konis.

"Not possible," said Rhyaz. "I'm positive he was telling the truth when he said he didn't know where they were. That's leaving aside the fact that he won't be able to get his hands on a deep space vessel and a crew willing to take him."

"Shuttles land at the spaceport every day," Lijou pointed out.

"Very few are capable of taking him beyond our orbit, and we've sewn up the spaceport tighter than a demonfish's arse. No one gets in without a body check and a pass; the perimeter is under heavy surveillance, and every craft is guarded from the moment it lands till it takes off again."

"Same with the estate," agreed Garras. "We're not taking any risks."

"What about Keeza?" asked Lijou. "She'd begun to remember Zhyaf and the fact he'd been tampering with her mind. That's a good indication she's managed to break her programming. Surely once she remembers she'll try to frustrate him and find a way to help us?"

Rhyaz sighed. "That's another complication. We finally got the report on how his herb is affecting her. At least we think it's the herb. There's his bite to be taken into account, too."

"What effect is it having?" asked Garras.

"Basically, stimulating her aggression to an almost psychotic level, and inducing mind-altering states just as it did with Kaid in its other forms."

"I thought the herb had a calmative effect on Kezule. She's out of the center now, away from the herb, beginning to remember her past. Surely all that will return her system to normal?" asked Lijou, a worried look on his face.

"I can only tell you about its effect on Keeza, not Kezule. We have no clear information on that yet. That damned Valtegan is a walking chemical factory, apparently able to control his body to a degree that's difficult for us to comprehend! I'm afraid we can't assume Keeza will be anything but a continuing risk to us. It'll take time for her to normalize, and we don't have that. Kezule could decide to head for the estate anyway on the premise Zhyaf was lying about them being away. Keeza herself could goad him into such a course of action as a revenge attack for what's been done to her."

"What about the search?" asked Konis. "I thought you'd found the aircar. There must have been tracks to indicate which way they headed."

"We did. It was abandoned apart from Zhyaf's body. Supplies and clothing had been taken, but there was no sign of them. Trails for a short distance to the north, then nothing. We've got very little chance of locating them in the forest now that it's well into spring—increased tree canopy, too many heat sources, you name it. It is a game reserve, after all. All we can do is guard the forest perimeter and hope to get him when he emerges."

"But the Taykui Forest is vast!" exclaimed Konis. "How can you hope to patrol it's perimeter?"

"We can't, but we can have outposts at every estate or village, then at regular intervals in between. We haven't exactly got an option, Konis. It has to be done. Commander Chuz is already implementing it with the help of General Raiban and ourselves."

"But Keeza's an innocent in all this!" said Lijou. "She's in this predicament because of us!"

"She killed two guards," reminded Rhyaz.

"Because of the chemicals in her blood, and because we put her in there in the first place," objected the priest. "You can't order her shot on sight, Rhyaz. You have to give her a chance!"

"We will have teams with tranquilizer guns standing by," agreed Rhyaz, "But our first concern is safety. We must stop them at all costs."

Lijou got to his feet and began pacing round the office. "It's our fault," he said. "We should never have agreed to this experiment!"

Konis stirred. "I'm equally responsible, Lijou, but we had to go ahead. We needed the information we've gotten because of her. There was no other option at the time. Rhyaz, please make every effort to take the female alive. Lijou is right. We owe her that at least."

Rhyaz nodded. "That goes without saying, Master Konis."

* * *

Captain Kishasayzar's distinctive voice filled the *Hkariyash*'s mess area. "Sholans, go to Trader Chikoi's lounge for briefing."

"Not another of Assadou's damned briefings," Carrie groaned as she got up from the dining table. "We've had more in the last three days than in the month it took to get here!"

"He's Chemerian," said Kusac. "The closer we get to landing on Jalna, the more paranoid he becomes. See it from his viewpoint. By being involved in this mission, he's risking his House's trade contracts in this whole sector. And as I said, from the looks of the *Hkariyash*, they're lucrative contracts. Not many Sumaan captains have indentured vessels of this caliber. Kishasayzar is being kept busy by Assadou."

"He's got as much to lose as Assadou, but you don't hear him complaining," said Carrie, heading round the corner to the Chemerian's quarters.

"It's not in their nature to say much. What they think is another matter, one they don't tend to communicate with other species."

"I still can't understand why they didn't tell us about Jalna."

"Not all the Sumaan know about it. Only those families contracted to Chemerian Houses come here, Carrie, and the Sumaan never discuss their employer's business," he said patiently.

"Why don't they go there on their own? They're Alliance members, traders in their own right."

"Not exactly," he said, palming the lounge door lock. "The Chemerians brought them into the Alliance a couple of hundred years ago, funding them and leasing them ships. Most Sumaan Captains are mortgaged to the hide to one House or another, trying to buy out their ships and become independent. They're getting there slowly. There're about half a dozen independent Sumaan ships around at the moment."

"So they're totally dependent on their employers? Upset them and they get no work?"

"And their debt to the House increases. You got it," he nodded as the door slid back.

"They're sharp traders," Carrie muttered. "Why don't your people do something about it?"

"It's a legitimate business practice," he whispered, nudging her into the room.

Conrad, Quin, and Kaid were already there. They joined them on the settee opposite Assadou, who, as usual, was flanked by his two personal guards.

Gods, it must cost him a small fortune in retainer's fees! Do they even have to sleep in that artificial forest he calls a suite? she sent to Kusac.

Kusac patted her hand. *Calm down, the waiting's almost over. We'll be landing shortly.*

She subsided with a few mental grumbles.

The door opened again to admit T'Chebbi, pelt still damp and a towel in her hands as she continued to rub at her hair.

"Apologies. Dye needed darkening," she said, quickly taking one of the chairs. "Briefing not expected when was one earlier today."

Assadou frowned in her direction, his large ears crinkling in disapproval. He turned his head, saucerlike eyes looking unblinkingly at them.

"As we enter Jalna's atmosphere, Captain will initiate a

ies of maneuvers to indicate our craft in difficulties. Will
ke a forced landing to drop two Humans posing as Jalni-
s, then, after suitable time, take off and head for the
aceport. There we land more conventionally."

I really needed to hear this yet again, sent Carrie, using
mental channel they could all pick up.

He's being direct even for him, was Quin's comment. *He
ust be worried.*

A change in the wind worries them. Kaid's thought held
underlying purr of amusement. *Our Captain will execute*
s maneuvers without risk to us; he's one of the best. Don't
t drawn up into Assadou's paranoia.

"You make your way to the Port town and see what
n discover about Valtegans," continued the Chemerian,
aware of their silent conversation.

The rebellion, corrected Kusac. *And the missing people.*
hey are our main concern. Through these rebels, in particu-
r one called Strick, we may get news of Jo's group up
Kaladar.

Don't rush things, warned Kaid. *We have all the time we*
ed. The Hkariyash *will be berthed here for some time*
ndergoing repairs for this engine failure we're about to
cperience.

You're not the only professionals, Kaid. Conrad's tone
as acerbic. I told you, we've quite a bit of experience of
ur own in special military ops back on Earth.

Kusac sighed inwardly. Since Kaid had joined them, Con-
ad had, for no apparent reason, started developing an an-
agonistic attitude toward the older Sholan.

That's why I asked for you. Kaid's thought was unruffled
s he turned a calm gaze on the taller of the two men.

Cool it, Conrad, sent Quin. *We got a job to do.*

"You," said Assadou, pinning Carrie with a stare, "must
ose as members of my crew and . . ."

"Initiate engine failure in three minutes. Each person in
cceleration couch in sixty seconds," said the captain over
he comm.

Assadou's ears started to fold over at the edges. "Too
oon, fool of a captain! Not finished briefing!" His voice
vas high-pitched with tension as he activated his powered
chair. It rose swiftly from the ground, and he circled it to
head for the inner door, followed by his two guards.

"Leader Aldatan, your people I will see after seco
landing!"

With a low sound of anger, Carrie got up and head
out into the main crew area. Kusac followed, reaching (
to rest his hand on the back of her neck and knead t
tensed muscles there. "At least we won't have the pleasu
of his company all the way back," he said quietly. "We
rendezvous with one of our own ships a short jump fro
here."

"Where?" she asked, sitting down on one of the padd
reclining seats.

"The satellite orbiting Chemer," he said, helping her fa
ten the restraint harness. "AlRel is determined to have
permanent Sholan presence in Chemerian space now th
we have them at a severe disadvantage over this matte
They've kept us out until now." The warning klaxon bega
to sound just as he finished and he had to dive for h
own couch.

How long the uneven acceleration, followed by the sic
ening stalls and swoops lasted, Kusac couldn't tell. Final
with a screeching of metal, they came to a grinding, slit
ering halt on the ground. All the while, over the ship
comm, they could hear the terse exchange between the
ship and the Jalnian Port official.

They sat there patiently until the shuddering in the hu
finally subsided. As soon as they'd been given the all clea
Conrad and Quin were off their couches and heading fo
the main air lock, stopping only to grab their packs from
locker beside the exit.

"Be seeing you," said Quin with a wave as he followe
Conrad down the ramp.

"No assistance required," repeated their comm office
firmly in a patois of the local language. "Repairs underway
Take off imminent."

As the outer hatch closed, the smell of ozone and sea
weed filled the ship.

"He managed a beach landing," said Kaid, looking ove
at Kusac with a grin. "Told you he was good."

"I get the feeling that some of his fancy flying was fo
real," said Carrie as they listened to Kishasayzar snappin
out terse commands to his crew.

The Port official was cursing them graphically, threaten

them with fines for breaking the treaty by landing out-
e of the designated zone. Patiently the Sumaan comm
icer repeated the message, not deviating from their
ver story.

A figure appeared at the doorway opposite them. Six feet
l to his shoulders, the crewman's crested head sat on top
a long sinuous neck. This neck was now curved down-
ard, bringing his head level with his shoulders.

"Captain apologize delay. Bird blocked intake. Make
ess." The lips on his muzzlelike face pulled back in a
imace of distaste. "Trying to remove it now." Turning,
retreated to the bridge, his thick tail held close against
e back of his legs.

"I wonder if Chemerians get travel sick," said Carrie
ftly. "Hope they do."

T'Chebbi gave a snort of amusement.

"What? There's got to be justice somewhere along the
ie!" Carrie said.

"I'm afraid they don't," said Kaid, "but if it's any conso-
tion, he'll have been terrified throughout our approach in
ise we really were suffering an engine failure. That's prob-
bly why Kishasayzar sent someone to tell us what had
appened rather than announce it."

They waited patiently while each thruster was tested.
ine of them made some peculiar noises before finally set-
ing into an almost soundless hum. Within a few minutes,
ie craft rose ponderously into the air and headed for the
paceport.

This landing, while nowhere near as dramatic as their
ast, was also troubled in order to sustain their cover. At
ast they were safely berthed and while the engines were
hut down, Kusac released himself from his couch. As he
tood up, he realized the internal gravity had been cut and
hey were now experiencing the slightly lighter Jalnian
conditions.

"We'd better head back to the lounge and Assadou," he
said as the others began to get to their feet.

"Must we?" groaned Carrie, stumbling slightly. Kaid
reached out a steadying hand which she accepted gratefully.

Assadou's guards stood on either side of the outer door
his time. At their approach, one of them activated the
ock, opening the door. Assadou was already there.

As they entered, they were aware of the long apprais
look that he gave them.

"Look like U'Churians," he said.

They did. T'Chebbi and Kaid were both as dark-pel
as Kusac now, and all three of them had fur that wa
good four inches long. It added bulk to their already i
pressive size, making them seem larger than normal.

"Even clothing is right," the Chemerian added.

U'Churian traders dressed to individual taste, the ba
garment being a mid-thigh length tunic held in by
pouched belt through which a diagonal leather baldric w
worn across one shoulder. From this, a sword could eith
be back-slung or suspended at waist level.

"Can you use swords?" Assadou asked.

"It's part of our basic training as Warriors," said Kai

Assadou dipped his head forward in acceptance, the
looked specifically at Carrie. "The Human, can she al
use them?"

"Your government thinks so," said Carrie dryly, stari
unblinkingly at him. "They requested us personally."

The Chemerian's ears quivered briefly in annoyance, ar
he looked back at Kusac.

You shouldn't bait him, sent Kaid, his tone gent
reproving.

*Why not? He's been a pain in the butt with all h
briefings!*

"Remember, my profession is dealing with Lord Brade
gan. Many years it takes me to build training reputatio
here. Do not destroy it. Sample goods, if needed, I hav
for your use, but are valuable. Do not give them wastefull
You remember our escape plan?"

Kusac nodded. "We've been over it a score of times,
he said with an amused glance at Carrie. "We'll do ou
jobs, you just arrange for us to get passes to take us ou
of the Port and up to the mountains, Assadou."

"Spacers not allowed out," the Chemerian objected, ear
once more beginning to tremble and curl inward. "Tol
you this several times."

"Then get us an interview with him so we can argu
our case."

Assadou let his breath out in a nervous sigh. "Will try
I will be at hotel inside this perimeter. And remember

ak only Jalnian! If use Sholan between yourselves, will
noticed!"

Carrie looked offended. "We're telepaths! We use mind-
ech when we need to keep our conversations private!"

"I know!" Assadou said, beginning to wring his hands in
tation. This time his ears did curl over until they were
dly visible against the side of his head. "Apologies! Am
cerned for safety of us all! If you should be discovered,
n I will be involved, too!"

"Believe me," said Kusac sharply, beginning to get as
tated as Carrie, "we value our hides as much as you do
rs! Now, unless there is anything really urgent you need
discuss with us, Trader Assadou, we need to go and
lect our packs and debark!"

"Go, then!" he said, urging them away from him with
id hand movements. "Contact me only if necessary!"

"Meet in five minutes at the port air lock," said Kusac
they left Assadou's suite.

Kusac had to grin to himself as Carrie almost danced
ck to their room. He could feel her jubilation. At last
ey were doing something concrete. He was, if truth be
d, as pleased as she was at the prospect of getting away
m the Chemerian. Assadou might have stayed in his own
arters throughout the trip, but he'd made his presence
own regularly.

"If anyone's going to give us away, it'll be him," said
arrie once they were in the privacy of their own room.
e headed for her locker, digging out her backpack and
ancing round the room a final time to make sure she'd
t forgotten anything.

"He shouldn't. Beyond arranging the permit, all he has
do is continue his normal trading." He went over to his
wn locker, pulling out his pack and their swords. "Come
ver and I'll fasten your sword on for you."

Stopping only long enough to stow her energy pistol in
s holster, she joined him, standing patiently while he se-
red the scabbard to the retaining rings. When he'd fin-
hed, she rotated her shoulders and reached up to readjust
e baldric, settling the weight of the blade more
mfortably.

He turned, fastening his own at waist level. "Check you
an draw it quickly if . . ." He stopped as he saw the flicker
f light on the steel blade that pointed at his throat.

"I have," she said, grinning up at him as she sheathed it.

He smiled back as he tied off the scabbard and stood "What am I to do with you?" he asked, pulling her ch for a moment. "Like Jack says, you have the face of (of Terra's angels and the soul of a warrior."

She ran her hand across his cheek, smoothing down long pelt. "What you usually do. Just love me," she wl pered, flicking his nose gently, then ducking away from h "Let's go! I want to get off this ship and onto firm grou again! I want to see the sky! I've had a bellyful Assadou!"

He turned back to his locker, drawing out the rifle a slinging it over his shoulder. "You won't see much, l afraid. It's night here."

She grasped his arm as he opened the door, holding or him. "It's an alien world, Kusac! The first I've visite Aren't you even a bit excited?"

"Don't know that excited is the word for it," he said they joined the other two. "Curious, certainly."

Kaid and T'Chebbi were standing with their rifles reac looking concerned. "Kishasayzar says there's trouble ot side. Port authorities warned us not to get involved, it's private matter."

"What kind of trouble?" asked Kusac, unslinging his gu Kaid shook his head. "No more information. His cre are already checking it out." Turning, he activated tl outer air lock.

One of the Sumaan was there, obviously standing guar "Is safe," he said, turning his neck and looking down them as they approached. "Rebels try to board cargo un Port Controllers chase. We see they not board *Hkariyash*

Now they could hear the sound of angry voices shoutir to each other. Kaid, rifle ready, took the lead, wit T'Chebbi behind him as they began to descend to the su face of Jalna.

It was still dusk, and by the last remnants of light the were able to see the figures running toward the warehouse on their right. They were closely followed by a group (four Sumaan and three others.

"U'Churians," said Carrie from her position behin T'Chebbi.

"Looks like our cover will be put to the test sooner tha

thought," said Kaid dryly. "Let's hope the scent neutral-
works on U'Churian noses."

If it doesn't, you're all going to have to do what Vanna
gested, keep coming to me for hugs," said Carrie with
ervous laugh, not taking her eyes off the pursuit. "You
say Human scent is stronger than yours. Have you no-
d how many Sumaan there are around here?"

'Mercenaries take work where they can find it," Kaid
ninded her, obliquely referring to his years in exile from
Brotherhood.

'Is bad, this," said T'Chebbi. "If they catch them and
y talk, give names of leaders, could compromise our
ssion."

'Kris said they belong to cells for that reason," said
id. "I don't think they'll let themselves be taken."

Energy pulses lit up the gathering darkness, and screams
1g out.

"Let's hope Strick wasn't one of them," said Kusac.

"Not likely. He organizes the caravans and works mainly
thin the perimeter. He'd be too cautious of his privileged
sition to risk it in a venture like this. I'll wager it wasn't
els, only renegade dock crew trying to steal."

They waited until the bodies were brought out and
aded onto one of the Controllers' ground sleds. People
re returning to their craft and their posts now that the
citement was over. Still keeping his rifle at the ready,
usac took the time to look around him.

He counted seven craft besides theirs within the inner
rimeter, mostly, as the Chemerians had said, powered
rgo pods or short-range shuttles. There was one other
acecraft, though. Larger than them, it stood two berths
vay. The design was unfamiliar.

"U'Churian," said Kaid, indicating with his rifle barrel
e two black-furred people still standing looking their way.
Could be watching the gate, but I don't think so."

"Not the gate," said Carrie. "Us. Definitely."

Kusac glanced over his shoulder at her. "You can pick
em up from here?"

"The surface thoughts, yes."

"Can you read either of them? Pick up the language to
ake sure those recordings of Ambassador Taira's are
ccurate?"

"I'll try," she said, leaning back against him for sup[p]
while she gently probed at the U'Churian's mind.

On the pad beside his ship, Tirak's head swung sudde
round to look at his companion.

"Captain?" asked Sheeowl, her face creased in conce
"What is it?"

Turning, he hurried up the ramp back into the *Profit* w
her hard on his heels.

"Captain! What is it?" she demanded, catching him
the arm and pulling him to a halt.

His eyes blazed with anger he could barely contain. "/
other such as that Kate!" he snarled. "A mind reader!'

"Telepath," she corrected him automatically, using
Sholan word. "Another Human?"

"Yes! She touched my mind, tried to read me! She ca
in on the Sumaan ship," he said, heading for the up[p]
decks where his guests were being held. "I need to kn[ow]
where that ship came from! Get Manesh onto it."

Sheeowl sprinted after him. "Where are you going? N
to the kids, Captain, it isn't their fault!"

"Yes, to them! I need her to stop this happening aga
and if she won't do it willingly, I'll . . ."

"Captain, they're children!" she warned him again.

"I'll shake her till every tooth in her head rattles,"
finished with another snarl of anger.

Shocked, Carrie almost dropped her pistol. "He sens[e]
me!"

Kusac watched the retreating U'Churians with intere
"He did, didn't he? Can you still pick him up?"

She shook her head. "No. He's angry and confused—h[is]
thoughts are too jumbled for me to make sense of ther
He recognized the touch of a telepath, though. That mu[ch]
I did get before he panicked."

"The touch of a telepath can be intimidating the fir
time," said Kaid. "Where could he have felt it before? A
his own kind Talented?"

"Too many coincidences," said T'Chebbi. "Most like[ly]
he's met one of our missing ones. Need to speak to him.

"Did he know it was you?" asked Kusac.

"I couldn't tell."

Kusac felt a heavy hand on his shoulder and looked up to find Captain Kishasayzar looming behind him.

"We debark now," he said. "Rooms are already booked for you at the inn we use this night. Port Controllers wish to speak with me later about landing *Hkariyash*. Merchant Chikoi goes to their office already."

Reaching past Kusac, he stretched a bony arm in the direction of the starboard air lock where Assadou was emerging from the shadow of the ship. His powered chair was now docked in a sled with room for his Sumaan guards to stand behind him. It was speeding toward the gateway.

"Rifles to be left on the ship. Sidearms only allowed, and blades. Give, and I will pass them back for stowage."

Kusac glanced at Kaid, who merely shrugged. They handed their rifles to Kishasayzar who in turn passed them back into the *Hkariyash*.

Kusac hefted his pack over his shoulder and continued down the steps. At the bottom, they waited for the rest of the crew, then began walking toward the illuminated spacers town that existed between the two perimeter fences.

"It looks exciting and exotic, and it's so warm after Shola!" murmured Carrie as they came closer to the gateway.

T'Chebbi snorted. "Doesn't smell good."

"I expect we'll quickly become desensitized," said Kusac as the sharp sounds and smells reached him. He wrinkled his nose in distaste. The underlying odors of poor drainage and sanitation were overlaid with the aromas of food vendors' wares. A sudden gust from behind them added the heavy smell of machine oil to the noxious combination.

Beside him, Carrie sniffed, her enhanced senses picking it up, too. "I hope so, but it still *looks* exotic!"

Lights strung above the stalls swayed in the breeze, sending dancing shadows over the holders. Beyond them were the ever present shops and taverns common to all ports.

"Get used to it," said T'Chebbi. "All same. Seen one, seen 'em all."

"This is my first, T'Chebbi. I refuse to be put off," she said firmly. *Kusac, do we need to read the guard to check the language?*

No need. Our Jalnian at least will be accurate because of Kris sending it to Vryaka.

Assadou could be seen heading away from the gate to

the east where a modern building stood several hundred yards away from an imposing stone tower. Access to both buildings was also controlled by guards and a checkpoint like the one for the spacers' town. They were set in the wide area between the two perimeter fences.

"A hotel for those merchants and traders who can afford to use it," said Kaid, following her gaze. "Assadou's staying there. The other is Lord Bradogan's residence."

"Thought Assadou was seeing the Controllers."

"He is," confirmed Kishasayzar, his neck snaking down to gaze at her. "There is office there, too."

"What's the history of the place? Who found it and built the Port?"

Kusac looked at the Sumaan. "Captain? Do you know?"

His head swiveled to look at Kusac before he returned his gaze to Carrie. "U'Churians say the Port built on old site some two hundred years ago, Alliance time. Built by TeLaxaud, Cabbars, and U'Churians. Controlled inside by us and U'Churians, and in spacers' town, by Lord Bradogan."

"TeLaxaud. Don't remember hearing of them before," said Kaid, slowing down as they came to the gates.

"Come rarely. Cargo unit in now but leaving in few hours."

"Why build a port they don't use often?" asked Carrie, stopping behind the group of Sumaan. She reached into the thigh pocket of her one-piece jumpsuit for her ID and landing papers.

The captain's mouth opened vertically, exposing teeth like tombstones and a thick, pink tongue as he smiled. "Are aliens, unlike Sholans and Sumaan; who knows their motives?" He made a jerky, guttural sound which Kusac realized with surprise was laughter. This was a trait in the Sumaan he'd been unaware of despite his dealings with them through AlRel.

Everything's different in the field, sent Kaid, a touch of humor in his mental tone. *As you should know, you come across the strangest allies.*

"Cabbars—they're the vegetarians, aren't they?" Kusac asked.

"Yes. Two cargo units of theirs are being here, but seeing them in spacers' town not usual." He held his three-fingered hands about a meter apart. "Short people; long bodies but

lose to ground. Dangerous for them." He let his hands
drop again and pointed to his large clawed feet. "Say we
might step on them." Again the strange laugh. "Hotel keep
lower level rooms for them. Crews often gather there."

With barely a glance at their papers, the guard waved
the Sumaan crew through. Then it was their turn and Kaid,
T'Chebbi at his side, stepped up first.

Where's the dog Jo's party warned us about? asked
Carrie.

Looking around, Kusac noticed several Jalnians with
large quadruped creatures on the end of leashes, patrolling
the dead area between the fences. *To your left, twenty meters away. They've got several of them. Must be used for
tracking and hunting, too. Vicious looking brutes,* he added.

He could see the creature's head was on a level with
the nearest Jalnian's waist. Round its neck was a ruff of
stiff spines.

Gods, it's huge! It does look like a wolf, Carrie sent. *A
wild one at that.* She shivered.

An equally cursory glance at Kaid's and T'Chebbi's papers had been enough for the guard, and he waved them
through.

Kaid turned to look at Carrie, his eyes glowing slightly
in the gathering darkness. *That is the creature you mistook
for Dzaka on the* Khalossa? He was grinning broadly and
she could sense his amusement.

He frightened me! she sent in justification. *I wasn't used
to Sholans then.*

"Papers," the guard said, holding his hand out imperi-
ously for them. His eyes roamed across Carrie's slim figure,
noticing the sword pommel protruding above her left
shoulder.

They handed them over and waited.

Armed to the teeth with an array of bladed weapons, the
guard still carried a pulse rifle slung negligently over one
shoulder and a pistol in the holster at his hip. His face, an
old battle scar creasing one swarthy cheek, looked Human
but there were subtle differences to the planes.

Kusac's papers were given the same cursory glance and
returned. Carrie's documents, however, he retained.

Trouble, she sent to her mate.

We expected this, he replied, standing his ground to wait
for her.

"You're Jalnian," said the guard, his voice deep and gravelly. He reached out to take hold of a lock of her hair, rubbing it between callused fingers. "No aliens like you exist. Posing as one is a serious offense. These papers are a forgery. I reckon you're one of the rebels we've been hunting. You should have waited an hour, then perhaps we could have come to some arrangement." Mouth widening in a slow smile that held no warmth, he let her hair go. "Carrying weapons, too. Women face the death penalty for that alone."

"She's a Solnian," said Kusac. "First of her kind to visit Jalna. Look at her papers."

The guard glanced at him, frowning. "Collaborating to smuggle her in? That's serious, Trader. I suggest you leave the lady to me and get on your way." His free hand moved to rest negligently on his pistol butt.

"Look at her eyes," said Kusac. "What Jalnian has eyes like hers?"

Taking her roughly by the chin, the guard tilted her face up and studied it. "Her eyes look normal to me," he said, beginning to get angry.

Kaid reached out and took Carrie by the arm, pulling her into the full glare of the gatehouse lighting. "Now look."

Again the guard took hold of her face. Carrie's irises shrank rapidly to narrow vertical slits rimmed with a faint touch of amber. Her dark brown eyes blazed back furiously at him as she reached up to catch his hand and twist it away. As the guard yelped in pain, she released him.

"Solnian, is she?" he snarled, looking at her papers. "I'd keep a close watch on her if I were you, or you'll lose your comm officer to one of the Port's whorehouses! Many a man would pay good money to beat some decent respect into the likes of her!"

Radiating fury in every direction, Carrie snatched her papers from him and stalked through the gate.

Kusac let his own anger show as his hackles rose around his face and neck. "She's under my protection," he growled, his voice a low, menacing rumble. He opened his mouth, lips curling back to reveal an array of carnivore's teeth that stood out starkly against his black pelt. "I have no fears for her safety." Then he followed her.

As if by some unspoken agreement, the Sholans found

emselves at the center of their Sumaan crew as they
rned toward the lights of the spacers' town.

From beside him, Kishasayzar's head snaked down to
ok at Kusac. "Though unwelcome, the guard's advice is
und. She is too like the Jalnians for comfort. Had your
ate been of your own species, would not be this prob-
m." There was a curious look on his face, but he didn't
ursue the matter.

"We anticipated this," said Kusac, replying in the same
lnian-based patois they'd grown used to using with the
umaan. "Carrie, now might be a good time to try pro-
cting the discouragement field we've been working on.
ry not to direct it at us."

Carrie nodded and gradually there grew about her an
lien coldness, an air of grim purpose, that though it wasn't
irected at them was felt by everyone.

Tone it down a bit, advised Kusac as their Sumaan col-
eagues made startled noises and looked at her in
uzzlement.

It was put to the test almost immediately as a couple of
runken Jalnians came out of one of the nearby inns.
aughing, they staggered backward into the center of the
roup, knocking into Kusac, then Carrie. One of them
urned to apologize, but the look on his face swiftly
hanged to one of horror as he caught sight of Carrie glow-
ring at him, gun half drawn. Then he saw her companions.

"Your pardons, Lady," he stammered, backing off hur-
iedly, dragging his friend with him.

As he reholstered his own weapon, Kusac realized Kaid
nd T'Chebbi had been just as trigger ready as himself.
They were all twitchy because of the episode at the gate.

*Good, but try toning it down a little. It'll be too strong
for the inn,* he sent to her.

As Carrie reduced the force of her sending, the Sumaan
egan to relax. *It's just a matter of fine tuning.*

The main street in the shanty town wasn't wide. One
side, that nearest the inner perimeter fence, belonged to
the stalls selling all manner of foods and trinkets. On the
other, the permanent buildings stood—the inns, the taverns
offering entertainments, the various shops and currency ex-
changes. The milling, bustling crowd of aliens and Jalnian
port workers parted easily for their Sumaan escort and

within a few minutes they had reached their destination
the inn usually frequented by the crew of the *Hkariyash*

"Stay with us for the moment," said Kishasayzar quiet
in Kusac's ear as they threaded their way through the J
nian section of the tap room to the area where the spac
crews were seated. "The U'Churians will approach y
soon. They are a curious species, unable to keep the
snouts out of business not concerning them. A bit like you
selves. Your tale will carry more conviction if you a
seated with us."

"A sensible suggestion," agreed Kusac as they followe
the captain over to a partially vacant table where anoth
Sumaan crew sat.

As they settled themselves on the benches, Kusac w
aware of Carrie mentally scanning the nearest group
U'Churians.

Found one. Link, and we'll have their language.

Kusac strengthened their mental link, letting her use hi
as a reservoir of energy. Kaid's mind, brought in by Carri
joined them, and on the extreme outer fringes, he cou
just sense T'Chebbi. Moments later, the chatter from th
U'Churian tables began to make sense.

I don't think T'Chebbi got it all. Will you make sure? sh
asked, raising a weary hand to rub her eyes as she let th
intense link fade. *She's not quite sensitive enough to absor
it without help.*

T'Chebbi's surprised look made him smile as he redi
the transfer carefully, mindful of the fact that she wasn
a telepath.

"Is good," she nodded. 'Have it now."

A barmaid came over and took their orders and whil
they waited for the food and drinks to arrive, friendly rela
tions were established with their table companions an
news began to pass between the two crews.

During their meal, one of the U'Churians padded up be
side Kusac. Resting a huge pawlike hand on the table, h
bent down toward him.

"Mind if I join you?"

Kusac nudged Carrie in the ribs and they slid up the
bench to accommodate him.

"You're from the *Hkariyash*, I see," he said, pointing t
the emblem they all wore on their clothing. "Working fo
the Chemerians. Why?"

"My family wish it," he replied with a shrug of feigned difference. This was the cover story the Chemerian auorities had provided for them. He prayed it wouldn't me unstuck. It wasn't unknown for the younger males in ading U'Churian families to be apprenticed to a Chemer- n to study the language and to learn the art of trading. he price of such tuition was high, but when balanced ainst the future gains, it was acceptable.

The U'Churian nodded and indicated Carrie, leaning past usac to sniff the air in her direction. His mobile nose, ore of a muzzle than the Sholan's, wrinkled with the ef- rt. "This one. Does she travel with you?"

"She does. Like me, she learns the trade."

He sat back again. "I don't recognize the scent. She nells too strongly of you and . . ." He indicated the Su- aan. "A new species? She's not Jalnian, I'll wager that. hey wouldn't let their women become involved in ading."

"A Solnian. The first of her kind to visit Jalna. Assadou hekoi says she's an honored visitor in his House. Her eople hope to be trading in the open market here soon, o she travels with us to see what goods are preferred." arefully he touched the edges of the other's mind with is, backing off hurriedly as he sensed a strong mental bar- ier that prevented any contact.

"I'm Tirak, Captain of the *Profit*. Like you, we're stuck ere with engine troubles."

"Kusac," he said, then introduced the others. They'd de- ided to use their own names as the sound of them was lose enough to be acceptable. He saw Tirak's brow raise uestioningly and from his newly acquired knowledge of J'Churian culture, he added, "We're from the Outlands."

Tirak nodded again. "What goods do they bring here? Anything new?"

"Some unusual beverages, both alcoholic and nonalco- olic, drugs, technology, and craft work. The usual range."

"The same but different," agreed Tirak. Lowering his voice, he said conspiratorially, "You and your followers will oin us later for some relaxation in the town?"

"Maybe," said Kusac. "Business first, and I have to look after her personally."

The eye ridge disappeared into the mane of hair this

time. "There are more interesting females in the Po
They'll keep you warmer than this one has."

Fighting hard not to grin at Carrie's outraged though
Kusac shrugged expressively. "Duty. I have to keep th
one sweet tempered."

Tirak gave a deep throated laugh. 'Duty can be carri
too far! I'll leave you to your cold comfort. When you g
bored, get a Jalnian to sweeten her and join us. As I sai
we're here for a while." As he rose, he clasped Kus;
briefly on the shoulder before rejoining his own table.

How dare he! How'd he know anyway? she demanded

Their sense of smell is sharper than ours, Kusac sent pl;
catingly, touching her hand briefly. *He can smell our scen
on each other. He knows we're paired at the moment.*

That's to the good, sent Kaid. *He's less likely to be susp
cious of us.*

She muttered audibly under her breath as she spoone
the last of her stew into her mouth and pushed the bov
aside.

*Keep touching us, bumping into us all, you know the kin
of behavior I mean,* sent Kaid. *That way we'll all have
similar alibi.*

*I can't be seen as an effective warrior and a clinging vin
was her tart reply. *You and T'Chebbi will have to do som
bumping into me yourselves!*

Not a problem, sent Kaid urbanely.

Kusac turned to the captain, grasping him by the arm t
attract his attention.

"Now that we've landed, I'm in charge of this venture
no matter what Assadou has said. I need you to behave a
you normally do when on leave here, but keep your ear
and eyes open for news of any Sholans on the planet, o
anything to do with the Valtegans."

"You have our help until it conflicts with our contrac
with Assadou. It is surprising that given all the Valtegan;
on Keiss, not one of them spoke of their purpose before
dying. Perhaps you should have been firmer with them."

Kusac tried not to wince. The Sumaan could be less thar
gentle when policing Alliance disputes, and worse wher
fighting their own kind. "We used telepaths, but foun
nothing of any use before they died," he said.

The captain sighed. "We trade here for many years anc
never hear of the Valtegans until their two visits just over

a year ago. They have not returned since. I feel we'll learn little about them. As for your people, to be slaves here for that length of time . . ." He left the sentence unfinished.

"We couldn't come sooner," said Kaid quietly, feeling stirrings of anger and suppressing it. "The authorities should have accepted another team instead of waiting for us."

The captain looked at him in surprise. "You should take no offense. I merely state a fact, not make a judgment."

"The delay annoys us all, Kishasayzar. Retrieving our people should have been a priority, but the Chemerians wanted the information on the Valtegans more and refused to allow another team to come to Jalna on a rescue mission."

"The Chemerians do not understand warriors," hissed Kishasayzar, coming as near to criticism of his employers as one of his kind would ever countenance. "We will see what we can discover. We stay here only one night, but you will find us in here at dusk every evening."

"We need to head up to our rooms now," Kusac said, getting to his feet. "We've work we must do. I assume that during the day there will be someone on board working on our engine failure." He emphasized the last two words.

"Yes. We will be ready when needed. Now I must go to see the Port Controller."

"Will there be trouble?" asked T'Chebbi.

Kishasayzar shrugged. "They can do nothing. Is another ship like us as Captain Tirak told you. A fine, no more, and not paid by us!" He grinned.

"Good. We'll join you for the evening meal tomorrow and see if you've any news."

They stopped at the bar to collect their keys, then headed up the rickety steps to the bedrooms. The building was made of timber, crudely but solidly constructed. In the passageway, oil lamps sat on high shelves, shedding pools of light that relieved the darkness only a little.

"I'll go first," said Kaid, holding his hand out for the key. "No point in taking chances."

Kusac mentally checked the room for intruders before Kaid unlocked it. When they entered, they found a lamp had been lit for them and in the grate, a small fire burned. Furniture was sparse. A wooden chair at either side of the fire, a small table, and a chest at the foot of the double bed was all it contained. The one window was shuttered against the night air.

T'Chebbi headed for the window, opening it to check for alternative exits. "Can get out here if need to," she said, closing and latching it again, satisfied they were secure. "Looks out onto back yard," she said. "If necessary, can climb down from here. There's a pipe beside the window. Best keep it closed lest others use it as entrance."

"But the heat," moaned Carrie. "Why do they have a fire in this weather?"

"Ignore it. We have to," said Kaid. He was at the other side of the room, trying the door set there. "It connects us to you," he said, opening it. "I suggest we keep it unlocked in case of emergencies."

"Sounds wise," agreed Kusac, going over to look into the room. It was identical to theirs apart from the two single beds. "We'll knock if we have news from Quin and Conrad for you."

T'Chebbi followed Kaid into the room.

"See you at first meal if not before," said Kaid, closing the door.

Carrie had carried the lamp over to the bed and was turning down the covers, examining the bedding. "I just hope it isn't flea-infested," she muttered, flinging the covers back up.

Kusac took the lamp from her and set it on the night table before throwing his pack down on the bed. "Stop fretting. If fleas are the worst of our worries, then we're doing well." Pulling his sword free, he slung it, then his belt and baldric beside the pack.

"Bring one of the blankets over," he said, squatting in front of the fire. "I want us to be comfortable while we work. Having said that," he muttered, standing up and reaching up under his tunic.

Carrie watched him in surprise. "What *are* you doing?" she asked, beginning to laugh at his antics.

"Getting this damned underwear off!" he said, pulling the decorated cord tie free and grabbing for the offending breech cloth as, unsupported, it began to fall down.

"It isn't that funny," he said, looking over at her. "How anyone can stand to wear these things is beyond me!"

"Modesty," she laughed. "They need to wear them, you don't. Imagine being . . ." she began.

"I can imagine it myself," he growled, throwing the garment onto the chest.

Still chuckling as she moved his belongings aside, Carrie pulled the top cover free and threw it over in his direction before taking off her own weapons and belt. By the time she joined him, he'd spread the blanket over the floor in front of the fire and was sitting there, leaning against the heavy chair.

"Sit with your back to me," he said, reaching up to tug her down beside him. He pulled her closer until she was leaning against his chest.

She sighed, and he could feel the tension drain out of her. Wriggling a little, she made herself more comfortable, then leaned her head back against his shoulder.

"Are you relaxed enough?" he asked gently, his voice soft in her ear.

She nodded.

"Then let's search and see if we can find any Sholans apart from ourselves nearby."

Their minds linked and Carrie focused their thoughts on the area surrounding the Port. Even among so many aliens, if there was a pattern that was uniquely Sholan, they'd find it. For a long time they searched, quartering the area mentally, almost as if they could see the spaceport spread out below them like a map. Once there was something, almost a flicker, but it faded, lost among new alien presences they'd never sensed before.

"Not U'Churian or Sumaan," said Carrie, finally giving up.

"The Cabbars? Kishasayzar said there were some in Port," Kusac hazarded.

"Possible. Shall we look for Quin, then stop for tonight?"

He licked the edge of her ear. "Are you sure you're up to it?"

"I'm fine," she said, beginning to still her mind again. She reached for Quin's mental signature, seeing his face before her, then sent their combined thoughts in his direction.

Almost instantly, they sensed his presence.

We're in a village some ten miles from the Port. Found ourselves a reasonable inn to put up in. Decent beer and the food's edible. The locals are friendly enough and have ac-

cepted us as Jalnians. I don't anticipate any problems. How's it with you?

Fine. We've acquired a working knowledge of U'Churian now. Kusac will send it to you, replied Carrie.

Kusac increased the contact, taking control of it before gradually beginning to transfer what Carrie had learned from the U'Churian at the inn. It took a little time but was helped by the fact that they'd used the method before to transfer knowledge between them on the inward journey to Jalna.

Assadou's supposed to be trying to arrange passes and a Trade mission for us, hopefully to Kaladar. If he does, I'll need you two along. Get as much information as you can in the next day or two, then move on to the village outside the Port. That's where they hire people for the caravans.

We'll move as fast as possible, but if we're going to get their trust, we have to take it easy.

Do what you can. I'll be in touch.

The contact was broken, leaving Kusac and Carrie alone. He blinked, once more aware of the glow from the fire and the lamp. Carrie, her eyes closed, was lying exhausted against him. Lowering his head, he licked her gently below the ear, receiving only the faintest of smiles by way of response.

"When all I get is a smile, then I know you're tired," he said, rubbing his cheek against hers.

Too tired to even talk, came the faint thought.

"Then let me get up. I've something in my bag that should help," he said, waiting till she moved forward before scrambling to his feet.

Bending down, he lifted her up and carried her over to the bed, putting her down carefully amid the various swords and bags. He touched her face briefly.

"You really are exhausted, aren't you? I knew we had left Shola too soon. You haven't gotten your strength back yet."

"I'm fine," she retorted sharply as he leaned across her to dig in his bag. "I don't want one of Vanna's stimulants," she warned as he drew out a small package.

"I should think not," he replied with a grin. "They're only for emergencies. All you need is a good night's rest."

A packet of homemade biscuits landed in her lap. With

a cry of delight she snatched them up. Opening the pack, she took one out and began to munch it.

"They're your mother's, aren't they? I'd recognize them anywhere." She helped herself to a second.

Kusac moved their belongings onto the chest at the end of the bed. "I only brought a few with me, but we should be able to find something in the market to replace them. Even dried fruit will raise our depleted blood sugar levels when we've been working." He handed Carrie her pistol. "Keep it under the pillow. You never know when you might need it. You settle down and I'll see to updating Kaid and T'Chebbi."

"Finding those four missing Sholans might prove impossible, Kusac," she said. "If this Strick and the rebellion know nothing about them, we may have to concentrate on pulling Jo's team out."

"It's early days yet. I don't want to give up on them unless we have no option. Once we have Jo's people safe on the *Hkariyash,* then we can take more time to locate them."

"We might not get out of the Port a second time."

"Wait and see what Quin comes up with first," he said, heading over to the connecting door.

* * *

Jo sat at the table in the Great Hall letting the sound of chatter and laughter fade until she barely noticed it. These twice weekly evenings were a strain on them all. After a day spent working in the drafty, poorly lit converted stable, fending off Belamor's insistent questions, she would have preferred the peace and quiet of their chambers upstairs. A tap on her shoulder brought her out of her reverie and back to reality. Looking up, she found herself face-to-face with Taradain. His face was flushed, and she remembered noticing he'd been drinking heavily.

"I want to talk to you," he said in a low voice.

"What is it, Taradain?"

"Not here. Take a walk with me."

"Forget it." She turned back to the table.

His hand clamped on her shoulder, fingers digging into her flesh. "*Not* here. Outside, and don't draw attention to me by refusing."

She looked up at him, mouth opening to answer him when he abruptly bent down.

"You want your friend to die?" he hissed in her ear. "Hear what I have to say first."

"Not outside," she said flatly, suppressing Rezac's anger by walling her mind off from his.

"To the second pillar then," he conceded. "And in the name of the Gods, look like you're *pleased* to be with me!"

She got to her feet, allowing the young Jalnian to take her by the elbow and draw her toward the end of the table.

"Smile, dammit," he muttered, a fake grin plastered on his face as he bowed to his father.

Kris was sending to her, too, wanting to know what she was doing. With a quick, *Later,* she thrust him aside.

"What do you want, Taradain?" she asked as they stopped by the pillar. Around the Hall, several other people had gotten up and were gathered in small groups talking; she and Taradain were not attracting too much attention.

"You," he said bluntly. "The alien woman is dying. She needs to get back to her own kind. I'll help them escape, if you remain here with me."

She looked at him, speechless with shock. "Your help would be wonderful, Taradain," she said, "but you know I need to be with Rezac."

"Don't give me that rubbish about the dependence between your people because I don't believe it! No matter what my father says, I'm not stupid. I know you don't want me, that's why I'm prepared to help your friends—for a price."

"You're drunk!" she said in disgust. "What you're suggesting is immoral. *If* I agreed, you'd have a shell, a body, not me. Is that what you really want?"

His face darkened with anger. "'I'll take you any way I can! Because of you I've been held up to ridicule by my father and all the court! This way I get back my pride, and have you! Well? Do you agree or not?"

Jo ran through their options. There weren't many. The caravan should be due any day now. Staying behind with Taradain was not a sensible option, but if all else failed . . . "I'll need to think about it," she said, turning away.

Taradain caught hold of her by the wrist. "No! Decide now or I withdraw my offer."

"I told you, I can't stay. I need to be with Rezac," she said angrily, hitting his hand away. "If I'm separated from him, I'll die!"

"And I told you, don't treat me like a fool! You can't have a dependence on him, you're too different." He caught hold of her wrist again.

"It's true whether you believe it or not, and I don't intend to prove it to you. Now let go of me, Taradain!" she hissed.

He pulled her closer till they were eye to eye, searching her face. "You believe it, though, don't you? What if I prove it wrong?"

"You can't."

"What happens? Do you sicken and die, or just . . . die?" he demanded.

"What's the difference?" she snapped. "I can't and won't stay and that's an end to it!"

"If you sicken first, then I'll let you return to him, and still help you all escape."

"What?" She stopped struggling and looked at him.

"I'll return you and still help you escape. Dammit, I don't want to cause your death! I'm not some kind of monster!"

"Why?" She was confused.

"Because I'll have gained my honor in front of these sheep!" he snarled. "Now, do you accept or not? My father's looking at us. You've run out of time. Yes or no?"

An icy calm settled on her. Their freedom, in exchange for sleeping with Taradain. She'd done it before with the Valtegans, and at least the Jalnians were almost human. Rezac was more alien than Taradain. If he let her return and helped them all escape, it was worth it. If.

"I can only stay three days, then I have to go back to him." She was amazed at how calm her voice sounded. "And you have to make sure he gets an adequate supply of the same food as is served in the Hall." She'd been sneaking what food she could to Rezac, but it wasn't really enough.

"Three days, then—and the food—but during that time, you'll look like you're enjoying my company. Agreed?"

"Agreed," she said through gritted teeth.

His hand reached for the back of her neck, holding her

still while he leaned forward to kiss her. "Starting right now!" he hissed.

Like a sleeper, she lifted her face to his and forced herself to respond. He had the good sense not to push her and the kiss was short.

He drew back and took hold of her hand. "I'll send for your belongings."

"I'll go. I need to tell them . . ."

"No! Not tonight. Tonight you come with me. Tomorrow you can tell them."

"Tonight?" She hadn't though he'd demand her company immediately. It made sense: he was preventing the others from persuading her to refuse.

"Enough talk, my father's calling us," he said, starting to walk back to the table. When she didn't come, he stopped and turned round to her. "Dammit! You want to ruin this already? You've just agreed to be my lover, try and act like it's real!"

She forced herself to move, forced a smile to her lips as she let him lead her back to the top table.

"Taradain! What's this?" Killian demanded loudly. "You still forcing yourself on my guest? She made it plain she doesn't want you!" A chorus of laughter spread round the room.

Flushing again, the young man waited till it stopped. "No, Father. The lady has changed her mind. She wants me to have her belongings brought to my room."

Killian looked at her with a raised eyebrow.

Jo felt Taradain's fingernails digging into her hand. She forced a brighter smile on her face. "If you would be so kind," she said quietly.

The Lord looked from her to Kris then back. "You wish to move in with my son?" he asked incredulously.

"She just said so," snapped Taradain, drawing her closer to his side and putting a proprietary arm round her waist.

"I'll hear it from the lady," said Killian mildly.

"Yes," she said, feeling her face starting to burn with embarrassment. At the edges of her mind, she could feel both Rezac and Kris clamoring. She needed every ounce of willpower she possessed to keep them at bay. "It's what I wish, Lord Killian. Please have my things sent to your son's room."

Killian sat back in his chair, fingering his beard thought-

lly before turning and gesturing to one of the guards bend him. The soldier approached and bent down to hear
s orders. Nodding, he left the Hall.

"It is being seen to," he said. "I have to admit you've
rprised me, Taradain. Don't let us detain you any longer.
ou are excused from the table. You and your lovely com-
nion may retire."

"Thank you," said Taradain, sketching a bow and tug-
ng on Jo's hand, warning her to do the same. Turning,
led her from the room. As they passed between the
ge double doors, the silence behind them was broken by
sudden babble of excited voices.

What the hell's she doing? Rezac demanded of Kris.
Leaving with Taradain, the Human sent. *She says she
ants her things taken to his room. I can't reach her any
ore than you can! God knows what she's up to, but it
ppears she's going with him willingly.*
Do something! Stop her! Rezac raged.
*There's nothing I can do! She'll be doing it for a reason,
nd if I interfere, it could cost us our lives!*
If I were there . . . Rezac began.
*You'd do what? Just remember she's our leader, Rezac.
he knows what she's doing, even if we don't.*
I'll not have my . . .
Your what? Kris' mental tone was incandescent. *She
oesn't belong to you! Sleeping with the enemy is what she's
ained to do!*

Abruptly, Rezac's presence was gone.

Taradain's chamber was not unlike theirs. Untidier, the
re still burning even on a spring night, but the same in all
mportant respects save one. It was on the first floor, and
here was a window. Shivering, Jo waited for the young
nan to close the door then rounded on him. "This is despi-
able of you," she said. "To use my friend's life as a means
f forcing me to sleep with you is utterly despicable."

Ignoring her, he walked over to the table and picked up
he bottle of wine standing there. Two goblets stood side
y side and into these he emptied the bottle.

Picking them up, he held one out to her. "Drink. It helps
ull the senses."

She noticed his hand was shaking slightly. "I don't w
your damned wine!"

"You humiliated me in front of my father that day!"
said, slamming her drink back down on the table. "Th
was no need for what you did!"

"*I* humiliated *you*? You forced yourself into our bedroo

Raising his goblet, he emptied it and set it back on
table. "So what? You led me to believe you were a la
when you're nothing better than one of the women w
sell themselves in the taverns for the price of an ale!"

"I'm no prostitute!"

"You sleep with that . . ." He stopped, lost for a wc
to describe Rezac. "Animal!"

"He's no animal! I told you, we're bound together.
need each other!"

"And you need me!" he said, covering the distance b
tween them in three strides. Grasping her by the shoulde
he shook her. "I'm going to be risking everything for yc
you'd better be worth it," he snarled. "How difficult can
be to pretend you're enjoying it? At least I look like o
of you!"

The next day at around noon, the door to their chambe
opened, admitting Taradain and Jo. Kris felt and hea
Rezac's building anger, and reached out to take hold of
arm warningly.

Hear what she has to say first, he sent to the Sholan.

Her face looked strained as she came over to them.

"Well, hello," Kris drawled, standing up. "Wondered
you were going to join us." He reached for her mind b
met only the barrier again.

"Listen to me," she said in Jalnian, her voice so low it w
barely audible. "I only have a few minutes. Taradain h
agreed to help us. Be ready to leave in two days' time. He
see the guards are dealt with and lead us down to an o
tunnel that'll bring us up outside the castle wall. Horses w
be waiting. From then, it's up to us. He says the carava
arrives tonight. In two days it leaves. He suggests we shou
try to join it."

"Two days?" Kris repeated, catching her eye.

"Two," she repeated, holding his gaze unflinchingly. "B
ready." She looked at Rezac. "Cause no trouble, Reza
Just have Zashou ready, you hear me?"

Rezac continued to growl, the sound low and menacing.
"Do you hear me?" she repeated.

"I hear." His voice was almost a snarl.

"I have to go," she said, turning away.

Rezac lunged out and caught hold of her. "Jo," he began.

She shook herself free. "Two days, Rezac," she said in
olan. "Don't make this have been for nothing."

"With you gone, and cutting yourself off mentally, I feel
like a sickness! If he keeps you here . . ."

"He won't," she said. "Don't let the Jalnians see what it
es to you. It'll be enough that he thinks it's harming me."

Taradain strode over to her, grasping her by the arm.
Don't use that outlandish tongue. I want to hear what
u're saying!"

Rezac snarled, the noise rising as he opened his mouth
roar his anger. Kris stepped between them, grasping hold
Rezac as Davies ran to help.

"I don't know what deal you made with her, Taradain,"
id Kris, "but you harm her and . . ."

"And what?" he asked, pulling Jo back with him toward
e door. "You're captives, remember?"

"We'll have nothing left to lose," snarled Rezac, strug-
ing between the two Humans. "Return her within two
ays, or by Varza, I will shred you and nail what's left of
ur hide to my wall!"

"Brave words! You wouldn't make it past the guards,"
ardain said, hand fumbling behind him for the latch.

When they'd gone, Kris released the enraged Sholan.
Violence won't help," he said sharply. "You go on the
arpath now and you'll ruin any hopes we have of help
om Taradain."

"He's using her!"

"And she agreed to it!" said Kris.

"She had no right to . . ."

"She had every right! Stop acting like a fool, Rezac!
ashou's getting worse, we have to take any opportunity we
an to escape! The cost justifies saving lives, and only Jo
ould decide to pay the price, not us!"

"She's done it before, we told you, she told you," said
avies, releasing him.

Rezac let out a low sound of anguish, turning away from

them. "She'd just begun to forget that life, to enjoy be loved! You think I didn't see the bruises on her wrists?

Kris caught Davies' eye. He lifted his shoulders in a m gesture. "She wasn't good when she came back from a to at Geshader or Tashkerra," he said quietly. "She had spend some time in our sick bay. The Valtegans were gentle with our women. She can cope."

"There's nothing we can do, Rezac, except not screw up for her," said Kris, reaching out to touch the oth comfortingly.

"When we escape, I will have that one," Rezac snarl turning round. "I will kill him before we leave!"

"You'll leave him alone! For all we know, Jo asked h to help us! You have no proof of any coercion! We ta what's offered and leave! If he fails to return Jo, tha another matter. Now let's get back to work. Killian con turn up at any time and we don't want him thinking we not doing our best for him."

As Jo had said, the caravan arrived that evening. T courtyard was a hive of bustling activity as stalls were put for the following day. That night, they ate up in their cha bers, the noise from the caravans still drifting up to them.

Jo remained mentally unreachable by either of them, b at the evening meal the following night, after Railin's stori Kris had the opportunity to exchange a few words with he

"How are you?" he asked. "Rezac saw bruises on yo We've been worried."

She frowned. "Bruises?"

"Your wrists." Kris indicated them.

"Oh, those," she said, looking at her wrist. "I got the the night we talked at the pillar. It's nothing."

"You sure? You don't look well. Don't cut us off, J You're making both you and Rezac suffer Link deprivatio If you keep it up, neither of you will be in a fit state do anything."

She raised her head to look him squarely in the fac "You think I want either of you there, inside my head, this time?"

"I'll stay out, but let Rezac back. I honestly think you' making it worse for both of you. I've never seen him s worried."

She considered it for a moment. "Very well, I'll open th

k a fraction, enough for him to be aware of me, no
re. Tell him not to force a greater contact."

'I'll speak to him. Railin says he'll not interfere in our
ns and the caravan will wait for us ten miles outside the
vn. They'll organize trouble with one of the wagons and
ed to stop to fix it."

She nodded absently as she saw Taradain returning. "No
re, please. Rezac should have a package for you. Our
. Taradain got it back for us."

"How's he going to get away with this? Surely his fa-
r's going to know he's responsible."

'He's got it covered," she said, putting on a smile and
ginning to get to her feet. "We'll come for you late to-
orrow night," she murmured. "Be ready."

* * *

Morning saw the four of them sharing breakfast down-
irs in the tap room. At this time of day, with only the
acers there, it was quiet. Their Sumaan crew was just leav-
g for the *Hkariyash* to work on the engines. A message
om Assadou was handed to them by one of the servants:
rrie and Kusac were to meet with the Chemerian at the
eventh hour in the Port Hotel. Meanwhile, they were to
scover which Lords currently had agents in the Port. They
re usually to be found in the Meeting Point Tavern.

Kaid and T'Chebbi decided they would return to the ship.
stensibly they'd help with repairs, but actually they'd use
e opportunity to poke around the maintenance sheds, look-
g for spares in the hope of hearing some useful gossip.

Carrie and Kusac took the time to amble down the
wn's only street as tourists—spacers on leave for a few
ys with money in their pockets to burn. Most of the stalls
ere already doing a brisk trade and despite having just
eakfasted, they found the smells of cooked food too good
ignore. They stopped at one selling meat rolls and con-
nued on their way, munching contentedly.

"These are good," said Carrie, stopping to catch a hand-
l of crumbs as a corner of flaking pastry fell.

"Popular, too," agreed Kusac, cramming the last piece into
s mouth. "That's usually a sign of good food. We need to
atch what we eat here, though. The last thing we need is to
e laid low because of an infection from the local food."

She murmured an assent before letting out an "Oh!" of

surprise and heading straight for a stall selling knives of
types from kitchen utensils to jeweled eating knives. So
ten minutes and a lot of spirited haggling later, Carrie
bought an eating knife. Six inches in length, narrow of bla
it ended in a lethal point. The tang had been encased wit
wood so black it resembled ebony, contrasting vividly v
the polished steel quillons. The pommel was a single tran
cent milky-white stone with a heart of lilac-colored vein
that spread in tendrils toward the surface.

As she ambled along fastening its plain black scabb
to her belt, Kusac took her by the arm, drawing her tow
the buildings opposite the stalls.

"Meeting Point," he said, tilting his chin and flicking
ear in the direction of the sign overhead.

This tavern was obviously intended for business u
Wide rectangular tables with roomy padded benches a
wooden armchairs were set in individually walled alcov
It was a far cry from the scarred wooden dining tables a
plain benches at their inn. Several of the alcoves, their
bles covered with papers, were already occupied by Suma
and U'Churian crews deep in conversation.

They made their way to the bar, ordered a couple
ales, then went to find somewhere to sit. Before they sett
themselves, a shadow loomed over them. Looking
Kusac saw Captain Tirak.

"I had not thought to see you again so soon," the capt.
said. "Join us. I presume you're here to locate the varic
agents."

"We are indeed," said Kusac, beginning to rise. "
would be a pleasure to join you."

Carrie looked up at him as she rose to her feet, notici
that as she did, the U'Churian gave a small start of surpri:
As they headed over to where two of his crew sat, s
probed gently at the edges of his mind. Once more she n
the mental barrier. Switching her attention, as she smil
in greeting and sat down again beside Kusac, she touch
the minds of the other two. Again the same barrier. It w
uniform for the three of them.

Crude but effective, sent Kusac. *You're right, though. It is.
a natural one. I'd say they've come across telepaths already.*

More than that, his was the mind I touched when
landed here. There was no barrier then, sent Carrie.

*Curious and curiouser. We'd do well to be on our guard
th them.*

"Sheeowl and Manesh," Tirak said, indicating his two
ew members. "If I remember, you're Carrie and Kusac."

Kusac nodded.

Their ales arrived and as they tasted them, Carrie pulled
face.

"Not to your liking?" asked Sheeowl, pushing her tankard
rward. "Try this. It's a local hot beverage and more pleas-
t than the recycled dishwater they serve here."

Carrie tasted it gingerly, a smile of surprise crossing her
ce. "It's like chocolate!"

Sheeowl raised her brows. "Chocolate?" she asked. "A
lnian drink?"

"Similar. Ours needs sweetening as it's quite bitter. This
much more pleasant."

Sheeowl looked toward the bar and, raising her hand,
dicated her drink and held up two digits. "Share one with
e," she said.

Tirak turned back to Kusac. "Agents. What goods are
u after this trip?"

"Not after. I'm to sound out the market available for
lnian crafts."

"Ah. New markets," he nodded. "Anything that might
terest us?"

Kusac shrugged. "Tastes differ. Doubtless when Assa-
ou's finished showing our samples to the Jalnian agents,
e'll make them available to the interested captains."

Tirak sighed. "As usual, we'll get to see the tag ends that
o one else wants. Nothing changes." He took a drink of
is own ale. "Sound business practice, though, considering
ost of us have our cargoes already spoken for. Few of us
ave the money to buy extra goods. This damned backwa-
r planet runs a cash only system, no credits."

"Sarak's and Haram's agents just came in, Captain,"
aid Manesh.

Tirak looked over to where the two wealthily dressed
alnians were standing by the alcove nearest the door.
They'll come over to us at some point," he said. "We
ave goods for them on board the *Profit*. I'll introduce you,
f you wish."

"How many Lords does Bradogan allow to trade here?"
sked Carrie.

Tirak turned to her in surprise. "Your command of c language is excellent," he said.

"I had plenty of time to learn it during the journey her she replied, catching his eye in a long stare before blin ing slowly.

"Ten," he replied, breaking the contact and blinking r: idly a couple of times.

They don't like sustained eye contact, she sent to Kus:

"They pay quite high taxes to Bradogan for the privile of trading with us," Tirak continued. "The agents live a work in the town, coming here regularly to deal with : Are you after someone specific?"

"Assadou wants us to meet with them all, give them c sales pitch and see who's interested. Then we'll set up meeting for them with Assadou."

"Wait here long enough and they'll all turn up," s: Sheeowl, taking the drinks from the servant and handling h a couple of coins. "They watch for the new arrivals and co here to meet them. They already know there's a new spec wanting to trade." She pushed a tankard over to Carrie.

"The bulk of our cargo is cloth for Lord Turna and he due to meet us at some point this morning. You're welcom to remain with us during our business meeting." He sh another glance across the table at Carrie. "Perhaps yo companion will learn by listening to our bargaining."

"She's a pretty shrewd negotiator in her own right," sa Kusac wryly. "But knowledge of the local agents and ho they operate would be very useful. We'll accept your off with thanks."

"Cloth," said Carrie thoughtfully, sipping her warm drin "If I remember correctly, cloth is not something your wor is known for; rather, it's a product you import in bulk."

"Ordinarily, you'd be correct," said Manesh, "but this a cargo of open weave cloth suitable for using for preserve meats and such like. It's a trial order. Lord Turna wants : see if it's cheaper and better for the job than the loc product he uses."

Trick question, I think, sent Carrie. *I sensed their surpris in their body language when they realized I knew about th cloth. Watch them, they're definitely suspicious of us alread*

By midafternoon, Carrie was unable to contain her imp: tience any longer. *I've had enough. Let's head for the hot*

*and Assadou. It must be about time to leave anyway. And
once those three agents spread the word that we're here with
new goods, the others should come looking for us.*

You're right.

Kusac tapped Tirak gently on the arm to draw his
attention.

Pausing in his writing, Tirak looked up at them.

"We have to leave now," Kusac said. "Time for us to
met with Trader Assadou. If any agents should ask for us,
we'll be eating at the inn tonight."

"I'll pass the message on. If there's room at our table,
join us."

"We will, and many thanks for your help today."

Tirak shrugged. "You're welcome. At the end of the day,
Home benefits from all of us who learn to trade
effectively."

Sheeowl watched them leave. "Why are you befriending
them?" she asked. "I'd have thought you'd rather keep
them at a distance."

"Keep your friends close, and your enemies closer," said
Tirak, bending his head again to his paperwork. "Damn,
but I'll be glad when this world's opened up fully! All this
hard cash and paper forms!" He glanced at Manesh. "Did
you check on the cryo units before we left?"

"Yes, Captain, you've asked me that already today. The
young people are fine. Mrowbay is a competent medic; you
have no need to worry."

Tirak growled briefly in annoyance. "I like putting them
there as little as the rest of you, but what option have we?
I want to find out what's going on here and the last thing
we need is two innocent-looking spies in our midst! Hell,
they can probably sit and chat with us as nice as you please
and be mentally telling that pair," he indicated the door by
which Kusac and Carrie had just left, "that they've been
tortured and abused by us! You tell me what other option
we had?" he demanded, looking at them in turn.

"You know my opinion, Captain," said Manesh. "They
should have been there from the first."

Sheeowl sighed. "You're right, of course, and they aren't
really children, as Manesh says. I suppose putting them in
cryo is in their best interest as it prevents them from feeling
they should get involved."

"Captain, I think I should point out that it is possible that the two females are not from the same species. After all, the eyes of the one called Carrie are very different from Kate's," said Manesh.

"You saw them, too?" Tirak gave an involuntary shiver. "Uncanny, eyes like that in such a face and body. I'm inclined to believe they're both Humans."

"Or both Solnians," said Sheeowl.

"Humans," said Manesh. "This Kusac and the other two are posing as U'Churians so they're obviously working covertly. Kate and Taynar aren't. I say we hear the truth from them."

"Nothing has changed, I want all four of them kept under surveillance as we discussed last night. I want to know what's going on here. At least we're a few steps ahead of them. We can be pretty sure that it involves the Valtegans, and rescuing that female in the *Spacer's Haven*. I'd trade my tail to get a look at that crashed craft! I'm sure it's a crucial factor."

"Didn't the female tell you much?" asked Sheeowl with a grin as she took a sip of her drink.

Tirak shot her an angry look. "No, she refused to talk about her past."

"So, did you?" she prompted, eyes like saucers looking at him innocently over the top of her tankard.

Tirak gave a rumble of annoyance and shoved his empty one across the table to her. "I paid for information, not sex! Do something useful. Get me another drink."

When she'd left, he found Manesh still regarding him. "Might have been useful to get that close to her. You can learn a lot about a species from their intimate habits."

"What's with this sudden intrusion into my privacy?" Tirak demanded, ears flicking edge on then lying sideways. "Go follow them! See they *are* heading for the Port Hotel!"

"Sayuk is doing that," Manesh replied urbanely. "Two of us will attract their attention. I am better in here, watching to see if anyone takes an unusual interest in this Solnian cargo."

With a hiss of annoyance, Tirak resumed his scribbling.

CHAPTER 15

"What d'you want?" asked Jeran, not bothering to look up from the container he was checking.

"May the sun shine on you today," said T'Chebbi quietly in Sholan.

Jeran froze, then swung round to see who'd spoken. The look of surprised hope faded slightly as he looked at what he thought were two U'Churians. "You shouldn't be here," he said cautiously in the same language. "Off-worlders aren't allowed in here."

"You're quite a distance from home yourself," said Kaid. "Sholans don't usually travel this far."

Jeran moved closer to them, reaching out to touch the gray tunic the male wore. Closing his eyes briefly, he sniffed the air. "Sholans. Gods, you *are* Sholans, and Brotherhood! I'd all but given up hope! The others, have you found the others yet? How'd you get here? Has Miroshi recovered?" The questions came tumbling out as he grasped Kaid's forearm with both hands.

"You are first," said T'Chebbi.

"She was so ill, I was afraid she'd die!" He stopped, realizing what she'd said. "Only me? I'm the first?"

Kaid loosened Jeran's grip, clasping him by the arm and drawing him back into the shadows from which they'd come.

Stopping only to pick up his clipboard, T'Chebbi followed them.

"If the others are alive, we'll find them," Kaid said reassuringly. "We don't know much about you, not even your names. Only that there were four of you."

Jeran began to sway as he passed a shaking hand over his forehead. "Four. Yes, there are four of us."

T'Chebbi guided him to a container, urging him to sit

down. Putting her hand against his neck, she checked his pulse. "Is only shock," she said. "Which one are you?"

"Jeran Khesrey, Life-Support engineer from Szurtha," he said automatically. His eye ridges met in a frown as he looked at her tunic. "Gray with purple? Only telepaths can wear purple, Miroshi told me."

Kaid squatted down in front of him. "Some of the Brothers are telepaths. Is Miroshi a telepath? We heard there were two."

Jeran turned to Kaid again. "Yes, a truthsayer from the offices. We were on our way from the Chakuu Mining Corporation moonbase to Szurtha on leave when they took us. I guess we were the lucky ones?"

Kaid nodded. "They destroyed Szurtha and Khyaal."

Jeran closed his eyes. T'Chebbi put a comforting hand on his shoulder. "All gone?" he whispered. "No one left?"

"Nothing," said Kaid. "I'm sorry, but I have to push you now. We may not have long before we're disturbed. The other two. What are their names?"

"Tallis Vrenga, he's the other telepath. He was one of the supervisors. And Tesha Freyash. She was in communications. I don't know where they are. They separated us, sold us off like livestock. . . ."

T'Chebbi gave him a small shake. "Enough," she said not unkindly. "Soon it will be over. Not yet, we have others to find, but soon."

"Can you leave this area?" asked Kaid.

"No, they keep me here because they know I'm an engineer. I check cargoes but if they need me to work on anything, I'm available."

"Do you get called on often?"

Jeran shrugged. "Rarely. They don't want the U'Churians to see me and start asking questions. You know there are Sumaan here?"

"They only involve themselves in their employers' business," said Kaid. "They're true mercenaries." He looked across at T'Chebbi. "Maybe our ship has life-support problems, eh?"

"Assuredly. Smelled burning seals when they tested it this morning."

"Ever worked on Sumaan systems?" he asked the young male.

Jeran's ears were pricked forward now, listening to their every word. "No, but how different can they be?" he asked.

Kaid let his mouth fall open in a grin as he stood up. "We'll be in touch. Do nothing to draw attention to yourself in the meantime. We have more than you to rescue." He turned to leave, then stopped.

Can you receive me? he sent, studying Jeran's face.

"What is it?" he asked, looking puzzled.

"Nothing," said Kaid, grasping him by the shoulder. "Stay strong. As she said, it'll soon be over." *Pity. It would have been useful,* he thought to himself.

A puzzled look crossed Jeran's face and he shook his head. As he did, the pendant he wore glinted at the neck of his tunic. "Did you say something?" he asked.

Kaid could do nothing but stare speechlessly at the green stone.

Following his gaze, T'Chebbi gave a small grunt of surprise. "What is it?" she asked Jeran, pointing at his pendant.

Surprised, Jeran lifted it up and held it out by the length of its thong for her to see. "A local talisman. We all have to wear them."

"Talisman for what?" asked Kaid in a hushed voice. He couldn't believe what he was seeing. A Valtegan la'quo stone here, on Jalna? "How could it be possible?"

"Excuse me?" Jeran, obviously confused, looked from one to the other.

"Is nothing for you to be concerned about," reassured T'Chebbi, reaching out her hand for it. "Can we borrow?"

"I can't," said Jeran, face creasing in concern as his hand closed over the pendant. "The Jalnians insist I wear it. They say it protects me from the madness that comes at this time of year."

"Take it off for a moment, please," said Kaid, finding his voice again. "Let T'Chebbi hold it. We won't keep it, you have my word. We've seen its like before."

"Where?" Interested now, Jeran took it off and handed it to the Sister.

Can you hear me now? sent Kaid, this time forcing the contact.

Jeran took a step back, catching his heels on the container behind him and sitting down heavily. "Better than when Miroshi does it! You *are* a telepath! But how? Brothers can't . . ."

"Can now," said T'Chebbi grimly, holding the pendant close for Kaid to see. "Don't touch it," she warned him.

The sound of distant voices could be heard coming toward the warehouse. Kaid reached out a finger. "I have to," he said, his voice equally grim. As his finger grazed the surface, he felt the familiar wave of nausea and weakness pass through him. "La'quo," he said. "Without a doubt. Give it back to him, T'Chebbi, we've got to leave." Vartra's bones! It was too much for him to take in right now. He forced himself to concentrate on what was necessary. "Leave it off when you can," he said to Jeran. "We can't contact you if you're wearing it. Remember what we said, wait for work on the Sumaan vessel *Hkariyash*. When it comes, take it. We'll have time to talk then."

The pendant spun through the air toward him and Jeran lunged to catch it. When he looked up, they were gone.

The voices had gotten closer and were quite audible now. "I don't care what you thought you saw, you're not authorized to go into the warehouses!" He knew that voice. It was the supervisor.

"You want one of those tarnachs roaming round free?" demanded the other. The spacer patois had a distinctive U'Churian burr to it.

Jeran snatched up his clipboard and, at a run, headed back to the consignment he'd been checking. A tarnach running free! It wasn't possible! They were barely controllable at the best of times.

"No tarnachs around here," said the guard at the entrance. "All the beasts but those on patrol are in the kennels. You been drinking too much ale, spacer!"

"I tell you, we saw a tarnach!" The door burst open and two U'Churians pushed their way in. They stopped dead, looking at Jeran.

A moment, then the female recovered herself. "Did a tarnach come in here?" she demanded of him.

"No, Lady," said Jeran. Then on impulse, "I did hear something snuffling around outside when they took their break fifteen minutes ago."

"Break? What break?" demanded the supervisor rounding angrily on the guards.

The female's mouth widened in a slow grin and she tilted

an ear at him. "We owe you," she mouthed at him, then spun round and stalked back to her companion. "Was here, but didn't come in," she said. "Our cargo is safe." With that, they went, leaving the supervisor and the two guards shouting at each other.

*   *   *

After the coolness of the air-conditioning in the *Meeting Point,* going outside felt like walking into a furnace. The crowds on the street were beginning to thin as the Jalnians who lived and worked in the town headed back to their homes to prepare the evening meal. Several of the daytime stalls were beginning to pack up, leaving their pitches for the night traders.

Did you learn anything of interest? Kusac asked as they made their way toward the checkpoint for the Port Hotel and Lord Bradogan's Keep.

A few things. I know how to make both Jalnians and U'Churians uneasy in my company. They dislike seeing a hunter's eyes in a humanoid face. Their curiosity vanishes rather quickly!

Useful, agreed Kusac. *Sholans don't seem to mind. I wonder why it affects the Jalnians and the U'Churians?*

Possibly because they're used to each others' species, whereas the majority of Sholans we know met me before any other Humans.

Could be. Have your pass ready, he sent as they approached the gates. Reaching into one of the pouches on his belt, he pulled his papers out, handing them to the guard. Carrie did the same.

The Jalnian studied them for a moment, returning Kusac's while taking a second look at Carrie's. A quick glance at her face then his eyes slid back to the pass. Hurriedly he returned it to her, waving them through.

I get the feeling he doesn't want us to linger. Kusac's tone was amused as he put his papers away.

Told you, came Carrie's smug reply.

Through the high, electrified fence they could see that the spaceport was fairly quiet in comparison to when they'd arrived the day before and, taking their time, they ambled leisurely over to the hotel.

The Keep looks very plain, Kusac observed. *Featureless. Just four sides and a large entrance with steps.*

It's a fortress. They were designed to be as siege proof as possible. At least they were on Earth, she amended. *Your enemy would camp outside the keep, unable to get in, while you were safe inside with all the livestock and water you needed.*

That was how they fought? Kusac looked at her in surprise. *Strange way to fight a battle.*

The point was, there was only one way in—through the front doors—and they were protected by a portcullis—a large metal gate that was lowered down in front of the doors when the keep was being attacked. It's an old building, so Bradogan's land must have been contested many times over the last few hundred years. Look, on the wall above the door. Those narrow slits are for archers to look through. They can shoot down on the attackers without being at risk themselves. Same with the crenellated wall right up at the top.

Built as a stronghold against any enemies. He guards himself well.

Doesn't he just, she agreed as they drew closer to the hotel.

This building was unashamedly modern, owing much of its design to the advanced technology of its visiting aliens. Passing the ubiquitous Jalnian guards, they pushed open the large transparent doors and entered the main foyer. Their eyes were instantly assaulted by a confusion of functional ship design overlaid with barbaric opulence.

Ouch, sent Carrie, looking round and wincing. *At least they've got air-conditioning!*

Kusac grunted in agreement. *I need it with this longer pelt. I'd be prepared to stay here for that alone.*

The lobby, set to the left of a staircase, was illuminated by a transparent domed ceiling. Crimson carpeting led the way to the reception area where, behind a plain functional counter, a Jalnian in brightly colored robes stood on duty. An array of comm controls could be seen behind him.

Floor-length crimson velvet curtains, looped at midpoint with golden ropes, lined the pale gray walls. Apparently placed at random, groups of matching crimson and gilt easy chairs sat around ornately carved low wooden tables. Between them, tubs of flowering plants, their blooms a riot of clashing colors, had been placed in the hope of creating an atmosphere of quiet and privacy.

This was designed by people who have no concept of re-

ixation, sent Kusac as they made their way over to the ~~r~~eceptionist.

I prefer our inn, even if it is hotter, she replied as they ~~a~~pproached the counter.

"What can I do for you, Trader?" the receptionist asked, ~~e~~yes narrowing as he looked past Carrie to Kusac. There ~~w~~as an edge of condescension in his voice.

"Inform Trader Assadou Chikoi that his agent and the ~~S~~olnian Representative are here," said Kusac, flexing his ~~c~~laws as he rested his hand on the counter.

"Solnian Representative?" The man glanced back at ~~C~~arrie.

"No one could fault your hearing," said Kusac, beginning ~~t~~o tap the surface with a claw tip.

"Certainly, honored Representatives," he said, dipping ~~h~~is head in a gesture of respect as he backed away to reach ~~h~~is comm. A few moments later he turned back to them. ~~"~~Trader Assadou is expecting you, Representatives," he ~~s~~aid. He indicated the stairs. "First floor, suite ten. Or there ~~i~~s an elevator around the corner."

Kusac nodded and turned toward the stairs, took hold of ~~C~~arrie's arm. *That son of a she-jegget thought you were ~~a~~ qwene!* he sent, his hand tightening protectively as he ~~s~~hepherded her toward the stairs.

How was he to know different? I think you're overreacting ~~a~~ little.

Kusac gave a brief, muted growl as they started up the ~~s~~teps. *I don't have to like it.*

They nodded briefly to the Sumaan who opened the door ~~t~~o them. Assadou was sitting in state in a large armchair, ~~w~~ell propped up with soft cushions. A drink and a plate of ~~C~~hemerian fruits sat on the table in front of him.

"Sit, sit," Assadou said, indicating the settee. "You are ~~p~~rompt, that is good. Is all well where you lodge?"

"Fine," said Kusac, speaking in Sholan. "I presume the ~~r~~oom is clear of listening devices?"

Assadou turned to look at the Sumaan behind him.

"Is clear," the guard confirmed.

"Have you managed to accomplish anything with regard ~~t~~o our permits?"

"Have only just arrived! Need time settling in, making ~~a~~ppropriate gestures of goodwill!" Assadou exclaimed.

"Have no idea how to conduct true business, you Sholar Too much haste!"

"Assadou, we're not sitting around waiting for a wee while you and Bradogan send polite messages to ea other," said Carrie. "We have to get moving now! Th longer we delay, the greater the chance of us bei discovered."

Assadou's ears twitched slightly at the edges. "When p like that, perhaps haste is not unseemly," he agreed relu tantly. "I send message, with Solnian trinket to whet h appetite for more. Then he will ask that I come to hir You, perhaps, could accompany me. But unlikely you g permit. He dislikes spacers on Jalna."

"We *will* accompany you," said Kusac. "We spent tl day at the *Meeting Point*. The Lord we want is Killian, b he seems to have no agent here at present."

Assadou inclined his head in agreement. "Is so. I di cover agent is regrettably on way to Kaladar with carava Not back in Port for several weeks."

"That's what I was afraid of. Unfortunately, I've alread put the word around the agents we did meet that you hav a cargo of new goods from Sol to show them," said Kusa "I've said I'm authorized to set up a meeting between yc and any of them who wish to examine the goods fc themselves."

"You wish me to sell the bulk of our Terran items t this Lord Killian's agent," surmised Assadou. "I can ho out for better prices and delay sale till he returns."

"I'm not happy about waiting that long," said Kusac.

"If not able to go to Kaladar, then next city is Galrayir Lord Tarolyn is favorite of Lord Bradogan. Maybe tha would do? Cannot wait for long, as you say. When tradin, must cut losses and take next best thing to what you wish.

We could always leave the caravan and head for the hill either on the way there or back. Maybe even make it loo like we were taken in the night by bandits, suggested Carri

Possibly a better option than sitting waiting for Killian agent to appear, agreed Kusac. "The goods are transporte in wagons, aren't they?" he asked.

Assadou nodded. "They travel in a caravan for prote tion. There are many bandits in the Jalnian hills."

"Then it wouldn't seem amiss if you insisted that two c your people traveled with this caravan to ensure that th oods arrive safely, and to gauge for themselves how the Ilnian Lord and his family react to the new trade items," id Kusac. "That might persuade Bradogan to give us ar permits."

"This could be suggested," agreed Assadou. "Lord Bra-ogan keeps strict watch on who goes in and out of the ort town, and aliens are rarely permitted to set foot on ie real Jalna."

"Rarely," said Carrie, frowning at him. "Last I heard it as never."

Assadou began to blink rapidly, a sure sign of embar-ssment. "Is not something that happens often. Who in ght mind wishes to go among such violent people?"

"Haven't seen any sign of their violence yet," said Kusac differently. "They seem as normal as Chemerians to me." The look he received was pure hate as Assadou pulled imself up to his full seated height of three feet. "Chemeri-is peaceful! Not violent, not kill one another!"

"No, you get the Sumaan to do it for you," he snapped, aning forward. "Sholans have tempers, too, Trader. ou'd do well to remember that! Sholan High Command ill not be impressed that you continue to tell us half-uths. We work together, your government said, and to-ether means you tell us everything! Now, just how difficult it for you to get us our permits?"

"Can be done," said Assadou stiffly, his ears quivering ith suppressed rage.

"How quickly?"

"Today. I send message now."

"Do it," ordered Kusac, sitting back. "We'll wait till you ave a reply."

With a chittering sound of displeasure, Assadou gave a eries of short commands in his own language to the Su-aan on his right. The guard disappeared into the inner oom, emerging minutes later with a small case of writing nplements. Hurriedly, Assadou scrawled a note, then dis-atched him to the Keep with it and a small wooden casket.

"Is done. We wait."

Carrie looked pointedly at the table. "Refreshments ould be nice."

Again the ears quivered, then common sense got the pper hand. "Am failing in duty as host. Please, help your-

selves," he said, his tone, if not gracious, at least mo
normal for a Chemerian.

Carrie got up and headed over to the dispenser unit
see what it served.

"What are your plans once you reach Kaladar?" Ass
dou asked Kusac.

He stirred in his seat. "Rescue our people."

"What of the Valtegans?" Assadou demanded. "That
our prime reason for bringing you here at such vast ri
and expense!"

"We hope they'll have discovered something at the cra
site, but we'll never know unless we get them safely out
Kaladar," said Kusac smoothly.

"Your rescue attempt. You will try nothing hazardo
that will involve me, will you?" Assadou was suddenly ne
vous. "Where will you hide these people? How will yo
get them into the Port without discovery?"

"We're working on that now," said Carrie, coming ba
with two mugs of coffee. "Didn't know you liked th
Assadou."

"We're not going to take any unnecessary risks, belie
me, Assadou."

"I hope not," replied the Chemerian acidly. "I val
my life!"

"As do we," murmured Kusac, taking his mug from Ca
rie with a nod of thanks. "I'd like our journey to Galray
set up as soon as possible."

Assadou made a gesture of assent. "I will have my cre
bring the Terran trade items from the ship today. If Lo
Bradogan grants you the permits, likely you will be free
journey on the next caravan leaving for there. That yo
can arrange at the Port Agency office by the gatehouse in
the spacers town."

"If you continue to call them Terran goods instead
Solnian, you're the one most likely to blow our cover
Carrie said warningly, sipping her drink. "Rememb
you'll go down with the rest of us."

A look of distress passed over Assadou's face and I
squeezed his eyes shut in obvious horror. "Apologies," I
whispered. "I will not forget again. Solnian."

Their wait was not long. Within fifteen minutes, the S
maan was back, bearing an invitation to meet lord Brad
gan later that evening.

As Carrie and Kusac went through the lobby on their way out, they passed a Jalnian of obvious importance seated in one of the chairs. A guard of some half a dozen armed men accompanied him.

Carrie glanced briefly in his direction. Tall and loose-limbed, there was an implicit arrogance in the way he lounged in his chair. She could feel his gaze following them as they made their way to the exit. The hairs on the back of her neck started to prickle and she found herself anxious to leave.

What is it? Kusac demanded, turning to her once they were outside.

Something and nothing, she replied, shivering again. *Who do you think he was?*

Probably Lord Bradogan, he sent, taking her arm and squeezing it gently. *He disturbs you?*

He has a predatory look about him, she replied, comforted by the contact.

We'll take no chances with him, Kusac assured her.

* * *

"Well?" asked Tirak as Giyesh slipped into the seat opposite him at the *Travelers Inn*. He could tell by the set of her ears that she had news.

"The two Sholans are here now, waiting for their friends. They found another one, one we'd missed," she said.

"Where?"

"In the last warehouse, checking cargo. A male. Nice looking, too. Pale colored pelt that makes his muscles stand out," she said, smiling reminiscently.

Tirak snorted in annoyance. "You were supposed to . . ."

"He covered our asses with his supervisor and the guards," she added hastily. "We barged past them into the warehouse saying we'd seen a loose tarnach. That's when we saw him."

"That should have been enough for them to throw the doors wide," said Mrowbay.

"You kept the Sholans in sight all day?" asked Tirak.

She nodded. "They spent the morning going from ship to ship, chatting to the various crews. Even stopped at the *Profit*. Were asking how good the Port engineers were in maintenance. Then in the afternoon, they headed over to

the workshops, spent some time there, doubled back
hind the sheds and made for the end warehouse. I rec
they were looking for him all along."

"Do you think you could get in to speak to this n
again?" asked Tirak.

Giyesh looked aslant at him, the smile returning. "O
might be able to do that. Did find out he'd not one of
staff, he's property. Owned by Lord Bradogan."

"I've heard they buy and sell their own folk," nod
Tirak. "No one else would want to with their record
violence. Four of them there were, I found out today fr
Lord Sarak's agent. Sold by the Valtegans. Seems th
Sholans know a fair bit about the Valtegans, more than
do." He drummed his fingers on the table thoughtfu
"There's a lot more going on than we thought. Move c
fully, people. I don't want them suspecting that w
watching them."

"The Jalnians have started checking the locals at
gates," said Mrowbay. "Making sure they're wearing th
green pendants."

"He wore one," said Giyesh.

"They'd automatically make him wear it," said Mrowb
"Doesn't mean he's susceptible to the sickness. Proba
making sure he eats only Port food, too, same with
female. Be as bad for them as if one of us ran amok. Im
ine the damage we'd do before they stopped us."

"The Solnian and her partner have arrived and are cc
ing over, Captain," said Sayuk quietly.

"After we've eaten, see if you can reach that male ag
Giyesh," said Tirak. "I'll try and get our new friends
come with us tonight, visit the *Haven* where this Te
female works."

"Tesha? Nice name," murmured Sheeowl.

Tirak shot her an angry look but had no time for m
as the Sholan group came up to them.

"May we join you?" asked Kusac.

Tirak gestured to the remaining places at the ta
"Help yourselves. Have you met all of my crew?"

Conversation flowed easily throughout the meal, with
U'Churians willing to tell them more about the vari
goods they traded in. Jalna's main export, apparently, v
fabrics. Top of their range was one woven from a fiber

ong and light that from its description it rivaled Terran

Carrie took the small sample that Tirak handed her. "It's believably soft," she said, rubbing it gently between her gers. "It's warm, almost feels alive, and so soft! This uld sell well on any world."

"And it's cheap to buy," said Tirak. "Our family owns franchise for it. We were one of the first to start trading re. My forefather was astute enough to realize that what Jalnian peasants wear would be a luxury for the wealthy ck home. Jalnian dyes are magnificent, too. There's a ninosity about them that we just cannot duplicate. We port this jotha in a variety of different shades as well as ir basic unbleached cream."

"I want some of this," said Carrie, handing the sample ck to him. "Is it all as fine a weave as this?"

"It comes in many weaves," said Sheeowl. "From so fine almost invisible, to so thick you could walk on it!"

"She exaggerates," said Tirak. "If you're seriously inter-ed, I can have samples brought over for you."

"I'm serious," she said. "Is your supply capable of ex-nding to accommodate us as well?"

"Depends whether you wish to sell a luxury item or not."
This fabric could help bring in the revenues we need to self-sufficient, Carrie sent to Kusac. *Can we trade in it ce we're not in the Merchants Guild?*

We're En'Shalla; we belong to no Guild, he replied. *We ed to establish ourselves and I'd rather we made our living ding in luxury goods than from the lives of our Clan. rras has the skills we need. Yes, make a preliminary deal th him now, I'll guide you.*

She smiled, lifting her tankard of Jalnian chocolate. "You n't expect me to tell you that, do you? Put a contract gether for me to review, with samples of the fabric and ices. I'll look it over during the next few days and we n discuss it further."

Tirak raised an eyebrow. "You sound very sure."

"I know my market, Captain Tirak," she said, her voice deep purr of amusement. "What else do you buy from re?"

"A fermented grain beverage and raw gemstones." He g into one of his waist pouches and brought out a clear

stone with a scintillating heart the color of a lapiz. "Th‸
a polished one," he added. "I keep it as a luck piece."

She held it up to the light, turning it first one way t‸
another to see the colors shift.

"It's beautiful. What's it called?" she asked, handin‸
back to him.

"They call it the Sky Tears," he said, returning it ‸
his pocket.

"Are they expensive?"

"They value them highly here so they aren't che‸
Worked stones are expensive, but if you buy the raw o‸
you can't be sure that they'll polish up well."

Ask if they trade in green stones—like the la'quo, s‸
Kaid.

Unable to hide her start of surprise, Carrie slopped so‸
of her drink on the table. She put the tankard down ‸
flexed her hand as if it were sore.

"Wrist still hurting?" asked Kaid sympathetically, se‸
ing to Kusac at the same time.

"A little," she said then turned back to the U'Churi‸
"What other raw gems do you get?"

"Is there a particular color that you're looking for?"
asked, taking a drink of his ale.

"Purple ones, and perhaps green," she said. "For ‸
own use."

Tirak picked up her new eating knife and handed it ‸
her. "Nothing darker than the stone you have in this, ‸
afraid," he said regretfully. "And no green ones at all. P‸
haps our native gems might interest you, but I expect Ku‸
has shown them to you already."

"Trade with U'Chur is not my province," she said. "I ‸
been given the task of seeing what I find of interest ‸
Jalna."

"I heard the Jalnians also trade in drugs," said Kaid.

Tirak shot him a hard look. "Some ships do. I don't.‸

Kaid shook his head. "I'm not interested myself, but t‸
is my first trip here. I had heard rumors."

"Drugs from other worlds are always available on ‸
black market. I believe the risk is too great, unless they ‸
been medically researched and prepared for use by on‸
own species." He turned to look at Carrie. "A warning ‸
you. Don't be tempted to buy any consumable goods fr‸
Jalna. Their land is poison as far as any non-Jalnian ‸

oncerned. And the poison goes into everything they eat
nd drink, drugs included," he added, glancing briefly at
aid.

"Poisoned?" asked Kusac. "In what way?"

Tirak shrugged. "I'm no scientist. It's enough that we
now it."

"You eat food here. Why it not affect you?" asked
'Chebbi.

"The food in the traders' town is either imported by
pacers like us, or comes from the estates of Lord Tarolyn.
his is the only land free of it. We import food for sale to
Bradogan's allies."

La'quo! sent Kaid. *I didn't get chance to tell you. Jeran,
he one we found, was wearing a la'quo stone as a pendant.
They all wear it to prevent the madness, he says.*

Kusac's wrist comm buzzed a warning. He looked apolo-
etically at Tirak. "We have to go," he said. "An appointment with Lord Bradogan."

Tirak nodded. "A pity. I had hoped you'd join us tonight.
We might even find a diversion to suit the Solnian's taste."
He grinned, showing a mouthful of teeth that rivaled
Kusac's.

"I think not," said Carrie. "We've work to do. You know
now it is with these Chemerians—they work you every hour
he Gods send."

Tirak nodded in agreement. "Another time. Will you go
o the *Meeting Point* tomorrow?"

"We'll be there at some point," said Kusac as he got to
his feet. "Enjoy your evening."

As they all threaded their way out, Kusac sent to Kaid.
You found one? Jeran? Where?

*At the last warehouse. He's an engineer. We stopped at
the ship before coming here. Kishasayzar is going to request
him to fix our life-support systems. Jeran told us all Port
workers wear talismans to ward off the madness.*

And are the talismans la'quo stones? sent Carrie.

Definitely. I touched it to make sure.

You shouldn't have taken such a risk, sent Kusac as they
emerged out into the Jalnian night. *You know it affects
you badly.*

Only way to be positive.

They moved in close to the wall, stopping for a momen
to talk.

"When he took his talisman off, Kusac, he could hea
me mind-speak," said Kaid. "He said Miroshi spoke to hin
like that, so he's obviously got some sensitivity. I told hin
to keep the talisman off whenever he could so we coul
reach him."

Kusac nodded. "You think the la'quo is responsible fo
this poisoning of the soil?"

Kaid nodded. "I'm sure. They use the stone to caln
themselves, prevent the violence, just as the Valtegans usec
it on us in the past. And you can't have the stones withou
the plant having been grown here at some point."

"A stone for nearly everyone on Jalna," murmured Car
rie. "That's one hell of a lot of plants."

"Isn't it?" said Kaid.

"Is big step from what you say stone does to the plan
causing violence," pointed out T'Chebbi. "Only know i
calms you, no more. Something else involved here."

"We know more. We know the la'quo in various form:
affects the Chemerians, us, the Valtegans and the Jalnians—it bridges species differences," said Kaid. "And we
know the soil has been poisoned."

"And that the Valtegans visit occasionally to take soil
and plant samples," said Carrie. "It all points to the plant
and the Valtegans being responsible for whatever has pol-
luted the soil, and the Valtegans know about it."

"Lots of plants," said T'Chebbi. "So many stones, perhaps use Jalna to grow this plant like a farm."

"What?" Kaid turned to look at her.

"They farm plant on Jalna," she repeated. "So many
alien plants that it puts alien chemicals in soil, pollutes it."

"And through the soil, as Tirak said, it gets into everything," said Kusac. "A hallucinogenic plant. No wonder the
people on Jalna are violent."

"Something else," said Carrie, her tone somber. "It sup-
presses telepathy. That's why we can't reach our people.
They've been eating the local food for over six months.
The Gods know what else it's done to them!"

Kusac glanced at his wrist unit. "We have to go. We're
supposed to be at the Keep to meet Assadou now. We've
got an interview with Bradogan, hopefully to get our permits. You and T'Chebbi see if you can find Strick and make

ontact with him. We'll meet you back at the inn when
we're through. Take care."

Kaid nodded.

"So they're looking for these green stones, eh?" mut-
ered Tirak, swirling the dregs of his ale around in his tankard. "Mrowbay, you keep an eye on our two Sholans
onight. Sheeowl, you follow the other pair to the Keep.
Giyesh . . ."

"With pleasure, Captain," she purred, stretching as she
got to her feet. "Nayash, I could do with your help to locate
him. Rather have some backup if I'm wandering around
the Port at night."

Tirak watched them disperse thoughtfully. "I wonder
what they're up to at the Keep at this time of night?" He
looked up at Mrowbay and Manesh. "You go and see if
you can find out who bought the other two. I think I'll pay
another visit to Tesha, see if she'll talk to me this time."

"You're late," said the servant who was waiting for them
at the gatehouse. He hustled them past the guards and on
toward the high arched doorway that led into the Keep.

As they passed under it, Kusac looked up, seeing the
metal spikes that formed the base of the raised portcullis.
"You were right about that," he murmured, drawing her
attention to it.

"Universal constant—like the wheel," she said. "I've noticed lots of them on . . . back home," she said, a shiver
running through her as she realized she'd almost said Shola.

"Lord Bradogan is waiting," said the servant, his tone
reproachful as they slowed down to look around the entrance hall. "We must hurry."

They followed him across to the stone staircase at the
far side of the hall. As they climbed, their footsteps echoed
eerily in the narrow stairwell. The wall on their left ended
and abruptly, they found themselves in a well lit anteroom.
There was nothing in the way of furniture and across from
them they could see Assadou perched uncomfortably on a
chest. Only one of his Sumaan retainers accompanied him
this time.

He looks like a child, thought Carrie as they crossed the
wooden floor to join him.

They're arboreal, remember? sent Kusac. *His legs are*

short and really only suited to gripping tree branches. That'
why he uses a powered chair. And the gravity is too heav
for him.

Is he going to walk in?

Kusac shrugged as they stopped opposite the obviousl*
distressed Chemerian.

"Wait here," said the servant, disappearing through *
doorway.

"You're late!" said Assadou, wringing his hands, th*
edges of his large ears quivering uncontrollably. "You re*
quest this audience! Why you not here on time? Keeping
Lord Bradogan waiting like this is *most* unacceptable!"

"It was unavoidable, Assadou," said Kusac, looking
down at the small being. "We're only a couple of minute*
late, nothing to be so concerned about."

Carrie sighed with relief as the door opened, preventing
Assadou from replying.

The servant held it wide for them. "Lord Bradogan wil
see you now."

"Can I help you, Assadou?" Kusac asked as the Chemerian began to push himself off the chest.

"Can manage," he snapped, steadying himself against i*
before beginning to walk painfully and slowly into the
inner chamber.

As he moved away from it, the Sumaan bent to retrieve*
the chest.

Bradogan insists that Assadou walk in, sent Carrie furiously. *He's humiliating him on purpose!*

We were warned about Bradogan, replied Kusac. *It's bad*
enough that Assadou has to put up with being treated like
this, but for us to see it too . . . Had I known, I wouldn't
have humiliated him further by offering to help. I should
have checked. His tone was regretful.

Their progress was by necessity slow and Carrie took the
opportunity to look around her. Like Kusac, she was aware
of Bradogan's presence, but she was damned if she was
going to acknowledge it until she had to.

This is how I always imagined a castle should look, she
sent to Kusac. The walls had been faced with panels of rich
brown wood with heavy decorative tapestries hung at regular intervals, their colors were a glowing testament to Tirak's earlier praise. Mainly of hunting scenes, they featured
men on their riding beasts accompanied by packs of some

anine creature more domesticated than the tarnachs used
s guard dogs outside in the Port.

Ornately carved sideboards and chests were set against
the walls, with an occasional highbacked plain chair be-
ween them. Lighting, though modern, was subdued and
entler on her eyes than that they'd encountered so far.

Now, Carrie looked ahead to the long table. Behind it
Bradogan lounged, with studied indifference. It was the
man they'd seen earlier, and being closer to him did nothing to dispel her instinctive dislike and wariness.

A youngish man, probably in his thirties, Carrie surmised. His face had a lean hardness about it which the
neatly trimmed beard and mustache only accentuated. As
they drew to a stop in front of him, he sat up in his chair,
resting his elbow on the padded arm. Cool brown eyes regarded them impassively.

From one end of the table, a scribe looked up. "Trader
Assadou Chikoi, Lord Bradogan, seeking a permit for his
agent and the Solnian Representative to accompany a cargo
containing his goods to Lord Tarolyn of Galrayin."

Bradogan rested his chin on his hand and surveyed the
small Chemerian in front of him. "Why do you think it
necessary for these people to accompany your cargo?" he
asked. "Aren't my soldiers enough guarantee for you?"

"Is valuable cargo, Lord Bradogan," said Assadou, inclining his upper body as low as it would go. "New trade
goods from Sol. The female," he indicated Carrie, "is Representative from there."

Bradogan's dark brows met in a frown. "Why wasn't I
apprised of this world before, Trader? And of the visiting
Representative? You make me appear inhospitable by your
own lack of courtesy."

"We only arrived last night, Lord. Sent word today."
Assadou's ears were beginning to curl and uncurl all along
the outer edges as he became more nervous. "Give you
assurances that insult not intentional." He turned to Carrie,
grasping her by the hand and tugging her forward. "Solnian
Representative, Lord Bradogan. Carrie Aldatan."

His hand trembled as it clutched her, tugging firmly
downward to let her know a sign of her respect was
required.

"Lord Bradogan," she said, inclining her head in his di-

rection. Though he concealed it well, she could feel h
intense interest in her.

"A pleasure to welcome you to Jalna, Carrie Aldatan.
he said. "Had the Trader informed me of your arrival ea
lier, I would have invited you to dine with me tonigh
Perhaps tomorrow evening?" His voice was quiet an
deep. Persuasive.

Let him see the predator in your eyes, sent Kusac.

"My schedule is tight, Lord Bradogan," she said, lookin
directly at him and increasing her discouragement fiel
"My people wish me to assess the potential market for ou
goods, then return. They are anxious to formalize trad
agreements with your people."

Surprise made him sit up, then look away. "Anothe
time," he said, turning his attention to Assadou. "Why hav
I seen none of the Solnian trade goods?" he demanded.

The Chemerian gestured to his guard, who stepped for
ward to place the chest on the table in front of Bradogan
Unfastening the catch, he opened the lid.

"Are for you, Lord Bradogan. A gift from Sol."

Bradogan leaned forward and pulled the chest closer
"Tallis!" he called. "Your opinion is required."

The floor length curtain behind Bradogan parted anc
Tallis stepped into the room. Walking round behind hi
Lord, he stopped at his left hand, looking over at Carrie
and Kusac before examining the contents of the chest.

Carrie almost forgot to breathe as she watched the Sho
lan telepath. She didn't dare send to Kusac in case Talli:
picked it up. Their constant Leska Link they could little
about, but Tallis seemed totally unaware of it. In fact, if he
was using his Talent, she couldn't sense it at all.

La'quo, sent Kusac. *He'll be wearing a talisman. Try him
carefully. Reading aliens is your gift. The drug is affecting
his Talent.*

Tallis took a sample of silk from the chest, running i
through his hands before passing it to Bradogan. "Our
jotha is superior," he murmured. Next he took out a small
case containing a necklace of amber beads. As he held it
up toward one of the lights, Bradogan reached out and
took it from him, examining each bead closely.

Carrie took advantage of the moment to reach for Tallis'
mind. She could sense nothing, no activity where there
should have been. Puzzled, she widened her search, looking

n mental wavelengths that belonged in the personal ranges
hey used. Nothing from him, but Kaid was there.

*Touch him. The talisman blocks it. It worked with Jeran
ʌho isn't even a telepath,* sent Kaid.

Moving closer, Carrie reached into the chest, her hand
,oing straight for the box containing the pearls. "Let me
how you these," she said, lifting the lid and picking up
ʌne of the larger ones. Holding it between forefinger and
humb, she let him look before putting it into his waiting
)alm. Continuing to hold his hand, she pushed the pearl
around, letting him see the faint iridescent colors.

"A freshwater pearl," she said. "From one of our river-
dwelling mollusks."

The contact was enough. She tightened her hold, taking
control of his mind.

*Tallis. Stay calm or we're all lost. Help is here. Tonight,
ʌhen you retire, take off the talisman. It prevents us from
contacting you. We'll speak then. Do you understand?*

Yes. The thought was faint but unmistakable.

Gradually Carrie released her hold till Tallis was once
more in control of himself. The pearl in his palm wobbled
toward the edge of his hand and would have fallen off had
she not caught it. Returning it to the box, she set it down
on the table and stepped back beside Kusac.

"We have nothing like that on Jalna," said Tallis, his
voice a trifle shaky. He turned to his Lord. "These are
handsome gifts, Lord Bradogan. Lord Tarolyn will certainly
be interested in them. I would grant them the permits."

Bradogan nodded and signaled to the scribe. "Write
them a permit."

"I thank you, Lord Bradogan. I'm glad our gifts are
pleasing," said Assadou, bowing in thanks.

"Next time, bring Representative Aldatan to me sooner,
Assadou," he said. "I trust your trip to Galrayin will be
uneventful, Representative. Despite Assadou's fears, most
of them are," he said, smiling at Carrie.

She watched while Assadou bowed low again, a gesture
that was beyond the capability of his fragile body. Anger
rose in her, hers and Kusac's.

The scribe passed the document to Bradogan for him to
sign and seal. That done, Bradogan held it out to Carrie. As
she reached for it, he withdrew it, making her step closer to
take it from him.

"Till we next meet," he said, this time holding her ga:
and smiling.

Carrie inclined her head, making no effort to tug th
permit from him until he released it. "My thanks, Lor
Bradogan," she said, turning and walking swiftly to th
door at the far end of the chamber. She had to force herse
not to wrench the knob off in her hurry to leave. In th
anteroom, she paced back and forth impatiently till Kus;
and Assadou joined her. Like a silent shadow, the Sumaa
shut the door behind them and waited.

"You endanger all by your hasty exit!" hissed the angi
Chemerian. "Why you not wait, show proper respect fc
Lord? He give you what you want! Is fine way to sho•
thanks!"

Carrie rounded angrily on him, just managing to kee
her voice low. "Don't make me start, Assadou! You ma
be able to abase yourself before someone like that, but
will not! I've had enough of your smarmy attitude to hir
and your arrogance to us! You'd do well to remember
few realities of life! Now leave me alone, or by Vartra, I'
snap that scrawny little neck of yours! I've been lookir
for an excuse to do it for weeks!" She turned on her hee
and stalked down the stairs to the hall below.

Assadou looked nervously at Kusac. "Is volatile," h
ventured. "Had not thought her capable of this."

"Be thankful you are a Chemerian," said Kusac, hi
voice a low rumble of annoyance as he moved toward th•
stairs. "She would never attack one smaller than herself."

The sound of raised voices drifted up from below.

"Go after her," begged Assadou. "She get herself anc
us into trouble with that temper!"

"No. Those who cross her get into trouble, Assadou,"
he growled, starting downstairs.

By the time he reached the entrance, a small crowd o:
soldiers from the guardroom had gathered. Carrie stood tc
one side, massaging her knuckles. Ignoring them, he joinec
her and together they left the Keep.

"What happened?" he asked as they passed through the
gates into the spacers town.

"One of them propositioned me, much the same way
Bradogan did," she said shortly. "Was stupid enough to try
and take hold of me."

"Uh huh." He walked beside her as she pushed her way

through the throng toward the *Travelers Inn*. "He's dead, then."

Startled, she glanced at him. "No," she grinned, her anger dissipating. "Broken wrist only."

"We'll stay clear of Bradogan," he said.

"I want something strong to wash the taste of that place out of my mouth," she muttered. "That male is just so . . . disgusting! I have no love for our tree-climbing Trader, but to treat him like that was calculated cruelty!"

"They're bound to have spirits for sale," said Kusac, pushing a Jalnian out of his way as the man stumbled against him. His torrent of abuse followed them, getting fainter as they approached the inn.

Carrie pushed the door open and headed for the bar. They'd just gotten there when a fight broke out in the center of the Jalnian area. Instantly, Kusac pushed her to one side, making sure he was between her and the trouble.

Sensing someone standing beside her, she looked round to find Tirak by her elbow.

"It's always bad at this time of year," he said. "The heat only makes it worse. Best to let them get on with it. Bradogan's men will be along any time. They're used to it."

"I thought the talismans were supposed to prevent it, or is this just an ordinary brawl?"

"From the looks of it, no. The Jalnians have only just started preventing anyone without a talisman from entering the town."

The brawl, which had originally involved three people, had spread and was boiling toward them.

Tirak took hold of her arm. "I think we move to our own area," he said, nodding toward the direction from which he'd come.

Carrie pulled free and opened her mouth as Kusac's hand clamped down on her shoulder, tightening warningly.

"Good idea," he said, pushing her in front of himself as they accompanied Tirak. "Thank you for coming over." *You're picking up their anger, cub. Tirak's looking out for you, that's all.*

With ulterior motives!

No matter. He'd do nothing to hurt you. Increase your shielding, you're too sensitive to these Jalnians.

The hand on her shoulder moved slightly till it was hidden beneath her hair, then she felt his touch become gen-

tler as his fingers caressed her throat, sending the magic
the Link flowing through them both. She groaned as the
minds began to become one, causing Tirak to turn rour
in concern.

"What happened?" he asked, looking from one to th
other.

"Nothing," said Carrie hastily.

"We have work to see to tomorrow that'll keep us on th
ship," said Kusac. *This explains a lot,* he sent. *No wond
Bradogan and that guard showed an interest in you, to so
nothing of Tirak! Turn your damper up to full.*

It is! I think we better leave. She looked round, hoverir
between sitting and standing.

No. It'll draw attention to us, he sent, pushing her dov
onto the seat before sitting down himself.

"Ah," said Tirak, moving round to resume his place ;
the table. He nodded toward the door. "Bradogan's me
are here. And one of mine," he added, seeing Sheeov
returning.

Carrie used the excuse of turning round to move close
to Kusac. Though they'd had Link days on the ship, ther
had at least been privacy. On this alien world, there wa
none, and they were on a mission. Knowing this didn
make it easier, she thought, resting her hand on his leg
They were so used to being able to touch each other tha
trying to remember not to was extremely difficult.

Kusac's hand covered hers, their fingers interlacing. Ou
of sight under the table like this, with the distraction c
Bradogan's men breaking up the fight, they weren't likel
to be noticed.

*There's something about you at this time, a glow tha
makes you even more desirable,* he sent. *We'll stay a fev
minutes, no more, then go upstairs.*

Not to the ship?

*Not tonight, not with these spates of violence. We'll leav
early and spend the day in our quarters.*

As she smiled at him, she realized Tirak was watchin
her closely. *Tirak!*

I know. He let her go and turned to glance at the fight
Bradogan's guards had descended indiscriminately on any
one involved or in the vicinity of the fight and were haulin
them out into the street.

Tirak's mouth split open in a grin. "I think your friend as more on her mind than sitting talking tonight."

"Just a little nervous," Kusac said. "Not used to bar rawls."

"If she intends to become a trader, she'd better get used o them," Tirak said, beckoning one of the servants over. Bring three kirris," he said.

"Kirris? They have kirris here?" asked Kusac, his tone urprised.

"The Chemerians will export their drinks anywhere," aid Tirak. "It's good for stiffening the spine," he said to Carrie.

Why did you have to say I was nervous? she asked, her mental tone irritable.

Simplest answer. The fight had me *worried.*

Sheeowl joined them. "I thought you were going elsewhere, Captain," she said.

"I did, but the lady was off duty tonight. You should ome with me tomorrow," he said to Kusac. "There are ome interesting females at the *Spacer's Haven*."

Kusac snorted, waiting till the returning servant had put lown the drinks and been paid before continuing. "I've no nterest in these Jalnian females."

"Not Jalnian. You wouldn't be when you have such a peautiful companion of your own," said Tirak gallantly, passing a glass to Carrie then one to Kusac. "But one like us, perhaps?"

Kusac froze with the glass halfway to his mouth. "An U'Churian?" he said in disbelief.

"Not U'Churian, but like enough to pass as one of us. That's her value here, that she seems one of us."

"She has a name, this female?" he asked, sipping his drink.

"Tesha, if memory serves me. She's certainly popular."

In a whorehouse? Gods, we have to get her out as soon as possible, Kusac!

"I'd be pleased to keep Carrie company if you wished to visit her," Tirak added.

Kusac's fur had started to rise despite his efforts to control himself. "I think not. This Solnian I prefer to keep to myself," he said, a low growl underlying his words as his free hand clenched into a fist on the table.

"She would be safe with me," said Tirak, all trace of h
smile gone. "I intended company only, I assure you."

"Thank you for the offer," said Carrie, aware one c
them had to defuse the situation. "I know I'd be safe i
your company, but I can look after myself!" She caugh
Sheeowl's eye and grinned at her.

The U'Churian female smiled back. "I think our captai
is concerned because of your resemblance to Jalnian fe
males. The Jalnian men here tend to assume that an unac
companied female is fair game. They wouldn't stop lon
enough to realize you're not of their species."

Carrie sighed. "I understand, and again, I thank you
Captain Tirak. My safety is Kusac's responsibility and h
takes it very seriously."

Kusac's hackles had lowered and he'd forced himself t
relax. "If I misunderstood you, Captain, I apologize," h
said stiffly. "Perhaps another night we could go there."

"Kaid's back," said Carrie, glancing over her shoulder a
she sensed his presence within her mind strengthening. "I
you want to stay and talk for a while, he could see m
upstairs," she said to Kusac. *Stay and put his suspicions t
rest. I think he may well have guessed we're of the sam
species as Tesha.*

*There's something about this world I don't like. This i
not like me at all! From now on, we only eat food tha
comes from the ship, and stick to drinks we know aren'
Jalnian, like this kirris,* he sent.

Coming up behind her, Kaid put a hand on her shoulder
"Did you get what you wanted from Assadou?" he askec
her as T'Chebbi nodded to the U'Churians.

"No problem," she replied.

He looked at Kusac. *I sensed what happened. Stay down
here for perhaps five minutes. T'Chebbi and I'll take Carrie
up now. Unless you want to go to the ship? Would be safe
enough with four of us.*

Kusac hesitated.

"We're needed on the ship," said Kaid. "Sorry to break
up the evening, but Kishasayzar was most insistent I fetch
you both."

Relieved, Carrie gulped down her drink and got to her
feet. "Thank you for your hospitality," she said, offering
her hand to Tirak. "We'll catch you later tomorrow." As

irak held out his hand, she briefly touched fingertips then
urned to leave.

"They're as much a couple as Taynar and Kate," said
heeowl, watching them thread their way toward the door.
His reaction proved it."

"That's what I was hoping for," said Tirak, leaning back
a his seat. "And it came immediately after I mentioned
ue Sholan female's name. I'll swear he recognized it. And
uere was the kirris."

"Kirris?" Sheeowl frowned, wrinkling her nose. "What
bout it?"

"He was surprised they sell it on Jalna. Those double-
ealing Chemerians are definitely involved with the
holans."

"What do you plan to do?"

Tirak pushed himself up from his seat and held his hand
ut to her, pulling her up when she accepted it. "I think
ve take a stroll over to the *Profit*."

Chapter 16

"We're picking up their violence, Kaid," said Kusac as the
passed through the gateway into the spaceport. "It's affec
ing us, making us argumentative. You must have felt
too."

"A little. Not enough for me to have mentioned it," h
said. "Likely you're feeling it more acutely because ther
are two of you, and it's the beginning of your Link day."

"There's three of us," said Carrie, looking up at him. "I
your reasoning is right, you should be feeling it more tha
you are."

"La'quo makes him unconscious," pointed out T'Chebb
"Not you. Remember when he touched collar, before goin
to Margins? Was same in warehouse. Not affect either c
you that way. Sedates him, not you. That why he not fee
the anger."

"That's probably it," agreed Kaid as they made their wa
past the first landing pad.

Carrie stopped dead, turning back to look. "Correct m
if I'm wrong, but aren't those shuttles there? Short hoj
cargo shuttles, like the one we have in the *Hkariyash*?"

"They weren't there earlier," frowned Kaid. "They're
only for atmospheric work from the looks of them. No
powerful enough to reach orbit. I'll look into it tomorrow
If they've got shuttles going in and out of here acros:
Jalna . . ."

"We can use our own shuttle," said Carrie in a hushec
voice. "This caravan journey isn't necessary."

"We can't go heading out across Jalna in a shuttle, bu
a short trip might be possible," said Kusac, catching her b
the arm and drawing her on toward the *Hkariyash*. "I think
we should make another attempt to contact Jo's party now
we know a lot more about what's happening here. Our

xtra sensitivity at this time may be just what's needed to p the balance and make contact possible."

"I can help if necessary," said Kaid as they approached ae cargo ramp. "It's about time I began to pull my weight s a telepath."

"There'll be opportunities enough, don't worry. Just as ou worked me at Stronghold, I'll make sure you do a fair hare," Kusac grinned, stopping in front of the hatch.

T'Chebbi thumbed the palm lock and the hatch slid back o admit them. First in, she waited by the control panel till hey were all in, then sealed it behind them.

"We found the second and third Sholans," said Carrie. Tallis, the telepath, is with Bradogan in the Keep, working s a truthsayer of sorts, and Tesha is in a brothel in the own."

"A brothel?" murmured Kaid as they made for the ele-ator up to the crew quarters. "Logical, I suppose, with so nany U'Churians here. Do you know which one?"

"Spacer's Haven," said Kusac. "Tirak keeps asking me o go there with him. I'm sure he suspects something."

"He does. Everywhere we go, one of his crew seems to ave business in the same vicinity," said Kaid. "They're good, but not that good. I need to know if it's simple curi-sity or something more."

The elevator gave a slight shudder as it ground to a halt. The cool air of the crew quarters was welcome to them all after the heat outside.

Carrie breathed deeply as she stepped out into the corri-lor. "Recycled air! Never thought I'd be glad to smell it again after so long on this ship."

T'Chebbi snorted with amusement. "Told you you'd get used to smells of town."

"It's the heat more than anything," Carrie said. "D'you realize we can have showers? And sleep in comfort? Not need to worry about whether or not to leave the window shuttered for fear of thieves? Or whether there are bugs?"

Kaid stopped outside their door. "Is that electronic or organic bugs?" he asked with a grin.

"Either!" she said, reaching a hand up to touch his cheek. "Good night, Kaid," she said, then turned to open their door. As it slid back, she disappeared inside.

"We had Tallis to contact tonight," said Kusac, hovering for a moment longer. "You can see to him if you wish."

Kaid nodded. "From what Jeran said, he's not a powerful telepath, but there's no point in exposing him to your Link. Carrie said you got the passes. For Kaladar?"

"No, only for Galrayin, I'm afraid. It's the main lowland town, and its lord—Tarolyn—is Bradogan's favorite. Kil-lian's agent is on his way inland with a caravan at present and this was our best option. We can head out with the next shipment to Galrayin. At least it gets us legitimately halfway to the mountains."

"Better than waiting," agreed Kaid. "See how you get on reaching Jo, then we can look at our options. Meanwhile, I'll see to organizing the caravan and visiting Tesha. If I call in at the *Haven* first thing in the morning, I might be able to see her before she starts work."

"Can you manage all that on your own?" asked Kusac, looking from Kaid to T'Chebbi.

The Sholan female grinned. "No problem. Better I go see Tesha, though. Kaid could fall asleep with all la'quo around!"

"Huh!" said Kaid, throwing a slightly irritated look at her. "Not likely."

Kusac grinned. "I'll leave it to you to sort out between you. We should be able to meet you tomorrow evening for third meal. Here, I think, given the presence of la'quo in everything Jalnian we eat or drink."

"In the mess, then," said Kaid, moving off down the corridor.

"Good night," said Kusac.

Outside their room, T'Chebbi stopped, looking at Kaid. "If you prefer, I can use Humans' room at night," she said. "We got space for you to be alone now."

Kaid hesitated. They'd had to share quarters on the outward journey because of a lack of rooms, and at the inn as well, but now he had a choice. So did she. They still weren't lovers and had only shared a bed a couple of times since they'd left Shola. "Your belongings are here," he said.

"Mostly at inn. Is not a problem."

"It's up to you, T'Chebbi. It doesn't bother me sharing the room. Where do you want to sleep?" he asked.

She shrugged. "Is only that this is their Link day, and know it affects you, too. Don't want you to feel I have to be in same room."

It did affect him, there was no point denying it. Just enough for him to want female company of his own during that time, and it wasn't fair to T'Chebbi that she happened to be the one who was there.

He palmed the door open. "How about we discuss this inside?" he asked, acutely aware they were standing in the corridor where any of the Sumaan crew could overhear them.

"All right," she agreed, preceding him into the room.

He shut the door, thinking through what he wanted, what was right and fair for both of them as he took off his weapons and laid them on the chair. "Would you like to stay?" he asked. "Not because of their Link, not because of anything except that I want *you* to stay?"

She looked up at him, tilting her head on one side. "You asking me to stay *not* because of them?"

"Yes. Because of you."

"Stay as what?" she asked. "I stay to keep you company if you want."

"More. To share my bed," he said, reaching out to touch her cheek.

She moved to one side, letting his hand slide past her. "No."

He looked at her in surprise.

"No," she said again. "You keep shutting me up, Kaid. Not this time. I want you more than just occasionally."

He began to speak but she gestured him to silence.

"I not shut up this time, Kaid," she said firmly, walking over to her bed and sitting down on it. "Know you have Tallis to mind-speak, but deal with this first. Is distracting me, making my work more difficult. Need to know where I am with you."

If it was bothering her to that extent, the matter had to have an airing. They were both professional enough to know, and admit, their own limits. He had been putting her off—because he knew what she would ask, and he hadn't been ready to answer her. There was no avoiding it any longer. "I'll listen to you now, T'Chebbi," he said, following her over.

"Know you like me. Like you, too, but want more. Want you as my lover. Don't want to change how we are, how often we're together," she continued. "Just want to know I matter enough to you, like you do to me."

"You do matter to me, T'Chebbi," he said, aware that what she was asking of him was only fair. He'd done his best not to take advantage of her willingness to be with him when he needed her company, but it was an easy habit to fall into.

"Know you need her, but I think you need me, too."

He could feel her distress at being so direct with him, but he knew she needed a measure of security from him. "I know," he said quietly. "But I'm part of a Triad, I have a life-mate. You should find someone who can give you more than I can, T'Chebbi. You deserve it. Being only my lover wouldn't be fair to you."

"That's *my* decision, but you don't ask me!" she said, ears going flat in distress as she looked down at her hands.

He smiled wryly. "I'm rather good at doing that," he admitted. He sat on the edge of his bed, facing her. Reaching out, he took her by the hand. "This really isn't a good time to discuss it, T'Chebbi. Their Link makes it difficult for me to separate my needs from the Link we share."

"Is never good time with you," she muttered, drawing her hand away from him. "Always you tell me, *not now*. Had enough *not nows*. What stopping you? Either you want me or you don't." Her voice cracked slightly then recovered. "Is easy, can't see problem."

"It's not easy. Easy is to say yes and not worry about the consequences." He wanted her, but a commitment? As troubled as his thoughts had been lately, he'd given no time to thinking of her when obviously he should have.

She looked up. "I would accept that. Not expecting guarantees. Don't have to be your Companion." She hesitated. "Unless you think I'm not good enough."

He caught her hand again. "Never that! I had no idea I meant so much to you," he said, holding her gaze. He turned her hand so he could lick her palm again. "As my lover."

Her ears flicked up and round, flaring to catch his every word. "What?"

"Be my lover, T'Chebbi," he whispered. "I should have asked you long ago, but I thought you deserved more than just being a Companion."

Reaching out with her other hand, she grasped a handful of the longer fur on his jawline. "So stupid, you males. Is *you* I want, have always wanted," she said quietly. "Right from time you came back for me so long ago. You think we need the show and the symbols of relationships when is only the person and their caring for you that matters to us." She pulled him closer, hands cupping his face as they kissed. Then she pushed him away.

"Now you mind-speak Tallis," she purred. "While I get first shower!"

"You conniving little she-jegget," he said with a grin, watching her jump to her feet and skip off to the shower, shedding sword, pistol, and weapons belt as she went.

She stopped to wave an admonishing finger at him. "Work, Kaid, then we play." Her voice held a purr of sheer devilment and he wondered what he'd let himself in for.

About time, came Carrie's lazy thought through their private lesser link. *You need each other, Kaid. And I need a bond-sister to help keep you two males in line!*

He laughed and T'Chebbi raised an eye ridge at him.

"Carrie says she needs a bond-sister to help keep me and Kusac in line," he explained.

T'Chebbi nodded vigorously, grinning. "She's right," then ducked out of sight, laughing as a pillow came sailing in her direction.

Good to hear her laugh, sent Kusac. *She's someone very special, Kaid. You're lucky to have her. May you both be very happy.*

Kaid leaned back on his bed as their contact faded, leaving only the small warmth of Carrie's presence at the edges of his mind. Life as an En'Shalla telepath was very different from what he'd imagined, but one thing Carrie had taught him was that while he could rationalize as much as he wanted, ultimately it was his feelings he had to listen to.

"Tallis!" T'Chebbi called from the bathing room.

Sighing, he began to recite the litany of Relaxation, preparing himself for making contact with the telepath at Bradogan's Keep.

Tallis, he sent, using the mental wavelength Carrie had discovered earlier. He reached for the Sholan's unique mental pattern. *Tallis!*

Faintly he heard a response. *I am here.*

Are you alone? Is it safe to speak? he asked, strengthening the contact.

It's safe. Lord Bradogan has dismissed me for the night. But you're not the one I heard earlier!

I was there. Help is at hand, but you must wait for now. We have others to see to first.

The others. Have you found them? Is Miroshi all right? I've heard nothing from her for so long!

We've found two more, Jeran and Tesha, but not Miroshi. Do you know what became of her?

She was so ill—never recovered from what the Valtegans did to us. The Lord couldn't sell her, so he gave her to one of his males. It's so good to hear another like myself. To have been trapped inside my own mind with silence for so long!

The contact was fading again as Tallis began to lose his focus.

Which one did Bradogan give her to? Kaid asked, once more feeding energy into Tallis' sending. This was tiring him more than he'd thought, but then they'd all expected Tallis to be more powerful than he was. Obviously he was lying to Bradogan and it was just sheer luck he'd not yet been discovered.

Which one? If I tell you, you'll have no need of me, sent Tallis, his tone becoming sly. *What of me? When will you take me away from this place? I won't wait here while you pick the others up! My position is dangerous—at any time the Lord could discover I can't read his visitors as well as I say I can!*

This one was going to be trouble, he just knew it. What could he say that would buy them some time by putting Tallis' mind at rest? *The sooner we find her, the sooner we can move all of you. We need to find out more about the Valtegans who brought you here.*

Why? They're gone now. We're the ones who need help! Your duty is to rescue us, return us to Szurtha!

Kaid hesitated, then decided to tell him. *Szurtha is gone, along with Khyaal. Everything living destroyed by those who took you prisoner.*

There was silence for the space of several heartbeats. *Gone, all gone?*

Yes. We must find out more about them. What did they want with you? Why did they take you?

All dead? My Clan—none left . . .

His thoughts were breaking up, becoming unfocused and incoherent. There was no point in pursuing the conversation now, Kaid realized. It would take some time for him to come to terms with what had happened.

Tallis! Leave the talisman off at night so I can contact you again. Tallis! It was no good, he'd gone.

Sighing, Kaid gave up and let himself relax into an exhausted heap. A touch on his cheek made him jump. T'Chebbi was leaning over him. She sat back as he rubbed at his eyes.

"You been asleep," she said. "Did you mind-speak with Tallis?"

"Yes, I spoke to him," he said, yawning. "He's going to cause trouble. He's faking it—hardly capable of reading a report, let alone someone's mind! He's trying to get clever with us, refusing to tell me where Miroshi is unless we pull him out first."

"Can we?"

"From the heart of Bradogan's Keep? Not an option. We're going to have to make sure he stays quiet, though. When he heard what had happened to his home, he broke contact. Hit him hard."

"Talk it over with Kusac in the morning," she said. "You want to bathe or sleep? Looks like you need sleep more."

"I do," he said, his eyes closing despite his efforts to keep them open. "It took a lot of energy because his sending was so weak." He heard her getting up and reached out to stop her, looping an arm around her waist to pull her down beside him.

"Tomorrow," she said, letting him hold her close and bury his head against her shoulder. "We got plenty time, you and I."

Her pelt was still damp from the shower. "You smell nice." He nuzzled his face lower. "Something I have to do first," he mumbled, stifling another yawn. Then his jaws closed over her larynx, tightening slowly till she lifted her chin. He released her. "Just wanted to be sure," he yawned again, arms tightening around her. "Damn that bloody Tallis! No right to disrupt our lives like this," he mumbled as he drifted off to sleep.

* * *

"Captain's looking for you," said Mrowbay as Giyesh passed the sickbay door. "Didn't expect you to stay out all night."

"That was silly of him," she said, leaning against the doorpost. "By the way, can tell you Taynar's not an immature male. They're all built like that—until aroused."

"And I expect you did a fair job of arousing this Jeran," said Tirak from behind her.

She whirled round. "Captain! Didn't expect you to be up so early."

"You took unnecessary risks, Giyesh," he said, a rumble of anger underlining his displeasure. "Not only could you have been discovered, but he could have harmed you. We know very little about these Sholans."

"I bribed the guard, Captain, and Jeran—he's been here so long! They've kept the four of them apart for months. He was desperate for the company of someone who looked like him."

"My office, now," he said firmly, ears flicking in anger.

Schooling ears and tail into positions of apology, she followed the captain across the corridor and through the air lock to his office.

Sitting behind his desk, he regarded her. "I sent you to talk to the male, nothing more, Giyesh. Did you stop to think what would have happened if the guard had alerted the Port Controller? How we would have explained your presence with him? Too much hinges on what we're doing here to have it risked by the actions of one female unable to control herself! I wasn't joking when I said he could have harmed you. Just because these Sholans resemble us doesn't make them any less alien than the Sumaan!"

"Yes, Captain," she said, hanging her head. "I'm sorry, Captain, but if you'd been there!" She raised her eyes and looked him straight in the face. "We all know you saw the one called Tesha. They have to be safe if you could sleep with her!"

Tirak's face took on a thunderous look. "You all know *what*?" he demanded. "I did nothing but speak to her. I told you all that, dammit! I can't get that close to an alien!"

She was confused. "But, we thought . . ."

"I know what you thought! You'd all do well to actually listen to me sometimes!" he thundered.

"I'm sorry, Captain," she said, looking at her feet, wishing the floor would open up and swallow her. "It's just that Nayash reckoned you . . ." She ground to a halt, realizing that nothing she could say would make her night's excursion any better in Tirak's eyes. She was only clawing a deeper hole for herself.

"I hope that after risking everything, you found out something more worthwhile than a comparison of U'Churian and Sholan male anatomy!" he snarled.

Now she really wished the floor would swallow her! Ears flattened backward, tail drooping to the floor, she mumbled, "Yes, Captain."

"Well, get on with it!"

"The Valtegans sold the four of them to Bradogan about a year ago, as best he can reckon it."

"We know that already!"

"I found out they were captured while traveling from their moon to the planet on leave. There was a fleet of vessels, ones they'd never seen before. Other craft were being destroyed but theirs was held and boarded and they were taken captives."

Tirak had sat back in his seat and was looking less angry. "A fleet, eh?"

She nodded. "They'd never seen the Valtegans before, didn't know they existed. Obviously they couldn't speak the language either so they didn't know what was wanted of them."

"Why were they taken?"

"He doesn't know. It was a military ship, Jeran said. The general had them beaten and even used drugs on them, but they told him nothing, even when they could understand enough of the language."

"What were they trying to find out?"

"They were never completely sure," she said. "Jeran was puzzled about that. What surprised him was the Valtegans fear of them."

Tirak leaned forward. "Fear? Of captives?"

"Yes. They were terrified of them. Kept them chained in some temple they had on board, with an object that they considered holy."

"Are you telling me that the Valtegans captured them, beat them, and kept them chained up because they're afraid of them?"

"I'm only telling you what he told me, Captain. Jeran refused to talk about it after that. Said he'd told me too much already."

Tirak sat back in his chair, clasping his hands on his desk.

"So what did you find out about his people from your more—intimate—association with him?"

Giyesh looked at the floor again, scuffing one foot against the other in acute embarrassment. She could feel the skin around her nose and eyes begin to prickle with heat.

"You weren't so reticent with Mrowbay!"

"Is different," she mumbled. "He's crew, like me."

"Do I have to wait for your gossip to get back to me?" he demanded. "You weren't so damned bashful with this Jeran!"

"He's not a mind-speaker," she said, picking on one innocent fact. "Few of them are. Telepaths, he called them. Said two of the others were telepaths."

"What else?"

Gods! What does he want to know? she thought in a panic. "He's a nice person, Captain! I don't know what else to say! He was so alone, so pleased to be with another like himself, and a female! Just an ordinary person trapped here, wanting to go home." She stopped, remembering something from the night before. "Home. When I asked him if he wanted to go home, he went very quiet," she said slowly. "It was as if there was nothing for him to go back to. That fleet. Do you think they destroyed his world, Captain?"

"I think we've uncovered a nest of poison stingers here," he said grimly, "and that the only ones who know what's going on are these Sholans. You're dismissed, Giyesh," he said, losing interest in her as he began to scratch his left ear in a gesture she knew well.

"Yes, Captain," she said, backing out of his office before he could change his mind.

* * *

After their first meal, Kaid and T'Chebbi headed out to the town. While Kaid went on to the *Spacers Haven,* she stopped at the Port Controller's office. Already there was a small crowd of people waiting, mainly Jalnian agents with one U'Churian and herself. As she searched her memory for a name to put to the familiar face, the other female got up and came over to her.

"Manesh," she said, holding her hand out, palm up.

T'Chebbi nodded and ignored the hand, clasping the other by the wrist instead. Telepath greeting. Why use that?

Where had she learned it? Then she remembered that Carrie had used it the night before with Tirak.

"Thought you touched hands," said Manesh, returning the gesture.

"Solnian way," she said. "Not ours. You got business here?" she asked, leaning against the wall.

"Some. Organizing a caravan for our cargo to Galrayin. Got to get Controller to allocate us space on next one out. You?"

"Same," said T'Chebbi shortly. She could have done without the U'Churian present. Hoped she didn't stay to hear what their business was.

"How long you here for?" asked Manesh.

"A while," said T'Chebbi. "Till ship repaired. Why so busy at this hour?" she asked.

"Morgil, the Controller, is late," she said. "There's much speculation as to what's keeping him."

A commotion at the door made her turn to look as a Jalnian, his head sporting a large bandage, came in. Trailing behind him were a young male and a couple of locals demanding to know what had happened.

"She finally did it," said someone beside her. "Hey, Morgil she got you, didn't she? That's what you get for foolin' around with that moth-eaten creature! Said she'd be the death of you one day!"

Laughter greeted his remark.

"Tell us what happened," said another. "What she do? Try to knock some sense into that thick head of yours?"

"No, she brained him for coming back drunk last night!" laughed a third. "Didn't you see him? So drunk he could barely stand!"

"You can keep your mouth shut, Faisal, if you want that cargo to reach your lord this side of harvest," Morgil snapped as he pushed his way through the agents to his door. "I got nothing to say to you lot about anythin'." He fumbled with his key at the lock, finally getting the door open.

"Aw, come on, Morgil, tell us what happened," said the one called Faisal. "Could do with a laugh this morning."

He turned, glowering at them all. "Think you're so funny, don't you? Well, laugh at this one. Some of you live outside like me, don't you? Well, she's gotten loose." Hands on hips, he waited for their reaction.

There was a stunned silence.

"Not so funny now, is it?" he said, looking round them all. "Watch yourselves when you hear a noise in the night. It could be her, a sneakin' into your kitchen for food. And if it is, the Gods help you if you disturb her!" He pointed to his head. "Cos that's what she did to me for only tellin' her to wash the pans right!" He turned and went into his office, waiting till his clerk scuttled in behind him, then he closed the door firmly.

"She's loose? Hell's teeth! I hope he's told Bradogan about it," said Faisal, looking decidedly uncomfortable. "Don't want one like that roaming around loose. All those teeth and claws, and her half wild as it is!"

T'Chebbi turned to Manesh. "What's this about?" she demanded. "You know who they mean?"

Manesh shrugged. "No idea. Your guess is as good as mine."

T'Chebbi grabbed hold of Faisal by the front of his robe. "What you talking about?" she asked, hauling him closer and lifting him slightly off the ground. "Who hit him? Who got loose?"

"Hey," the Jalnian said, a terrified look crossing his face. "No need to get angry with me! I had nothing to do with it. Wasn't one of your kind anyway, so don't know why you're getting so fired up about it!"

"What wasn't one of my kind?" she growled.

"The female! Morgil's female servant! One he says got loose!" he said, plucking at T'Chebbi's hand.

She felt a hand on her arm and turned to snarl at whoever had the temerity to interfere. It was Manesh.

"I'd put him down," she said quietly. "You can bet Bradogan's men will be on their way here. Not a good idea for this male to make a complaint about you."

There was sense in what she said. T'Chebbi turned back to the Jalnian and dropped him on his feet. Opening her mouth, she smiled pleasantly. "Am sorry. Was only curious. Meant no harm to you," she said, rearranging the front of his robes.

He batted her hand away, frowning as he backed off. "No need to be so insistent," he muttered, turning away from her to his friends. "Bloody aliens," she heard him say. "Think they own the place just because they trade here."

"Another one like us," said Manesh thoughtfully, glancing at T'Chebbi. "That's unusual. Wonder where they come from?"

"They? He said one female," said T'Chebbi, watching her closely. "You know of others like this one?"

The U'Churian blinked, obviously taken aback by the question and unsure how to answer it. "No, I know of no others. I meant they as in her species."

"How you so sure she's not one of us taken hostage?"

"Not possible," said Manesh firmly. "Would have been reported, we'd all know about it. No ship would leave one of its crew behind in the first place. Would be a bloodbath to rescue her rather than that."

"Probably right," T'Chebbi agreed holding the other's gaze. "Not good to come between a ship and her crew."

Manesh looked away, distinctly uneasy.

Good, thought T'Chebbi. *Let them think is a crew member of ours. Maybe then they not interfere.*

What with the delay caused by Bradogan's men questioning Morgil, it took a good two hours before her turn came. After sending word to Assadou at the Hotel, she headed for their inn, checking upstairs to see that their belongings were safe before finding herself a seat in which to wait for Kaid. He wasn't long in joining her. When he sat down opposite, she pushed a drink across to him.

He raised a questioning eye ridge at her.

"Is some Chemerian dishwater they call ale, but is safe to drink," she said. "Got them to open fresh sealed container so know it wasn't watered down."

Nodding, he picked it up gratefully, taking a long drink. "Needed that," he said, putting the tankard down. "When do we leave?"

"Tomorrow," she said. "Next caravan in two weeks."

"Tomorrow? That's short notice."

She flicked an ear in assent. "Sent word to Assadou to get cargo ready. Need to let Kusac and Carrie know, also Quin and Conrad."

"Weren't we supposed to contact them last night?"

"Kusac will have seen to that. They contact him, don't they?"

Kaid nodded. "I'd better let them know now," he said.

"You can contact them from here with all the noise?" she asked in surprise.

"Yes. I have a permanent link—only a small one—with Carrie. All I have to do is strengthen it. I thought you knew."

"Never asked, and you never said. Not my business. Before you do, I might have found the last one. A female like us was with the Port Controller. Last night she knocked him unconscious and escaped. Bradogan's men search for her in shantytown outside Port—town where caravans leave from."

"We're missing a female," he said, taking another sip of his drink.

"Manesh was there. We talked about missing crew members. She said if was U'Churian, be a bloodbath to get her back. I let her think these four might be crew members of ours."

"She'll have gotten the point, then."

"Yes," T'Chebbi grinned. "She understood. No U'Churians in here are there? I think they decide not to follow me. How you get on? See this Tesha?"

"Yes, briefly. Had to pay for the privilege, though," he grimaced.

She laughed, making him look at her in surprise. "Not tempted, were you?"

He reached out across the table to touch the hand that held her tankard. "It's good to hear you laugh like that," he said quietly.

She shrugged, grinning. "Were you?"

He sat back. "With you and Carrie to contend with? Not likely! I spent the time asking her about the Valtegans. From what she could gather, they wanted to know how many worlds we had. Of course, it took them weeks to even understand what they were being asked, and even when they did, they decided their safest option was to pretend ignorance. From Tesha's description of what happened, they were taken by the ship that controlled Keiss. It must have returned around the time we arrived to liberate that world. The Valtegans had them dragged up to the bridge one at a time to identify our craft on their screens. Being civilians, and from the colonies, they'd no idea what our fleet looked like so they couldn't have told them anyway."

"If Valtegans so scared of us they'd suicide, probably beat them just for being Sholan."

"I came to that conclusion, too. Tesha was bought by the Ialnian who owns the *Haven,* and she's kept closely guarded. We're going to need to break her out, the same with Jeran and Tallis," he sighed. "And we can't do it till we get back from rescuing Jo's group. Let's hope Quin's had some luck in locating this rebellion. If they could spring Jo's party out of Kaladar, even if we're en route to Galrayin, it would make life so much simpler."

"We take communicator with us, then if trouble we can get Kishasayzar's folk to get them out, take off, and meet us," said T'Chebbi.

"That's our last-ditch option," agreed Kaid, "but we'd all prefer not to use it."

"We're done here, why we not head back to ship and eat?" she suggested. "Am hungry. Can contact Carrie and Kusac in person then."

"Might as well," he said, finishing his drink. "No point in disturbing them too early. It's not as if they can do much about getting ready to leave until later."

*   *   *

"I can't do it, I tell you! He's increased the security earlier than I expected!" said Taradain angrily, flinging himself down on his bed and glowering at her.

She sat by the fire in the easy chair, a blanket wrapped around her as she shivered uncontrollably. Waves of nausea passed through her, making her feel like she was about to throw up, and to crown it all, her head ached abominably.

"Then take me back now," she said, her voice low. "You know I'm ill, and you know why. You've sat and watched me since dawn. You must know I'm only getting worse."

"I can't take you out looking like this," he said. "Some good that'll do my reputation! I offered to fetch Arnor, but you'd have none of him!"

He was right, dammit. In her current state, she doubted if she could make it to the Lesser Hall without collapsing. She'd expected nothing like this, though. Searching through the memories inherited from both Rezac and Zashou, she'd realized it was what Kris had said, Link deprivation, but on a level comparable with a full Leska Link.

Taradain got up and came over to her. "Let me at least get something to settle your stomach from Arnor, even if you won't see him," he said. "I have to take you back to your friends and I can't when you're this bad."

She nodded, instantly wishing she hadn't as the pounding in her head increased. As he left, she knew she'd no option but to contact Rezac and ask for his help. She no longer mattered, but their plans for escape were in shreds, and Railin had to be contacted before his caravan left.

There was no way she could relax enough to mind-speak Rezac, but she could open their Link again. Gradually she released the block she'd put on his presence. His response was instant.

Gods, Jo, you should have called me sooner! His tone was gentle, something she'd not expected. *You thought I'd be angry with you?* Now she felt his remorse, but more importantly, she could feel his strength flowing into her, pushing the weakness back.

Rezac, what I've done's been for nothing. Killian has increased the security again because of the violence yesterday. Taradain refuses to help now.

Is he holding you against your will? His anger flared briefly but was as quickly smothered.

No, but . . .

The Link deprivation, he sent. *You're too ill to come to me! Gods!*

I'm better now, she sent hastily, *just speaking to you . . .*

I know. The suddenness of his love surrounding her caught her unaware, and she began to cry.

Jo, for the Gods sake, get him to bring you back now! I can't help you at this distance!

She scrubbed at her face with her hands, ashamed at her weakness.

Not weak! Never that! What you've tried to do, Jo . . . His sending was fierce and threatened to overwhelm her. Sensing this, he immediately toned it down.

I can't, Rezac. He won't take me through the castle like this.

Then make *him! Take over his mind!*

I can't! She was shocked at the suggestion. *To control his mind, force him to do what I want . . .*

What's he doing to you? Rezac demanded. *He's threatening your life, Jo! Let me do it if you won't. I can control him through you, if you'll let me.*

She rested her head against the back of her chair. She was sick and tired, and all this was too much for her.

You can't give up now, he pleaded, his tone gentle again. *A few minutes, that's all it will take, no more. Get him to bring you to us at the stables. I'm there. They had to allow me out to test the circuits. Their weapon is almost complete.*

The laser? We're leaving them a working laser?

The first time he uses it will be the last. Rezac's tone was grim. *We've rigged it to blow in a controlled explosion. Kris insisted as few lives be lost as possible. If you can come here, even briefly, I can make you better—until we have the time to be alone again.*

But our escape? she asked. *How will we escape?*

Kris talks to Railin now. Trust us, Jo, as we've trusted you. I know you're our leader, but the best of leaders suffer injuries and have to pass command to their seconds.

He was right. She wasn't fit to lead them now. The thought of passing command to them was so tempting. The constant stress and worry were not making her present condition any easier. To give it over to Kris and Rezac, if they could bury their differences, *their* lack of trust of each other . . .

I'll work with him, you have my word on it, Jo. To step down is no weakness. Rather it's a strength, as when you came to me just now. She could feel his respect for her, a respect he let her know she'd earned despite his prejudices.

Do it, she sent, surrendering her mind to his with a relief that went to the heart of her being.

In the stable, Rezac waited impatiently for Jo and Taradain to arrive. It took ten heart-stopping minutes, but at last they heard the voices of the guards outside.

"Link with me now, Kris," murmured Rezac from where he stood against the stable wall. *That's it. Now this is what you must maintain. Can you sense it? Have you his pattern? When I tell you, just hold him like this so he can't regain control of his mind. Seeing to Jo will take me perhaps five minutes, then I can work directly on him.*

The door opened and Jo came in first. Davies was at her side, supporting her as he helped her over to Rezac.

Now, sent Rezac, letting his grip on Taradain's mind go. He monitored Kris for a moment, then, satisfied, he nodded to Davies and reached out to take hold of her.

Rezac's presence, which had dominated her mind while he controlled Taradain, began to fade and once more she was herself—but the Link to him remained as intense as ever. His arms closed round her and he drew her out of sight of the others into the adjacent stall.

At his touch, the cool fire surged through her, blending their minds into one. Memories flowed between them as frantically he licked at her face, catching her tears of relief even as they fell. Gradually the merging slowed, leaving them once more to their own separate identities.

In its wake came the compulsion, but Rezac worked to push it aside, knowing there was no time for that now. *Sit,* he sent, urging her down onto the pile of clean animal bedding that lay on the floor. *I need to try and heal you. Jo, no matter what happens, never shut me out like this again. You only make matters worse by depriving us of our Link.*

This isn't supposed to happen, she sent, stumbling to her knees, the voluminous skirts of her dress tangled round her legs. *It's too strong, too intense!*

I know, he replied, catching hold of her and easing her down onto the yielding surface. *It's because you shut me out. Now be still, we haven't long. Let me work.*

She rested her head against his chest, the coarse wool of his robe rough against her cheek. Needing to touch him, she pushed her hand along his arm, up inside his wide sleeve.

Rezac was finding it almost impossible to control the compulsion as her scent, stronger because she'd been feverish, began to make him light-headed. Reality, though, kept him focused on their predicament. With a grunt of discomfort, he moved her so she wasn't pressing against his groin.

No! We can't do that now! she sent, suddenly as aware as he of his arousal.

Be still, Jo! He tightened his arms as she began to pull away from him. *Do you think I'm some youngling unable to control myself? Time for that later—when we can enjoy it.* There was a flash of humor from him. *I want a hurried pairing as little as you do, believe me. But we must take this a little way to complete the healing.*

She forced herself to relax, feeling his presence within her mind increase again as gently he tilted her face up to his and began to kiss her.

Link with me. Remember our last time together, he sent. *elive the memories. It should be enough.* As she did, beveen them grew an echo of the compulsion and carefully fostered it, using it to simulate their joining till she egan to respond as if it were real. It was unfair, a liberty e had no right to take, but he could think of no other olution. Her actions had created the need for them to pair nd that was impossible under these circumstances.

His only consolation was that his torment was worse as e dared not get swept up in her pleasure. He still had aradain to deal with and he couldn't do that if he allowed imself to be drained by making love to her.

Rezac, you said we wouldn't . . . Her thought was a wail f anguish as she lay poised between the imaginary sensual orld he'd created for her, and the reality of the stable ith the others only a few feet away.

Hush, he sent, knowing it needed only a small push for to be over for her. His frustration would take longer to o. *We aren't. This is not real, it's only within your mind.* hen he pushed her, gently, lovingly, over the edge, stifling er cries and her body against his so the others would ot know.

When at last she was still, he let her go. *Are you better?* e asked anxiously, wiping her forehead with his hand. *I'm orry, Jo, I could think of nothing else that would dispel the Link deprivation.*

She lay there, clutching his robe, exhausted but clear of ead, the nausea and the Link-induced fever gone.

"Jo, are you better?" he repeated, ears flattening with is anxiety, afraid she might never forgive him for what e'd done.

She nodded slowly, avoiding his eyes. *That was unfair. Would you rather have . . .*

No! She hid her face against him, beginning to cry silently, her shoulders shaking with the violence of her sobs, her thoughts a confusion of jumbled emotions.

"Jo," he said softly, holding her tight. "A little longer and we're done here. We'll be on our way home, trust me. We can do it, I know we can. You can."

"I've had enough, Rezac," she said, her voice indistinct through her sobs. "This place, you, our Link, it's too much for me!"

"Hush," he said, rocking her gently, trying to still his

own rising panic because he didn't know what to say or d
to comfort her. "It's strange for me, too. You're strong,
know you can cope just a little longer."

"I can't, not any more!"

Davies appeared at the side of the stall, the concern obvi
ous on his face. "Kris needs you to hurry," he said. "Ca
I do anything?"

Rezac shook his head, gesturing to him to leave. Whe
he'd gone, he lifted Jo up till she faced him. "*This* is m
leader?" he asked, lacing his voice with sarcasm. "This sod
den Human, dressed in female clothes that reveal more o
her body than they conceal?"

He felt the anger surge through her as she pulled awa
from him, trying to fold her arms over the low neckline o
her dress. Before she could, he tightened his grip. "*Use* tha
anger, Jo! Use it to strengthen yourself, as I do!"

She stopped, realizing what he'd done.

"Gods, Jo, you're a warrior as fiery as any I've faced,
he said, putting everything he could of his feelings for he
into a sending. "You hold us together, Sholans and Hu
mans both. Don't fall apart on us now. When it's over," he
took a deep breath, "then you can call on us for everything
you want. Rant and rave at us if you must, but until then,
we need you! *I* need you!" He tightened his hands round
her arms and pulled her close enough to nip at her lips
before kissing her.

The hair growing at the sides of his neck was grasped
firmly as she pulled him away. Letting out a short yowl of
pain, he looked down at her.

"What am I supposed to do about you?" she demanded.
"That stunt you pulled was utterly reprehensible, manipula
tive, seductive . . ." She stopped, having run out of words.

He grinned and leaned forward to lick her nose. *And
worked!* "If you'll let me go . . . ?"

She released him, and with his help, climbed to her feet.

"I have to work on Taradain now," he said, his voice
deepening with a rumble of anger.

She put a restraining hand on his arm. "Rezac, he did
nothing to hurt me," she said. "What he offered, it was
because of his father's ridicule of him. He only wanted to
prove him wrong. He was concerned for me. His intentions
were to help us."

"More than the body can be hurt," he said, his hand

ghtening briefly on her arm. "You'd only just begun to
orget the past, Jo."

She leaned against him, reaching up to caress his face.
Rezac, I'm all right. *We* are all right. Treat him gently, he
eally did try to help us. We still have a chance because of
im. God knows, what he's going through now is punish-
nent enough!"

His rumble continued as they began to walk back to the
nain area. "You're our leader, Jo. I'll do as you wish, but
on't ask me to like it!"

"Rezac!" she whispered. He stopped, looking round at
er questioningly. "I love you Rezac."

He smiled, a slow one that lit his whole face and was
ransmitted to every line of his body. *I swear you'd distract
he very Gods themselves, Jo Edwards,* he sent.

* * *

The demands of their Link would not be put off, and it
was late morning before they were able to try and search
or Jo. Kusac helped Carrie pull the pillows and blankets
rom the beds to make a nest for themselves on the floor.
Leaning against the bed, once again Kusac provided the
physical support for his mate.

*Do you remember Jo's mental pattern? Hold it in the front
of your mind. That's good. Now we search for it. Range
wider, Carrie, wider than we have before.*

Slowly, they widened their search, letting the power of
their Link blend their minds once more into one.

We must change the wavelength, came their thought.
Allow for the drift caused by the la'quo.

It was as if they were reaching for the impossible, this
searching for one mind in an area so wide and full of the
violence of the alien drug.

Filter it. Rise above these thoughts.

The portion that was Carrie grew impatient and reached
within them for the power that was the gestalt. It erupted
instantly, surging through their mind to be grasped by Carrie and flung outward like a signal, looking for the tiny
spark that was Jo.

From what had seemed a dark and barren landscape,
suddenly a faint glow of energy emerged. Like a beacon it
began to slowly pulse, guiding them toward it.

There!

The glow swelled, filling their mind until Jo's presenc
was suddenly with them.

Jo!

Hesitantly, she answered them. *Carrie? Kusac? Recognizing* them, the contact flared and strengthened as Reza
joined her.

*Jo, you're Linked! To Rezac? A Triad with Rezac an.
Zashou?*

Thank God you've found us! We need your help, Carrie

Let me, Jo, came Rezac's thought, and within second
they knew all that had happened.

Follow your plan, they sent. *We travel to Galrayin our
selves tomorrow. We'll meet you outside the city. Keep lis
tening for us, we'll contact you again tomorrow with th
details.*

You'll be waiting? sent Rezac. *Zashou is bad. I fear fo
her.*

We'll be there, they sent as they let the contact fade.

Chapter 17

As well as contacting Jo, we told Quin to head for the ort," said Kusac, helping himself to more bread from the late in the center of the table.

Kaid nodded. "We've got news, too," he said. "Kisha-ayzar found out for us that shuttles, piloted by the Su-aan, collect the Port town's food supplies from Lord 'arolyn and occasionally run the odd errand for Bradogan. 'here's a landing pad outside Galrayin."

Kusac sat up. "Really? Then we've an excuse to take our huttle there."

"We have. Kishasayzar says he'll provide us with a pilot. Ashay's his name. All we have to do is see to the Landing Controller, make sure he thinks we're doing a favor for Bradogan because we broke the law in landing the ship nere."

"Not a problem," said Carrie. "If I can get a clear view of the man, I can link and make him believe what we want."

"T'Chebbi and I worked out a plan while we were wait-ng for you. You leave as arranged with the caravan—you'll pe outriders on riding beasts—and once you're a decent distance from the Port, you head off on your own to ren-dezvous with the shuttle. You then head straight for Galrayin."

"On the way we can contact Jo and make sure we meet up with her," said Kusac nodding. "Not at the landing pad, I think. We don't want to attract attention to ourselves."

"It should be all right. It's apparently in the middle of nowhere. Just a hard surfaced area capable of supporting a shuttle."

"I take it I pull the same trick to get us back into the Port," said Carrie, picking up her mug of coffee. "That takes care of Jo and the others. What about Tesha, Jeran and Tallis? To say nothing of the missing Miroshi?"

"We need a diversion to get them out. Jeran is the easiest. We can leave him till last as he's in this area. Tesha i a little more difficult. It's Tallis that's going to be the problem," said Kaid.

"Came up with solution that should see to both," said T'Chebbi, getting up and going over to the dispenser. She punched the buttons, waiting for her drink to be served. "Incendiaries in the *Haven*. We go there early tomorrow morning. Is open then for drinks. Plant devices where cause fire that seem worse than is. Then when you return, we trigger them by remote and in confusion get Tesha out. We also burn the place," she said, her tone one of grim satisfaction as she turned back to collect her drink.

Carrie looked to Kaid questioningly, but he shook his head. *Don't ask*, he sent to her and Kusac. *When she wishes, if she wishes, she'll tell you.*

"How does that get Tallis out?" she asked instead.

"When you signal us you've arrived at the Port, I'll send to Tallis, telling him that when Bradogan sends his men out to deal with the fire, he's to make his way to the shuttle landing pad and wait for one of us. We'll have Kishasayzar and two of his crew posted at the gate on this side waiting for him. Conrad and Quin could wait there on the Jalnian side. It's my bet that the fire will cause the town to be evacuated anyway. The spacers will certainly want to get back to their craft because of the danger of sparks and secondary fires. And there's a fuel dump out in one of the warehouses."

"I take it there's no real danger," said Kusac.

"I can mix the incendiaries very precisely," said Kaid. "We brought everything we need. I'm including an explosive effect so when they ignite, it'll sound far worse than it actually is. However, the danger is real. If they have inadequate fire fighting facilities, which I doubt in a complex this size, then it could get out of control."

"At end of day," said T'Chebbi, sipping her drink, "we take every precaution, but our responsibility is to our own."

"So we land our shuttle right outside here, get everyone off, then what?"

"No, it lands inside *Hkariyash*, and you don't unload.

eave it to the crew," said Kaid. "You join T'Chebbi and
e outside and we head for Jeran."

"Why do it immediately after we land?" asked Carrie.
Why not wait till after everyone's unloaded and when Jer-
n's arrived to work on the life-support systems?"

"Too much chance of others in the control office ques-
oning our shuttle's return," said Kaid. "When we go out,
'll be early morning, the Controller will be tired, near the
nd of his shift—you know the scenario as well as I."

"That still leaves Miroshi," said Kusac.

"We can ask Conrad and Quin to keep an eye out for
er. Beyond that, there's little we can do. Remember, in a
nonth, the starship *Rhijissoh* will arrive to open formal
irst Contact negotiations with Jalna and the aliens who
ade here. They'll be able to ask for help locating her."

"Given the nature of Bradogan, I don't think he'll coop-
rate with us," said Carrie. "Trade, yes, on this same lim-
ed scale."

"Maybe the rebellion will have succeeded by then, you
ever know," said Kusac. "Talking of which, we've Strick
o contact and give those medical supplies Jo promised to
im."

"Set aside and waiting. It's pretty basic stuff, given that
ve don't know their physiology. There's some all-species
tuff in there but it's labeled in Jalnian for them to test
irst in case the la'quo has made them allergic to anything
ll our Alliance members can use."

"Did you contact Jeran, tell him we'll be in touch?"
asked Kusac.

"Better," grinned T'Chebbi. "Should be below now with
Kisha and crew. Only here for another couple of hours,
hough," she said, checking her wrist unit. "Then Sumaan
guard who brought him returns."

Kusac raised an eye ridge. "Kisha, is it? Wonder what
our captain will make of that."

T'Chebbi shrugged. "Didn't seem to mind. Just grinned
and laughed. He has a sense of humor, that one. Needs it,
working with Assadou!"

"Oh, I told Assadou to move back here," said Kaid.
"Much as I'm sure you'd like us to leave him behind, Carrie, we can't."

She shrugged. "We'll only have his company for a short

time before we transfer to one of our own ships. I can live with it."

Kusac pushed himself away from the table. "I'd like to go and have a look round our shuttle," he said. "Double check everything and pick up some provisions to take with us tomorrow on the caravan. Check where everything is. We need to make it look as though we are going to be traveling overland and back with them."

"Need to choose what weapons you want as well," Kaid said, getting to his feet. "You'll be searched to make sure you take nothing above the normal Jalnian tech level. I got some nice self-assembly pistols and rifles. Broken down you'd not guess what they were. I suggest you take one of each and put them together as soon as you can."

T'Chebbi led the way down to the cargo bay. Kaid chose to fall back beside Carrie.

"Y'know, I wish I had her long hair," said Carrie, watching the other female's single plait bob against her hips as she walked.

"Huh?"

Carrie looked up at him. "T'Chebbi. You wanted to talk to me about her."

"Yes, but . . ."

"Kaid, I meant what I sent last night. She's part of our family now, not just a Clan member, and I'm glad she is. We've gotten close. She must have had a rough time before you brought her to Stronghold. No one could have guessed she'd been a Consortia. She hides it well."

"You must have gotten close," he said as he felt her take his hand. "She kept that from me until very recently. Even I'm only beginning to know about her past."

"I won't ask her," she reassured him, stopping for a moment. "I chose my family, Kaid. I chose Kusac, and I chose you as my life-mates. You chose T'Chebbi as your lover and I choose to have her as my bond-sister. Now stop fretting!" she said, reaching up to rest her hand against his neck and caress it. "Stop worrying about my Human side!"

She felt his relief as he bent to kiss her briefly before they continued down the corridor to the cargo lift.

"What does worry me is that in a few hours you'll be face to face with the father you've never seen," she said. "You're going to find it difficult to avoid each other as

's one of us, more so now he has a Triad relationship
th Jo."

Kaid shrugged. "A biological act, nothing more. He was
aware of my existence, still is. I was the result of my
other's choice. I see no need to tell him."

"It's a bit more complex than that, and you don't know
ow he felt about your mother. He may well have cared
r her. Aren't you even curious?"

"Perhaps a little," was the last he'd say on the matter.

*   *   *

Rezac sat waiting impatiently for Jo. Rescue was so close.
he Sholans and Carrie had come for them, all they had
 do was get out of this castle and down to the lowland
wn of Galrayin. Beside him, Zashou sat wrapped in a
lanket. Her once lustrous blonde hair and pelt were dull,
nd her face looked thin and haggard.

"I'm afraid, Rezac," she said. "I don't think I'll make it
 this town. I'll never stay on the beast."

"You're sharing one with me," he said gently, reaching
ut to touch her cheek. "I'll hold you in front of me. You
on't be able to fall."

"I'm too pregnant to be riding," she whispered. "I know I
am!"

"You don't know for sure. You'll be fine, Zashou." He
vas glad their Link had dimmed with her increasing preg-
ancy. Because now she couldn't feel his fears for her.
None of them had any experience with parenthood but he
vas afraid she had the right of it.

We're coming, he heard Jo send to him. He roused him-
elf, easing away from Zashou and standing up. "They're
ere," he whispered to Kris and Davies.

Together they headed for the door, waiting for the guard
o open it. When he did, Kris reached out and grasped the
nan by the throat, pulling him into the room as Rezac
larted outside to deal with the other.

Davies dealt the startled soldier a swift thump on the
back of the head with one of their heavier tools. Stunned,
ne fell to his knees, dropping his spear which Kris leaped
forward to catch. Another blow, and he fell to the floor
senseless.

Outside, one cuff to the side of the head from Rezac's
paw and the other guard fell against the wall, sliding down

it into an unconscious heap. Looping his hands under the man's arms, Rezac hauled him into their chamber, dropped him, then returned swiftly to Jo's side.

Taradain's face was frozen in a look of bland politeness but his eyes were fully dilated and staring out at Rezac in sheer terror.

"Is the conditioning holding?" he asked her, touching her face briefly to reassure himself she was all right.

"Yes, but I'm holding him, too," she said, her voice sounding strained.

"I'll take over," he said. "Kris is helping Zashou."

She nodded, releasing her hold on him, and sagged briefly against the wall.

Moments later, the others joined them. Davies shut the chamber door, turning the key that still sat in the lock. Removing it, he lifted his robe and placed it in his pants pocket.

"It'll take them a while to get them out," he said with satisfaction, moving up to the front to be with Jo.

She led the way down to the level below, waiting at the foot of the stairs while Rezac checked mentally to see if the way was clear. Turning left, they headed quickly down the corridor, stopping at the second door on the right.

Empty. And it is the Queen's chamber, sent Rezac. *Despite my conditioning, Taradain's aware of what's happening, so I can follow his thoughts.*

Davies pushed the door open a fraction, peering into the room before opening it wider. They followed him in, blinking at the sudden glare of his flashlight.

"Taradain was as good as his word about our stuff," he said. "Everything there bar the gun. Where now, Jo?" he asked, playing the beam around the obviously unused room.

She preceded him, going over to the large, ornate bed. A carved wooden panel formed the headboard and it was over this that she began to run her fingers, obviously looking for some catch or depression. There was a click, then a faint rumbling sound came from the wall to her right.

Davies shone the torch on it to reveal a slowly widening black gap. "Now that's what I call a secret passage," he murmured, stepping up to it and peering inside. "Queen's Chamber, eh? The Queen who had this built must have had some love life!" Then her remembered Taradain. "Not

at I meant to infer that it might be your mother," he
ded hastily. "Anyone can see this is an old tunnel."

"Two hundred years old." said Jo. "She was a so-called
rgin queen whose exploits were the talk of her generation.
e left her crown to her cousin, Taradain's three or four
nes great aunt."

"Hurry up," hissed Rezac. "We haven't any time to lose!
e've got a four hour start if no one checks on the guards
fore then!"

Davies stepped cautiously into the gap, shining his torch
wn the passage before sticking his head back out. "It's
e. Cobwebs here and there, wood paneling on one side,
one on the other. We'd best keep very quiet. We've no
ay of knowing who's in the rooms on the other side."

"What about Taradain?" asked Jo.

"Bind and gag him and take him with us," said Rezac.
We can't afford the energy to monitor him."

The tunnel seemed to stretch for miles as, stumbling
long in almost pitch-blackness, they followed the bobbing
ght of Davies' torch. Stairs there were, two flights of them,
ading down, their surfaces treacherous because of the un-
ven treads. Finally they saw a faint glow ahead of them:
was Railin's lantern.

"You made it," he said, a relieved smile splitting his face.
hen he saw the two Sholans.

Rezac was past caring what anyone thought of them. Za-
hou was on the point of collapse. He'd had to carry her
r the last part of their journey. Staggering out of the
unnel entrance, to his surprise, he found willing hands
eady to take his burden from him. A water container was
ffered to him.

Parched, he leaned against the rocks and drank his fill
vhile Railin's soldiers saw to Zashou and the others. When
e'd finished, Railin came up to him, placing his hand on
is arm and urging him to one side.

"Your wife," he said quietly. "No one said she was preg-
ant. We must ride hard and fast if we're to outrun Killian.
You risk the child's life, perhaps even hers."

"We have no choice," said Rezac. "Believe me, if we
ad, we'd take it. We're linked in a way that makes our
ives dependent on each other. If she dies, so do I. And
nless we meet up with our friends, she *will* die."

"Where are you to meet these friends?" Railin asked. "How will they get you to the Port?"

"They have a shuttle," said Jo, joining them. "They' meet us at the pad outside Galrayin. It isn't guarded, is it?"

"No, there's nothing there to guard until our caravan are there. but if they have a shuttle, can't they come close than Galrayin? The ride will be too much for her, believe me. I have children of my own, and from the look of her she's near her time."

"Six weeks," said Jo.

Railin shook his head. "Too close at twice the time. Can you not use this mind-speaking to contact them, ask them to meet you sooner?"

Jo looked at Rezac. "I'll try," he said, reaching out to take Jo by the hand. "Link with me, Jo," he said tiredly tugging her till she rested against him. With a sigh, he leaned his head on her shoulder, letting go of the block he'd been trying to keep on their Link compulsion.

Instantly, their minds merged, sweeping them up in a kaleidoscope of memories and sensations. They fought to control it, using it to focus a sending to Carrie, but they sensed only the sleeping minds of those who'd come to rescue them. Exhausted and suffering from the effects of holding back a Link day, Rezac broke the connection abruptly before it took them down a path they couldn't yet tread.

I daren't hold you any longer, he sent to Jo, resolutely pushing her away. "We can't reach them, they're asleep," he said to Railin.

The older man nodded sympathetically. "Then we must ride with all speed. We only have a few hours grace before Killian discovers the imprisoned guards and learns that his son is missing."

"What do we do with Taradain?" Jo asked.

"We'll leave him with the caravan as we pass it," said Railin. "He'll be safe with them and it's the first place Killian will look. He'll not harm the caravaneers, so they take no risk in looking after him for us."

Nodding, Jo picked up her skirts and began to walk toward the others. "Did Taradain return my clothes?" she asked of Davies.

"Yes. Do you want to change here?" he asked in surprise as he reached into his backpack for her coveralls.

"Damned right, I do," she said firmly, beginning to un-
ce her dress at the side as she turned her back to him.
Undo the back, please. I want to forget we ever stayed
ere."

*　　*　　*

An hour before dawn, Ashay, the Sumaan pilot chosen
y Kishasayzar, warmed up the engines of the shuttle rest-
ng in the hold of the *Hkariyash*. Kaid had run through the
ontrols with him earlier. Nice little craft, she was. Ashay
as proud to be trusted with flying her. Concealed guns
ere but a button's touch away, and as for speed—she com-
ared with ground to space vessels of twice the size. Be-
eath her hull were hidden many things that did not by
ghts belong in such a vehicle, and his captain as well as
he Sholan, had given her to him to pilot on this most
nportant mission.

Lips curled back in a happy grin, Ashay let the craft rise
ff the deck and gently nosed her out of the *Hkariyash*'s
argo hold into the Jalnian night. He took her higher, open-
ng a comm link to the Port. He knew what to say, and he
ould stick to it. Briefly, his finger hovered over the firing
utton. No, they wouldn't need him to shoot his way out.
He sighed. Stealth was acceptable in a warrior, but fighting
vas best. Maybe he'd get the chance to shoot his way back
n, though. His marksmanship might yet save the day.

Then he remembered what his captain had said. His was
a peaceful mission. Unless he was ordered to do any shoot-
ng, he should refrain from opening fire on those who
vould willfully thwart his purpose. He sighed and got ready
o respond to the Jalnian voice that demanded answers
rom him over his comm. A warrior could dream,
couldn't he?

The shuttle had left as planned and now, as Carrie and
Kusac headed back to the ship, it was time to gather their
belongings and join the caravan. They didn't need much,
but they were carrying their own drinking water and food
in packs that would tie onto saddles.

Kaid and T'Chebbi came with them as far as the outer
gates. The permit was only for them and the guard would
not allow the two Sholans to pass through for long enough
to see their friends depart.

The small shantytown was a hive of quiet, efficient activity as the caravan, which had been loaded earlier that evening, gathered in a line, waiting for the guards and outriders hired to protect it. The draft animals stood patiently: They knew they had a long haul ahead of them, they weren't in a hurry to leave. Not so the riding beast Carrie's pranced and danced beneath her, pawing the ground with impatience.

At last the command to move came, and slowly, the wagons jolted forward as the beasts took up the slack and began to pull.

Kaid looked at his wrist unit as they walked back to the ship. "We can stay awake and eat an early meal, or go back to bed and sleep a little longer," he said. "What do you want to do?"

"Sleep," yawned T'Chebbi. "Be fresher when we need it. If I stay up now, might fall asleep at wrong time."

*   *   *

Jo signaled frantically to Railin to slow down till she could shout across at him.

"We must stop! Zashou's gone into labor!"

He signed to his men and within moments their headlong flight had ground to a halt. Turning her beast around, she urged it back to Rezac's side and dismounted. Kris' and Davies' willing hands had already taken Zashou from him.

"Over here!" called one of Railin's soldiers, beckoning to a small grassy knoll a few feet away.

While Kris carried Zashou over, Davies helped Rezac down from his beast. He was hardly able to stand and needed Davies' and Jo's support to make the short walk to where Kris had laid Zashou in the grass.

"She's gone into premature labor," said Jo, terrified for them both as Zashou, wracked with pain, began to whimper. Rezac suddenly sagged and they had to grab him before he fell. "Their Link's come back," she said. "He's suffering her pain, too! Rezac, you should have told us sooner!"

"She wouldn't let me," he said, staggering slightly as they lowered him to the ground. He reached out for Zashou, drawing her close so her head and shoulders were cradled on his lap. His eyes, dimmed with his Leska's pain, looked

) at her. "What of you, Jo? Do you feel it too? Are you
l right?"

She crouched down beside them, taking Zashou's hand
a hers, wiping the sweat-soaked tendrils of hair back from
:r face. "I'm fine, I feel nothing Rezac. But I don't know
ow to help her!"

"Try contacting them again. They must be awake now,"
e said, shuddering and closing his eyes as another spasm
racked them both.

She waited till the contraction had passed before with-
rawing her hand from Zashou's and moving away from
iem. Railin was waiting.

"We can't go on," she said. "I'm going to try reaching
iem again. Railin, I know nothing about childbirth. I don't
now how to help her!"

Railin turned to his men. They stood with their beasts a
lecent distance away from them, watching the road for
igns of pursuit. Though daylight, it was not long after dawn
nd still cool.

"Lanris! You birthed your last child, didn't you? Over
iere and help us! Jored, collect all our water and bring it
iere!" He turned back to Jo as he began rolling up his
leeves. "You get on with what you have to do, we'll take
:are of her," he said, patting her comfortingly on the
houlder.

Dazed, she nodded, watching as he strode purposefully
)ver to Zashou and Rezac.

"Lord Tarolyn," said the one called Lanris as he rushed
)ver. "We know nothing about her kind. She may not be
:he same as us," he began.

"Rubbish! All young come into the world the same way,"
said Railin brusquely, glancing back apologetically at Jo.
"Get some of your gear stripped off, man, and lend a
iand!"

"Lord Tarolyn," said Jo, looking in confusion to the
soldiers.

The nearest one nodded. "Lord Railin Tarolyn, Lady.
Our Lord."

Jo found herself suddenly sitting on the ground looking
into the blurry face of the soldier who'd just answered her.
His face cleared as she blinked up at him. He held the
spout of a waterskin to her lips.

"Drink, Lady. You just fainted, that's all."

She held onto the skin, drinking greedily till her thirst was quenched, then pushed it aside. "Does he do this often?" she asked.

The soldier looked from her to his Lord then back, and he grinned. "That he does, Lady. Says it keeps him in touch with what's going on. It'll be the death of him and us, one day, being as we're his special guards. But there's worse jobs, as they say."

A yowl of pain from Zashou brought her back to what she was supposed to be doing. With a smile, the soldier offered to help her to her feet. She shook her head. "I'm better sitting down now," she said.

A shadow falling across her made her look up as Kris approached and squatted down beside her. "I'm not much use back there, but I can help you reach Carrie," he said. "Rezac says to tell you now he's Linked with Zashou, he knows the cub's dead."

"Oh, no. To go through all this pain and have no child at the end," said Jo, sadness for them both welling up inside her. She sighed. "I'd be glad of your help, Kris."

Sitting beside her, he offered her his hand. She took it. It was cool, his skin rough and alien to her touch, so used was she now to Rezac's furred hand. Mentally, she reached for Kris, establishing a link so she could use his energy to power their search.

The shuttle, sent Kusac, reining in his beast as they rounded the hill. It sat beside the track some thirty meters away.

And exactly where we said. Well done for Ashay, Carrie replied as she slowed her mount.

The cabin air lock opened to reveal Ashay standing in the doorway, rifle slung in a ready position, grinning at them.

"Good time, you make," he called out.

Their mounts, nervous enough with Sholan scent, began to snicker in terror as they caught Ashay's predator's smell.

"Beasts not like Sumaan," he said, his tone regretful. "Sad. I like to touch them. See if their hide is as soft as it looks."

They dismounted, grabbing their packs then releasing the animals. They needed no encouragement. Nostrils flaring, with tiny shrieks of fear, they were gone.

Running to the vehicle, Carrie grasped Ashay's outstretched hand first. He seemed to give only a gentle pull and she was sailing through the air to land with a jolt on the deck beside him. She'd just time to clear the entrance before Kusac was beside her.

They headed into the cargo area where the containers substantiating their claim to have been picking up goods were stowed.

"Five minutes, Ashay," said Kusac to their pilot as the young Sumaan closed the air lock behind them. "Good navigating. You were right on target."

He joined Carrie, helping her release and stow the inner bulkhead that concealed their tiny medical facility. While she locked the drop-down treatment bed into place and located the various drugs and hypos, he continued releasing sections of paneling that formed the seating for their passengers. The craft was capable of seating ten in the back plus three up front. A multipurpose vehicle, it was a military prototype outfitted to their specifications for this mission.

Carrie, satisfied that all she needed was at hand, headed back up front where Ashay was observing them in wonder.

"Amazing what you can find behind bulkheads, isn't it, Ashay?" she said with a grin.

"Indeed. Had I not been seeing it for myself, I would not be believing it."

She settled herself in one of the remaining front seats and had just finished fastening her safety restraint when she sensed Jo's presence.

Carrie, thank God you're there! We need your help. Zashou's in premature labor; there's no way we can make the rendezvous.

We're with the shuttle now. Where are you?

Fifteen miles northeast of Galrayin, on the caravan trail from Kaladar. How soon can you get here?

Leaning forward, Carrie punched several buttons on the nav screen display. Beside her she felt the thumps of Ashay resuming his pilot's seat and Kusac joining her.

"Ten minutes if I go fast," said Ashay, beginning to start his ignition sequence.

"Make it five," said Kusac.

Between five and ten minutes, she sent to Jo.

The cub's dead, Carrie, but Zashou and Rezac are bad.

We know what to expect, Jo, sent Kusac. *Carrie had our cub in the field like this.*

You have a cub?

A daughter. We'll talk later, Jo, sent Carrie.

Carrie, one more thing. Railin—he's Lord Tarolyn, leader of the rebellion.

With only another three customers, the *Haven* was quiet at this time of morning, and it was cool. Already the heat outside had built up to a level that promised another scorching day. Kaid and T'Chebbi collected their drinks and headed to a table off to one side of the entrance.

As she sat down, T'Chebbi pressed something to the table's underside. "Two," she said.

Kaid nodded and turned to look toward the window. "I think I see something," he said, getting up. "Back in a moment." He made a show of peering out before he returned.

"Three," he said.

"How many more?" T'Chebbi asked as she sipped at her ale and grimaced.

"Another couple ought to do it," he said, leaning across the table toward her. A slightly glazed look came over his face for a moment, then he refocused on her.

"Carrie?"

He nodded. "They're on their way again. Zashou's in shock but stabilizing, and Rezac's fine now that she's been given psi suppressants."

"The cub?"

He shook his head. "Dead. Malformed, too, which made it worse for Zashou. Never would have survived. Must be the effects of this damned la'quo. They'll be here in fifteen minutes."

T'Chebbi nodded. "Is for the best, then. This telepathy is useful," she said, in an attempt to change the conversation. "Makes mission easier. No batteries to get wet, run out, or comms to break down."

"Has its uses, but anyone can use a comm, only the telepaths can use their Talent. Knock them out and your line of communication has gone."

She made a grudging sound of agreement. "Is good backup then."

"Definitely. What you think, one over by the game machine?" he nodded his chin toward a long holo machine set off-center from the main seating area.

"Think I see what games it has," she said.

While she was away, his wrist comm warbled in a pattern of sound he'd given to Strick as a signal to let him know when his folk were ready.

"Our local is ready," he said when she returned. "Quin and Conrad are watching for the shuttle and he says he can see Kisha." He grinned briefly at her. "We're ready, all we do now is wait."

Nearer the time, they ambled up to the window, looking through it as if watching for a friend. T'Chebbi loosened her outer robe, letting it fall open.

"Is getting hot," she said.

"Mmm," he said, watching how the street and the spaceport were beginning to come to life. They were going to need the extra support not only of Strick, but of Tarolyn and his soldiers on the shuttle.

We're in, Kaid, sent Carrie, *but a wagon's blocking us. We can't get into the* Hkariyash. *We have to land to the left of the main ramp.*

Get Jo's party in, then have Tarolyn's males move it. He let the connection drop, turning to T'Chebbi.

"We go."

They headed across the room toward the stairs. As they started up them, Kaid slapped another device on the wall.

Catching sight of them, the barkeep began to yell. "Hey, where the hell you think you're going? That's off limits to you at this time of day!"

Ignoring him, they took the stairs two at a time, pausing at the top only long enough to trigger the incendiaries. As they turned the corner into the corridor to Tesha's room, they heard them blow simultaneously, a bang that shook the whole building.

"You sure you got the mix right?" asked T'Chebbi as they stopped outside Tesha's door.

It flew open, and the Sholan female ran straight into them. Pushing her back into the room, they closed the door behind them. A klaxon went off. Then, in the distance, they heard the wail of the Port's siren start to build.

"You," she said, recognizing Kaid.

T'Chebbi pulled the robe off and handed it to her. "Put it on. Not much time to get you out, so hurry."

She stood looking at them, holding the robe, too stunned to move.

"You ready to go home, to Shola?" Kaid asked her.

"Home? Yes!" she said, suddenly galvanized into action. As she pulled the robe on, tying it with the attached belt, she looked from one to the other. "I take it the fire's your doing?"

"Shuttle's just landed beside the *Hkariyash*, Captain," said Giyesh from her post monitoring the outside vid screen.

Tirak was there in seconds. "What the hell? The Human, and the Sholan? They've been outside the Port?" He could hardly believe his eyes. "Jalnian soldiers coming off her, too? What the hell are they up to?"

The sound of the Port siren, relayed automatically through all ship comms, wailed throughout the *Profit*.

"*Fire*? Pan the camera along the town, Giyesh," he ordered. "I want to know where that fire is." He watched in silence till the *Haven* was in view. On the rooftop of the next building he could see, amid the swirling smoke, three tiny figures. "It's them! It's got to be them," he snarled. "Arm yourselves. I want everyone outside in sixty seconds. We're going to the *Hkariyash*. *I want to know what the hell's going on!* Manesh, seal the ship behind us!" He turned and ran for the arms locker.

"Captain, the fire!" wailed Giyesh.

"Move it! That fire's been rigged, there's no real danger!"

Bradogan was in the entrance hall of the Keep as the siren went off. He stood to one side, out of the way of the guard as they streamed out for the town. Fire drills had been drummed into them; there was no need for him to concern himself yet.

Accompanied by his personal guard, he made his way outside to the perimeter fence to watch the proceedings. The fire appeared to be at the far end. One of the taverns, doubtless. People were abandoning vehicles and wagons, beginning to stream out of the town and back into the Port, returning to their ships. Then something caught his eye. A shuttle, outside the Sumaan ship? He'd requested no shuttles, and certainly none should have landed anywhere but on the pad! He narrowed his eyes. The design was unfamiliar, not one belonging to the Port. Then he saw them, the U'Churian with the Solnian female. They, in the company of another two U'Churians, were heading toward one of the warehouses at a run. But the night watch had told him they'd left at dawn on the caravan for Galrayin!

He turned to the nearest guard. "Take half a dozen men over to that shuttle," he said, pointing to it. "Place the crew under arrest until I join you. The rest of you, follow me."

Pulling his gun, he began to run toward the gate. So they thought they'd played him for a fool, did they? They were about to find out just how wrong they were!

Tirak and his crew arrived just as Bradogan's guards decided the only way to implement their orders was to open fire on the shuttle. Caught in the open with Zashou in his arms, Rezac was an easy target. He was not prepared for the arrival of three burly people looking so like Sholans that it defied belief.

They placed themselves between him and the attacking Jalnians, and hauled him behind the shuttle to safety. Face to face with Tirak, there was little he could do.

"Sholan?" asked Tirak.

He nodded.

"Is she injured?" The question was a bit redundant Tirak realized even as he asked it. The female was obviously far from well.

Rezac looked at him blankly. He couldn't understand a word.

"Take them to the *Profit,*" Tirak ordered Mrowbay and turned his attention back to what was happening on the other side of the shuttle.

As he did, the air lock on the port side opened. A phrase in what they recognized as the Human language was yelled at them. The words they couldn't understand.

"Lower your weapons," Tirak said quietly to Mrowbay, Nayash, and Giyesh.

Tirak turned around as, guns trained on them, the three Humans dropped to the ground.

Again they spoke and this time Tirak spread his hands in a gesture he hoped would convey his inability to under

stand them. Suddenly a blinding pain hit him between the
eyes, almost making him black out. It lasted perhaps a minute then was gone.

"Not again," he moaned, putting his hands to his head
and massaging his temples. "You damned telepaths are a
pain in the ass!"

"He's met both our kinds," said Jo to Rezac.

Tirak lifted his head. "Thank the Gods someone understands us!"

Jo looked at him. "We understand each other," she said
coldly, pointing her gun at Mrowbay. "Let him go. What
do you want with us?"

"We've come to help," said Tirak. "You're cut off from
your ship. Take her to ours. We've med facilities onboard."

A shriek rang out as someone was hit. Jo looked at the
others, then back to Rezac. "Your choice," she said. "It's
not safe here and we can't get on the ship."

The siren continued to shriek its warning as Rezac
hesitated.

Tirak searched his mind for something he could say that
would break the deadlock. "His partner. You're his Human
partner," he said. "Linked mentally, aren't you? We'll not
keep him from you, you have my word. I know you'll die
if separated. If we stand here like this any longer, we'll *all*
die!" he added.

Rezac nodded. "We'll go," he said. "Are you coming,
Jo?"

She shook her head. "I'll stay and fight. You go on, I'll
see you when it's over."

Mrowbay took Rezac by the arm again. "Come," he said,
urging him gently. "We know something of the Sholan system. I am a medic, I can treat her."

"Jo!" Rezac called out as she turned away. *For the Gods
sake, take care, Jo! I don't want to lose you either.*

She nodded, turning her back on him as she faced the
others.

As they ran across the spaceport to the warehouses, Carrie looked briefly over her shoulder. "Gods, there's a fight
over at the ship!"

Forget it! sent Kaid. *Remember your training. Focus on
what we have to do.*

Dodging round the abandoned wagons, they came to the warehouse where Jeran was kept.

Skidding to a halt, Kaid hammered on the wooden doors. 'Jeran! You there?"

"Yes! What's happening?"

"Diversion, that's all. Stand back. Going to shoot the door open," Kaid yelled over the sound of the siren. Checking to see that the others were behind him, he aimed at the lock and fired. Splinters of wood flew everywhere and the door slowly creaked open.

Kusac ran forward, pulling it wide enough for Jeran to push through.

From the rear, Carrie glanced around, realizing that the figures she'd assumed were running for the Port gates were getting closer—far too close. *Bradogan!* she sent. *Heading for us with a half dozen guards!*

Kaid spun round, looking for cover for them. "The wagon! Head for it!"

T'Chebbi grabbed Jeran by the arm and pushing him in front of her, ran for the wagon.

Shots rang out, ricocheting off the ground and the partially open warehouse door.

Flattening himself against the wall, Kaid returned fire, his weapon sending bursts of energy toward the leading figures. One stopped, falling back slightly as the others scattered and passed him.

Carrie lifted her gun and aimed. As she pressed the trigger, she felt a sudden warmth at her side. Surprise made her shot go wide but she kept her attention to the men in front of her.

Carrie, run for the wagon, sent Kaid. *We'll cover you!*

The fire increased, sending Bradogan and his men scattering for cover. Pushing herself away from the wall, she began to run, aware of the two males close on her heels. A sudden pain in her ribs made her stumble and she pressed her hand to her side, surprised to find that it came away damp.

Behind the wagon, she had time to catch her breath. Now her side was starting to hurt. She looked down, seeing blood beginning to stain her coveralls. "Oh, hell," she said quietly.

Bullets zinged around them as she crouched there, wondering what to do. Seeing her so still, T'Chebbi glanced round, seeing the blood.

"How bad?" she asked.

"Dunno," said Carrie. "Doesn't hurt."

"Stay down with Jeran," she said, moving over to cover her.

"Ashay!" yelled Jo. "What can you see?"

"Bradogan's men still shooting at us!" he yelled down.

Jo tapped her foot on the ground, thinking furiously. Fighting was breaking out all over the Port now. They couldn't go on like this. One of Tirak's crew was down already. If she remembered right, when they'd come in there had been an empty bay beside them. There was a clear line of sight straight to the huge stone Keep between the two perimeter fences.

"Your friends are in trouble, too," said Tirak, grasping her arm and pointing down toward the far end.

She looked. A group of Bradogan's men had them pinned down behind a wagon. Suddenly her mind was made up. "Boost me up," she said to Davies, pointing back to the shuttle air lock above them

"What?"

"Boost me up, dammit!"

He did and as she scrambled back into the cockpit of the shuttle, she turned. "Pull all our people back," she ordered. "I'm settling this one now."

Davis grabbed at Tirak. "Better do as she says. She's going to start up the shuttle."

"*What?*" Then a grin lit his face. "I like this female," he said, swinging round to yell to his crew.

"Ashay," she said, throwing herself into the seat beside him. "How'd you like to end this fight?" She scanned the area ahead carefully. None of their people were in the line of fire.

Ashay looked expectantly at her. "Start her up, move her round, and open fire on Bradogan's men," she said.

Ashay's mouth opened slowly, lips curling back in a grin. "We fire on enemy?" His tone was hopeful.

"I'm afraid so," she said. "Try to only take them out, don't use anything too heavy. No missiles, okay? And for God's sake, don't hit the *Hkariyash!*"

"Definitely no hitting *Hkariyash*," Ashay agreed with a

shudder as he lifted the shuttle into the air and swung her about.

Seeing that Jo had matters well under control, Tirak regrouped his crew. Davies and Kris joined them as the sound of the shuttle's bursts of rapid fire almost deafened them. Pointing to the far end, they headed off at a run, ducking behind the landing bays and out of sight. From the corner of his eye, Tirak saw a shape, like a shadow, pacing them. He risked a glance sideways and blinked. Nothing. Dismissing it from his mind, he focused on the threat to the small group of Sholans ahead of them.

They stopped at the *Profit,* easing their way down between it and the adjacent craft. Ahead of them they could see Bradogan and his men, hiding behind an abandoned grav sled.

"We'll pick a few off first," Tirak said, "then see if Bradogan will surrender."

"We've got friendly cross fire," said Kusac, looking to his right as the second volley of shots came in.

"I noticed," said Kaid. "Hold fire. Let's see what they can do. We're running low on power. Better save it just in case."

A yell of pain rang out from Bradogan's direction.

"Sounds like they got one."

T'Chebbi bent down to Carrie, taking her knife out. "I check that wound now," she said.

"Wound?" said Kusac, swinging round to look at her. "You're wounded?"

"Doesn't hurt," she said, pushing T'Chebbi away even as she continued to block the pain off behind her mental shield. "It's nothing, honestly. Just winged me."

Firmly, T'Chebbi pushed her hands aside and began cutting the bloodstained entry hole to her coveralls to get a better look at her wound.

Shots were still being fired, but they were sporadic and none were coming in their direction.

Torn between concern for his Leska and the knowledge of the danger they still faced, Kusac forced himself to turn away. *Why didn't I know? I should have felt it!*

Kusac, it doesn't hurt now, and didn't when it happened.

It was Bradogan. Bastard aimed at me on purpose. Then she yelped as T'Chebbi touched the hole in her side.

"Kaid, is small entry wound, no exit. Bullet still inside," said T'Chebbi.

"Take over," he said. He waited till she'd relieved him then bent down to check for himself.

"What is it, Kaid?" demanded Kusac, glancing down.

"Bullet's still inside her," Kaid said, gently probing the wound as Carrie tried not to moan.

Voices could be heard shouting to each other.

"Is over, now," said T'Chebbi. "Tirak was one helping us! With Davies and Kris." She bent down to hand something to him. "Is what Bradogan used."

Kusac joined them, the fight, Bradogan, all forgotten in his concern for Carrie. "Show me," he said, holding out his hand.

Kaid nodded and T'Chebbi leaned over to place a deformed bullet in his hand. "Soft tipped bullets," she said. "Not good."

Kusac's hand closed around the projectile.

"She'll be fine, with the right treatment," said Kaid, looking him straight in the eye. *Need to know exactly where it is before it can be removed by surgery. We don't have those facilities. The nearest ones will be at our rendezvous.*

They heard footsteps and looked up to find Tirak standing there.

"Got this habit of following us," said T'Chebbi, getting to her feet.

"Be glad I do," said Tirak with a grin. It faded swiftly as he saw Carrie. "Injured?" he asked.

Kusac held out his hand, opening it to show him the bullet.

"I got a medic on my ship, good facilities," he said. "Your injured Sholan female is already there."

"Bullet's still inside her," said Kaid, bending to pick Carrie up.

She pushed him away and began to struggle to her feet before he could stop her. "I'm fine. You're all making a fuss about nothing," she said. Then the blood drained from her face and she began to crumple.

Kaid caught her, sweeping her up in his arms as he looked at Kusac, who had collapsed against the wagon.

Hkariyash hasn't the facilities," he said. "I don't know what Tirak has, but without surgery soon, she'll die."

"Cryo," said Tirak, grasping Kaid by the arm. "I have cryo units. Can put her—him, too, if necessary—in cryo till we reach your ship."

"Cryo units are free, Captain," said Mrowbay. "I started bringing the young pair out when I took the Sholan female to sick bay."

"Take her there," said Kusac, pushing himself upright with an effort of willpower. "I want to see Bradogan."

He pushed T'Chebbi aside as she tried to stop him, rounding the wagon till he faced the captive Lord.

"You I will kill with my bare hands," he snarled, advancing slowly on him.

Out from between the ships, a dark shape came running, uttering an unearthly howl that stopped even Kusac in his tracks. Straight as an arrow it headed for Bradogan. Launching itself, it sprang, landing full on the Jalnian's chest, its weight wrenching him from the guards and bearing him to the ground.

The two U'Churians sprang back, watching in horror as the screaming man was savagely attacked.

A shot rang out and the creature stiffened, then fell limply across Bradogan's equally still form.

Jeran moved forward. "Miroshi?" he said. "Oh, Gods, it's Miroshi!"

"Miroshi?" demanded T'Chebbi. "Why she do this to Bradogan?"

"Because of what he did to her," said Jeran, bending down to touch the dead female. "She was ill," he said, looking up at Kaid. "I told you that. He gave her to his men one night because he was angry with her. There was nothing we could have done to help."

The sound of an approaching shuttle drowned out any hope of further conversation. It stopped to let Jo descend, then turned and headed back down to the other end of the spaceport.

She rushed over to Kaid. "Not Carrie," she said, touching her face. "Oh, God, not Carrie!"

"Bradogan's dead." said Jeran, standing up. "She got her revenge."

Tirak decided enough time had been wasted. "We need

to get Carrie to sick bay," he said, taking hold of Kusac's arm. "Are you done here? Have you got all your people?"

Kusac looked at Jo.

"Yes, all accounted for," she said, looking over to him. "Rezac and Zashou are on the *Profit*, the rest of us are here or on the *Hkariyash*."

"Including Tallis?"

"Yes, he made his break while Bradogan was after you, and managed to reach the *Hkariyash*."

"You said you need to reach a rendezvous. Where?" asked Tirak.

"Chemerian home world," said Kaid.

"We can get you there in two weeks. Is that fast enough? Let's go, now, before any more fighting starts. You can talk to your ship from mine while we see to the injured."

"We're coming," said Kusac, leaning on Davies for support.

"I'll go on the *Hkariyash*," said Kris. "We don't need to get back quickly."

"Same with me," said Davies as he helped Kusac toward the *Profit*. "We'll keep you posted on what happens. Next few days could be quite interesting as Railin takes over from Bradogan."

As Mrowbay prepared to seal the cryo units, Kaid reached out to touch Kusac's hand. Already the premed had taken effect and his friend was drifting into unconsciousness.

"Two weeks, Kaid," he said, his voice barely audible. "Find out what Tirak was up to in that time. I'll want to know."

"I'll find out," he reassured him, standing back for the unit to be sealed. He turned away, moving to Carrie's.

"She never came round," said Mrowbay, joining him.

Kaid touched her cheek. "Sleep well," he whispered.

Lisanne Norman

☐ TURNING POINT   UE2575—$5.99

When a human-colonized world falls under the sway of imperialistic aliens, there is scant hope of salvation from far-distant Earth. Instead, their hopes rest upon an underground rebellion and the intervention of a team of catlike aliens.

☐ FORTUNE'S WHEEL   UE2675—$5.99

Carrie was the daughter of the human governor of the colony planet Keiss. Kusac was the son and heir of the Sholan Clan Lord. Both were telepaths and the bond they formed was compounded equally of love and mind power. But now they were about to be thrust into the heart of an interstellar conflict, as factions on both their worlds sought to use their powers for their own ends . . .

☐ FIRE MARGINS   UE2718—$6.99

A new race is about to be born on the Sholan homeworld, and it may cause the current unstable political climate to explode. Only through exploring the Sholan's long-buried and purposely forgotten past can Carrie and Kusac hope to find the path to survival, not only for their own people, but for Sholans and humans as well.

☐ RAZOR'S EDGE   UE2766—$6.99

Still adjusting to the revelations about its past, the Sholan race must now also face the increasing numbers and independence of the new human-Sholan telepathic pairs. Meanwhile, Carrie, Kusac, Kaid, and T'Chebbi are sent to the planet Jalna on a rescue mission that will see them caught up in the midst of a local revolution . . . even as they uncover a shocking truth that threatens both their species!

More Top-Flight Science Fiction and Fantasy from
C.J. CHERRYH

ANTASY

|] THE DREAMING TREE | UE2782—$6.99 |

ourney to a transitional time in the world, as the dawn
f mortal man brings about the downfall of elven magic,
n the complete *Ealdwood* novels, finally together in one
olume with an all new ending.

SCIENCE FICTION

] FOREIGNER	UE2637—$5.99
] INVADER	UE2687—$5.99
] INHERITOR	UE2728—$6.99

THE MORGAINE CYCLE

] GATE OF IVREL (BOOK 1)	UE2321—$4.50
] WELL OF SHIUAN (BOOK 2)	UE2322—$4.50
] FIRES OF AZEROTH (BOOK 3)	UE2323—$4.50
] EXILE'S GATE (BOOK 4)	UE2254—$5.50

Elizabeth Forrest

☐ **PHOENIX FIRE** UE2515—$4.99
As the legendary Phoenix awoke, so too did an ancient Chinese demon—and Los Angeles was destined to become the final battle ground in their millenia-old war.

☐ **DARK TIDE** UE2560—$4.99
The survivor of an accident at an amusement pier is forced to return to the town where it happened. And slowly, long buried memories start to resurface, and all his nightmares begin to come true . . .

☐ **DEATH WATCH** UE2648—$5.99
McKenzie Smith has been targeted by a mastermind of evil who can make virtual reality into the ultimate tool of destructive power. Stalked in both the real and virtual worlds, can McKenzie defeat an assassin who can strike out anywhere, at any time?

☐ **KILLJOY** UE2695—$5.99
Given experimental VR treatments, Brand must fight a constant battle against the persona of a serial killer now implanted in his brain. But Brand would soon learn that there were even worse things in the world—like the unstoppable force of evil and destruction called KillJoy

☐ **BRIGHT SHADOW** UE2695—$5.99
When a clandestie FBI invasion of a cult ranch blows up, Vernon Spense manages to rescue one little girl, Jennifer. Though Spense finds what he thinks is a safe haven for her, to one man she's far too important to let go. Either he will get her back or he'll make sure she's beyond everyone's reach. And to that end, he will eliminate Spense or anyone who gets in his way. . . .
